THE
THOMAS WOLFE
READER

THE

THOMAS WOLFE

READER

Edited, with an Introduction and Notes, by
C. HUGH HOLMAN

New York

CHARLES SCRIBNER'S SONS

c/1

CONTENTS

v

THE
THOMAS WOLFE
READER

C. HUGH HOLMAN

INTRODUCTION

THOMAS WOLFE possessed a singularly delicate sensory perception, a remarkably retentive memory, a passionate concern with the nature of experience, a deep patriotic strain, a commitment to self-expression, and a powerful rhetorical style. These elements combined in his work to produce a vast, sprawling epic of one man's experience in America. At his death in 1938, just before his thirty-eighth birthday, Wolfe had published two long novels, a collection of short stories and short novels, and an essay on literary method. He left behind an enormous mass of manuscript out of which his editor shaped two more novels and another collection of short pieces.

At no time since that October day in 1929 when *Look Homeward, Angel* first appeared have critics seriously questioned the lyric power and the skill with words which Wolfe possessed. Yet his works have raised fundamental questions about his sense of form, and criticism has labored almost endlessly over his structure and the propriety of his direct use of autobiography. All these works have a common subject and one almost universally recognized as Wolfe's own experience in his world presented under the transparent disguises of two protagonists, Eugene Gant and George Webber. Although this subject is treated in a mixture of literary modes, a potpourri of dramatic scenes, narrative passages, tone poems, rhetorical incantations, and satirical social sketches, the works, after *Look Homeward, Angel,* are seemingly portions of one vast but unfinished "book."

Look Homeward, Angel has the structure of an apprenticeship novel, recounting in a chronological pattern a youth's growth into maturity. As a unified novel, it is Wolfe's most successful single effort. Throughout the remainder of his career he groped toward other controlling forms with only limited success. *Of Time and the River,* his second novel, is almost an anthology of separate items, many of them originally published as short stories, sketches, and short novels, organized around the loosely defined theme of "the search for a father." His two posthumous novels are assemblies of materials left at his death. The result is that Thomas Wolfe at his best is the author of a fine first novel and of a group of magnificently executed fragments which he originally published as short stories and short novels and which he left, when he died, without having adequately fitted into large organic wholes. As a writer of short novels and short stories, he was surprisingly effective. Most of his formal failures are on the level of large works.

Thomas Wolfe's life formed the broad pattern of his vast "book." He was born into a middle class family in Asheville, North Carolina, a small town nestled in the first ranges of the Blue Ridge Mountains and destined to undergo a rapid burgeoning into a resort city. His father was from Pennsylvania, his mother from the North Carolina mountains. He attended the state university at Chapel Hill at a time when it was beginning its growth from a sleepy liberal arts college into an important regional university and research center. At Chapel Hill he was one of the first of the Carolina Playmakers, a student dramatic group which, under the guidance of Professor Frederick Koch, was working seriously at the writing and production of regional and folk plays. Wolfe's first literary efforts were one-act plays based on life in his mountain region and written for the Playmakers group.

From the University of North Carolina he went to Harvard where he studied drama under Professor George Pierce Baker in the "47 Workshop" and took an A. M. degree in English literature under John Livingston Lowes, from whom he absorbed the theory of the romantic imagination which Lowes was working out for *The Road to Xanadu,* his study of Coleridge's mind. From that time on Wolfe was to attempt to fill his "well of unconscious cerebration" with the materials from which his art was to flow—experiences, sights, sounds, people, books, and all the materials of art, both immediate and vicarious.

When Wolfe's efforts at establishing a career as a playwright met with steady rebuffs from producers, he took a job as an instructor in English at the Washington Square College of New York University, where he taught intermittently from 1924 until 1930. The boy from the Carolina mountain town had made the traditional American pilgrimage to the city. In 1925 he made his first trip to Europe and met Mrs. Aline Bernstein, a theatrical designer eighteen years his senior, with whom he had a love affair which was a central experience of his life. The following year he returned to Europe and began writing a novel. The book was completed in 1928, and accepted for publication by Maxwell E. Perkins, of Charles Scribner's Sons, after being rejected by several publishers. Wolfe worked closely with Perkins in shaping the long manuscript into a publishable form, and thus began perhaps the best-known author-editor relationship in American letters. Perkins was to work with Wolfe with increasing closeness from this time on until Wolfe, spurred on by the charges of critics that the editor was doing too much of the author's work and by irritations growing out of some libel suits, severed his relations with Scribner's in 1937.

Look Homeward, Angel was received in Asheville as a calculated affront to the town, and Wolfe was shocked by the angry denunciations which arose over the book. Once more he sailed for Europe, and returned to begin in Brooklyn the long struggle toward a new book. In the years between 1930 and 1934 he tried again and again to find a pattern for the work, and he wrote for it thousands of pages of material containing hundreds of episodes. Many of these episodes were self-contained units which he published as short stories. Others were organized as longer units and were published as short novels. At least two of his major fictional achievements belong to this period: "The Web of Earth" and "A Portrait of Bascom Hawke," both short novels published in *Scribner's Magazine*. In 1934 at the insistence of Perkins, Wolfe began organizing the materials he had into a second novel, *Of Time and the River*. The account of the reception of *Look Homeward, Angel* and the writing of *Of Time and the River* is given in detail in *The Story of a Novel*, Wolfe's disarmingly frank account of his struggles toward form. In 1935 he cleared the deck, so to speak, by assembling in a collection called *From Death to Morning* several of the stories and short novels which he had published in *Scribner's Magazine* but had not reworked into his second novel.

In 1937 he returned to Asheville, now a respected son rather than a despised reprobate, but he soon found that he could not live and work there happily and concluded that "you can't go home again." Before the year had ended, he had severed his relations with Scribner's and signed a contract with Harper and Brothers. He began the preparation of a new long work, determined now to achieve an objectivity which he had lacked in his earlier books. To this end he scrapped Eugene Gant, the protagonist of *Look Homeward, Angel* and *Of Time and the River,* and began writing about George Webber. When, in May, 1938, he left a huge bulk of manuscript with his new editor and started on a trip to the west, he regarded the new book as by no means complete. On this trip he contracted pneumonia in Seattle, was finally brought to the Johns Hopkins Hospital

in Baltimore, and there he died on September 15, 1938, of tuberculosis of the brain, resulting from the release of old tubercle bac-
teria in his lungs.

The pattern of his life was a pattern of ever-widening circles.
From his hill-locked home town, to a state university just beginning
to reach out to find its place in the national scene, to the city, and
finally to Europe, Wolfe moved in a steadily expanding world. A
similar expansion was present in his work. He began in an intensely
personal lyric cry in *Look Homeward, Angel,* moved on to an attempt to realize his nation through himself in *Of Time and the
River,* and came at the end to a satiric social criticism in *You Can't
Go Home Again.*

Actually Wolfe was struggling throughout his career toward some
solution to the problems posed in America for the democratic and
yet patriotic artist. As Alexis de Tocqueville had perceived in 1830,
"In democratic communities, where men are all insignificant and
very much alike, each man instantly sees all his fellows when he
surveys himself. The poets of democratic ages, therefore, can never
take any man in particular as the subject of a piece. . . ." Walt
Whitman had attempted to sing the nature of America by celebrating the American whom he knew best, hoping to find in his own
generic experiences an image of a national Self. Thomas Wolfe attempted much the same objective. Caught in the essentially romantic
theory of art which holds that the artist must express himself, the
patriotic poet must experience a catholicity of life in order to give
expression to a self representative of the nation. Hence Wolfe's
intense preoccupation with experience and feeling.

Yet, having given expression to this national self, usually through
a powerful evocation of time, place, and action, employing to its
fullest his intensely sensuous style—almost literally rubbing the objects of experience against the reader's nerve-ends—Wolfe seldom
felt that the evocation of feeling was enough. He added rhetorical exhortation and explanation, reasserting in rhythmic prose the
meaning of what he had earlier given powerfully in dramatic scene.
Among his ardent admirers there has been little agreement about
which of these "voices"—the dramatic or the rhetorical—is the better; for some see his strength as being primarily the result of the
force with which he brings the world of the senses to bear vicariously

upon the reader, evoking a response that is almost physical, while others find in his dithyrambic chants and his rhetorical incantations a power of language that is for them his chief strength.

But, in any case, the quality, aside from his almost dizzying command of language, that is most impressive about Wolfe's writing is his power of characterization. His protagonists—whether Eugene Gant or George Webber—are essentially the focal points of a broadgauged experience of the world. They are uniquely "a part of all that they have seen" and their American experience is basically the record of the world through which they pass. Both are young men of sharp perceptions and enormous gusto for life, so that experience impresses them with unusual force and magnitude. Each possesses the gift of a permanent child-like wonder, the ability to respond freshly to primary experiences, to see a person or smell a flower or hear a movement as though it were breaking through some barrier to be recorded for the first time. The result is that the portrayals of their worlds are drawn very large, tending toward the tremendous and the grotesque. This intensity sometimes becomes almost overpowering; it can, on occasion, raise the trivial to the level of absurd exaggeration.

Yet neither Eugene nor George is as important as the people whom they meet, watch with startled and child-like wonder, and record with an intense delight in variety. W. O. Gant, Eliza Gant, brother Ben, sister Helen, Laura James, Abraham Jones, the Coulson family, Esther Jack, Dick Prosser, Randy Shepperson, Nebraska Crane —these are all vividly realized people, caught in action and permanently imprisoned in the amber of Wolfe's language. Paradoxically, to know this most autobiographical of authors is to know a wealth of fully-realized characters of many types, classes, and locales.

The experiences of Eugene Gant and George Webber are bound together through certain recurrent themes. One of his central themes is loneliness. To be an American is to be lonely and restlessly moving beneath vast skies, Wolfe asserts. The barriers that are erected around the individual effectively shut him off from all communication. The original title of *Look Homeward, Angel* was "The Building of a Wall." The theme of *Of Time and the River* is the "search for a father." One of Wolfe's most successful short novels—one which he wanted to issue as a separate book—is entitled *No Door*. When his characters grow out from home they find that "you can't go home again." The search for communion and for communication is obsessive in Wolfe's work, and he repeatedly asserted that it was central to the American experience.

Another theme is time. If he has a philosophical concern in these works, it seems to be centered in the nature of time, and in the relations among past and present and "time immutable." In *The Story of a Novel* he is quite explicit about the centrality of time to the structure and meaning of his work, and in place after place in his fiction he tries to bring past into present through memory and to project them both against the backdrop of eternity. A story like "The Lost Boy" is centered squarely on this problem of time.

Death is another recurrent theme in his work. It seems always to hover over his mutable world, and some of his most impressive scenes are concerned with its coming. The deaths of Ben Gant and of W. O. Gant are as fine dramatic scenes as he ever wrote. And death is central to a short story like "Child by Tiger" or "Dark in the Forest, Strange as Time" or even to a rhetorical meditation like "The Hollow Men."

All of these concerns are extremely romantic, as indeed Wolfe himself was. Yet he could turn an angry and satiric eye on the world around him. His portrait of the members of Professor Hatcher's playwriting class is etched in acid. His portrait of Libya Hill in the real estate boom is close in spirit and method to the work of Sinclair Lewis, whom he greatly admired.

While these themes remained fairly constant in Wolfe's work and while his use of language and subject underwent only gradual changes, there was a steady development in his work of a sense of the outer world. He began as a youthful lyric writer, celebrating the intense and uniquely personal response of the self to the morning freshness of the earth. He gradually developed a larger view that centered itself increasingly in a national ideal. In *Look Homeward, Angel* he was largely content to revel in the "meadows of sensation." By the time of the later works, he was attempting, as he wrote in a letter to Perkins in 1930, the representation of "the whole consciousness of his people and nation . . . every sight, sound and memory of the people." The motive force shifts from representing a person to using that person to express the elements of a universal experience, or at least an experience common to most Americans.

And the American experience seemed to him to demand a new

use of language and new art forms. Thus, Wolfe takes his place in the long pattern of American writers struggling to find an adequate form and substance for the native character and the democratic ideal. In one sense he is the poet whom Emerson demanded but could not find and about whom he said:

> . . . Dante's praise is that he dared to write his autobiography in colossal cipher, or into universality. We have yet no genius in America, with tyrannous eye, which knew the value of our incomparable materials, and saw, in the barbarism and materialism of the times, another carnival of the same gods whose picture he so much admires in Homer; then in the Middle Ages; then in Calvinism. Banks and tariffs, the newspaper and caucus, Methodism and Unitarianism, are flat and dull to dull people, but rest on the same foundations of wonder as the town of Troy and the temple of Delphi, and are as swiftly passing away. Our long-rolling, our stumps and their politics, our fisheries, our Negroes and Indians, our boasts and our repudiations, the wrath of rogues and the pusillanimity of honest men, the northern trade, the southern planting, the western clearing, Oregon and Texas, are yet unsung. Yet America is a poem in our eyes; its ample geography dazzles the imagination, and it will not wait long for metres.

Whitman attempted in poetry to fill Emerson's demand. Thomas Wolfe is, after Whitman, perhaps the closest pursuer of this objective of the national poet. As Wolfe says in *The Story of a Novel,* ". . . in the cultures of Europe and of the Orient the American artist can find no antecedent scheme, no structural plan, no body of tradition that can give his own work the validity and truth that it must have. . . . the labor of a complete and whole articulation, the discovery of an entire universe and of a complete language, is the task that lies before him."

In his search for a new articulation by which to express the "enormous space and energy of American life," Wolfe brought a trained and sophisticated literary mind to bear. He was an early disciple of H. G. Wells, a follower and imitator of James Joyce, both in *Ulysses* and in the "Work in Progress" that became *Finnegans Wake,* an admirer of Sinclair Lewis, of Dostoievski, who supplanted Dickens in his affections while he was an undergraduate, and of Proust. The whole range of English poetry fascinated him. Milton and Shakespeare, Wordsworth and Coleridge he echoed and paraphrased again and again. Donne he admired and Eliot's verse he knew and quoted.

When Wolfe was writing badly his pages sometimes seem like a pastiche of other writers. At his best, Wolfe's style and structure are enriched by an allusiveness that has depth and subtlety.

Wolfe's writing methods, by which he fashioned units of his perception into dramatic scenes, episodes, essays, or prose poems and then attempted to fit them into larger structures, resulted in an obscuring of the outlines of his larger schemes. The result is that we are often confronted with vast shadowy plans that are at best dimly seen or with rhetorical exhortations unsupported by the novelist's customary demonstration through action. Yet a portion of our confusion results from the mammoth size and uncertain organization of books like *Of Time and the River, The Web and the Rock,* and *You Can't Go Home Again.* It might be helpful to look at Wolfe's work as having a pattern not unlike Faulkner's, whose short stories have their significant parts to play in the larger legend of Yoknapatawpha County and are sometimes later incorporated in larger forms, yet retain an integrity of their own. Much less of Wolfe's national epic is available to us than there is of Faulkner's; Wolfe's legend lacks the historical definition which Faulkner's has; we often have to act in the faith that meaningful relationships exist among the parts of his large volumes without being able fully to see them. Yet none of these things should exclude us from an appreciation of Wolfe's skill, range, and variety as a writer of short dramatic episodes and of essays and prose poems.

Wolfe's experiments in search of new "structural plans" were almost all on a scale larger than individual scenes. It was in the organization of materials, in efforts at counterpoint between episodes, and the creation of multiple senses of time that he worked hardest. The short novel which he called "Proustian," *The Party at Jack's,* is starkly direct in its telling, fixed almost entirely in the forward moving events of a single night. This work is Proustian not in its use of memory or sensory detail but in its attempt structurally to join representatives from a great range of society. In fact, however, it is in his presentation of the precise content of specific scenes with a convincing richness of detail and a sense of great vitality that Wolfe appears best, and here his methods are essentially those of the traditional rather than the experimental novelist.

In this Reader, groups of self-contained units from Thomas

Wolfe's work are given in an effort to present him in his representative moods, manners, and moments, with a view to showing the richness and the variety that exist in the sprawling volumes which constitute his vast but incomplete "book." The selections are given in the order in which they appear in the books from which they are taken, and the books appear in the order of their initial publication. Such a presentation will, I hope, allow the reader to follow Wolfe's career as it develops, giving some sense of its changing style, its modifications of subject matter, and its deepening of theme. For the sake of maintaining a reasonable length and because they are readily available in their original form, the short novels are not reprinted. This Reader is, therefore, a collection of units which are essentially short stories, essays, and prose poems. It contains, however, a large proportion of his best known passages and most of his memorable characters. The collection demonstrates Wolfe's strength, his variety, and his great skill with language. His intention of producing an epic expression of his native land can be seen here at least in shadowy outline.

In such relatively brief units as these, Wolfe worked with artistic control and often with great success, producing some of the most distinguished prose passages of our century. Such units as those here selected can best be approached, however, not in terms of distinct literary genres but as the expressions of a gifted writer working in what is essentially the bardic tradition. It is my hope that any readers who meet him for the first time in these brief encounters will be led to make his further acquaintance as a novelist, not only in his larger well-known works but in his short novels as well.

THE STORY OF A NOVEL

THOMAS WOLFE prepared a long preface to *Of Time and the River,* expressing his gratitude to Maxwell E. Perkins for the assistance he had given in the final preparation of the novel and describing the processes by which it had been written, but Perkins would not allow it to be used in the book. When Wolfe was invited to be a "visiting novelist" at a writer's conference at the University of Colorado in August, 1935, he used this unpublished preface as the basis for his public lecture. In his opinion, he "did the job up pretty brown," although it took him an hour and forty minutes to deliver the long address.

The manuscript of the speech, after some cutting by his agent, Elizabeth Nowell, was published as a serial in the *Saturday Review of Literature* on December 14, 21, and 28, 1935. Then, after some further editing and expansion by Wolfe, it was issued by Charles Scribner's Sons as a small book in April, 1936, under the title *The Story of a Novel.*

The Story of a Novel is a remarkably frank and engagingly humble account of Wolfe's ambitions, methods, and struggles as a writer. It demonstrates that he was a reasonably accurate self-critic and that he had a clear-eyed vision of his weaknesses and his strengths as a writer. Since its publication it has been a primary document in the examination of Wolfe's work, an indispensable tool for all who want even a casual knowledge of his literary ideals and artistic methods. It is also a literary essay of very high intrinsic merit.

The account given in it of the assistance Wolfe received from Perkins proved to be a weapon for those who felt that he was lacking in form and too dependent on his editor. In the *Saturday Review of Literature* for April 25, 1936, Bernard DeVoto, in a front page article entitled "Genius Is Not Enough," attacked the book and its author, accusing Wolfe of leaving to "the Scribner's assembly line" many of the primary tasks which a novelist should perform for himself. This review and other expressions of similar opinions were partially responsible for Wolfe's decision to part company with Scribner's and to seek a new editor.

The text of *The Story of a Novel* here reproduced is that of the first edition (New York: Charles Scribner's Sons, 1936) .

THE STORY OF A NOVEL

AN EDITOR, who is also a good friend of mine, told me about a year ago that he was sorry he had not kept a diary about the work that both of us were doing, the whole stroke, catch, flow, stop, and ending, the ten thousand fittings, changings, triumphs, and surrenders that went into the making of a book. This editor remarked that some of it was fantastic, much incredible, all astonishing, and he was also kind enough to say that the whole experience was the most interesting he had known during the twenty-five years he had been a member of the publishing business.

I propose to tell about this experience. I cannot tell any one how to write books; I cannot attempt to give any one rules whereby he will be enabled to get his books published by publishers or his stories accepted by high-paying magazines. I am not a professional writer; I am not even a skilled writer; I am just a writer who is on the way to learning his profession and to discovering the line, the structure, and the articulation of the language which I must discover if I do the work I want to do. It is for just this reason, because I blunder, because every energy of my life and talent is still involved in this process of discovery, that I am speaking as I speak here. I am going to tell the way in which I wrote a book. It will be intensely personal. It was the most intense part of my life for several years. There is nothing very literary about it. It is a story of sweat and pain and despair and partial achievement. I don't know how to write a story yet. I don't know how to write a novel yet. But I have learned something about myself and about the work of writing, and if I can, I am going to try to tell what it is.

I don't know when it occurred to me first that I would be a writer. I suppose that like a great many other children in this country of my generation, I may have thought that it would be a fine thing because a writer was a man like Lord Byron or Lord Tennyson or Longfellow or Percy Bysshe Shelley. A writer was a man who was far away like these people I have mentioned, and since I was myself an American and an American not of the wealthy or university-going sort of people, it seemed to me that a writer was a man from a kind of remote people that I could never approach.

I think this has happened to us all—or almost all of us here in America. We're still more perturbed by the strangeness of the writing profession than any other people I have known on the earth. It is for this reason, I think, that one finds among a great number of our people, I mean the laboring, farming sort of people from which I came, a kind of great wonder and doubt and romantic feeling about writers so that it is hard for them to understand that a writer may be one of them and not a man far away like Lord Byron or Tennyson or Percy Bysshe Shelley. Then there is another kind of American who has come from the more educated, university-going kind of people, and these people also become fascinated with the glamor and difficulty of writing, but in a different way. They get more involved or fancy than the most involved and fancy European people of this sort. They become more "Flauberty" than Flaubert. They establish little magazines that not only split a hair with the best of them, but they split more hairs than Europeans think of splitting. The Europeans say: "Oh God, where did these people, these aesthetic Americans, ever come from?" Well, we have known it all. I think all of us who have tried to write in this country may have fallen in between these two groups of well meaning and misguided people, and if we become writers finally, it is in spite of each of them.

I don't know how I became a writer, but I think it was because of a certain force in me that had to write and that finally burst through and found a channel. My people were of the working class of people. My father, a stonecutter, was a man with a great respect and veneration for literature. He had a tremendous memory, and he loved poetry, and the poetry that he loved best was naturally of the rhetorical kind that such a man would like. Nevertheless it was good poetry, Hamlet's Soliloquy, "Macbeth," Mark Antony's Funeral Oration, Grey's "Elegy," and all the rest of it. I heard it all as a child; I memorized and learned it all.

He sent me to college to the state university. The desire to write, which had been strong during all my days in high school, grew stronger still. I was editor of the college paper, the college magazine, etc., and in my last year or two I was a member of a course in playwriting which had just been established there. I wrote several little one-act plays, still thinking I would become a lawyer or a newspaper man, never daring to believe I could seriously become a writer. Then I went to Harvard, wrote some more plays there, became obsessed with the idea that I had to be a playwright, left Harvard, had my plays rejected, and finally in the autumn of 1926, how, why, or in what manner I have never exactly been able to determine, but probably because the force in me that had to write at length sought out its channel, I began to write my first book in London. I was living all alone at that time. I had two rooms—a bedroom and a sitting room —in a little square in Chelsea in which all the houses had that familiar, smoked brick and cream-yellow-plaster look of London houses. They looked exactly alike.

As I say, I was living alone at that time and in a foreign country. I did not know why I was there or what the direction of my life should be, and that was the way I began to write my book. I think that is one of the hardest times a writer goes through. There is no standard, no outward judgment, by which he can measure what he has done. By day I would write for hours in big ledgers which I had bought for the purpose; then at night I would lie in bed and fold my hands behind my head and think of what I had done that day and hear the solid, leather footbeat of the London bobby as he came by my window, and remember that I was born in North Carolina and wonder why the hell I was now in London lying in the darkened bed, and thinking about words I had that day put down on paper. I would get a great, hollow, utterly futile feeling inside me, and then I would get up and switch on the light and read the words I had written that day, and then I would wonder: why am I here now? why have I come?

By day there would be the great, dull roar of London, the gold, yellow, foggy light you have there in October. The manswarmed and old, weblike, smoky London! And I loved the place, and I loathed it and abhorred it. I knew no one there, and I had been a child in North Carolina long ago, and I was living there in two rooms in the huge octopal and illimitable web of that overwhelming city. I did not know why I had come, why I was there.

I worked there every day with such feelings as I have described, and came back to America in the winter and worked here. I would teach all day and write all night, and finally about two and a half years after I had begun the book in London, I finished it in New York.

I should like to tell about this, too. I was very young at the time, and I had the kind of wild, exultant vigor which a man has at that period of his life. The book took hold of me and possessed me. In a way, I think it shaped itself. Like every young man, I was strongly under the influence of writers I admired. One of the chief writers at that time was Mr. James Joyce with his book *Ulysses*. The book that I was writing was much influenced, I believe, by his own book, and yet the powerful energy and fire of my own youth played over and, I think, possessed it all. Like Mr. Joyce, I wrote about things that I had known, the immediate life and experience that had been familiar to me in my childhood. Unlike Mr. Joyce, I had no literary experience. I had never had anything published before. My feeling toward writers, publishers, books, that whole fabulous far-away world, was almost as romantically unreal as when I was a child. And yet my book, the characters with which I had peopled it, the color and the weather of the universe which I had created, had possessed me, and so I wrote and wrote with that bright flame with which a young man writes who never has been published, and who yet is sure all will be good and must go well. This is a curious thing and hard to tell about, yet easy to understand in every writer's mind. I wanted fame, as every youth who ever wrote must want it, and yet fame was a shining, bright, and most uncertain thing.

The book was finished in my twenty-eighth year. I knew no publishers and no writers. A friend of mine took the huge manuscript— it was about 350,000 words long—and sent it to a publisher whom she knew. In a few days, a week or two, I received an answer from this man saying that the book could not be published. The gist of what he said was that his house had published several books like it the year before, that all of them had failed, and that, further, the book in its present form was so amateurish, autobiographical, and unskilful that a publisher could not risk a chance on it. I was, myself, so depressed and weary by this time, the illusion of creation which had sustained me for two and a half years had so far worn off, that I believed what the man said. At that time I was a teacher in one of New York's great universities, and when the year came to a close, I went abroad. It was only after I had been abroad almost six months that news came to me from another publisher in America that he had read my manuscript and would like to talk to me about it as soon as I came home.

I came home on New Year's Day that year. The next day I called up the publisher who had written me. He asked me if I would come to his office and talk to him. I went at once, and before I had left his office that morning, I had signed a contract and had a check for five hundred dollars in my hand.

It was the first time, so far as I can remember, that any one had concretely suggested to me that anything I had written was worth as much as fifteen cents, and I know that I left the publisher's office that day and entered into the great swarm of men and women who passed constantly along Fifth Avenue at 48th Street and presently I found myself at 110th Street, and from that day to this I have never known how I got there.

For the next six or eight months I taught at the university and worked upon the manuscript of my book with this editor. The book appeared in the month of October, 1929. The whole experience still had elements of that dream-like terror and unreality that writing had had for me when I had first begun it seriously and had lain in my room in London with my hands below my head and thought, why am I here? The awful, utter nakedness of print, that thing which is for all of us so namelessly akin to shame, came closer day by day. That I had wanted this exposure, I could not believe. It seemed to me that I had shamelessly exposed myself and yet that subtle drug of my desire and my creating held me with a serpent's eye, and I could do no other. I turned at last to this editor who had worked with me and found me, and I asked him if he could foretell the end and verdict of my labor. He said that he would rather tell me nothing, that he could not prophesy or know what profit I would have. He said, "All that I know is that they cannot let it go, they cannot ignore it. The book will find its way."

And that fairly describes what happened. I have read in recent months that this first book was received with what is called a "storm of critical applause," but this really did not happen. It got some wonderful reviews in some places; it got some unfavorable reviews in others, but it unquestionably did have a good reception for a first book, and what was best of all, as time went on, it continued to make friends among people who read books. It continued to sell over a period of four or five years in the publisher's edition, and later in a cheaper edition, The Modern Library, it renewed its life and began to sell again. The upshot of it was that after the publication of this book in the autumn of 1929, I found myself with a position as a writer. And here one of the first of my great lessons as a writer began.

Up to this time I had been a young man who wanted to be a writer more than anything on earth and who had created his first book in a great blaze of illusion which a young writer must feel when he has no evidence except his hope to drive him on. Now, in a certain measure, this had changed. I had been a writer in hope and in desire before and now I was a writer in fact. I would read about myself, for example, as one of the "younger American writers." I was a person who, some of the critics said, was to be watched. They were looking forward to my future book with interest and with a certain amount of apprehension. Here, too, my education as a writer was increasing all the time. Now, indeed, I could hear myself discussed, and somehow the fact was far more formidable than I had dreamed that it could be. It worried me, confused me, gave me a strange feeling of guilt and responsibility. I was a young American writer, and they had hopes and fears about my future, and what would I do, or would it be anything, nothing, much, or little? Would the faults which they had found in my work grow worse or would I conquer them? Was I another flash in the pan? Would I come through? What would happen to me?

I let it worry me. I would go home at night and look around my room and see that morning's coffee cup still unwashed and books on the floor and a shirt where I had thrown it the night before and great stacks of manuscript and everything so common and familiar looking and so disorderly, and then I would think that I was now "a young American writer"; that somehow I was practising an imposture on my readers and my critics because my shirt looked the way it did and my books and my bed—not, you understand, because they were disorderly, common, familiar, but just because they looked the way they did.

But now another fact began to gnaw a way into my consciousness.

The critics had begun to ask questions about the second book, and so now I had to think about the second one as well. I had always wanted to think about the second one and the thirty-second one and the fifty-second one. I had been sure that I had a hundred books in me, that all of them would be good, that each of them would make me famous. But here again was a strange and jolting transition from wild hope and exultant conviction; and plain, blazing fact remained. Now that I had actually written one book and *they,* the actual readers and critics who had read it, were looking for a second, I was up against it. I was not up against it the way I dreaded, I was just up against it cold and hard as one comes up against a wall. I was a writer. I had made the writer's life my life; there was no going back; I had to go on. What could I do? After the first book there had to be a second book. What was the second book to be about? Where would it come from?

This inexorable fact, although it became more and more pressing, did not bother me so much at first. Rather I was concerned with many other things that had to do with the publication of that first book, and as before, I had foreseen none of them. In the first place, I had not foreseen one fact which becomes absolutely plain after a man has written a book, but which he cannot foresee until he has written one. This fact is that one writes a book not in order to remember it, but in order to forget it, and now this fact was evident. As soon as the book was in print, I began to forget about it, I wanted to forget about it, I didn't want people to talk to me or question me about it. I just wanted them to leave me alone and shut up about it. And yet I longed desperately for my book's success. I wanted it to have the position of proud esteem and honor in the world that I longed for it to have—I wanted, in short, to be a successful and a famous man, and I wanted to lead the same kind of obscure and private life I'd always had and not to be told about my fame and success.

From this problem, another painful and difficult situation was produced. I had written my book, more or less, directly from the experience of my own life, and, furthermore, I now think that I may have written it with a certain naked intensity of spirit which is likely to characterize the earliest work of a young writer. At any rate, I can honestly say that I did not foresee what was to happen. I was surprised not only by the kind of response my book had with the critics and the general public, I was most of all surprised with the response it had in my native town. I had thought there might be a hundred people in that town who would read the book, but if there were a hundred outside of the negro population, the blind, and the positively illiterate who did not read it, I do not know where they are. For months the town seethed with a fury of resentment which I had not believed possible. The book was denounced from the pulpit by the ministers of the leading churches. Men collected on street corners to denounce it. For weeks the women's clubs, bridge parties, teas, receptions, book clubs, the whole complex fabric of a small town's social life was absorbed by an outraged clamor. I received anonymous letters full of vilification and abuse, one which threatened to kill me if I came back home, others which were merely obscene. One venerable old lady, whom I had known all my life, wrote me that although she had never believed in lynch law, she would do nothing to prevent a mob from dragging my "big overgroan karkus" across the public square. She informed me further, that my mother had taken to her bed "as white as a ghost" and would "never rise from it again."

There were many other venomous attacks from my home town and for the first time I learned another lesson which every young writer has got to learn. And that lesson is the naked, blazing power of print. At that time it was for me a bewildering and almost overwhelming situation. My joy at the success my book had won was mixed with bitter chagrin at its reception in my native town. And yet I think I learned something from that experience, too. For the first time I was forced to consider squarely this problem: where does the material of an artist come from? What are the proper uses of that material, and how far must his freedom in the use of that material be controlled by his responsibility as a member of society? This is a difficult problem, and I have by no means come to the bottom of it yet. Perhaps I never shall, but as a result of all the distress which I suffered at that time and which others may have suffered on account of me, I have done much thinking and arrived at certain conclusions.

My book was what is often referred to as an autobiographical novel. I protested against this term in a preface to the book upon the grounds that any serious work of creation is of necessity autobiographical and that few more autobiographical works than *Gulliver's Travels* has ever been written. I added that Dr. Johnson had remarked that a man might turn over half the volumes in his library to make a single book, and that in a similar way, a novelist might turn over half the characters in his native town to make a single figure for his novel. In spite of this the people in my native town were not persuaded or appeased, and the charge of autobiography was brought against me in many other places.

As I have said, my conviction is that all serious creative work must be at bottom autobiographical, and that a man must use the material and experience of his own life if he is to create anything that has substantial value. But I also believe now that the young writer is often led through inexperience to a use of the materials of life which are, perhaps, somewhat too naked and direct for the purpose of a work of art. The thing a young writer is likely to do is to confuse the limits between actuality and reality. He tends unconsciously to describe an event in such a way because it actually happened that way, and from an artistic point of view, I can now see that this is wrong. It is not, for example, important that one remembers a beautiful woman of easy virtue as having come from the state of Kentucky in the year 1907. She could perfectly well have come from Idaho or Texas or Nova Scotia. The important thing really is only to express as well as possible the character and quality of the beautiful woman of easy virtue. But the young writer, chained to fact and to his own inexperience, as yet unliberated by maturity, is likely to argue, "she must be described as coming from Kentucky because that is where she actually did come from."

In spite of this, it is impossible for a man who has the stuff of creation in him to make a literal transcription of his own experience. Everything in a work of art is changed and transfigured by the personality of the artist. And as far as my own first book is concerned, I can truthfully say that I do not believe that there is a single page of it that is true to fact. And from this circumstance, also, I learned another curious thing about writing. For although my book was not true to fact, it was true to the general experience of the town I came from and I hope, of course, to the general experience of all men living. The best way I can describe the situation is this: it was as if I were a sculptor who had found a certain kind of clay with which to model. Now a farmer who knew well the neighborhood from which this clay had come might pass by and find the sculptor at his work and say to him, "I know the farm from which you got that clay." But it would be unfair of him to say, "I know the figure, too." Now I think what happened in my native town is that having seen the clay, they became immediately convinced that they recognized the figure, too, and the results of this misconception were so painful and ludicrous that the telling of it is almost past belief.

It was my experience to be assured by people from my native town not only that they remembered incidents and characters in my first book, which may have had some basis in actuality, but also that they remembered incidents which so far as I know had no historical basis whatever. For example, there was one scene in the book in which a stonecutter is represented as selling to a notorious woman of the town a statue of a marble angel which he has treasured for many years. So far as I know, there was no basis in fact for this story, and yet I was informed by several people later that they not only remembered the incident perfectly, but had actually been witnesses to the transaction. Nor was this the end of the story. I heard that one of the newspapers sent a reporter and a photographer to the cemetery and a photograph was printed in the paper with a statement to the effect that the angel was the now famous angel which had stood upon the stonecutter's porch for so many years and had given the title to my book. The unfortunate part of this proceeding was that I had never seen or heard of this angel before, and that this angel was, in fact, erected over the grave of a well known Methodist lady who had died a few years before and that her indignant family had immediately written the paper to demand a retraction of its story, saying that their mother had been in no way connected with the infamous book or the infamous angel which had given the infamous book its name. Such, then, were some of the unforseen difficulties with which I was confronted after the publication of my first book.

Month was passing into month; I had had a success. The way was opened to me. There was only one thing for me to do and that was work, and I was spending my time consuming myself with anger, grief, and useless passion about the reception the book had had in my native town, or wasting myself again in exuberant elation because of the critics and the readers' praise, or in anguish and bitterness because of their ridicule. For the first time, I realized the nature of one of the artist's greatest conflicts, and was faced with the need of meeting it. For the first time I saw not only that the artist must live and sweat and love and suffer and enjoy as other men, but that the artist must also work as other men and that furthermore, he must work even while these common events of life are going on. It seems a simple and banal assertion, but I learned it hardly, and in one of the worst moments of my life. There is no such thing as an artistic vacuum; there is no such thing as a time when the artist may work in a delightful atmosphere, free of agony that other men must know, or if the artist ever does find such a time, it is something not to be hoped for, something not to be sought for indefinitely.

At any rate, while my life and energy were absorbed in the emotional vortex which my first book had created, I was getting almost no work done on the second. And now I was faced with another fundamental problem which every young writer must meet squarely if he is to continue. How is a man to get his writing done? How long should he work at writing, and how often? What kind of method, if any, must he find in following his work? I suddenly found myself face to face with the grim necessity of constant, daily work. And as simple as this discovery may seem to every one, I was not prepared for it. A young writer without a public does not feel the sense of necessity, the pressure of time, as does a writer who has been published and who must now begin to think of time schedules, publishing seasons, the completion of his next book. I realized suddenly with a sense of definite shock that I had let six months go by since the publication of my first book and that, save for a great many notes and fragments, I had done nothing. Meanwhile, the book continued to sell slowly but steadily, and in February, 1930, about five months after its publication, I found it possible to resign from the faculty of New York University and devote my full time to the preparation of a second book. That spring I was also fortunate enough to be awarded the Guggenheim Fellowship which would enable me to live and work abroad for a year. And accordingly at the beginning of May, I went abroad again.

I was in Paris for a couple of months, until the middle of July, and although I now compelled myself to work for four or five hours a day, my effort at composition was still confused and broken, and there was nothing yet that had the structural form and unity of a book. The life of the great city fascinated me as it had always done, but also aroused all the old feelings of naked homelessness, rootlessness, and loneliness which I have always felt there. It was, and has always remained for me, at least, the most homesick city in the world; the place where I have felt mostly an alien and a stranger, and certainly for me as fascinating and seductive as the city is, it has never been a good place to work. But here I would like to say something about places to work because that is another problem which causes young writers a great deal of doubt, uncertainty, and confusion, and I think, uselessly.

I had gone through the whole experience and now I was almost done with it. I had come to Paris first six years before, a youth of twenty-four, filled with all the romantic faith and foolishness which many young men at that time felt when they saw Paris. I had come there that first time, so I told myself, to work, and so glamorous was the magic name of Paris at that time, that I really thought one could work far better there than any anywhere on earth; that it was a place where the very air was impregnated with the energies of art; where the artist was bound to find a more fortunate and happy life than he could possibly find in America. Now I had come to see that this was wrong. I had come to understand very plainly that what many of us were doing in those years when we fled from our own country and sought refuge abroad was not really looking for a place to work, but looking for a place where we could escape from work; that what we were really fleeing from in those years was not the Philistinism, the materialism, and ugliness in American life which we said we were fleeing from, but from the necessity of grappling squarely with ourselves and the necessity of finding in ourselves, somehow, the stuff to live by, to get from our own lives and our own experience the substance of our art which every man who ever wrote a living thing has had to get out of himself and without which he is lost.

The place to work! Yes, the place to work *was* Paris; it *was* Spain; it *was* Italy and Capri and Majorca, but great God, it was also Keokuk, and Portland, Maine, and Denver, Colorado, and Yancey County, North Carolina, and wherever we might be, if work was there within us at the time. If this was all that I had learned from these voyages to Europe, if the price of all this wandering had been just this simple lesson, it would have been worth the price, but that was not all. I had found out during these years that the way to discover one's own country was to leave it; that the way to find America was to find it in one's heart, one's memory, and one's spirit, and in a foreign land.

I think I may say that I discovered America during these years abroad out of my very need of her. The huge gain of this discovery seemed to come directly from my sense of loss. I had been to Europe five times now; each time I had come with delight, with maddening eagerness to return, and each time how, where, and in what way I did not know, I had felt the bitter ache of homelessness, a desperate long-ing for America, an overwhelming desire to return.

During that summer in Paris, I think I felt this great homesick-ness more than ever before, and I really believe that from this emo-tion, this constant and almost intolerable effort of memory and desire, the material and the structure of the books I now began to write were derived.

The quality of my memory is characterized, I believe, in a more than ordinary degree by the intensity of its sense impressions, its power to evoke and bring back the odors, sounds, colors, shapes, and feel of things with concrete vividness. Now my memory was at work night and day, in a way that I could at first neither check nor control and that swarmed unbidden in a stream of blazing pageantry across my mind, with the million forms and substances of the life that I had left, which was my own, America. I would be sitting, for example, on the terrace of a café watching the flash and play of life before me on the Avenue de l'Opéra and suddenly I would re-member the iron railing that goes along the boardwalk at Atlantic City. I could see it instantly just the way it was, the heavy iron pipe; its raw, galvanized look; the way the joints were fitted together. It was all so vivid and concrete that I could feel my hand upon it and know the exact dimensions, its size and weight and shape. And sud-denly I would realize that I had never seen any railing that looked like this in Europe. And this utterly familiar, common thing would suddenly be revealed to me with all the wonder with which we dis-cover a thing which we have seen all our life and yet have never known before. Or again, it would be a bridge, the look of an old iron bridge across an American river, the sound the train makes as it goes across it; the spoke-and-hollow rumble of the ties below; the look of the muddy banks; the slow, thick, yellow wash of an Amer-ican river; an old flat-bottomed boat half filled with water stogged in the muddy bank; or it would be, most lonely and haunting of all the sounds I know, the sound of a milk wagon as it entered an American street just at the first gray of the morning, the slow and lonely clopping of the hoof upon the street, the jink of bottles, the sudden rattle of a battered old milk can, the swift and hurried footsteps of the milkman, and again the jink of bottles, a low word spoken to his horse, and then the great, slow, clopping hoof receding into silence, and then quietness and a bird song rising in the street again. Or it would be a little wooden shed out in the country two miles from my home town where people waited for the street car, and I could see and feel again the dull and rusty color of the old green paint and see and feel all of the initials that had been carved out with jackknives on the planks and benches within the shed, and smell the warm and sultry smell so resinous and so thrilling, so filled with a strange and nameless excitement of an unknown joy, a coming prophecy, and hear the street car as it came to a stop, the moment of brooding, drowzing silence; a hot thrum and drowsy stitch at three o'clock; the smell of grass and hot sweet clover; and then the sudden sense of absence, loneliness and departure when the street car had gone and there was nothing but the hot and drowsy stitch at three o'clock again.

Or again, it would be an American street with all its jumble of a thousand ugly architectures. It would be Montague Street or Fulton Street in Brooklyn, or Eleventh Street in New York, or other streets where I had lived; and suddenly I would see the gaunt and savage webbing of the elevated structure along Fulton Street, and how the light swarmed through in dusty, broken bars, and I could remember the old, familiar rusty color, that incomparable rusty color that gets into so many things here in America. And this also would be like something I had seen a million times and lived with all my life.

I would sit there, looking out upon the Avenue de l'Opéra and my life would ache with the whole memory of it; the desire to see it again; somehow to find a word for it; a language that would tell its shape, its color, the way we have all known and felt and seen it. And when I understood this thing, I saw that I must find for myself the tongue to utter what I knew but could not say. And from the moment of that discovery, the line and purpose of my life was shaped. The end toward which every energy of my life and talent would be henceforth directed was in such a way as this defined. It was as if I had discovered a whole new universe of chemical elements and had begun to see certain relations between some of them but had by no means begun to organize the whole series into a harmonious and coherent union. From this time on, I think my efforts might be described as the effort to complete that organization, to discover that articulation for which I strove, to bring about that final coherent union. I know that I have failed thus far in doing so, but I believe I understand pretty thoroughly just where the nature of my failure lies, and of course my deepest and most earnest hope is that the time will come when I shall not fail.

At any rate, from this time on the general progress of the three books which I was to write in the next four and a half years could be fairly described in somewhat this way. It was a progress that began in a whirling vortex and a creative chaos and that proceeded slowly at the expense of infinite confusion, toil, and error toward clarification and the articulation of an ordered and formal structure. An extraordinary image remains to me from that year, the year I spent abroad when the material of these books first began to take on an articulate form. It seemed that I had inside me, swelling and gathering all the time, a huge black cloud, and that this cloud was loaded with electricity, pregnant, crested, with a kind of hurricane violence that could not be held in check much longer; that the moment was approaching fast when it must break. Well, all I can say is that the storm did break. It broke that summer while I was in Switzerland. It came in torrents, and it is not over yet.

I cannot really say the book was written. It was something that took hold of me and possessed me, and before I was done with it— that is, before I finally emerged with the first completed part—it seemed to me that it had done for me. It was exactly as if this great black storm cloud I have spoken of had opened up and, mid flashes of lightning, was pouring from its depth a torrential and ungovernable flood. Upon that flood everything was swept and borne along as by a great river. And I was borne along with it.

There was nothing at first which could be called a novel. I wrote about night and darkness in America, and the faces of the sleepers in ten thousand little towns; and of the tides of sleep and how the rivers flowed forever in the darkness. I wrote about the hissing glut of tides upon ten thousand miles of coast; of how the moonlight blazed down on the wilderness and filled the cat's cold eye with blazing yellow. I wrote about death and sleep, and of that enfabled rock of life we call the city. I wrote about October, of great trains that thundered through the night, of ships and stations in the morning; of men in harbors and the traffic of the ships.

I spent the winter of that year in England from October until March, and here perhaps because of the homely familiarity of the English life, the sense of order and repose which such a life can give one, my work moved forward still another step from this flood tide chaos of creation. For the first time the work began to take on the lineaments of design. These lineaments were still confused and broken, sometimes utterly lost, but now I really did get the sense at last that I was working on a great block of marble, shaping a figure which no one but its maker could as yet define, but which was emerging more and more into the sinewy lines of composition.

From the beginning—and this was one fact that in all my times of hopelessness returned to fortify my faith in my conviction—the idea, the central legend that I wished my book to express had not changed. And this central idea was this: the deepest search in life, it seemed to me, the thing that in one way or another was central to all living was man's search to find a father, not merely the father of his flesh, not merely the lost father of his youth, but the image of a strength and wisdom external to his need and superior to his hunger, to which the belief and power of his own life could be united.

Yet I was terribly far away from the actual accomplishment of a book—how far away I could not at that time foresee. But four more years would have to pass before the first of a series of books on which I was now embarked would be ready for the press, and if I could have known that in those next four years there would be packed a hundred lives of birth and death, despair, defeat, and triumph and the sheer exhaustion of a brute fatigue, I do not know whether or not I could have found the power within myself to continue. But I was still sustained by the exuberant optimism of youth. My temperament, which is pessimistic about many things, has always been a curiously sanguine one concerning time, and although more than a year had now gone by and I had done no more than write great chants on death and sleep, prepare countless notes and trace here

and there the first dim outlines of a formal pattern, I was confident
that by the spring or the fall of the next year my book would somehow miraculously be ready.

So far as I can describe with any accuracy, the progress of that
winter's work in England was not along the lines of planned design, but along this line that I have mentioned—writing some of
the sections which I knew would have to be in the book. Meanwhile
what was really going on in my whole creative consciousness, during
all this time, although I did not realize it at the moment, was this:
What I was really doing, what I had been doing all the time since
my discovery of my America in Paris the summer before, was to
explore day by day and month by month with a fanatical intensity,
the whole material domain of my resources as a man and as a writer.
This exploration went on for a period which I can estimate con-
servatively as two years and a half. It is still going on, although not
with the same all-absorbing concentration, because the work it led
to, the work that after infinite waste and labor it helped me wonderfully to define, that work has reached such a state of final definition that the immediate task of finishing it is the one that now occupies the energy and interest of my life.

In a way, during that period of my life, I think I was like the
Ancient Mariner who told the Wedding Guest that his frame was
wrenched by the woeful agony which forced him to begin his tale
before it left him free. In my own experience, my wedding guests
were the great ledgers in which I wrote, and the tale which I told
to them would have seemed, I am afraid, completely incoherent,
as meaningless as Chinese characters, had any reader seen them. I
could by no means hope to give a comprehensive idea of the whole
extent of this labor because three years of work and perhaps a million and a half words went into these books. It included everything
from gigantic and staggering lists of the towns, cities, counties, states,
and countries I had been in, to minutely thorough, desperately
evocative descriptions of the undercarriage, the springs, wheels,
flanges, axle rods, color, weight, and quality of the day coach of an
American railway train. There were lists of the rooms and houses
in which I had lived or in which I had slept for at least a night,
together with the most accurate and evocative descriptions of those
rooms that I could write—their size, their shape, the color and de-

sign of the wallpaper, the way a towel hung down, the way a chair creaked, a streak of water rust upon the ceiling. There were countless charts, catalogues, descriptions that I can only classify here under the general heading of Amount and Number. What were the total combined populations of all the countries in Europe and America? In how many of those countries had I had some personal and vital experience? In the course of my twenty-nine or thirty years of living, how many people had I seen? How many had I passed by on the streets? How many had I seen on trains and subways, in theatres, at baseball or football games? With how many had I actually had some vital and illuminating experience, whether of joy, pain, anger, pity, love, or simple casual companionship, however brief?

In addition, one might come upon other sections under some such cryptic heading as "Where now?" Under such a heading as this, there would be brief notations of those thousands of things which all of us have seen for just a flash, a moment in our lives, which seem to be of no consequence whatever at the moment that we see them, and which live in our minds and hearts forever, which are somehow pregnant with all the joy and sorrow of the human destiny, and which we know, somehow, are therefore more important than many things of more apparent consequences. "Where now?" Some quiet steps that came and passed along a leafy night-time street in summer in a little town down South long years ago; a woman's voice, her sudden burst of low and tender laughter; then the voices and the footsteps going, silence, the leafy rustle of the trees. "Where now?" Two trains that met and paused at a little station at some little town at some unknown moment upon the huge body of the continent; a girl who looked and smiled from the window of the other train; another passing in a motor car on the streets of Norfolk; the winter boarders in a little boarding house down South twenty years ago; Miss Florrie Mangle, the trained nurse; Miss Jessie Rimmer, the cashier at Reed's drug store; Doctor Richards, the clairvoyant; the pretty girl who cracked the whip and thrust her head into the lion's mouth with Johnny J. Jones Carnival and Combined Shows.

"Where now?" It went beyond the limits of man's actual memory. It went back to the farthest adyt of his childhood before conscious

memory had begun, the way he thought he must have felt the sun
one day and heard Peagram's cow next door wrenching the coarse
grass against the fence, or heard the street car stop upon the hill
above his father's house at noon; and Earnest Peagram coming home
to lunch, his hearty voice in midday greeting; and then the street
car going, the sudden lonely green-gold silence of the street car's
absence and an iron gate slamming, then the light of that lost day
fades out. "Where now?" He can recall no more and does not know
if what he has recalled is fact or fable or a fusion of the two. Where
now—in these great ledger books, month after month, I wrote such
things as this, not only the concrete, material record of man's ordered memory, but all the things he scarcely dares to think he has
remembered; all the flicks and darts and haunting lights that flash
across the mind of man that will return unbidden at an unexpected
moment: a voice once heard; a face that vanished; the way the sunlight came and went; the rustling of a leaf upon a bough; a stone,
a leaf, a door.

It may be objected, it has been objected already by certain critics,
that in such research as I have here attempted to describe there is
a quality of intemperate excess, an almost insane hunger to devour
the entire body of human experience, to attempt to include more,
experience more, than the measure of one life can hold, or than the
limits of a single work of art can well define. I readily admit the
validity of this criticism. I think I realize as well as any one the
fatal dangers that are consequent to such a ravenous desire, the
damage it may wreak upon one's life and on one's work. But having
had this thing within me, it was in no way possible for me to reason
it out of me, no matter how cogently my reason worked against it.
The only way I could meet it was to meet it squarely, not with reason
but with life.

It was part of my life; for many years it was my life; and the only
way I could get it out of me was to live it out of me. And that is what
I did. I have not wholly succeeded in that purpose yet, but I have
succeeded better than I at one time dared to hope. And now I really
believe that so far as the artist is concerned, the unlimited extent of
human experience is not so important for him as the depth and
intensity with which he experiences things. I also know now that
it is a great deal more important to have known one hundred living

men and women in New York, to have understood their lives, to have got, somehow, at the root and source from which their natures came than to have seen or passed or talked with 7,000,000 people upon the city streets. And what finally I should most like to say about this research which I have attempted to describe is this: That foolish and mistaken as much of it may seem, the total quality, end, and impact of that whole experience was not useless or excessive. And from my own point of view, at least, it is in its whole implication the one thing I may have to tell about my experience as a writer which may be of some concrete value to other people. I consider this experience on the whole the most valuable and practical in my whole writing life thus far. With all the waste and error and confusion it led me into, it brought me closer to a concrete definition of my resources, a true estimate of my talents at this period of my life, and, most of all, toward a rudimentary, a just-beginning, but a living apprehension of the articulation I am looking for, the language I have got to have if, as an artist, my life is to proceed and grow, than any other thing that has ever happened to me.

I know the door is not yet open. I know the tongue, the speech, the language that I seek is not yet found, but I believe with all my heart that I have found the way, have made a channel, am started on my first beginning. And I believe with all my heart, also, that each man for himself and in his own way, each man who ever hopes to make a living thing out of the substances of his one life, must find that way, that language, and that door—must find it for himself as I have tried to do.

When I returned to America in the spring of 1931, although I had three or four hundred thousand words of material, I had nothing that could be published as a novel. Almost a year and a half had elapsed since the publication of my first book and already people had begun to ask that question which is so well meant, but which as year followed year was to become more intolerable to my ears than the most deliberate mockery: "Have you finished your next book yet?" "When is it going to be published?"

At this time I was sure that a few months of steady work would bring the book to completion. I found a place, a little basement flat in the Assyrian quarter in South Brooklyn, and there I went about my task.

The spring passed into the summer; the summer, into autumn. I was working hard, day after day, and still nothing that had the unity and design of a single work appeared. October came and with it a second full year since the publication of my first book. And now, for the first time, I was irrevocably committed so far as the publication of my book was concerned. I began to feel the sensation of pressure, and of naked desperation, which was to become almost maddeningly intolerable in the next three years. For the first time I began to realize that my project was much larger than I thought it would be. I had still believed at the time of my return from Europe that I was writing a single book, which would be comprised within the limits of about 200,000 words. Now as scene followed scene, as character after character came into being, as my understanding of my material became more comprehensive, I discovered that it would be impossible to write the book I had planned within the limits I had thought would be sufficient.

All of this time I was being baffled by a certain time element in the book, by a time relation which could not be escaped, and for which I was now desperately seeking some structural channel. There were three time elements inherent in the material. The first and most obvious was an element of actual present time, an element which carried the narrative forward, which represented characters and events as living in the present and moving forward into an immediate future. The second time element was of past time, one which represented these same characters as acting and as being acted upon by all the accumulated impact of man's experience so that each moment of their lives was conditioned not only by what they experienced in that moment, but by all that they had experienced up to that moment. In addition to these two time elements, there was a third which I conceived as being time immutable, the time of rivers, mountains, oceans, and the earth; a kind of eternal and unchanging universe of time against which would be projected the transience of man's life, the bitter briefness of his day. It was the tremendous problem of these three time elements that almost defeated me and that cost me countless hours of anguish in the years that were to follow.

As I began to realize the true nature of the task I had set for myself, the image of the river began to haunt my mind. I actually felt that I had a great river thrusting for release inside of me and that I had to find a channel into which its flood-like power could pour. I knew I had to find it or I would be destroyed in the flood of my own creation, and I am sure that every artist who ever lived has had the same experience.

Meanwhile, I was being baffled by a fixed and impossible idea whose error at the time I did not fully apprehend. I was convinced at that time that this whole gigantic plan had to be realized within the limits of a single book which would be called "The October Fair." It was not until more than a year had passed, when I realized finally that what I had to deal with was material which covered almost 150 years in history, demanded the action of more than 2000 characters, and would in its final design include almost every racial type and social class of American life, that I realized that even the pages of a book of 200,000 words were wholly inadequate for the purpose.

How did I finally arrive at this conclusion? I think it is not too much to say that I simply wrote myself into it. During all that year, I was writing furiously, feeling now the full pressure of inexorable time, the need to finish something. I wrote like mad; I finished scene after scene, chapter after chapter. The characters began to come to life, to grow and multiply until they were numbered by the hundreds, but so huge was the extent of my design, as I now desperately realized, that I can liken these chapters only to a row of lights which one sometimes sees at night from the windows of a speeding train, strung out across the dark and lonely countryside.

I would work furiously day after day until my creative energies were utterly exhausted, and although at the end of such a period I would have written perhaps as much as 200,000 words, enough in itself to make a very long book, I would realize with a feeling of horrible despair that what I had completed was only one small section of a single book.

During this time I reached that state of naked need and utter isolation which every artist has got to meet and conquer if he is to survive at all. Before this I had been sustained by that delightful illusion of success which we all have when we dream about the books we are going to write instead of actually doing them. Now I was face to face with it, and suddenly I realized that I had committed my life and my integrity so irrevocably to this struggle that I must conquer now or be destroyed. I was alone with my own work, and now I knew that I had to be alone with it, that no one could help me with it now no matter how any one might wish to help. For the first time I realized another naked fact which every artist must know, and that is that in a man's work there are contained not only the seeds of life, but the seeds of death, and that that power of creation which sustains us will also destroy us like a leprosy if we let it rot stillborn in our vitals. I had to get it out of me somehow. I saw that now. And now for the first time a terrible doubt began to creep into my mind that I might not live long enough to get it out of me, that I had created a labor so large and so impossible that the energy of a dozen lifetimes would not suffice for its accomplishment.

During this time, however, I was sustained by one piece of inestimable good fortune. I had for a friend a man of immense and patient wisdom and a gentle but unyielding fortitude. I think that if I was not destroyed at this time by the sense of hopelessness which these gigantic labors had awakened in me, it was largely because of the courage and patience of this man. I did not give in because he would not let me give in, and I think it is also true that at this particular time he had the advantage of being in the position of a skilled observer at a battle. I was myself engaged in that battle, covered by its dust and sweat and exhausted by its struggle, and I understood far less clearly than my friend the nature and the progress of the struggle in which I was engaged. At this time there was little that this man could do except observe, and in one way or another keep me at my task, and in many quiet and marvelous ways he succeeded in doing this.

I was now at the place where I must produce, and even the greatest editor can do little for a writer until he has brought from the secret darkness of his own spirit into the common light of day the completed concrete accomplishment of his imagining. My friend, the editor, has likened his own function at this painful time to that of a man who is trying to hang on to the fin of a plunging whale, but hang on he did, and it is to his tenacity that I owe my final release.

Meanwhile, my creative power was functioning at the highest

intensity it had ever known. I wrote at times without belief that I would ever finish, with nothing in me but black despair, and yet I wrote and wrote and could not give up writing. And it seemed that despair itself was the very goad that urged me on, that made me write even when I had no belief that I would ever finish. It seemed to me that my life in Brooklyn, although I had been there only two and a half years, went back through centuries of time, through ocean depths of black and bottomless experience which no ordinary scale of hours would ever measure. People have sometimes asked me what happened to my life during these years. They have asked me how I ever found time to know anything that was going on in the world about me when my life was so completely absorbed by this world of writing. Well, it may seem to be an extraordinary fact, but the truth is that never in my whole life have I lived so fully, have I shared so richly in the common life of man as I did during these three years when I was struggling with the giant problem of my own work.

For one thing, my whole sensory and creative equipment, my powers of feeling and reflection—even the sense of hearing, and above all, my powers of memory, had reached the greatest degree of sharpness that they had ever known. At the end of the day of savage labor, my mind was still blazing with its effort, could by no opiate of reading, poetry, music, alcohol, or any other pleasure, be put at rest. I was unable to sleep, unable to subdue the tumult of these creative energies, and as a result of this condition, for three years I prowled the streets, explored the swarming web of the million-footed city and came to know it as I had never done before. It was a black time in the history of the nation, a black time in my own life and, I suppose, it is but natural that my own memory of it now should be a pretty grim and painful one.

Everywhere around me, during these years, I saw the evidence of an incalculable ruin and suffering. My own people, the members of my own family, had been ruined, had lost all the material wealth and accumulation of a lifetime in what was called the "depression." And that universal calamity had somehow struck the life of almost every one I knew. Moreover, in this endless quest and prowling of the night through the great web and jungle of the city, I saw, lived, felt, and experienced the full weight of that horrible human calamity.

I saw a man whose life had subsided into a mass of shapeless and filthy rags, devoured by vermin; wretches huddled together for a little warmth in freezing cold squatting in doorless closets upon the foul seat of a public latrine within the very shadow, the cold shelter of palatial and stupendous monuments of wealth. I saw acts of sickening violence and cruelty, the menace of brute privilege, a cruel and corrupt authority trampling ruthlessly below its feet the lives of the poor, the weak, the wretched, and defenseless of the earth.

And the staggering impact of this black picture of man's inhumanity to his fellow man, the unending repercussions of these scenes of suffering, violence, oppression, hunger, cold, and filth and poverty going on unheeded in a world in which the rich were still rotten with their wealth left a scar upon my life, a conviction in my soul which I shall never lose.

And from it all, there has come as the final deposit, a burning memory, a certain evidence of the fortitude of man, his ability to suffer and somehow to survive. And it is for this reason now that I think I shall always remember this black period with a kind of joy that I could not at that time have believed possible, for it was during this time that I lived my life through to a first completion, and through the suffering and labor of my own life came to share those qualities in the lives of people all around me. And that is another thing which the making of a book has done for me. It has given my life that kind of growth which I think the fulfilment of each work does give the artist's life, and insofar as I have known these things, I think that they have added to my stature.

The early winter of 1933 arrived and with it, it seemed to me, the final doom of an abysmal failure. I still wrote and wrote, but blindly, hopelessly, like an old horse who trots around in the unending circle of a treadmill and knows no other end nor purpose for his life than this. If I slept at night, it was to sleep an unceasing nightmare of blazing visions that swept across my fevered and unresting mind. And when I woke, it was to wake exhausted, not knowing anything but work, lashing myself on into a hopeless labor, and so furiously at it through the day; and then night again, a frenzied prowling of a thousand streets, and so to bed and sleepless sleep again, the nightmare pageantry to which my consciousness lay chained a spectator.

There was a kind of dream which I can only summarize as dreams of Guilt and Time. Chameleon-like in all their damnable and unending fecundities, they restored to me the whole huge world that I had known, the billion faces and the million tongues, and they restored it to me with the malevolent triumph of a passive and unwanted ease. My daily conflict with Amount and Number, the huge accumulations of my years of struggle with the forms of life, my brutal and unending efforts to record upon my memory each brick and paving stone of every street that I had ever walked upon, each face of every thronging crowd in every city, every country with which my spirit had contested its savage and uneven struggle for supremacy —they all returned now—each stone, each street, each town, each country—yes, even every book in the library whose loaded shelves I had tried vainly to devour at college—they returned upon the wings of these mighty, sad, and somehow quietly demented dreams— I saw and heard and knew them all at once, was instantly without pain or anguish, with the calm consciousness of God, master of the whole universe of life against whose elements I had contended vainly for all-knowledge for so many years. And the fruit of that enormous triumph, the calm and instant passivity of that inhuman and demented immortality, was somehow sadder and more bitter than the most galling bitterness of defeat in my contention with the multitudes of life had ever been.

For above that universe of dreams there shone forever a tranquil, muted, and unchanging light of time. And through the traffic of those thronging crowds—whose faces, whose whole united and divided life was now instantly and without an effort of the will, my *own*—there rose forever the sad unceasing murmurs of the body of this life, the vast recessive fadings of the shadow of man's death that breathes forever with its dirge-like sigh around the huge shores of the world.

And *beyond, beyond*—forever *above, around, behind* the vast and tranquil consciousness of my spirit that now held the earth and all her elements in the huge clasp of its effortless subjection—there dwelt forever the fatal knowledge of my own inexpiable *guilt*.

I did not know what I had done—I only knew that I had ruinously forgotten time, and by so doing had betrayed my brother men.
I had been long from home—why, how, or in what way, I could not
know—but drugged there in the drowsy fumes of some green country of the witches' magic, with something in me dark and full of
grief I could not quite remember. And suddenly I was home again—
walking alone beneath that light of tranquil, quiet, and unchanging
brown, walking the roads, the hill-slopes, and the streets of my familiar country—sometimes the *exact* and *actual* lineaments of home,
my childhood, and my native town, so that not only all that I had
known and remembered—each familiar street and face and house
and every cobblestone upon the pavement—but countless things I
never knew that I had seen, or had forgotten that I ever knew—a
rusty hinge upon the cellar door, the way a stair creaked, or an old
cracked blister of brown paint upon the woodwork by the grate, an
oak tree trunk upon the hill all hollowed out upon one side by a
knotted hole, the glazed pattern of the glass in the front door, the
brass handle of a street-car brake-control, quite rubbed to silver on
one side by the hard grip of the motorman, and covered by a cloth
tobacco sack—such things as these, together with a million others,
returned now to torment my sleep.

And even more than these, more, more familiar even than these
scenes of memory and inheritance, were those landscapes that somehow had been *derived* from them—the streets, the towns, the houses
and the faces that I saw and imagined not the way they *were,* but the
way they *should* be in the unfathomed, strange, and unsuspected
logics of man's brain and heart—and that were, on this account,
more real than real-ness, and more true than home.

I had been long from home—I had grown old in some evil and
enchanted place, I had allowed my life to waste and rot in the sloth-
ful and degrading surfeits of Circean time. And now my life was
lost—my work undone—I had betrayed my home, my friends, my
people in the duties of some solemn and inviolable trust—and suddenly I was home again, and *silence* was my answer!

They did not look at me with looks of bitterness and hate, they
did not lash me with the fierce opprobrium of scorn, or curse me
with the menaces of vengeance and reprisal—oh, if they had, what
balm of anguish and of judgment even curses would have had!—

but instead their look was silence, and their tongue was mute. And again, again, I walked the streets of that familiar town, and after years of absence saw again the features of familiar faces, and heard familiar words, the sounds of well-known voices once again, and with a still and deep amazement saw the shift and interplay of action, the common familiarity of day, the traffic of the streets, and saw that it was all as it had always been, I had forgotten nothing—until I passed them, and death fell.

I walked among them, and their movements ceased, I walked among them, and their tongues were still, I walked among them and they neither moved nor spoke until I passed, and if they looked at me, their eyes were blank with silence and no memory; there was no reproach, no grief, and no contempt, there was no bitterness and scorn—if I had died, there should at least have been the ghost of memory, but it was as if I never had been born. And so I passed them by, and everywhere I trod was death, and when I had gone by, behind me I could hear their voices start again; the clamours of the street, and all the traffic of bright day awoke—but only after I had passed them by!

And so the whole town flowed around me, was behind me, and at once, without a bridge or instant of transition, I was walking on a barren road, across the huge sweep of a treeless waste and barren vacancy and that tranquil, sad and fatal light shone on me from the horror of a planetary vacancy, the lidless and remorseless eye of an unperturbed sky that ate into my naked spirit constantly the acid of unuttered shame.

Another and more pertinent variety of these dreams of Guilt and Time would take this form: It seemed to me that I had gone abroad, was living there, and yet was conscious that I was still employed as an instructor at the university. Remote from all the violence and turmoil of America, the harsh impact of its daily life, remote too from the rasping jargon of the university, its corridors packed with swarthy faces, loud with strident tongues, away from all the jar and rush and hurly-burly of its fevered life, its unwholesome tensions and its straining nerves, I lived my life in foreign luxuries of green and gold. I dreamed my life away in ancient Gothic towns, or in the pleasant romance of a château country, my spirit slid from land to land, from one enchantment to another, my life was passing by in spells of drowsy magic—and yet I was forever haunted by a consciousness of Time and Guilt, the obscure gnawing of forsaken trust. And suddenly I would seem to wake into a full and frenzied consciousness: I had been gone from home a year—my classes at the university had been waiting on me—and instantly I was there again, rushing through those swarming corridors, hurrying frantically from one classroom to another, trying desperately to find the classes I had so forgotten. There was a grotesque and horrible quality of humor in these dreams, which unfortunately I could not appreciate: I was somehow convinced my forlorn classes had been seeking for me for a year, I saw them searching through the mazes of the corridors, prowling among the swarming myriads of their 30,000 fellow students, sitting in patient dejection at the hours appointed for our meetings in classrooms where their absent teacher never entered. And finally—and most horrible of all—I saw the mounting pile of unmarked student themes—those accursed themes that grew in number week by week—that piled up in mountainous and hopeless accumulations—whose white backs were hideously innocent of the scrawled comment with which I had once—tormented by twin agonies of boredom and conscience—covered every scrap of their surface. And now it was too late! Even a month, two weeks, a week— some miracle of time and frenzied labor—might have served somehow to retrieve myself—but now it was the last day of the term, the last class ended, the last irrevocable moment of salvation had gone by. I found myself suddenly standing there in the offices of the English faculty, struck dumb with horror, confronted by the great white mountain of those unmarked themes. I turned, a ring of silent forms encircled me, not staring, not harsh with scorn or anger, and not thrusting close, but just looking at me with the still surveyal of their condemnation. My little Jews stood first, their dark eyes fixed on me with a dejected but unwavering reproach, and behind them stood the jury of my peers, the outer circle of instructors.

They were all there—students, instructors, friends, enemies, and the huge damnation of that pile of unmarked themes—there was no word spoken, nothing but their quiet look of inflexible and unpardoning accusal.

This dream returned to torture sleep a hundred times: Each time I would awake from it in a cold sweat of anguish and of horror, and so strong was the impression of the dream, so real and terrible the spell of its conviction, that sometimes I would wake out of this dream and lie for minutes in cold terror while my mind fought with the phantoms of my sleep to argue me back into reality.

Nor were these dreams of Guilt and Time the only ones: my mind and memory in sleep blazed with a fiery river of unending images: the whole vast reservoirs of memory were exhumed and poured into the torrents of this fiery flood, a million things, once seen and long forgotten, were restored and blazed across my vision in this stream of light—and a million million things unseen, the faces, cities, streets, and landscapes yet unseen and long imagined—the unknown faces yet more real than these that I had known, the unheard voices more familiar than the voices I had heard forever, the unseen patterns, masses, shapes and landscapes in their essence far more real than any actual or substantial fact that I had ever known—all streamed across my fevered and unresting mind the flood of their unending pageantry—and suddenly I knew that it would never end.

For sleep was dead forever, the merciful, dark and sweet oblivions of childhood sleep. The worm had entered at my heart, the worm lay coiled and feeding at my brain, my spirit, and my memory—I knew that finally I had been caught in my own fire, consumed by my own hungers, impaled on the hook of that furious and insatiate desire that had absorbed my life for years. I knew, in short, that one bright cell in the brain or heart or memory would now blaze on forever—by night, by day, through every waking, sleeping moment of my life, the worm would feed and the light be lit,—that no anodyne of food or drink, or friendship, travel, sport or women could ever quench it, and that nevermore until death put its total and conclusive darkness on my life, could I escape.

I knew at last I had become a writer: I knew at last what happens to a man who makes the writer's life his own.

Such was the state my life had come to in the early winter of 1933, and even at that moment, although I could not see it, the end of my huge labor was in sight. In the middle of December of that year the editor, of whom I have spoken, and who, during all this tormented period, had kept a quiet watch upon me, called me to his home and calmly informed me that my book was finished. I could only look at him with stunned surprise, and finally I only could tell him out of the depth of my own hopelessness, that he was mistaken, that the book was not finished, that it could never be completed, that I could write no more. He answered with the same quiet finality that the book was finished whether I knew it or not, and then he told me to go to my room and spend the next week in collecting in its proper order the manuscript which had accumulated during the last two years.

I followed his instructions, still without hope and without belief. I worked for six days sitting in the middle of the floor surrounded by mountainous stacks of typed manuscript on every side. At the end of a week I had the first part of it together, and just two days before Christmas, 1933, I delivered to him the manuscript of "The October Fair," and a few days later, the manuscript of "The Hills Beyond Pentland." The manuscript of "The Fair" was, at that time, something over 1,000,000 words in length. He had seen most of it in its dismembered fragments during the three preceding years, but now, for the first time, he was seeing it in its sequential order, and once again his intuition was right; he had told me the truth when he said that I had finished the book.

It was not finished in any way that was publishable or readable. It was really not a book so much as it was the skeleton of a book, but for the first time in four years the skeleton was all there. An enormous labor of revision, weaving together, shaping, and, above all, cutting remained, but I had the book now so that nothing, not even the despair of my own spirit, could take it from me. He told me so, and suddenly I saw that he was right.

I was like a man who is drowning and who suddenly, at the last gasp of his dying effort, feels earth beneath his feet again. My spirit was borne upward by the greatest triumph it had ever known, and although my mind was tired, my body exhausted, from that moment on I felt equal to anything on earth.

It was evident that many problems were before us, but now we had the thing, and we welcomed the labor before us with happy confidence. In the first place there was the problem of the book's gigantic length. Even in this skeletonized form the manuscript of "The October Fair" was about twelve times the length of the average novel or twice the length of *War and Peace*. It was manifest, therefore, that it would not only be utterly impossible to publish such a manuscript in a single volume, but that even if it were published in several volumes, the tremendous length of such a manuscript would practically annihilate its chances of ever finding a public which would read it.

This problem now faced us, and the editor grappled with it immediately. As his examination of the manuscript of "The October Fair" proceeded, he found that the book did describe two complete and separate cycles. The first of these was a movement which described the period of wandering and hunger in a man's youth. The second cycle described the period of greater certitude, and was dominated by the unity of a single passion. It was obvious, therefore, that what we had in the two cyclic movements of this book was really the material of two completely different chronicles, and although the second of the two was by far the more finished, the first cycle, of course, was the one which logically we ought to complete and publish first, and we decided on this course.

We took the first part first. I immediately prepared a minutely thorough synopsis which described not only the course of the book from first to last, but which also included an analysis of those chapters which had been completed in their entirety, of those which were completed only in part, and of those which had not been written at all, and with this synopsis before us, we set to work immediately to prepare the book for press. This work occupied me throughout the whole of the year 1934. The book was completed at the beginning of 1935, and was published in March of that year under the title of *Of Time and the River*.

In the first place, the manuscript, even in its unfinished form, called for the most radical cutting, and because of the way in which the book had been written, as well as the fatigue which I now felt, I was not well prepared to do by myself the task that lay ahead of us.

Cutting had always been the most difficult and distasteful part of writing to me; my tendency had always been to write rather than to cut. Moreover, whatever critical faculty I may have had concerning my own work had been seriously impaired, for the time being at least, by the frenzied labor of the past four years. When a man's work has poured from him for almost five years like burning lava from a volcano; when all of it, however superfluous, has been given fire and passion by the white heat of his own creative energy, it is very difficult suddenly to become coldly surgical, ruthlessly detached.

To give a few concrete illustrations of the difficulties that now confronted us: The opening section of the book describes the journey of a train across the State of Virginia at night. Its function in the book is simply to introduce some of the chief characters, to indicate a central situation, to give something of the background from which the book proceeds, and perhaps through the movement of the train across the stillness of the earth to establish a certain beat, evoke a certain emotion which is inherent to the nature of the book. Such a section, therefore, undoubtedly serves an important function, but in proportion to the whole purport of the book, its function is a secondary one and must be related to the whole book in a proportionate way.

Now in the original version, the manuscript which described the journey of the train across Virginia at night was considerably longer than the average novel. What was needed was just an introductory chapter or two, and what I had written was over 100,000 words in length, and this same difficulty, this lack of proportion, was also evident in other parts of the manuscript.

What I had written about the great train was really good. But what I had to face, the very bitter lesson that every one who wants to write has got to learn, was that a thing may in itself be the finest piece of writing one has ever done, and yet have absolutely no place in the manuscript one hopes to publish. This is a hard thing, but it must be faced, and so we faced it.

My spirit quivered at the bloody execution. My soul recoiled before the carnage of so many lovely things cut out upon which my heart was set. But it had to be done, and we did it.

The first chapter in the original manuscript, a chapter which the editor, himself, admitted was as good a single piece of writing as I had ever done, was relentlessly kicked out, and the reason it was kicked out was that it was really not a true beginning for the book but merely something which led up to the true beginning; therefore it had to go. And so it went all up and down the line. Chapters 50,000 words long were reduced to ten or fifteen thousand words, and having faced this inevitable necessity, I finally acquired a kind of ruthlessness of my own, and once or twice, myself, did more cutting than my editor was willing to allow.

Another fault that has always troubled me in writing is that I have often attempted to reproduce in its entirety the full flood and fabric of a scene in life itself. Thus, in another section of the book, four people were represented as talking to each other for four hours without a break or intermission. All were good talkers; often all talked, or tried to talk, at the same time. The talk was wonderful and living talk because I knew the life and character and the vocabulary of all these people from its living source, and I had forgotten nothing. Yet all the time, all that was actually happening in this scene was that a young woman had got out of her husband's motor car and gone into her mother's house and kept calling to the impatient man outside every time he honked his horn, "All right. All right. I'll be with you in five minutes." These five minutes really lengthened into four hours, while the unfortunate man outside honked upon his horn, and while the two women and two young men of the same family inside carried on a torrential discourse and discussed exhaustively the lives and histories of almost everyone in town, their memories of the past, adventures of the present, and speculations of the future. I put it all down in the original manuscript just as I had seen and known and lived it a thousand times, and even if I do say so myself, the nature of the talk, the living vitality and character of the language, the utter naturalness, the floodtide river of it all was wonderful, but I had made four people talk 80,000 words—200 printed pages of close type in a minor scene of an enormous book, and of course, good as it was, it was all wrong and had to go.

Such, then, were some of our major difficulties with the manuscript we had in hand, and although since its publication there have been many declarations to the effect that the book would have benefited by a much more radical cutting, the cutting we did do was much more drastic than I had dreamed was possible.

Meanwhile I was proceeding at full speed with the work of completing my design, finishing the unfinished parts and filling in the transition links which were essential.

This in itself was an enormous job and kept me writing all day long as hard as I could go for a full year. Here again the nature of my chief fault was manifest. I wrote too much again. I not only wrote what was essential, but time and time again my enthusiasm for a good scene, one of those enchanting vistas which can open up so magically to a man in the full flow of his creation, would overpower me, and I would write thousands of words upon a scene which contributed nothing of vital importance to a book whose greatest need already was ruthless condensation.

During the course of this year, I must have written well over a half million words of additional manuscript, of which, of course, only a small part was finally used.

The nature of my method, the desire fully to explore my material, had led me into another error. The whole effect of those five years of incessant writing had been to make me feel not only that everything had to be used, but that everything had to be told, that nothing could be implied. Therefore, at the end, there were at least a dozen additional chapters which I felt had to be completed to give the book its final value. A thousand times I debated this question desperately with my editor. I told him that these chapters had to go in simply because I felt the book would not be complete without them, and with every argument he had, he tried to show me that I was wrong. I see now that on the whole he was right about it, but at the time I was so inextricably involved in my work, that I did not have the detachment necessary for a true appraisal.

The end came suddenly—the end of those five years of torment and incessant productivity. In October I took a trip to Chicago, a two weeks' vacation, my first in over a year. When I returned I found that my editor had quietly and decisively sent the manuscript to the press, the printers were already at work on it, the proof was beginning to come in. I had not foreseen it; I was desperate, bewildered. "You can't do it," I told him, "the book is not yet finished. I must have six months more on it."

To this he answered that the book was not only finished, but that if I took six months more on it, I would then demand another six months and six months more beyond that, and that I might very well become so obsessed with this one work that I would never get it published. He went on to say, and I think with complete justice, that such a course was wrong for me. I was not, he said, a Flaubert kind of writer. I was not a perfectionist. I had twenty, thirty, almost any numbers of books in me, and the important thing was to get them produced and not to spend the rest of my life in perfecting one book. He agreed that with six months' additional work upon the book, I might achieve a certain finish and completeness, but he did not think that the benefit would be nearly as great as I thought it would be, and his own deep conviction was that the book should be published at once without further delay, that I should get it out of me, forget about it, turn my life to the final completion of the work which was already prepared and ready, waiting for me. He told me, furthermore, exactly what the nature of the criticism would be, the criticism of its length, its adjectives, its overabundance, but he told me not to despair.

He told me finally that I would go on and do better work, that I would learn to work without so much confusion, waste, and useless torment, that my future books would more and more achieve the unity, sureness, and finality that every artist wants his work to have, but that I had to learn in the way I had learned, groping, struggling, finding my own way for myself, that this was the only way to learn.

In January, 1935, I finished the last of my revisions on the proof; the first printed copies came from the press in February. The book was released for final publication early in March. I was not here when it came out. I had taken a ship for Europe the week before, and as the ship got farther and farther from the American shores, my spirits sank lower and lower, reaching, I think, the lowest state of hopeless depression they had ever known. This, I believe, was largely a physical reaction, the inevitable effect of relaxation upon a human organism which had for five years been strained to its utmost limit. My life seemed to me to be like a great spring which had been taut for years and which was now slowly uncoiling from its tension. I had the most extraordinary sense of desolation I had ever known when I thought about my book. I had never realized until now how close I had been to it, how much a part of me it had become, and now that it had been taken away from me, my life felt utterly futile, hollow as a shell. And now that the book was gone, now that there was nothing more that I could do about it, I felt the most abysmal sensation of failure. I have always been somewhat afraid of print, although print is a thing I have tried so hard to achieve. Yet it is literally true that with everything I have ever written, I have felt when the hour of naked print drew nigh a kind of desperation and have even entreated my publisher not only to defer the publication of my book until another season, but have asked the editors of magazines to put off the publication of a story for another month or two until I had a chance to work on it some more, do something to it, I was not always sure what.

Now I had an overwhelming sense of shame greater than any I had felt before. I felt as if I had ruinously exposed myself as a pitiable fool who had no talent and who once and for all had completely vindicated the prophecies of the critics who had felt the first book was just a flash in the pan. It was in this frame of mind that I arrived in Paris on March 8, the day the book was to be published in America. I had come away to forget about it, and yet I thought about it all the time. I walked the streets from dawn to dark, from night to morning, at least a dozen times in two short weeks I heard the celebration of mass at Sacré Coeur, and then would walk the streets again and come back to my hotel at ten o'clock and lie upon the bed, and still I could not sleep.

After several days of this, I steeled myself to go to the office of the travel agency where a message might be waiting for me. I found a cablegram there. It was from my publisher, and it said simply: "Magnificent reviews somewhat critical in ways expected, full of greatest praise." I read it the first time with a feeling of almost intolerable joy but as I continued to read and reread it, the old dark doubt began to creep across my mind and by the time night had come I was convinced that this wonderful cable was just a sentence of doom, and that my editor, out of the infinite compassion of his spirit, had taken this means of breaking the news to me that my book was a colossal failure.

Three days passed in which I prowled the streets of Paris like a maddened animal, and of those three days I could later remember almost nothing. At the end of that time I sent a frenzied cablegram to that editor in which I told him I could stand anything better than this state of damnable uncertainty and pleaded with him to

give me the blunt truth no matter how bitter it might be. His answer to this cable was such that I could no longer doubt him or the
reception which the book had had at home.

This completes, as far as I can remember it, the story of the making of a book and what happened to its maker. I know it is too long
a story; I know, also, that it must seem to be a story filled with the
record of a man's blunders and ludicrous mistakes, but simply because it is that kind of story, I hope that it may have some value.
It is a story of the artist as a man and as a worker. It is a story of
the artist as a man who is derived out of the common family of earth
and who knows all the anguish, error, and frustration that any man
alive can know.

The life of the artist at any epoch of man's history has not been an
easy one. And here in America, it has often seemed to me, it may well
be the hardest life that man has ever known. I am not speaking of
some frustration in our native life, some barrenness of spirit, some
arid Philistinism which contends against the artist's life and which
prevents his growth. I do not speak of these things because I do not
put the same belief in them that I once did. I am speaking as I have
tried to speak from first to last in the concrete terms of the artist's
actual experience, of the nature of the physical task before him. It
seems to me that the task is one whose physical proportions are vaster
and more difficult here than in any other nation on the earth. It is
not merely that in the cultures of Europe and of the Orient the
American artist can find no antecedent scheme, no structural plan,
no body of tradition that can give his own work the validity and
truth that it must have. It is not merely that he must make somehow
a new tradition for himself, derived from his own life and from the
enormous space and energy of American life, the structure of his own
design; it is not merely that he is confronted by these problems; it is
even more than this, that the labor of a complete and whole articulation, the discovery of an entire universe and of a complete language,
is the task that lies before him.

Such is the nature of the struggle to which henceforth our lives
must be devoted. Out of the billion forms of America, out of the
savage violence and the dense complexity of all its swarming life;
from the unique and single substance of this land and life of ours,

must we draw the power and energy of our own life, the articulation of our speech, the substance of our art.

For here it seems to me in hard and honest ways like these we may find the tongue, the language, and the conscience that as men and artists we have got to have. Here, too, perhaps, must we who have no more than what we have, who know no more than what we know, who are no more than what we are, find our America. Here, at this present hour and moment of my life, I seek for mine.

FROM

LOOK HOMEWARD, ANGEL

THOMAS WOLFE's first novel is the detailed, sensuous, and intense record of the childhood, youth, and young manhood of Eugene Gant. Its dramatic frame is centered in the world of childhood in its relations to family and town. Its progression, aside from the simple chronology of the mounting days from birth to graduation from college, is that of the discovery of the self and the world. In reading it one is caught up in the sharp impressions of youth and rushed along toward that moment of self-realization with which it ends. Wolfe's many admirers who view him as primarily a nostalgic chronicler of a lost childhood and of pristine delight in the manifold shapes, colors, odors, sounds, and textures of experience find *Look Homeward, Angel* to be his best and most satisfying work.

Yet, however intense Eugene's experience of his world, the characters who dominate much of the novel are the members of his family, and in one sense the book is a family chronicle as much as it is a personal testament. And in its skeptical and often satiric view of the mountain town in which the events of Eugene's life occur, the book takes its place, along with works of Sinclair Lewis and Sherwood Anderson, in the American writer's "revolt against the village."

The selections from the book which follow represent these various aspects of the novel and attempt to present its principal themes and moods. W. O. Gant, the father, is given space to define himself; the village is satirically presented through the Joycean journey homeward on an April afternoon; the three most celebrated dramatic actions—the selling of the stone angel, the love affair with Laura James, and the death of Ben Gant—are given in full; and representative episodes in the progress of Eugene's maturing sense of the nature of his world are presented.

Only one incident in the novel was published before the book's appearance; that was "An Angel on the Porch," which was extracted from the novel for publication as a short story in the August, 1929, issue of *Scribner's Magazine*. Except for "An Angel on the Porch," the titles given the selections are mine and not Wolfe's. Neither chapters nor parts of the novel itself have titles.

The text of the selections is that of *Look Homeward, Angel* (New York: Charles Scribner's Sons, 1929). "A Window on All Time" is from pages 2-8 of that edition; "The Return of the Far-Wanderer" from pages 70-80; "The Meadows of Sensation" from pages 81-87; "An Angel on the Porch" from pages 262-269; "The Paper Route" from pages 294-306; "The World of Books" from pages 307-315; "April in Altamont" from pages 324-348; "Louise in Charleston" from pages 357-369; "Love in the Enchanted Wood" from pages 427-461; "The Death of Ben Gant" from pages 536-583; and "The Vision in the Square" from pages 617-626.

A WINDOW ON ALL TIME

. . . a stone, a leaf, an unfound door; of a stone, a leaf, a door. And of all the forgotten faces.

Naked and alone we came into exile. In her dark womb we did not know our mother's face; from the prison of her flesh have we come into the unspeakable and incommunicable prison of this earth.

Which of us has known his brother? Which of us has looked into his father's heart? Which of us has not remained forever prison-pent? Which of us is not forever a stranger and alone?

O waste of loss, in the hot mazes, lost, among bright stars on this most weary unbright cinder, lost! Remembering speechlessly we seek the great forgotten language, the lost lane-end into heaven, a stone, a leaf, an unfound door. Where? When?

O lost, and by the wind grieved, ghost, come back again.

A DESTINY that leads the English to the Dutch is strange enough; but one that leads from Epsom into Pennsylvania, and thence into the hills that shut in Altamont over the proud coral cry of the cock, and the soft stone smile of an angel, is touched by that dark miracle of chance which makes new magic in a dusty world.

Each of us is all the sums he has not counted: subtract us into nakedness and night again, and you shall see begin in Crete four thousand years ago the love that ended yesterday in Texas.

The seed of our destruction will blossom in the desert, the alexin of our cure grows by a mountain rock, and our lives are haunted by a Georgia slattern, because a London cutpurse went unhung. Each moment is the fruit of forty thousand years. The minute-winning days, like flies, buzz home to death, and every moment is a window on all time.

This is a moment:

An Englishman named Gilbert Gaunt, which he later changed to Gant (a concession probably to Yankee phonetics), having come to Baltimore from Bristol in 1837 on a sailing vessel, soon let the profits of a public house which he had purchased roll down his improvident gullet. He wandered westward into Pennsylvania, eking out a dangerous living by matching fighting cocks against the champions of country barnyards, and often escaping after a night spent in a village jail, with his champion dead on the field of battle, without the clink of a coin in his pocket, and sometimes with the print of a farmer's big knuckles on his reckless face. But he always escaped, and coming at length among the Dutch at harvest time he was so touched by the plenty of their land that he cast out his anchors there. Within a year he married a rugged young widow with a tidy farm who like all the other Dutch had been charmed by his air of travel, and his grandiose speech, particularly when he did Hamlet in the manner of the great Edmund Kean. Every one said he should have been an actor.

The Englishman begot children—a daughter and four sons—lived easily and carelessly, and bore patiently the weight of his wife's harsh but honest tongue. The years passed, his bright somewhat staring eyes grew dull and bagged, the tall Englishman walked with a gouty shuffle: one morning when she came to nag him out of sleep she found him dead of an apoplexy. He left five children, a mortgage and —in his strange dark eyes which now stared bright and open—something that had not died: a passionate and obscure hunger for voyages.

So, with this legacy, we leave this Englishman and are concerned hereafter with the heir to whom he bequeathed it, his second son, a boy named Oliver. How this boy stood by the roadside near his mother's farm, and saw the dusty Rebels march past on their way to Gettysburg, how his cold eyes darkened when he heard the great name of Virginia, and how the year the war had ended, when he was still fifteen, he had walked along a street in Baltimore, and seen within a little shop smooth granite slabs of death, carved lambs and cherubim, and an angel poised upon cold phthisic feet, with a smile of soft stone idiocy—this is a longer tale. But I know that his cold and shallow eyes had darkened with the obscure and passionate hunger that had lived in a dead man's eyes, and that had led from Fenchurch Street past Philadelphia. As the boy looked at the big angel with the carved stipe of lilystalk, a cold and nameless excitement possessed him. The long fingers of his big hands closed. He felt that he wanted, more than anything else in the world, to carve delicately with a chisel. He wanted to wreak something dark and unspeakable in him into cold stone. He wanted to carve an angel's head.

Oliver entered the shop and asked a big bearded man with a wooden mallet for a job. He became the stone cutter's apprentice.

He worked in that dusty yard five years. He became a stone cutter. When his apprenticeship was over he had become a man.

He never found it. He never learned to carve an angel's head. The dove, the lamb, the smooth joined marble hands of death, and letters fair and fine—but not the angel. And of all the years of waste and loss—the riotous years in Baltimore, of work and savage drunkenness, and the theatre of Booth and Salvini, which had a disastrous effect upon the stone cutter, who memorized each accent of the noble rant, and strode muttering through the streets, with rapid gestures of the enormous talking hands—these are blind steps and gropings of our exile, the painting of our hunger as, remembering speechlessly, we seek the great forgotten language, the lost lane-end into heaven, a stone, a leaf, a door. Where? When?

He never found it, and he reeled down across the continent into the Reconstruction South—a strange wild form of six feet four with cold uneasy eyes, a great blade of nose, and a rolling tide of rhetoric, a preposterous and comic invective, as formalized as classical epithet, which he used seriously, but with a faint uneasy grin around the corners of his thin wailing mouth.

He set up business in Sydney, the little capital city of one of the middle Southern states, lived soberly and industriously under the attentive eye of a folk still raw with defeat and hostility, and finally, his good name founded and admission won, he married a gaunt tubercular spinstress, ten years his elder, but with a nest egg and an unshakable will to matrimony. Within eighteen months he was a howling maniac again, his little business went smash while his foot stayed on the polished rail, and Cynthia, his wife—whose life, the natives said, he had not helped to prolong—died suddenly one night after a hemorrhage.

So, all was gone again—Cynthia, the shop, the hard-bought praise of soberness, the angel's head—he walked through the streets at dark, yelling his pentameter curse at Rebel ways, and all their indolence; but sick with fear and loss and penitence, he wilted under the town's reproving stare, becoming convinced, as the flesh wasted on his own gaunt frame, that Cynthia's scourge was doing vengeance now on him.

He was only past thirty, but he looked much older. His face was yellow and sunken; the waxen blade of his nose looked like a beak.

He had long brown mustaches that hung straight down mournfully. His tremendous bouts of drinking had wrecked his health. He was thin as a rail and had a cough. He thought of Cynthia now, in the lonely and hostile town, and he became afraid. He thought he had tuberculosis and that he was going to die.

So, alone and lost again, having found neither order nor establishment in the world, and with the earth cut away from his feet, Oliver resumed his aimless drift along the continent. He turned westward toward the great fortress of the hills, knowing that behind them his evil fame would not be known, and hoping that he might find in them isolation, a new life, and recovered health.

The eyes of the gaunt spectre darkened again, as they had in his youth.

All day, under a wet gray sky in October, Oliver rode westward across the mighty state. As he stared mournfully out the window at the great raw land so sparsely tilled by the futile and occasional little farms, which seemed to have made only little grubbing patches in the wilderness, his heart went cold and leaden in him. He thought of the great barns of Pennsylvania, the ripe bending of golden grain, the plenty, the order, the clean thrift of the people. And he thought of how he had set out to get order and position for himself, and of the rioting confusion of his life, the blot and blur of years, and the red waste of his youth.

By God! he thought. I'm getting old! Why here?

The grisly parade of the spectre years trooped through his brain. Suddenly, he saw that his life had been channelled by a series of accidents: a mad Rebel singing of Armageddon, the sound of a bugle on the road, the mule-hoofs of the army, the silly white face of an angel in a dusty shop, a slut's pert wiggle of her hams as she passed by. He had reeled out of warmth and plenty into this barren land: as he stared out the window and saw the fallow unworked earth, the great raw lift of the Piedmont, the muddy red clay roads, and the slattern people gaping at the stations—a lean farmer gangling above his reins, a dawdling Negro, a gap-toothed yokel, a hard sallow woman with a grimy baby—the strangeness of destiny stabbed him with fear. How came he here from the clean Dutch thrift of his youth into this vast lost earth of rickets?

The train rattled on over the reeking earth. Rain fell steadily. A brakeman came draftily into the dirty plush coach and emptied a scuttle of coal into the big stove at the end. High empty laughter shook a group of yokels sprawled on two turned seats. The bell tolled mournfully above the clacking wheels. There was a droning interminable wait at a junction-town near the foot-hills. Then the train moved on again across the vast rolling earth.

Dusk came. The huge bulk of the hills was foggily emergent. Small smoky lights went up in the hillside shacks. The train crawled dizzily across high trestles spanning ghostly hawsers of water. Far up, far down, plumed with wisps of smoke, toy cabins stuck to bank and gulch and hillside. The train toiled sinuously up among gouged red cuts with slow labor. As darkness came, Oliver descended at the little town of Old Stockade where the rails ended. The last great wall of the hills lay stark above him. As he left the dreary little station and stared into the greasy lamplight of a country store, Oliver felt that he was crawling, like a great beast, into the circle of those enormous hills to die.

The next morning he resumed his journey by coach. His destination was the little town of Altamont, twenty-four miles away beyond the rim of the great outer wall of the hills. As the horses strained slowly up the mountain road Oliver's spirit lifted a little. It was a gray-golden day in late October, bright and windy. There was a sharp bite and sparkle in the mountain air: the range soared above him, close, immense, clean, and barren. The trees rose gaunt and stark: they were almost leafless. The sky was full of windy white rags of cloud; a thick blade of mist washed slowly around the rampart of a mountain.

Below him a mountain stream foamed down its rocky bed, and he could see little dots of men laying the track that would coil across the hill toward Altamont. Then the sweating team lipped the gulch of the mountain, and, among soaring and lordly ranges that melted away in purple mist, they began the slow descent toward the high plateau on which the town of Altamont was built.

In the haunting eternity of these mountains, rimmed in their enormous cup, he found sprawled out on its hundred hills and hollows a town of four thousand people.

There were new lands. His heart lifted.

THE RETURN OF THE FAR-WANDERER

THIS journey to California was Gant's last great voyage. He made it two years after Eliza's return from St. Louis, when he was fifty-six years old. In the great frame was already stirring the chemistry of pain and death. Unspoken and undefined there was in him the knowledge that he was at length caught in the trap of life and fixity, that he was being borne under in this struggle against the terrible will that wanted to own the earth more than to explore it. This was the final flare of the old hunger that had once darkened in the small gray eyes, leading a boy into new lands and toward the soft stone smile of an angel.

And he returned from nine thousand miles of wandering, to the bleak bare prison of the hills on a gray day late in winter.

In the more than eight thousand days and nights of this life with Eliza, how often had he been wakefully, soberly and peripatetically conscious of the world outside him between the hours of one and five A.M.? Wholly, for not more than nineteen nights—one for the birth of Leslie, Eliza's first daughter; one for her death twenty-six months later, cholera infantis; one for the death of Major Tom Pentland, Eliza's father, in May, 1902; one for the birth of Luke; one, on the train westbound to Saint Louis, en route to Grover's death; one for the death in the Playhouse (1893) of Uncle Thaddeus Evans, an aged and devoted Negro; one, with Eliza, in the month of March, 1897, as deathwatch to the corpse of old Major Isaacs; three at the end of the month of July, 1897, when it was thought that Eliza, withered to a white sheeting of skin upon a bone frame, must die of typhoid; again in early April, 1903, for Luke, typhoid death near; one for the death of Greeley Pentland, aged twenty-six, congenital scrofulous tubercular, violinist, Pentlandian punster, petty check-forger, and six weeks' jailbird; three nights, from the eleventh to the fourteenth of January, 1905, by the rheumatic crucifixion of his right side, participant in his own grief, accuser of himself and his God; once in February, 1896, as deathwatch to the remains of Sandy Duncan, aged eleven; once in September, 1895, penitentially alert and shamefast in the City "calaboose"; in a room of the Keeley Institute at Piedmont, North Carolina, June 7, 1896; on March 17,

1906, between Knoxville, Tennessee, and Altamont, at the conclusion of a seven weeks' journey to California.

How looked the home-earth then to Gant the Far-Wanderer? Light crept gayly, melting on the rocky river, the engine smoke streaked out on dawn like a cold breath, the hills were big, but nearer, nearer than he thought. And Altamont lay gray and withered in the hills, a bleak mean wintry dot. He stepped carefully down in squalid Toytown, noting that everything was low, near, and shrunken as he made his Gulliverian entry. He had a roof-and-gulley high conviction; with careful tucked-in elbows he weighted down the heated Toytown street-car, staring painfully at the dirty pasteboard *pebbledash* of the Pisgah Hotel, the brick and board cheap warehouses of Depot Street, the rusty clapboard flimsiness of the Florence (Railway Men's) Hotel, quaking with beef-fed harlotry.

So small, so small, so small, he thought. I never believed it. Even the hills here. I'll soon be sixty.

His sallow face, thin-flanked, was hang-dog and afraid. He stared wistful-sullenly down at the rattan seat as the car screeched round into the switch at the cut and stopped; the motorman, smoke-throated, slid the door back and entered with his handle. He closed the door and sat down yawning.

"Where you been, Mr. Gant?"

"California," said Gant.

"Thought I hadn't seen you," said the motorman.

There was a warm electric smell and one of hot burnt steel.

But two months dead! But two months dead! Ah, Lord! So it's come to this. Merciful God, this fearful, awful, and damnable climate. Death, death! Is it too late? A land of life, a flower land. How clear the green clear sea was. And all the fishes swimming there. Santa Catalina. Those in the East should always go West. How came I here? Down, down—always down, did I know where? Baltimore, Sydney—In God's name, why? The little boat glass-bottomed, so you could look down. She lifted up her skirts as she stepped down. Where now? A pair of pippins.

"Jim Bowles died while you were gone, I reckon," said the motorman.

"What!" howled Gant. "Merciful God!" he clucked mournfully downward. "What did he die of?" he asked.

"Pneumonia," said the motorman. "He was dead four days after he was took down."

"Why, he was a big healthy man in the prime of life," said Gant. "I was talking to him the day before I went away," he lied, convincing himself permanently that this was true. "He looked as if he had never known a day's sickness in his life."

"He went home one Friday night with a chill," said the motorman, "and the next Tuesday he was gone."

There was a crescent humming on the rails. With his thick glove finger he pushed away a clearing in the window-coated ice scurf and looked smokily out on the raw red cut-bank. The other car appeared abruptly at the end of the cut and curved with a skreeking jerk into the switch.

"No, sir," said the motorman, sliding back the door, "you never know who'll go next. Here to-day and gone to-morrow. Hit gits the big 'uns first sometimes."

He closed the door behind him and jerkily opened three notches of juice. The car ground briskly off like a wound toy.

In the prime of life, thought Gant. Myself like that some day. No, for others. Mother almost eighty-six. Eats like a horse, Augusta wrote. Must send her twenty dollars. Now in the cold clay, frozen. Keep till Spring. Rain, rot, rain. Who got the job? Brock or Saul Gudger? Bread out of my mouth. Do me to death—the stranger. Georgia marble, sandstone base, forty dollars.

> "A gracious friend from us is gone,
> A voice we loved is fled,
> But faith and memory lead us on:
> He lives; he is not dead."

Four cents a letter. Little enough, God knows, for the work you do. My letters the best. Could have been a writer. Like to draw too. And all of mine! I would have heard if anything—he would have told me. I'll never go that way. All right above the waist. If anything happens it will be down below. Eaten away. Whisky holes through all your guts. Pictures in Cardiac's office of man with cancer. But several doctors have to agree on it. Criminal offense if they don't. But, if worse comes to worst—all that's outside. Get it before it gets up in you. Still live. Old man Haight had a flap in his belly. Ladled

it out in a cup. McGuire—damned butcher. But he can do anything. Cut off a piece here, sew it on there. Made the Hominy man
a nose with a piece of shinbone. Couldn't tell it. Ought to be possible. Cut all the strings, tie them up again. While you wait. Sort
of job for McGuire—rough and ready. They'll do it some day. After
I'm gone. Things standing thus, unknown—but kill you maybe.
Bull's too big. Soon now the Spring. You'd die. Not big enough. All
bloody in her brain. Full filling fountains of bull-milk. Jupiter and
what's-her-name.

But westward now he caught a glimpse of Pisgah and the western
range. It was more spacious there. The hills climbed sunward to the
sun. There was width to the eye, a smoking sun-hazed amplitude,
the world convoluting and opening into the world, hill and plain,
into the west. The West for desire, the East for home. To the east
the short near mile-away hills reeked protectively above the town.
Birdseye, Sunset. A straight plume of smoke coiled thickly from
Judge Buck Sevier's smut-white clapboard residence on the decent
side of Pisgah Avenue, thin smoke-wisps rose from the nigger shacks
in the ravine below. Breakfast. Fried brains and eggs with streaky
rashers of limp bacon. Wake, wake, wake, you mountain grills!
Sleeps she yet, wrapped dirtily in three old wrappers in stale, airless
yellow-shaded cold. The chapped hands sick-sweet glycerined. Gum-
headed bottles, hairpins, and the bits of string. No one may enter
now. Ashamed.

A paper-carrier, number 7, finished his route on the corner of
Vine Street, as the car stopped, turned eastwards now from Pisgah
Avenue toward the town core. The boy folded, bent, and flattened
the fresh sheets deftly, throwing the block angularly thirty yards
upon the porch of Shields the jeweller; it struck the boarding and
bounded back with a fresh plop. Then he walked off with fatigued
relief into time toward the twentieth century, feeling gratefully
the ghost-kiss of absent weight upon his now free but still leaning
right shoulder.

About fourteen, thought Gant. That would be Spring of 1864.
The mule camp at Harrisburg. Thirty a month and keep. Men
stank worse than mules. I was in third bunk on top. Gil in second.
Keep your damned dirty hoof out of my mouth. It's bigger than a
mule's. That was the man. If it ever lands on you, you bastard, you'll

think it is a mule's, said Gil. Then they had it. Mother made us go. Big enough to work, she said. Born at the heart of the world, why here? Twelve miles from Gettysburg. Out of the South they came. Stove-pipe hats they had stolen. No shoes. Give me a drink, son. That was Fitzhugh Lee. After the third day we went over. Devil's Den. Cemetery Ridge. Stinking piles of arms and legs. Some of it done with meat-saws. Is the land richer now? The great barns bigger than the houses. Big eaters, all of us. I hid the cattle in the thicket. Belle Boyd, the Beautiful Rebel Spy. Sentenced to be shot four times. Took the despatches from his pocket while they danced. Probably a little chippie.

Hog-chitlins and hot cracklin' bread. Must get some. The whole hog or none. Always been a good provider. Little I ever had done for me.

The car still climbing, mounted the flimsy cheap-boarded brown-gray smuttiness of Skyland Avenue.

America's Switzerland. The Beautiful Land of the Sky. Jesus God! Old Bowman said he'll be a rich man some day. Built up all the way to Pasadena. Come on out. Too late now. Think he was in love with her. No matter. Too old. Wants her out there. No fool like— White bellies of the fish. A spring somewhere to wash me through. Clean as a baby once more. New Orleans, the night Jim Corbett knocked out John L. Sullivan. The man who tried to rob me. My clothes and my watch. Five blocks down Canal Street in my night-gown. Two A.M. Threw them all in a heap—watch landed on top. Fight in my room. Town full of crooks and pickpockets for prize-fight. Make good story. Policeman half hour later. They come out and beg you to come in. Frenchwomen. Creoles. Beautiful Creole heiress. Steamboat race. Captain, they are gaining. I will not be beaten. Out of wood. Use the bacon she said proudly. There was a terrific explosion. He got her as she sank the third time and swam to shore. They powder in front of the window, smacking their lips at you. For old men better maybe. Who gets the business there? Bury them all above ground. Water two feet down. Rots them. Why not? All big jobs. Italy. Carrara and Rome. Yet Brutus is an hon-or-able man. What's a Creole? French and Spanish. Has she any nigger blood? Ask Cardiac?

The car paused briefly at the car-shed, in sight of its stabled brothers. Then it moved reluctantly past the dynamic atmosphere of the Power and Light Company, wheeling bluntly into the gray frozen ribbon of Hatton Avenue, running gently up hill near its end into the frore silence of the Square.

Ah, Lord! Well do I remember. The old man offered me the whole piece for $1,000 three days after I arrived. Millionaire to-day if—

The car passed the Tuskegee on its eighty-yard climb into the Square. The fat slick worn leather-chairs marshalled between a fresh-rubbed gleaming line of brass spittoons squatted massively on each side of the entry door, before thick sheets of plate-glass that extended almost to the sidewalks with indecent nearness.

Many a fat man's rump upon the leather. Like fish in a glass case. Travelling man's wet chewed cigar, spit-limp on his greasy lips. Staring at all the women. Can't look back long. Gives advantage.

A Negro bellboy sleepily wafted a gray dust-cloth across the leather. Within, before the replenished crackle-dance of the wood-fire, the night-clerk sprawled out in the deep receiving belly of a leather divan.

The car reached the Square, jolted across the netting of north-south lines, and came to a halt on the north side, facing east. Scurfing a patch away from the glazed window, Gant looked out. The Square in the wan-gray frozen morning walled round him with frozen un-natural smallness. He felt suddenly the cramped mean fixity of the Square: this was the one fixed spot in a world that writhed, evolved, and changed constantly in his vision, and he felt a sick green fear, a frozen constriction about his heart because the centre of his life now looked so shrunken. He got very definitely the impression that if he flung out his arms they would strike against the walls of the mean three-and-four-story brickbuilt buildings that flanked the Square raggedly.

Anchored to earth at last, he was hit suddenly by the whole cumu-lation of sight and movement, of eating, drinking, and acting that had gathered in him for two months. The limitless land, wood, field, hill, prairie, desert, mountain, the coast rushing away below his eyes, the ground that swam before his eyes at stations, the remembered ghosts of gumbo, oysters, huge Frisco seasteaks, tropical fruits swarmed with the infinite life, the ceaseless pullulation of the sea. Here only, in his unreal-reality, this unnatural vision of what he had known for twenty years, did life lose its movement, change, color.

The Square had the horrible concreteness of a dream. At the far southeastern edge he saw his shop: his name painted hugely in dirty scaly white across the brick near the roof: W. O. Gant—Marbles, Tombstones, Cemetery Fixtures. It was like a dream of hell, when a man finds his own name staring at him from the Devil's ledger; like a dream of death, when he who comes as mourner finds himself in the coffin, or as witness to a hanging, the condemned upon the scaffold.

A sleepy Negro employed at the Manor Hotel clambered heavily up and slumped into one of the seats reserved for his race at the back. In a moment he began to snore gently through his blubbered lips.

At the east end of the Square, Big Bill Messler, with his vest half-unbuttoned over his girdled paunch-belly, descended slowly the steps of the City Hall, and moved soundingly off with country leisure along the cold-metallic sidewalk. The fountain, ringed with a thick bracelet of ice, played at quarter-strength a sheening glut of ice-blue water.

Cars droned separately into their focal positions; the carmen stamped their feet and talked smokily together; there was a breath of beginning life. Beside the City Hall, the firemen slept above their wagons: behind the bolted door great hoofs drummed woodenly.

A dray rattled across the east end of the Square before the City Hall, the old horse leaning back cautiously as he sloped down into the dray market by the oblique cobbled passage at the southeast that cut Gant's shop away from the market and "calaboose." As the car moved eastward again, Gant caught an angular view of Niggertown across this passage. The settlement was plumed delicately with a hundred tiny fumes of smoke.

The car sloped swiftly now down Academy Street, turned, as the upper edge of the Negro settlement impinged steeply from the valley upon the white, into Ivy Street, and proceeded north along a street bordered on one side by smutty pebble-dash cottages, and on the other by a grove of lordly oaks, in which the large quaking plaster pile of old Professor Bowman's deserted School for Young Ladies loomed desolately, turning and stopping at the corner, at the top of the Woodson Street hill, by the great wintry, wooden, and deserted barn of the Ivy Hotel. It had never paid.

Gant kneed his heavy bag before him down the passage, depositing it for a moment at the curbing before he descended the hill. The unpaved frozen clay fell steeply and lumpily away. It was steeper, shorter, nearer than he thought. Only the trees looked large. He saw Duncan come out on his porch, shirtsleeved, and pick up the morning paper. Speak to him later. Too long now. As he expected, there was a fat coil of morning smoke above the Scotchman's chimney, but none from his own.

He went down the hill, opening his iron gate softly, and going around to the side entrance by the yard, rather than ascend the steep veranda steps. The grape vines, tough and barren, writhed about the house like sinewy ropes. He entered the sitting-room quietly. There was a strong odor of cold leather. Cold ashes were strewn thinly in the grate. He put his bag down and went back through the wash-room into the kitchen. Eliza, wearing one of his old coats, and a pair of fingerless woollen gloves, poked among the embers of a crawling little fire.

"Well, I'm back," Gant said.

"Why, what on earth!" she cried as he knew she would, becoming flustered and moving her arms indeterminately. He laid his hand clumsily on her shoulder for a moment. They stood awkwardly without movement. Then he seized the oil-can, and drenched the wood with kerosene. The flame roared up out of the stove.

"Mercy, Mr. Gant," cried Eliza, "you'll burn us up!"

But, seizing a handful of cut sticks and the oil-can, he lunged furiously towards the sitting-room.

As the flame shot roaring up from the oiled pine sticks, and he felt the fire-full chimney-throat tremble, he recovered joy. He brought back the width of the desert; the vast yellow serpent of the river, alluvial with the mined accretions of the continent; the rich vision of laden ships, masted above the sea-walls, the world-nostalgic ships, bearing about them the filtered and concentrated odors of the earth, sensual Negroid rum and molasses, tar, ripening guavas, bananas, tangerines, pineapples in the warm holds of tropical boats, as cheap, as profuse, as abundant as the lazy equatorial earth and all its women; the great names of Louisiana, Texas, Arizona, Colorado, California; the blasted fiend-world of the desert, and the terrific boles of trees, tunnelled for the passage of a coach; water that fell from a mountain-top in a smoking noiseless coil, internal boiling lakes flung skywards by the punctual respiration of the earth, the multitudinous torture in form of granite oceans, gouged depthlessly by canyons, and iridescent with the daily chameleon-shift beyond man, beyond nature, of terrific colors, below the un-human iridescence of the sky.

Eliza, still excited, recovering speech, followed him into the sitting-room, holding her chapped gloved hands clasped before her stomach while she talked.

"I was saying to Steve last night, 'It wouldn't surprise me if your papa would come rolling in at any minute now'—I just had a feeling, I don't know what you'd call it," she said, her face plucked inward by the sudden fabrication of legend, "but it's pretty strange when you come to think of it. I was in Garret's the other day ordering some things, some vanilla extract, soda and a pound of coffee when Aleck Carter came up to me. 'Eliza,' he said, 'when's Mr. Gant coming back—I think I may have a job for him?' 'Why, Aleck,' I said, 'I don't much expect him before the first of April.' Well, sir, what do you know—I had no sooner got out on the street—I suppose I must have been thinking of something else, because I remember Emma Aldrich came by and hollered to me and I didn't think to answer her until she had gone on by, so I called out just as big as you please to her, 'Emma!'—the thing flashed over me all of a sudden—I was just as sure of it as I'm standing here—'what do you think? Mr. Gant's on his way back home'."

Jesus God! thought Gant. It's begun again.

Her memory moved over the ocean-bed of event like a great octopus, blindly but completely feeling its way into every seacave, rill, and estuary, focussed on all she had done, felt and thought, with sucking Pentlandian intentness, for whom the sun shone, or grew dark, rain fell, and mankind came, spoke, and died, shifted for a moment in time out of its void into the Pentlandian core, pattern and heart of purpose.

Meanwhile, as he laid big gleaming lumps of coal upon the wood, he muttered to himself, his mind ordering in a mounting sequence, with balanced and climactic periods, his carefully punctuated rhetoric.

Yes, musty cotton, baled and piled under long sheds of railway sidings; and odorous pine woodlands of the level South, saturated with brown faery light, and broken by the tall straight leafless poles of trees; a woman's leg below an elegantly lifted skirt mounting to a carriage in Canal Street (French or Creole probably) ; a white arm curved reaching for a window shade, French-olive faces window-glimmering, the Georgia doctor's wife who slept above him going out, the unquenchable fish-filled abundance of the unfenced, blue, slow cat-slapping lazy Pacific; and the river, the all-drinking, yellow, slow-surging snake that drained the continent. His life was like that river, rich with its own deposited and onward-borne agglutinations, fecund with its sedimental accretions, filled exhaustlessly by life in order to be more richly itself, and this life, with the great purpose of a river, he emptied now into the harbor of his house, the sufficient haven of himself, for whom the gnarled vines wove round him thrice, the earth burgeoned with abundant fruit and blossom, the fire burnt madly.

"What have you got for breakfast?" he said to Eliza.

"Why," she said, pursing her lips meditatively, "would you like some eggs?"

"Yes," said he, "with a few rashers of bacon and a couple of pork sausages."

He strode across the dining-room and went up the hall.

"Steve! Ben! Luke! You damned scoundrels!" he yelled. "Get up!"

Their feet thudded almost simultaneously upon the floor.

"Papa's home!" they shrieked.

Mr. Duncan watched butter soak through a new-baked roll. He looked through his curtain angularly down, and saw thick acrid smoke biting heavily into the air above Gant's house.

"He's back," said he, with satisfaction.

So, at the moment looking, Tarkington of the paints said: "W. O.'s back."

Thus came he home, who had put out to land westward, Gant the Far-Wanderer.

THE MEADOWS OF SENSATION

EUGENE was loose now in the limitless meadows of sensation: his sensory equipment was so complete that at the moment of perception of a single thing, the whole background of color, warmth, odor, sound, taste established itself, so that later, the breath of hot dandelion brought back the grass-warm banks of Spring, a day, a place, the rustling of young leaves, or the page of a book, the thin exotic smell of tangerine, the wintry bite of great apples; or, as with *Gulliver's Travels,* a bright windy day in March, the spurting moments of warmth, the drip and reek of the earth-thaw, the feel of the fire.

He had won his first release from the fences of home—he was not quite six, when, of his own insistence, he went to school. Eliza did not want him to go, but his only close companion, Max Isaacs, a year his senior, was going, and there was in his heart a constricting terror that he would be left alone again. She told him he could not go: she felt, somehow, that school began the slow, the final loosening of the cords that held them together, but as she saw him slide craftily out the gate one morning in September and run at top speed to the corner where the other little boy was waiting, she did nothing to bring him back. Something taut snapped in her; she remembered his furtive backward glance, and she wept. And she did not weep for herself, but for him: the hour after his birth she had looked in his dark eyes and had seen something that would brood there eternally, she knew, unfathomable wells of remote and intangible loneliness: she knew that in her dark and sorrowful womb a stranger had come to life, fed by the lost communications of eternity, his own ghost, haunter of his own house, lonely to himself and to the world. O lost.

Busy with the ache of their own growing-pains, his brothers and sisters had little time for him: he was almost six years younger than Luke, the youngest of them, but they exerted over him the occasional small cruelties, petty tormentings by elder children of a younger, interested and excited by the brief screaming insanity of his temper when, goaded and taunted from some deep dream, he would seize a carving knife and pursue them, or batter his head against the walls.

They felt that he was "queer"—the other boys preached the smug cowardice of the child-herd, defending themselves, when their persecutions were discovered, by saying they would make a "real boy" of him. But there grew up in him a deep affection for Ben who stalked occasionally and softly through the house, guarding even then with scowling eyes, and surly speech, the secret life. Ben was a stranger: some deep instinct drew him to his child-brother, a portion of his small earnings as a paper-carrier he spent in gifts and amusement for Eugene, admonishing him sullenly, cuffing him occasionally, but defending him before the others.

Gant, as he watched his brooding face set for hours before a firelit book of pictures, concluded that the boy liked books, more vaguely, that he would make a lawyer of him, send him into politics, see him elected to the governorship, the Senate, the presidency. And he unfolded to him time after time all the rude American legendry of the country boys who became great men because they were country boys, poor boys, and hard-working farm boys. But Eliza thought of him as a scholar, a learned man, a professor, and with that convenient afterthought that annoyed Gant so deeply, but by which she firmly convinced herself, she saw in this book-brooder the fruit of her own deliberate design.

"I read every moment I could get the chance the summer before he was born," she said. And then, with a complacent and confidential smile which, Gant knew, always preceded some reference to her family, she said: "I tell you what: it may all come out in the Third Generation."

"The Third Generation be Goddamned!" answered Gant furiously.

"Now, I want to tell you," she went on thoughtfully, speaking with her forefinger, "folks have always said that his grandfather would have made a fine scholar if—"

"Merciful God!" said Gant, getting up suddenly and striding about the room with an ironical laugh. "I might have known that it would come to this! You may be sure," he exclaimed in high excitement, wetting his thumb briefly on his tongue, "that if there's any credit to be given I won't get it. Not from you! You'd rather die than admit it! No, but I'll tell you what you will do! You'll brag about that miserable old freak who never did a hard day's work in his life."

"Now, I wouldn't be so sure of that if I were you," Eliza began, her lips working rapidly.

"Jesus God!" he cried, flinging about the room with his customary indifference to reasoned debate. "Jesus God! What a travesty! A travesty on Nature! Hell hath no fury like a woman scorned!" he exclaimed, indefinitely but violently, and then as he strode about he gave way to loud, bitter, forced laughter.

Thus, pent in his dark soul, Eugene sat brooding on a fire-lit book, a stranger in a noisy inn. The gates of his life were closing him in from their knowledge, a vast aerial world of fantasy was erecting its fuming and insubstantial fabric. He steeped his soul in streaming imagery, rifling the book-shelves for pictures and finding there such treasures as *With Stanley in Africa,* rich in the mystery of the jungle, alive with combat, black battle, the hurled spear, vast snake-rooted forests, thatched villages, gold and ivory; or Stoddard's *Lectures,* on whose slick heavy pages were stamped the most-visited scenes of Europe and Asia; a Book of Wonder, with enchanting drawings of all the marvels of the age—Santos Dumont in his balloon, liquid air poured from a kettle, all the navies of the earth lifted two feet from the water by an ounce of radium (Sir William Crookes), the building of the Eiffel Tower, the Flatiron Building, the stick-steered automobile, the submarine. After the earthquake in San Francisco there was a book describing it, its cheap green cover lurid with crumbling towers, shaken spires, toppling many-storied houses plunging into the splitting flame-jawed earth. And there was another called *Palaces of Sin,* or *The Devil in Society,* purporting to be the work of a pious millionaire, who had drained his vast fortune in exposing the painted sores that blemish the spotless-seeming hide of great position, and there were enticing pictures showing the author walking in a silk hat down a street full of magnificent palaces of sin.

Out of this strange jumbled gallery of pictures the pieced-out world was expanding under the brooding power of his imagination; the lost dark angels of the Doré "Milton" swooped into cavernous Hell beyond this upper earth of soaring or toppling spires, machine wonder, maced and mailed romance. And, as he thought of his future liberation into this epic world, where all the color of life blazed brightest far away from home, his heart flooded his face with lakes of blood.

He had heard already the ringing of remote church bells over a countryside on Sunday night; had listened to the earth steeped in the brooding of dark, and the million-noted little night things; and he had heard thus the far retreating wail of a whistle in a distant valley, and faint thunder on the rails; and he felt the infinite depth and width of the golden world in the brief seductions of a thousand multiplex and mixed mysterious odors and sensations, weaving, with a blinding interplay and aural explosions, one into the other.

He remembered yet the East India Tea House at the Fair, the sandalwood, the turbans, and the robes, the cool interior and the smell of India tea; and he had felt now the nostalgic thrill of dew-wet mornings in Spring, the cherry scent, the cool clarion earth, the wet loaminess of the garden, the pungent breakfast smells and the floating snow of blossoms. He knew the inchoate sharp excitement of hot dandelions in young Spring grass at noon; the smell of cellars, cobwebs, and built-on secret earth; in July, of watermelons bedded in sweet hay, inside a farmer's covered wagon; of cantaloupe and crated peaches; and the scent of orange rind, bitter-sweet, before a fire of coals. He knew the good male smell of his father's sitting-room; of the smooth worn leather sofa, with the gaping horse-hair rent; of the blistered varnished wood upon the hearth; of the heated calf-skin bindings; of the flat moist plug of apple tobacco, stuck with a red flag; of wood-smoke and burnt leaves in October; of the brown tired autumn earth; of honey-suckle at night; of warm nasturtiums; of a clean ruddy farmer who comes weekly with printed butter, eggs and milk; of fat limp underdone bacon and of coffee; of a bakery-oven in the wind; of large deep-hued stringbeans smoking-hot and seasoned well with salt and butter; of a room of old pine boards in which books and carpets have been stored, long closed; of Concord grapes in their long white baskets.

Yes, and the exciting smell of chalk and varnished desks; the smell of heavy bread-sandwiches of cold fried meat and butter; the smell of new leather in a saddler's shop, or of a warm leather chair; of honey and of unground coffee; of barrelled sweet-pickles and cheese and all the fragrant compost of the grocer's; the smell of stored apples in the cellar, and of orchard-apple smells, of pressed-cider pulp; of pears ripening on a sunny shelf, and of ripe cherries stewing with sugar on hot stoves before preserving; the smell of whittled wood, of all young lumber, of sawdust and shavings; of peaches stuck with cloves and pickled in brandy; of pine-sap, and green pine-needles; of a horse's pared hoof; of chestnuts roasting, of bowls of nuts and raisins; of hot cracklin, and of young roast pork; of butter and cinnamon melting on hot candied yams.

Yes, and of the rank slow river, and of tomatoes rotten on the vine; the smell of rain-wet plums and boiling quinces; of rotten lily-pads; and of foul weeds rotting in green marsh scum; and the exquisite smell of the South, clean but funky, like a big woman; of soaking trees and the earth after heavy rain.

Yes, and the smell of hot daisy-fields in the morning; of melted puddling-iron in a foundry; the winter smell of horse-warm stables and smoking dung; of old oak and walnut; and the butcher's smell of meat, of strong slaughtered lamb, plump gouty liver, ground pasty sausages, and red beef; and of brown sugar melted with slivered bitter chocolate; and of crushed mint leaves, and of a wet lilac bush; of magnolia beneath the heavy moon, of dogwood and laurel; of an old caked pipe and Bourbon rye, aged in kegs of charred oak; the sharp smell of tobacco; of carbolic and nitric acids; the coarse true smell of a dog; of old imprisoned books; and the cool fern-smell near springs; of vanilla in cake-dough; and of cloven ponderous cheeses.

Yes, and of a hardware store, but mostly the good smell of nails; of the developing chemicals in a photographer's dark-room; and the young-life smell of paint and turpentine; of buckwheat batter and black sorghum; and of a Negro and his horse, together; of boiling fudge; the brine smell of pickling vats; and the lush undergrowth smell of southern hills; of a slimy oyster-can, of chilled gutted fish; of a hot kitchen Negress; of kerosene and linoleum; of sarsaparilla and guavas; and of ripe autumn persimmons; and the smell of the wind and the rain; and of the acrid thunder; of cold starlight, and the brittle-bladed frozen grass; of fog and the misted winter sun; of seed-time, bloom, and mellow dropping harvest.

And now, whetted intemperately by what he had felt, he began, at school, in that fecund romance, the geography, to breathe the mixed odors of the earth, sensing in every squat keg piled on a pier-head a treasure of golden rum, rich port, fat Burgundy; smelling the jungle growth of the tropics, the heavy odor of plantations, the salt-fish smell of harbors, voyaging in the vast, enchanting, but un-perplexing world.

Now the innumerable archipelago had been threaded, and he stood, firm-planted, upon the unknown but waiting continent.

He learned to read almost at once, printing the shapes of words immediately with his strong visual memory; but it was weeks later before he learned to write, or even to copy, words. The ragged spume and wrack of fantasy and the lost world still floated from time to time through his clear schoolday morning brain, and although he followed accurately all the other instruction of his teacher, he was walled in his ancient unknowning world when they made letters. The children made their sprawling alphabets below a line of models, but all he accomplished was a line of jagged wavering spear-points on his sheet, which he repeated endlessly and rapturously, unable to see or understand the difference.

"I have learned to write," he thought.

Then, one day, Max Isaacs looked suddenly, from his exercise, on Eugene's sheet, and saw the jagged line.

"That ain't writin'," said he.

And clubbing his pencil in his warted grimy hand, he scrawled a copy of the exercise across the page.

The line of life, that beautiful developing structure of language that he saw flowing from his comrade's pencil, cut the knot in him that all instruction failed to do, and instantly he seized the pencil, and wrote the words in letters fairer and finer than his friend's. And he turned, with a cry in his throat, to the next page, and copied it without hesitation, and the next, the next. They looked at each other a moment with that clear wonder by which children accept miracles, and they never spoke of it again.

"That's writin' now," said Max. But they kept the mystery caged between them.

Eugene thought of this event later; always he could feel the opening gates in him, the plunge of the tide, the escape; but it happened like this one day at once. Still midget-near the live pelt of the earth, he saw many things that he kept in fearful secret, knowing that revelation would be punished with ridicule. One Saturday in Spring, he stopped with Max Isaacs above a deep pit in Central Avenue where city workmen were patching a broken watermain. The clay walls of their pit were much higher than their heads; behind their huddled backs there was a wide fissure, a window in the earth which opened on some dark subterranean passage. And as the boys looked, they gripped each other suddenly, for past the fissure slid the flat head of an enormous serpent; passed, and was followed by a scaled body as thick as a man's; the monster slid endlessly on into the deep earth and vanished behind the working and unwitting men. Shaken with fear they went away, they talked about it then and later in hushed voices, but they never revealed it.

THE ANGEL ON THE PORCH

ONE afternoon in the young summer, Gant leaned upon the rail, talking to Jannadeau. He was getting on to sixty-five, his erect body had settled, he stooped a little. He spoke of old age often, and he wept in his tirades now because of his stiffened hand. Soaked in pity, he referred to himself as "the poor old cripple who has to provide for them all."

The indolence of age and disintegration was creeping over him. He now rose a full hour later, he came to his shop punctually, but he spent long hours of the day extended on the worn leather couch of his office, or in gossip with Jannadeau, bawdy old Liddell, Cardiac, and Fagg Sluder, who had salted away his fortune in two big buildings on the Square and was at the present moment tilted comfortably in a chair before the fire department, gossiping eagerly with members of the ball club, whose chief support he was. It was after five o'clock, the game was over.

Negro laborers, grisly with a white coating of cement, sloped down past the shop on their way home. The draymen dispersed slowly, a slouchy policeman loafed down the steps of the city hall picking his teeth, and on the market side, from high grilled windows, there came the occasional howls of a drunken Negress. Life buzzed slowly like a fly.

The sun had reddened slightly, there was a cool flowing breath from the hills, a freshening relaxation over the tired earth, the hope, the ecstasy of evening in the air. In slow pulses the thick plume of fountain rose, fell upon itself, and slapped the pool in lazy rhythms. A wagon rattled leanly over the big cobbles; beyond the firemen, the grocer Bradley wound up his awning with slow creaking revolutions.

Across the Square, at its other edge, the young virgins of the eastern part of town walked lightly home in chattering groups. They came to town at four o'clock in the afternoon, walked up and down the little avenue several times, entered a shop to purchase small justifications, and finally went into the chief drugstore, where the bucks of the town loafed and drawled in lazy alert groups. It was their club, their brasserie, the forum of the sexes. With confident smiles the young men detached themselves from their group and strolled back to booth and table.

"Hey theah! Wheahd you come from?"

"Move ovah theah, lady. I want to tawk to you."

Eyes as blue as Southern skies looked roguishly up to laughing gray ones, the winsome dimples deepened, and the sweetest little tail in dear old Dixie slid gently over on the polished board.

Gant spent delightful hours now in the gossip of dirty old men—their huddled bawdry exploded in cracked high wheezes on the Square. He came home at evening stored with gutter tidings, wetting his thumb and smiling slyly as he questioned Helen hopefully:

"She's no better than a regular little chippie—eh?"

"Ha-ha-ha-ha," she laughed mockingly. "Don't you wish you knew?"

His age bore certain fruits, emoluments of service. When she came home in the evening with one of her friends, she presented the girl with jocose eagerness to his embrace. And, crying out paternally, "Why, bless her heart! Come kiss the old man," he planted bristling mustache kisses on their white throats, their soft lips, grasping the firm meat of one arm tenderly with his good hand and cradling them gently. They shrieked with throaty giggle-twiddles of pleasure because it tuh-tuh-tuh-tuh-*tickled* so.

"Ooh! Mr. Gant! What-whah-whah!"

"Your father's such a nice man," they said. "Such lovely manners."

Helen's eyes fed fiercely on them. She laughed with husky-harsh excitement.

"Hah-ha-ha! He likes that, doesn't he? It's too bad, old boy, isn't it? No more monkey business."

He talked with Jannadeau, while his fugitive eyes roved over the east end of the Square. Before the shop the comely matrons of the town came up from the market. From time to time they smiled, seeing him, and he bowed sweepingly. Such lovely manners.

"The King of England," he observed, "is only a figurehead. He doesn't begin to have the power of the President of the United States."

"His power is severely li*mite*d," said Jannadeau gutturally, "by custom but not by statute. In actua*lity* he is still one of the most powerful monarchs in the world." His thick black fingers probed carefully into the viscera of a watch.

"The late King Edward for all his faults," said Gant, wetting his thumb, "was a smart man. This fellow they've got now is a nonentity and a nincompoop." He grinned faintly, craftily, with pleasure at the big words, glancing slily at the Swiss to see if they had told.

His uneasy eyes followed carefully the stylish carriage of "Queen" Elizabeth's well clad figure as she went down by the shop. She smiled pleasantly, and for a moment turned her candid stare upon smooth marble slabs of death, carved lambs and cherubim. Gant bowed elaborately.

"Good-evening, madam," he said.

She disappeared. In a moment she came back decisively and mounted the broad steps. He watched her approach with quickened pulses. Twelve years.

"How's the madam?" he said gallantly. "Elizabeth, I was just telling Jannadeau you were the most stylish woman in town."

"Well, that's mighty sweet of you, Mr. Gant," she said in her cool poised voice. "You've always got a word for every one."

She gave a bright pleasant nod to Jannadeau, who swung his huge scowling head ponderously around and muttered at her.

"Why, Elizabeth," said Gant, "you haven't changed an inch in fifteen years. I don't believe you're a day older."

She was thirty-eight and pleasantly aware of it.

"Oh, yes," she said laughing. "You're only saying that to make me feel good. I'm no chicken any more."

She had a pale clear skin, pleasantly freckled, carrot-colored hair, and a thin mouth live with humor. Her figure was trim and strong

—no longer young. She had a great deal of energy, distinction, and elegance in her manner.

"How are all the girls, Elizabeth?" he asked kindly.

Her face grew sad. She began to pull her gloves off.

"That's what I came to see you about," she said. "I lost one of them last week."

"Yes," said Gant gravely, "I was sorry to hear of that."

"She was the best girl I had," said Elizabeth. "I'd have done anything in the world for her. We did everything we could," she added. "I've no regrets on that score. I had a doctor and two trained nurses by her all the time."

She opened her black leather handbag, thrust her gloves into it, and pulling out a small bluebordered handkerchief, began to weep quietly.

"Huh-huh-huh-huh-huh," said Gant, shaking his head. "Too bad, too bad, too bad. Come back to my office," he said. They went back and sat down. Elizabeth dried her eyes.

"What was her name?" he asked.

"We called her Lily—her full name was Lillian Reed."

"Why, I knew that girl," he exclaimed. "I spoke to her not over two weeks ago."

"Yes," said Elizabeth, "she went like that—one hemorrhage right after another, down here." She tapped her abdomen. "Nobody ever knew she was sick until last Wednesday. Friday she was gone." She wept again.

"T-t-t-t-t," he clucked regretfully. "Too bad, too bad. She was pretty as a picture."

"I couldn't have loved her more, Mr. Gant," said Elizabeth, "if she had been my own daughter."

"How old was she?" he asked.

"Twenty-two," said Elizabeth, beginning to weep again.

"What a pity! What a pity!" he agreed. "Did she have any people?"

"No one who would do anything for her," Elizabeth said. "Her mother died when she was thirteen—she was born out here on the Beetree Fork—and her father," she added indignantly, "is a mean old bastard who's never done anything for her or any one else. He didn't even come to her funeral."

"He will be punished," said Gant darkly.

"As sure as there's a God in heaven," Elizabeth agreed, "he'll get what's coming to him in hell. The old bastard!" she continued virtuously, "I hope he rots!"

"You can depend upon it," he said grimly. "He will. Ah, Lord." He was silent a moment while he shook his head with slow regret.

"A pity, a pity," he muttered. "So young." He had the moment of triumph all men have when they hear some one has died. A moment, too, of grisly fear. Sixty-four.

"I couldn't have loved her more," said Elizabeth, "if she'd been one of my own. A young girl like that, with all her life before her."

"It's pretty sad when you come to think of it," he said. "By God, it is."

"And she was such a fine girl, Mr. Gant," said Elizabeth, weeping softly. "She had such a bright future before her. She had more opportunities than I ever had, and I suppose you know"—she spoke modestly—"what I've done."

"Why," he exclaimed, startled, "you're a rich woman, Elizabeth —damned if I don't believe you are. You own property all over town."

"I wouldn't say that," she answered, "but I've got enough to live on without ever doing another lick of work. I've had to work hard all my life. From now on I don't intend to turn my hand over."

She regarded him with a shy pleased smile, and touched a coil of her fine hair with a small competent hand. He looked at her attentively, noting with pleasure her firm uncorseted hips, moulded compactly into her tailored suit, and her cocked comely legs tapering to graceful feet, shod in neat little slippers of tan. She was firm, strong, washed, and elegant—a faint scent of lilac hovered over her: he looked at her candid eyes, lucently gray, and saw that she was quite a great lady.

"By God, Elizabeth," he said, "you're a fine-looking woman."

"I've had a good life," she said. "I've taken care of myself."

They had always known each other—since first they met. They had no excuses, no questions, no replies. The world fell away from them. In the silence they heard the pulsing slap of the fountain, the high laughter of bawdry in the Square. He took a book of models from the desk, and began to turn its slick pages. They showed modest blocks of Georgia marble and Vermont granite.

"I don't want any of those," she said impatiently. "I've already made up my mind. I know what I want."

He looked up surprised. "What is it?"

"I want the angel out front."

His face was shocked and unwilling. He gnawed the corner of his thin lip. No one knew how fond he was of the angel. Publicly he called it his White Elephant. He cursed it and said he had been a fool to order it. For six years it had stood on the porch, weathering, in all the wind and the rain. It was now brown and fly-specked. But it had come from Carrara in Italy, and it held a stone lily delicately in one hand. The other hand was lifted in benediction, it was poised clumsily upon the ball of one phthisic foot, and its stupid white face wore a smile of soft stone idiocy.

In his rages, Gant sometimes directed vast climaxes of abuse at the angel. "Fiend out of Hell!" he roared. "You have impoverished me, you have ruined me, you have cursed my declining years, and now you will crush me to death, fearful, awful, and unnatural monster that you are."

But sometimes when he was drunk he fell weeping on his knees before it, called it Cynthia, and entreated its love, forgiveness, and blessing for its sinful but repentant boy. There was laughter from the Square.

"What's the matter?" said Elizabeth. "Don't you want to sell it?"

"It will cost you a good deal, Elizabeth," he said evasively.

"I don't care," she answered, positively. "I've got the money. How much do you want?"

He was silent, thinking for a moment of the place where the angel stood. He knew he had nothing to cover or obliterate that place— it left a barren crater in his heart.

"All right," he said. "You can have it for what I paid for it—$420."

She took a thick sheaf of banknotes from her purse and counted the money out for him. He pushed it back.

"No. Pay me when the job's finished and it has been set up. You want some sort of inscription, don't you?"

"Yes. There's her full name, age, place of birth, and so on," she said, giving him a scrawled envelope. "I want some poetry, too— something that suits a young girl taken off like this."

He pulled his tattered little book of inscriptions from a pigeonhole, and thumbed its pages, reading her a quatrain here and there. To each she shook her head. Finally, he said: "How's this one, Elizabeth?" He read:

> She went away in beauty's flower,
> Before her youth was spent;
> Ere life and love had lived their hour
> God called her, and she went.
>
> Yet whispers Faith upon the wind:
> No grief to her was given.
> She left *your* love and went to find
> A greater one in heaven.

"Oh, that's lovely—lovely," she said. "I want that one."

"Yes," he agreed, "I think that's the best one."

In the musty cool smell of his little office they got up. Her gallant figure reached his shoulder. She buttoned her kid gloves over the small pink haunch of her palms and glanced about her. His battered sofa filled one wall, the line of his long body was printed in the leather. She looked up at him. His face was sad and grave. They remembered.

"It's been a long time, Elizabeth," he said.

They walked slowly to the front through aisled marbles. Sentinelled just beyond the wooden doors, the angel leered vacantly down. Jannadeau drew his great head turtlewise a little further into the protective hunch of his burly shoulders. They went out on to the porch.

The moon stood already, like its own phantom, in the clear washed skies of evening. A little boy with an empty paper-delivery bag swung lithely by, his freckled nostrils dilating pleasantly with hunger and the fancied smell of supper. He passed, and for a moment, as they stood at the porch edge, all life seemed frozen in a picture: the firemen and Fagg Sluder had seen Gant, whispered, and were now looking toward him; a policeman, at the high side-porch of the Police Court, leaned on the rail and stared; at the near edge of the central grass-plot below the fountain, a farmer bent for water at a bubbling jet, rose dripping, and stared; from the Tax Collector's office, City Hall, upstairs, Yancey, huge, meaty, shirtsleeved, stared. And in that second the slow pulse of the fountain was suspended, life was held, like an arrested gesture, in photographic abeyance, and Gant felt himself alone move deathward in a world of seemings as, in 1910, a man might find himself again in a picture taken on the grounds of the Chicago Fair, when he was thirty and his mustache black, and, noting the bustled ladies and the derbied men fixed in the second's pullulation, remember the dead instant, seek beyond the borders for what was there (he knew); or as a veteran who finds himself upon his elbow near Ulysses Grant, before the march, in pictures of the Civil War, and sees a dead man on a horse; or I should say, like some completed Don, who finds himself again before a tent in Scotland in his youth, and notes a cricket-bat long lost and long forgotten, the face of a poet who has died, and young men and the tutor as they looked that Long Vacation when they read nine hours a day for "Greats."

Where now? Where after? Where then?

THE PAPER ROUTE

TOWARD the beginning of Eugene's fourteenth year, when he had been a student at Leonard's for two years, Ben got work for him as a paper carrier. Eliza grumbled at the boy's laziness. She complained that she could get him to do little or nothing for her. In fact, he was not lazy, but he hated all the dreariness of boarding-house routine. Her demands on him were not heavy, but they were frequent and unexpected. He was depressed at the uselessness of effort in Dixieland, at the total erasure of all daily labor. If she had given him position, the daily responsibility of an ordered task, he could have fulfilled it with zeal. But her own method was much too random: she wanted to keep him on tap for an occasional errand, and he did not have her interest.

Dixieland was the heart of her life. It owned her. It appalled him.

When she sent him to the grocer's for bread, he felt wearily that the bread would be eaten by strangers, that nothing out of the effort of their lives grew younger, better, or more beautiful, that all was erased in a daily wash of sewage. She sent him forth in the rank thicket of her garden to hoe out the swarming weeds that clustered about her vegetables, which flourished, as did all the earth, under her careless touch. He knew, as he chopped down in a weary frenzy, that the weeds would grow again in the hot sun-stench, that her vegetables—weeded or not—would grow fat and be fed to her boarders, and that her life, hers alone, would endure to something. As he looked at her, he felt the weariness and horror of time: all but her must die in a smothering Sargasso. Thus, flailing the clotted earth drunkenly, he would be brought to suddenly by her piercing scream from the high back porch, and realize that he had destroyed totally a row of young bladed corn.

"Why, what on earth, boy!" she fretted angrily, peering down at him through a shelving confusion of wash-tubs, limp drying stockings, empty milk-bottles, murky and unwashed, and rusty lard-buckets. "I'll vow!" she said, turning to Mr. Baskett, the Hattiesburg cotton merchant, who grinned down malarially through his scraggly mustaches, "what am I going to do with him? He's chopped down every stock of corn in the row."

"Yes," Mr. Baskett said, peering over, "and missed every weed. Boy," he added judicially, "you need two months on a farm."

The bread that I fetch will be eaten by strangers. I carry coal and split up wood for fires to warm them. Smoke. *Fuimus fumus.* All of our life goes up in smoke. There is no structure, no creation in it, not even the smoky structure of dreams. Come lower, angel; whisper in our ears. We are passing away in smoke and there is nothing to-day but weariness to pay us for yesterday's toil. How may we save ourselves?

He was given the Niggertown route—the hardest and least profitable of all. He was paid two cents a copy for weekly deliveries, given ten per cent of his weekly collections, and ten cents for every new subscription. Thus, he was able to earn four or five dollars a week. His thin undeveloped body drank sleep with insatiable thirst, but it was now necessary for him to get up at half-past three in the morning with darkness and silence making an unreal humming in his drugged ears.

Strange aerial music came fluting out of darkness, or over his slow-wakening senses swept the great waves of symphonic orchestration. Fiend-voices, beautiful and sleep-loud, called down through darkness and light, developing the thread of ancient memory.

Staggering blindly in the whitewashed glare, his eyes, sleepcorded opened slowly as he was born anew, umbilically cut, from darkness. Waken, ghost-eared boy, but into darkness. Waken, phantom, O into us. Try, try, O try the way. Open the wall of light. Ghost, ghost, who is the ghost? O lost. Ghost, ghost, who is the ghost? O whisper-tongued laughter. Eugene! Eugene! Here, O here, Eugene. Here, Eugene. The way is here, Eugene. Have you forgotten? The leaf, the rock, the wall of light. Lift up the rock, Eugene, the leaf, the stone, the unfound door. Return, return.

A voice, sleep-strange and loud, forever far-near, spoke.

Eugene!

Spoke, ceased, continued without speaking, to speak. In him spoke. Where darkness, son, is light. Try, boy, the word you know remember. In the beginning was the logos. Over the border the borderless green-forested land. Yesterday, remember?

Far-forested, a horn-note wound. Sea-forested, water-far, the grotted coral sea-far horn-note. The pillioned ladies witch-faced in bottle-green robes saddle-swinging. Merwomen unscaled and lovely in sea-floor colonnades. The hidden land below the rock. The flitting wood-girls growing into bark. Far-faint, as he wakened, they besought him with lessening whir. Then deeper song, fiend-throated, wind-shod. Brother, O brother! They shot down the brink of darkness, gone on the wind like bullets. O lost, and by the wind grieved, ghost, come back again.

He dressed and descended the stairs gently to the back porch. The cool air, charged with blue starlight, shocked his body into wakefulness, but as he walked townward up the silent streets, the strange ringing in his ears persisted. He listened like his own ghost, to his footsteps, heard from afar the winking flicker of the street-lamps, saw, from sea-sunk eyes, the town.

There sounded in his heart a solemn music. It filled the earth, the air, the universe; it was not loud, but it was omnipresent, and it spoke to him of death and darkness, and of the focal march of all who lived or had lived, converging on a plain. The world was filled with silent marching men: no word was spoken, but in the heart of each there was a common knowledge, the word that all men knew and had forgotten, the lost key opening the prison gates, the lane-end into heaven, and as the music soared and filled him, he cried: "I will remember. When I come to the place, I shall know."

Hot bands of light streamed murkily from the doors and windows of the office. From the press-room downstairs there was an ascending roar as the big press mounted to its capacity. As he entered the office and drank in the warm tides of steel and ink that soaked the air, he awoke suddenly, his light-drugged limbs solidifying with a quick shock, as would some aerial spirit, whose floating body corporealizes the instant it touches earth. The carriers, waiting in a boisterous line, filed up to the circulation manager's desk, depositing their collections, cold handfuls of greasy coin. Seated beneath a green-shaded light, he ran swiftly down their books, totalling up their figures and counting nickels, dimes, and pennies into little spooned trays of a drawer. Then he gave to each a scrawled order for his morning quota.

They ran downstairs, eager as whippets to be off, brandishing their slips at a sullen counter whose black fingers galloped accurately across the stiff ridges of a great sheaf. He allowed them two "extras." If the carrier was not scrupulous, he increased his number of spare copies by keeping on his book the names of a half-dozen discontinued subscribers. These surplus copies were always good for coffee and pie with the lunchman, or as tribute to a favorite policeman, fireman, or motorman.

In the press-pit Harry Tugman loafed under their stare comfortably, a fat trickle of cigarette smoke coiling from his nostrils. He glanced over the press with professional carelessness, displaying his powerful chest with its thick bush, which lay a dark blot under his sweat-wet under-shirt. An assistant pressman climbed nimbly among roaring pistons and cylinders, an oil-can and a bunch of waste in his hand. A broad river of white paper rushed constantly up from the cylinder and leaped into a mangling chaos of machinery whence it emerged a second later, cut, printed, folded and stacked, sliding along a board with a hundred others in a fattening sheaf.

Machine-magic! Why not men, like that? Doctor, surgeon, poet, priest—stacked, folded, printed.

Harry Tugman cast away his wet fragment of cigarette with a luxurious grimace. The carriers eyed him reverently. Once he had knocked a sub-pressman down for sitting in his chair. He was Boss. He got $55 a week. If he was not pleased he could get work at any time on the *New Orleans Times-Picayune,* the *Louisville Courier Journal,* the *Atlanta Constitution,* the *Knoxville Sentinel,* the *Norfolk Pilot.* He could travel.

In a moment more they were out on the streets, hobbling along rapidly under the accustomed weight of the crammed canvas bags.

He was most desperately afraid of failure. He listened with constricted face to Eliza's admonition.

"Spruce up, boy! Spruce up! Make them think you are somebody!"

He had little confidence in himself; he recoiled in advance from the humiliation of dismissal. He feared the sabre-cut of language, and before his own pride he drew back and was afraid.

For three mornings he accompanied the retiring carrier, gathering his mind to focal intensity while he tried to memorize each stereotyped movement of the delivery, tracing again and again the labyrinthine web of Niggertown, wreaking his plan out among the sprawled chaos of clay and slime, making incandescent those houses to which a paper was delivered, and forgetting the others. Years later, alone in darkness, when he had forgotten the twisted anarchy of that pattern, he still remembered a corner where he left his bag while he climbed a spur of hill, a bank down which he clambered to three rotting shacks, a high porched house into which accurately he shot his folded block of news.

The retiring carrier was a robust country boy of seventeen who had been given better employment at the paper office. His name was Jennings Ware. He was tough, good-humored, a little cynical, and he smoked a great many cigarettes. He was clothed in vitality and comfort. He taught his pupil when and where to expect the prying face of "Foxy," how to escape discovery under the lunchroom counter, and how to fold a paper and throw it with the speed and accuracy of a ball.

In the fresh pre-natal morning they began their route, walking down the steep hill of Valley Street into tropical sleep, past the stabled torpor of black sleepers, past all the illicit loves, the casual and innumerable adulteries of Niggertown. As the stiff block of paper thudded sharply on the flimsy porch of a shack, or smacked the loose boarding of a door, they were answered by a long sullen moan of discontent. They sniggered.

"Check this one off," said Jennings Ware, "if you can't collect next time. She owes for six weeks now."

"This one," he said, flipping a paper quietly on a door mat, "is good pay. They're good niggers. You'll get your money every Wednesday."

"There's a High Yaller in here," he said, hurling the paper against the door with a whizzing smack and smiling, as a young full-meated woman's yell of indignation answered, a thin devil's grin. "You can have that if you want it."

A wan smile of fear struggled across Eugene's mouth. Jennings Ware looked at him shrewdly, but did not press him. Jennings Ware was a good-hearted boy.

"She's a pretty good old girl," he said. "You've got a right to a few dead-heads. Take it out in trade."

They walked on down the dark unpaved street, folding papers rapidly during the intervals between delivery.

"It's a hell of a route," said Jennings Ware. "When it rains it's terrible. You'll go into mud up to your knees. And you can't collect from half the bastards." He hurled a paper viciously.

"But, oh man" he said, after a moment. "If you want Jelly Roll you've come to the right place. I ain't kidding you!"

"With—with niggers?" Eugene whispered, moistening his dry lips. Jennings Ware turned his red satirical face on him.

"You don't see any Society Belles around here, do you?" he said.

"Are niggers good?" Eugene asked in a small dry voice.

"Boy!" The word blew out of Jennings Ware's mouth like an explosion. He was silent a moment.

"There ain't nothing better," he said.

At first, the canvas strap of the paper-bag bit cruelly across his slender shoulders. He strained against the galling weight that pulled him earthwards. The first weeks were like a warring nightmare: day after day he fought his way up to liberation. He knew all the sorrow of those who carry weight; he knew, morning by morning, the aerial ecstasy of release. As his load lightened with the progress of his route, his leaning shoulder rose with winged buoyancy, his straining limbs grew light: at the end of his labor his flesh, touched sensuously by fatigue, bounded lightly from the earth. He was Mercury chained by fardels, Ariel bent beneath a pack: freed, his wingshod feet trod brightness. He sailed in air. The rapier stars glinted upon his serfdom: dawn reddened on release. He was like a sailor drowned within the hold, who gropes to life and morning through a hatch; a diver twined desperately in octopal feelers, who cuts himself from death and mounts slowly from the sea-floor into light.

Within a month a thick hummock of muscle hardened on his shoulder: he bent jubilantly into his work. He had now no fear of failure. His heart lifted like a proud crested cock. He had been dropped among others without favor, and he surpassed them. He was a lord of darkness; he exulted in the lonely sufficiency of his work. He walked into the sprawled chaos of the settlement, the rifleman of news for sleeping men. His fast hands blocked the crackling sheet, he swung his lean arm like a whip. He saw the pale stars drown, and ragged light break open on the hills. Alone, the only man alive, he began the day for men, as he walked by the shuttered windows and heard the long denned snore of the tropics. He walked amid this close thick sleep, hearing again the ghostly ring of his own feet, and the vast orchestral music of darkness. As the gray tide of morning surged westward he awoke.

And Eugene watched the slow fusion of the seasons; he saw the royal processional of the months; he saw the summer light eat like a river into dark; he saw dark triumph once again; and he saw the minute-winning days, like flies, buzz home to death.

In summer, full day had come before he finished: he walked home in a world of wakenings. The first cars were grouped on the Square as he passed, their new green paint giving them the pleasant appearance of fresh toys. The huge battered cans of the milkmen glinted cleanly in the sun. Light fell hopefully upon the swarthy greasiness of George Chakales, nightman of the Athens Cafe. The Hellenic Dawn. And in Uneeda No. 1, upon the Square, Eugene sat, washing an egg-sandwich down with long swallows of pungent coffee, stooled in a friendly company of motormen, policemen, chauffeurs, plasterers, and masons. It was very pleasant, he felt, to complete one's work when all the world was beginning theirs. He went home under singing trees of birds.

In autumn, a late red moon rode low in the skies till morning. The air was filled with dropping leaves, there was a solemn thunder of great trees upon the hills; sad phantasmal whisperings and the vast cathedral music deepened in his heart.

In winter, he went down joyously into the dark howling wind, leaning his weight upon its advancing wall as it swept up a hill; and when in early Spring the small cold rain fell from the reeking sky he was content. He was alone.

He harried his deficient subscribers for payment, with a wild tenacity. He accepted their easy promises without question; he hunted them down in their own rooms, or in the rooms of a neighbor, he pressed so doggedly that, at length, sullenly or good-humoredly, they paid a part of their debt. This was more than any of his predecessors had accomplished, but he fretted nervously over his accounts until he found that he had become, for the circulation manager, the exemplar for indolent boys. As he dumped his desperately gathered pile of "chicken feed" upon the man's desk, his employer would turn accusingly to a delinquent boy, saying:

"Look at that! He does it every week! Niggers, too!"

His pallid face would flame with joy and pride. When he spoke to the great man his voice trembled. He could hardly speak.

As the wind yelled through the dark, he burst into maniacal laughter. He leaped high into the air with a scream of insane exultancy, burred in his throat idiot animal-squeals, and shot his papers terrifically into the flimsy boarding of the shacks. He was free. He was alone. He heard the howl of a train-whistle, and it was not so far away. In the darkness he flung his arm out to the man on the rails, his goggled brother with steel-steady rail-fixed eyes.

He did not shrink so much, beneath the menace of the family fist. He was more happily unmindful of his own unworthiness.

Assembled with three or four of the carriers in the lunchroom, he learned to smoke: in the sweet blue air of Spring, as he sloped down to his route, he came to know the beauty of Lady Nicotine, the de-

lectable wraith who coiled into his brain, left her poignant breath
in his young nostrils, her sharp kiss upon his mouth.

He was a sharp blade.

The Spring drove a thorn into his heart, it drew a wild cry from
his lips. For it, he had no speech.

He knew hunger. He knew thirst. A great flame rose in him. He
cooled his hot face in the night by bubbling water jets. Alone, he
wept sometimes with pain and ecstasy. At home the frightened silence of his childhood was now touched with savage restraint. He
was wired like a race-horse. A white atom of inchoate fury would
burst in him like a rocket, and for a moment he would be cursing
mad.

"What's wrong with him? Is it the Pentland crazy streak coming
out?" Helen asked, seated in Eliza's kitchen.

Eliza moulded her lips portentously for some time, shaking her
head slowly.

"Why," she said, with a cunning smile, "don't you know, child?"

His need for the Negroes had become acute. He spent his afternoons after school combing restlessly through the celled hive of Niggertown. The rank stench of the branch, pouring its thick brown
sewage down a bed of worn boulders, the smell of wood-smoke and
laundry stewing in a black iron yard-pot, and the low jungle cadences
of dusk, the forms that slid, dropped, and vanished, beneath a twinkling orchestration of small sounds. Fat ropes of language in the dusk,
the larded sizzle of frying fish, the sad faint twanging of a banjo, and
the stamp, far-faint, of heavy feet; voices Nilotic, river-wailing, and
the greasy light of four thousand smoky lamps in shack and tenement.

From the worn central butte round which the colony swarmed,
the panting voices of the Calvary Baptist Church mounted, in an
exhausting and unceasing frenzy, from seven o'clock until two in
the morning, in their wild jungle wail of sin and love and death.
The dark was hived with flesh and mystery. Rich wells of laughter
bubbled everywhere. The catforms slid. Everything was immanent.
Everything was far. Nothing could be touched.

In this old witch-magic of the dark, he began to know the awful
innocence of evil, the terrible youth of an ancient race; his lips slid
back across his teeth, he prowled in darkness with loose swinging

arms, and his eyes shone. Shame and terror, indefinable, surged through him. He could not face the question in his heart.

A good part of his subscription list was solidly founded among decent and laborious darkies—barbers, tailors, grocers, pharmacists, and ginghamed black housewives, who paid him promptly on a given day each week, greeted him with warm smiles full of teeth, and titles of respect extravagant and kindly: "Mister," "Colonel," "General," "Governor," and so on. They all knew Gant.

But another part—the part in which his desire and wonder met— were "floaters," young men and women of precarious means, variable lives, who slid mysteriously from cell to cell, who peopled the night with their flitting stealth. He sought these phantoms fruitlessly for weeks, until he discovered that he might find them only on Sunday morning, tossed like heavy sacks across one another, in the fetid dark of a tenement room, a half-dozen young men and women, in a snoring exhaustion of whisky-stupor and sexual depletion.

One Saturday evening, in the fading red of a summer twilight, he returned to one of these tenements, a rickety three-story shack, that cropped its two lower floors down a tall clay bank at the western ledge, near the whites. Two dozen men and women lived here. He was on the search for a woman named Ella Corpening. He had never been able to find her: she was weeks behind in her subscriptions. But her door stood open to-night: a warm waft of air and cooking food came up to him. He descended the rotten steps that climbed the bank.

Ella Corpening sat facing the door in a rocking chair, purring lazily in the red glow of a little kitchen range, with her big legs stretched comfortably out on the floor. She was a mulatto of twenty-six years, a handsome woman of Amazonian proportions, with smooth tawny skin.

She was dressed in the garments of some former mistress: she wore a brown woollen skirt, patent-leather shoes with high suede tops pearl-buttoned, and gray silk hose. Her long heavy arms shone darkly through the light texture of a freshly laundered white shirtwaist. A lacing of cheap blue ribbon gleamed across the heavy curve of her breasts.

There was a bubbling pot of cabbage and sliced fat pork upon the stove.

"Paper boy," said Eugene. "Come to collect."

"Is you de boy?" drawled Ella Corpening with a lazy movement of her arm. "How much does I owe?"

"$1.20," he answered. He looked meaningfully at one extended leg, where, thrust in below the knee, a wadded bank-note gleamed dully.

"Dat's my rent money," she said. "Can't give you dat. Dollah-twenty!" She brooded. "Uh! Uh!" she grunted pleasantly. "Don't seem lak it ought to be dat much."

"It is, though," he said, opening his account book.

"It mus' is," she agreed, "if de book says so."

She meditated luxuriously for a moment.

"Does you collec' Sunday mawnin'?" she asked.

"Yes," he said.

"You come roun' in de mawnin'," she said hopefully. "I'll have somethin' fo' yuh, sho. I'se waitin' fo' a white gent'man now. He's goin' gib me a dollah."

She moved her great limbs slowly, and smiled at him. Forked pulses beat against his eyes. He gulped dryly: his legs were rotten with excitement.

"What's—what's he going to give you a dollar for?" he muttered, barely audible.

"Jelly Roll," said Ella Corpening.

He moved his lips twice, unable to speak. She got up from her chair.

"What yo' want?" she asked softly. "Jelly Roll?"

"Want to see—to see!" he gasped.

She closed the door opening on the bank and locked it. The stove cast a grated glow from its open ashpan. There was a momentary rain of red cinders into the pit.

Ella Corpening opened the door beyond that, leading to another room. There were two dirty rumpled beds; the single window was bolted and covered by an old green shade. She lit a smoky little lamp, and turned the wick low.

There was a battered little dresser with a mottled glass, from which the blistered varnish was flaking. Over the screened hearth, on a low mantel, there was a Kewpie doll, sashed with pink ribbon, a vase with fluted edges and gilt flowers, won at a carnival, and a paper of pins. A calendar, also, by courtesy of the Altamont Coal and Ice Company, showing an Indian maid paddling her canoe down an alley of paved moonlight, and a religious motto in flowered scroll-work, framed in walnut: *God Loves Them Both.*

"What yo' want?" she whispered, facing him.

Far off, he listened to the ghost of his own voice.

"Take off your clothes."

Her skirt fell in a ring about her feet. She took off her starched waist. In a moment, save for her hose, she stood naked before him.

Her breath came quickly, her full tongue licked across her mouth.

"Dance!" he cried. "Dance!"

She began to moan softly, while an undulant tremor flowed through her great yellow body; her hips and her round heavy breasts writhed slowly in a sensual rhythm.

Her straight oiled hair fell across her neck in a thick shock. She extended her arms for balance, the lids closed over her large yellow eyeballs. She came near him. He felt her hot breath on his face, the smothering flood of her breasts. He was whirled like a chip in the wild torrent of her passion. Her powerful yellow hands gripped his slender arms round like bracelets. She shook him to and fro slowly, fastening him tightly against her pelt.

He strained back desperately against the door, drowning in her embrace.

"Get-'way nigger. Get-'way," he panted thickly.

Slowly she released him: without opening her eyes, moaning, she slid back as if he had been a young tree. She sang, in a wailing minor key, with unceasing iteration:

"Jelly Roll! J-e-e-e-ly Roll!—"

her voice falling each time to a low moan.

Her face, the broad column of her throat, and her deep-breasted torso were rilled with sweat. He fumbled blindly for the door, lunged across the outer room and, gasping, found his way into the air. Her chant, unbroken and undisturbed by his departure, followed him up the flimsy steps. He did not pause to get his breath until he came to the edge of the market square. Below him in the valley, across on the butte, the smoky lamps of Niggertown flared in the dusk. Faint laughter, rich, jungle-wild, welled up from hived darkness. He heard lost twangling notes, the measured thump of distant feet; beyond, above, more thin, more far than all, the rapid wail of sinners in a church.

THE WORLD OF BOOKS

Ἐντεῦθεν ἐξελαύνει σταθμοὺς τρεῖς παρασάγγας πεντεκαίδεκα ἐπὶ τὸν Εὐφράτην ποταμὸν·

HE DID not tell the Leonards that he was working in the early morning. He knew they would oppose his employment, and that their opposition would manifest itself in the triumphant argument of lowered grades. Also, Margaret Leonard, he knew, would talk ominously of health undermined, of the promise of future years destroyed, of the sweet lost hours of morning sleep that could never be regained. He was really more robust now than he had ever been. He was heavier and stronger. But he sometimes felt a gnawing hunger for sleep: he grew heavy at mid-day, revived in the afternoon, but found it difficult to keep his sleepy brain fixed on a book after eight o'clock in the evening.

He learned little of discipline. Under the care of the Leonards he came even to have a romantic contempt for it. Margaret Leonard had the marvelous vision, of great people, for essences. She saw always the dominant color, but she did not always see the shadings. She was an inspired sentimentalist. She thought she "knew boys": she was proud of her knowledge of them. In fact, however, she had little knowledge of them. She would have been stricken with horror if she could have known the wild confusion of adolescence, the sexual nightmares of puberty, the grief, the fear, the shame in which a boy broods over the dark world of his desire. She did not know that every boy, caged in from confession by his fear, is to himself a monster.

She did not have knowledge. But she had wisdom. She found immediately a person's quality. Boys were her heroes, her little gods. She believed that the world was to be saved, life redeemed, by one of them. She saw the flame that burns in each of them, and she guarded it. She tried somehow to reach the dark gropings toward light and articulation, of the blunt, the stolid, the shamefast. She spoke a calm low word to the trembling racehorse, and he was still.

Thus, he made no confessions. He was still prison-pent. But he turned always to Margaret Leonard as toward the light: she saw the unholy fires that cast their sword-dance on his face, she saw the hunger and the pain, and she fed him—majestic crime!—on poetry.

Whatever of fear or shame locked them in careful silence, whatever decorous pretense of custom guarded their tongues, they found release in the eloquent symbols of verse. And by that sign, Margaret was lost to the good angels. For what care the ambassadors of Satan, for all the small fidelities of the letter and the word, if from the singing choir of earthly methodism we can steal a single heart—lift up, flame-tipped, one great lost soul to the high sinfulness of poetry?

The wine of the grape had never stained her mouth, but the wine of poetry was inextinguishably mixed with her blood, entombed in her flesh.

By the beginning of his fifteenth year Eugene knew almost every major lyric in the language. He possessed them to their living core, not in a handful of scattered quotations, but almost line for line. His thirst was drunken, insatiate: he added to his hoard entire scenes from Schiller's *William Tell,* which he read by himself in German; the lyrics of Heine, and several folk songs. He committed to memory the entire passage in the *Anabasis,* the mounting and triumphal Greek which described the moment when the starving remnant of the Ten Thousand had come at length to the sea, and sent up their great cry, calling it by name. In addition, he memorized some of the sonorous stupidities of Cicero, because of the sound, and a little of Caesar, terse and lean.

The great lyrics of Burns he knew from music, from reading, or from hearing Gant recite them. But "Tam O'Shanter" Margaret Leonard read to him, her eyes sparkling with laughter as she read:

"In hell they'll roast thee like a herrin'."

The shorter Wordsworth pieces he had read at grammar school. "My heart leaps up," "I wandered lonely as a cloud," and "Behold her, single in the field," he had known for years; but Margaret read him the sonnets and made him commit "The world is too much with us" to memory. Her voice trembled and grew low with passion when she read it.

He knew all the songs in Shakespeare's plays, but the two that moved him most were: "O mistress mine, where are you roaming?" which blew a far horn in his heart, and the great song from *Cymbeline*: "Fear no more the heat o' the sun." He had tried to read all the sonnets, and failed, because their woven density was too much for his experience, but he had read, and forgotten, perhaps half of them, and remembered a few which burned up from the page, strangely, immediately, like lamps for him.

Those that he knew were: "When, in the chronicle of wasted time," "To me, fair friend, you never can be old," "Let me not to the marriage of true minds," "The expense of spirit in a waste of shame," "When to the sessions of sweet silent thought," "Shall I compare thee to a summer's day?" "From you have I been absent in the spring," and "That time of year thou mayest in me behold," the greatest of all, which Margaret brought him to, and which shot through him with such electric ecstasy when he came to "Bare ruined choirs, where late the sweet birds sang," that he could hardly hold his course unbroken through the rest of it.

He read all the plays save *Timon, Titus Andronicus, Pericles, Coriolanus,* and *King John,* but the only play that held his interest from first to last was *King Lear.* With most of the famous declamatory passages he had been familiar, for years, by Gant's recitation, and now they wearied him. And all the wordy pinwheels of the clowns, which Margaret laughed at dutifully, and exhibited as specimens of the master's swingeing wit, he felt vaguely were very dull. He never had any confidence in Shakespeare's humor—his Touchstones were not only windy fools, but dull ones.

"For my part I had rather bear with you than bear you; yet I should bear no cross if I did bear you, for I think you have no money in your purse."

This sort of thing reminded him unpleasantly of the Pentlands. The Fool in "Lear" alone he thought admirable—a sad, tragic, mysterious fool. For the rest, he went about and composed parodies, which, with a devil's grin, he told himself would split the sides of posterity. Such as: "Aye, nuncle, an if Shrove Tuesday come last Wednesday, I'll do the capon to thy cock, as Tom O'Ludgate told the shepherd when he found the cowslips gone. Dost bay with two throats, Cerberus? Down, boy, down!"

The admired beauties he was often tired of, perhaps because he had heard them so often, and it seemed to him, moreover, that Shakespeare often spoke absurdly and pompously when he might better have spoken simply, as in the scene where, being informed by the Queen of the death of his sister by drowning, Laertes says:

> "Too much of water hast thou, poor Ophelia,
> And therefore I forbid my tears."

You really can't beat that (he thought). Aye, Ben! Would he had blotted a hundred! A thousand!

But he was deep in other passages which the elocutionist misses, such as the terrible and epic invocation of Edmund, in *King Lear,* drenched in evil, which begins:

> "Thou, Nature, art my goddess,"

and ends,

> "Now, gods, stand up for bastards."

It was as dark as night, as evil as Niggertown, as vast as the elemental winds that howled down across the hills: he chanted it in the black hours of his labor, into the dark and the wind. He understood; he exulted in its evil—which was the evil of earth, of illicit nature. It was a call to the unclassed; it was a cry for those beyond the fence, for rebel angels, and for all of the men who are too tall.

He knew nothing of the Elizabethan drama beyond Shakespeare's plays. But he very early came to know a little of the poetry of Ben Jonson, whom Margaret looked on as a literary Falstaff, condoning, with the familiar weakness of the schoolmarm, his Gargantuan excesses as a pardonable whimsy of genius.

She was somewhat academically mirthful over the literary bacchanalia, as a professor in a Baptist college smacks his lips appetizingly and beams ruddily at his classes when he reads of sack and porter

and tankards foaming with the musty ale. All this is part of the liberal tradition. Men of the world are broadminded. Witness Professor
Albert Thorndyke Firkins, of the University of Chicago, at the Falcon
in Soho. Smiling bravely, he sits over a half-pint of bitter beer, in
the company of a racing tout, a swaybacked barmaid, broad in the
stern, with adjustable teeth, and three companionable tarts from
Lisle street, who are making the best of two pints of Guinness. With
eager impatience he awaits the arrival of G. K. Chesterton and E. V.
Lucas.

"O rare Ben Jonson!" Margaret Leonard sighed with gentle laughter. "Ah, Lord!"

"My God, boy!" Sheba roared, snatching the suggested motif of
conversation out of the air, and licking her buttered fingers noisily
as she stormed into action. "God bless him!" Her hairy red face
burned like clover, her veinous eyes were tearful bright. "God bless
him, 'Gene! He was as English as roast beef and a tankard of musty
ale!"

"Ah, Lord!" sighed Margaret. "He was a genius if ever there was
one." With misty eyes she gazed far off, a thread of laughter on her
mouth. "Whee!" she laughed gently. "Old Ben!"

"And say, 'Gene!" Sheba continued, bending forward with a fat
hand gripped upon her knee. "Do you know that the greatest tribute
to Shakespeare's genius is from his hand?"

"Ah, I tell you, boy!" said Margaret, with darkened eyes. Her voice
was husky. He was afraid she was going to weep.

"And yet the fools!" Sheba yelled. "The mean little two-by-two
pusillanimous swill-drinking fools—"

"Whee!" gently Margaret moaned. John Dorsey turned his chalk-
white face to the boy and whined with vacant appreciation, winking
his head pertly. Ah absently!

"—for that's all they are, have had the effrontery to suggest that he
was jealous."

"Pshaw!" said Margaret impatiently. "There's nothing in that."

"Why, they don't know what they're talking about!" Sheba turned
a sudden grinning face upon him. "The little upstarts! It takes us to
tell 'em, 'Gene," she said.

He began to slide floorwards out of the wicker chair. John Dorsey slapped his meaty thigh, and bent forward whining inchoately, drooling slightly at the mouth.

"The Lord a' mercy!" he wheezed, gasping.

"I was talking to a feller the other day," said Sheba, "a lawyer that you'd think might know a *little* something, and I used a quotation out of *The Merchant of Venice* that every schoolboy knows—'The quality of mercy is not strained.' The man looked at me as if he thought I was crazy!"

"Great heavens!" said Margaret in a still voice.

"I said, 'Look here, Mr. So-and-so, you may be a smart lawyer, you may have your million dollars that they say you have, but there are a lot of things you don't know yet. There are a lot of things money can't buy, my sonny, and one of them is the society of cult-shered men and women.' "

"Why, pshaw!" said Mr. Leonard. "What do these little whipper-snappers know about the things of the mind? You might as well expect some ignorant darky out in the fields to construe a passage in Homer." He grasped a glass half full of clabber, on the table, and tilting it intently in his chalky fingers, spooned out a lumpy spilth of curds which he slid, quivering, into his mouth. "No, sir!" he laughed. "They may be Big Men on the tax collector's books, but when they try to associate with educated men and women, as the feller says, 'they—they—' " he began to whine, " 'why, they just ain't nothin'.' "

"What shall it profit a man," said Sheba, "if he gain the whole world, and lose—"

"Ah, Lord!" sighed Margaret, shaking her smoke-dark eyes. "I tell you!"

She told him. She told him of the Swan's profound knowledge of the human heart, his universal and well-rounded characterization, his enormous humor.

"Fought a long hour by Shrewsbury clock!" She laughed. "The fat rascal! Imagine a man keeping the time!"

And, carefully: "It was the custom of the time, 'Gene. As a matter of fact, when you read some of the plays of his contemporaries you see how much purer he is than they are." But she avoided a word, a line, here and there. The slightly spotty Swan—muddied a little by custom. Then, too, the Bible.

The smoky candle-ends of time. Parnassus As Seen From Mount

Sinai: Lecture with lantern-slides by Professor McTavish (D.D.) of Presbyterian College.

"And observe, Eugene," she said, "he never made vice attractive."

"Why didn't he?" he asked. "There's Falstaff."

"Yes," she replied, "and you know what happened to him, don't you?"

"Why," he considered, "he died!"

"You see, don't you?" she concluded, with triumphant warning.

I see, don't I? The wages of sin. What, by the way, are the wages of virtue? The good die young.

> Boo-hoo! Boo-hoo! Boo-hoo!
> I really feel so blue!
> I was given to crime,
> And cut off in my prime
> When only eighty-two.

"Then, note," she said, "how none of his characters stand still. You can see them grow, from first to last. No one is the same at the end as he was in the beginning."

In the beginning was the word. I am Alpha and Omega. The growth of Lear. He grew old and mad. There's growth for you.

This tin-currency of criticism she had picked up in a few courses at college, and in her reading. They were—are, perhaps, still—part of the glib jargon of pedants. But they did her no real injury. They were simply the things people said. She felt, guiltily, that she must trick out her teaching with these gauds: she was afraid that what she had to offer was not enough. What she had to offer was simply a feeling that was so profoundly right, so unerring, that she could no more utter great verse meanly than mean verse well. She was a voice that God seeks. She was the reed of demonic ecstasy. She was possessed, she knew not how, but she knew the moment of her possession. The singing tongues of all the world were wakened into life again under the incantation of her voice. She was inhabited. She was spent.

She passed through their barred and bolted boy-life with the direct stride of a spirit. She opened their hearts as if they had been lockets. They said: "Mrs. Leonard is sure a nice lady."

He knew some of Ben Jonson's poems, including the fine Hymn to Diana, "Queen and huntress, chaste and fair," and the great tribute to Shakespeare which lifted his hair at

". . . But call forth thundering Æschylus,
Euripides and Sophocles to us."—

and caught at his throat at:

"He was not for an age, but for all time!
And all the Muses still were in their prime . . ."

The elegy to little Salathiel Pavy, the child actor, was honey from the lion's mouth. But it was too long.

Of Herrick, sealed of the tribe of Ben, he knew much more. The poetry sang itself. It was, he thought later, the most perfect and unfailing lyrical voice in the language—a clean, sweet, small, unfaltering note. It is done with the incomparable ease of an inspired child. The young men and women of our century have tried to recapture it, as they have tried to recapture Blake and, a little more successfully, Donne.

Here a little child I stand
Heaving up my either hand;
Cold as paddocks though they be,

Here I lift them up to Thee,
For a benison to fall
On our meat and on us all. Amen.

There was nothing beyond this—nothing that surpassed it in precision, delicacy, and wholeness.

Their names dropped musically like small fat bird-notes through the freckled sunlight of a young world: prophetically he brooded on the sweet lost bird-cries of their names, knowing they never would return. Herrick, Crashaw, Carew, Suckling, Campion, Lovelace, Dekker. O sweet content, O sweet, O sweet content!

He read shelves of novels: all of Thackeray, all the stories of Poe and Hawthorne, and Herman Melville's *Omoo* and *Typee,* which he found at Gant's. Of *Moby Dick* he had never heard. He read a half-dozen Coopers, all of Mark Twain, but failed to finish a single book of Howells or James.

He read a dozen of Scott, and liked best of all *Quentin Durward*, because the descriptions of food were as bountiful and appetizing as any he had ever read.

APRIL IN ALTAMONT

A LIGHT wind of April fanned over the hill. There was a smell of burning leaves and rubble around the school. In the field on the hill flank behind the house a plowman drove his big horse with loose clanking traces around a lessening square of dry fallow earth. Gee, woa. His strong feet followed after. The big share bit cleanly down, cleaving a deep spermy furrow of moist young earth along its track.

John Dorsey Leonard stared fascinated out the window at the annual rejuvenation of the earth. Before his eyes the emergent nymph was scaling her hard cracked hag's pelt. The golden age returned.

Down the road a straggling queue of boys were all gone into the world of light. Wet with honest sweat, the plowman paused at the turn, and wiped the blue shirting of his forearm across his beaded forehead. Meanwhile, his intelligent animal, taking advantage of the interval, lifted with slow majesty a proud flowing tail, and added his mite to the fertility of the soil with three moist oaty droppings. Watching, John Dorsey grunted approvingly. They also serve who only stand and wait.

"Please, Mr. Leonard," said Eugene, carefully choosing his moment, "can I go?"

John Dorsey Leonard stroked his chin absently, and stared sightlessly at his book. Others abide our question, thou art free.

"Huh?" he purred vaguely. Then, with a high vacant snigger he turned suddenly, and said:

"You rascal, you! See if Mrs. Leonard wants you." He fastened his brutal grip with keen hunger into the boy's thin arm. April is the cruelest of months. Eugene winced, moved away, and then stood quietly, checked by memory of the old revolt from awe.

He found Margaret in the library reading to the children from *The Water Babies.*

"Mr. Leonard says to ask you if I can go?" he said.

And her eyes were darkened wholly.

"Yes, you scamp. Go on," she said. "Tell me, boy," she coaxed, softly, "can't you be a little bit better?"

"Yes'm," he promised, easily. "I'll try." Say not the struggle naught availeth.

She smiled at his high mettled prancing nervousness.

"In hell they'll roast thee like a herrin'," she said gently. "Get out of here."

He bounded away from the nunnery of the chaste breast and quiet mind.

As he leaped down the stairs into the yard he heard Dirk Barnard's lusty splashing bathtub solo. Sweet Thames, run softly till I end my song. Tyson Leonard, having raked into every slut's corner of nature with a thin satisfied grin, emerged from the barn with a cap full of fresh eggs. A stammering cackle of protest followed him from angry hens who found too late that men betray. At the barnside, under the carriage shed, "Pap" Rheinhart tightened the bellyband of his sad-dled brown mare, swinging strongly into the saddle, and with a hard scramble of hoofs, came up the hill, wheeled in behind the house, and drew up by Eugene.

"Jump on, 'Gene," he invited, patting the mare's broad rump. "I'll take you home."

Eugene looked up at him grinning.

"You'll take me nowhere," he said. "I couldn't sit down for a week last time."

"Pap" boomed with laughter.

"Why, pshaw, boy!" he said. "That was nothing but a gentle little dog-trot."

"Dog-trot your granny," said Eugene. "You tried to kill me."

"Pap" Rheinhart turned his wry neck down on the boy with grave dry humor.

"Come on," he said gruffly. "I'm not going to hurt you. I'll teach you how to ride a horse."

"Much obliged, Pap," said Eugene ironically. "But I'm thinking of using my tail a good deal in my old age. I don't want to wear it out while I'm young."

Pleased with them both, "Pap" Rheinhart laughed loud and deep, spat a brown quid back over the horse's crupper, and, digging his heels in smartly, galloped away around the house, into the road. The horse bent furiously to his work, like a bounding dog. With four-hooved thunder he drummed upon the sounding earth. *Quadrupedante putrem sonitu quatit ungula campum.*

At the two-posted entry, by the bishop's boundary, the departing students turned, split quickly to the sides, and urged the horseman on with shrill cries. "Pap" bent low, with loose-reined hands above the horsemane, went through the gate like the whiz of a cross-bow. Then, he jerked the mare back on her haunches with a dusty skid of hoofs, and waited for the boys to come up.

"Hey!" With high bounding exultancy Eugene came down the road to join them. Without turning, stolid Van Yeats threw up his hand impatiently and greeted the unseen with a cheer. The others turned, welcoming him with ironical congratulation.

" 'Highpockets,' " said "Doc" Hines, comically puckering his small tough face, "how'd you happen to git out on time?" He had an affected, high-pitched nigger drawl. When he spoke he kept one hand in his coat pocket, fingering a leather thong loaded with buckshot.

"J. D. had to do his spring plowing," said Eugene.

"Well, if it ain't ole Handsome," said Julius Arthur. He grinned squintily, revealing a mouthful of stained teeth screwed in a wire clamp. His face was covered with small yellow pustulate sores. How begot, how nourished?

"Shall we sing our little song for Handsome Hal?" said Ralph Rolls to his copesmate Julius. He wore a derby hat jammed over his pert freckled face. As he spoke he took a ragged twist of tobacco from his pocket and bit off a large chew with a rough air of relish.

"Want a chew, Jule?" he said.

Julius took the twist, wiped off his mouth with a loose male grin, and crammed a large quid into his cheek.

He brought me roots of relish sweet.

"Want one, Highpockets?" he asked Eugene, grinning.

I hate him that would upon the rack of this tough world stretch me out longer.

"Hell," said Ralph Rolls. "Handsome would curl up and die if he ever took a chew."

In Spring like torpid snakes my enemies awaken.

At the corner of Church Street, across from the new imitation Tudor of the Episcopal church, they paused. Above them, on the hill, rose the steeples of the Methodist and Presbyterian churches. Ye antique spires, ye distant towers!

"Who's going my way?" said Julius Arthur. "Come on, 'Gene. The car's down here. I'll take you home."

"Thanks, but I can't," said Eugene. "I'm going up-town." Their curious eyes on Dixieland when I get out.

"You going home, Villa?"

"No," said George Graves.

"Well, keep Hal out of trouble," said Ralph Rolls.

Julius Arthur laughed roughly and thrust his hand through Eugene's hair. "Old Hairbreadth Hal," he said. "The cutthroat from Saw-Tooth Gap!"

"Don't let 'em climb your frame, son," said Van Yeats, turning his quiet pleasant face on Eugene. "If you need help, let me know."

"So long, boys."

"So long."

They crossed the street, mixing in nimble horse-play, and turned down past the church along a sloping street that led to the garages. George Graves and Eugene continued up the hill.

"Julius is a good boy," said George Graves. "His father makes more money than any other lawyer in town."

"Yes," said Eugene, still brooding on Dixieland and his clumsy deceptions.

A street-sweeper walked along slowly uphill, beside his deep wedge-bodied cart. From time to time he stopped the big slow-footed horse and, sweeping the littered droppings of street and gutter into a pan, with a long-handled brush, dumped his collections into the cart. Let not Ambition mock their useful toil.

Three sparrows hopped deftly about three fresh smoking globes of horse-dung, pecking out tidbits with dainty gourmandism. Driven away by the approaching cart, they skimmed briskly over to the bank, with bright twitters of annoyance. One too like thee, tameless, and swift, and proud.

George Graves ascended the hill with a slow ponderous rhythm, staring darkly at the ground.

"Say, 'Gene!" he said finally. "I don't believe he makes that much."

Eugene thought seriously for a moment. With George Graves, it was necessary to resume a discussion where it had been left off three days before.

"Who?" he said, "John Dorsey? Yes, I think he does," he added, grinning.

"Not over $2,500, anyway," said George Graves gloomily.

"No—three thousand, three thousand!" he said, in a choking voice.

George Graves turned to him with a sombre, puzzled smile. "What's the matter?" he asked.

"O you fool! You damn fool!" gasped Eugene. "You've been thinking about it all this time."

George Graves laughed sheepishly, with embarrassment, richly.

From the top of the hill at the left, the swelling unction of the Methodist organ welled up remotely from the choir, accompanied by a fruity contralto voice, much in demand at funerals. Abide with me.

Most musical of mourners, weep again!

George Graves turned and examined the four large black houses, ascending on flat terraces to the church, of Paston Place.

"That's a good piece of property, 'Gene," he said. "It belongs to the Paston estate."

Fast falls the even-tide. Heaves the proud harlot her distended breast, in intricacies of laborious song.

"It will all go to Gil Paston some day," said George Graves with virtuous regret. "He's not worth a damn."

They had reached the top of the hill. Church Street ended levelly a block beyond, in the narrow gulch of the avenue. They saw, with quickened pulse, the little pullulation of the town.

A negro dug tenderly in the round loamy flowerbeds of the Presbyterian churchyard, bending now and then to thrust his thick fingers gently in about the roots. The old church, with its sharp steeple, rotted slowly, decently, prosperously, like a good man's life, down into its wet lichened brick. Eugene looked gratefully, with a second's pride, at its dark decorum, its solid Scotch breeding.

"I'm a Presbyterian," he said. "What are you?"

"An Episcopalian, when I go," said George Graves with irreverent laughter.

"To hell with these Methodists!" Eugene said with an elegant, disdainful face. "They're too damn common for us." God in three persons—blessed Trinity. "Brother Graves," he continued, in a fat well-oiled voice, "I didn't see you at prayer-meeting Wednesday night. Where in Jesus' name were you?"

With his open palm he struck George Graves violently between his meaty shoulders. George Graves staggered drunkenly with high resounding laughter.

"Why, Brother Gant," said he, "I had a little appointment with one of the Good Sisters, out in the cow-shed."

Eugene gathered a telephone pole into his wild embrace, and threw one leg erotically over its second foot-wedge. George Graves leaned his heavy shoulder against it, his great limbs drained with laughter.

There was a hot blast of steamy air from the Appalachian Laundry across the street and, as the door from the office of the washroom opened, they had a moment's glimpse of negresses plunging their wet arms into the liquefaction of their clothes.

George Graves dried his eyes. Laughing wearily, they crossed over.

"We oughtn't to talk like that, 'Gene," said George Graves reproachfully. "Sure enough! It's not right."

He became moodily serious rapidly. "The best people in this town are church members," he said earnestly. "It's a fine thing."

"Why?" said Eugene, with an idle curiosity.

"Because," said George Graves, "you get to know all the people who are worth a damn."

Worth being damned, he thought quickly. A quaint idea.

"It helps you in a business way. They come to know you and respect you. You won't get far in this town, 'Gene, without them. It pays," he added devoutly, "to be a Christian."

"Yes," Eugene agreed seriously, "you're right." To walk together to the kirk, with a goodly company.

He thought sadly of his lost sobriety, and of how once, lonely, he had walked the decent lanes of God's Scotch town. Unbidden they came again to haunt his memory, the shaven faces of good tradesmen, each leading the well washed kingdom of his home in its obedient ritual, the lean hushed smiles of worship, the chained passion of devotion, as they implored God's love upon their ventures, or delivered their virgin daughters into the holy barter of marriage. And from even deeper adyts of his brain there swam up slowly to the shores of his old hunger the great fish whose names he scarcely knew—whose names, garnered with blind toil from a thousand books, from Augustine, himself a name, to Jeremy Taylor, the English metaphysician, were brief evocations of scalded light, electric, phosphorescent, illuminating by their magic connotations the vast far depths of ritual and religion: They came—Bartholomew, Hilarius, Chrysostomos, Polycarp, Anthony, Jerome, and the forty martyrs of Cappadocia who walked the waves—coiled like their own green shadows for a moment, and were gone.

"Besides," said George Graves, "a man ought to go anyway. Honesty's the best policy."

Across the street, on the second floor of a small brick three-story building that housed several members of the legal, medical, surgical, and dental professions, Dr. H. M. Smathers pumped vigorously with his right foot, took a wad of cotton from his assistant, Miss Lola Bruce, and thrusting it securely into the jaw of his unseen patient, bent his fashionable bald head intently. A tiny breeze blew back the thin curtains, and revealed him, white-jacketed, competent, drill in hand.

"Do you feel that?" he said tenderly.

"Wrogd gdo gurk!"

"Spit!" With thee conversing, I forget all time.

"I suppose," said George Graves thoughtfully, "the gold they use in people's teeth is worth a lot of money."

"Yes," said Eugene, finding the idea attractive, "if only one person in ten has gold fillings that would be ten million in the United States alone. You can figure on five dollars' worth each, can't you?"

"Easy!" said George Graves. "More than that." He brooded lusciously a moment. "That's a lot of money," he said.

In the office of the Rogers-Malone Undertaking Establishment the painful family of death was assembled, "Horse" Hines, tilted back in a swivel chair, with his feet thrust out on the broad window-ledge, chatted lazily with Mr. C. M. Powell, the suave silent partner. How sleep the brave, who sink to rest. Forget not yet.

"There's good money in undertaking," said George Graves. "Mr. Powell's well off."

Eugene's eyes were glued on the lantern face of "Horse" Hines. He beat the air with a convulsive arm, and sank his fingers in his throat.

"What's the matter?" cried George Graves.

"They shall not bury me alive," he said.

"You can't tell," George Graves said gloomily. "It's been known to happen. They've dug them up later and found them turned over on their faces."

Eugene shuddered. "I think," he suggested painfully, "they're supposed to take out your insides when they embalm you."

"Yes," said George Graves more hopefully, "and that stuff they use would kill you anyway. They pump you full of it."

With shrunken heart, Eugene considered. The ghost of old fear, that had been laid for years, walked forth to haunt him.

In his old fantasies of death he had watched his living burial, had foreseen his waking life-in-death, his slow, frustrated efforts to push away the smothering flood of earth until, as a drowning swimmer claws the air, his mute and stiffened fingers thrust from the ground a call for hands.

Fascinated, they stared through screen-doors down the dark central corridor, flanked by jars of weeping ferns. A sweet funereal odor of carnations and cedar-wood floated on the cool heavy air. Dimly, beyond a central partition, they saw a heavy casket, on a wheeled trestle, with rich silver handles and velvet coverings. The thick light faded there in dark.

"They're laid out in the room behind," said George Graves, lowering his voice.

To rot away into a flower, to melt into a tree with the friendless bodies of unburied men.

At this moment, having given to misery all he had (a tear), the very Reverend Father James O'Haley, S.J., among the faithless faithful only he, unshaken, unseduced, unterrified, emerged plumply from the chapel, walked up the soft aisle rug with brisk short-legged strides, and came out into the light. His pale blue eyes blinked rapidly for a moment, his plump uncreased face set firmly in a smile of quiet benevolence; he covered himself with a small well-kept hat of black velvet, and set off toward the avenue. Eugene shrank back gently as the little man walked past him: that small priestly figure in black bore on him the awful accolade of his great Mistress, that smooth face had heard the unutterable, seen the unknowable. In this remote outpost of the mighty Church, he was the standard-bearer of the one true faith, the consecrate flesh of God.

"They don't get any pay," said George Graves sorrowfully.

"How do they live, then?" Eugene asked.

"Don't you worry!" said George Graves, with a knowing smile. "They get all that's coming to them. He doesn't seem to be starving, does he?"

"No," said Eugene, "he doesn't."

"He lives on the fat of the land," said George Graves. "Wine at every meal. There are some rich Catholics in this town."

"Yes," said Eugene. "Frank Moriarty's got a pot full of money that he made selling licker."

"Don't let them hear you," said George Graves, with a surly laugh. "They've got a family tree and a coat of arms already."

"A beer-bottle rampant on a field of limburger cheese, gules," said Eugene.

"They're trying to get the Princess Madeleine into Society," said George Graves.

"Hell fire!" Eugene cried, grinning. "Let's let her in, if that's all she wants. We belong to the Younger Set, don't we?"

"You may," said George Graves, reeling with laughter, "but I don't. I wouldn't be caught dead with the little pimps."

"Mr. Eugene Gant was the host last night at a hot wienie roast given to members of the local Younger Set at Dixieland, the beautiful old ancestral mansion of his mother, Mrs. Eliza Gant."

George Graves staggered. "You oughtn't to say that, 'Gene," he gasped. He shook his head reproachfully. "Your mother's a fine woman."

"During the course of the evening, the Honorable George Graves, the talented scion of one of our oldest and wealthiest families, the Chesterfield Graveses, ($10 a week and up), rendered a few appropriate selections on the jews-harp."

Pausing deliberately, George Graves wiped his streaming eyes, and blew his nose. In the windows of Bain's millinery store, a waxen nymph bore a confection of rakish plumes upon her false tresses, and extended her simpering fingers in elegant counterpoise. Hats For Milady. O that those lips had language.

At this moment, with a smooth friction of trotting rumps, the death-wagon of Rogers-Malone turned swiftly in from the avenue, and wheeled by on ringing hoofs. They turned curiously and watched it draw up to the curb.

"Another Redskin bit the dust," said George Graves.

Come, delicate death, serenely arriving, arriving.

"Horse" Hines came out quickly on long flapping legs, and opened the doors behind. In another moment, with the help of the two men on the driver's seat, he had lowered the long wicker basket gently, and vanished, quietly, gravely, into the fragrant gloom of his establishment.

As Eugene watched, the old fatality of place returned. Each day, he thought, we pass the spot where some day we must die; or shall I, too, ride dead to some mean building yet unknown? Shall this bright clay, the hillbound, die in lodgings yet unbuilt? Shall these eyes, drenched with visions yet unseen, stored with the viscous and interminable seas at dawn, with the sad comfort of unfulfilled Arcadias, seal up their cold dead dreams upon a tick, as this, in time, in some hot village of the plains?

He caught and fixed the instant. A telegraph messenger wheeled vigorously in from the avenue with pumping feet, curved widely into the alley at his right, jerking his wheel up sharply as he took the curb and coasted down to the delivery boy's entrance. And post o'er land and ocean without rest. Milton, thou shouldst be living at this hour.

Descending the dark stairs of the Medical Building slowly, Mrs. Thomas Hewitt, the comely wife of the prominent attorney (of Arthur, Hewitt, and Grey), turned out into the light, and advanced slowly toward the avenue. She was greeted with flourishing gestures of the hat by Henry T. Merriman (Merriman and Merriman), and Judge Robert C. Allan, professional colleagues of her husband. She smiled and shot each quickly with a glance. Pleasant is this flesh. When she had passed they looked after her a moment. Then they continued their discussion of the courts.

On the third floor of the First National Bank building on the right hand corner, Fergus Paston, fifty-six, a thin lecherous mouth between iron-gray dundrearies, leaned his cocked leg upon his open window, and followed the movements of Miss Bernie Powers, twenty-two, crossing the street. Even in our ashes live their wonted fires.

On the opposite corner, Mrs. Roland Rawls, whose husband was manager of the Peerless Pulp Company (Plant No. 3), and whose father owned it, emerged from the rich seclusion of Arthur N. Wright, jeweller. She clasped her silver mesh bag and stepped into her attendant Packard. She was a tall black-haired woman of thirty-three with a good figure: her face was dull, flat, and Mid-western.

"She's the one with the money," said George Graves. "He hasn't a damn thing. It's all in her name. She wants to be an opera singer."

"Can she sing?"

"Not worth a damn," said George Graves. "I've heard her. There's your chance, 'Gene. She's got a daughter about your age."

"What does she do?" said Eugene.

"She wants to be an actress," said George Graves, laughing throatily.

"You have to work too damn hard for your money," said Eugene.

They had reached the corner by the Bank, and now halted, indecisively, looking up the cool gulch of afternoon. The street buzzed with a light gay swarm of idlers: the faces of the virgins bloomed in and out like petals on a bough. Advancing upon him, an inch to the second, Eugene saw, ten feet away, the heavy paralyzed body of old Mr. Avery. He was a very great scholar, stone-deaf, and seventy-eight years old. He lived alone in a room above the Public Library. He had neither friends nor connections. He was a myth.

"Oh, my God!" said Eugene. "Here he comes!"

It was too late for escape.

Gasping a welcome, Mr. Avery bore down on him, with a violent shuffle of his feet and a palsied tattoo of his heavy stick which brought him over the intervening three yards in forty seconds.

"Well, young fellow," he panted, "how's Latin?"

"Fine," Eugene screamed into his pink ear.

"*Poeta nascitur, non fit,*" said Mr. Avery, and went off into a silent wheeze of laughter which brought on a fit of coughing strangulation. His eyes bulged, his tender pink skin grew crimson, he roared his terror out in a phlegmy rattle, while his goose-white hand trembled frantically for his handkerchief. A crowd gathered. Eugene quickly drew a dirty handkerchief from the old man's pocket, and thrust it into his hands. He tore up from his convulsed organs a rotting mass, and panted rapidly for breath. The crowd dispersed somewhat dejectedly.

George Graves grinned darkly. "That's too bad," he said. "You oughtn't to laugh, 'Gene." He turned away, gurgling.

"Can you conjugate?" gasped Mr. Avery. "Here's the way I learned:

> *"Amo, amas,*
> I love a lass.
> *Amat,*
> He loves her, too."

Quivering with tremors of laughter, he launched himself again. Because he could not leave them, save by the inch, they moved off several yards to the curb. Grow old along with me!

"That's a damn shame," said George Graves, looking after him and shaking his head. "Where's he going?"

"To supper," said Eugene.

"To supper!" said George Graves. "It's only four o'clock. Where does he eat?"

Not where he eats, but where he is eaten.

"At the Uneeda," said Eugene, beginning to choke. "It takes him two hours to get there."

"Does he go every day?" said George Graves, beginning to laugh.

"Three times a day," Eugene screamed. "He spends all morning going to dinner, and all afternoon going to supper."

A whisper of laughter came from their weary jaws. They sighed like sedge.

At this moment, dodging briskly through the crowd, with a loud and cheerful word for every one, Mr. Joseph Bailey, secretary of the Altamont Chamber of Commerce, short, broad, and ruddy, came by them with a hearty gesture of the hand:

"Hello, boys!" he cried. "How're they going?" But before either of them could answer, he had passed on, with an encouraging shake of his head, and a deep applauding *"That's* right."

"What's right?" said Eugene.

But before George Graves could answer, the great lung specialist,

Dr. Fairfax Grinder, scion of one of the oldest and proudest families in Virginia, drove in viciously from Church Street, with his sinewy length of six feet and eight inches coiled tensely in the deep pit of his big Buick roadster. Cursing generally the whole crawling itch of Confederate and Yankee postwar rabbledom, with a few special parentheses for Jews and niggers, he drove full tilt at the short plump figure of Joe Zamschnick, men's furnishings ("Just a Whisper Off The Square").

Joseph, two yards away from legal safety, hurled himself with a wild scream headlong at the curb. He arrived on hands and knees, but under his own power.

"K-hurses!" said Eugene. "Foiled again."

'Twas true! Dr. Fairfax Grinder's lean bristled upper lip drew back over his strong yellow teeth. He jammed on his brakes, and lifted his car round with a complete revolution of his long arms. Then he roared away through scattering traffic, in a greasy blue cloud of gasoline and burnt rubber.

Joe Zamschnick frantically wiped his gleaming bald head with a silk handkerchief and called loudly on the public to bear witness.

"What's the matter with him?" said George Graves, disappointed. "He usually goes up on the sidewalk after them if he can't get them on the street."

On the other side of the street, attracting no more than a languid stare from the loafing natives, the Honorable William Jennings Bryan paused benevolently before the windows of the H. Martin Grimes Bookstore, allowing the frisking breeze to toy pleasantly with his famous locks. The tangles of Neaera's hair.

The Commoner stared carefully at the window display which included several copies of *Before Adam,* by Jack London. Then he entered, and selected a dozen views of Altamont and the surrounding hills.

"He may come here to live," said George Graves. "Dr. Doak's offered to give him a house and lot in Doak Park."

"Why?" said Eugene.

"Because the advertising will be worth a lot to the town," said George Graves.

A little before them, that undaunted daughter of desires, Miss Elizabeth Scragg, emerged from Woolworth's Five and Ten Cent Store, and turned up toward the Square. Smiling, she acknowledged the ponderous salute of Big Jeff White, the giant half-owner of the Whitstone hotel, whose fortunes had begun when he had refused to return to his old comrade, Dickson Reese, the embezzling cashier, ninety thousand dollars of entrusted loot. Dog eat dog. Thief catch thief. It is not growing like a tree, in bulk doth make man better be.

His six-and-a-half-foot shadow flitted slowly before them. He passed, in creaking number twelves, a massive smooth-jawed man with a great paunch girdled in a wide belt.

Across the street again, before the windows of the Van W. Yeats Shoe Company, the Reverend J. Brooks Gall, Amherst ('61), and as loyal a Deke as ever breathed, but looking only sixty of his seventy-three years, paused in his brisk walk, and engaged in sprightly monologue, three of his fellow Boy Scouts—the Messrs. Lewis Monk, seventeen, Bruce Rogers, thirteen, and Malcolm Hodges, fourteen. None knew as well as he the heart of a boy. He, too, it seems, had once been one himself. Thus, as one bright anecdote succeeded, or suggested, a half-dozen others, they smiled dutifully, with attentive respect, below the lifted barrier of his bristly white mustache, into the gleaming rhyme of his false teeth. And, with rough but affectionate camaraderie, he would pause from time to time to say: "Old Male!" or "Old Bruce!" gripping firmly his listener's arm, shaking him gently. Pallidly, on restless feet, they smiled, plotting escape with slant-eyed stealth.

Mr. Buse, the Oriental rug merchant, came around the corner below them from Liberty Street. His broad dark face was wreathed in Persian smiles. I met a traveller from an antique land.

In the Bijou Cafe for Ladies and Gents, Mike, the counter man, leaned his hairy arms upon the marble slab, and bent his wrinkled inch of brow upon a week-old copy of *Atlantis*. Fride Chicken Today with Sweet Potatos. Hail to thee, blithe spirit, bird thou never wert. A solitary fly darted swiftly about the greasy cover of a glass humidor, under which a leathery quarter of mince pie lay weltering. Spring had come.

Meanwhile, having completed twice their parade up and down the street from the Square to the post-office, the Misses Christine Ball, Viola Powell, Aline Rollins, and Dorothy Hazzard were accosted outside Wood's Drug Store by Tom French, seventeen, Roy Duncan, nineteen, and Carl Jones, eighteen.

"Where do you think you're going?" said Tom French, insolently. Gayly, brightly, in unison, they answered:

"Hey—ee!"

"Hay's seven dollars a ton," said Roy Duncan, and immediately burst into a high cackle of laughter, in which all the others joined, merrily.

"You craz-ee!" said Viola Powell tenderly. Tell me, ye merchants' daughters, did ye see another creature fair and wise as she.

"Mr. Duncan," said Tom French, turning his proud ominous face upon his best friend, "I want you to meet a friend of mine, Miss Rollins."

"I think I've met this man somewhere before," said Aline Rollins. Another Splendor on his mouth alit.

"Yes," said Roy Duncan, "I go there often."

His small tight freckled impish face was creased again by his high cackle. All I could never be. They moved into the store, where drouthy neibors neibors meet, through the idling group of fountain gallants.

Mr. Henry Sorrell (It Can Be Done), and Mr. John T. Howland (We Sell Lots and Lots of Lots), emerged, beyond Arthur N. Wright's, jeweller, from the gloomy dusk of the Gruner Building. Each looked into the subdivisions of the other's heart; their eyes kept the great Vision of the guarded mount as swiftly they turned into Church Street where Sorrell's Hudson was parked.

White-vested, a trifle paunchy, with large broad feet, a shaven moon of red face, and abundant taffy-colored hair, the Reverend John Smallwood, pastor of the First Baptist Church, walked heavily up the street, greeting his parishioners warmly, and hoping to see his Pilot face to face. Instead, however, he encountered the Honorable William Jennings Bryan, who was coming slowly out of the bookstore. The two close friends greeted each other affectionately, and, with a firm friendly laying on of hands, gave each to each the Christian aid of a benevolent exorcism.

"Just the man I was looking for," said Brother Smallwood. In silence, slowly, they shook hands for several seconds. Silence was pleased.

"That," observed the Commoner with grave humor, "is what I thought the Great American People said to me on three occasions." It was a favorite jest—ripe with wisdom, mellowed by the years, yet, withal, so characteristic of the man. The deep furrows of his mouth widened in a smile. Our master—famous, calm, and dead.

Passed, on catspaw rubber tread, from the long dark bookstore, Professor L. B. Dunn, principal of Graded School No. 3, Montgomery Avenue. He smiled coldly at them with a gimlet narrowing of his spectacled eyes. The tell-tale cover of *The New Republic* peeked from his pocket. Clamped under his lean and freckled arm were new library copies of *The Great Illusion,* by Norman Angell, and *The Ancient Grudge,* by Owen Wister. A lifelong advocate of a union of the two great English-speaking (sic) nations, making together irresistibly for peace, truth, and righteousness in a benevolent but firm authority over the less responsible elements of civilization, he passed, the Catholic man, pleasantly dedicated to the brave adventuring of minds and the salvaging of mankind. Ah, yes!

"And how are you and the Good Woman enjoying your sojourn in the Land of the Sky?" said the Reverend John Smallwood.

"Our only regret," said the Commoner, "is that our visit here must be measured by days and not by months. Nay, by years."

Mr. Richard Gorman, twenty-six, city reporter of *The Citizen,* strode rapidly up the street, with proud cold news-nose lifted. His complacent smile, hard-lipped, loosened into servility.

"Ah, there, Dick," said John Smallwood, clasping his hand affectionately, and squeezing his arm, "Just the man I was looking for. Do you know Mr. Bryan?"

"As fellow newspaper men," said the Commoner, "Dick and I have been close friends for—how many years is it, my boy?"

"Three, I think sir," said Mr. Gorman, blushing prettily.

"I wish you could have been here, Dick," said the Reverend Smallwood, "to hear what Mr. Bryan was saying about us. The good people of this town would be mighty proud to hear it."

"I'd like another statement from you before you go, Mr. Bryan," said Richard Gorman. "There's a story going the rounds that you may make your home with us in the future."

When questioned by a *Citizen* reporter, Mr. Bryan refused either to confirm or deny the rumor:

"I may have a statement to make later," he observed with a significant smile, "but at present I must content myself by saying that if I could have chosen the place of my birth, I could not have found a fairer spot than this wonderland of nature."

Earthly Paradise, thinks Commoner.

"I have travelled far in my day," continued the man who had been chosen three times by a great Party to contend for the highest honor within the gift of the people. "I have gone from the woods of Maine to the wave-washed sands of Florida, from Hatteras to Halifax, and from the summits of the Rockies to where Missouri rolls her turgid flood, but I have seen few spots that equal, and none that surpass, the beauty of this mountain Eden."

The reporter made notes rapidly.

The years of his glory washed back to him upon the rolling tides of rhetoric—the great lost days of the first crusade when the money barons trembled beneath the shadow of the Cross of God, and Bryan! Bryan! Bryan! Bryan! burned through the land like a comet. Ere I was old. 1896. Ah, woeful *ere,* which tells me youth's no longer here.

Foresees Dawn of New Era.

When pressed more closely by the reporter as to his future plans, Mr. Bryan replied:

"My schedule is completely filled, for months to come, with speaking engagements that will take me from one end of the country to the other, in the fight I am making for the reduction of the vast armaments that form the chief obstacle to the reign of peace on earth, good-will to men. After that, who knows?" he said, flashing his famous smile. "Perhaps I shall come back to this beautiful region, and take up my life among my good friends here as one who, having fought the good fight, deserves to spend the declining years of his life not only within sight, but within the actual boundaries, of the happy land of Canaan."

Asked if he could predict with any certainty the date of his proposed retirement, the Commoner answered characteristically with the following beautiful quotation from Longfellow:

> "When the war-drum throbbed no longer,
> And the battle-flags were furled
> In the Parliament of man,
> The Federation of the world."

The magic cell of music—the electric piano in the shallow tiled lobby of Altamont's favorite cinema, the Ajax, stopped playing with firm, tinny abruptness, hummed ominously for a moment, and without warning commenced anew. It's a long way to Tipperary. The world shook with the stamp of marching men.

Miss Margaret Blanchard and Mrs. C. M. McReady, the druggist's drugged wife who, by the white pitted fabric of her skin, and the wide bright somnolence of her eyes, on honey-dew had fed too often, came out of the theatre and turned down toward Wood's pharmacy.

To-day: Maurice Costello and Edith M. Story in *Throw Out the Lifeline*, a Vitagraph Release.

Goggling, his great idiot's head lolling on his scrawny neck, wearing the wide-rimmed straw hat that covered him winter and summer, Willie Goff, the pencil merchant, jerked past, with inward lunges of his crippled right foot. The fingers of his withered arm pointed stiffly toward himself, beckoning to him, and touching him as he walked with stiff jerking taps, in a terrible parody of vanity. A gaudy handkerchief with blue, yellow and crimson patterns hung in a riotous blot from his breast-pocket over his neatly belted gray Norfolk jacket, a wide loose collar of silk barred with red and orange stripes flowered across his narrow shoulders. In his lapel a huge red carnation. His thin face, beneath the jutting globular head, grinned constantly, glutting his features with wide, lapping, receding, returning, idiot smiles. For should he live a thousand years, he never will be out of humor. He burred ecstatically at the passers-by, who grinned fondly at him, and continued down to Wood's where he was greeted with loud cheers and laughter by a group of young men who loitered at the fountain's end. They gathered around him boisterously, pounding his back and drawing him up to the fountain. Pleased, he looked at them warmly, gratefully. He was touched and happy.

"What're you having, Willie?" said Mr. Tobias Pottle.

"Give me a dope," said Willie Goff to the grinning jerker, "a dope and lime."

Pudge Carr, the politician's son, laughed hilariously. "Want a dope and lime, do you, Willie?" he said, and struck him heavily on the back. His thick stupid face composed itself.

"Have a cigarette, Willie," he said, offering the package to Willie Goff.

"What's yours?" said the jerker to Toby Pottle.

"Give me a dope, too."

"I don't want anything," said Pudge Carr. Such drinks as made them nobly wild, not mad.

Pudge Carr held a lighted match to Willie's cigarette, winking slowly at Brady Chalmers, a tall, handsome fellow, with black hair, and a long dark face. Willie Goff drew in on his cigarette, lighting it with dry smacking lips. He coughed, removed the weed, and held it awkwardly between his thumb and forefinger, looking at it, curiously.

They sputtered with laughter, involved and lost in clouds of fume, and guzzling deep, the boor, the lackey, and the groom.

Brady Chalmers took Willie's colored handkerchief gently from his pocket and held it up for their inspection. Then he folded it carefully and put it back.

"What are you all dressed up about, Willie?" he said. "You must be going to see your girl."

Willie Goff grinned cunningly.

Toby Pottle blew a luxurious jet of smoke through his nostrils. He was twenty-four, carefully groomed, with slick blond hair, and a pink massaged face.

"Come on, Willie," he said, blandly, quietly, "you've got a girl, haven't you?"

Willie Goff leered knowingly; at the counter-end, Tim McCall, twenty-eight, who had been slowly feeding cracked ice from his cupped fist into his bloated whisky-fierce jowls, collapsed suddenly, blowing a bright rattling hail upon the marble ledge.

"I've got several," said Willie Goff. "A fellow's got to have a little Poon-Tang, hasn't he?"

Flushed with high ringing laughter, they smiled, spoke respectfully, uncovered before Miss Tot Webster, Miss Mary McGraw, and Miss Martha Cotton, older members of the Younger Set. They called for stronger music, louder wine.

"How do you do?"

"Aha! Aha!" said Brady Chalmers to Miss Mary McGraw. "Where were *you* that time?"

"*You'll* never know," she called back. It was between them—their little secret. They laughed knowingly with joy of possession.

"Come on back, Pudge," said Euston Phipps, their escort. "You too, Brady." He followed the ladies back—tall, bold, swagger—a young alcoholic with one sound lung. He was a good golfer.

Pert boys rushed from the crowded booths and tables to the fountain, coming up with a long slide. They shouted their orders rudely, nagging the swift jerkers glibly, stridently.

"All right, son. Two dopes and a mint limeade. Make it snappy."

"Do you work around here, boy?"

The jerkers moved in ragtime tempo, juggling the drinks, tossing scooped globes of ice-cream into the air and catching them in glasses, beating swift rhythms with a spoon.

Seated alone, with thick brown eyes above her straw regardant, Mrs. Thelma Jarvis, the milliner, drew, in one swizzling guzzle, the last beaded chain of linked sweetness long drawn out from the bottom of her glass. Drink to me only with thine eyes. She rose slowly, looking into the mirror of her open purse. Then, fluescent, her ripe limbs moulded in a dress of silk henna, she writhed carefully among the crowded tables, with a low rich murmur of contrition. Her voice was ever soft, gentle, and low—an excellent thing in a woman. The high light chatter of the tables dropped as she went by. For God's sake, hold your tongue and let me love! On amber undulant limbs she walked slowly up the aisle past perfume, stationery, rubber goods, and toilet preparations, pausing at the cigar counter to pay her check. Her round, melon-heavy breasts nodded their heads in slow but sprightly dance. A poet could not but be gay, in such a jocund company.

But—at the entrance, standing in the alcove by the magazine rack, Mr. Paul Goodson, of the Dependable Life, closed his long grinning, dish-face abruptly, and ceased talking. He doffed his hat without effusiveness, as did his companion, Coston Smathers, the furniture man (you furnish the girl, we furnish the house). They were both Baptists.

Mrs. Thelma Jarvis turned her warm ivory stare upon them, parted her full small mouth in a remote smile, and passed, ambulant. When she had gone they turned to each other, grinning quietly. We'll be waiting at the river. Swiftly they glanced about them. No one had seen.

Patroness of all the arts, but particular sponsor for Music, Heavenly Maid, Mrs. Franz Wilhelm Von Zeck, wife of the noted lung specialist, and the discoverer of Von Zeck's serum, came imperially from the doors of the Fashion Mart, and was handed tenderly into the receiving cushions of her Cadillac by Mr. Louis Rosalsky. Benevolently but distantly she smiled down upon him: the white parchment of his hard Polish face was broken by a grin of cruel servility curving up around the wings of his immense putty-colored nose. Frau Von Zeck settled her powerful chins upon the coarse shelving of her Wagnerian breasts and, her ponderous gaze already dreaming on remote philanthropies, was charioted smoothly away from the devoted tradesman. *Nur wer die Sehnsucht kennt, weiss was Ich leide.*

Mr. Rosalsky returned into his store.

For the third time the Misses Mildred Shuford, Helen Pendergast, and Mary Catherine Bruce drove by, clustered together like unpicked cherries in the front seat of Miss Shuford's Reo. They passed, searching the pavements with eager, haughty eyes, pleased at their proud appearance. They turned up Liberty Street on their fourth swing round the circle. Waltz me around again, Willie.

"Do you know how to dance, George?" Eugene asked. His heart was full of bitter pride and fear.

"Yes," said George Graves absently, "a little bit. I don't like it." He lifted his brooding eyes.

"Say, 'Gene," he said, "how much do you think Dr. Von Zeck is worth?"

He answered Eugene's laughter with a puzzled sheepish grin.

"Come on," said Eugene. "I'll match you for a drink."

They dodged nimbly across the narrow street, amid the thickening afternoon traffic.

"It's getting worse all the time," said George Graves. "The people who laid the town out didn't have any vision. What's it going to be like, ten years from now?"

"They could widen the streets, couldn't they?" said Eugene.

"No. Not now. You'd have to move all the buildings back. Wonder how much it would cost?" said George Graves thoughtfully.

"And if we don't," Professor L. B. Dunn's precise voice sounded its cold warning, "their next move will be directed against us. You may yet live to see the day when the iron heel of militarism is on your neck, and the armed forces of the Kaiser do the goose-step up and down this street. When that day comes—"

"I don't put any stock in those stories," said Mr. Bob Webster rudely and irreverently. He was a small man, with a gray, mean face, violent and bitter. A chronic intestinal sourness seemed to have left its print upon his features. "In my opinion, it's all propaganda. Those Germans are too damn good for them, that's all. They're beginning to call for calf-rope."

"When that day comes," Professor Dunn implacably continued, "remember what I told you. The German government has imperialistic designs upon the whole of the world. It is looking to the day when it shall have all mankind under the yoke of Krupp and Kultur. The fate of civilization is hanging in the balance. Mankind is at the crossroads. I pray God it shall not be said that we were found wanting. I pray God that this free people may never suffer as little Belgium suffered, that our wives and daughters may not be led off into slavery or shame, our children maimed and slaughtered."

"It's not our fight," said Mr. Bob Webster. "I don't want to send my boys three thousand miles across the sea to get shot for those foreigners. If they come over here, I'll shoulder a gun with the best of them, but until they do they can fight it out among themselves. Isn't that right, Judge?" he said, turning toward the party of the third part, Judge Walter C. Jeter, of the Federal Circuit, who had fortunately been a close friend of Grover Cleveland. Ancestral voices prophesying war.

"Did you know the Wheeler boys?" Eugene asked George Graves. "Paul and Clifton?"

"Yes," said George Graves. "They went away and joined the French army. They're in the Foreign Legion."

"They're in the aviation part of it," said Eugene. "The Lafayette Eskydrill. Clifton Wheeler has shot down more than six Germans."

"The boys around here didn't like him," said George Graves. "They thought he was a sissy."

Eugene winced slightly at the sound of the word.

"How old was he?" he asked.

"He was a grown man," said George. "Twenty-two or three."

Disappointed, Eugene considered his chance of glory. (*Ich bin ja noch ein Kind.*)

"—But fortunately," continued Judge Walter C. Jeter deliberately, "we have a man in the White House on whose farseeing statesmanship we can safely rely. Let us trust to the wisdom of his leadership, obeying, in word and spirit, the principles of strict neutrality, accepting only as a last resort a course that would lead this great nation again into the suffering and tragedy of war, which," his voice sank to a whisper, "God forbid!"

Thinking of a more ancient war, in which he had borne himself gallantly, Colonel James Buchanan Pettigrew, head of the Pettigrew Military Academy (Est. 1789), rode by in his open victoria, behind an old Negro driver and two well-nourished brown mares. There was a good brown smell of horse and sweat-cured leather. The old Negro snaked his whip gently across the sleek trotting rumps, growling softly.

Colonel Pettigrew was wrapped to his waist in a heavy rug, his shoulders were covered with a gray Confederate cape. He bent forward, leaning his old weight upon a heavy polished stick, which his freckled hands gripped upon the silver knob. Muttering, his proud powerful old head turned shakily from side to side, darting fierce splintering glances at the drifting crowd. He was a very parfit gentil knight.

He muttered.

"Suh?" said the Negro, pulling in on his reins, and turning around.

"Go on! Go on, you scoundrel!" said Colonel Pettigrew.

"Yes, suh," said the Negro. They drove on.

In the crowd of loafing youngsters that stood across the threshold of Wood's pharmacy, Colonel Pettigrew's darting eyes saw two of his own cadets. They were pimply youths, with slack jaws and a sloppy carriage.

He muttered his disgust. Not the same! Not the same! Nothing the same! In his proud youth, in the only war that mattered, Colonel Pettigrew had marched at the head of his own cadets. There were 117, sir, all under nineteen. They stepped forward to a man . . . until not a single commissioned officer was left . . . 36 came back . . . since 1789 . . . it must go on! . . . 19, sir—all under one hundred and seventeen . . . must . . . go . . . on!

His sagging cheek-flanks trembled gently. The horses trotted out of sight around the corner, with a smooth-spoked rumble of rubber tires.

George Graves and Eugene entered Wood's pharmacy and stood up to the counter. The elder soda-jerker, scowling, drew a sopping rag across a puddle of slop upon the marble slab.

"What's yours?" he said irritably.

"I want a chock-lut milk," said Eugene.

"Make it two," added George Graves.

O for a draught of vintage that hath been cooled a long age in the deep-delvèd earth!

LOUISE IN CHARLESTON

IN THE autumn, at the beginning of his fifteenth year—his last year at Leonard's—Eugene went to Charleston on a short excursion. He found a substitute for his paper route.

"Come on!" said Max Isaacs, whom he still occasionally saw. "We're going to have a good time, son."

"Yeah, man!" said Malvin Bowden, whose mother was conducting the tour. "You can still git beer in Charleston," he added with a dissipated leer.

"You can go swimmin' in the ocean at the Isle of Palms," said Max Isaacs. Then, reverently, he added: "You can go to the Navy Yard an' see the ships."

He was waiting until he should be old enough to join the navy. He read the posters greedily. He knew all the navy men at the enlistment office. He had read all the booklets—he was deep in naval lore. He knew to a dollar the earnings of firemen, second class, of radio men, and of all kinds of C. P. O.'s

His father was a plumber. He did not want to be a plumber. He wanted to join the navy and see the world. In the navy, a man was given good pay and a good education. He learned a trade. He got good food and good clothing. It was all given to him free, for nothing.

"H'm!" said Eliza, with a bantering smile. "Why, say, boy, what do you want to do that for? You're my baby!"

It had been years since he was. She smiled tremulously.

"Yes'm," said Eugene. "Can I go? It's only for five days. I've got the money." He thrust his hand into his pocket, feeling.

"I tell you what!" said Eliza, working her lips, smiling. "You may wish you had that money before this winter's over. You're going to need new shoes and a warm overcoat when the cold weather comes. You must be mighty rich. I wish I could afford to go running off on a trip like that."

"Oh, my God!" said Ben, with a short laugh. He tossed his cigarette into one of the first fires of the year.

"I want to tell you, son," said Eliza, becoming grave, "you've got to learn the value of a dollar or you'll never have a roof to call your own. I want you to have a good time, boy, but you mustn't squander your money."

"Yes'm," said Eugene.

"For heaven's sake!" Ben cried. "It's the kid's own money. Let him do what he likes with it. If he wants to throw it out the damned window, it's his own business."

She clasped her hands thoughtfully upon her waist and stared away, pursing her lips.

"Well, I reckon it'll be all right," she said. "Mrs. Bowden will take good care of you."

It was his first journey to a strange place alone. Eliza packed an old valise carefully, and stowed away a box of sandwiches and eggs. He went away at night. As he stood by his valise, washed, brushed, excited, she wept a little. He was again, she felt, a little farther off. The hunger for voyages was in his face.

"Be a good boy," she said. "Don't get into any trouble down there." She thought carefully a moment, looking away. Then she went down in her stocking, and pulled out a five-dollar bill.

"Don't waste your money," she said. "Here's a little extra. You may need it."

"Come here, you little thug!" said Ben. Scowling, his quick hands worked busily at the boy's stringy tie. He jerked down his vest, slipping a wadded ten-dollar bill into Eugene's pocket. "Behave yourself," he said, "or I'll beat you to death."

Max Isaacs whistled from the street. He went out to join them.

There were six in Mrs. Bowden's party: Max Isaacs, Malvin Bowden, Eugene, two girls named Josie and Louise, and Mrs. Bowden.

Josie was Mrs. Bowden's niece and lived with her. She was a tall beanpole of a girl with a prognathous mouth and stick-out grinning teeth. She was twenty. The other girl, Louise, was a waitress. She was small, plump, a warm brunette. Mrs. Bowden was a little sallow woman with ratty brown hair. She had brown worn-out eyes. She was a dressmaker. Her husband, a carpenter, had died in the Spring. There was a little insurance money. That was how she came to take the trip.

Now, by night, he was riding once more into the South. The day-coach was hot, full of the weary smell of old red plush. People dozed painfully, distressed by the mournful tolling of the bell, and the grinding halts. A baby wailed thinly. Its mother, a gaunt wisp-haired mountaineer, turned the back of the seat ahead, and bedded the child on a spread newspaper. Its wizened face peeked dirtily out of its swaddling discomfort of soiled jackets and pink ribbon. It wailed and slept. At the front of the car, a young hill-man, high-boned and red, clad in corduroys and leather leggings, shelled peanuts steadily, throwing the shells into the aisle. People trod through them with a sharp masty crackle. The boys, bored, paraded restlessly to the car-end for water. There was a crushed litter of sanitary drinking-cups upon the floor, and a stale odor from the toilets.

The two girls slept soundly on turned seats. The small one breathed warmly and sweetly through moist parted lips.

The weariness of the night wore in upon their jaded nerves, lay upon their dry hot eyeballs. They flattened noses against the dirty windows, and watched the vast structure of the earth sweep past— clumped woodlands, the bending sweep of the fields, the huge flowing lift of the earth-waves, cyclic intersections bewildering—the American earth—rude, immeasurable, formless, mighty.

His mind was bound in the sad lulling magic of the car wheels. Clackety-clack. Clackety-clack. Clackety-clack. Clackety-clack. He thought of his life as something that had happened long ago. He had found, at last, his gateway to the lost world. But did it lie before or behind him? Was he leaving or entering it? Above the rhythm of the wheels he thought of Eliza's laughter over ancient things. He saw a brief forgotten gesture, her white broad forehead, a ghost of old grief in her eyes. Ben, Gant—their strange lost voices. Their sad laughter. They swam toward him through green walls of fantasy.

They caught and twisted at his heart. The green ghost-glimmer of their faces coiled away. Lost. Lost.

"Let's go for a smoke," said Max Isaacs.

They went back and stood wedged for stability on the closed platform of the car. They lighted cigarettes.

Light broke against the east, in a murky rim. The far dark was eaten cleanly away. The horizon sky was barred with hard fierce strips of light. Still buried in night, they looked across at the unimpinging sheet of day. They looked under the lifted curtain at brightness. They were knifed sharply away from it. Then, gently, light melted across the land like dew. The world was gray.

The east broke out in ragged flame. In the car, the little waitress breathed deeply, sighed, and opened her clear eyes.

Max Isaacs fumbled his cigarette awkwardly, looked at Eugene, and grinned sheepishly with delight, craning his neck along his collar, and making a nervous grimace of his white fuzz-haired face. His hair was thick, straight, the color of taffy. He had blond eyebrows. There was much kindness in him. They looked at each other with clumsy tenderness. They thought of the lost years at Woodson Street. They saw with decent wonder their awkward bulk of puberty. The proud gate of the years swung open for them. They felt a lonely glory. They said farewell.

Charleston, fat weed that roots itself on Lethe wharf, lived in another time. The hours were days, the days weeks.

They arrived in the morning. By noon, several weeks had passed, and he longed for the day's ending. They were quartered in a small hotel on King Street—an old place above stores, with big rooms. After lunch, they went out to see the town. Max Isaacs and Malvin Bowden turned at once toward the Navy Yard. Mrs. Bowden went with them. Eugene was weary for sleep. He promised to meet them later.

When they had gone, he pulled off his shoes and took off his coat and shirt, and lay down to sleep in a big dark room, into which the warm sun fell in shuttered bars. Time droned like a sleepy October fly.

At five o'clock, Louise, the little waitress, came to wake him. She, too, had wanted to sleep. She knocked gently at the door. When he did not answer, she opened it quietly and came in, closing it behind her. She came to the side of the bed and looked at him for a moment.

"Eugene!" she whispered. "Eugene."

He murmured drowsily, and stirred. The little waitress smiled and sat down on the bed. She bent over him and tickled him gently in the ribs, chuckling to see him squirm. Then she tickled the soles of his feet. He wakened slowly, yawning, rubbing sleep from his eyes.

"What is it?" he said.

"It's time to go out there," she said.

"Out where?"

"To the Navy Yard. We promised to meet them."

"Oh, damn the Navy Yard!" he groaned. "I'd rather sleep."

"So would I!" she agreed. She yawned luxuriously, stretching her plump arms above her head. "I'm so sleepy. I could stretch out anywhere." She looked meaningly at the bed.

He wakened at once, sensuously alert. He lifted himself upon one elbow: a hot torrent of blood swarmed through his cheeks. His pulses beat thickly.

"We're all alone up here," said Louise smiling. "We've got the whole floor to ourselves."

"Why don't you lie down and take a nap, if you're still sleepy?" he asked. "I'll wake you up," he added, with gentle chivalry.

"I've got such a little room. It's hot and stuffy. That's why I got up," said Louise. "What a nice big room you've got!"

"Yes," he said. "It's a nice big bed, too." They were silent a waiting moment.

"Why don't you lie down here, Louise?" he said, in a low unsteady voice. "I'll get up," he added hastily, sitting up. "I'll wake you."

"Oh, no," she said, "I wouldn't feel right."

They were again silent. She looked admiringly at his thin young arms.

"My!" she said. "I bet you're strong."

He flexed his long stringy muscles manfully, and expanded his chest.

"My!" she said. "How old are you, 'Gene?"

He was just at his fifteenth year.

"I'm going on sixteen," he said. "How old are you, Louise?"

"I'm eighteen," she said. "I bet you're a regular heart-breaker, 'Gene. How many girls have you got?"

"Oh—I don't know. Not many," he said truthfully enough. He wanted to talk—he wanted to talk madly, seductively, wickedly. He would excite her by uttering, in grave respectful tones, honestly, matter-of-factly, the most erotic suggestions.

"I guess you like the tall ones, don't you?" said Louise. "A tall fellow wouldn't want a little thing like me, would he? Although," she said quickly, "you never know. They say opposites attract each other."

"I don't like tall girls," said Eugene. "They're too skinny. I like them about your size, when they've got a good build."

"Have I got a good build, 'Gene?" said Louise, holding her arms up and smiling.

"Yes, you have a pretty build, Louise—a fine build," said Eugene earnestly. "The kind I like."

"I haven't got a pretty face. I've got an ugly face," she said invitingly.

"You haven't got an ugly face. You have a pretty face," said Eugene firmly. "Anyway, the face doesn't matter much with me," he added, subtly.

"What do you like best, 'Gene?" Louise asked.

He thought carefully and gravely.

"Why," he said, "a woman ought to have pretty legs. Sometimes a woman has an ugly face, but a pretty leg. The prettiest legs I ever saw were on a High Yellow."

"Were they prettier than mine?" said the waitress, with an easy laugh.

She crossed her legs slowly and displayed her silk-shod ankle.

"I don't know, Louise," he said, staring critically. "I can't see enough."

"Is that enough?" she said, pulling her tight skirt above her calves.

"No," said Eugene.

"Is that?" she pulled her skirt back over her knees, and displayed her plump thighs, gartered with a ruffled band of silk and red rosettes. She thrust her small feet out, coyly turning the toes in.

"Lord!" said Eugene, staring with keen interest at the garter. "I never saw any like that before. That's pretty." He gulped noisily. "Don't those things hurt you, Louise?"

"Uh-huh," she said, as if puzzled, "why?"

"I should think they'd cut into your skin," he said. "I know mine do if I wear them too tight. See."

He pulled up his trousers' leg and showed his young gartered shank, lightly spired with hair.

Louise looked, and felt the garter gravely with a plump hand. "Mine don't hurt me," she said. She snapped the elastic with a ripe smack. "See!"

"Let me see," he said. He placed his trembling fingers lightly upon her garter.

"Yes," he said unsteadily. "I see."

Her round young weight lay heavy against him, her warm young face turned blindly up to his own. His brain reeled as if drunken, he dropped his mouth awkwardly upon her parted lips. She sank back heavily on the pillows. He planted dry and clumsy kisses upon her mouth, her eyes, in little circles round her throat and face. He fumbled at the throat-hook of her waist, but his fingers shook so violently that he could not unfasten it. She lifted her smooth hands with a comatose gesture, and unfastened it for him.

Then he lifted his beet-red face, and whispered tremulously, not knowing well what he said:

"You're a nice girl, Louise. A pretty girl."

She thrust her pink fingers slowly through his hair, drew back his face into her breasts again, moaned softly as he kissed her, and clutched his hair in an aching grip. He put his arms around her and drew her to him. They devoured each other with young wet kisses, insatiate, unhappy, trying to grow together in their embrace, draw out the last distillation of desire in a single kiss.

He lay sprawled, scattered and witless with passion, unable to collect and focus his heat. He heard the wild tongueless cries of desire, the inchoate ecstasy that knows no gateway of release. But he knew fear—not the social fear, but the fear of ignorance, of discovery. He feared his potency. He spoke to her thickly, wildly, not hearing himself speak.

"Do you want me to? Do you want me to, Louise?"

She drew his face down, murmuring:

"You won't hurt me, 'Gene? You wouldn't do anything to hurt me, honey? If anything happens—" she said drowsily.

He seized the straw of her suggestion.

"I won't be the first. I won't be the one to begin you. I've never started a girl off," he babbled, aware vaguely that he was voicing an approved doctrine of chivalry. "See here, Louise!" he shook her—she seemed drugged. "You've got to tell me before—. I won't do *that!* I may be a bad fellow, but nobody can say I ever did that. Do you hear!" His voice rose shrilly; his face worked wildly; he was hardly able to speak.

"I say, do you hear? Am I the first one, or not? You've got to answer! Did you ever—before?"

She looked at him lazily. She smiled.

"No," she said.

"I may be bad, but I won't do that." He had become inarticulate; his voice went off into a speechless jargon. Gasping, stammering, with contorted and writhing face, he sought for speech.

She rose suddenly, and put her warm arms comfortingly around him. Soothing and caressing him, she drew him down on her breast. She stroked his head, and talked quietly to him.

"I know you wouldn't, honey. I know you wouldn't. Don't talk. Don't say anything. Why, you're all excited, dear. There. Why, you're shaking like a leaf. You're high-strung, honey. That's what it is. You're a bundle of nerves."

He wept soundlessly into her arm.

He became quieter. She smiled, and kissed him softly.

"Put on your clothes," said Louise. "We ought to get started if we're going out there."

In his confusion he tried to draw on a pair of Mrs. Bowden's cast-off pumps. Louise laughed richly, and thrust her fingers through his hair.

At the Navy Yard, they could not find the Bowdens nor Max Isaacs. A young sailor took them over a destroyer. Louise went up a railed iron ladder with an emphatic rhythm of her shapely thighs. She showed her legs. She stared impudently at a picture of a chorus lady, cut from the *Police Gazette*. The young sailor rolled his eyes aloft with an expression of innocent debauchery. Then he winked heavily at Eugene.

The deck of the Oregon.

"What's that for?" said Louise, pointing to the outline in nails of Admiral Dewey's foot.

"That's where he stood during the fight," said the sailor.

Louise put her small foot within the print of the greater one. The sailor winked at Eugene. You may fire when you are ready, Gridley.

"She's a nice girl," said Eugene.

"Yeah," said Max Isaacs. "She's a nice lady." He craned his neck awkwardly, and squinted. "About how old is she?"

"She's eighteen," said Eugene.

Malvin Bowden stared at him.

"You're crazy!" said he. "She's twenty-one."

"No," said Eugene, "she's eighteen. She told me so."

"I don't care," said Malvin Bowden, "she's no such thing. She's twenty-one. I reckon I ought to know. My folks have known her for five years. She had a baby when she was eighteen."

"Aw!" said Max Isaacs.

"Yes," said Malvin Bowden, "a travelling man got her in trouble. Then he ran away."

"Aw!" said Max Isaacs. "Without marryin' her or anything?"

"He didn't do nothing for her. He ran away," said Malvin Bowden. "Her people are raising the kid now."

"Great Day!" said Max Isaacs slowly. Then, sternly, he added, "A man who'd do a thing like that ought to be shot."

"You're right!" said Malvin Bowden.

They loafed along the Battery, along the borders of ruined Camelot.

"Those are nice old places," said Max Isaacs. "They've been good houses in their day."

He looked greedily at wrought-iron gateways; the old lust of his childhood for iron-scraps awoke.

"Those are old Southern mansions," said Eugene, reverently.

The bay was still: there was a green stench of warm standing water.

"They've let the place run down," said Malvin. "It's no bigger now than it was before the Civil War."

No, sir, and, by heaven, so long as one true Southern heart is left alive to remember Appomattox, Reconstruction, and the Black parliaments, we will defend with our dearest blood our menaced, but sacred, traditions.

"They need some Northern capital," said Max Isaacs sagely. They all did.

An old woman, wearing a tiny bonnet, was led out on a high veranda from one of the houses, by an attentive Negress. She seated herself in a porch rocker and stared blindly into the sun. Eugene looked at her sympathetically. She had probably not been informed by her loyal children of the unsuccessful termination of the war. United in their brave deception, they stinted themselves daily, reining in on their proud stomachs in order that she might have all the luxury to which she had been accustomed. What did she eat? The wing of a chicken, no doubt, and a glass of dry sherry. Meanwhile, all the valuable heirlooms had been pawned or sold. Fortunately, she was almost blind, and could not see the wastage of their fortune. It was very sad. But did she not sometimes think of that old time of the wine and the roses? When knighthood was in flower?

"Look at that old lady," whispered Malvin Bowden.

"You can *tell* she's a lady," said Max Isaacs. "I bet she's never turned a hand over."

"An old family," said Eugene gently. "The Southern aristocracy."

An old Negro came by, fringed benevolently by white whiskers. A good old man—an ante-bellum darkey. Dear Lord, their number was few in these unhappy days.

Eugene thought of the beautiful institution of human slavery, which his slaveless maternal ancestry had fought so valiantly to preserve. Bress de Lawd, Marse! Ole Mose doan' wan' to be free niggah. How he goan' lib widout marse? He doan' wan' stahve wid free niggahs. Har, har, har!

Philanthropy. Pure philanthropy. He brushed a tear from his een.

They were going across the harbor to the Isle of Palms. As the boat churned past the round brick cylinder of Fort Sumter, Malvin Bowden said:

"They had the most men. If things had been even, we'd have beaten them."

"They didn't beat us," said Max Isaacs. "We wore ourselves out beating them."

"We were defeated," said Eugene, quietly, "not beaten."

Max Isaacs stared at him dumbly.

"Aw!" he said.

They left the little boat, and ground away toward the beach in a streetcar. The land had grown dry and yellow in the enervation of the summer. The foliage was coated with dust: they rattled past cheap summer houses, baked and blistered, stogged drearily in the sand. They were small, flimsy, a multitudinous vermin—all with their little wooden sign of lodging. "The Ishkabibble," "Seaview," "Rest Haven," "Atlantic Inn,"—Eugene looked at them, reading with weariness the bleached and jaded humor of their names.

"There are a lot of boarding-houses in the world," said he.

A hot wind of beginning autumn rustled dryly through the long parched leaves of stunted palms. Before them rose the huge rusted spokes of a Ferris Wheel. St. Louis. They had reached the beach.

Malvin Bowden leaped joyously from the car.

"Last one in's a rotten egg!" he cried, and streaked for the bath-house.

"Kings! I've got kings, son," yelled Max Isaacs. He held up his crossed fingers. The beach was bare: two or three concessions stood idly open for business. The sky curved over them, a cloudless blue burnished bowl. The sea offshore was glazed emerald: the waves rode heavily in, thickening murkily as they turned with sunlight and sediment to a beachy yellow.

They walked slowly down the beach toward the bathhouse. The tranquil, incessant thunder of the sea made in them a lonely music. Seawards, their eyes probed through the seething glare.

"I'm going to join the navy, 'Gene," said Max Isaacs. "Come on and go with me."

"I'm not old enough," said Eugene. "You're not, either."

"I'll be sixteen in November," said Max Isaacs defensively.

"That's not old enough."

"I'm going to lie to get in," said Max Isaacs. "They won't bother you. You can get in. Come on."

"No," said Eugene. "I can't."

"Why not?" said Max Isaacs. "What are you going to do?"

"I'm going to college," said Eugene. "I'm going to get an education and study law."

"You'll have lots of time," said Max Isaacs. "You can go to college when you come out. They teach you a lot in the navy. They give you a good training. You go everywhere."

"No," said Eugene. "I can't."

But his pulse throbbed as he listened to the lonely thunder of the sea. He saw strange dusky faces, palm frondage, and heard the little tinkling sounds of Asia. He believed in harbors at the end.

Mrs. Bowden's niece and the waitress came out on the next car. After his immersion he lay, trembling slightly under the gusty wind, upon the beach. A fine tang of salt was on his lips. He licked his clean young flesh.

Louise came from the bathhouse and walked slowly toward him. She came proudly, her warm curves moulded into her bathing-suit: her legs were covered with stockings of green silk.

Far out, beyond the ropes, Max Isaacs lifted his white heavy arms, and slid swiftly through a surging wall of green water. His body glimmered greenly for a moment; he stood erect wiping his eyes and shaking water from his ears.

Eugene took the waitress by the hand and led her into the water. She advanced slowly, with little twittering cries. An undulant surge rolled in deceptively, and rose suddenly to her chin, drinking her breath. She gasped and clung to him. Initiated, they bucked deliciously through a roaring wall of water, and, while her eyes were still closed, he caught her to him with young salty kisses.

Presently they came out, and walked over the wet strip of beach into the warm loose sand, bedding their dripping bodies gratefully in its warmth. The waitress shivered: he moulded sand over her legs and hips, until she was half buried. He kissed her, stilling his trembling lips upon her mouth.

"I like you! I like you a lot!" he said.

"What did they tell you about me?" she said. "Did they talk about me?"

"I don't care," he said. "I don't care about that. I like you."

"You won't remember me, honey, when you start going with the girls. You'll forget about me. Some day you'll see me, and you won't even know me. You won't recognize me. You'll pass without speaking."

"No," he said. "I'll never forget you, Louise. So long as I live."

Their hearts were filled with the lonely thunder of the sea. She kissed him. They were hill-born.

LOVE IN THE ENCHANTED WOOD

THERE was at Dixieland a girl named Laura James. She was twenty-one years old. She looked younger. She was there when he came back.

Laura was a slender girl, of medium height, but looking taller than she was. She was very firmly moulded: she seemed fresh and washed and clean. She had thick hair, very straight and blonde, combed in a flat bracelet around her small head. Her face was white, with small freckles. Her eyes were soft, candid, cat-green. Her nose was a little too large for her face: it was tilted. She was not pretty. She dressed very simply and elegantly in short plaid skirts and waists of knitted silk.

She was the only young person at Dixieland. Eugene spoke to her with timid hauteur. He thought her plain and dull. But he began to sit with her on the porch at night. Somehow, he began to love her.

He did not know that he loved her. He talked to her arrogantly and boastfully as they sat in the wooden porch-swing. But he breathed the clean perfume of her marvellous young body. He was trapped in the tender cruelty of her clear green eyes, caught in the subtle net of her smile.

Laura James lived in the eastern part of the State, far east even of Pulpit Hill, in a little town built on a salt river of the great coastal plain. Her father was a wealthy merchant—a wholesale provisioner. The girl was an only child: she spent extravagantly.

Eugene sat on the porch rail one evening and talked to her. Before, he had only nodded, or spoken stiffly a word or two. They began haltingly, aware painfully of gaps in their conversation.

"You're from Little Richmond, aren't you?" he said.

"Yes," said Laura James, "do you know any one from there?"

"Yes," said he, "I know John Bynum and a boy named Ficklen. They're from Little Richmond, aren't they?"

"Oh, Dave Ficklen! Do you know him? Yes. They both go to Pulpit Hill. Do you go there?"

"Yes," he said, "that's where I knew them."

"Do you know the two Barlow boys? They're Sigma Nus," said Laura James.

He had seen them. They were great swells, football men.
"Yes, I know them," he said, "Roy Barlow and Jack Barlow."
"Do you know 'Snooks' Warren? He's a Kappa Sig."
"Yes. They call them Keg Squeezers," said Eugene.
"What fraternity are you?" said Laura James.
"I'm not any," he said painfully. "I was just a Freshman this year."
"Some of the best friends I have never joined fraternities," said
Laura James.

They met more and more frequently, without arrangement, until
by silent consent they met every night upon the porch. Sometimes
they walked along the cool dark streets. Sometimes he squired her
clumsily through the town, to the movies, and later, with the uneasy
pugnacity of youth, past the loafing cluster at Wood's. Often he took
her to Woodson Street, where Helen secured for him the cool privacy
of the veranda. She was very fond of Laura James.

"She's a nice girl. A lovely girl. I like her. She's not going to take
any beauty prizes, is she?" She laughed with a trace of good-natured
ridicule.

He was displeased.

"She looks all right," he said. "She's not as ugly as you make out."

But she *was* ugly—with a clean lovely ugliness. Her face was
freckled lightly, over her nose and mouth: her features were eager,
unconscious, turned upward in irregular pertness. But she was exquisitely made and exquisitely kept: she had the firm young line of
Spring, budding, slender, virginal. She was like something swift, with
wings, which hovers in a wood—among the feathery trees suspected,
but uncaught, unseen.

He tried to live before her in armor. He showed off before her.
Perhaps, he thought, if he were splendid enough, she would not see
the ugly disorder and meanness of the world he dwelt in.

Across the street, on the wide lawn of the Brunswick—the big
brick gabled house that Eliza once had coveted—Mr. Pratt, who
crawled in that mean world in which only a boarding-house husband
can exist, was watering wide green spaces of lawn with a hose. The
flashing water motes gleamed in the red glare of sunset. The red light
fell across the shaven pinched face. It glittered on the buckles of his
arm-bands. Across the walk, on the other lobe of grass, several men
and women were playing croquet. There was laughter on the vine-

hid porch. Next door, at the Belton, the boarders were assembled on the long porch in bright hash-house chatter. The comedian of the Dixie Ramblers arrived with two chorus girls. He was a little man, with the face of a weasel and no upper teeth. He wore a straw hat with a striped band, and a blue shirt and collar. The boarders gathered in around him. In a moment there was shrill laughter.

Julius Arthur sped swiftly down the hill, driving his father home. He grinned squintily and flung his arm up in careless greeting. The prosperous lawyer twisted a plump Van Dyked face on a wry neck curiously. Unsmiling, he passed.

A Negress in the Brunswick struck on the several bells of a Japanese gong. There was a scramble of feet on the porch; the croquet players dropped their mallets and walked rapidly toward the house. Pratt wound his hose over a wooden reel.

A slow bell-clapper in the Belton sent the guests in a scrambling drive for the doors. In a moment there was a clatter of heavy plates and a loud foody noise. The guests on the porch at Dixieland rocked more rapidly, with low mutters of discontent.

Eugene talked to Laura in thickening dusk, sheeting his pain in pride and indifference. Eliza's face, a white blur in the dark, came up behind the screen.

"Come on out, Mrs. Gant, and get a breath of fresh air," said Laura James.

"Why no-o, child. I can't now. Who's that with you?" she cried, obviously flustered. She opened the door. "Huh? Heh? Have you seen 'Gene? Is it 'Gene?"

"Yes," he said. "What's the matter?"

"Come here a minute, boy," she said.

He went into the hall.

"What is it?" he asked.

"Why, son, what in the world! I don't know. You'll have to do something," she whispered, twisting her hands together.

"What is it, mama? What are you talking about?" he cried irritably.

"Why—Jannadeau's just called up. Your papa's on a rampage again and he's coming this way. Child! There's no telling what he'll do. I've all these people in the house. He'll ruin us." She wept. "Go and try to stop him. Head him off if you can. Take him to Woodson Street."

He got his hat quickly and ran through the door.

"Where are you going?" asked Laura James. "Are you going off without supper?"

"I've got to go to town," he said. "I won't be long. Will you wait for me?"

"Yes," she said.

He leaped down on the walk just as his father lurched in from the street by the high obscuring hedge that shut the house from the spacious yard of the attorney Hall. Gant reeled destructively, across a border of lilies, on to the lawn, and strode for the veranda. He stumbled, cursing, on the bottom step and plunged forward in a sprawl upon the porch. The boy jumped for him, and half dragged, half lifted his great drunken body erect. The boarders shrank into a huddle with a quick scattering of chairs: he greeted them with a laugh of howling contempt.

"Are you there? I say, are you there? The lowest of the low— boarding-house swine! Merciful God! What a travesty! A travesty on Nature! That it should come to this!"

He burst into a long peal of maniacal laughter.

"Papa! Come on!" said Eugene in a low voice. He took his father cautiously by the sleeve. Gant flung him half across the porch with a gesture of his hand. As he stepped in again swiftly, his father struck at him with a flailing arm. He evaded the great mowing fist without trouble, and caught the falling body, swung from its own pivot, in his arms. Then quickly, before Gant could recover, holding him from behind, he rushed him toward the door. The boarders scattered away like sparrows. But Laura James was at the screen before him: she flung it open.

"Get away! Get away!" he cried, full of shame and anger. "You stay out of this." For a moment he despised her for seeing his hurt.

"Oh, let me help you, my dear," Laura James whispered. Her eyes were wet, but she was not afraid.

Father and son plunged chaotically down the wide dark hall, Eliza, weeping and making gestures, just before them.

"Take him in here, boy. Take him in here," she whispered, motioning to a large bed-room on the upper side of the house. Eugene propelled his father through a blind passage of bath room, and pushed him over on the creaking width of an iron bed.

"You damned scoundrel!" Gant yelled, again trying to reap him down with the long arm, "let me up or I'll kill you!"

"For God's sake, papa," he implored angrily, "try to quiet down. Every one in town can hear you."

"To hell with them!" Gant roared. "Mountain Grills—all of them, fattening upon my heart's-blood. They have done me to death, as sure as there's a God in heaven."

Eliza appeared in the door, her face contorted by weeping.

"Son, can't you do something to stop him?" she said. "He'll ruin us all. He'll drive every one away."

Gant struggled to stand erect when he saw her. Her white face stirred him to insanity.

"There it is! There! There! Do you see! The fiend-face I know so well, gloating upon my misery. Look at it! Look! Do you see its smile of evil cunning? Greeley, Will, The Hog, The Old Major! The Tax Collector will get it all, and I shall die in the gutter!"

"If it hadn't been for me," Eliza began, stung to retaliation, "you'd have died there long ago."

"Mama, for God's sake!" the boy cried. "Don't stand there talking to him! Can't you see what it does to him! Do something, in heaven's name! Get Helen! Where is she?"

"I'll make an end to it all!" Gant yelled, staggering erect. "I'll do for us both now."

Eliza vanished.

"Yes, sir, papa. It's going to be all right," Eugene began soothingly, pushing him back on the bed again. He dropped quickly to his knees, and began to draw off one of Gant's soft tongueless shoes, muttering reassurances all the time: "Yes, sir. We'll get you some good hot soup and put you to bed in a jiffy. Everything's going to be all right," the shoe came off in his hand and, aided by the furious thrust of his father's foot, he went sprawling back.

Gant got to his feet again and, taking a farewell kick at his fallen son, lunged toward the door. Eugene scrambled up quickly, and leaped after him. The two men fell heavily into the roughly grained plaster of the wall. Gant cursed, flailing about clumsily at his tormenter. Helen came in.

"Baby!" Gant wept, "they're trying to kill me. O Jesus, do something to save me, or I perish."

"You get back in that bed," she commanded sharply, "or I'll knock your head off."

Very obediently he suffered himself to be led back to bed and un-dressed. In a few minutes she was sitting beside him with a bowl of smoking soup. He grinned sheepishly as she spooned it into his opened mouth. She laughed—almost happily—thinking of the lost and irrevocable years. Suddenly, before he slept, he lifted himself strongly from the pillows that propped him, and with staring eyes, called out in savage terror:

"Is it a cancer? I say, is it a cancer?"

"Hush!" she cried. "No. Of course not! Don't be foolish."

He fell back exhausted, with eyes closed. But they knew that it was. He had never been told. The terrible name of his malady was never uttered save by him. And in his heart he knew—what they all knew and never spoke of before him—that it was, it was a cancer. All day, with fear-stark eyes, Gant had sat, like a broken statue, among his marbles, drinking. It was a cancer.

The boy's right hand bled very badly across the wrist, where his father's weight had ground it into the wall.

"Go wash it off," said Helen. "I'll tie it up for you."

He went into the dark bathroom and held his hand under a jet of lukewarm water. A very quiet despair was in his heart, a weary peace that brooded too upon the house of death and tumult, that flowed, like a soft exploring wind through its dark halls, bathing all things quietly with peace and weariness. The boarders had fled like silly sheep to the two houses across the street; they had eaten there, they were clustered there upon the porches, whispering. And their going brought him peace and freedom, as if his limbs had been freed from a shackling weight. Eliza, amid the slow smoke of the kitchen, wept more quietly over the waste of supper; he saw the black mourn-ful calm of the Negress's face. He walked slowly up the dark hall, with a handkerchief tied loosely round his wound. He felt suddenly the peace that comes with despair. The sword that pierces very deep had fared through the folds of his poor armor of pride. The steel had sheared his side, had bitten to his heart. But under his armor he had found himself. No more than himself could be known. No more than himself could be given. What he was—he was: evasion and pretense could not add to his sum. With all his heart he was glad.

By the door, in the darkness, he found Laura James.

"I thought you had gone with the others," he said.

"No," said Laura James, "how is your father?"

"He's all right now. He's gone to sleep," he answered. "Have you had anything to eat?"

"No," she said, "I didn't want it."

"I'll bring you something from the kitchen," he said. "There's plenty there." In a moment he added: "I'm sorry, Laura."

"What are you sorry for?" she asked.

He leaned against the wall limply, drained of his strength at her touch.

"Eugene. My dear," she said. She pulled his drooping face down to her lips and kissed him. "My sweet, my darling, don't look like that."

All his resistance melted from him. He seized her small hands, crushing them in his hot fingers, and devouring them with kisses.

"My dear Laura! My dear Laura!" he said in a choking voice. "My sweet, my beautiful Laura! My lovely Laura. I love you, I love you." The words rushed from his heart, incoherent, unashamed, foaming through the broken levees of pride and silence. They clung together in the dark, with their wet faces pressed mouth to mouth. Her perfume went drunkenly to his brain; her touch upon him shot through his limbs a glow of magic; he felt the pressure of her narrow breasts, eager and lithe, against him with a sense of fear—as if he had dishonored her—with a sickening remembrance of his defilement.

He held between his hands her elegant small head, so gloriously wound with its thick bracelet of fine blonde hair, and spoke the words he had never spoken—the words of confession, filled with love and humility.

"Don't go! Don't go! Please don't go!" he begged. "Don't leave, dear. Please!"

"Hush!" she whispered. "I won't go! I love you, my dear."

She saw his hand, wrapped in its bloody bandage: she nursed it gently with soft little cries of tenderness. She fetched a bottle of iodine from her room and painted the stinging cut with a brush. She wrapped it with clean strips of fine white cloth, torn from an old waist, scented with a faint and subtle perfume.

Then they sat upon the wooden swing. The house seemed to sleep in darkness. Helen and Eliza came presently from its very quiet depth.

"How's your hand, 'Gene?" Helen asked.

"It's all right," he said.

"Let me see! O-ho, you've got a nurse now, haven't you?" she said, with a good laugh.

"What's that? What's that? Hurt his hand? How'd you do that? Why, here—say—I've got the very thing for it, son," said Eliza, trying to bustle off in all directions.

"Oh, it's all right now, mama. It's been fixed," he said wearily, reflecting that she had the very thing always too late. He looked at Helen grinning:

"God bless our Happy Home!" he said.

"Poor old Laura!" she laughed, and hugged the girl roughly with one hand. "It's too bad you have to be dragged into it."

"That's all right," said Laura. "I feel like one of the family now anyhow."

"He needn't think he can carry on like this," said Eliza resentfully. "I'm not going to put up with it any longer."

"Oh forget about it!" said Helen wearily. "Good heavens, mama. Papa's a sick man. Can't you realize that?"

"Pshaw!" said Eliza scornfully. "I don't believe there's a thing in the world wrong with him but that vile licker. All his trouble comes from that."

"Oh—how ridiculous! How ridiculous! You can't tell me!" Helen exclaimed angrily.

"Let's talk about the weather," said Eugene.

Then they all sat quietly, letting the darkness soak into them. Finally Helen and Eliza went back into the house: Eliza went unwillingly, at the girl's insistence, casting back the doubtful glimmer of her face upon the boy and girl.

The wasting helve of the moon rode into heaven over the bulk of the hills. There was a smell of wet grass and lilac, and the vast brooding symphony of the million-noted little night things, rising and falling in a constant ululation, and inhabiting the heart with steady unconscious certitude. The pallid light drowned out the stars, it lay like silence on the earth, it dripped through the leafy web of the young maples, printing the earth with swarming moths of elvish light.

Eugene and Laura sat with joined hands in the slowly creaking swing. Her touch shot through him like a train of fire: as he put his arm around her shoulders and drew her over to him, his fingers touched the live firm cup of her breast. He jerked his hand away, as if he had been stung, muttering an apology. Whenever she touched him, his flesh got numb and weak. She was a virgin, crisp like celery —his heart shrank away from the pollution of his touch upon her. It seemed to him that he was much the older, although he was sixteen, and she twenty-one. He felt the age of his loneliness and his dark perception. He felt the gray wisdom of sin—a waste desert, but seen and known. When he held her hand, he felt as if he had already seduced her. She lifted her lovely face to him, pert and ugly as a boy's; it was inhabited by a true and steadfast decency, and his eyes were wet. All the young beauty in the world dwelt for him in that face that had kept wonder, that had kept innocency, that had lived in such immortal blindness to the terror and foulness of the world. He came to her, like a creature who had travelled its life through dark space, for a moment of peace and conviction on some lonely planet, where now he stood, in the vast enchanted plain of moonlight, with moonlight falling on the moonflower of her face. For if a man should dream of heaven and, waking, find within his hand a flower as token that he had really been there—what then, what then?

"Eugene," she said presently, "how old are you?"

His vision thickened with his pulse. In a moment he answered with terrible difficulty.

"I'm—just sixteen."

"Oh, you child!" she cried. "I thought you were more than that!"

"I'm—old for my age," he muttered. "How old are you?"

"I'm twenty-one," she said. "Isn't it a pity?"

"There's not much difference," he said. "I can't see that it matters."

"Oh, my dear," she said. "It does! It matters so much!"

And he knew that it did—how much he did not know. But he

had his moment. He was not afraid of pain, he was not afraid of loss. He cared nothing for the practical need of the world. He dared to say the strange and marvellous thing that had bloomed so darkly in him.

"Laura," he said, hearing his low voice sound over the great plain of the moon, "let's always love each other as we do now. Let's never get married. I want you to wait for me and to love me forever. I am going all over the world. I shall go away for years at a time; I shall become famous, but I shall always come back to you. You shall live in a house away in the mountains, you shall wait for me, and keep yourself for me. Will you?" he said, asking for her life as calmly as for an hour of her time.

"Yes, dear," said Laura in the moonlight, "I will wait for you forever."

She was buried in his flesh. She throbbed in the beat of his pulses. She was wine in his blood, a music in his heart.

"He has no consideration for you or any one else," Hugh Barton growled. He had returned late from work at his office, to take Helen home. "If he can't do better than this, we'll find a house of our own. I'm not going to have you get down sick on account of him."

"Forget about it," Helen said. "He's getting old."

They came out on the veranda.

"Come down to-morrow, honey," she said to Eugene. "I'll give you a real feed. Laura, you come too. It's not always like this, you know." She laughed, fondling the girl with a big hand.

They coasted away downhill.

"What a lovely girl your sister is," said Laura James. "Aren't you simply crazy about her?"

Eugene made no answer for a moment.

"Yes," he said.

"She is about you. Any one can see that," said Laura.

In the darkness he caught at his throat.

"Yes," he said.

The moon quartered gently across heaven. Eliza came out again, timidly, hesitantly.

"Who's there? Who's there?" she spoke into the darkness. "Where's 'Gene? Oh! I didn't know! Are you there, son?" She knew very well.

"Yes," he said.

"Why don't you sit down, Mrs. Gant?" asked Laura. "I don't see how you stand that hot kitchen all day long. You must be worn out."

"I tell you what!" said Eliza, peering dimly at the sky. "It's a fine night, isn't it? As the fellow says, a night for lovers." She laughed uncertainly, then stood for a moment in thought.

"Son," she said in a troubled voice, "why don't you go to bed and get some sleep? It's not good for you staying up till all hours like this."

"That's where I should be," said Laura James, rising.

"Yes, child," said Eliza. "Go get your beauty sleep. As the saying goes, early to bed and early to rise—"

"Let's all go, then. Let's all go!" said Eugene impatiently and angrily, wondering if she must always be the last one awake in that house.

"Why law, no!" said Eliza. "I can't, boy. I've all those things to iron."

Beside him, Laura gave his hand a quiet squeeze, and rose. Bitterly, he watched his loss.

"Good-night, all. Good-night, Mrs. Gant."

"Good-night, child."

When she had gone, Eliza sat down beside him, with a sigh of weariness.

"I tell you what," she said. "That feels good. I wish I had as much time as some folks, and could sit out here enjoying the air." In the darkness, he knew her puckering lips were trying to smile.

"Hm!" she said, and caught his hand in her rough palm. "Has my baby gone and got him a girl?"

"What of it? What if it were true?" he said angrily. "Haven't I a right as much as any one?"

"Pshaw!" said Eliza. "You're too young to think of them. I wouldn't pay any attention to them, if I were you. Most of them haven't an idea in the world except going out to parties and having a good time. I don't want my boy to waste his time on them."

He felt her earnestness beneath her awkward banter. He struggled in a chaos of confused fury, trying for silence. At last he spoke in a low voice, filled with his passion:

"We've got to have something, mama. We've got to have something, you know. We can't go on always alone—alone."

It was dark. No one could see. He let the gates swing open. He wept.

"I know!" Eliza agreed hastily. "I'm not saying—"

"My God, my God, where are we going? What's it all about? He's dying—can't you see it? Don't you know it? Look at his life. Look at yours. No light, no love, no comfort—nothing." His voice rose frantically: he beat on his ribs like a drum. "Mama, mama, in God's name, what is it? What do you want? Are you going to strangle and drown us all? Don't you own enough? Do you want more string? Do you want more bottles? By God, I'll go around collecting them if you say so." His voice had risen almost to a scream. "But tell me what you want. Don't you own enough? Do you want the town? What is it?"

"Why, I don't know what you're talking about, boy," said Eliza angrily. "If I hadn't tried to accumulate a little property none of you would have had a roof to call your own, for your papa, I can assure you, would have squandered everything."

"A roof to call our own!" he yelled, with a crazy laugh. "Good God, we haven't a bed to call our own. We haven't a room to call our own. We have not a quilt to call our own that might not be taken from us to warm the mob that rocks upon this porch and grumbles."

"Now, you may sneer at the boarders all you like—" Eliza began sternly.

"No," he said. "I can't. There's not breath or strength enough in me to sneer at them all I like."

Eliza began to weep.

"I've done the best I could!" she said. "I'd have given you a home if I could. I'd have put up with anything after Grover's death, but he never gave me a moment's peace. Nobody knows what I've been through. Nobody knows, child. Nobody knows."

He saw her face in the moonlight, contorted by an ugly grimace of sorrow. What she said, he knew, was fair and honest. He was touched deeply.

"It's all right, mama," he said painfully. "Forget about it! I know."

She seized his hand almost gratefully and laid her white face, still twisted with her grief, against his shoulder. It was the gesture of a child: a gesture that asked for love, pity, and tenderness. It tore up great roots in him, bloodily.

"Don't!" he said. "Don't, mama! Please!"

"Nobody knows," said Eliza. "Nobody knows. I need some one too. I've had a hard life, son, full of pain and trouble." Slowly, like a child again, she wiped her wet weak eyes with the back of her hand.

Ah, he thought, as his heart twisted in him full of wild pain and regret, she will be dead some day and I shall always remember this. Always this. This.

They were silent a moment. He held her rough hand tightly, and kissed her.

"Well," Eliza began, full of cheerful prophecy, "I tell you what: I'm not going to spend my life slaving away here for a lot of boarders. They needn't think it. I'm going to set back and take things as easy as any of them." She winked knowingly at him. "When you come home next time, you may find me living in a big house in Doak Park. I've got the lot—the best lot out there for view and location, far better than the one W. J. Bryan has. I made the trade with old Dr. Doak himself, the other day. Look here! What about!" She laughed. "He said, 'Mrs. Gant, I can't trust any of my agents with you. If I'm to make anything on this deal, I've got to look out. You're the sharpest trader in this town.' 'Why, pshaw! Doctor,' I said (I never let on I believed him or anything), 'all I want is a fair return on my investment. I believe in every one making his profit and giving the other fellow a chance. Keep the ball a-rolling!' I said, laughing as big as you please. 'Why, Mrs. Gant!' he said—" She was off on a lengthy divagation, recording with an absorbed gusto the interminable minutia of her transaction with the worthy Quinine King, with the attendant phenomena, during the time, of birds, bees, flowers, sun, clouds, dogs, cows, and people. She was pleased. She was happy.

Presently, returning to an abrupt reflective pause, she said: "Well, I may do it. I want a place where my children can come to see me and bring their friends, when they come home."

"Yes," he said, "yes. That would be nice. You musn't work all your life."

He was pleased at her happy fable: for a moment he almost believed in a miracle of redemption, although the story was an old one to him.

"I hope you do," he said. "It would be nice. . . . Go on to bed now, why don't you, mama? It's getting late." He rose. "I'm going now."

"Yes, son," she said, getting up. "You ought to. Well, good-night." They kissed with a love, for the time, washed clean of bitterness. Eliza went before him into the dark house.

But before he went to bed, he descended to the kitchen for matches. She was still there, beyond the long littered table, at her ironing board, flanked by two big piles of laundry. At his accusing glance she said hastily:

"I'm a-going. Right away. I just wanted to finish up these towels."

He rounded the table, before he left, to kiss her again. She fished into a button-box on the sewing-machine and dug out the stub of a pencil. Gripping it firmly above an old envelope, she scrawled out on the ironing board a rough mapping. Her mind was still lulled in its project.

"Here, you see," she began, "is Sunset Avenue, coming up the hill. This is Doak Place, running off here at right angles. Now this corner-lot here belongs to Dick Webster; and right here above it, at the very top is—"

Is, he thought, staring with dull interest, the place where the Buried Treasure lies. Ten paces N.N.E. from the Big Rock, at the roots of the Old Oak Tree. He went off into his delightful fantasy while she talked. What if there *was* a buried treasure on one of Eliza's lots? If she kept on buying, there might very well be. Or why not an oil-well? Or a coal-mine? These famous mountains were full (they said) of minerals. 150 Bbl. a day right in the backyard. How much would that be? At $3.00 a Bbl., there would be over $50.00 a day for every one in the family. The world is ours!

"You see, don't you?" she smiled triumphantly. "And right there is where I shall build. That lot will bring twice its present value in five years."

"Yes," he said, kissing her. "Good-night, mama. For God's sake, go to bed and get some sleep."

"Good-night, son," said Eliza.

He went out and began to mount the dark stairs. Benjamin Gant, entering at this moment, stumbled across a mission-chair in the hall. He cursed fiercely, and struck at the chair with his hand. Damn it! Oh damn it! Mrs. Pert whispered a warning behind him, with a fuzzy laugh. Eugene paused, then mounted softly the carpeted stair, so that he would not be heard, entering the sleeping-porch at the top of the landing on which he slept.

He did not turn on the light, because he disliked seeing the raw blistered varnish of the dresser and the bent white iron of the bed. It sagged, and the light was dim—he hated dim lights, and the large moths, flapping blindly around on their dusty wings. He undressed in the moon. The moonlight fell upon the earth like a magic unearthly dawn. It wiped away all rawness, it hid all sores. It gave all common and familiar things—the sagging drift of the barn, the raw shed of the creamery, the rich curve of the lawyer's crab-apple trees —a uniform bloom of wonder. He lighted a cigarette, watching its red glowing suspiration in the mirror, and leaned upon the rail of his porch, looking out. Presently, he grew aware that Laura James, eight feet away, was watching him. The moonlight fell upon them, bathing their flesh in a green pallor, and steeping them in its silence. Their faces were blocked in miraculous darkness, out of which, seeing but unseen, their bright eyes lived. They gazed at each other in that elfin light, without speaking. In the room below them, the light crawled to his father's bed, swam up the cover, and opened across his face, thrust sharply upward. The air of the night, the air of the hills, fell on the boy's bare flesh like a sluice of clear water. His toes curled in to grip wet grasses.

On the landing, he heard Mrs. Pert go softly up to bed, fumbling with blind care at the walls. Doors creaked and clicked. The house grew solidly into quiet, like a stone beneath the moon. They looked, waiting for a spell and the conquest of time. Then she spoke to him —her whisper of his name was only a guess at sound. He threw his leg across the rail, and thrust his long body over space to the sill of her window, stretching out like a cat. She drew her breath in sharply, and cried out softly, "No! No!" but she caught his arms upon the sills and held him as he twisted in.

Then they held each other tightly in their cool young arms, and kissed many times with young lips and faces. All her hair fell down about her like thick corn-silk, in a sweet loose wantonness. Her straight dainty legs were clad in snug little green bloomers, gathered in by an elastic above the knee.

They were locked limb to limb: he kissed the smooth sheen of her arms and shoulders—the passion that numbed his limbs was governed by a religious ecstasy. He wanted to hold her, and go away by himself to think about her.

He stooped, thrusting his arm under her knees, and lifted her up exultantly. She looked at him frightened, holding him more tightly.

"What are you doing?" she whispered. "Don't hurt me."

"I won't hurt you, my dear," he said. "I'm going to put you to bed. Yes. I'm going to put you to bed. Do you hear?" He felt he must cry out in his throat for joy.

He carried her over and laid her on the bed. Then he knelt beside her, putting his arm beneath her and gathering her to him.

"Good-night, my dear. Kiss me good-night. Do you love me?"

"Yes." She kissed him. "Good-night, my darling. Don't go back by the window. You may fall."

But he went, as he came, reaching through the moonlight exultantly like a cat. For a long time he lay awake, in a quiet delirium, his heart thudding fiercely against his ribs. Sleep crept across his senses with goose-soft warmth: the young leaves of the maples rustled, a cock sounded his distant elfin minstrelsy, the ghost of a dog howled. He slept.

He awoke with a high hot sun beating in on his face through the porch awnings. He hated to awake in sunlight. Some day he would sleep in a great room that was always cool and dark. There would be trees and vines at his windows, or the scooped-out lift of the hill. His clothing was wet with night-damp as he dressed. When he went downstairs he found Gant rocking miserably upon the porch, his hand gripped over a walkingstick.

"Good-morning," he said, "how do you feel?"

His father cast his uneasy flickering eyes on him, and groaned.

"Merciful God! I'm being punished for my sins."

"You'll feel better in a little," said Eugene. "Did you eat anything?"

"It stuck in my throat," said Gant, who had eaten heartily. "I couldn't swallow a bite. How's your hand, son?" he asked very humbly.

"Oh, it's all right," said Eugene quickly. "Who told you about my hand?"

"She said I had hurt your hand," said Gant sorrowfully.

"Ah-h!" said the boy angrily. "No. I wasn't hurt."

Gant leaned to the side and, without looking, clumsily, patted his son's uninjured hand.

"I'm sorry for what I've done," he said. "I'm a sick man. Do you need money?"

"No," said Eugene, embarrassed. "I have all I need."

"Come to the office to-day, and I'll give you something," said Gant. "Poor child, I suppose you're hard up."

But instead, he waited until Laura James returned from her morning visit to the city's bathing-pool. She came with her bathing-suit in one hand, and several small packages in the other. More arrived by Negro carriers. She paid and signed.

"You must have a lot of money, Laura?" he said. "You do this every day, don't you?"

"Daddy gets after me about it," she admitted, "but I love to buy clothes. I spend all my money on clothes."

"What are you going to do now?"

"Nothing—whatever you like. It's a lovely day to do something, isn't it?"

"It's a lovely day to do nothing. Would you like to go off somewhere, Laura?"

"I'd love to go off somewhere with you," said Laura James.

"That is the idea, my girl. That is the idea," he said exultantly, in throaty and exuberant burlesque. "We will go off somewhere alone—we will take along something to eat," he said lusciously.

Laura went to her room and put on a pair of sturdy little slippers. Eugene went into the kitchen.

"Have you a shoe-box?" he asked Eliza.

"What do you want that for?" she said suspiciously.

"I'm going to the bank," he said ironically. "I wanted something to carry my money in." But immediately he added roughly:

"I'm going on a picnic."

"Huh? Hah? What's that you say?" said Eliza. "A picnic? Who are you going with? That girl?"

"No," he said heavily, "with President Wilson, the King of England, and Dr. Doak. We're going to have lemonade—I've promised to bring the lemons."

"I'll vow, boy!" said Eliza fretfully. "I don't like it—your running off this way when I need you. I wanted you to make a deposit for me, and the telephone people will disconnect me if I don't send them the money to-day."

"O mama! For God's sake!" he cried annoyed. "You always need me when I want to go somewhere. Let them wait! They can wait a day."

"It's overdue," she said. "Well, here you are. I wish I had time to go off on picnics." She fished a shoe-box out of a pile of magazines and newspapers that littered the top of a low cupboard.

"Have you got anything to eat?"

"We'll get it," he said, and departed.

They went down the hill, and paused at the musty little grocery around the corner on Woodson Street, where they bought crackers, peanut butter, currant jelly, bottled pickles, and a big slice of rich yellow cheese. The grocer was an old Jew who muttered jargon into a rabbi's beard as if saying a spell against Dybbuks. The boy looked closely to see if his hands touched the food. They were not clean.

On their way up the hill, they stopped for a few minutes at Gant's. They found Helen and Ben in the dining-room. Ben was eating breakfast, bending, as usual, with scowling attention, over his coffee, turning from eggs and bacon almost with disgust. Helen insisted on contributing boiled eggs and sandwiches to their provision: the two women went back into the kitchen. Eugene sat at table with Ben, drinking coffee.

"O-oh my God!" Ben said at length, yawning wearily. He lighted a cigarette. "How's the Old Man this morning?"

"He's all right, I think. Said he couldn't eat breakfast."

"Did he say anything to the boarders?"

" 'You damned scoundrels! You dirty Mountain Grills! Whee—!' That was all."

Ben snickered quietly.

"Did he hurt your hand? Let's see."

"No. You can't see anything. It's not hurt," said Eugene, lifting his bandaged wrist.

"He didn't hit you, did he?" asked Ben sternly.

"Oh, no. Of course not. He was just drunk. He was sorry about it this morning."

"Yes," said Ben, "he's always sorry about it—after he's raised all the hell he can." He drank deeply at his cigarette, inhaling the smoke as if in the grip of a powerful drug.

"How'd you get along at college this year, 'Gene?" he asked presently.

"I passed my work. I made fair grades—if that's what you mean? I did better—this Spring," he added, with some difficulty. "It was hard getting started—at the beginning."

"You mean last Fall?"

Eugene nodded.

"What was the matter?" said Ben, scowling at him. "Did the other boys make fun of you?"

"Yes," said Eugene, in a low voice.

"Why did they? You mean they didn't think you were good enough for them? Did they look down on you? Was that it?" said Ben savagely.

"No," said Eugene, very red in the face. "No. That had nothing to do with it. I look funny, I suppose. I looked funny to them."

"What do you mean you look funny?" said Ben pugnaciously. "There's nothing wrong with you, you know, if you didn't go around looking like a bum. In God's name," he exclaimed angrily, "when did you get that hair cut last? What do you think you are: the Wild Man from Borneo?"

"I don't like barbers!" Eugene burst out furiously. "That's why! I don't want them to go sticking their damned dirty fingers in my mouth. Whose business is it, if I never get my hair cut?"

"A man is judged by his appearance to-day," said Ben sententiously. "I was reading an article by a big business man in *The Post* the other day. He says he always looks at a man's shoes before he gives him a job."

He spoke seriously, haltingly, in the same way that he read, without genuine conviction. Eugene writhed to hear his fierce condor prattle this stale hash of the canny millionaires, like any obedient parrot in a teller's cage. Ben's voice had a dull flat quality as he uttered these admirable opinions: he seemed to grope behind it all for some answer, with hurt puzzled eyes. As he faltered along, with scowling intensity, through a success-sermon, there was something poignantly moving in his effort: it was the effort of his strange and lonely spirit to find some entrance into life—to find success, position, companionship. And it was as if, spelling the words out with his mouth, a settler in the Bronx from the fat Lombard plain, should try to unriddle the new world by deciphering the World Almanac, or as if some woodsman, trapped by the winter, and wasted by an obscure and terrible disease, should hunt its symptoms and its cure in a book of Household Remedies.

"Did the Old Man send you enough money to get along on?" Ben asked. "Were you able to hold your own with the other boys? He can afford it, you know. Don't let him stint you. Make him give it to you, 'Gene."

"I had plenty," said Eugene, "all that I needed."

"This is the time you need it—not later," said Ben. "Make him put you through college. This is an age of specialization. They're looking for college-trained men."

"Yes," said Eugene. He spoke obediently, indifferently, the hard bright mail of his mind undinted by the jargon: within, the Other One, who had no speech, saw.

"So get your education," said Ben, scowling vaguely. "All the Big Men—Ford, Edison, Rockefeller—whether they had it or not, say it's a good thing."

"Why didn't you go yourself?" said Eugene curiously.

"I didn't have any one to tell me," said Ben. "Besides, you don't think the Old Man would give me anything, do you?" He laughed cynically. "It's too late now."

He was silent a moment; he smoked.

"You didn't know I was taking a course in advertising, did you?" he asked, grinning.

"No. Where?"

"Through the Correspondence School," said Ben. "I get my lessons every week. I don't know," he laughed diffidently, "I must be good at it. I make the highest grades they have—98 or 100 every time. I get a diploma, if I finish the course."

A blinding mist swam across the younger brother's eyes. He did not know why. A convulsive knot gathered in his throat. He bent his head quickly and fumbled for his cigarettes. In a moment he said:

"I'm glad you're doing it. I hope you finish, Ben."

"You know," Ben said seriously, "they've turned out some Big

Men. I'll show you the testimonials some time. Men who started with nothing: now they're holding down big jobs."

"I hope you do," said Eugene.

"So, you see you're not the only College Man around here," said Ben with a grin. In a moment, he went on gravely: "You're the last hope, 'Gene. Go on and finish up, if you have to steal the money. The rest of us will never amount to a damn. Try to make something out of yourself. Hold your head up! You're as good as any of them —a damn sight better than these little pimps about town." He became very fierce; he was very excited. He got up suddenly from the table. "Don't let them laugh at you! By God, we're as good as they are. If any of them laughs at you again, pick up the first damn thing you get your hand on and knock him down. Do you hear?" In his fierce excitement he snatched up the heavy carving steel from the table and brandished it.

"Yes," said Eugene awkwardly. "I think it's going to be all right now. I didn't know how to do at first."

"I hope you have sense enough now to leave those old hookers alone?" said Ben very sternly. Eugene made no answer. "You can't do that and be anything, you know. And you're likely to catch everything. This looks like a nice girl," he said quietly, after a pause. "For heaven's sake, fix yourself up and try to keep fairly clean. Women notice that, you know. Look after your fingernails, and keep your clothes pressed. Have you any money?"

"All I need," said Eugene, looking nervously toward the kitchen. "Don't, for God's sake!"

"Put it in your pocket, you little fool," Ben said angrily, thrusting a bill into his hand. "You've got to have some money. Keep it until you need it.

Helen came out on the high front porch with them as they departed. As usual, she had added a double heaping measure to what they needed. There was another shoe-box stuffed with sandwiches, boiled eggs, and fudge.

She stood on the high step-edge, with a cloth wound over her head, her gaunt arms, pitted with old scars, akimbo. A warm sunny odor of nasturtiums, loamy earth, and honeysuckle washed round them its hot spermy waves.

"O-ho! A-ha!" she winked comically. "I know something! I'm not as blind as you think, you know—" She nodded with significant jocularity, her big smiling face drenched in the curious radiance and purity that occasionally dwelt so beautifully there. He thought always when he saw her thus, of a sky washed after rain, of wide crystalline distances, cool and clean.

With a rough snigger she prodded him in the ribs:

"Ain't love grand! Ha-ha-ha-ha! Look at his face, Laura." She drew the girl close to her in a generous hug, laughing, Oh, with laughing pity, and as they mounted the hill, she stood there, in the sunlight, her mouth slightly open, smiling, touched with radiance, beauty, and wonder.

They mounted slowly toward the eastern edge of town, by the long upward sweep of Academy Street, which bordered the Negro settlement sprawled below it. At the end of Academy Street, the hill loomed abruptly; a sinuous road, well paved, curved up along the hillside to the right. They turned into this road, mounting now along the eastern edge of Niggertown. The settlement fell sharply away below them, rushing down along a series of long clay streets. There were a few frame houses by the roadside: the dwellings of Negroes and poor white people, but these became sparser as they mounted. They walked at a leisurely pace up the cool road speckled with little dancing patches of light that filtered through the arching trees and shaded on the left by the dense massed foliage of the hill. Out of this green loveliness loomed the huge raw turret of a cement reservoir: it was streaked and blotted cooly with watermarks. Eugene felt thirsty. Further along, the escape from a smaller reservoir roared from a pipe in a foaming hawser, as thick as a man's body.

They climbed sharply up, along a rocky trail, avoiding the last long corkscrew of the road, and stood in the gap, at the road's summit. They were only a few hundred feet above the town: it lay before them with the sharp nearness of a Sienese picture, at once close and far. On the highest ground, he saw the solid masonry of the Square, blocked cleanly out in light and shadow, and a crawling toy that was a car, and men no bigger than sparrows. And about the Square was the treeless brick jungle of business—cheap, ragged, and ugly, and beyond all this, in indefinite patches, the houses where all the people lived, with little bright raw ulcers of suburbia further off, and the healing and concealing grace of fair massed trees. And below them, weltering up from the hollow along the flanks and shoulders of the hill, was Niggertown. There seemed to be a kind of centre at the Square, where all the cars crawled in and waited, yet there was no purpose anywhere.

But the hills were lordly, with a plan. Westward, they widened into the sun, soaring up from buttressing shoulders. The town was thrown up on the plateau like an encampment: there was nothing below him that could resist time. There was no idea. Below him, in a cup, he felt that all life was held: he saw it as might one of the old schoolmen writing in monkish Latin a Theatre of Human Life; or like Peter Breughel, in one of his swarming pictures. It seemed to him suddenly that he had not come up on the hill from the town, but that he had come out of the wilderness like a beast, and was staring now with steady beast-eye at this little huddle of wood and mortar which the wilderness must one day repossess, devour, cover over.

The seventh from the top was Troy—but Helen had lived there; and so the German dug it up.

They turned from the railing, with recovered wind, and walked through the gap, under Philip Roseberry's great arched bridge. To the left, on the summit, the rich Jew had his cattle, his stables, his horses, his cows, and his daughters. As they went under the shadow of the bridge Eugene lifted his head and shouted. His voice bounded against the arch like a stone. They passed under and stood on the other side of the gap, looking from the road's edge down into the cove. But they could not yet see the cove, save for green glimmers. The hillside was thickly wooded, the road wound down its side in a white perpetual corkscrew. But they could look across at the fair wild hills on the other side of the cove, cleared half-way up their flanks with ample field and fenced meadow, and forested above with a billowing sea of greenery.

The day was like gold and sapphires: there was a swift flash and sparkle, intangible and multifarious, like sunlight on roughened water, all over the land. A rich warm wind was blowing, turning all the leaves back the same way, and making mellow music through all the lutestrings of flower and grass and fruit. The wind moaned, not with the mad fiend-voice of winter in harsh boughs, but like a fruitful woman, deep-breasted, great, full of love and wisdom; like Demeter unseen and hunting through the world. A dog bayed faintly in the cove, his howl spent and broken by the wind. A cowbell tinkled gustily. In the thick wood below them the rich notes of birds fell from their throats, straight down, like nuggets. A woodpecker drummed on the dry unbarked hole of a blasted chestnut-tree. The blue gulf of the sky was spread with light massy clouds: they cruised like swift galleons, tacking across the hills before the wind, and darkening the trees below with their floating shadows.

The boy grew blind with love and desire: the cup of his heart was glutted with all this wonder. It overcame and weakened him. He grasped the girl's cool fingers. They stood leg to leg, riven into each other's flesh. Then they left the road, cutting down across its loops along steep wooded paths. The wood was a vast green church; the bird-cries fell like plums. A great butterfly, with wings of blue velvet streaked with gold and scarlet markings, fluttered heavily before them in freckled sunlight, tottering to rest finally upon a spray of dogwood. There were light skimming noises in the dense under-growth to either side, the swift bullet-shadows of birds. A garter snake, greener than wet moss, as long as a shoelace and no thicker than a woman's little finger, shot across the path, its tiny eyes bright with terror, its small forked tongue playing from its mouth like an electric spark. Laura cried out, drawing back in sharp terror; at her cry he snatched up a stone in a wild lust to kill the tiny creature that shot at them, through its coils, the old snake-fear, touching them with beauty, with horror, with something supernatural. But the snake glided away into the undergrowth and, with a feeling of strong shame, he threw the stone away. "They won't hurt you," he said.

At length, they came out above the cove, at a forking of the road. They turned left, to the north, toward the upper and smaller end. To the south, the cove widened out in a rich little Eden of farm and pasture. Small houses dotted the land, there were green meadows and a glint of water. Fields of young green wheat bent rhythmically under the wind; the young corn stood waist-high, with light clash-ing blades. The chimneys of Rheinhart's house showed above its obscuring grove of maples; the fat dairy cows grazed slowly across the wide pastures. And further below, half tree-and-shrub-hidden, lay the rich acres of Judge Webster Tayloe. The road was thickly coated with white dust; it dipped down and ran through a little brook. They crossed over on white rocks, strewn across its bed. Several ducks, scarcely disturbed by their crossing, waddled up out of the clear water and regarded them gravely, like little children in white choir aprons. A young country fellow clattered by them in a buggy filled with empty milk-cans. He grinned with a cordial red face, saluting them with a slow gesture, and leaving behind an odor of milk and sweat and butter. A woman, in a field above them, stared curiously with shaded eyes. In another field, a man was mowing with a scythe, moving into the grass like a god upon his enemies, with a reaping hook of light.

They left the road near the head of the cove, advancing over the fields on rising ground to the wooded cup of the hills. There was a powerful masculine stench of broad dock-leaves, a hot weedy odor. They moved over a pathless field, knee-high in a dry stubbly waste, gathering on their clothes clusters of brown cockle-burrs. All the field was sown with hot odorous daisies. Then they entered the wood again, mounting until they came to an island of tender grass, by a little brook that fell down from the green hill along a rocky ferny bed in bright cascades.

"Let's stop here," said Eugene. The grass was thick with dandelions: their poignant and wordless odor studded the earth with yellow magic. They were like gnomes and elves, and tiny witchcraft in flower and acorn.

Laura and Eugene lay upon their backs, looking up through the high green shimmer of leaves at the Caribbean sky, with all its fleet of cloudy ships. The water of the brook made a noise like silence. The town behind the hill lay in another unthinkable world. They forgot its pain and conflict.

"What time is it?" Eugene asked. For, they had come to a place where no time was. Laura held up her exquisite wrist, and looked at her watch.

"Why!" she exclaimed, surprised. "It's only half-past twelve!"

But he scarcely heard her.

"What do I care what time it is!" he said huskily, and he seized the lovely hand, bound with its silken watch-cord, and kissed it. Her long cool fingers closed around his own; she drew his face down to her mouth.

They lay there, locked together, upon that magic carpet, in that paradise. Her gray eyes were deeper and clearer than a pool of clear water; he kissed the little freckles on her rare skin; he gazed reverently at the snub tilt of her nose; he watched the mirrored dance of the sparkling water over her face. All of that magic world—flower and field and sky and hill, and all the sweet woodland cries, sound and sight and odor—grew into him, one voice in his heart, one tongue in his brain, harmonious, radiant, and whole—a single passionate lyrical noise.

"My dear! Darling! Do you remember last night?" he asked fondly, as if recalling some event of her childhood.

"Yes," she gathered her arms tightly about his neck, "why do you think I could forget it?"

"Do you remember what I said—what I asked you to do?" he insisted eagerly.

"Oh, what are we going to do? What are we going to do?" she moaned, turning her head to the side and flinging an arm across her eyes.

"What is it? What's the matter? Dear?"

"Eugene—my dear, you're only a child. I'm so old—a grown woman."

"You're only twenty-one," he said. "There's only five years' difference. That's nothing."

"Oh!" she said. "You don't know what you're saying. It's all the difference in the world."

"When I'm twenty, you'll be twenty-five. When I'm twenty-six, you'll be thirty-one. When I'm forty-eight, you'll be fifty-three. What's that?" he said contemptuously. "Nothing."

"Everything," she said, "everything. If I were sixteen, and you twenty-one it would be nothing. But you're a boy and I'm a woman. When you're a young man I'll be an old maid; when you grow old I shall be dying. How do you know where you'll be, what you'll be doing five years from now?" she continued in a moment. "You're only a boy—you've just started college. You have no plans yet. You don't know what you're going to do."

"Yes, I do!" he yelled furiously. "I'm going to be a lawyer. That's what they're sending me for. I'm going to be a lawyer, and I'm going

into politics. Perhaps," he added with gloomy pleasure, "you'll be
sorry then, after I make a name for myself." With bitter joy he
foresaw his lonely celebrity. The Governor's Mansion. Forty rooms.
Alone. Alone.

"You're going to be a lawyer," said Laura, "and you're going every·
where in the world, and I'm to wait for you, and never get married.
You poor kid!" She laughed softly. "You don't know what you're
going to do."

He turned a face of misery on her; brightness dropped from the
sun.

"You don't care?" he choked. "You don't care?" He bent his head
to hide his wet eyes.

"Oh, my dear," she said, "I do care. But people don't live like
that. It's like a story. Don't you know that I'm a grown woman? At
my age, dear, most girls have begun to think of getting married.
What—what if I had begun to think of it, too?"

"Married!" The word came from him in a huge gasp of horror as
if she had mentioned the abominable, proposed the unspeakable.
Then, having heard the monstrous suggestion, he immediately accepted it as a fact. He was like that.

"So! That's it!" he said furiously. "You're going to get married,
eh? You have fellows, have you? You go out with them, do you?
You've known it all the time, and you've tried to fool me."

Nakedly, with breast bare to horror, he scourged himself, knowing in the moment that the nightmare cruelty of life is not in the
remote and fantastic, but in the probable—the horror of love, loss,
marriage, the ninety seconds treason in the dark.

"You have fellows—you let them feel you. They feel your legs,
they play with your breasts, they—" His voice became inaudible
through strangulation.

"No. No, my dear. I haven't said so," she rose swiftly to a sitting
position, taking his hands. "But there's nothing unusual about getting married, you know. Most people do. Oh, my dear! Don't look
like that! Nothing has happened. Nothing! Nothing!"

He seized her fiercely, unable to speak. Then he buried his face
in her neck.

"Laura! My dear! My sweet! Don't leave me alone! I've been
alone! I've always been alone!"

"It's what you want, dear. It's what you'll always want. You couldn't stand anything else. You'd get so tired of me. You'll forget this ever happened. You'll forget me. You'll forget—forget."

"Forget! I'll never forget! I won't live long enough."

"And I'll never love any one else! I'll never leave you! I'll wait for you forever! Oh, my child, my child!"

They clung together in that bright moment of wonder, there on the magic island, where the world was quiet, believing all they said. And who shall say—whatever disenchantment follows—that we ever forget magic, or that we can ever betray, on this leaden earth, the apple-tree, the singing, and the gold? Far out beyond that timeless valley, a train, on the rails for the East, wailed back its ghostly cry: life, like a fume of painted smoke, a broken wrack of cloud, drifted away. Their world was a singing voice again: they were young and they could never die. This would endure.

He kissed her on her splendid eyes; he grew into her young Mænad's body, his heart numbed deliciously against the pressure of her narrow breasts. She was as lithe and yielding to his sustaining hand as a willow rod—she was bird-swift, more elusive in repose than the dancing watermotes upon her face. He held her tightly lest she grow into the tree again, or be gone amid the wood like smoke.

Come up into the hills, O my young love. Return! O lost, and by the wind grieved, ghost, come back again, as first I knew you in the timeless valley, where we shall feel ourselves anew, bedded on magic in the month of June. There was a place where all the sun went glistering in your hair, and from the hill we could have put a finger on a star. Where is the day that melted into one rich noise? Where the music of your flesh, the rhyme of your teeth, the dainty languor of your legs, your small firm arms, your slender fingers, to be bitten like an apple, and the little cherry-teats of your white breasts? And where are all the tiny wires of finespun maidenhair? Quick are the mouths of earth, and quick the teeth that fed upon this loveliness. You who were made for music, will hear music no more: in your dark house the winds are silent. Ghost, ghost, come back from that marriage that we did not foresee, return not into life, but into magic, where we have never died, into the enchanted wood, where we still lie, strewn on the grass. Come up into the hills, O my young love: return. O lost, and by the wind grieved, ghost, come back again.

One day, when June was coming to its end, Laura James said to him:

"I shall have to go home next week." Then, seeing his stricken face, she added, "but only for a few days—not more than a week."

"But why? The summer's only started. You will burn up down there."

"Yes. It's silly, I know. But my people expect me for the Fourth of July. You know, we have an enormous family—hundreds of aunts, cousins, and in-laws. We have a family re-union every year—a great barbecue and picnic. I hate it. But they'd never forgive me if I didn't come."

Frightened, he looked at her for a moment.

"Laura! You're coming back, aren't you?" he said quietly.

"Yes, of course," she said. "Be quiet."

He was trembling violently; he was afraid to question her more closely.

"Be quiet," she whispered, "quiet!" She put her arms around him.

He went with her to the station on a hot mid-afternoon. There was a smell of melted tar in the streets. She held his hand beside her in the rattling trolley, squeezing his fingers to give him comfort, and whispering from time to time:

"In a week! Only a week, dear."

"I don't see the need," he muttered. "It's over 400 miles. Just for a few days."

He passed the old one-legged gateman on the station platform very easily, carrying her baggage. Then he sat beside her in the close green heat of the pullman until the train should go. A little electric fan droned uselessly above the aisle; a prim young lady whom he knew, arranged herself amid the bright new leather of her bags. She returned his greeting elegantly, with a shade of refined hauteur, then looked out the window again, grimacing eloquently at her parents who gazed at her raptly from the platform. Several prosperous merchants went down the aisle in expensive tan shoes that creaked under the fan's drone.

"Not going to leave us, are you, Mr. Morris?"

"Hello, Jim. No, I'm running up to Richmond for a few days."

But even the gray weather of their lives could not deaden the excitement of that hot chariot to the East.

" 'Board!"

He got up trembling.

"In a few days, dear." She looked up, taking his hand in her small gloved palms.

"You will write as soon as you get there? Please!"

"Yes. To-morrow—at once."

He bent down suddenly and whispered, "Laura—you will come back. You will come back!"

She turned her face away and wept bitterly. He sat beside her once more; she clasped him tightly as if he had been a child.

"My dear, my dear! Don't forget me ever!"

"Never. Come back. Come back."

The salt print of her kiss was on his mouth, his face, his eyes. It was, he knew, the guttering candle-end of time. The train was in motion. He leaped blindly up the passage with a cry in his throat.

"Come back again!"

But he knew. Her cry followed him, as if he had torn something from her grasp.

Within three days he had his letter. On four sheets of paper, bordered with victorious little American flags, this:

"My dear: I got home at half-past one, just too tired to move. I couldn't sleep on the train at all last night, it seemed to get hotter all the way down. I was so blue when I got here, I almost cried. Little Richmond is too ghastly for words—everything burned up and every one gone away to the mountains or the sea. How can I ever stand it even for a week!" (Good! he thought. If the weather holds, she will come back all the sooner.) "It would be heaven now to get one breath of mountain air. Could you find your way back to our place in the valley again?" (Yes, even if I were blind, he thought.) "Will you promise to look after your hand until it gets well? I worried so after you had gone, because I forgot to change the bandage yesterday. Daddy was glad to see me: he said he was not going to let me go again but, don't worry, I'll have my own way in the end. I always do. I don't know any one at home any more—all of the boys have enlisted or gone to work in the shipyards at Norfolk. Most of the girls I know are getting married, or married already. That leaves only the kids." (He winced. As old as I am, maybe older.) "Give my love to Mrs. Barton, and tell your mother I said she must not work so hard in that hot kitchen. And all the little cross-marks at the bottom are for you. Try to guess what they are.

LAURA."

He read her prosy letter with rigid face, devouring the words more hungrily than if they had been lyrical song. She would come back! She would come back! Soon.

There was another page. Weakened and relaxed from his excitement, he looked at it. There he found, almost illegibly written, but at last in her own speech, as if leaping out from the careful aimlessness of her letter, this note:

"July 4.

"Richard came yesterday. He is twenty-five, works in Norfolk. I've been engaged to him almost a year. We're going off quietly to Norfolk to-morrow and get married. My dear! My dear! I couldn't tell you! I tried to, but couldn't. I didn't want to lie. Everything else was true. I meant all I said. If you hadn't been so young, but what's the use of saying that? Try to forgive me, but please don't forget me. Good-by and God bless you. Oh, my darling, it was heaven! I shall never forget you."

When he had finished the letter, he re-read it, slowly and carefully. Then he folded it, put it in his inner breast-pocket, and leaving Dixieland, walked for forty minutes, until he came up in the gap over the town again. It was sunset. The sun's vast rim, blood-red, rested upon the western earth, in a great field of murky pollen. It sank beyond the western ranges. The clear sweet air was washed with gold and pearl. The vast hills melted into purple solitudes: they were like Canaan and rich grapes. The motors of cove people toiled up around the horse-shoe of the road. Dusk came. The bright winking lights in the town went up. Darkness melted over the town like dew: it washed out all the day's distress, the harsh confusions. Low wailing sounds came faintly up from Niggertown.

And above him the proud stars flashed into heaven: there was one, so rich and low, that he could have picked it, if he had climbed the hill beyond the Jew's great house. One, like a lamp, hung low above the heads of men returning home. (O Hesperus, you bring us all good things.) One had flashed out the light that winked on him the night that Ruth lay at the feet of Boaz; and one on Queen Isolt; and one on Corinth and on Troy. It was night, vast brooding night, the mother of loneliness, that washes our stains away. He was washed in the great river of night, in the Ganges tides of redemption. His bitter wound was for the moment healed in him: he turned his face upward to the proud and tender stars, which made him a god and a grain of dust, the brother of eternal beauty and the son of death—alone, alone.

"Ha-ha-ha-ha!" Helen laughed huskily, prodding him in the ribs. "Your girl went and got married, didn't she? She fooled you. You got left."

"Wh-a-a-a-t!" said Eliza banteringly, "has my boy been—as the fellow says" (she sniggered behind her hand) "has my boy been a-courtin'?" She puckered her lips in playful reproach.

"Oh, for God's sake," he muttered angrily, "What fellow says!"

His scowl broke into an angry grin as he caught his sister's eye. They laughed.

"Well, 'Gene," said the girl seriously, "forget about it. You're only a kid yet. Laura is a grown woman."

"Why, son," said Eliza with a touch of malice, "that girl was fooling you all the time. She was just leading you on."

"Oh, stop it, please."

"Cheer up!" said Helen heartily. "Your time's coming. You'll forget her in a week. There are plenty more, you know. This is puppy love. Show her that you're a good sport. You ought to write her a letter of congratulation."

"Why, yes," said Eliza, "I'd make a big joke of it all. I wouldn't let on to her that it affected me. I'd write her just as big as you please and laugh about the whole thing. I'd show them! That's what I'd—"

"Oh, for God's sake!" he groaned, starting up. "Leave me alone, won't you?"

He left the house.

THE DEATH OF BEN GANT

ONE drizzling evening at six o'clock, when he returned to the room that he occupied with Heston, he found a telegram. It read: "Come home at once. Ben has pneumonia. Mother."

There was no train until the next day. Heston quieted him during the evening with a stiff drink of gin manufactured from alcohol taken from the medical laboratory. Eugene was silent and babbled incoherently by starts: he asked the medical student a hundred questions about the progress and action of the disease.

"If it were double pneumonia she would have said so. Doesn't it seem that way to you? Hey?" he demanded feverishly.

"I should think so," said Heston. He was a kind and quiet boy.

Eugene went to Exeter the next morning to catch the train. All through a dreary gray afternoon it pounded across the sodden State. Then, there was a change and a terrible wait of several hours at a junction. Finally, as dark came, he was being borne again toward the hills.

Within his berth he lay with hot sleepless eyes, staring out at the black mass of the earth, the bulk of the hills. Finally, in the hours after midnight, he dropped into a nervous doze. He was wakened by the clatter of the trucks as they began to enter the Altamont yards. Dazed, half-dressed, he was roused by the grinding halt, and a moment later was looking out through the curtains into the grave faces of Luke and Hugh Barton.

"Ben's very sick," said Hugh Barton.

Eugene pulled on his shoes and dropped to the floor stuffing his collar and tie into a coat pocket.

"Let's go," he said. "I'm ready."

They went softly down the aisle, amid the long dark snores of the sleepers. As they walked through the empty station toward Hugh Barton's car, Eugene said to the sailor:

"When did you get home, Luke?"

"I came in last night," he said. "I've been here only a few hours."

It was half-past three in the morning. The ugly station settlement lay fixed and horrible, like something in a dream. His strange and sudden return to it heightened his feeling of unreality. In one of the cars lined at the station curbing, the driver lay huddled below his blanket. In the Greek's lunch-room a man sat sprawled faced downward on the counter. The lights were dull and weary: a few burned with slow lust in the cheap station-hotels.

Hugh Barton, who had always been a cautious driver, shot away with a savage grinding of gears. They roared townward through the rickety slums at fifty miles an hour.

"I'm afraid B-B-B-Ben is one sick boy," Luke began.

"How did it happen?" Eugene asked. "Tell me."

He had taken influenza, they told Eugene, from one of Daisy's children. He had moped about, ill and feverish, for a day or two, without going to bed.

"In that G-g-g-god dam cold barn," Luke burst out. "If that boy dies it's because he c-c-c-couldn't keep warm."

"Never mind about that now," Eugene cried irritably, "go on."

Finally he had gone to bed, and Mrs. Pert had nursed him for a day or two.

"She was the only one who d-d-d-did a damn thing for him," said the sailor. Eliza, at length, had called in Cardiac.

"The d-d-damned old quack," Luke stuttered.

"Never mind! Never mind!" Eugene yelled. "Why dig it up now? Get on with it!"

After a day or two, he had grown apparently convalescent, and Cardiac told him he might get up if he liked. He got up and moped about the house for a day, in a cursing rage, but the next day he lay a-bed, with a high fever. Coker at length had been called in, two days before—

"That's what they should have done at the start," growled Hugh Barton over his wheel.

"Never mind!" screamed Eugene. "Get on with it."

And Ben had been desperately ill, with pneumonia in both lungs, for over a day. The sad prophetic story, a brief and terrible summary of the waste, the tardiness, and the ruin of their lives, silenced them for a moment with its inexorable sense of tragedy. They had nothing to say.

The powerful car roared up into the chill dead Square. The feeling of unreality grew upon the boy. He sought for his life, for the bright lost years, in this mean cramped huddle of brick and stone.

Ben and I, here by the City Hall, the Bank, the grocery-store (he thought) . Why here? In Gath or Ispahan. In Corinth or Byzantium. Not here. It is not real.

A moment later, the big car sloped to a halt at the curb, in front of Dixieland. A light burned dimly in the hall, evoking for him chill memories of damp and gloom. A warmer light burned in the parlor, painting the lowered shade of the tall window a warm and mellow orange.

"Ben's in that room upstairs," Luke whispered, "where the light is."

Eugene looked up with cold dry lips to the bleak front room upstairs, with its ugly Victorian bay-window. It was next to the sleeping-porch where, but three weeks before, Ben had hurled into the darkness his savage curse at life. The light in the sickroom burned grayly, bringing to him its grim vision of struggle and naked terror.

The three men went softly up the walk and entered the house. There was a faint clatter from the kitchen, and voices.

"Papa's in here," said Luke.

Eugene entered the parlor and found Gant seated alone before a bright coal-fire. He looked up dully and vaguely as his son entered.

"Hello, papa," said Eugene, going to him.

"Hello, son," said Gant. He kissed the boy with his bristling cropped mustache. His thin lip began to tremble petulantly.

"Have you heard about your brother?" he snuffled. "To think that this should be put upon me, old and sick as I am. O Jesus, it's fearful—"

Helen came in from the kitchen.

"Hello, Slats," she said, heartily embracing him. "How are you, honey? He's grown four inches more since he went away," she jeered, sniggering. "Well, 'Gene, cheer up! Don't look so blue. While there's life there's hope. He's not gone yet, you know." She burst into tears, hoarse, unstrung, hysterical.

"To think that this must come upon me," Gant sniffled, responding mechanically to her grief, as he rocked back and forth on his cane and stared into the fire. "O boo-hoo-hoo! What have I done that God should—"

"You shut up!" she cried, turning upon him in a blaze of fury. "Shut your mouth this minute. I don't want to hear any more from you! I've given my life to you! Everything's been done for you, and

you'll be here when we're all gone. You're not the one who's sick."
Her feeling toward him had, for the moment, gone rancorous and
bitter.

"Where's mama?" Eugene asked.

"She's back in the kitchen," Helen said. "I'd go back and say hello
before you see Ben if I were you." In a low brooding tone, she continued: "Well, forget about it. It can't be helped now."

He found Eliza busy over several bright bubbling pots of water
on the gas-stove. She bustled awkwardly about, and looked surprised
and confused when she saw him.

"Why, what on earth, boy! When'd you get in?"

He embraced her. But beneath her matter-of-factness, he saw the
terror in her heart: her dull black eyes glinted with bright knives of
fear.

"How's Ben, mama?" he asked quietly.

"Why-y," she pursed her lips reflectively, "I was just saying to
Doctor Coker before you came in. 'Look here,' I said. 'I tell you
what, I don't believe he's half as bad off as he looks. Now, if only we
can hold on till morning. I believe there's going to be a change for
the better.' "

"Mama, in heaven's name!" Helen burst out furiously. "How
can you bear to talk like that? Don't you know that Ben's condition
is critical? Are you never going to wake up?"

Her voice had its old cracked note of hysteria.

"Now, I tell you, son," said Eliza, with a white tremulous smile,
"when you go in there to see him, don't make out as if you knew
he was sick. If I were you, I'd make a big joke of it all. I'd laugh
just as big as you please and say, 'See here, I thought I was coming
to see a sick man. Why, pshaw!' (I'd say) 'there's nothing wrong
with you. Half of it's only imagination!' "

"O mamma! for Christ's sake!" said Eugene frantically. "For
Christ's sake!"

He turned away, sick at heart, and caught at his throat with his
fingers.

Then he went softly upstairs with Luke and Helen, approaching
the sick-room with a shrivveled heart and limbs which had gone cold
and bloodless. They paused for a moment, whispering, before he
entered. The wretched conspiracy in the face of death filled him
with horror.

"N-n-n-now, I wouldn't stay but a m-m-m-minute," whispered Luke. "It m-m-might make him nervous."

Eugene, bracing himself, followed Helen blindly into the room. "Look who's come to see you," her voice came heartily. "It's High-pockets."

For a moment Eugene could see nothing, for dizziness and fear. Then, in the gray shaded light of the room, he descried Bessie Gant, the nurse, and the long yellow skull's-head of Coker, smiling wearily at him, with big stained teeth, over a long chewed cigar. Then, under the terrible light which fell directly and brutally upon the bed alone, he saw Ben. And in that moment of searing recognition he saw, what they had all seen, that Ben was dying.

Ben's long thin body lay three-quarters covered by the bedding; its gaunt outline was bitterly twisted below the covers, in an attitude of struggle and torture. It seemed not to belong to him, it was somehow distorted and detached as if it belonged to a beheaded criminal. And the sallow yellow of his face had turned gray; out of this granite tint of death, lit by two red flags of fever, the stiff black furze of a three-day beard was growing. The beard was somehow horrible; it recalled the corrupt vitality of hair, which can grow from a rotting corpse. And Ben's thin lips were lifted, in a constant grimace of torture and strangulation, above his white somehow dead-looking teeth, as inch by inch he gasped a thread of air into his lungs.

And the sound of this gasping—loud, hoarse, rapid, unbelievable, filling the room, and orchestrating every moment in it—gave to the scene its final note of horror.

Ben lay upon the bed below them, drenched in light, like some enormous insect on a naturalist's table, fighting, while they looked at him, to save with his poor wasted body the life that no one could save for him. It was monstrous, brutal.

As Eugene approached, Ben's fear-bright eyes rested upon the younger brother for the first time and bodilessly, without support, he lifted his tortured lungs from the pillow, seizing the boy's wrists fiercely in the hot white circle of his hands, and gasping in strong terror like a child: "Why have you come? Why have you come home, 'Gene?"

The boy stood white and dumb for a moment, while swarming pity and horror rose in him.

"They gave us a vacation, Ben," he said presently. "They had to close down on account of the flu."

Then he turned away suddenly into the black murk, sick with his poor lie, and unable to face the fear in Ben's gray eyes.

"All right, 'Gene," said Bessie Gant, with an air of authority. "Get out of here—you and Helen both. I've got one crazy Gant to look after already. I don't want two more in here." She spoke harshly, with an unpleasant laugh.

She was a thin woman of thirty-eight years, the wife of Gant's nephew, Gilbert. She was of mountain stock: she was coarse, hard, and vulgar, with little pity in her, and a cold lust for the miseries of sickness and death. These inhumanities she cloaked with her professionalism, saying:

"If I gave way to my feelings, where would the patient be?"

When they got out into the hall again, Eugene said angrily to Helen:

"Why have you got that death's-head here? How can he get well with her around? I don't like her!"

"Say what you like—she's a good nurse." Then, in a low voice, she said: "What do you think?"

He turned away, with a convulsive gesture. She burst into tears, and seized his hand.

Luke was teetering about restlessly, breathing stentorously and smoking a cigarette, and Eliza, working her lips, stood with an attentive ear cocked to the door of the sick-room. She was holding a useless kettle of hot water.

"Huh? Hah? What say?" asked Eliza, before any one had said anything. "How is he?" Her eyes darted about at them.

"Get away! Get away! Get away!" Eugene muttered savagely. His voice rose. "Can't you get away?"

He was infuriated by the sailor's loud nervous breathing, his large awkward feet. He was angered still more by Eliza's useless kettle, her futile hovering, her "huh?" and "hah?"

"Can't you see he's fighting for his breath? Do you want to strangle him? It's messy! Messy! Do you hear?" His voice rose again.

The ugliness and discomfort of the death choked him; and the swarming family, whispering outside the door, pottering uselessly around, feeding with its terrible hunger for death on Ben's strangulation, made him mad with alternate fits of rage and pity.

Indecisively, after a moment, they went downstairs, still listening for sounds in the sick-room.

"Well, I tell you," Eliza began hopefully. "I have a feeling, I don't know what you'd call it—" She looked about awkwardly and found herself deserted. Then she went back to her boiling pots and pans.

Helen, with contorted face, drew him aside, and spoke to him in whispered hysteria, in the front hall.

"Did you see that sweater she's wearing? Did you see it? It's filthy!" Her voice sank to a brooding whisper. "Did you know that he can't bear to look at her? She came into the room yesterday, and he grew perfectly sick. He turned his head away and said 'O Helen, for God's sake, take her out of here.' You hear that, don't you. Do you hear? He can't stand to have her come near him. He doesn't want her in the room."

"Stop! Stop! For God's sake, stop!" Eugene said, clawing at his throat.

The girl was for the moment insane with hatred and hysteria.

"It may be a terrible thing to say, but if he dies I shall hate her. Do you think I can forget the way she's acted? Do you?" Her voice rose almost to a scream. "She's let him die here before her very eyes. Why, only day before yesterday, when his temperature was 104, she was talking to Old Doctor Doak about a lot. Did you know that?"

"Forget about it!" he said frantically. "She'll always be like that! It's not her fault. Can't you see that? O God, how horrible! How horrible!"

"Poor old mama!" said Helen, beginning to weep. "She'll never get over this. She's scared to death! Did you see her eyes? She knows, of course she knows!"

Then suddenly, with mad brooding face, she said: "Sometimes I think I hate her! I really think I hate her." She plucked at her large chin, absently. "Well, we mustn't talk like this," she said. "It's not right. Cheer up. We're all tired and nervous. I believe he's going to get all right yet."

Day came gray and chill, with a drear reek of murk and fog. Eliza bustled about eagerly, pathetically busy, preparing breakfast. Once she hurried awkwardly upstairs with a kettle of water, and stood for a second at the door as Bessie Gant opened it, peering in at the terrible bed, with her white puckered face. Bessie Gant blocked her further entrance, and closed the door rudely. Eliza went away making flustered apologies.

For, what the girl had said was true, and Eliza knew it. She was not wanted in the sick-room; the dying boy did not want to see her. She had seen him turn his head wearily away when she had gone in. Behind her white face dwelt this horror, but she made no confession, no complaint. She bustled around doing useless things with an eager matter-of-factness. And Eugene, choked with exasperation at one moment, because of her heavy optimism, was blind with pity the next when he saw the terrible fear and pain in her dull black eyes. He rushed toward her suddenly, as she stood above the hot stove, and seized her rough worn hand, kissing it and babbling helplessly.

"O mama! Mama! It's all right! It's all right! It's all right."

And Eliza, stripped suddenly of her pretenses, clung to him, burying her white face in his coat sleeve, weeping bitterly, helplessly, grievously, for the sad waste of the irrevocable years—the immortal hours of love that might never be relived, the great evil of forgetfulness and indifference that could never be righted now. Like a child she was grateful for his caress, and his heart twisted in him like a wild and broken thing, and he kept mumbling:

"It's all right! It's all right! It's all right!"—knowing that it was not, could never be, all right.

"If I had known. Child, if I had known," she wept, as she had wept long before at Grover's death.

"Brace up!" he said. "He'll pull through yet. The worst is over."

"Well, I tell you," said Eliza, drying her eyes at once, "I believe it is. I believe he passed the turning-point last night. I was saying to Bessie——"

The light grew. Day came, bringing hope. They sat down to breakfast in the kitchen, drawing encouragement from every scrap of cheer doctor or nurse would give them. Coker departed, non-committally optimistic. Bessie Gant came down to breakfast and was professionally encouraging.

"If I can keep his damn family out of the room, he may have some chance of getting well."

They laughed hysterically, gratefully, pleased with the woman's abuse.

"How is he this morning?" said Eliza. "Do you notice any improvement?"

"His temperature is lower, if that's what you mean."

They knew that a lower temperature in the morning was a fact of no great significance, but they took nourishment from it: their diseased emotion fed upon it—they had soared in a moment to a peak of hopefulness.

"And he's got a good heart," said Bessie Gant. "If that holds out, and he keeps fighting, he'll pull through."

"D-d-don't worry about his f-f-fighting," said Luke, in a rush of eulogy. "That b-b-boy'll fight as long as he's g-g-got a breath left in him."

"Why, yes," Eliza began, "I remember when he was a child of seven—I know I was standing on the porch one day—the reason I remember is Old Mr. Buckner had just come by with some butter and eggs your papa had——"

"O my God!" groaned Helen, with a loose grin. "Now we'll get it."

"Whah—whah!" Luke chortled crazily, prodding Eliza in the ribs.

"I'll vow, boy!" said Eliza angrily. "You act like an idiot. I'd be ashamed!"

"Whah—whah—whah!"

Helen sniggered, nudging Eugene.

"Isn't he crazy, though? Tuh-tuh-tuh-tuh-tuh." Then, with wet eyes, she drew Eugene roughly into her big bony embrace.

"Poor old 'Gene. You always got on together, didn't you? You'll feel it more than any of us."

"He's not b-b-buried yet," Luke cried heartily. "That boy may be here when the rest of us are pushing d-d-daisies."

"Where's Mrs. Pert?" said Eugene. "Is she in the house?"

A strained and bitter silence fell upon them.

"I ordered her out," said Eliza grimly, after a moment. "I told her exactly what she was—a whore." She spoke with the old stern judiciousness, but in a moment her face began to work and she burst into tears. "If it hadn't been for that woman I believe he'd be well and strong to-day. I'll vow I do!"

"Mama, in heaven's name!" Helen burst out furiously. "How dare you say a thing like that? She was the only friend he had: when he was taken sick she nursed him hand and foot. Why, the idea! The idea!" she panted in her indignation. "If it hadn't been for Mrs. Pert he'd have been dead by now. Nobody else did anything for him. You were willing enough, I notice, to keep her here and take her money until he got sick. No, sir!" she declared with emphasis. "Personally, I like her. I'm not going to cut her now."

"It's a d-d-d-damn shame!" said Luke, staunch to his goddess. "If it hadn't been for Mrs. P-P-P-Pert and you, Ben would be S. O. L. Nobody else around here gave a damn. If he d-d-d-dies, it's because he didn't get the proper care when it would have done him some good. There's always been too d-d-damn much thought of saving a nickel, and too d-d-damn little about flesh and blood!"

"Well, forget about it!" said Helen wearily. "There's one thing sure: I've done everything I could. I haven't been to bed for two days. Whatever happens, I'll have no regrets on that score." Her voice was filled with a brooding ugly satisfaction.

"I know you haven't! I know that!" The sailor turned to Eugene in his excitement, gesticulating. "That g-g-girl's worked her fingers to the bone. If it hadn't been for her—" His eyes got wet; he turned his head away and blew his nose.

"Oh, for Christ's sake!" Eugene yelled, springing up from the table. "Stop it, won't you! Let's wait till later."

In this way, the terrible hours of the morning lengthened out, while they spent themselves trying to escape from the tragic net of frustration and loss in which they were caught. Their spirits soared to brief moments of insane joy and exultancy, and plunged into black pits of despair and hysteria. Eliza alone seemed consistently hopeful. Trembling with exacerbated nerves, the sailor and Eugene paced the lower hall, smoking incessant cigarettes, bristling as they approached each other, ironically polite when their bodies touched. Gant dozed in the parlor or in his own room, waking and sleeping by starts, moaning petulantly, detached, vaguely aware only of the meaning of events, and resentful because of the sudden indifference to him. Helen went in and out of the sick-room constantly, dominating the dying boy by the power of her vitality, infusing him with moments of hope and confidence. But when she came out, her hearty cheerfulness was supplanted by the strained blur of hysteria; she wept, laughed, brooded, loved, and hated by turns.

Eliza went only once into the room. She intruded with a hotwater bag, timidly, awkwardly, like a child, devouring Ben's face with her dull black eyes. But when above the loud labor of his breath his bright eyes rested on her, his clawed white fingers tightened their grip in the sheets, and he gasped strongly, as if in terror:

"Get out! Out! Don't want you."

Eliza left the room. As she walked she stumbled a little, as if her feet were numb and dead. Her white face had an ashen tinge, and her dull eyes had grown bright and staring. As the door closed behind her, she leaned against the wall and put one hand across her face. Then, in a moment, she went down to her pots again.

Frantically, angrily, with twitching limbs they demanded calm and steady nerves from one another; they insisted that they keep away from the sick-room—but, as if drawn by some terrible magnet, they found themselves again and again outside the door, listening, on tip-toe, with caught breath, with an insatiate thirst for horror, to the hoarse noise of his gasping as he strove to force air down into his strangled and cemented lungs. And eagerly, jealously, they sought entrance to the room, waiting their turn for carrying water, towels, supplies.

Mrs. Pert, from her refuge in the boarding-house across the street, called Helen on the phone each half-hour, and the girl talked to her while Eliza came from the kitchen into the hall, and stood, hands folded, lips pursed, with eyes that sparkled with her hate.

The girl cried and laughed as she talked.

"Well . . . that's all right, Fatty. . . . You know how I feel about it. . . . I've always said that if he had one true friend in the world, it's you . . . and don't think we're *all* ungrateful for what you've done. . . ."

During the pauses, Eugene could hear the voice of the other woman across the wires, sobbing.

And Eliza said, grimly: "If she calls up again you let me talk to her. I'll fix her!"

"Good heavens, mama!" Helen cried angrily. "You've done enough already. You drove her out of the house when she'd done more for him than all his family put together." Her big strained features worked convulsively. "Why, it's ridiculous!"

Within Eugene, as he paced restlessly up and down the hall or prowled through the house a-search for some entrance he had never found, a bright and stricken thing kept twisting about like a trapped bird. This bright thing, the core of him, his Stranger, kept twisting its head about, unable to look at horror, until at length it gazed stead-fastly, as if under a dreadful hypnosis, into the eyes of death and darkness. And his soul plunged downward, drowning in that deep pit: he felt that he could never again escape from this smothering flood of pain and ugliness, from the eclipsing horror and pity of it all. And as he walked, he twisted his own neck about, and beat the air with his arm like a wing, as if he had received a blow in his kidneys. He felt that he might be clean and free if he could only escape into a single burning passion—hard, and hot, and glittering—of love, hatred, terror, or disgust. But he was caught, he was strangling, in the web of futility—there was no moment of hate that was not touched by a dozen shafts of pity: impotently, he wanted to seize them, cuff them, shake them, as one might a trying brat, and at the same time to caress them, love them, comfort them.

As he thought of the dying boy upstairs, the messy ugliness of it—as they stood whimpering by while he strangled—choked him with fury and horror. The old fantasy of his childhood came back to him: he remembered his hatred of the semi-private bathroom, his messy discomfort while he sat at stool and stared at the tub filled with dirty wash, sloppily puffed and ballooned by cold gray soapy water. He thought of this as Ben lay dying.

Their hopes revived strongly in the forenoon when word came to them that the patient's temperature was lower, his pulse stronger, the congestion of the lungs slightly relieved. But at one o'clock, after a fit of coughing, he grew delirious, his temperature mounted, he had increasing difficulty in getting his breath. Eugene and Luke raced to Wood's pharmacy in Hugh Barton's car, for an oxygen tank. When they returned, Ben had almost choked to death.

Quickly they carried the tank into the room, and placed it near his head. Bessie Gant seized the cone, and started to put it over Ben's mouth, commanding him to breathe it in. He fought it away tiger-ishly: curtly the nurse commanded Eugene to seize his hands.

Eugene gripped Ben's hot wrists: his heart turned rotten. Ben rose wildly from his pillows, wrenching like a child to get his hands free, gasping horribly, his eyes wild with terror:

"No! No! 'Gene! 'Gene! No! No!"

Eugene caved in, releasing him and turning away, white-faced, from the accusing fear of the bright dying eyes. Others held him: he was given temporary relief. Then he became delirious again.

By four o'clock it was apparent that death was near. Ben had brief periods of consciousness, unconsciousness, and delirium—but most of the time he was delirious. His breathing was easier, he hummed snatches of popular songs, some old and forgotten, called up now from the lost and secret adyts of his childhood; but always he returned, in his quiet humming voice, to a popular song of war-time —cheap, sentimental, but now tragically moving: "Just a Baby's Prayer at Twilight,"

> ". . . when lights are low.
> Poor baby's years"

Helen entered the darkening room.

> "Are filled with tears."

The fear had gone out of his eyes: above his gasping he looked gravely at her, scowling, with the old puzzled child's stare. Then, in a moment of fluttering consciousness, he recognized her. He grinned beautifully, with the thin swift flicker of his mouth.

"Hello, Helen! It's Helen!" he cried eagerly.

She came from the room with a writhen and contorted face, holding the sobs that shook her until she was half-way down the stairs.

As darkness came upon the gray wet day, the family gathered in the parlor, in the last terrible congress before death, silent, waiting. Gant rocked petulantly, spitting into the fire, making a weak whining moan from time to time. One by one, at intervals, they left the room, mounting the stairs softly, and listening outside the door of the sick-room. And they heard Ben, as, with incessant humming repetition, like a child, he sang his song,

> "There's a mother there at twilight
> Who's glad to know—"

Eliza sat stolidly, hands folded, before the parlor fire. Her dead white face had a curious carven look; the inflexible solidity of madness.

"Well," she said at length, slowly, "you never know. Perhaps this is the crisis. Perhaps—" her face hardened into granite again. She said no more.

Coker came in and went at once, without speaking, to the sick-room. Shortly before nine o'clock Bessie Gant came down.

"All right," she said quietly. "You had all better come up now. This is the end."

Eliza got up and marched out of the room with a stolid face. Helen followed her: she was panting with hysteria, and had begun to wring her big hands.

"Now, get hold of yourself, Helen," said Bessie Gant warningly. "This is no time to let yourself go."

Eliza went steadily upstairs, making no noise. But, as she neared the room, she paused, as if listening for sounds within. Faintly, in the silence, they heard Ben's song. And suddenly, casting away all pretense, Eliza staggered, and fell against the wall, turning her face into her hand, with a terrible wrenched cry:

"O God! If I had known! If I had known!"

Then, weeping with bitter unrestraint, with the contorted and ugly glimace of sorrow, mother and daughter embraced each other. In a moment they composed themselves, and quietly entered the room.

Eugene and Luke pulled Gant to his feet and supported him up the stairs. He sprawled upon them, moaning in long quivering ex-halations.

"Mer-ci-ful God! That I should have to bear this in my old age. That I should—"

"Papa! For God's sake!" Eugene cried sharply. "Pull yourself together! It's Ben who's dying—not us! Let's try to behave decently to him for once."

This served to quiet Gant for a moment. But as he entered the room, and saw Ben lying in the semi-conscious coma that precedes death, the fear of his own death overcame him, and he began to moan again. They seated him in a chair, at the foot of the bed, and he rocked back and forth, weeping:

"O Jesus! I can't bear it! Why must you put this upon me? I'm old and sick, and I don't know where the money's to come from. How are we ever going to face this fearful and croo-el winter? It'll cost a thousand dollars before we're through buying him, and I don't know where the money's to come from." He wept affectedly with sniffling sobs.

"Hush! hush!" cried Helen, rushing at him. In her furious anger, she seized him and shook him. "You damned old man you, I could kill you! How dare you talk like that when your son's dying? I've wasted six years of my life nursing you, and you'll be the last one to go!" In her blazing anger, she turned accusingly on Eliza:

"You've done this to him. You're the one that's responsible. If you hadn't pinched every penny he'd never have been like this. Yes, and Ben would be here, too!" She panted for breath for a moment. Eliza made no answer. She did not hear her.

"After this, I'm through! I've been looking for you to die—and Ben's the one who has to go." Her voice rose to a scream of exasperation. She shook Gant again. "Never again! Do you hear that, you selfish old man? You've had everything—Ben's had nothing. And now he's the one to go. I hate you!"

"Helen! Helen!" said Bessie Gant quietly. "Remember where you are."

"Yes, that means a lot to us," Eugene muttered bitterly.

Then, over the ugly clamor of their dissension, over the rasp and snarl of their nerves, they heard the low mutter of Ben's expiring breath. The light had been re-shaded: he lay, like his own shadow, in all his fierce gray lonely beauty. And as they looked and saw his bright eyes already blurred with death, and saw the feeble beating flutter of his poor thin breast, the strange wonder, the dark rich miracle of his life surged over them its enormous loveliness. They grew quiet and calm, they plunged below all the splintered wreckage of their lives, they drew together in a superb communion of love and valiance, beyond horror and confusion, beyond death.

And Eugene's eyes grew blind with love and wonder: an enormous organ-music sounded in his heart, he possessed them for a moment, he was a part of their loveliness, his life soared magnificently out of the slough of pain and ugliness. He thought:

"That was not all! That really was not all!"

Helen turned quietly to Coker, who was standing in shadow by the window, chewing upon his long unlighted cigar.

"Is there nothing more you can do? Have you tried everything? I mean—*everything?*"

Her voice was prayerful and low. Coker turned toward her slowly, taking the cigar between his big stained fingers. Then, gently, with his weary yellow smile, he answered: "Everything. Not all the king's horses, not all the doctors and nurses in the world, can help him now."

"How long have you known this?" she said.

"For two days," he answered. "From the beginning." He was silent for a moment. "For ten years!" he went on with growing energy. "Since I first saw him, at three in the morning, in the Greasy Spoon, with a doughnut in one hand and a cigarette in the other. My dear, dear girl," he said gently as she tried to speak, "we can't turn back the days that have gone. We can't turn life back to the hours when our lungs were sound, our blood hot, our bodies young. We are a flash of fire—a brain, a heart, a spirit. And we are three-cents worth of lime and iron—which we cannot get back."

He picked up his greasy black slouch hat, and jammed it carelessly upon his head. Then he fumbled for a match and lit the chewed cigar.

"Has everything been done?" she said again. "I want to know! Is there anything left worth trying?"

He made a weary gesture of his arms.

"My dear girl!" he said. "He's drowning! Drowning!"

She stood frozen with the horror of his pronouncement.

Coker looked for a moment at the gray twisted shadow on the bed. Then, quietly, sadly, with tenderness and tired wonder, he said: "Old Ben. When shall we see *his* like again?"

Then he went quietly out, the long cigar clamped firmly in his mouth.

In a moment, Bessie Gant, breaking harshly in upon their silence with ugly and triumphant matter-of-factness, said: "Well, it will be a relief to get this over. I'd rather be called into forty outside cases than one in which any of these damn relations are concerned. I'm dead for sleep."

Helen turned quietly upon her.

"Leave the room!" she said. "This is our affair now. We have the right to be left alone."

Surprised, Bessie Gant stared at her for a moment with an angry, resentful face. Then she left the room.

The only sound in the room now was the low rattling mutter of

Ben's breath. He no longer gasped; he no longer gave signs of consciousness or struggle. His eyes were almost closed; their gray flicker was dulled, coated with the sheen of insensibility and death. He lay quietly upon his back, very straight, without sign of pain, and with a curious upturned thrust of his sharp thin face. His mouth was firmly shut. Already, save for the feeble mutter of his breath, he seemed to be dead—he seemed detached, no part of the ugly mechanism of that sound which came to remind them of the terrible chemistry of flesh, to mock at illusion, at all belief in the strange passage and continuance of life.

He was dead, save for the slow running down of the worn-out machine, save for that dreadful mutter within him of which he was no part. He was dead.

But in their enormous silence wonder grew. They remembered the strange flitting loneliness of his life, they thought of a thousand forgotten acts and moments—and always there was something that now seemed unearthly and strange: he walked through their lives like a shadow—they looked now upon his gray deserted shell with a thrill of awful recognition, as one who remembers a forgotten and enchanted word, or as men who look upon a corpse and see for the first time a departed god.

Luke, who had been standing at the foot of the bed, now turned to Eugene nervously, stammering in an unreal whisper of wonder and disbelief:

"I g-g-g-guess Ben's gone."

Gant had grown very quiet: he sat in the darkness at the foot of the bed, leaning forward upon his cane, escaped from the revery of his own approaching death, into the waste land of the past, blazing back sadly and poignantly the trail across the lost years that led to the birth of his strange son.

Helen sat facing the bed, in the darkness near the windows. Her eyes rested not on Ben but on her mother's face. All by unspoken consent stood back in the shadows and let Eliza repossess the flesh to which she had given life.

And Eliza, now that he could deny her no longer, now that his fierce bright eyes could no longer turn from her in pain and aversion, sat near his head beside him, clutching his cold hand between her rough worn palms.

She did not seem conscious of the life around her. She seemed under a powerful hypnosis: she sat very stiff and erect in her chair, her white face set stonily, her dull black eyes fixed upon the gray cold face.

They sat waiting. Midnight came. A cock crew. Eugene went quietly to a window and stood looking out. The great beast of night prowled softly about the house. The walls, the windows seemed to bend inward from the thrusting pressure of the dark. The low noise in the wasted body seemed almost to have stopped. It came infrequently, almost inaudibly, with a faint fluttering respiration.

Helen made a sign to Gant and Luke. They rose and went quietly out. At the door she paused, and beckoned to Eugene. He went to her.

"You stay here with her," she said. "You're her youngest. When it's over come and tell us."

He nodded, and closed the door behind her. When they had gone, he waited, listening for a moment. Then he went to where Eliza was sitting. He bent over her.

"Mama!" he whispered. "Mama!"

She gave no sign that she had heard him. Her face did not move; she did not turn her eyes from their fixed stare.

"Mama!" he said more loudly. "Mama!"

He touched her. She made no response.

"Mama! Mama!"

She sat there stiffly and primly like a little child.

Swarming pity rose in him. Gently, desperately, he tried to detach her fingers from Ben's hand. Her rough clasp on the cold hand tightened. Then, slowly, stonily, from right to left, without expression, she shook her head.

He fell back, beaten, weeping, before that implacable gesture. Suddenly, with horror, he saw that she was watching her own death, that the unloosening grip of her hand on Ben's hand was an act of union with her own flesh, that, for her, Ben was not dying—but that a part of *her,* of *her* life, *her* blood, *her* body, was dying. Part of her, the younger, the lovelier, the better part, coined in her flesh, borne and nourished and begun with so much pain there twenty-six years before, and forgotten since, was dying.

Eugene stumbled to the other side of the bed and fell upon his knees. He began to pray. He did not believe in God, nor in Heaven or Hell, but he was afraid they might be true. He did not believe in angels with soft faces and bright wings, but he believed in the dark spirits that hovered above the heads of lonely men. He did not believe in devils or angels, but he believed in Ben's bright demon to whom he had seen him speak so many times.

Eugene did not believe in these things, but he was afraid they might be true. He was afraid that Ben would get lost again. He felt that no one but he could pray for Ben now: that the dark union of their spirits made only *his* prayers valid. All that he had read in books, all the tranquil wisdom he had professed so glibly in his philosophy course, and the great names of Plato and Plontinus, of Spinoza and Immanuel Kant, of Hegel and Descartes, left him now, under the mastering surge of his wild Celtic superstition. He felt that he must pray frantically as long as the little ebbing flicker of breath remained in his brother's body.

So, with insane sing-song repetition, he began to mutter over and over again: "Whoever You Are, be good to Ben to-night. Show him the way . . . Whoever You Are, be good to Ben to-night. Show him the way . . ." He lost count of the minutes, the hours: he heard only the feeble rattle of dying breath, and his wild synchronic prayer.

Light faded from his brain, and consciousness. Fatigue and powerful nervous depletion conquered him. He sprawled out on the floor, with his arms pillowed on the bed, muttering drowsily. Eliza, unmoving, sat across the bed, holding Ben's hand. Eugene, mumbling, sank into an uneasy sleep.

He awoke suddenly, conscious that he had slept, with a sharp quickening of horror. He was afraid that the little fluttering breath had now ceased entirely, that the effect of his prayer was lost. The body on the bed was almost rigid: there was no sound. Then, unevenly, without rhythm, there was a faint mutter of breath. He knew it was the end. He rose quickly and ran to the door. Across the hall, in a cold bedroom, on two wide beds, Gant, Luke, and Helen lay exhausted.

"Come," cried Eugene. "He's going now."

They came quickly into the room. Eliza sat unmoving, oblivious of them. As they entered the room, they heard, like a faint expiring sigh, the final movement of breath.

The rattling in the wasted body, which seemed for hours to have given over to death all of life that is worth saving, had now ceased. The body appeared to grow rigid before them. Slowly, after a moment, Eliza withdrew her hands. But suddenly, marvellously, as if his resurrection and rebirth had come upon him, Ben drew upon the air in a long and powerful respiration; his gray eyes opened. Filled with a terrible vision of all death to the dark spirit who had brooded upon each footstep of his pillows without support—a flame, a light, a glory—joined at length in death to the dark spirit who had brooded upon each footstep of his lonely adventure on earth; and, casting the fierce sword of his glance with utter and final comprehension upon the room haunted with its gray pageantry of cheap loves and dull consciences and on all those uncertain mummers of waste and confusion fading now from the bright window of his eyes, he passed instantly, scornful and unafraid, as he had lived, into the shades of death.

We can believe in the nothingness of life, we can believe in the nothingness of death and of life after death—but who can believe in the nothingness of Ben? Like Apollo, who did his penance to the high god in the sad house of King Admetus, he came, a god with broken feet, into the gray hovel of this world. And he lived here a stranger, trying to recapture the music of the lost world, trying to recall the great forgotten language, the lost faces, the stone, the leaf, the door.

O Artemidorus, farewell!

In that enormous silence, where pain and darkness met, some birds were waking. It was October. It was almost four o'clock in the morning. Eliza straightened out Ben's limbs, and folded his hands across his body. She smoothed out the rumpled covers of the bed, and patted out the pillows, making a smooth hollow for his head to rest in. His flashing hair, cropped close to his well-shaped head, was crisp and crinkly as a boy's, and shone with bright points of light. With a pair of scissors, she snipped off a little lock where it would not show.

"Grover's was black as a raven's without a kink in it. You'd never have known they were twins," she said.

They went downstairs to the kitchen.

"Well, Eliza," said Gant, calling her by name for the first time in thirty years, "you've had a hard life. If I'd acted different, we might have got along together. Let's try to make the most of what time's left. Nobody is blaming you. Taking it all in all, you've done pretty well."

"There are a great many things I'd like to do over again," said Eliza gravely. She shook her head. "We never know."

"We'll talk about it some other time," said Helen. "I guess every one is worn out. I know I am. I'm going to get some sleep. Papa, go on to bed, in heaven's name! There's nothing you can do now. Mama, I think you'd better go, too—"

"No," said Eliza, shaking her head. "You children go on. I couldn't sleep now anyway. There are too many things to do. I'm going to call up John Hines now."

"Tell him," said Gant, "to spare no expense. I'll foot the bills."

"Well," said Helen, "whatever it costs, let's give Ben a good funeral. It's the last thing we can ever do for him. I want to have no regrets on that score."

"Yes," said Eliza, nodding slowly. "I want the best one that money will buy. I'll make arrangements with John Hines when I talk to him. You children go on to bed now."

"Poor old 'Gene," said Helen, laughing. "He looks like the last rose of summer. He's worn out. You pile in and get some sleep, honey."

"No," he said, "I'm hungry. I haven't had anything to eat since I left the university."

"Well, for G-G-G-Gods sake!" Luke stuttered. "Why didn't you speak, idiot? I'd have got you something. Come on," he said, grinning. "I wouldn't mind a bite myself. Let's go uptown and eat."

"Yes," said Eugene. "I'd like to get out for a while from the bosom of the family circle."

They laughed crazily. He poked around the stove for a moment, peering into the oven.

"Huh? Hah? What are you after, boy?" said Eliza suspiciously.

"What you got good to eat, Miss Eliza?" he said, leering crazily at her. He looked at the sailor: they burst into loud idiot laughter, pronging each other in the ribs. Eugene picked up a coffee-pot half-filled with a cold weak wash, and sniffed at it.

"By God!" he said. "That's one thing Ben's out of. He won't have to drink mama's coffee any more."

"Whah-whah-whah!" said the sailor.

Gant grinned, wetting a thumb.

"You ought to be ashamed of yourself," said Helen, with a hoarse snigger. "Poor old Ben!"

"Why, what's wrong with that coffee?" said Eliza, vexed. "It's *good* coffee."

They howled. Eliza pursed her lips for a moment.

"I don't like that way of talking, boy," she said. Her eyes blurred suddenly. Eugene seized her rough hand and kissed it.

"It's all right, mama!" he said. "It's all right. I didn't mean it!" He put his arms around her. She wept, suddenly and bitterly.

"Nobody ever knew him. He never told us about himself. He was the quiet one. I've lost them both now." Then, drying her eyes, she added:

"You boys go get something to eat. A little walk will do you good. And, say," she added, "why don't you go by *The Citizen* office? They ought to be told. They've been calling up every day to find out about him."

"They thought a lot of that boy," said Gant.

They were tired, but they all felt an enormous relief. For over a day, each had known that death was inevitable, and after the horror of the incessant strangling gasp, this peace, this end of pain touched them all with a profound, a weary joy.

"Well, Ben's gone," said Helen slowly. Her eyes were wet, but she wept quietly now, with gentle grief, with love. "I'm glad it's over. Poor old Ben! I never got to know him until these last few days. He was the best of the lot. Thank God, he's out of it now."

Eugene thought of death now, with love, with joy. Death was like a lovely and tender woman, Ben's friend and lover, who had come to free him, to heal him, to save him from the torture of life.

They stood there together, without speaking, in Eliza's littered kitchen, and their eyes were blind with tears, because they thought of lovely and delicate death, and because they loved one another.

Eugene and Luke went softly up the hall, and out into the dark. Gently, they closed the big front door behind them, and descended the veranda steps. In that enormous silence, birds were waking. It was a little after four o'clock in the morning. Wind pressed the boughs. It was still dark. But above them the thick clouds that had covered the earth for days with a dreary gray blanket had been torn open. Eugene looked up through the deep ragged vault of the sky and saw the proud and splendid stars, bright and unwinking. The withered leaves were shaking.

A cock crew his shrill morning cry of life beginning and awaking. The cock that crew at midnight (thought Eugene) had an elfin ghostly cry. His crow was drugged with sleep and death: it was like a far horn sounding under sea; and it was a warning to all the men who are about to die, and to the ghosts that must go home.

But the cock that crows at morning (he thought), has a voice as shrill as any fife. It says, we are done with sleep. We are done with death. O waken, waken into life, says his voice as shrill as any fife. In that enormous silence, birds were waking.

He heard the cock's bright minstrelsy again, and by the river in the dark, the great thunder of flanged wheels, and the long retreating wail of the whistle. And slowly, up the chill deserted street, he heard the heavy ringing clangor of shod hoofs. In that enormous silence, life was waking.

Joy awoke in him, and exultation. They had escaped from the prison of death; they were joined to the bright engine of life again. Life, ruddered life, that would not fail, began its myriad embarkations.

A paper-boy came briskly, with the stiff hobbled limp that Eugene knew so well, down the centre of the street, hurling a blocked paper accurately upon the porch of the Brunswick. As he came opposite Dixieland, he moved in to the curb, tossing his fresh paper with a careful plop. He knew there was sickness in the house.

The withered leaves were shaking.

Eugene jumped to the sidewalk from the sodded yard. He stopped the carrier.

"What's your name, boy?" he said.

"Tyson Smathers," said the boy, turning upon him a steady Scotch-Irish face that was full of life and business.

"My name is 'Gene Gant. Did you ever hear of me?"

"Yes," said Tyson Smathers, "I've heard of you. You had number 7."

"That was a long time ago," said Eugene, pompously, grinning. "I was just a boy."

In that enormous silence, birds were waking.

He thrust his hand into a pocket and found a dollar-bill.

"Here," he said. "I carried the damn things once. Next to my brother Ben, I was the best boy they ever had. Merry Christmas, Tyson."

"It ain't Christmas yet," said Tyson Smathers.

"You're right, Tyson," said Eugene, "but it will be."

Tyson Smathers took the money, with a puzzled, freckled grin. Then he went on down the street, throwing papers.

The maples were thin and sere. Their rotting leaves covered the ground. But the trees were not leafless yet. The leaves were quaking. Some birds began to chatter in the trees. Wind pressed the boughs, the withered leaves were shaking. It was October.

As Luke and Eugene turned up the street toward town, a woman came out of the big brick house across the street, and over the yard toward them. When she got near, they saw she was Mrs. Pert. It was October, but some birds were waking.

"Luke," she said fuzzily. "Luke? Is it Old Luke?"

"Yes," said Luke.

"And 'Gene? Is it old 'Gene?" She laughed gently, patting his hand, peering comically at him with her bleared oaken eyes, and swaying back and forth gravely, with alcoholic dignity. The leaves, the withered leaves, were shaking, quaking. It was October, and the leaves were shaking.

"They ran old Fatty away, 'Gene," she said. "They won't let her come in the house any more. They ran her away because she liked Old Ben. Ben. Old Ben." She swayed gently, vaguely collecting her thought. "Old Ben. How's Old Ben, 'Gene?" she coaxed. "Fatty wants to know.

"I'm m-m-m-mighty sorry, Mrs. P-P-P-Pert . . ." Luke began.

Wind pressed the boughs, the withered leaves were quaking.

"Ben's dead," said Eugene.

She stared at him for a moment, swaying on her feet.

"Fatty liked Ben," she said gently, in a moment. "Fatty and Old Ben were friends."

She turned and started unsteadily across the street, holding one hand out gravely, for balance.

In that enormous silence, birds were waking. It was October, but some birds were waking.

Then Luke and Eugene walked swiftly townward, filled with great joy because they heard the sounds of life and daybreak. And as they walked, they spoke often of Ben, with laughter, with old pleasant memory, speaking of him not as of one who had died, but as of a brother who had been gone for years, and was returning home. They spoke of him with triumph and tenderness, as of one who had defeated pain, and had joyously escaped. Eugene's mind groped awkwardly about. It fumbled like a child, with little things.

They were filled with a deep and tranquil affection for each other: they talked without constraint, without affectation, with quiet confidence and knowledge.

"Do you remember," Luke began, "the t-t-t-time he cut the hair of Aunt Pett's orphan boy—Marcus?"

"He—used—a chamber-pot—to trim the edges," Eugene screamed, waking the street with wild laughter.

They walked along hilariously, greeting a few early pedestrians with ironical obsequiousness, jeering pleasantly at the world in brotherly alliance. Then they entered the relaxed and weary offices of the paper which Ben had served so many years, and gave their stick of news to the tired man there.

There was regret, a sense of wonder, in that office where the swift record of so many days had died—a memory that would not die, of something strange and passing.

"Damn! I'm sorry! He was a great boy!" said the men.

As light broke grayly in the empty streets, and the first car rattled up to town, they entered the little beanery where he had spent, in smoke and coffee, so many hours of daybreak.

Eugene looked in and saw them there, assembled as they had been many years before, like the nightmare ratification of a prophecy: McGuire, Coker, the weary counter-man, and, at the lower end, the press-man, Harry Tugman.

Luke and Eugene entered, and sat down at the counter.

"Gentlemen, gentlemen," said Luke sonorously.

"Hello, Luke," barked McGuire. "Do you think you'll ever have any sense? How are you, son? How's school?" he said to Eugene. He stared at them for a moment, his wet cigarette plastered comically on his full sag lip, his bleared eyes kindly and drunken.

"General, how's the boy? What're you drinking these days—turpentine or varnish?" said the sailor, tweaking him roughly in his larded ribs. McGuire grunted.

"Is it over, son?" said Coker quietly.

"Yes," said Eugene.

Coker took the long cigar from his mouth and grinned malarially at the boy.

"Feel better, don't you, son?" he said.

"Yes," said Eugene. "A hell of a lot."

"Well, Eugenics," said the sailor briskly, "what are you eating?"

"What's the man got?" said Eugene, staring at the greasy card. "Have you got any young roast whale left?"

"No," said the counter-man. "We did have some, but we run out."

"How about the fricasseed bull?" said Luke. "Have you got any of that?"

"You don't need any one to fricassee your bull, son," said Mc-Guire. "You've got plenty as it is."

Their bull-laughter bellowed in the beanery.

With puckered forehead, Luke stuttered over the menu.

"F-f-f-fried chicken à la Maryland," he muttered. "A la Maryland?" he repeated as if puzzled. "Now, ain't that nice?" he said, looking around with mincing daintiness.

"Bring me one of your this week's steaks," said Eugene, "well done, with a meat-axe and the sausage-grinder."

"What do you want the sausage-grinder for, son?" said Coker.

"That's for the mince pie," said Eugene.

"Make it two," said Luke, "with a coupla cups of Mock-a, just like mother still makes."

He looked crazily around at Eugene, and burst into loud whah-whahs, prodding him in the ribs.

"Where they got you stationed now, Luke?" said Harry Tugman, peering up snoutily from a mug of coffee.

"At the p-p-p-present time in Norfolk at the Navy Base," Luke answered, "m-m-making the world safe for hypocrisy."

"Do you ever get out to sea, son?" said Coker.

"Sure!" said Luke. "A f-f-five-cent ride on the street-car brings me right out to the beach."

"That boy has had the makings of a sailor in him ever since he wet the bed," said McGuire. "I predicted it long ago."

Horse Hines came in briskly, but checked himself when he saw the two young men.

"Look out!" whispered the sailor to Eugene, with a crazy grin. "You're next! He's got his fishy eye glued on you. He's already getting you measured up for one."

Eugene looked angrily around at Horse Hines, muttering. The sailor chortled madly.

"Good-morning, gentlemen," said Horse Hines, in an accent of refined sadness. "Boys," he said, coming up to them sorrowfully, "I was mighty sorry to hear of your trouble. I couldn't have thought more of that boy if he'd been my own brother."

"Don't go on, Horse," said McGuire, holding up four fat fingers of protest. "We can see you're heart-broken. If you go on, you may get hysterical with your grief, and break right out laughing. We couldn't bear that, Horse. We're big strong men, but we've had hard lives. I beg of you to spare us, Horse."

Horse Hines did not notice him.

"I've got him over at the place now," he said softly. "I want you boys to come in later in the day to see him. You won't know he's the same person when I'm through."

"God! An improvement over nature," said Coker. "His mother will appreciate it."

"Is this an undertaking shop you're running, Horse," said McGuire, "or a beauty parlor?"

"We know you'll d-d-do your best, Mr. Hines," said the sailor with ready earnest insincerity. "That's the reason the family got you."

"Ain't you goin' to eat the rest of your steak?" said the counterman to Eugene.

"Steak! Steak! It's not steak!" muttered Eugene. "I know what it is now." He got off the stool and walked over to Coker. "Can you save me? Am I going to die? Do I look sick, Coker?" he said in a hoarse mutter.

"No, son," said Coker. "Not sick—crazy."

Horse Hines took his seat at the other end of the counter. Eugene, leaning upon the greasy marble counter, began to sing:

> "Hey, ho, the carrion crow,
> Derry, derry, derry, derr—oh!"

"Shut up, you damn fool!" said the sailor in a hoarse whisper, grinning.

> "A carrion crow sat on a rock,
> Derry, derry, derry, derr—oh!"

Outside, in the young gray light, there was a brisk wakening of life. A street-car curved slowly into the avenue, the motorman leaning from his window and shifting the switch carefully with a long rod, blowing the warm fog of his breath into the chill air. Patrolman Leslie Roberts, sallow and liverish, slouched by anæmically, swinging his club. The negro man-of-all-work for Wood's Pharmacy walked briskly into the post-office to collect the morning mail. J. T. Stearns, the railway passenger-agent, waited on the curb across the street for the depot car. He had a red face, and he was reading the morning paper.

"There they go!" Eugene cried suddenly. "As if they didn't know about it!"

"Luke," said Harry Tugman, looking up from his paper, "I was certainly sorry to hear about Ben. He was one fine boy." Then he went back to his sheet.

"By God!" said Eugene. "This is news!"

He burst into a fit of laughter, gasping and uncontrollable, which came from him with savage violence. Horse Hines glanced craftily up at him. Then he went back to his paper.

The two young men left the lunch-room and walked homeward through the brisk morning. Eugene's mind kept fumbling with little things. There was a frosty snap and clatter of life upon the streets, the lean rattle of wheels, the creak of blinds, a cold rose-tint of pearled sky. In the Square, the motormen stood about among their cars, in loud foggy gossip. At Dixieland, there was an air of exhaustion, of nervous depletion. The house slept; Eliza alone was stirring, but she had a smart fire crackling in the range, and was full of business.

"You children go and sleep now. We've all got work to do later in the day."

Luke and Eugene went into the big dining-room which Eliza had converted into a bed-room.

"D-d-d-damn if I'm going to sleep upstairs," said the sailor angrily. "Not after this!"

"Pshaw!" said Eliza. "That's only superstition. It wouldn't bother me a bit."

The brothers slept heavily until past noon. Then they went out again to see Horse Hines. They found him with his legs comfortably disposed on the desk of his dark little office, with its odor of weeping ferns, and incense, and old carnations.

He got up quickly as they entered, with a starchy crackle of his hard boiled shirt, and a solemn rustle of his black garments. Then he began to speak to them in a hushed voice, bending forward slightly.

How like Death this man is (thought Eugene). He thought of the awful mysteries of burial—the dark ghoul-ritual, the obscene communion with the dead, touched with some black and foul witch-magic. Where is the can in which they throw the parts? There is a restaurant near here. Then he took the cold phthisic hand, freckled on its back, that the man extended, with a sense of having touched something embalmed. The undertaker's manner had changed since the morning: it had become official, professional. He was the alert marshal of their grief, the efficient master-of-ceremonies. Subtly he made them feel there was an order and decorum in death: a ritual of mourning that must be observed. They were impressed.

"We thought we'd like to s-s-s-see you f-f-f-first, Mr. Hines, about the c-c-c-c-casket," Luke whispered nervously. "We're going to ask your advice. We want you to help us find something appropriate."

Horse Hines nodded with grave approval. Then he led them softly back, into a large dark room with polished waxen floors where, amid a rich dead smell of wood and velvet, upon wheeled trestles, the splendid coffins lay in their proud menace.

"Now," said Horse Hines quietly, "I know the family doesn't want anything cheap."

"No, sir!" said the sailor positively. "We want the b-b-b-best you have."

"I take a personal interest in this funeral," said Horse Hines with gentle emotion. "I have known the Gant and Pentland families for thirty years or more. I have had business dealings with your father for nigh on to twenty years."

"And I w-w-want you to know, Mr. Hines, that the f-f-f-family appreciates the interest you're taking in this," said the sailor very earnestly.

He likes this, Eugene thought. The affection of the world. He must have it.

"Your father," continued Horse Hines, "is one of the oldest and most respected business men in the community. And the Pentland family is one of the wealthiest and most prominent."

Eugene was touched with a moment's glow of pride.

"You don't want anything shoddy," said Horse Hines. "I know that. What you get ought to be in good taste and have dignity. Am I right?"

Luke nodded emphatically.

"That's the way we feel about it, Mr. Hines. We want the best you have. We're not pinching p-p-p-pennies where Ben's concerned," he said proudly.

"Well, then," said Horse Hines, "I'll give you my honest opinion. I could give you this one cheap," he placed his hand upon one of the caskets, "but I don't think it's what you want. Of course," he said, "it's good at the price. It's worth the money. It'll give you service, don't worry. You'll get value out of it—"

Now there's an idea, thought Eugene.

"They're all good, Luke. I haven't got a bad piece of stock in the place. But—"

"We want something b-b-b-better," said Luke earnestly. He turned to Eugene. "Don't you think so, 'Gene?"

"Yes," said Eugene.

"Well," said Horse Hines, "I could sell you this one," he indicated the most sumptuous casket in the room. "They don't come better than that, Luke. That's the top. She's worth every dollar I ask for her."

"All right," said Luke. "You're the judge. If that's the best you've g-g-g-got, we'll take it."

No, no! thought Eugene. You mustn't interrupt. Let him go on.

"But," said Horse Hines relentlessly, "there's no need for you to take that one, either. What you're after, Luke, is dignity and simplicity. Is that right?"

"Yes," said the sailor meekly, "I guess you're right at that, Mr. Hines."

Now we'll have it, thought Eugene. This man takes joy in his work.

"Well, then," said Horse Hines decisively, "I was going to suggest to you boys that you take this one." He put his hand affectionately upon a handsome casket at his side.

"This is neither too plain nor too fancy. It's simple and in good taste. Silver handles, you see—silver plate here for the name. You can't go wrong on this one. It's a good buy. She'll give you value for every dollar you put into it."

They walked around the coffin, staring at it critically.

After a moment, Luke said nervously:

"How—wh—wh—wh-what's the price of this one?"

"That sells for $450," said Horse Hines. "But," he added, after a moment's dark reflection, "I'll tell you what I'll do. Your father and I are old friends. Out of respect for the family, I'll let you have it at cost—$375."

"What do you say, 'Gene?" the sailor asked. "Does it look all right to you?"

Do your Christmas shopping early.

"Yes," said Eugene, "let's take it. I wish there were another color. I don't like black," he added. "Haven't you got any other color?"

Horse Hines stared at him a moment.

"Black *is* the color," he said.

Then, after a moment's silence, he went on:

"Would you boys care to see the body?"

"Yes," they said.

He led them on tiptoe down the aisle of the coffins, and opened a door to a room behind it. It was dark. They entered and stood with caught breath. Horse Hines switched on a light and closed the door.

Ben, clad in his best suit of clothes, a neat one of dark gray-black, lay in rigid tranquillity upon a table. His hands, cold and white, with clean dry nails, withered a little like an old apple, were crossed loosely on his stomach. He had been closely shaved: he was immaculately groomed. The rigid head was thrust sharply upward, with a ghastly counterfeit of a smile: there was a little gum of wax at the nostrils, and a waxen lacing between the cold firm lips. The mouth was tight, somewhat bulging. It looked fuller than it ever had looked before.

There was a faint indefinably cloying odor.

The sailor looked with superstition, nervously, with puckered forehead. Then he whispered to Eugene:

"I g-g-guess that's Ben, all right."

Because, Eugene thought, it is not Ben, and we are lost. He looked at the cold bright carrion, that bungling semblance which had not even the power of a good wax-work to suggest its image. Nothing of Ben could be buried here. In this poor stuffed crow, with its pathetic barbering, and its neat buttons, nothing of the owner had been left. All that was there was the tailoring of Horse Hines, who now stood by, watchfully, hungry for their praise.

No, this is not Ben (Eugene thought). No trace of him is left in this deserted shell. It bears no mark of him. Where has he gone? Is this his bright particular flesh, made in his image, given life by his unique gesture, by his one soul? No, he is gone from that bright flesh. This thing is one with all carrion; it will be mixed with the earth again. Ben? Where? O lost!

The sailor, looking, said:

"That b-b-b-boy sure suffered." Suddenly, turning his face away into his hand, he sobbed briefly and painfully, his confused stammering life drawn out of its sprawl into a moment of hard grief.

Eugene wept, not because he saw Ben there, but because Ben had gone, and because he remembered all the tumult and the pain.

"It is over now," said Horse Hines gently. "He is at peace."

"By God, Mr. Hines," said the sailor earnestly, as he wiped his eyes on his jacket, "that was one g-g-great boy."

Horse Hines looked raptly at the cold strange face.

"A fine boy," he murmured as his fish-eye fell tenderly on his work. "And I have tried to do him justice."

They were silent for a moment, looking.

"You've d-d-done a fine job," said the sailor. "I've got to hand it to you. What do you say, 'Gene?"

"Yes," said Eugene, in a small choking voice. "Yes."

"He's a b-b-b-bit p-p-p-pale, don't you think?" the sailor stammered, barely conscious of what he was saying.

"Just a moment!" said Horse Hines quickly, lifting a finger. Briskly he took a stick of rouge from his pocket, stepped forward, and deftly, swiftly, sketched upon the dead gray cheeks a ghastly rose-hued mockery of life and health.

"There!" he said, with deep satisfaction; and, rouge-stick in hand, head critically cocked, like a painter before his canvas, he stepped back into the terrible staring prison of their horror.

"There are artists, boys, in every profession," Horse Hines continued in a moment, with quiet pride, "and though I do say it myself, Luke, I'm proud of my work on this job. Look at him!" he exclaimed with sudden energy, and a bit of color in his gray face. "Did you ever see anything more natural in your life?"

Eugene turned upon the man a grim and purple stare, noting with pity, with a sort of tenderness, as the dogs of laughter tugged at his straining throat the earnestness and pride in the long horse-face.

"Look at it!" said Horse Hines again in slow wonder. "I'll never beat that again! Not if I live to be a million! That's art, boys!"

A slow strangling gurgle escaped from Eugene's screwed lips. The sailor looked quickly at him, with a crazy suppressed smile.

"What's the matter?" he said warningly. "Don't, fool!" His grin broke loose.

Eugene staggered across the floor and collapsed upon a chair, roaring with laughter while his long arms flapped helplessly at his sides. "Scuse!" he gasped. "Don't mean to—A-r-rt! Yes! Yes! That's it!" he screamed, and he beat his knuckles in a crazy tattoo upon the polished floor. He slid gently off the chair, slowly unbuttoning his vest, and with a languid hand loosening his necktie. A faint gurgle came from his weary throat, his head lolled around on the floor languidly, tears coursed down his swollen features.

"What's wrong with you? Are you c-c-c-crazy?" said the sailor, all a-grin.

Horse Hines bent sympathetically and assisted the boy to his feet. "It's the strain," he said knowingly to the sailor. "The pore fellow has become hysterical."

So, to Ben dead was given more care, more time, more money than had ever been given to Ben living. His burial was a final gesture of irony and futility: an effort to compensate carrion death for the unpaid wage of life—love and mercy. He had a grand funeral. All the Pentlands sent wreaths, and came with their separate clans, bringing along with their hastily assumed funeral manners a smell of recent business. Will Pentland talked with the men about politics, the war, and trade conditions, paring his nails thoughtfully, pursing his lips and nodding in his curiously reflective way, and occasionally punning with a birdy wink. His pleased self-laughter was mixed with Henry's loud guffaw. Pett, older, kinder, gentler than Eugene had ever seen her, moved about with a rustling of gray silk, and a relaxed bitterness. And Jim was there, with his wife, whose name Eugene forgot, and his four bright hefty daughters, whose names he confused, but who had all been to college and done well, and his son, who had been to a Presbyterian college, and had been expelled for advocating free love and socialism while editor of the college paper. Now he played the violin, and loved music, and helped his father with the business: he was an effeminate and mincing young man, but of the breed. And there was Thaddeus Pentland, Will's bookkeeper, the youngest and poorest of the three. He was a man past fifty, with a pleasant red face, brown mustaches, and a gentle placid manner. He was full of puns and pleased good-nature, save when he quoted from Karl Marx and Eugene Debs. He was a Socialist, and had once received eight votes for Congress. He was there with his garrulous wife (whom Helen called Jibber-Jibber) and his two daughters, languid good-looking blondes of twenty and twenty-four.

There they were, in all their glory—that strange rich clan, with its fantastic mixture of success and impracticality, its hard monied sense, its visionary fanaticism. There they were, in their astonishing contradictions: the business man who had no business method, and yet had made his million dollars; the frantic antagonist of Capital who had given the loyal service of a lifetime to the thing he denounced; the wastrel son, with the bull vitality of the athlete, a great laugh, animal charm—no more; the musician son, a college rebel, intelligent, fanatic, with a good head for figures; insane miserliness for oneself, lavish expenditure for one's children.

There they were, each with the familiar marking of the clan— broad nose, full lips, deep flat cheeks, deliberate pursed mouths, flat drawling voices, flat complacent laughter. There they were, with their enormous vitality, their tainted blood, their meaty health, their sanity, their insanity, their humor, their superstition, their meanness, their generosity, their fanatic idealism, their unyielding materialism. There they were, smelling of the earth and Parnassus—

that strange clan which met only at weddings or funerals, but which was forever true to itself, indissoluble and forever apart, with its melancholia, its madness, its mirth: more enduring than life, more strong than death.

And as Eugene looked, he felt again the nightmare horror of destiny: he was of them—there was no escape. Their lust, their weakness, their sensuality, their fanaticism, their strength, their rich taint, were rooted in the marrow of his bones.

But Ben, with the thin gray face (he thought) was not a part of them. Their mark was nowhere on him.

And among them, sick and old, leaning upon his cane, moved Gant, the alien, the stranger. He was lost and sorrowful, but sometimes, with a flash of his old rhetoric, he spoke of his grief and the death of his son.

The women filled the house with their moaning. Eliza wept almost constantly; Helen by fits, in loose hysterical collapse. And all the other women wept with gusto, comforting Eliza and her daughter, falling into one another's arms, wailing with keen hunger. And the men stood sadly about, dressed in their good clothes, wondering when it would be over. Ben lay in the parlor, bedded in his expensive coffin. The room was heavy with the incense of the funeral flowers.

Presently the Scotch minister arrived: his decent soul lay above all the loud posturings of grief like a bolt of hard clean wool. He began the service for the dead in a dry nasal voice, remote, monotonous, cold, and passionate.

Then, marshalled by Horse Hines, the pallbearers, young men from the paper and the town, who had known the dead man best, moved slowly out, gripping the coffin-handles with their nicotined fingers. In proper sequence, the mourners following, lengthening out in closed victorias that exhaled their funeral scent of stale air and old leather.

To Eugene came again the old ghoul fantasy of a corpse and cold pork, the smell of the dead and hamburger steak—the glozed corruption of Christian burial, the obscene pomps, the perfumed carrion. Slightly nauseated, he took his seat with Eliza in the carriage, and tried to think of supper.

The procession moved off briskly to the smooth trotting pull of the velvet rumps. The mourning women peered out of the closed carriages at the gaping town. They wept behind their heavy veils, and looked to see if the town was watching. Behind the world's great mask of grief, the eyes of the mourners shone through with a terrible and indecent hunger, an unnameable lust.

It was raw October weather—gray and wet. The service had been short, as a precaution against the pestilence which was everywhere. The funeral entered the cemetery. It was a pleasant place, on a hill. There was a good view of the town. As the hearse drove up, two men who had been digging the grave, moved off. The women moaned loudly when they saw the raw open ditch.

Slowly the coffin was lowered onto the bands that crossed the grave.

Again Eugene heard the nasal drone of the Presbyterian minister. The boy's mind fumbled at little things. Horse Hines bent ceremoniously, with a starched crackle of shirt, to throw his handful of dirt into the grave. "Ashes to ashes—" He reeled and would have fallen in if Gilbert Gant had not held him. He had been drinking. "I am the resurrection and the life—" Helen wept constantly, harshly and bitterly. "He that believeth in me—" The sobs of the women rose to sharp screams as the coffin slid down upon the bands into the earth.

Then the mourners got back into their carriages and were driven briskly away. There was a fast indecent hurry about their escape. The long barbarism of burial was at an end. As they drove away, Eugene peered back through the little glass in the carriage. The two grave-diggers were already returning to their work. He watched until the first shovel of dirt had been thrown into the grave. He saw the raw new graves, the sere long grasses, noted how quickly the mourning wreaths had wilted. Then he looked at the wet gray sky. He hoped it would not rain that night.

It was over. The carriages split away from the procession. The men dropped off in the town at the newspaper office, the pharmacy, the cigar-store. The women went home. No more. No more.

Night came, the bare swept streets, the gaunt winds. Helen lay before a fire in Hugh Barton's house. She had a bottle of chloroform liniment in her hand. She brooded morbidly into the fire, reliving the death a hundred times, weeping bitterly and becoming calm again.

"When I think of it, I hate her. I shall never forget. And did you hear her? Did you? Already she's begun to pretend how much he loved her. But you can't fool me! I know! He wouldn't have her around. You saw that, didn't you? He kept calling for me. I was the only one he'd let come near him. You know that, don't you?"

"You're the one who always has to be the goat," said Hugh Barton sourly. "I'm getting tired of it. That's what has worn you out. If they don't leave you alone, I'm going to take you away from here."

Then he went back to his charts and pamphlets, frowning importantly over a cigar, and scrawling figures on an old envelope with a stub of pencil gripped between his fingers.

She has him trained, too, Eugene thought.

Then, hearing the sharp whine of the wind, she wept again.

"Poor old Ben," she said. "I can't bear to think of him out there to-night."

She was silent for a moment, staring at the fire.

"After this, I'm through," she said. "They can get along for themselves. Hugh and I have a right to our own lives. Don't you think so?"

"Yes," said Eugene. I'm merely the chorus, he thought.

"Papa's not going to die," she went on. "I've nursed him like a slave for six years, and he'll be here when I'm gone. Every one was expecting papa to die, but it was Ben who went. You never can tell. After this, I'm through."

Her voice had a note of exasperation in it. They all felt the grim trickery of Death, which had come in by the cellar while they waited at the window.

"Papa has no right to expect it of me!" she burst out resentfully. "He's had his life. He's an old man. We have a right to ours as well as any one. Good heavens! Can't they realize that! I'm married to Hugh Barton! I'm *his* wife!"

Are you? thought Eugene. Are you?

But Eliza sat before the fire at Dixieland with hands folded, reliving a past of tenderness and love that never had been. And as the wind howled in the bleak street, and Eliza wove a thousand fables of that lost and bitter spirit, the bright and stricken thing in the boy twisted about in horror, looking for escape from the house of death. No more! No more! (it said). You are alone now. You are lost. Go find yourself, lost boy, beyond the hills.

This little bright and stricken thing stood up on Eugene's heart and talked into his mouth.

O but I can't go now, said Eugene to it. (Why not? it whispered.) Because her face is so white, and her forehead is so broad and high, with the black hair drawn back from it, and when she sat there at the bed she looked like a little child. I can't go now and leave her here alone. (She is alone, it said, and so are you.) And when she purses up her mouth and stares, so grave and thoughtful, she is like a little child. (You are alone now, it said. You must escape, or you will die.) It is all like death: she fed me at her breast, I slept in the same bed with her, she took me on her trips. All of that is over now, and each time it was like a death. (And like a life, it said to him. Each time that you die, you will be born again. And you will die a hundred times before you become a man.) I can't! I can't! Not now—later, more slowly. (No. Now, it said.) I am afraid. I have nowhere to go. (You must find the place, it said.) I am lost. (You must hunt for yourself, it said.) I am alone. Where are you? (You must find me, it said.)

Then, as the bright thing twisted about in him, Eugene heard the whine of the bleak wind about the house that he must leave, and the voice of Eliza calling up from the past the beautiful lost things that never happened.

"—and I said, 'Why, what on earth, boy, you want to dress up warm around your neck or you'll catch your death of cold.' "

Eugene caught at his throat and plunged for the door.

"Here, boy! Where are going?" said Eliza, looking up quickly.

"I've got to go," he said in a choking voice. "I've got to get away from here."

Then he saw the fear in her eyes, and the grave troubled child's stare. He rushed to where she sat and grasped her hand. She held him tightly and laid her face against his arm.

"Don't go yet," she said. "You've all your life ahead of you. Stay with me just a day or two."

"Yes, mama," he said, falling to his knees. "Yes, mama." He hugged her to him frantically. "Yes, mama. God bless you, mama. It's all right, mama. It's all right."

Eliza wept bitterly.

"I'm an old woman," she said, "and one by one I've lost you all.

He's dead now, and I never got to know him. O son, don't leave me yet. You're the only one that's left: you were my baby. Don't go! Don't go." She laid her white face against his sleeve.

It is not hard to go (he thought). But when can we forget?

It was October and the leaves were quaking. Dusk was beginning. The sun had gone, the western ranges faded in chill purple mist, but the western sky still burned with ragged bands of orange. It was October.

Eugene walked swiftly along the sinuous paved curves of Rutledge Road. There was a smell of fog and supper in the air: a warm moist blur at window-panes, and the pungent sizzle of cookery. There were mist-far voices, and a smell of burning leaves, and a warm yellow blur of lights.

He turned into an unpaved road by the big wooden sanitarium. He heard the rich kitchen laughter of the Negroes, the larded sizzle of food, the dry veranda coughing of the lungers.

He walked briskly along the lumpy road, with a dry scuffling of leaves. The air was a chill dusky pearl: above him a few pale stars were out. The town and the house were behind him. There was a singing in the great hill-pines.

Two women came down the road and passed him. He saw that they were country women. They were dressed rustily in black, and one of them was weeping. He thought of the men who had been laid in the earth that day, and of all the women who wept. Will they come again? he wondered.

When he came to the gate of the cemetery he found it open. He went in quickly and walked swiftly up the winding road that curved around the crest of the hill. The grasses were dry and sere; a wilted wreath of laurel lay upon a grave. As he approached the family plot, his pulse quickened a little. Some one was moving slowly, deliberately, in among the grave-stones. But as he came up he saw that it was Mrs. Pert.

"Good-evening, Mrs. Pert," said Eugene.

"Who is it?" she asked, peering murkily. She came to him with her grave unsteady step.

"It's 'Gene," he said.

"Oh, is it Old 'Gene?" she said. "How are you, 'Gene?"

"Pretty well," he said. He stood awkwardly, chilled, not knowing how to continue. It was getting dark. There were long lonely preludes to winter in the splendid pines, and a whistling of wind in the long grasses. Below them, in the gulch, night had come. There was a Negro settlement there—Stumptown, it was called. The rich voices of Africa wailed up to them their jungle dirge.

But in the distance, away on their level and above, on other hills, they saw the town. Slowly, in twinkling nests, the lights of the town went up, and there were frost-far voices, and music, and the laughter of a girl.

"This is a nice place," said Eugene. "You get a nice view of the town from here."

"Yes," said Mrs. Pert. "And Old Ben's got the nicest place of all. You get a better view right here than anywhere else. I've been here before in the daytime." In a moment she went on. "Old Ben will turn into lovely flowers. Roses, I think."

"No," said Eugene, "dandelions—and big flowers with a lot of thorns on them."

She stood looking about fuzzily for a moment, with the blurred gentle smile on her lips.

"It is getting dark, Mrs. Pert," said Eugene hesitantly. "Are you out here alone?"

"Alone? I've got Old 'Gene and Old Ben here, haven't I?" she said.

"Maybe we'd better go back, Mrs. Pert?" he said. "It's going to turn cold to-night. I'll go with you."

"Fatty can go by herself," she said with dignity. "Don't worry, 'Gene. I'll leave you alone."

"That's all right," said Eugene, confused. "We both came for the same reason, I suppose."

"Yes," said Mrs. Pert. "Who'll be coming here this time next year, I wonder? Will Old 'Gene come back then?"

"No," said Eugene. "No, Mrs. Pert. I shall never come here again."

"Nor I, 'Gene," she said. "When do you go back to school?"

"To-morrow," he said.

"Then Fatty will have to say good-bye," she said reproachfully. "I'm going away too."

"Where are you going?" he asked, surprised.

"I'm going to live with my daughter in Tennessee. You didn't know Fatty was a grandmother, did you?" she said, with her soft blurred smile. "I've a little grandson two years old."

"I'm sorry to see you go," Eugene said.

Mrs. Pert was silent a moment, rocking vaguely upon her feet.

"What did they say was wrong with Ben?" she asked.

"He had pneumonia, Mrs. Pert," said Eugene.

"Oh, pneumonia! That's it!" She nodded her head wisely as if satisfied. "My husband's a drug salesman, you know, but I never can remember all the things that people have. Pneumonia."

She was silent again, reflecting.

"And when they shut you up in a box and put you in the ground, the way they did Old Ben, what do they call that?" she asked with a soft inquiring smile.

He did not laugh.

"They call that death, Mrs. Pert."

"Death! Yes, that's it," said Mrs. Pert brightly, nodding her head in agreement. "That's one kind, 'Gene. There are some other kinds, too. Did you know that?" She smiled at him.

"Yes," said Eugene. "I know that, Mrs. Pert."

She stretched out her hands suddenly to him, and clasped his cold fingers. She did not smile any more.

"Good-bye, my dear," she said. "We both knew Ben, didn't we? God bless you."

Then she turned and walked away down the road, at her portly uncertain gait, and was lost in the gathering dark.

The great stars rode proudly up into heaven. And just over him, just over the town, it seemed, there was one so rich and low he could have touched it. Ben's grave had been that day freshly sodded: there was a sharp cold smell of earth there. Eugene thought of Spring, and the poignant and wordless odor of the elvish dandelions that would be there. In the frosty dark, far-faint, there was the departing wail of a whistle.

And suddenly, as he watched the lights wink cheerfully up in the town, their warm message of the hived life of men brought to him a numb hunger for all the words and the faces. He heard the far voices and laughter. And on the distant road a powerful car, bending around the curve, cast over him for a second, over that lonely hill of the dead, its great shaft of light and life. In his numbed mind, which for days now had fumbled curiously with little things, with little things alone, as a child fumbles with blocks or with little things, a light was growing.

His mind gathered itself out of the wreckage of little things: out of all that the world had shown or taught him he could remember now only the great star above the town, and the light that had swung over the hill, and the fresh sod upon Ben's grave, and the wind, and far sounds and music, and Mrs. Pert.

Wind pressed the boughs, the withered leaves were shaking. It was October, but the leaves were shaking. A star was shaking. A light was waking. Wind was quaking. The star was far. The night, the light. The light was bright. A chant, a song, the slow dance of the little things within him. The star over the town, the light over the hill, the sod over Ben, night over all. His mind fumbled with little things. Over us all is something. Star, night, earth, light . . . light . . . O lost! . . . a stone . . . a leaf . . . a door . . . O ghost! . . . a light . . . a song . . . a light . . . a light swings over the hill . . . over us all . . . a star shines over the town . . . over us all . . . a light.

We shall not come again. We never shall come back again. But over us all, over us all, over us all is—something.

Wind pressed the boughs; the withered leaves were shaking. It was October, but some leaves were shaking.

A light swings over the hill. (We shall not come again.) And over the town a star. (Over us all that shall not come again.) And over the day the dark. But over the darkness—what?

We shall not come again. We never shall come back again.

Over the dawn a lark. (That shall not come again.) And wind and music far. O lost! (It shall not come again.) And over your mouth the earth. O ghost! But, over the darkness—what?

Wind pressed the boughs; the withered leaves were quaking.

We shall not come again. We never shall come back again. It was October, but we never shall come back again.

When will they come again? When will they come again?

The laurel, the lizard, and the stone will come no more. The women weeping at the gate have gone and will not come again. And pain and pride and death will pass, and will not come again. And light and dawn will pass, and the star and the cry of a lark will pass, and will not come again. And we shall pass, and shall not come again.

What things will come again? O Spring, the cruellest and fairest of the seasons, will come again. And the strange and buried men will come again, in flower and leaf the strange and buried men will come again, and death and the dust will never come again, for death and the dust will die. And Ben will come again, he will not die again, in flower and leaf, in wind and music far, he will come back again.

O lost, and by the wind grieved, ghost, come back again!

It had grown dark. The frosty night blazed with great brilliant stars. The lights in the town shone with sharp radiance. Presently, when he had lain upon the cold earth for some time, Eugene got up and went away toward the town.

Wind pressed the boughs; the withered leaves were shaking.

THE VISION IN THE SQUARE

THE Square lay under blazing moonlight. The fountain pulsed with a steady breezeless jet: the water fell upon the pool with a punctual slap. No one came into the Square.

The chimes of the bank's clock struck the quarter after three as Eugene entered from the northern edge, by Academy Street.

He came slowly over past the fire department and the City Hall. On Gant's corner, the Square dipped sharply down toward Niggertown, as if it had been bent at the edge.

Eugene saw his father's name, faded, on the old brick in moonlight. On the stone porch of the shop, the angels held their marble posture. They seemed to have frozen, in the moonlight.

Leaning against the iron railing of the porch, above the sidewalk, a man stood smoking. Troubled and a little afraid, Eugene came over. Slowly, he mounted the long wooden steps, looking carefully at the man's face. It was half-obscured in shadow.

"Is there anybody there?" said Eugene.

No one answered.

But, as Eugene reached the top, he saw that the man was Ben.

Ben stared at him a moment without speaking. Although Eugene could not see his face very well under the obscuring shadow of his gray felt hat, he knew that he was scowling.

"Ben?" said Eugene doubtfully, faltering a little on the top step. "Is it you, Ben?"

"Yes," said Ben. In a moment, he added in a surly voice: "Who did you think it was, you little idiot?"

"I wasn't sure," said Eugene somewhat timidly. "I couldn't see your face."

They were silent a moment. Then Eugene, clearing his throat in his embarrassment, said: "I thought you were dead, Ben."

"Ah-h!" said Ben contemptuously, jerking his head sharply upward. "Listen to this, won't you?"

He drew deeply on his cigarette: the spiral fumes coiled out and melted in the moon-bright silence.

"No," he said in a moment, quietly. "No, I am not dead."

Eugene came up on the porch and sat down on a limestone base, up-ended. Ben turned, in a moment, and climbed up on the rail, bending forward comfortably upon his knees.

Eugene fumbled in his pockets for a cigarette, with fingers that were stiff and trembling. He was not frightened: he was speechless with wonder and strong eagerness, and afraid to betray his thoughts to ridicule. He lighted a cigarette. Presently he said, painfully, hesitantly, in apology:

"Ben, are you a ghost?"

Ben did not mock.

"No," he said. "I am not a ghost."

There was silence again, while Eugene sought timorously for words.

"I hope," he began presently, with a small cracked laugh, "I hope, then, this doesn't mean that I'm crazy?"

"Why not?" said Ben, with a swift flickering grin. "Of course you're crazy."

"Then," said Eugene slowly, "I'm imagining all this?"

"In heavens name!" Ben cried irritably. "How should I know? Imagining all what?"

"What I mean," said Eugene, "is, are we here talking together, or not?"

"Don't ask me," said Ben. "How should I know?"

With a strong rustle of marble and a cold sigh of weariness, the angel nearest Eugene moved her stone foot and lifted her arm to a higher balance. The slender lily stipe shook stiffly in her elegant cold fingers.

"Did you see that?" Eugene cried excitedly.

"Did I see what?" said Ben, annoyed.

"Th-th-that angel there!" Eugene chattered, pointing with a trembling finger. "Did you see it move? It lifted its arm."

"What of it?" Ben asked irritably. "It has a right to, hasn't it? You know," he added with biting sarcasm, "there's no law against an angel lifting its arm if it wants to."

"No, I suppose not," Eugene admitted slowly, after a moment. "Only, I've always heard—"

"Ah! Do you believe all you hear, fool?" Ben cried fiercely. "Because," he added more calmly, in a moment, drawing on his cigarette, "you're in a bad way if you do."

There was again silence while they smoked. Then Ben said:

"When are you leaving, 'Gene?"

"To-morrow," Eugene answered.

"Do you know why you are going, or are you just taking a ride on the train?"

"I know! Of course—I know why I'm going!" Eugene said angrily, confused. He stopped abruptly, bewildered, chastened. Ben continued to scowl at him. Then, quietly, with humility, Eugene said:

"No, Ben. I don't know why I'm going. Perhaps you're right. Perhaps I just want a ride on the train."

"When are you coming back, 'Gene?" said Ben.

"Why—at the end of the year, I think," Eugene answered.

"No," said Ben, "you're not."

"What do you mean, Ben?" Eugene said, troubled.

"You're not coming back, 'Gene," said Ben softly. "Do you know that?"

There was a pause.

"Yes," said Eugene, "I know it."

"Why aren't you coming back?" said Ben.

Eugene caught fiercely at the neckband of his shirt with a clawed hand.

"I want to go! Do you hear!" he cried.

"Yes," said Ben. "So did I. Why do you want to go?"

"There's nothing here for me," Eugene muttered.

"How long have you felt like this?" said Ben.

"Always," said Eugene. "As long as I can remember. But I didn't know about it until you—" He stopped.

"Until I what?" said Ben.

There was a pause.

"You are dead, Ben," Eugene muttered. "You must be dead. I saw you die, Ben." His voice rose sharply. "I tell you, I saw you die. Don't you remember? The front room upstairs that the dentist's wife has now? Don't you remember, Ben? Coker, Helen, Bessie Gant who nursed you, Mrs. Pert? The oxygen tank? I tried to hold your hands together when they gave it to you." His voice rose to a scream. "Don't you remember? I tell you, you are dead, Ben."

"Fool," said Ben fiercely. "I am not dead."

There was a silence.

"Then," said Eugene very slowly, "which of us is the ghost, I wonder?"

Ben did not answer.

"Is this the Square, Ben? Is it you I'm talking to? Am I really here or not? And is this moonlight in the Square? Has all this happened?"

"How should I know?" said Ben again.

Within Gant's shop there was the ponderous tread of marble feet. Eugene leaped up and peered through the broad sheet of Jannadeau's dirty window. Upon his desk the strewn vitals of a watch winked with a thousand tiny points of bluish light. And beyond the jeweller's fenced space, where moonlight streamed into the ware-room through the tall side-window, the angels were walking to and fro like huge wound dolls of stone. The long cold pleats of their raiment rang with brittle clangor; their full decent breasts wagged in stony rhythms, and through the moonlight, with clashing wings, the marble cherubim flew round and round. With cold ewe-bleatings the carved lambs grazed stiffly across the moon-drenched aisle.

"Do you see it?" cried Eugene. "Do you see it, Ben?"

"Yes," said Ben. "What about it? They have a right to, haven't they?"

"Not here! Not here!" said Eugene passionately. "It's not right, here! My God, this is the Square! There's the fountain! There's the City Hall! There's the Greek's lunch-room."

The bank-chimes struck the half hour.

"And there's the bank," he cried.

"That makes no difference," said Ben.

"Yes," said Eugene, "it does!"

I am thy father's spirit, doomed for a certain term to walk the night—

"But not here! Not here, Ben!" said Eugene.

"Where?" said Ben wearily.

"In Babylon! In Thebes! In all the other places. But not here!" Eugene answered with growing passion. "There is a place where all things happen! But not here, Ben!"

My gods, with bird-cries in the sun, hang in the sky.

"Not here, Ben! It is not right!" Eugene said again.

The manifold gods of Babylon. Then, for a moment, Eugene stared at the dark figure on the rail, muttering in protest and disbelief: "Ghost! Ghost!"

"Fool," said Ben again, "I tell you I am not a ghost."

"Then, what are you?" said Eugene with strong excitement. "You are dead, Ben."

In a moment, more quietly, he added: "Or do men die?"

"How should I know," said Ben.

"They say papa is dying. Did you know that, Ben?" Eugene asked.

"Yes," said Ben.

"They have bought his shop. They are going to tear it down and put up a skyscraper here."

"Yes," said Ben, "I know it."

We shall not come again. We never shall come back again.

"Everything is going. Everything changes and passes away. To-morrow I shall be gone and this—" he stopped.

"This—what?" said Ben.

"This will be gone or—O God! Did all this happen?" cried Eugene.

"How should I know, fool?" cried Ben angrily.

"What happens, Ben? What really happens?" said Eugene. "Can you remember some of the same things that I do? I have forgotten the old faces. Where are they, Ben? What were their names? I forget the names of people I knew for years. I get their faces mixed. I get their heads stuck on other people's bodies. I think one man has said what another said. And I forget—forget. There is something I have lost and have forgotten. I can't remember, Ben."

"What do you want to remember?" said Ben.

A stone, a leaf, an unfound door. And the forgotten faces.

"I have forgotten names. I have forgotten faces. And I remember little things," said Eugene. "I remember the fly I swallowed on the peach, and the little boys on tricycles at Saint Louis, and the mole on Grover's neck, and the Lackawanna freight-car, number 16356, on a siding near Gulfport. Once, in Norfolk, an Australian soldier on his way to France asked me the way to a ship; I remember that man's face."

He stared for an answer into the shadow of Ben's face, and then he turned his moon-bright eyes upon the Square.

And for a moment all the silver space was printed with the thousand forms of himself and Ben. There, by the corner in from Academy Street, Eugene watched his own approach; there, by the City Hall, he strode with lifted knees; there, by the curb upon the step, he stood, peopling the night with the great lost legion of himself— the thousand forms that came, that passed, that wove and shifted in unending change, and that remained unchanging Him.

And through the Square, unwoven from lost time, the fierce bright horde of Ben spun in and out its deathless loom. Ben, in a thousand moments, walked the Square: Ben of the lost years, the forgotten days, the unremembered hours; prowled by the moonlit façades; vanished, returned, left and rejoined himself, was one and many— deathless Ben in search of the lost dead lusts, the finished enterprise, the unfound door—unchanging Ben multiplying himself in form, by all the brick façades entering and coming out.

And as Eugene watched the army of himself and Ben, which were not ghosts, and which were lost, he saw himself—his son, his boy, his lost and virgin flesh—come over past the fountain, leaning against the loaded canvas bag, and walking down with rapid crippled stride past Gant's toward Niggertown in young pre-natal dawn. And as he passed the porch where he sat watching, he saw the lost child-face below the lump ragged cap, drugged in the magic of unheard music, listening for the far-forested horn-note, the speechless almost captured pass-word. The fast boy-hands folded the fresh sheets, but the fabulous lost face went by, steeped in its incantations.

Eugene leaped to the railing.

"You! You! My son! My child! Come back! Come back!"

His voice strangled in his throat: the boy had gone, leaving the memory of his bewitched and listening face turned to the hidden world. O lost!

And now the Square was thronging with their lost bright shapes, and all the minutes of lost time collected and stood still. Then, shot from them with projectile speed, the Square shrank down the rails of destiny, and was vanished with all things done, with all forgotten shapes of himself and Ben.

And in his vision he saw the fabulous lost cities, buried in the drifted silt of the earth—Thebes, the seven-gated, and all the temples of the Daulian and Phocian lands, and all Oenotria to the Tyrrhene gulf. Sunk in the burial-urn of earth he saw the vanished cultures: the strange sourceless glory of the Incas, the fragments of lost epics upon a broken shard of Gnossic pottery, the buried tombs of the Memphian kings, and imperial dust, wound all about with gold and rotting linen, dead with their thousand bestial gods, their mute unwakened *ushabtii,* in their finished eternities.

He saw the billion living of the earth, the thousand billion dead: seas were withered, deserts flooded, mountains drowned; and gods and demons came out of the South, and ruled above the little rocket-flare of centuries, and sank—came to their Northern Lights of death, the muttering death-flared dusk of the completed gods.

But, amid the fumbling march of races to extinction, the giant rhythms of the earth remained. The seasons passed in their majestic processionals, and germinal Spring returned forever on the land— new crops, new men, new harvests, and new gods.

And then the voyages, the search for the happy land. In his moment of terrible vision he saw, in the tortuous ways of a thousand alien places, his foiled quest of himself. And his haunted face was possessed of that obscure and passionate hunger that had woven its shuttle across the seas, that had hung its weft among the Dutch in Pennsylvania, that had darkened his father's eyes to impalpable desire for wrought stone and the head of an angel. Hill-haunted, whose vision of the earth was mountain-walled, he saw the golden cities sicken in his eye, the opulent dark splendors turn to dingy gray. His brain was sick with the million books, his eyes with the million pictures, his body sickened on a hundred princely wines.

And rising from his vision, he cried: "I am not there among the cities. I have sought down a million streets, until the goat-cry died within my throat, and I have found no city where I was, no door where I had entered, no place where I had stood."

Then, from the edges of moon-bright silence, Ben replied: "Fool, why do you look in the streets?"

Then Eugene said: "I have eaten and drunk the earth, I have been lost and beaten, and I will go no more."

"Fool," said Ben, "what do you want to find?"

"Myself, and an end to hunger, and the happy land," he answered. "For I believe in harbors at the end. O Ben, brother, and ghost, and stranger, you who could never speak, give me an answer now!"

Then, as he thought, Ben said: "There is no happy land. There is no end to hunger."

"And a stone, a leaf, a door? Ben?" Spoke, continued without speaking, to speak. "Who are, who never were, Ben, the seeming of my brain, as I of yours, my ghost, my stranger, who died, who never lived, as I? But if, lost seeming of my dreaming brain, you have what I have not—an answer?"

Silence spoke. ("I cannot speak of voyages. I belong here. I never got away," said Ben.)

"Then I of yours the seeming, Ben? Your flesh is dead and buried in these hills: my unimprisoned soul haunts through the million streets of life, living its spectral nightmare of hunger and desire. Where, Ben? Where is the world?"

"Nowhere," Ben said. "*You* are your world."

Inevitable catharsis by the threads of chaos. Unswerving punctuality of chance. Apexical summation, from the billion deaths of possibility, of things done.

"I shall save one land unvisited," said Eugene. *Et ego in Arcadia.*

And as he spoke, he saw that he had left the million bones of cities, the skein of streets. He was alone with Ben, and their feet were planted on darkness, their faces were lit with the cold high terror of the stars.

On the brink of the dark he stood, with only the dream of the cities, the million books, the spectral images of the people he had loved, who had loved him, whom he had known and lost. They will not come again. They never will come back again.

With his feet upon the cliff of darkness, he looked and saw the lights of no cities. It was, he thought, the strong good medicine of death.

"Is this the end?" he said. "Have I eaten life and have not found him? Then I will voyage no more."

"Fool," said Ben, "*this* is life. You have been nowhere."

"But in the cities?"

"There are none. There is one voyage, the first, the last, the only one."

"On coasts more strange than Cipango, in a place more far than Fez, I shall hunt him, the ghost and haunter of myself. I have lost the blood that fed me; I have died the hundred deaths that lead to life. By the slow thunder of the drums, the flare of dying cities, I have come to this dark place. And this is the true voyage, the good one, the best. And now prepare, my soul, for the beginning hunt. I will plumb seas stranger than those haunted by the Albatross."

He stood naked and alone in darkness, far from the lost world of the streets and faces; he stood upon the ramparts of his soul, before the lost land of himself; heard inland murmurs of lost seas, the far interior music of the horns. The last voyage, the longest, the best.

"O sudden and impalpable faun, lost in the thickets of myself, I will hunt you down until you cease to haunt my eyes with hunger. I heard your foot-falls in the desert, I saw your shadow in old buried cities, I heard your laughter running down a million streets, but I did not find you there. And no leaf hangs for me in the forest; I shall lift no stone upon the hills; I shall find no door in any city. But in the city of myself, upon the continent of my soul, I shall find the forgotten language, the lost world, a door where I may enter, and music strange as any ever sounded; I shall haunt you, ghost, along the labyrinthine ways until—until? O Ben, my ghost, an answer?"

But as he spoke, the phantom years scrolled up their vision, and only the eyes of Ben burned terribly in darkness, without an answer.

And day came, and the song of waking birds, and the Square, bathed in the young pearl light of morning. And a wind stirred lightly in the Square, and, as he looked, Ben, like a fume of smoke, was melted into dawn.

And the angels on Gant's porch were frozen in hard marble silence, and at a distance life awoke, and there was a rattle of lean wheels, a slow clangor of shod hoofs. And he heard the whistle wail along the river.

Yet, as he stood for the last time by the angels of his father's porch, it seemed as if the Square already were far and lost; or, I should say, he was like a man who stands upon a hill above the town he has left, yet does not say "The town is near," but turns his eyes upon the distant soaring ranges.

FROM

OF TIME AND THE RIVER

OF TIME AND THE RIVER is a mammoth book which continues the story of Eugene Gant. It opens as he leaves Altamont for Harvard, follows him there, then to New York City where he teaches, and to Europe where his friendship with his Harvard friend, Francis Starwick, ends and he falls frustratingly in love with a girl named Ann, and concludes as he meets Esther on the ship back to America. The book is actually an anthology of materials out of Eugene Gant's experience. It contains some of Wolfe's finest writing; it also contains most of the passages which are cited as examples of his failure to control his material, his tendency toward ineffectual rhetoric and bombast, and his almost endless elaboration of scenes. It is the least known of all Wolfe's works, because relatively few of its readers struggle through to its conclusion; and this is a pity, for it contains many of Wolfe's most magnificent passages.

The following selections from the novel attempt to capture its many different moods and subjects, to present some of its memorable characters, and to give examples of Wolfe's prose poems at their best. They range from the Joycean passage on the thundering, north-bound train, through such dramatically powerful episodes as the death of W. O. Gant, the incident at the Coulson's in England, and the events on the train to Orleans, to the satiric portrait gallery of the students in Professor Hatcher's celebrated drama course.

Relatively little of this material was published prior to its appearance in *Of Time and the River*. "The House of the Far and the Lost" was published as a short story in *Scribner's Magazine*, August, 1934, in virtually the same form in which it appears in the novel. It was originally written, however, as an episode in the short novel *No Door* but was removed because of its length when the short novel was published in *Scribner's Magazine*, July, 1933. "The Sun and the Rain" was published in *Scribner's Magazine*, May, 1934. A portion of the selection here entitled "The Dream of Time" appeared as "The Names of the Nation" in the *Modern Monthly*, December, 1934. Except for "The House of the Far and the Lost" and "The Sun and the Rain," the titles given the following selections are mine rather than Wolfe's, although "Flight Before Fury" is the title of the entire section of the novel of which the selection here given is a portion, and the selections grouped under the title "The Dream of Time" are from the section of the novel which Wolfe entitled "Kronos and Rhea: The Dream of Time."

The text of all the selections is from *Of Time and the River*

(New York: Charles Scribner's Sons, 1935) . "Flight Before Fury" is from pages 68-76; "The Place of Deathless Moments" from pages 155-160; "The Death of W. O. Gant" from pages 210-268; "Professor Hatcher's Celebrated Course" from pages 130-135; 167-175, 282-304, 309-324; "A Portrait of Abraham Jones" from pages 440-447, 454-468, 491-497; "The House of the Far and the Lost" from pages 619-627, 637-652; "The Sun and the Rain" from pages 797-802; and "The Dream of Time" from pages 853-870, 880-886, 892-893.

FLIGHT BEFORE FURY

SO HERE they are now, three atoms on the huge breast of the indifferent earth, three youths out of a little town walled far away within the great rim of the silent mountains, already a distant, lonely dot upon the immense and sleeping visage of the continent. Here they are—three youths bound for the first time towards their image of the distant and enchanted city, sure that even though so many of their comrades had found there only dust and bitterness, the shining victory will be theirs. Here they are hurled onward in the great projectile of the train across the lonely visage of the ever-lasting earth. Here they are—three nameless grains of life among the manswarm ciphers of the earth, three faces of the million faces, three drops in the unceasing flood—and each of them a flame, a light, a glory, sure that his destiny is written in the blazing stars, his life shone over by the fortunate watches of the moon, his fame nourished and sustained by the huge earth, whose single darling charge he is, on whose immortal stillness he is flung onward in the night, his glorious fate set in the very brain and forehead of the fabulous, the unceasing city, of whose million-footed life he will tomorrow be a part.

Therefore they stand upon the rocking platform of the train, wild and dark and jubilant from the fierce liquor they have drunk, but more wild and dark and jubilant from the fury swelling in their hearts, the mad fury pounding in their veins, the savage, exultant and unutterable fury working like a madness in the adyts of their soul. And the great wheels smash and pound beneath their feet, the great wheels pound and smash and give a rhyme to madness, a tongue to hunger and desire, a certitude to all the savage, drunken, and exultant fury that keeps mounting, rising, swelling in them all the time!

Click, clack, clackety-clack; click, clack, clackety-clack; click, clack, clackety-clack; clackety-clackety-clack!

Hip, hop, hackety-hack; stip, step, rackety-rack; come and fetch it, come and fetch it, hickety hickety hack!

Rock, reel, smash, and swerve; hit it, hit it, on the curve; steady, steady, does the trick, keep her steady as a stick; eat the earth, eat the earth, slam and slug and beat the earth, and let her whir-r, and let her pur-r, at eighty per-r!

—Whew-w!

—Wow!

—God-dam!

—Put 'er there, boy!

—Put 'er there—whah!—*whah-h!* you ole long-legged frowsle-headed son-of-a-bitch!

—Whoop-ee! Whah-*whah-h!* Why, Go-d-d-damn!

—Whee! Vealer rog?

—Wadja say? Gant hearya!

—I say 'ja vealer rog? Wow! Pour it to her, son! Give 'er the gas! We're out to see the world! Run her off the god-damn track, boy! We don't need no rail, do we?

—Hell no! Which way does this damn train go, anyway, after it leaves Virginia?

—Maryland.

—Maryland my—! I don't want to go to Maryland! To hell with Mary's land! Also to hell with Mary's lamb and Mary's calf and Mary's blue silk underdrawers! Good old Lucy's the girl for me—the loosier the better! Give me Lucy any day! Good old Lucy Bowles, God bless her—she's the pick of the crowd, boys! Here's to Lucy!

Robert! Art there, boy?

—Aye, aye, sir! Present!

—Hast seen the damsel down in Lower Seven?

—I' sooth, sir, that I have! A comely wench, I trow!

—Peace, fool! Don't think, proud Princocke, thou canst snare this dove of innocence into the nets of infamous desire with stale reversions of thy wit! Out, out, vile lendings! An but thou carried'st at thy shunken waist what monstrous tun of guts thou takest for a brain 'twould so beslubber this receiving earth with lard as was not seen 'twixt here and Nottingham since butter shrove! Out, out upon you, scrapings of the pot! A dove, a doe, it is a faultless swan, I say, a pretty thing!

Now Virginia lay dreaming in the moonlight. In Louisiana bayous the broken moonlight shivers the broken moonlight quivers the light of many rivers lay dreaming in the moonlight beaming in the moonlight dreaming in the moonlight moonlight moonlight seeming in the moonlight moonlight moonlight to be gleaming to be streaming in the moonlight moonlight moonlight moonlight moonlight moonlight moonlight moonlight

—Mo-hoo-oonlight-oonlight oonlight oonlight oonlight oonlight oonlight oonlight oonlight oonlight

—To be seeming to be dreaming in the moonlight!

WHAM!
SMASH!
—Now! God-dam, let her have it! Wow-w!

With slamming roar, hoarse waugh, and thunderbolted light, the southbound train is gone in one projectile smash of wind-like fury, and the open empty silence of its passing fills us, thrills us, stills us with the vision of Virginia in the moonlight, with the dream-still magic of Virginia in the moon.

And now, as if with recollected force, the train gains power from the train it passed, leaps, gathers, springs beneath them, smashes on with recollected demon's fury in the dark . . .

With slam-bang of devil's racket and God-dam of curse—give us the bottle, drink, boys, drink!—the power of Virginia lies compacted in the moon. To you, God-dam of devil's magic and slam-bang of drive, fireflame of the terrific furnace, slam of rod, storm-stroke of pistoned wheel and thunderbolt of speed, great earth-devourer, city-bringer—hail!

To you, also, old glint of demon hawkeyes on the rail and the dark gloved hand of cunning—you, there, old bristle-crops!—Tom Wilson, H. F. Cline, or T. J. Johnson—whatever the hell your name is——

CASEY JONES! Open the throttle, boy, and let her rip! Boys, I'm a belly-busting bastard from the State of old Catawba—a rootin' tootin' shootin' son-of-a-bitch from Saw Tooth Gap in Buncombe— why, God help this lovely bastard of a train—it is the best damned train that ever turned a wheel since Casey Jones's father was a pup —why, you sweet bastard, run! Eat up Virginia!—Give her the throttle, you old goggle-eyed son-of-a-bitch up there!—Pour it to her! Let 'er have it, you nigger-Baptist bastard of a shoveling fire-man—let 'er rip!—Wow! By God, we'll be in Washington for breakfast!

—Why, God bless this lovely bastard of a train! It is the best damned train that ever pulled a car since Grant took Richmond!—

Which way does the damn thing go?—Pennsylvania?—Well, that's
all right! Don't you say a word against Pennsylvania! My father
came from Pennsylvania, boys, he was the best damned man that
ever lived—He was a stonecutter and he's better than any son-of-a-
bitch of a plumber you ever saw—He's got a cancer and six doctors
and they can't kill him!—But to hell with going where we go!—
We're out to see the world, boy!—To hell with Baltimore, New
York, Boston! Run her off the God-damn rails! We're going West!
Run her through the woods—cross fields—rivers, through the hills!
Hell's pecker! But I'll shove her up the grade and through the gap,
no double-header needed!—Let's see the world now! Through
Nebraska, boy! Let's shove her through, now, you can do it!—Let's
run her through Ohio, Kansas, and the unknown plains! Come on,
you hogger, let's see the great plains and the fields of wheat—stop
off in Dakota, Minnesota, and the fertile places—Give us a minute
while you breathe to put our foot upon it, to feel it spring back
with the deep elastic feeling, 8000 miles below, unrolled and lavish,
depthless, different from the East.

Now Virginia lay dreaming in the moonlight! And on Florida's
bright waters the fair and lovely daughters of the Wilsons and the
Potters; the Cabots and the Lowells; the Weisbergs and O'Hares;
the Astors and the Goulds; the Ransoms and the Rands; the
Westalls and the Pattons and the Webbs; the Reynolds and Mc-
Raes; the Spanglers and the Beams; the Gudgers and the Blakes;
the Pedersons and Craigs—all the lovely daughters, the Robinsons
and Waters, the millionaires' sweet daughters, the Boston maids, the
Beacon Slades, the Back Bay Wades, all of the merchant, lawyer,
railroad and well-monied grades of Hudson River daughters in the
moon's bright living waters—lay dreaming in the moonlight, beaming in the moonlight, seeming in the moonlight, to be dreaming to
be gleaming in the moon.
    —Give 'em hell, son!
    —Here, give him another drink!—Attaboy! Drink her down!
    —Drink her down—drink her down—drink her down—damn
your soul—drink her down!
    —By God, I'll drink her down and flood the whole end of Vir-
ginia, I'll drown out Maryland, make a flood in Pennsylvania—I
tell you boys I'll float 'em, I'll raise 'em up, I'll bring 'em down

stream, now—I mean the Potters and the Waters, the rich men's lovely daughters, the city's tender daughters, the Hudson river daughters——

Lay dreaming in the moonlight, beaming in the moonlight, to be seeming to be beaming in the moonlight moonlight moonlight oonlight oonlight oonlight oonlight oonlight.

And Virginia lay dreaming in the moon.

Then the moon blazed down upon the vast desolation of the American coasts, and on all the glut and hiss of tides, on all the surge and foaming slide of waters on lone beaches. The moon blazed down on 18,000 miles of coast, on the million sucks and scoops and hollows of the shore, and on the great wink of the sea, that ate the earth minutely and eternally. The moon blazed down upon the wilderness, it fell on sleeping woods, it dripped through moving leaves, it swarmed in weaving patterns on the earth, and it filled the cat's still eye with blazing yellow. The moon slept over mountains and lay like silence in the desert, and it carved the shadows of great rocks like time. The moon was mixed with flowing rivers, and it was buried in the heart of lakes, and it trembled on the water like bright fish. The moon steeped all the earth in its living and unearthly substance, it had a thousand visages, it painted continental space with ghostly light; and its light was proper to the nature of all the things it touched: it came in with the sea, it flowed with the rivers, and it was still and living on clear spaces in the forest where no men watched.

And in woodland darkness great birds fluttered to their sleep—in sleeping woodlands strange and secret birds, the teal, the nightjar, and the flying rail went to their sleep with flutterings dark as hearts of sleeping men. In fronded beds and on the leaves of unfamiliar plants where the tarantula, the adder, and the asp had fed themselves asleep on their own poisons, and on lush jungle depths where green-golden, bitter red and glossy blue proud tufted birds cried out with brainless scream, the moonlight slept.

The moonlight slept above dark herds moving with slow grazings in the night, it covered lonely little villages; but most of all it fell upon the unbroken undulation of the wilderness, and it blazed on windows, and moved across the face of sleeping men.

Sleep lay upon the wilderness, it lay across the faces of the nations, it lay like silence on the hearts of sleeping men; and low upon lowlands, and high upon hills, flowed gently sleep, smooth-sliding sleep —sleep—sleep.

—Robert——

—Go on to bed, Gene, go to bed now, go to bed.

—There's shump'n I mush shay t'you——

—Damn fool! Go to bed!

—Go to bed, my balls! I'll go to bed when I'm God-damn good and ready! I'll not go to bed when there's shump'n I mush shay t'you——

—Go on to bed now, Gene. You had enough.

—Creasman, you're a good fellow maybe but I don't know you. . . . You keep out of this. . . . Robert . . . I'm gonna tell y' shump'n. . . . You made a remark t'night I didn' like—Prayin' for me, are they, Robert?

—You damn fool!—You don't know what you're talkin' 'bout! Go on to bed!——

—I'll go to bed, you bastard—I got shump'n to shay t'you!—Prayin' for me, are yuh?—Pray for yourself, y' bloody little Deke!

—Damn fool's crazy! Go on to bed now——

—I'll bed yuh, you son-of-a-bitch! What was it that y' said that day?——

—What day? You damned fool, you don't know what you're saying!

—I'll tell yuh what day!—Coming along Chestnut Street that day after school with you and me and Sunny Jim Curtis and Ed Petrie and Bob Pegram and Carl Hartshorn and Monk Paul—and the rest of those boys——

—You damn fool! Chestnut Street! I don't know what you're talking about!

—Yes, you do!—You and me and Bob and Carl and Irwin and Jim Homes and some other boys—'Member what y'said, yuh son-of-a-bitch? Old man English was in his yard there burning up some leaves and it was October and we were comin' along there after school and you could smell the leaves and it was after school and you said, "Here's Mr. Gant the tomb-stone cutter's son."

psychiatric

—You damn fool! I don't know what you're talking about!——

—Yes, you do, you cheap Deke son-of-a-bitch—Too good to talk to us on the street when you were sucking around after Bruce Martin or Steve Patton or Jack Marriot—but a life-long brother—oh! couldn't see enough of us, could you, when you were alone?

—The damn fool's crazy!

—Crazy, am I?—Well, we never had any old gummy grannies tied down and hidden in the attic—which is more than some people that I know can say!—you son-of-a-bitch—who do you think you are with your big airs and big Deke pin!—My people were better people than your crowd ever hoped to be—we've been here longer and we're better people—and as for the tombstone cutter's son, my father was the best damned stonecutter that ever lived—he's dying of cancer and all the doctors in the world can't kill him—he's a better man than any little ex-police court magistrate who calls himself a judge will ever be—and that goes for you too—you——

Why, you crazy fool! I never said anything about your father——

To hell with you, you damn little bootlicking——

Come on Gene come on you've had enough you're drunk now come on.

Why God-damn you to hell, I hate your guts you——

All right, all right—He's drunk! He's crazy—Come on, Bill! Leave him alone!—He don't know what he's doing——

All right. Good night, Gene. . . . Be careful now—See you in the morning, boy.

All right, Robert, I mean nothing against you—you——

All right!—All right!—Come on, Bill. Let him alone! Good night, Gene—Come on—let's go to bed!——

To bed to bed to bed to bed to bed! So, so, so, so, so! Make no noise, make no noise, draw the curtains; so, so, so. We'll go to supper i' the morning: so, so, so.

And Ile go to bedde at noone.

Alone, alone now, down the dark, the green, the jungle aisle between the dark drugged snorings of the sleepers. The pause, the stir, the sigh, the sudden shift, the train that now rumbles on through the dark forests of the dream-charged moon-enchanted mind its monotone of silence and forever: Out of these prison bands of clothes, now, rip, tear, toss, and haul while the green-curtained sleepers move from jungle depths and the even-pounding silence of eternity—into the stiff white sheets, the close, hot air, his long body crookedly athwart, lights out, to see it shining faintly in the coffined under-surface of the berth above—and sleepless, Virginia floating, dreamlike, in the still white haunting of the moon——

—At night, great trains will pass us in the timeless spell of an unsleeping hypnosis, an endless, and unfathomable stupefaction. Then suddenly in the unwaking never sleeping century of the night, the sensual limbs of carnal whited nakedness that stir with drowsy silken warmth in the green secrecies of Lower Seven, the slow swelling and lonely and swarmhaunted land—and suddenly, suddenly, silence and thick hardening lust of dark exultant joy, the dreamlike passage of Virginia!—Then in the watches of the night a pause, the sudden silence of up-welling night, and unseen faces, voices, laughter, and farewells upon a lonely little night-time station—the lost and lonely voices of Americans:—"Good-bye! Good-bye, now! Write us when you get there, Helen! Tell Bob he's got to write!—Give my love to Emily!—Good-bye, good-bye now—write us, soon!"—And then the secret, silken and subdued rustling past the thick green curtains and the sleepers, the low respectful Negroid tones of the black porter—and then the whistle cry, the tolling bell, the great train mounting to its classic monotone again, and presently the last lights of a little town, the floating void and loneliness of moon-haunted earth—Virginia!

Also, in the dream—thickets of eternal night—there will be huge steamings on the rail, the sudden smash, the wall of light, the sudden flarings of wild, roaring light upon the moon-haunted and dream-tortured faces of the sleepers!

—And finally, in that dark jungle of the night, through all the visions, memories, and enchanted weavings of the timeless and eternal spell of time, the moment of forever—there are two horsemen, riding, riding, riding in the night.

Who are they? Oh, we know them with our life and they will ride across the land, the moon-haunted passage of our lives forever. Their names are Death and Pity, and we know their face: our brother and our father ride ever beside us in the dream-enchanted spell and vista of the night; the hooves keep level time beside the rhythms of the train.

Horsed on the black and moon-maned steeds of fury, cloaked in the dark of night, the spell of time, dream-pale, eternal, they are rushing on across the haunted land, the moon-enchanted wilderness, and their hooves make level thunder with the train.

Pale Pity and Lean Death their names are, and they will ride forevermore the moon-plantations of Virginia keeping time time time to the level thunder of the train pounding time time time as with four-hooved thunder of phantasmal hooves they pound forever level with the train across the moon-plantations of Virginia.

Quadrupedante putrem sonitu quatit ungula campum as with storm-phantasmal hooves Lean Death and Pale Pity with quadrupedante putrem sonitu quatit ungula campum . . . campum . . . quadrupe dante . . . putrem . . . putrem . . . putrem putrem putrem as with sonitu quatit ungula campum quadrupedante putrem . . . putrem . . . putrem putrem putrem . . . putrem . . . putrem . . . putrem putrem putrem quadrupedante quadrupedante quadrupedante putrem putrem as with sonitu quatit ungula campum quadrupedante putrem . . . putrem . . . putrem putrem putrem . . . as with sonitu quatit ungula campum quadrupedante putrem . . . ungula campum . . . campum . . . ungula . . . ungula campum . . .

THE PLACE OF DEATHLESS MOMENTS

BUT this was the reason why these things could never be forgotten —because we are so lost, so naked and so lonely in America. Immense and cruel skies bend over us, and all of us are driven on forever and we have no home. Therefore, it is not the slow, the punctual sanded drip of the unnumbered days that we remember best, the ash of time; nor is it the huge monotone of the lost years, the unswerving schedules of the lost life and the well-known faces, that we remember best. It is a face seen once and lost forever in a crowd, an eye that looked, a face that smiled and vanished on a passing train, it is a prescience of snow upon a certain night, the laughter of a woman in a summer street long years ago, it is the memory of a single moon seen at the pine's dark edge in old October—and all of our lives is written in the twisting of a leaf upon a bough, a door that opened, and a stone.

For America has a thousand lights and weathers and we walk the streets, we walk the streets forever, we walk the streets of life alone.

It is the place of the howling winds, the hurrying of the leaves in old October, the hard clean falling to the earth of acorns. The place of the storm-tossed moaning of the wintry mountainside, where the young men cry out in their throats and feel the savage vigor, the rude strong energies; the place also where the trains cross rivers.

It is a fabulous country, the only fabulous country; it is the one place where miracles not only happen, but where they happen all the time.

It is the place of exultancy and strong joy, the place of the darkened brooding air, the smell of snow; it is the place of all the fierce, the bitten colors in October, when all of the wild, sweet woods flame up; it is also the place of the cider press and the last brown oozings of the York Imperials. It is the place of the lovely girls with good jobs and the husky voices, who will buy a round of drinks; it is the place where the women with fine legs and silken underwear lie in the pullman berth below you, it is the place of the dark-green snore of the pullman cars, and the voices in the night-time in Virginia.

It is the place where great boats are baying at the harbor's mouth, where great ships are putting out to sea; it is the place where great boats are blowing in the gulf of night, and where the river, the dark and secret river, full of strange time, is forever flowing by us to the sea.

The tugs keep baying in the river; at twelve o'clock the Berengaria *moans, her lights slide gently past the piers beyond Eleventh Street; and in the night a tall tree falls in Old Catawba, there in the hills of home.*

It is the place of autumnal moons hung low and orange at the frosty edges of the pines; it is the place of frost and silence; of the clean dry shocks and the opulence of enormous pumpkins that yellow on hard clotted earth; it is the place of the stir and feathery stumble of the hens upon their roost, the frosty, broken barking of the dogs, the great barnshapes and solid shadows in the running sweep of the moon-whited countryside, the wailing whistle of the fast express. It is the place of flares and steamings on the tracks, and the swing and bob and tottering dance of lanterns in the yards; it is the place of dings and knellings and the sudden glare of mighty engines over sleeping faces in the night; it is the place of the terrific web and spread and smouldering, the distant glare of Philadelphia and the solid rumble of the sleepers; it is also the place where the Transcontinental Limited is stroking eighty miles an hour across the continent and the small dark towns whip by like bullets, and there is only the fanlike stroke of the secret, immense and lonely earth again.

I have foreseen this picture many times: I will buy passage on the Fast Express.

It is the place of the wild and exultant winter's morning and the wind, with the powdery snow, that has been howling all night long; it is the place of solitude and the branches of the spruce and hemlock piled with snow; it is the place where the Fall River boats are tethered to the wharf, and the wild gray snow of furious, secret, and storm-white morning whips across them. It is the place of the lodge by the frozen lake and the sweet breath and amorous flesh of sinful woman; it is the place of the tragic and lonely beauty of New England; it is the place of the red barn and the sound of the stabled hooves and of bright tatters of old circus posters; it is the place of the immense and pungent smell of breakfast, the country sausages and the ham and eggs, the smoking wheat cakes and the fragrant coffee, and of lone hunters in the frosty thickets who whistle to their lop-eared hounds.

Where is old Doctor Ballard now with all his dogs? He held that they were sacred, that the souls of all the dear lost dead went into them. His youngest sister's soul sat on the seat beside him; she had long ears and her eyes were sad. Two dozen of his other cherished dead trotted around the buggy as he went up the hill past home. And that was eleven years ago, and I was nine years old; and I

*stared gravely out the window of my father's house at old Doctor
Ballard.*

It is the place of the straight stare, the cold white bellies and the
buried lust of the lovely Boston girls; it is the place of ripe brainless
blondes with tender lips and a flowery smell, and of the girls with
shapely arms who stand on ladders picking oranges; it is also the
place where large slow-bodied girls from Kansas City, with big legs
and milky flesh, are sent East to school by their rich fathers, and
there are also immense and lovely girls, with the grip of a passionate
bear, who have such names as Neilson, Lundquist, Jorgenson, and
Brandt.

*I will go up and down the country, and back and forth across the
country on the great trains that thunder over America. I will go out
West where States are square; Oh, I will go to Boise, and Helena
and Albuquerque. I will go to Montana and the two Dakotas and
the unknown places.*

It is the place of violence and sudden death; of the fast shots in
the night, the club of the Irish cop, and the smell of brains and
blood upon the pavement; it is the place of the small-town killings,
and the men who shoot the lovers of their wives; it is the place
where the Negroes slash with razors and the hillmen kill in the
mountain meadows; it is the place of the ugly drunks and the snarling voices and of foul-mouthed men who want to fight; it is the
place of the loud word and the foolish boast and the violent threat;
it is also the place of the deadly little men with white faces and the
eyes of reptiles, who kill quickly and casually in the dark; it is the
lawless land that feeds on murder.

*"Did you know the two Lipe girls?" he asked. "Yes," I said,
"They lived in Biltburn by the river, and one of them was drowned
in the flood. She was a cripple, and she wheeled herself along in a
chair. She was strong as a bull." "That's the girl," he said.*

It is the place of the crack athletes and of the runners who limber
up in March; it is the place of the ten-second men and the great
jumpers and vaulters; it is the place where Spring comes, and the
young birch trees have white and tender barks, of the thaw of the
earth, and the feathery smoke of the trees; it is the place of the burst
of grass and bud, the wild and sudden tenderness of the wilderness,
and of the crews out on the river and the coaches coming down be-

hind them in the motorboats, the surges rolling out behind when they are gone with heavy sudden wash. It is the place of the baseball players, and the easy lob, the soft spring smackings of the glove and mit, the crack of the bat; it is the place of the great batters, fielders, and pitchers, of the nigger boys and the white, drawling, shirt-sleeved men, the bleachers and the resinous smell of old worn wood; it is the place of Rube Waddell, the mighty untamed and ill-fated pitcher when his left arm is swinging like a lash. It is the place of the fighters, the crafty Jewish lightweights and the mauling Italians, Leonard, Tendler, Rocky Kansas, and Dundee; it is the place where the champion looks over his rival's shoulder with a bored expression.

I shall wake at morning in a foreign land thinking I heard a horse in one of the streets of home.

It is the place where they like to win always, and boast about their victories; it is the place of quick money and sudden loss; it is the place of the mile-long freights with their strong, solid, clank-ing, heavy loneliness at night, and of the silent freight of cars that curve away among raw piney desolations with their promise of new lands and unknown distances—the huge attentive gape of empti-ness. It is the place where the bums come singly from the woods at sunset, the huge stillness of the watertower, the fading light, the rails, secret and alive, and trembling with the oncoming train; it is the place of the great tramps, Oklahoma Red, Fargo Pete, and the Jersey Dutchman, who grab fast rattlers for the Western shore; it is the place of old blown bums who come up in October skirls of dust and wind and crumpled newspapers and beg, with canned heat on their breaths: "Help Old McGuire: McGuire's a good guy, kid. You're not so tough, kid: McGuire's your pal, kid: How about McGuire, McGuire—?"

It is the place of the poolroom players and the drug-store boys; of the town whore and her paramour, the tough town driver; it is the place where they go to the woods on Sunday and get up among the laurel and dogwood bushes and the rhododendron blossoms; it is the place of the cheap hotels and the kids who wait with chatter-ing lips while the nigger goes to get them their first woman; it is the place of the drunken college boys who spend the old man's money and wear fur coats to the football games; it is the place of the lovely girls up North who have rich fathers, of the beautiful wives of business men.

The train broke down somewhere beyond Manassas, and I went forward along the tracks with all the other passengers. "What's the matter?" I said to the engineer. "The eccentric strap is broken, son," he said. It was a very cold day, windy and full of sparkling sun. This was the farthest north I'd ever been, and I was twelve years old and on my way to Washington to see Woodrow Wilson inaugurated. Later I could not forget the face of the engineer and the words "eccentric strap."

It is the place of the immense and lonely earth, the place of fat ears and abundance where they grow cotton, corn, and wheat, the wine-red apples of October, and the good tobacco.

It is the place that is savage and cruel, but it is also the innocent place; it is the wild lawless place, the vital earth that is soaked with the blood of the murdered men, with the blood of the countless murdered men, with the blood of the unavenged and unremembered murdered men; but it is also the place of the child and laughter, where the young men are torn apart with ecstasy, and cry out in their throats with joy, where they hear the howl of the wind and the rain and smell the thunder and the soft numb spitting of the snow, where they are drunk with the bite and sparkle of the air and mad with the solar energy, where they believe in love and victory and think that they can never die.

It is the place where you come up through Virginia on the great trains in the night-time, and rumble slowly across the wide Potomac and see the morning sunlight on the nation's dome at Washington, and where the fat man shaving in the pullman washroom grunts, "What's this? What's this we're coming to—Washington?"—And the thin man glancing out the window says, "Yep, this is Washington. That's what it is, all right. You gettin' off here?"—And where the fat man grunts, "Who—me? Naw—I'm goin' on to Baltimore." It is the place where you get off at Baltimore and find your brother waiting.

Where is my father sleeping on the land? Buried? Dead these seven years? Forgotten, rotten in the ground? Held by his own great stone? No, no! Will I say, "Father" when I come to him? And will he call me, "Son"? Oh, no, he'll never see my face: we'll never speak except to say—

It is the place of the fast approach, the hot blind smoky passage, the tragic lonely beauty of New England, and the web of Boston; the place of the mighty station there, and engines passive as great cats, the straight dense plumes of engine smoke, the acrid and exciting smell of trains and stations, and of the man-swarm passing ever in its million-footed weft, the smell of the sea in harbors and the thought of voyages—and the place of the goat cry, the strong joy of our youth, the magic city, when we knew the most fortunate life on earth would certainly be ours, that we were twenty and could never die.

And always America is the place of the deathless and enraptured moments, the eye that looked, the mouth that smiled and vanished, and the word; the stone, the leaf, the door we never found and never have forgotten. And these are the things that we remember of America, for we have known all her thousand lights and weathers, and we walk the streets, we walk the streets forever, we walk the streets of life alone.

THE DEATH OF W. O. GANT

ONE afternoon early in May, Helen met McGuire upon the street. He had just driven in behind Wood's Pharmacy on Academy Street, and was preparing to go in to the prescription counter when she approached him. He got out of his big dusty-looking roadster with a painful grunt, slammed the door, and began to fumble slowly in the pockets of his baggy coat for a cigarette. He turned slowly as she spoke, grunted, "Hello, Helen," stuck the cigarette on his fat under-lip and lighted it, and then looking at her with his brutal, almost stupid, but somehow kindly glance, he barked coarsely:

"What's on your mind?"

"It's about Papa," she began in a low, hoarse and almost morbid tone—"Now I want to know if this last attack means that the end has come. You've got to tell me—we've got the right to know about it—"

The look of strain and hysteria on her big-boned face, her dull eyes fixed on him in a morbid stare, the sore on her large cleft chin, above all, the brooding insistence of her tone as she repeated phrases he had heard ten thousand times before suddenly rasped upon his frayed nerves, stretched them to the breaking point; he lost his air of hard professionalism and exploded in a flare of brutal anger:

"You want to know what? You've got a right to be told what? For God's sake,"—his tone was brutal, rasping, jeering—"pull yourself together and stop acting like a child." And then, a little more quietly, but brusquely, he demanded:

"All right. What do you want to know?"

"I want to know how long he's going to last," she said with morbid insistence. "Now, you're a doctor," she wagged her large face at him with an air of challenge that infuriated him, "and you ought to tell us. We've got to know!"

"Tell you! Got to know!" he shouted. "What the hell are you talking about? What do you expect to be told?"

"How long Papa has to live," she said with the same morbid insistence as before.

"You've asked me that a thousand times," he said harshly. "I've told you that I didn't know. He may live another month, he may be here a year from now—how can we tell about these things," he said in an exasperated tone, "particularly where your father is concerned. Helen, three or four years ago I might have made a prediction. I did make them—I didn't see how W. O. could go on six months longer. But he's fooled us all—you, me, the doctors at Johns Hopkins, every one who's had anything to do with the case. The man is dying from malignant carcinoma—he has been dying for years—his life is hanging by a thread, and the thread may break at any time—but when it is going to break I have no way of telling you."

"Ah-hah," she said reflectively. Her eyes had taken on a dull appeased look as he talked to her, and now she had begun to pluck at her large cleft chin. "Then you think—" she began.

"I think nothing," he shouted. "And for God's sake stop picking at your chin!"

For a moment he felt the sudden brutal anger that one sometimes feels toward a contrary child. He felt like taking her by the shoulders and shaking her. Instead, he took it out in words and scowling at her, said with brutal directness:

"Look here! . . . You've got to pull yourself together. You're becoming a mental case—do you hear me? You wander around like a person in a dream, you ask questions no one can answer, you demand answers no one can give—you work yourself up into hysterical frenzies and then you collapse and soak yourself with drugs, patent medicines, corn licker—anything that has alcohol in it—for days at a time. When you go to bed at night you think you hear voices talking to you, some one coming up the steps, the telephone. And really you hear nothing: there is nothing there. Do you know what that is?" he demanded brutally. "Those are symptoms of insanity—you're becoming unbalanced, if it keeps on they may have to send you to the crazy-house to take the cure."

"Ah-hah! Uh-huh!" she kept plucking at her big chin with an air of abstracted reflection, and with a curious look of dull appeasement in her eyes as if his brutal words had really given her some comfort. Then she suddenly came to herself, looked at him with clear eyes, and, her generous mouth touched at the corners with the big lewd tracery of her earthy humor, she sniggered hoarsely, and prodding him in his fat ribs with a big bony finger, she said:

"You think I've got 'em, do you? Well—" she nodded seriously in agreement, frowning a little as she spoke, but with the faint grin still legible around the corners of her mouth,—"I've often thought the same thing. You may be right," she nodded seriously again. "There are times when I do feel off—you know?—*queer*—looney—crazy—like there was a screw loose somewhere—Brrr!" and with the strange lewd mixture of frown and grin, she made a whirling movement with her finger towards her head. "What do you think it is?" she went on with an air of seriousness. "Now, I'd just like to know. What is it that makes me act like that? . . . Is it woman-business?" she said with a lewd and comic look upon her face. "Am I getting funny like the rest of them—now I've often thought the same—that maybe I'm going through a change of life—is that it? Maybe——"

"Oh, change of life be damned!" he said in a disgusted tone. "Here you are a young woman thirty-two years old and you talk to me about a change of life! That has about as much sense to it as a lot of other things you say! The only thing you change is your mind—and you do that every five minutes!" He was silent for a moment, breathing heavily and staring at her coarsely with his bloated and unshaven face, his veined and weary-looking eyes. When he spoke again his voice was gruff and quiet, touched with a burly, almost paternal tenderness:

"Helen," he said, "I'm worried about you—and not about your father. Your father is an old man now with a malignant cancer and with no hope of ever getting well again. He is tired of life, he wants to die—for God's sake why do you want to prolong his suffering, to try to keep him here in a state of agony, when death would be a merciful release for him? . . . I know there is no hope left for your father: he has been doomed for years, the sooner the end comes the better——"

She tried to speak but he interrupted her brusquely, saying:

"Just a minute. There's something that I want to say to you— for God's sake try to use it, if you can. The death of this old man seems strange and horrible to you because he is your father. It is as hard for you to think about his death as it is to think about the death of God Almighty; you think that if your father dies there will be floods and earthquakes and convulsions throughout nature. I assure you that this is not true. Old men are dying every second of the day, and nothing happens except they die——"

"Oh, but Papa was a wonderful man," she said. "I *know*! I *know*! Everybody who ever knew him said the same."

"Yes," McGuire agreed, "he was—he was one of the most remarkable men I ever knew. And that is what makes it all the harder now."

She looked at him eagerly, and said:

"You mean—his dying?"

"No, Helen," McGuire spoke quietly and with a weary patience "There's nothing very bad about his dying. Death seems so terrible to you because you know so little about it. But I have seen so much of death, I have seen so many people die—and I know there is really nothing very terrible about it, and about the death of an old man ravaged by disease there is nothing terrible at all. It seems terrible to those looking on—there are," he shrugged his fat shoulders, "there are sometimes—physical details that are unpleasant. But the old man knows little of all that: an old man dies as a clock runs down—he is worn out, has lost the will to live, he wants to die, and he just stops. That is all. And that will happen to your father."

"Oh, but it will be so strange now—so hard to understand!" she muttered with a bewildered look in her eyes. "We have expected him to die so many times—we have been fooled so often—and now I can't believe that it will ever happen. I thought that he would die in 1916, I never expected him to live another year; in 1918, the year that Ben died, none of us could see how he'd get through the winter—and then Ben died! No one had even thought of Ben—" her voice grew cracked and hoarse and her eyes glistened with tears. "We had forgotten Ben—every one was thinking about Papa—and then when Ben died, I turned against Papa for a time. For a while I was bitter against him—it seemed that I had done everything for this old man, that I had given him everything I had—my life, my strength, my energy—all because I thought that he was going to die —and then Ben, who had never been given anything—who had had nothing out of life—who had been neglected and forgotten by us all and who was the best one—the most decent one of the whole crowd—Ben was the one who had to go. For a time after his death I didn't care what happened—to Papa or to any one else. I was so bitter about Ben's death—it seemed so cruel, so rotten and unjust— that it had to be Ben of all the people in the world—only twenty-six years old and without a thing to show for his life—no love, no children, no happiness, cheated out of everything, when Papa had had so much—I couldn't stand the thought of it, even now I hate to go to Mama's house, it almost kills me to go near Ben's room, I've never been in it since the night he died—and somehow I was bitter against Papa! It seemed to me that he had cheated me, tricked me—at times I got so bitter that I thought that he was responsible in some way for Ben's death. I said I was through with him, that I would do nothing else for him, that I had done all that I intended to do, and that somebody else would have to take care of him. . . . But it all came back; he had another bad spell and I was afraid that he was going to die, and I couldn't stand the thought of it. . . . And it has gone on now so long, *year* after **year**, and *year* after year," she said in a frenzied tone, "always thinking that he couldn't last and seeing him come back again, that I couldn't believe that it would ever happen. I can't believe it now. . . . And what am I going to do?" she said hoarsely and desperately, clutching McGuire by the sleeve, "what am I going to do now if he really dies? What is there left for me in life with Papa gone?" Her voice was almost sobbing now with grief and desperation— "He's all I've got to live for, Doctor McGuire. I've got nothing out of life that I wanted or expected—it's all been so different from the way I thought it was—I've had nothing—no fame, no glory, no success, no children—everything has gone—Papa is all that I have left! If he dies what shall I do?" she cried frantically, shaking him by the sleeve. "That old man is all I've got—the only thing I've got left to live for; to keep him alive, to make him comfortable, to ease his pain, to see he gets good food and attention—somehow, somehow," she panted desperately, clasping her big bony hands in a gesture of unconscious but pitiable entreaty, and beginning to rock unsteadily on her feet as she spoke—"somehow, somehow, to keep life in him, to keep him here, not to let him go—that's all I've got to live for—what in the name of God am I going to do when that is taken from me?"

And she paused, panting and exhausted by her tirade, her big face strained and quivering, glaring at him with an air of frantic entreaty as if it was in his power to give the answers to these frenzied questions. And for a moment he said nothing; he just stood there looking at her with the coarse and brutal stare of his blotched face, his venous yellowed eyes, the wet cigarette stuck comically at the corner of one fat lip.

"What are you going to do?" he barked, presently. "You're going to get hold of yourself—pull yourself together—amount to something, be somebody!" He coughed chokingly to one side, for a moment there was just the sound of his thick short breathing, then he flung the cigarette away, and said quietly:

"Helen, for God's sake, don't throw your life away! Don't destroy the great creature that lies buried in you somewhere—wake it up, make it come to life. Don't talk to me of this old man's life as if it were your own——"

"It is, it is!" she said in a brooding tone of morbid fatality.

"It is not!" he said curtly, "unless you make it so—unless you play the weakling and the fool and throw yourself away. For God's sake, don't let that happen to you. I have seen it happen to so many people—some of them fine people like yourself, full of energy, imagination, intelligence, ability—all thrown away, frittered away like that," he flung fat fingers in the air—"because they did not have the guts to use what God had given them—to make a new life for themselves—to stand on their own feet and not to lean upon another's shoulder! . . . Don't die the death!" he rasped coarsely, staring at her with his brutal face. "Don't die the rotten, lousy, dirty death-in-life—the only death that's really horrible! For God's sake, don't betray life and yourself and the people who love you by dying that kind of death! I've seen it happen to so many people—and it was always so damned useless, such a rotten waste! That's what I was trying to say to you a few minutes ago—it's not the death of the dying that is terrible, it is the death of the living. And we always die that death for the same reason:—because our father dies, and takes from us his own life, his world, his time—and we haven't courage enough to make a new life, a new world for ourselves. I wonder if you know how often that thing happens—how often I have seen it happen—the wreck, the ruin, and the tragedy it has caused in life! When the father goes, the whole structure of the family life goes with him—and unless his children have the will, the stuff, the courage to make something of their own, they die, too. . . . With you, it's going to be very hard when your father dies; he was a man of great vitality and a strong personality who has left a deep impression on every one who knew him. And for seven years now, your father's death has been your life. . . . It has become a part of you, you have brooded over it, lived with it, soaked in it, been tainted by it—and now it is going to be hard for you to escape. But escape you must, and stand on your own feet—or you are lost. . . . Helen!" he barked sharply, and fixed her with his coarse and brutal stare—"listen to me:—your childhood, Woodson Street, getting your father over drunks, cooking for him, nursing him, feeding him, dressing and undressing him—I know about it all, I saw it all—and now!"—he paused, staring at her, then made a sudden gesture outward, palms downward, of his two thick hands—

"over, done for, gone forever! It's no good any more, it won't work any more, it can't be brought back any more—forget about it!"

"Oh, I can't! I can't!" she said desperately. "I can't give him up— I can't let him go—he's all I've got. Doctor McGuire," she said earnestly, "ever since I was a kid of ten and you first came to get Papa over one of his sprees, I've fairly worshipped you! I've always felt down in my heart that you were one of the most wonderful people—the most wonderful doctor—in the world! I've always felt that at the end you could do anying—perform a miracle—bring him back. For God's sake, don't go back on me now! Do something —anything you can—but save him, save him."

He was silent for a moment, and just stared at her with his yellow, venous eyes. And when he spoke his voice was filled with the most quiet and utter weariness of despair that she had ever heard:

"Save him?" he said. "My poor child, I can save no one—nothing —least of all myself."

And suddenly she saw that it was true; she saw that he was lost, that he was done for, gone, and that he knew it. His coarse and bloated face was mottled by great black purplish patches, his yellow weary eyes already had the look of death in them; the knowledge of death rested with an unutterable weariness in his burly form, was audible in the short thick labor of his breath. She saw instantly that he was going to die, and with that knowledge her heart was torn with a rending pity as if a knife had been driven through it and twisted there; all of the brightness dropped out of the day, and in that moment it seemed that the whole substance and structure of her life was gone.

The day was a shining one, full of gold and sapphire and sparkle, and in the distance, toward the east, she could see the sweet familiar green of hills. She knew that nothing had been changed at all, and yet even the brightness of the day seemed dull and common to her. It served only to make more mean and shabby the rusty buildings and the street before her. And the bright light filled her with a nameless uneasiness and sense of shame: it seemed to expose her, to show her imperfections nakedly, and instinctively she turned away from it into the drugstore, where there were coolness, artificial lights and gaiety, the clamor of voices and people that she knew. And she knew that most of them had come here for the same reason—because the place gave them a sort of haven, however brief and shabby, from the naked brightness of the day and their sense of indefinable uncertitude and shame—because "it was the only place there was to go."

Several young people, two girls and a boy were coming down among the crowded tables towards one of the mirrored booths against the wall, where another boy and girl were waiting for them. As they approached, she heard their drawling voices, talking "cute nigger-talk" as her mind contemptuously phrased it, the vapid patter phrased to a monotonous formula of "charm," inane, cheap, completely vulgar, and as if they had been ugly little monsters of some world of dwarfs she listened to them with a detached perspective of dislike and scorn.

One of the girls—the one already in the booth—was calling to the others in tones of playful protest, in her "cute," mannered, empty little voice:

"*Hey,* theah, you all! *Wheah* you been! Come *on,* heah, man!" she cried urgently and reproachfully toward the approaching youth— "We been lookin' up an' down faw you! What you been doin', anyhow?" she cried with reproachful curiosity. "We been *waitin'* heah an' waitin' heah until it seemed lak you nevah *would* come! We wuh about to give you up!"

"Child!" another of the girls drawled back, and made a languid movement of the hand—a move indicative of resignation and defeat. "Don't tawk! I thought we nevah would get away. . . . That Jawdan woman came in to see Mothah just as me an' Jim was fixin' to go out, an' child!"—again the languid movement of exhaustion and defeat—"when that woman gits stahted tawkin' you might as well give up! No one else can git a wuhd in edgeways. I'll declayah!" the voice went up, and the hand again made its languid movement of surrender—"I nevah huhd the lak of it in all mah days! That's the tawkinest woman that evah lived. You'd a-died if you could a-seen the way Jim looked. I thought he was goin' to pass right out befoah we got away from theah!"

"Lady," said Jim, who had as yet taken no part in the conversation, "you *said* it! It sho'ly is the truth! That sho is *one* tawkin' woman— an' I don't mean *maybe,* eithah!" He drawled these words out with an air of pert facetiousness, and then looked round him with a complacent smirk on his young, smooth, empty face to see if his display of wit had been noticed and properly appreciated.

And Helen, passing by, kept smiling, plucking at her chin abstractedly, feeling toward these young people a weary disgust that was tinged with a bitter and almost personal animosity.

"Awful little made up girls . . . funny-looking little boys . . . nothing to do but hang out here and loaf . . . walk up and down the street . . . and drink coca-cola all day long . . . and to think it seemed so wonderful to me when I was a kid, to dress up and go up town and come in here where Papa was. . . . How dull and cheap and dreary it all is!"

A little after three o'clock one morning in June, Hugh McGuire was seated at his desk in the little office which stood just to the left of the entrance hall at the Altamont Hospital, of which institution he was chief of staff and principal owner. McGuire's burly bloated form was seated in a swivel chair and sprawled forward, his fat arms resting on the desk which was an old-fashioned roll-top affair with a number of small cubby-holes above and with two parallel rows of drawers below. In the space below the desk and between the surgeon's fat legs there was a gallon jug of corn whiskey.

And on the desk there was a stack of letters which had also been delivered to him the day before. The letters had been written to one of McGuire's own colleagues by a certain very beautiful lady of the town, of whom it is only necessary to say that she was not McGuire's wife and that he had known her for a long time. The huge man—curiously enough, not only a devoted father and a loyal husband, but a creature whose devotion to his family had been desperately intensified by the bitter sense of his one unfaith—had been for many years obsessed by one of those single, fatal and irremediable passions which great creatures of this sort feel only once in life, and for just one woman. Now the obsession of that mad fidelity was gone—exploded in an instant by a spiderly scheme of words upon a page, a packet of torn letters in a woman's hand. Hence, this sense now of a stolid, slow, and cureless anguish in the man, the brutal deliberation of his drunkenness. Since finding these letters upon his desk when he had returned at seven o'clock the night before from his visit to Gant, McGuire had not left his office or moved in his chair, except to bend with a painful grunt from time to time, feel between his legs with a fat hand until he found the jug, and then, holding it with a bear-like solemnity between his paws, drink long and deep of the raw, fiery, and colorless liquid in the jug. He had done this very often, and now the jug was two-thirds empty. As he read, his mouth was half open and a cigarette was stuck on the corner of one fat lip, a look that suggested a comical drunken stupefaction. The hospital had long since gone to sleep, and in the little office there was no sound save the ticking of a clock and McGuire's short, thick, and stertorous breathing. Then when he had finished a letter, he would fold it carefully, put it back in its envelope, rub his thick fingers across the stubble of brown-reddish beard that covered his bloated and discolored face, reach with a painful grunt for the glass jug, drink, and open up another letter.

And from time to time he would put a letter down before he had finished reading it, take up a pen, and begin to write upon a sheet of broad hospital stationery, of which there was a pad upon the desk. And McGuire wrote as he read, slowly, painfully, carefully, with a fixed and drunken attentiveness, no sound except the minute and careful scratching of the pen in his fat hands, and the short, thick stertorous breathing as he bent over the tablet, his cigarette plastered comically at the edge of one fat lip.

McGuire would read the letters over and over, slowly, carefully, and solemnly. Burly, motionless and with no sound save for the short and stertorous labor of his breath he stared with drunken fixity at the pages which he held close before his yellowed eyes, his bloated face. He had read each letter at least a dozen times during the course of the long evening. And each time that he finished reading it, he would fold it carefully with his thick fingers, put it back into its envelope, bend and reach down between his fat legs with a painful grunt, fumble for the liquor jug, and then drink long and deep.

It seemed that a red-hot iron had been driven through his heart and twisted there; the liquor burned in his blood and guts like fire; and each time that he had finished reading that long letter, he would grunt, reach for the jug again, and then slowly and painfully begin to scrawl some words down on the pad before him.

He had done this at least a dozen times that night, and each time after a few scrawled lines, he would grunt impatiently, wad the paper up into a crumpled ball and throw it into the waste-paper basket at his side. Now, a little after three o'clock in the morning, he was writing steadily; there was no sound now in the room save for the man's thick short breathing, and the minute scratching of his pen across the paper. An examination of these wadded balls of paper, however, in the order in which they had been written, would have revealed perfectly the successive states of feeling in the man's spirit.

The first, which was written after his discovery of the letters, was just a few scrawled words without punctuation of grammatical co-herence, ending abruptly in an explosive splintered movement of the pen, and read simply and expressively as follows:

"You bitch you damned dirty trollop of a lying whore you——"

And this ended here in an explosive scrawl of splintered ink, and had been wadded up and thrown away into the basket.

Helen had lain awake for hours in darkness, in a strange coma-tose state of terror and hallucination. There was no sound save the sound of Barton's breathing beside her, but in her strange drugged state she would imagine she heard all kinds of sounds. And she lay there in the dark, her eyes wide open, wide awake, plucking at her large cleft chin abstractedly, in a kind of drugged hypnosis, think-ing like a child:

"What is that? . . . Some one is coming! . . . That was a car that stopped outside. . . . Now they're coming up the steps. . . . There's some one knocking at the door. . . . Oh, my God! . . . It's about Papa! . . . He's had another attack, they've come to get me . . . he's dead! . . . Hugh! Hugh! Wake up!" she said hoarsely, and seized him by the arm. And he woke, his sparse hair touselled, grumbling sleepily.

"Hugh! Hugh!" she whispered. "It's Papa—he's dying . . . they're at the door now! . . . oh, for heaven's sake, get up!" she almost screamed, in a state of frenzied despair and exasperation. "Aren't you good for anything! . . . Don't lie there like a dummy—Papa may be dying! Get up! Get up! There's some one at the door! My God, you can at least go and find out what it is! Oh, get up, get up,

I tell you! . . . Don't leave everything to me! You're a man—you can at least do that much!"—and by now her voice was almost sobbing with exasperation.

"Well, *all* right, *all* right!" he grumbled in a tone of protest, "I'm going! Only give me a moment to find my slippers and my bath-robe, won't you?"

And, hair still twisted, tall, bony, thin to emaciation, he felt around with his bare feet until he found his slippers, stepped gingerly into them, and put on his bath-robe, tying the cord around his waist, and looking himself over in the mirror carefully, smoothing down his rumpled hair and making a shrugging motion of the shoulders. And she looked at him with a tortured and exasperated glare, saying:

"Oh, slow, slow, slow! . . . My God, you're the slowest thing that ever lived! . . . I could walk from here to California in the time it takes you to get out of bed."

"Well, *I'm* going, *I'm* going," he said again with surly protest "I don't want to go to the front door naked—only give me a minute to get ready, won't you?"

"Then, go, go, go!" she almost screamed at him. "They've been there for fifteen minutes. . . . They're almost hammering the door down—for God's sake go and find out if they've come because of Papa, I beg of you."

And he went hastily, still preserving a kind of dignity as he stepped along gingerly in his bath-robe and thin pyjamaed legs. And when he got to the door, there was no one, nothing there. The street outside was bare and empty, the houses along the street dark and hushed with their immense and still attentiveness of night and silence and the sleepers, the trees were standing straight and lean with their still young leafage—and he came back again growling surlily.

"Ah-h, there's no one there! You didn't hear anything! . . . You imagined the whole thing!"

And for a moment her eyes had a dull appeased look, she plucked at her large cleft chin and said in an abstracted tone: "Ah-hah! . . . Well, come on back to bed, honey, and get some sleep."

"Ah, get some sleep!" he growled, scowling angrily as he took off his robe—and scuffed the slippers from his feet. "What chance do

I have to get any sleep any more with you acting like a crazy woman half the time?"

She snickered hoarsely and absently, still plucking at her chin, as he lay down beside her; she kissed him, and put her arms around him with a mothering gesture:

"Well, I know, Hugh," she said quietly, "you've had a hard time of it, but someday we will get away from it and live our own life. I know you didn't marry the whole damn family—but just try to put up with it a little longer: Papa has not got long to live, he's all alone over there in that old house—and she can't realize—she doesn't understand that he is dying—she'll never wake up to the fact until he's gone! I lie here at night thinking about it—and I can't go to sleep . . . I get funny notions in my head." As she spoke these words the dull strained look came into her eyes again, and her big-boned generous face took on the warped outline of hysteria —"You know, I get queer." She spoke the word in a puzzled and baffled way, the dull strained look becoming more pronounced— "I think of him over there all alone in that old house, and then I think they're coming for me—" she spoke the word "they" in this same baffled and puzzled tone, as if she did not clearly understand who "they" were—"I think the telephone is ringing, or that some one is coming up the steps and then I hear them knocking at the door, and then I hear them talking to me, telling me to come quick, he needs me—and then I hear him calling to me 'Baby! Oh, baby— come quick, baby, for Jesus' sake!' "

"You've been made the goat," he muttered, "you've got to bear the whole burden on your shoulders. You're cracking up under the strain. If they don't leave you alone I'm going to take you away from here."

"Do you think it's right?" she demanded in a frenzied tone again, responding thirstily to his argument. "Why, good heavens, Hugh! I've got a right to my own life the same as anybody else. Don't you think I have? I married *you!*" she cried, as if there were some doubt of the fact. "I wanted a home of my own, children, my own life— good heavens, we have a right to that just the same as any one else! Don't you think we have?"

"Yes," he said grimly, "and I'm going to see we get it. I'm tired of seeing you made the victim! If they don't give you some peace or quiet we'll move away from this town."

"Oh, it's not that I mind doing it for Papa," she said more quietly. "Good heavens, I'll do anything to make that poor old man happier. If only the rest of them—well, honey," she said, breaking off abruptly, "let's forget about it! It's too bad you've got to go through all this now, but it won't last forever. After Papa is gone, we'll get away from it. Some day we'll have a chance to lead our own lives together."

"Oh, it's all right about me, dear," the man said quietly, speaking the word "dear" in the precise and nasal way Ohio people have. He was silent for a moment, and when he spoke again, his lean seamed face and care-worn eyes were quietly eloquent with the integrity of devotion and loyalty that was of the essence of his life. "I don't mind it for myself—only I hate to see you get yourself worked up to this condition. I'm afraid you'll crack under the strain: that's all I care about."

"Well, forget about it. It can't be helped. Just try to make the best of it. Now go on back to sleep, honey, and try to get some rest before you have to get up."

And returning her kiss, with an obedient and submissive look on his lean face, he said quietly, "Good night, dear," turned over on his side and closed his eyes.

She turned the light out, and now again there was nothing but darkness, silence, the huge still hush and secrecy of night, her husband's quiet breath of sleep as he lay beside her. And again she could not sleep, but lay there plucking absently at her large cleft chin, her eyes open, turned upward into darkness in a stare of patient, puzzled, and abstracted thought.

For a long time now, McGuire had sat there without moving, sprawled out upon the desk in a kind of drunken stupor. About half-past three the telephone upon the desk began to ring, jangling the hospital silence with its ominous and insistent clangor, but the big burly figure of the man did not stir, he made no move to answer. Presently he heard the brisk heel-taps of Creasman, the night superintendent, coming along the heavy oiled linoleum of the corridor. She entered, glanced quickly at him, and saying, "Shall I take it?" picked up the phone, took the receiver from its hook, said "hello" and listened for a moment. He did not move.

In a moment, the night superintendent said quietly:

"Yes, I'll ask him."

When she spoke to him, however, her tone had changed completely from the cool professional courtesy of her speech into the telephone: putting the instrument down upon the top of the desk, and covering the mouth-piece with her hand, she spoke quietly to him, but with a note of cynical humor in her voice, bold, coarse, a trifle mocking.

"It's your wife," she said. "What shall I tell her?"

He regarded her stupidly for a moment before he answered.

"What does she want?" he grunted.

She looked at him with hard eyes touched with pity and regret.

"What do you think a woman wants?" she said. "She wants to know if you are coming home tonight."

He stared at her, and then grunted:

"Won't go home."

She took her hand away from the mouth-piece instantly, and taking up the phone again, spoke smoothly, quietly, with cool crisp courtesy:

"The doctor will not be able to go home tonight, Mrs. McGuire. He has to operate at seven-thirty. . . . Yes. . . . Yes. . . . At seven-thirty. . . . He has decided it is best to stay here until the operation is over. . . . Yes. . . . I'll tell him. . . . Thank *you.* . . . Good-bye."

She hung up quietly and then turning to him, her hands arched cleanly on starched hips, she looked at him for a moment with a bold sardonic humor.

"What did she say?" he mumbled thickly.

"Nothing," she said quietly. "Nothing at all. What else is there to say?"

He made no answer but just kept staring at her in his bloated drunken way with nothing but the numb swelter of that irremediable anguish in his heart. In a moment, her voice hardening imperceptibly, the nurse spoke quietly again:

"Oh, yes—and I forgot to tell you—you had another call tonight."

He moistened his thick lips, and mumbled:

"Who was it?"

"It was that woman of yours."

There was no sound save the stertorous labor of his breath; he

stared at her with his veined and yellow eyes, and grunted stolidly:
"What did she want?"

"She wanted to know if the doc-taw was theah," Creasman said in
a coarse and throaty parody of refinement. "And is he coming in
tonight? Really, I should like to know. . . . Ooh, yaas," Creasman
went on throatily, adding a broad stroke or two on her own account. "I simply must find out! I cawn't get my sleep in until I
do. . . . Well," she demanded harshly, "what am I going to tell her
if she calls again?"

"What did she say to tell me?"

"She said"—the nurse's tone again was lewdly tinged with parody
—"to tell you that she is having guests for dinner tomorrow night—
this evening—and that you simply *got* to be thöh, you, and your
wife, too—ooh, Gawd, yes!—the Reids are comin', don't-cherknow
—and if you are not thöh Gawd only knows what will happen!"

He glowered at her drunkenly for a moment, and then, waving
thick fingers at her in disgust, he mumbled:

"You got a dirty mouth . . . don't become you. . . . Unlady-like.
. . . Don't like a dirty-talkin' woman. . . . Never did. . . . Unbecomin'. . . . Unlady-like. . . . Nurses all alike . . . all dirty talkers
. . . don't like 'em."

"Oh, dirty talkers, your granny!" she said coarsely. "Now you
leave the nurses alone. . . . They're decent enough girls, most of 'em,
until they come here and listen to you for a month or two. . . . You
listen to me, Hugh McGuire; don't blame the nurses. When it
comes to dirty talking, you can walk off with the medals any day
in the week. . . . Even if I am your cousin, I had a good Christian
raising out in the country before I came here. So don't talk to me
about nurses' dirty talk: after a few sessions with you in the operat-
ing room even the Virgin Mary could use language to fit to make a
monkey blush. So don't blame it on the nurses. Most of them are
white as snow compared to you."

"You're dirty talkers—all of you," he muttered, waving his thick
fingers in her direction. "Don't like it. . . . Unbecomin' in a lady."

For a moment she did not answer, but stood looking at him, arms
akimbo on her starched white hips, a glance that was bold, hard,
sardonic, but somehow tinged with a deep and broad affection.

Then, taking her hands off her hips, she bent swiftly over him, reached down between his legs, and got the jug and lifting it up to the light in order to make her cynical inspection of its depleted contents more accurate, she remarked with ironic approbation:

"My, my! You're doing pretty well, aren't you? . . . Well, it won't be long *now*, will it?" she said cheerfully, and then turning to him abruptly and accusingly, demanded:

"Do you realize that you were supposed to call Helen Gant at twelve o'clock?" She glanced swiftly at the clock. "Just three and a half hours ago. Or did you forget it?"

He passed his thick hand across the reddish unshaved stubble of his beard.

"Who?" he said stupidly, "Where? What is it?"

"Oh, nothing to worry about," she said with a light hard humor. "Just a little case of carcinoma of the prostate. He's going to die anyway, so you've got nothing to worry about at all."

"Who?" he said stupidly again. "Who is it?"

"Oh, just a man," she said gaily. "An old, old man named Mr. Gant.—You've been his physician for twenty years, but maybe you've forgotten him. You know—they come and go; some live and others die—it's all right,—this one's going to die. They'll bury him —it'll all come out right one way or the other—so you've nothing to worry about at all. . . . Even if you kill him," she said cheerfully. "He's just an old, old man with cancer, and bound to die anyway, so promise me you won't worry about it too much, will you?"

She looked at him a moment longer; then, putting her hand under his fat chin, she jerked his head up sharply. He stared at her stupidly with his yellowed drunken eyes, and in them she saw the mute anguish of a tortured animal, and suddenly her heart was twisted with pity for him.

"Look here," she said, in a hard and quiet voice, "what's wrong with you?"

In a moment he mumbled thickly:

"Nothing's wrong with me."

"Is it the woman business again? For God's sake, are you never going to grow up, McGuire? Are you going to remain an overgrown schoolboy all your life? Are you going to keep on eating your heart out over a bitch who thinks that spring is here every time her hind end itches? Are you going to throw your life away, and let your work go to smash because some damned woman in the change of life has done you dirt! What kind of man are you, anyway?" she jeered. "Jesus God! If it's a woman that you want the woods are full of 'em. Besides," she added, "what's wrong with your own wife! She's worth a million of those flossy sluts."

He made no answer and in a moment she went on in a harsh and jeering tone that was almost deliberately coarse:

"Haven't you learned yet, with all you've seen of it, that a piece of tail is just a piece of tail, and that in the dark it doesn't matter one good God-damn whether it's brown, black, white, or yellow?"

Even as she spoke, something cold and surgical in his mind, which no amount of alcohol seemed to dull or blur, was saying accurately: "Why do they all feel such contempt for one another? What is it in them that makes them despise themselves?"

Aloud, however, waving his thick fingers at her in a gesture of fat disgust, he said:

"Creasman, you got a dirty tongue. . . . Don't like to hear a woman talk like that. . . . Never liked to hear a dirty-talkin' woman . . . You're no lady!"

"Ah-h! No lady!" she said bitterly, and let her hands fall in a gesture of defeat. "All right, you poor fool, if that's the way you feel about it, go ahead and drink yourself to death over your 'lady.' That's what's wrong with you."

And, muttering angrily, she left him. He sat there stupidly, without moving, until her firm heel-taps had receded down the silent hall, and he heard a door close. Then he reached down between his knees, and got the jug, and drank again. And again there was nothing in the place except the sound of silence, the rapid ticking of a little clock, the thick short breathing of the man.

Somewhere, far away, across the cool sweet silence of the night, Helen heard the sound of a train. For a moment she could hear the faint and ghostly tolling of its bell, the short explosive blasts of its hard labor, now muted almost into silence, now growing near, immediate as it labored out across the night from the enclosure of a railway cut down by the river's edge; and for an instant she heard the lonely wailing and receding cry of the train's whistle, and then the long heavy rumble of its wheels; and then nothing but silence, darkness, the huge hush and secrecy of night again.

And still plucking at her chin, thinking absently, but scarcely conscious of her thinking, like a child in revery, she thought:

"There is a freight-train going west along the river. Now, by the sound, it should be passing below Patton Hill, just across from where Riverside Park used to be before the flood came and washed it all away. . . . Now it is getting farther off, across the river from the casket factory. . . . Now it is almost gone, I can hear nothing but the sound of wheels . . . it is going west toward Boiling Springs . . . and after that it will come to Wilson City, Tennessee . . . and then to Dover. . . . Knoxville . . . Memphis—after that? I wonder where the train is going . . . where it will be tomorrow night? . . . Perhaps across the Mississippi River, and then on through Arkansas . . . perhaps to St. Louis . . . and then on to—what comes next?" she thought absently, plucking at her chin—"to Kansas City, I suppose . . . and then to Denver . . . and across the Rocky Mountains . . . and across the desert . . . and then across more mountains and then at last to California."

And still plucking at her chin, and scarcely conscious of her thought—not *thinking* indeed so much as reflecting by a series of broken but powerful images all cogent to a central intuition about life—her mind resumed again its sleepless patient speculation:

"How strange and full of mystery life is. . . . Tomorrow we shall all get up, dress, go out on the streets, see and speak to one another—and yet we shall know absolutely nothing about anyone else. . . . I know almost every one in town—the bankers, the lawyers, the butchers, the bakers, the grocers, the clerks in the stores, the Greek restaurant man, Tony Scarsati the fruit dealer, even the niggers down in Niggertown—I know them all, as well as their wives and children—where they came from, what they are doing, all the lies and scandals and jokes and mean stories, whether true or false, that are told about them—and yet I really know nothing about any of them. I know nothing about any one, not even about myself—" and suddenly, this fact seemed terrible and grotesque to her, and she thought desperately:

"What is wrong with people? . . . Why do we never get to know one another? . . . Why is it that we get born and live and die here in this world without ever finding out what any one else is like? . . . No, what is the strangest thing of all—why is it that all our efforts to know people in this world lead only to greater ignorance and confusion than before? We get together and talk, and say we think and feel and believe in such a way, and yet what we really think and feel and believe we never say at all. Why is this? We talk and talk in an effort to understand another person, and yet almost all we say is false: we hardly ever say what we mean or tell the truth —it all leads to greater misunderstanding and fear than before—it would be better if we said nothing. Tomorrow I shall dress and go out on the street and bow and smile and flatter people, laying it on with a trowel, because I want them to like me, I want to make 'a good impression,' to be a 'success'—and yet I have no notion what it is all about. When I pass Judge Junius Pearson on the street, I will smile and bow, and try to make a good impression on him, and if he speaks to me I shall almost fawn upon him in order to flatter my way into his good graces. Why? I do not like him, I hate his long pointed nose, and the sneering and disdainful look upon his face: I think he is 'looking down' on me—but I know that he goes with the 'swell' social set and is invited out to all the parties at Catawba House by Mrs. Goulderbilt and is received by them as a social equal. And I feel that if Junius Pearson should accept me as *his* social equal it would help me—get me forward somehow—make me a success—get *me* an invitation to Catawba House. And yet it would get me nothing; even if I were Mrs. Goulderbilt's closest friend, what good would it do me? But the people I really like and feel at home with are working people of Papa's kind. The people I really like are Ollie Gant, and old man Alec Ramsay, and big Mike Fogarty, and Mr. Jannadeau, and Myrtis, my little nigger servant girl, and Mr. Luther, the fish man down in the market, and the nigger Jacken, the fruit and vegetable man, and Ernest Peagram, and Mr. Duncan and the Tarkingtons—all the old neighbors down on Woodson Street—and Tony Scarsati and Mr. Pappas. Mr. Pappas is just a Greek lunchroom proprietor, but he seems to me to be one of the finest people I have ever known, and yet if Junius Pearson saw me talking to him I should try to make a joke out of it—to make a joke out of talking to a Greek who runs a restaurant. In the same way, when some of my new friends see me talking to people like Mr. Jannadeau or Mike Fogarty or Ollie or Ernest Pegram or the Tarkintons or the old Woodson Street crowd, I feel ashamed or embarrassed, and turn it off as a big joke. I laugh about Mr. Jannadeau and his dirty fin-

gers and the way he picks his nose, and old Alec Ramsay and Ernest
Pegram spitting tobacco while they talk, and then I wind up by
appearing to be democratic and saying in a frank and open manner
—'Well, I like them . . . I don't care what any one says' (when no
one has said anything!) , "I like them, and always have. If the truth
is told, they're just as good as any one else!'—as if there is any doubt
about it, and as if I should have to justify myself for being 'democratic.' Why 'democratic'? Why should I apologize or defend myself
for liking people when no one has accused me?

"I'm pushing Hugh ahead now all the time; he's tired and sick
and worn-out and exhausted—but I keep 'pushing him ahead' without knowing what it is we're pushing ahead toward, where it will all
wind up. What is it all about? I've pushed him ahead from Woodson Street up here to Weaver Street: and now this neighborhood has
become old-fashioned—the swell society crowd is all moving out to
Grovemont—opposite the golf-course; and now I'm pushing him to
move out there, build upon the lot we own, or buy a house. I've
'pushed' him and myself until now he belongs to the Rotary Club,
and I belong to the Thursday Literary Club, the Orpheus Society, the
Saturday Musical Guild, the Woman's Club, the Discussion Group,
and God knows what else—all these silly and foolish little clubs in
which we have no interest—and yet it would kill us if we did not
belong to them, we feel that they are a sign that we are 'getting
ahead.' Getting ahead to what?

"And it is the same with all of us: pretend, pretend, pretend—
show-off, show-off, show-off—try to keep up with the neighbors and
to go ahead of them—and never a word of truth; never a word of
what we really feel, and understand and know. The one who shouts
the loudest goes the farthest:—Mrs. Richard Jeter Ebbs sits up on
top of the whole heap, she goes everywhere and makes speeches;
people say 'Mrs. Richard Jeter Ebbs said so-and-so'—and all because
she shouts out everywhere that she is a lady and a member of an
old family and the widow of Richard Jeter Ebbs. And no one in
town ever met Richard Jeter Ebbs, they don't know who he was,
what he did, where he came from; neither do they know who Mrs.
Richard Jeter Ebbs was, or where she came from, or who or what her
family was.

"Why are we all so false, cowardly, cruel, and disloyal toward one another and toward ourselves? Why do we spend our days in doing useless things, in false-pretense and triviality? Why do we waste our lives—exhaust our energy—throw everything good away on falseness and lies and emptiness? Why do we deliberately destroy ourselves this way, when we want joy and love and beauty and it is all around us in the world if we would only take it? Why are we so afraid and ashamed when there is really nothing to be afraid and ashamed of? Why have we wasted everything, thrown our lives away, what is this horrible thing in life that makes us throw ourselves away—to hunt out death when what we want is life? Why is it that we are always strangers in this world, and never come to know one another, and are full of fear and shame and hate and falseness, when what we want is love? Why is it? Why? Why? Why?"

And with that numb horror of disbelief and silence and the dark about her, in her, filling her, it seemed to her suddenly that there was some monstrous and malevolent force in life that held all mankind in its spell and that compelled men to destroy themselves against their will. It seemed to her that everything in life—the things men did and said, the way they acted—was grotesque, perverse, and accidental, that there was no reason for anything.

A thousand scenes from her whole life, seen now with the terrible detachment of a spectator, and dark and sombre with the light of time, swarmed through her mind: she saw herself as a child of ten, hanging on grimly to her father, a thin fury of a little girl, during his sprees of howling drunkenness—slapping him in the face to make him obey her, feeding him hot soup, undressing him, sending for McGuire, "sobering him up" and forcing him to obey her when no one else could come near him. And she saw herself later, a kind of slavey at her mother's boarding house in St. Louis during the World's Fair, drudging from morn to night, a grain of human dust, an atom thrust by chance into the great roar of a distant city, or on an expedition as blind, capricious, and fatally mistaken as all life. Later, she saw herself as a girl in high school, she remembered her dreams and hopes, the pitiably mistaken innocence of her vision of the world; her grand ambitions to "study music," to follow a "career in grand opera"; later still, a girl of eighteen or twenty, amorous of life, thirsting for the great cities and voyages of the world, playing popular songs of the period—"Love Me and the World is Mine," "I Wonder Who's Kissing Her Now," "Till the Sands of the Desert

Grow Cold," and so on—for her father, as he sat, on summer evenings, on his porch; a little later, "touring" the little cities of the
South, singing and playing the popular "rhythm" and sentimental
ballads of the period in vaudeville and moving-picture houses. She
remembered how she had once been invited to a week-end house
party with a dozen other young men and women of her acquaintance, and of how she had been afraid to go, and how desperately
ashamed she was when she had "to go in swimming" with the others,
and to "show her figure," her long skinny legs, even when they were
concealed by the clumsy bathing dress and the black stockings of the
period. She remembered her marriage then, the first years of her life
with Barton, her tragic failure to have children, and the long horror
of Gant's last years of sickness—the years of sombre waiting, the
ever-impending terror of his death.

A thousand scenes from this past life flashed through her mind
now, as she lay there in the darkness, and all of them seemed grotesque, accidental and mistaken, as reasonless as everything in life.

And filled with a numb, speechless feeling of despair and nameless
terror, she heard, somewhere across the night, the sound of a train
again, and thought:

"My God! My God! What is life about? We are all living here in
darkness in ten thousand little towns—waiting, listening, hoping—
for what?"

And suddenly, with a feeling of terrible revelation, she saw the
strangeness and mystery of man's life; she felt about her in the darkness the presence of ten thousand people, each lying in his bed,
naked and alone, united at the heart of night and darkness, and
listening, as she, to the sounds of silence and of sleep. And suddenly
it seemed to her that she knew all these lonely, strange, and unknown watchers of the night, that she was speaking to them, and
they to her, across the fields of sleep, as they had never spoken
before, that she knew men now in all their dark and naked loneliness, without falseness and pretense as she had never known them.
And it seemed to her that if men would only listen in the darkness,
and send the language of their naked lonely spirits across the silence
of the night, all of the error, falseness and confusion of their lives
would vanish, they would no longer be strangers, and each would
find the life he sought and never yet had found.

"If we only could!" she thought. "If we only could!"

Then, as she listened, there was nothing but the huge hush of night and silence, and far away the whistle of a train. Suddenly the phone rang.

A few minutes after four o'clock that morning as McGuire lay there sprawled upon his desk, the phone rang again. And again he made no move to answer it: he just sat there, sprawled out on his fat elbows, staring stupidly ahead. Creasman came in presently, as the telephone continued to disturb the silence of the hospital with its electric menace and this time, without a glance at him, answered.

It was Luke Gant. At four o'clock his father had had another hemorrhage, he had lost consciousness, all efforts to awaken him had failed, they thought he was dying.

The nurse listened carefully for a moment to Luke's stammering and excited voice, which was audible across the wire even to McGuire. Then, with a troubled and uncertain glance toward the doctor's sprawled and drunken figure, she said quietly:

"Just a minute. I don't know if the doctor is in the hospital. I'll see if I can find him."

Putting her hand over the mouthpiece, keeping her voice low, she spoken urgently to McGuire:

"It's Luke Gant. He says his father has had another hemorrhage and that they can't rouse him. He wants you to come at once. What shall I tell him?"

He stared drunkenly at her for a moment, and then waving his finger at her in a movement of fat impatience, he mumbled thickly:

"Nothing to do. . . . No use. . . . Can't be stopped. . . . People expect miracles. . . . Over. . . . Done for. . . . Tell him I'm not here . . . gone home," he muttered, and sprawled forward on the desk again.

Quietly, coolly, the nurse spoke into the phone again:

"The doctor doesn't seem to be here at the hospital, Mr. Gant. Have you tried his house? I think you may find him at home."

"No, G-g-g-god-damn it!" Luke fairly screamed across the wire. "He's not at home. I've already t-t-tried to get him there. . . . N-n-n-now you look here, Miss Creasman!" Luke shouted angrily. "You c-c-can't kid me: I know where he is—He's d-d-down there at the hospital right now—wy-wy-wy—stinkin' drunk! You t-t-tell him,

G-g-g-god-damn his soul, that if he d-d-doesn't come, wy-wy-wy—
P-p-p-papa's in a bad way and and and f-f-frankly, I f'ink it's a
rotten shame for McGuire to act this way, wy-wy-wy after he's
b-b-been Papa's doctor all these years. F-f-frankly, I do!"

"Nothing to be done," mumbled McGuire. "No use. . . . All
over."

"I'll see what I can do, Mr. Gant," said Creasman quietly. "I'll let
the doctor know as soon as he comes in!"

"C-c-c-comes in, hell!" Luke stammered bitterly. "I'm c-c-comin'
down there myself and g-g-get him if I have to wy wy wy d-d-drag
him here by the s-s-scruff of his neck!" And he hung up the receiver
with a bang.

The nurse put the phone down on the desk, and turning to
McGuire, said:

"He's raving. He says if you don't go, he'll come for you and get
you himself. Can't you pull yourself together enough to go? If you
can't drive the car, I'll send Joe along to drive it for you—" Joe was
a Negro orderly in the hospital.

"What's the use?" McGuire mumbled thickly, a little angrily.
"What the hell do these people expect anyway? . . . I'm a doctor,
not a miracle man. . . . The man's gone, I tell you . . . the whole
gut and rectum is eaten away . . . he can't live over a day or two
longer at the most. . . . It's cruelty to prolong it: why the hell should
I try to?"

"All right," she said resignedly. "Do as you please. Only, he'll
probably be here for you himself in a few minutes. And since they
do feel that way about it, I think you might make the effort just to
please them."

"Ah-h," he muttered wearily. "People are all alike. . . . They all
want miracles."

"Are you just going to sit here all night?" she said with a rough
kindliness. "Aren't you going to try to get a little sleep before you
operate?"

He waved fat fingers at her, and did not look at her.

"Leave me alone," he mumbled; and she left him.

When she had gone, he fumbled for the jug and drank again. And
then, while time resumed its sanded drip, and he sat there in the
silence, he thought again of the old dying man whom he had known

first when he was a young doctor just beginning and with whom his own life had been united by so many strange and poignant memories. And thinking of Gant, the strangeness of the human destiny returned to haunt his mind; there was something that he could not speak, a wonder and a mystery he could not express.

He fumbled for the jug again, and holding it solemnly in his bearish paws, drained it. Then he sat for several minutes without moving. Finally, he got up out of his chair, grunting painfully, and fumbling for the walls, lurched out into the hall, and began to grope his way across the corridor toward the stairs. And the first step fooled him as it had done so many time before; he missed his step, even as a man stepping out in emptiness might miss, and came down heavily upon his knees. Then, pushing with his hands, he slid out peacefully on the oiled green linoleum, pillowed his big head on his arms with a comfortable grunt, and sprawled out flat, already half dead to the world. It was in this position—also a familiar one —that Creasman, who had heard his thump when falling, found him. And she spoke sharply and commandingly as one might speak to a little child:

"You get right up off that floor and march upstairs," she said. "If you want to sleep you're going to your room; you'll not disgrace us sleeping on that floor."

And like a child, as he had done so many times before, he obeyed her. In a moment, as her sharp command reached his drugged consciousness, he grunted, stirred, climbed painfully to his knees, and then, pawing carefully before him like a bear, unable or unwilling to stand up, he began to crawl slowly up the stairs.

And it was in this position, half-way up, pawing his burly and cumbersome way on hands and knees, that Luke Gant found him. Cursing bitterly, and stammering with wild excitement, the young man pulled him to his feet, Creasman sponged off the great bloated face with a cold towel and assisted by Joe Corpering, the Negro man, they got him down the stairs and out of the hospital into Luke's car.

Dawn was just breaking, a faint glimmer of blue-silver light, with the still purity of the earth, the sweet fresh stillness of the trees, the bird-song waking. The fresh sweet air, Luke's breakneck driving through the silent streets, the roaring motor—finally, the familiar and powerfully subdued emotion of a death chamber, the repressed hysteria, the pain and tension and the terror of shocked flesh, the aura of focal excitement around the dying man revived McGuire.

Gant lay still and almost lifeless on the bed, his face already tinged with the ghostly shade of death, his breath low, hoarse, faintly rattling, his eyes half-closed, comatose, already glazed with death.

McGuire sighted at his shining needle, and thrust a powerful injection of caffeine, sodium, and benzoate into the arm of the dying man. This served partially to revive him, got him through the low ebb of the dark, his eyes opened, cleared, he spoke again. Bright day and morning came, and Gant still lived. And with the light, their impossible and frenzied hopes came back again, as they have always been revived in desperate men. And Gant did not die that day. He lived on.

By the middle of the month Gant had a desperate attack; for four days now he was confined to bed, he began to bleed out of the bowels, he spent four sleepless days and night of agony, and with the old terror of death awake again and urgent, Helen telegraphed to Luke, who was in Atlanta, frantically imploring him to come home at once.

With the arrival of his son and under the stimulation of Luke's vital and hopeful nature, the old man revived somewhat: they got him out of bed, and into a new wheel-chair which they had bought for the purpose, and the day of his arrival Luke wheeled his father out into the bright June sunshine, and through the streets of the town, where he again saw friends, and renewed acquaintances he had not known in years.

The next day Gant seemed better. He ate a good breakfast, by ten o'clock he was up and Luke had dressed him, got him into the new wheel-chair and was wheeling him out on the streets again in the bright sunshine. All along the streets of the town people stopped and greeted the old man and his son, and in Gant's weary old brain there may perhaps have been a flicker of an old hope, a feeling that he had come to life again.

"Wy-wy-wy-wy, he's f-f-f-fine as silk!" Luke would sing out in answer to the question of some old friend or acquaintance, before his father had a chance to answer. "Aren't you, C-C-C-Colonel?

Wy-wy-wy-wy Lord God! Mr. P-p-p-p-parker, you couldn't k-k-k-kill him with a wy wy wy wy wy with a b-b-butcher's cleaver. He'll be here when you and I bofe are p-p-p-pushing daisies." And Gant, pleased, would smile feebly, puffing from time to time at a cigar in the unaccustomed, clumsy, and pitifully hopeful way sick men have.

Towards one o'clock Gant began to moan with pain again, and to entreat his son to make haste and take him home. When they got back before the house, Luke brought the wheel chair to a stop, and helped his father to get up. His stammering solicitude and over-extravagant offers of help served only to exasperate and annoy the old man who, still moaning feebly, and sniffling with trembling lip, said petulantly:

"No, no, no. Just leave me alone to try to get a moment's peace, I beg of you, I ask you, for Jesus' sake."

"Wy-wy-wy-wy, all right, P-p-p-papa," Luke stammered with earnest cheerfulness. "Wy-wy-wy, you're the d-d-d-doctor. Wy-wy, I'll just wheel the chair up on the porch and then I'll c-c-come back to your room and f-f-f-fix you up in a j-j-j-j-jiffy."

"Oh, Jesus, I don't care what you do. . . . Do what you like," Gant moaned. "I'm in agony. . . . O Jesus!" he wept. "It's fearful, it's awful, it's cruel—just leave me alone, I beg of you," he sniffled.

"Wy-wy-wy, yes, sir, P-p-p-papa—wy, you're the doctor," Luke said. "Can you make it by yourself all right?" he said anxiously, as his father, leaning heavily upon his cane, started up the stone steps toward the walk that led up to the house.

"Why, yes, now, son," Eliza, who had heard their voices and come out on the porch, now said diplomatically, seeing that Luke's well-meant but stammering solicitude had begun to irritate his father. "Mr. Gant doesn't want any help—you put the car up, son, and leave him alone, he's able to manage all right by himself."

And Luke, muttering respectfully, "Wy-wy-wy, yes, sir, P-p-p-papa, you're the d-d-doctor," stopped then, lifted the chair up to the walk, and began to push it toward the house, not however without a troubled glance at the old man who was walking slowly and feebly toward the porch steps. And for a moment, Eliza stood surveying them and then turned, to stand looking at her house reflectively before she entered it again, her hands clasped loosely at her waist, her lips pursed in a strong reflective expression in which the whole pride of possession, her living and inseparable unity with this gaunt old house, was powerfully evident.

It was at this moment while she stood planted there upon the sidewalk looking at the house, that the thing happened. Gant, still moaning feebly to himself, had almost reached the bottom of the steps when suddenly he staggered, a scream of pain and horror was torn from him; in that instant, the walking cane fell with a clatter to the concrete walk, his two great hands went down to his groin in a pitiable clutching gesture and crying out loudly: "O Jesus! Save me! Save me!" he fell to his knees, still clutching at his entrails with his mighty hands.

Even before Eliza got to him, her flesh turned rotten at the sight. Blood was pouring from him; the bright arterial blood was already running out upon the concrete walk, the heavy black cloth of Gant's trousers was already sodden, turning purplish with the blood; the blood streamed through his fingers, covering his great hands. He was bleeding to death through the genital organs.

Eliza rushed toward him at a strong clumsy gait; she tried to lift him, he was too big for her to handle, and she screamed to Luke for help. He came at once, running at top speed across the yard and, scarcely pausing in his stride, he picked up Gant's great figure in his arms—it felt as light and fleshless as a bundle of dry sticks—and turning to his mother, said curtly:

"Call Helen! Quick! I'll take him to his room and get his clothes off."

And holding the old man as if he were a child, he fairly raced up the steps and down the hall, leaving a trail of blood behind him as he went.

Eliza, scarcely conscious of what she did, paused just long enough to pick up Gant's black felt hat and walking stick which had fallen to the walk. Then, her face white and set as a block of marble, she rushed up the steps and down the hall toward the telephone. Now that the end had come, after all the years of agony and waiting, the knowledge filled her with an unbelievable, an incredulous horror. In another moment she was talking to her daughter:

"Oh, child, child," she said in a low tone of utter terror, "come quick! . . . Your father's bleeding to death!"

There was a gasp, a sob of anguish and surprise, half broken in the throat, the receiver was banged on the hook without an answer: within four minutes Helen had arrived, Barton, usually a deliberate and cautious driver, having taken the dangerous hills and curves between at murderous speed.

As she entered the hall, her mother had just finished phoning to McGuire. Without a word of greeting the two women rushed back through the rear hall towards Gant's room; when they got there Luke had already finished undressing him. Gant lay half propped on pillows still holding his great hands clutched around his genitals, the sheet beneath him was already soaked with blood, a red wet blot that spread horribly, sickeningly even as they looked. Gant's cold-gray eyes were bright with terror. As his daughter entered the room, he looked at her with the pitiable entreaty of a child, a look that tore at her heart, that begged her—the only one on earth who could, the only one who through black years of horror actually had —by some miracle of strength and grace to save him. And even as he looked at her with pitiable entreaty, she saw that he was gone, that he was dying, and that he knew it. Cold terror drank her heart; without a word she seized a towel, pulled his great hands away from that fount of jetting blood and covered him. By the time McGuire arrived, they had got a fresh sheet under him: but the spreading horror of the great red blot could not be checked, the sheet was soaking in bright blood the moment that they got it down.

McGuire came in and took one look, then turned toward the window, fumbling in his pocket for a cigarette. Helen came to him and seized him by his burly arms, unconsciously shaking him in the desperation of her entreaty.

"You've got to make it stop," she said hoarsely, "you've got to! You've got to!"

He stared at her for a moment, then stuck the cigarette in the corner of his thick lip, and barked coarsely:

"Stop what? What the hell do you think I am—Jehovah?"

"You've got to! You've got to!" she muttered again, her large gaunt face strained with hysteria—and then, suddenly, abruptly, quietly:

"What's to be done?"

He did not answer for a moment; he stared out the window, his coarse, bloated and brutally good face patched and mottled in late western light.

"You'd better wire the others," he grunted. "That is, if you want them here. Tell Steve and Daisy to come on. They may make it. Where's Eugene?"

"Boston."

He shrugged his burly shoulders and said nothing for a moment. "All right. Tell him to come on."

"How long?" she whispered.

Again he shrugged his burly shoulders, but made no answer. He lit his cigarette, and turned toward the bed: nothing could be heard except Luke's heavy and excited breathing. Both towel and sheet were red and wet again. Gant remained motionless, his great hands clasped upon the towel, his eyes bright with terror and pitiable entreaty. McGuire opened his old leather case, squinted at the needle and loaded it. Then, the cigarette still plastered on his fat lip, coiling smoke, he walked over to the bed and even as Gant raised his fear-bright eyes to him, he took him by his stringy arm, and grunting "All right, W. O.," he plunged the needle in above the elbow. Gant moaned a little, and relaxed insensibly after the needle had gone in: in a few minutes his eyes grew dull, and his great hands loosened in their clutch.

He bled incredibly. It was unbelievable that an old cancer-riddled spectre of a man should have so much blood in him. One has often heard the phrase "bled white," and that is literally what happened to him. Some liquid still came from him, but it was almost colorless, like water. There was no more blood left in him. And even then he did not die. Instead, as if to compensate him for all these years of agony and mortal terror, this bitter clutch on life so desperately relinquished, there came now a period of almost total peace and clarity. And Helen, grasping hope fiercely from that unaccustomed tranquillity, tried to hearten him and herself with futile words; she even seized him by his shoulders and shook him a little, saying:

"Why, you're all right! You're going to be all right now! The worst is over—you'll get well now! Don't you know it?"

And Gant covered her fingers with his own great hand and, smiling a little and shaking his head, looked at her, saying in a low and gentle voice:

"Oh, no, baby. I'm dying. It's all right now."

And in her heart, she knew at last that she was beaten; yet she would not give up. The final stop of that horrible flow of blood which had continued unabated for a day, the unaccustomed tranquil clarity of Gant's voice and mind, awakened in her again all the old unreasoning hopefulness of her nature, its desperate refusal to accept the ultimate.

"Oh," she said that night to Eliza, shaking her head with a strong movement of negation—"you can't tell me! Papa's not going to die yet! He'll pull through this just like he's pulled through all those other spells. Why, his mind is as clear and sound as a bell! He knows everything that's going on around him! He hasn't talked in years as he talked to me tonight—he was more like his old self than he's been since he took sick."

"Why, yes," Eliza answered instantly, eagerly catching up the drift of her daughter's talk, and pursuing it with the web-like, invincibly optimistic hopefulness of her own nature.

"Why, yes," she went on, pursing her lips reflectively and speaking in a persuasive manner. "And, see here, now!—Say!—Why, you know, I got to studyin' it over tonight and it's just occurred to me—now I'll tell you what *my* theory is! I believe that that old growth—that awful old thing—that—well, I suppose, now, you might say—that *cancer*," she said, making a gesture of explanation with her broad hand—"whatever it is, that awful old thing that has been eating away inside him there for years—" here she pursed her lips powerfully and shook her head in a short convulsive tremor of disgust—"well, now, I give it as my theory that the whole thing tore loose in him yesterday—when he had that attack—and," she paused deliberately, looked her daughter straight in the eyes, and went on with a slow and telling force—"and that he has simply gone and got that rotten old thing out of his system."

"Then, you mean—" Helen began eagerly, seizing at this fantastic straw as if it were the rock by which her drowning hope might be saved—"you mean, Mama——"

"Yes, sir!" said Eliza, shaking her head slowly and positively. "That's exactly what I mean! I think nature has taken its own course—I think nature has succeeded in doing what all the doctors and hospitals in the world were not able to do—for you can rest assured," and here she paused, looking her daughter gravely in the eyes—"you can rest assured that nature is the best physician in the end! Now, I've always said as much, and all the best authorities agree with me. Why, yes, now!—here!—say!—wasn't I readin' in the paper—oh! here along, you know a week or so ago—Doctor Royal S. Copeland!—yes, sir!—that was the very feller—why, he said, you know—" she went on in explanatory fashion.

"Oh, but, Mama!" Helen said, desperately, unable to make her mind believe this grotesque reasoning, and yet clutching at every word with a pleading entreaty that begged to be convinced.

"Oh, but, Mama, surely Wade Eliot and all those other men at Hopkins couldn't have been wrong! Why, Mama," she cried furiously, yet pleadingly—"you know they couldn't—after all these years—after taking him there for treatment a dozen times or more! Why, Mama, those men are *famous*—the greatest doctors in the world! Oh, surely not! Surely not!" she said desperately, and then gazed at Eliza pleadingly again.

"H'm!" said Eliza, pursing her lips with a little scornful smile. "It won't be the first time that a doctor has been wrong—I don't care how famous they may be! You can rest assured of that! It's always been my opinion that they're wrong about as often as they're right—only you can't prove it on 'em. They *bury* their mistakes." She was silent a moment, looking at her daughter in a sudden, straight and deadly fashion, with a little smile at the corners of her mouth. "Now, child, I want to tell you something. . . . I want to tell you what I saw today." Again she was silent, looking straight in her daughter's eyes, smiling her quiet little smile.

"What? What was it, Mama?" Helen demanded eagerly.

"Did you ever take a good look at that maple tree out front that stands on your right as you come in the house?"

"Why, no," Helen said in a bewildered tone. "How do you mean?"

"Well," said Eliza calmly, yet with a certain triumph in her voice, "you just take a good look at it tomorrow. That's all."

"But why—I can't see—how do you mean, Mama?"

"Now, child—" Eliza pursued her subject deliberately, with a ruminant relish of her strong pursed lips—"I was born and brought up in the country—close to the lap of Mother Earth, as the sayin' goes—and when it comes to *trees*—why, I reckon there's mighty little about 'em that I don't know. . . . Now here," she said abruptly, coming to the centre of her argument—"did you ever see a tree that had a big hollow gash down one side—that looked like it had all been eaten an' rotted out by some disease that had been destroyin' it?"

"Why, yes," Helen said, in a puzzled voice. "But I don't see yet——"

"Well, child, I'll tell you, then," said Eliza, both voice and worn brown eyes united in their portents of a grave and quiet earnestness —"that tree doesn't *always* die! You'll see trees that have had that happen to them—and they *cure* themselves! You can see where some old rotten growth has eaten into them—and then you can see where the tree has got the best of it—and grown up again—as sound and healthy as it *ever* was—around that old rotten growth. And that," she said triumphantly, "that is just exactly what has happened to that maple in the yard. Oh, you can *see* it!" she cried positively, at the same time making an easy descriptive gesture with her wide hand—"you can see where it has lapped right around that old growth—made a sort of fold, you know—and here it is just as sound and healthy as it ever was!"

"Then you mean?——"

"I mean," said Eliza in her straight and deadly fashion—"I mean that if a tree can do it, a *man* can do it—and I mean that if any man alive could do it your daddy is that man—for he's had as much strength and vitality as any man I ever saw—and *more* than a tree!" she cried. "Lord! I've seen him do enough to kill a *hundred* trees— the things *he's* done and managed to get over would kill the strongest tree that ever lived!"

"Oh, but Mama, surely not!" said Helen, laughing, and beginning to pluck at her chin in an abstracted manner, amused and tickled in spite of herself by her mother's extraordinary reasoning. "You know that a man is not built the same way as a tree!"

"Why," Eliza cried impatiently, "why not! They're both Nature's products, aren't they? Now, here," she said persuasively, "just stop and consider the thing for a moment. Just imagine for a moment that *you're* the tree." Here she took her strong worn fingers and traced a line down Helen's stomach. "Now," she went on persuasively, "you've got some kind of growth inside you—call it what you like—a tumor, a growth, a cancer—anything you will—and your *healthy* tissues get to work to get the *best* of that growth—to build up a wall around it—to destroy it—to replace it with sound tissues, weed it out! Now," she said, clenching her fingers in a loose but powerful clasp—"if a *tree* can do that, doesn't it stand to reason that a *man* can do the same! Why, I wouldn't doubt it for a moment!" she cried powerfully. "Not a bit of it."

Thus the two women talked together according to the laws of their nature—the one with an invincible and undaunted optimism that persuaded itself in the octopal pursuit of its own reasonings, the other clutching like a drowning person at a straw.

He had not heard from any of his family in some weeks but late that night, while he was reading in his room on Trowbridge Street, he received the following telegram from home: "Father very ill doctor says cannot live come at once." The telegram was signed by his mother.

He telephoned the railway information offices and was informed that there was a train for New York and the South in about an hour. If he hurried, he could make it. He did not have enough money for the fare, he knew that he might hunt up Starwick, Dodd, Professor Hatcher, or other people that he knew, and get the money, but the delay would make him miss the train. Accordingly, he appealed to the person he knew best in the house, and who would be, he thought, most likely to help him. This was Mr. Wang, the Chinese student.

Mr. Wang was as good-hearted as he was stupid and childlike and now, faced with the need of getting money at once, the boy appealed to him. Mr. Wang came to his door and blinked owlishly; behind him the room was a blur of smoke and incense, and the big cabinet victrola was giving forth for the dozenth time that evening the hearty strains of "Yes, We have No Bananas."

When Mr. Wang saw him, his round yellow face broke into a foolish crease of merriment, he began to shake his finger at the young man waggishly, and his throat already beginning to choke and squeak a little with his jest, he said:

"I s'ink lest night I see you with nice—" Something in the other's manner cut him short; he stopped, his round foolish face grew wondering and solemn, and in a doubtful and inquiring tone, he said:

"You say——?"

"Listen, Wang: I've just got this telegram from home. My father is very sick—they think that he is dying. I've got to get money to go home at once. I need fifty dollars: can you let me have it?"

As Mr. Wang listened, his sparkling eyes grew dull as balls of tar, his round yellow moon of face grew curiously impassive. When the boy had finished, the Chinese thrust his hands into the wide flowered sleeves of his dressing gown, and then with a curious formal stiffness said:

"Will you come in? Please."

The boy entered, and Mr. Wang, closing the door, turned, thrust his hand in his sleeves again, marched across the room to a magnificent teak-wood desk and opening a small drawer, took out a roll of bills, peeled off two twenties and a ten, and coming back to where his visitor was standing, presented the money to him with a stiff bow, and his round face still woodenly impassive, said again:

"Please."

The young man seized the money and saying, "Thank you, Wang, I'll send it to you as soon as I get home," ran back to his room and began to hurl clothing, shirts, socks, toilet articles, into his valise as hard as he could. He had just finished when there was a tapping on the door and the Chinese appeared again. He marched into the room with the same ceremonious formality that had characterized his former conduct and bowing stiffly again, presented the boy with two magnificent fans of peacock feathers of which the lacquered blades were delicately and beautifully engraved.

And bowing stiffly again, and saying, "Please!" he turned and marched out of the room, his fat hands thrust into the wide sleeves of the flowered dressing gown.

Thirty minutes later he was on his way, leaving behind him, in the care of Mrs. Murphy, most of his belongings—the notebooks, letters, books, old shoes, worn-out clothes and battered hats, the thousands of pages of manuscript that represented the accretions of two years—that immense and nondescript collection of past events, foredone accomplishment, and spent purposes, the very sight of which filled him with weariness and horror but which, with the huge acquisitive mania of his mother's blood, he had never been able to destroy.

In this way he left Cambridge and a life he had known for two years; instantly re-called, drawn back by the hand of death into the immediacy of a former life that had grown strange as dreams. It was toward the end of June, just a day or two before the commencement exercises at the university. That year he had been informed of his eligibility for the Master's degree—a degree he had neither sought nor known he had earned and, at the time he had received the telegram, he had been waiting for the formal exercises at which he would receive the degree—a wait prompted more by his total indecision as to his future purpose than by any other cause. Now, with explosive suddenness, his purpose had been shaped, decided for him, and with the old feeling of groping bewilderment, he surveyed the history of the last two years and wondered why he had come, why he was here, toward what blind goal he had been tending: all that he had to "show" for these years of fury, struggle, homelessness and hunger with an academic distinction which he had not aimed at, and on which he placed small value.

And it was in this spirit that he left the place. Rain had begun to fall that night, it fell now in torrential floods. The gay buntings and Japanese lanterns with which the Harvard Yard were already decked were reduced to sodden ruin, and as he raced towards the station in a taxi, the streets of Cambridge, and the old, narrow, twisted and familiar lanes of Boston were deserted—pools of wet light and glittering ribbons swept with storm.

When he got to the South station he had five minutes left to buy his ticket and get on his train. In spite of the lashing storm and the lateness of the hour, that magnificent station, which at that time—before the later "improvements" had reduced it to a glittering sterility of tile and marble—was one of the most thrilling and beautiful places in the world, was still busy with the tides of people that hurry forever through the great stations of America, and that no violence of storm can check.

The vast dingy sweep of the cement concourse outside the train-gates was pungent, as it had always been, with the acrid and powerfully exciting smell of engine smoke, and beyond the gates, upon a dozen tracks, great engines, passive and alert as cats, purred and panted softly, with the couched menace of their tremendous stroke. The engine smoke rose up straight in billowing plumes to widen under vaulting arches, to spread foggily throughout the enormous spaces of the grimy sheds. And beside the locomotives, he could see the burly denimed figures of the engineers, holding flaming torches and an oil-can in their hands as they peered and probed through the shining flanges of terrific pistoned wheels much taller than their heads. And forever, over the enormous cement concourse and down the quays beneath the powerful groomed attentiveness of waiting trains the tides of travellers kept passing, passing, in their everlasting change and weft, of voyage and return—of speed and space and movement, morning, cities, and new lands.

And caught up in the vaulting arches of those immense and grimy sheds he heard again the murmurous sound of time—that sound remote and everlasting, distilled out of all the movement, frenzy, and unceasing fury of our unresting lives, and yet itself detached, as calm and imperturbable as the still sad music of humanity, and which, made up out of our million passing lives, is in itself as fixed and everlasting as eternity.

They came, they paused and wove and passed and thrust and vanished in their everlasting tides, they streamed in and out of the portals of that enormous station in unceasing swarm; great trains steamed in to empty them, and others steamed out loaded with their nameless motes of lives, and all was as it had always been, moving, changing, swarming on forever like a river, and as fixed, unutterable in unceasing movement, and in changeless change as the great river is, and time itself.

And within ten minutes he himself, another grain of dust borne onward on this ceaseless tide, another nameless atom in this everlasting throng, another wanderer in America, as all his fathers were before him, was being hurled into the South again in the huge projectile of a train. The train swept swiftly down the gleaming rails, paused briefly at the Back-Bay station, then was on its way again, moving smoothly, powerfully, almost noiselessly now, through the outer stretches of the small dense web of Boston. The town swept smoothly past: old blanks of wall, and old worn brick, and sudden spokes of streets, deserted, lashed with rain, set at the curbs with glittering beetles of its wet machinery and empetalled with its wet and sudden blooms of life. The flushed spoke-wires crossed his vision, lost the moment that he saw them, his forever, gone, like all things else, and never to be captured, seen a million times, yet never known before—as haunting, fading, deathless as a dream, as brief as is the bitter briefness of man's days, as lost and lonely as his life upon the mighty breast of earth, and of America.

Then the great train, gathering now in speed, and mounting smoothly to the summit of its tremendous stroke, was running swiftly through the outskirts of the city, through suburbs and brief blurs of light and then through little towns and on into the darkness, the wild and secret loneliness of earth. And he was going home again into the South and to a life that had grown strange as dreams, and to his father who was dying and who had become a ghost and shadow of his father to him, and to the bitter reality of grief and death. And—how, why, for what reason he could not say—all he felt was the tongueless swelling of wild joy. It was the wild and secret joy that has no tongue, the impossible hope that has no explanation, the savage, silent, and sweet exultancy of night, the wild and lonely visage of the earth, the imperturbable stroke and calmness of the everlasting earth, from which we have been derived, wherein again we shall be compacted, on which all of us have lived alone as strangers, and across which, in the loneliness of night, we have been hurled onward in the projectile flight of mighty trains—America.

Then the great train was given to the night and darkness, the great train hurtled through the night across the lonely, wild, and secret earth, bearing on to all their thousand destinations its freight of unknown lives—some to morning, cities, new lands, and the joy of voyages, and some to known faces, voices, and the hills of home—but which to certain fortune, peace, security, and love, no man could say.

The news that Gant was dying had spread rapidly through the town and, as often happens, that news had brought him back to life again in the heart and living memory of men who had known him, and who had scarcely thought of him for years. That night—the night of his death—the house was filled with some of the men who had known him best since he came to the town forty years before.

Among these people were several of the prominent and wealthy business men of the community: these included, naturally, Eliza's brothers, William and James Pentland, both wealthy lumber dealers, as well as one of her younger brothers, Crockett, who was Will Pentland's bookkeeper, a pleasant, ruddy, bucolic man of fifty years. Among the other men of wealth and influence who had been Gant's friends there was Fagg Sluder, who had made a fortune as a contractor and retired to invest his money in business property, and to spend his time seated in an easy creaking chair before the fire department, in incessant gossip about baseball with the firemen and the young professional baseball players whose chief support he was, whose annual deficit he cheerfully supplied, and to whom he had given the local baseball park, which bore his name. He had been one of Gant's best friends for twenty years, he was immensely fond of him, and now, assembled in the broad front hall in earnest discussion with the Pentlands and Mike Fogarty, another of Gant's friends, and armed with the invariable cigar (despite his doctor's orders he smoked thirty or forty strong black cigars every day), which he chewed on, took out of his mouth, and put back again, with quick, short, unconscious movements, he could be heard saying in the rapid, earnest, stammering tone that was one of the most attractive qualities of his buoyant and constantly hopeful nature:

"I-I-I-I just believe he's going to pull right out of this and-and-and-get well! "Why-why-why-why-when I went in there tonight he spoke right up and-and-and knew me right away!" he blurted out, sticking the cigar in his mouth and chewing on it vigorously a moment—"why-why-why his mind is-is-is-is just as clear—as it always was—spoke right up, you know, says 'Sit down, Fagg'—shook hands with me—knew me right away—talked to me just the same way he always talked—says 'Sit down, Fagg. I'm glad to see you. How have you been?' he says—and-and-and—I just believe he's going to pull right out of this," Mr. Sluder blurted out,—"be damned if I don't—what do *you* say, Will?" and snatching his chewed cigar butt from his mouth he turned eagerly to Will Pentland for confirmation. And Will, who, as usual, had been paring his stubby nails during the whole course of the conversation, his lips pursed in their characteristic family grimace, now studied his clenched fingers for a moment, pocketed his knife and turning to Fagg Sluder, with a little bird-like nod and wink, and with the incomparable Pentland drawl, at once precise, and full of the relish of self-satisfaction, said:

"Well, if any man alive can do it, W. O. is that man. I've seen him time and again when I thought every breath would be his last—and he's got over it every time. I've always said," he went on precisely, and with a kind of deadly directness in his small compact and almost wizened face, "that he has more real vitality than any two men that I ever knew—he's got out of worse holes than this before— and he may do it again." He was silent a moment, his small packed face pursed suddenly in its animal-like grimace that had an almost savage ferocity and a sense of deadly and indomitable power.

Even more astonishing and troubling was the presence of these four older members of the Pentland family gathered together in his mother's hall. As they stood there talking—Eliza with her hands held in their loose and powerful clasp across her waist, Will intently busy with his finger-nails, Jim listening attentively to all that was said, his solid porcine face and small eyes wincing from time to time in a powerful but unconscious grimace, and Crockett, gentlest, ruddiest, most easy-going and dreamy of them all, speaking in his quiet drawling tone and stroking his soft brown mustaches in a gesture of quiet and bucolic meditation, Luke could not recall hav- ing seen so many of them together at one time and the astonishing enigma of their one-ness and variety was strikingly apparent.

What was it?—this indefinable tribal similarity that united these people so unmistakably. No one could say: it would have been difficult to find four people more unlike in physical appearance, more strongly marked by individual qualities. Whatever it was— whether some chemistry of blood and character, or perhaps some physical identity of broad and fleshy nose, pursed reflective lips and flat wide cheeks, or the energies of powerfully concentrated egotisms —their kinship with one another was astonishing and instantly apparent.

In a curious and indefinable way the two groups of men in the hallway had become divided: the wealthier group of prominent citizens, which was composed of the brothers, William, James, and Crockett Pentland, Mr. Sluder, and Eliza, stood in a group near the front hall door, engaged in earnest conversation. The second group, which was composed of working men, who had known Gant well, and worked for or with him—a group composed of Jannadeau the jeweller, old Alec Ramsay and Saul Gudger, who were stone-cutters, Gant's nephew, Ollie Gant, who was a plasterer, Ernest Pegram, the city plumber, and Mike Fogarty, who was perhaps Gant's closest friend, a building contractor—this group, composed of men who had all their lives done stern labor with their hands, and who were really the men who had known the stone-cutter best, stood apart from the group of prominent and wealthy men who were talking so earnestly to Eliza.

And in this circumstance, in this unconscious division, in the air of constraint, vague uneasiness and awkward silence that was evident among these working men, as they stood there in the hallway dressed in their "good clothes," nervously fingering their hats in their big hands, there was something immensely moving. The men had the look that working people the world over have always had when they found themselves suddenly gathered together on terms of social intimacy with their employers or with members of the governing class.

And Helen, coming out at this instant from her father's room into the hall, suddenly saw and felt the awkward division between these two groups of men, as she had never before felt or noticed it, as sharply as if they had been divided with a knife.

And, it must be admitted, her first feeling was an unworthy one— an instinctive wish to approach the more "important" group, to join her life to the lives of these "influential" people who represented to her a "higher" social level. She found herself walking towards the group of wealthy and prominent men at the front of the hall, and away from the group of working men who had really been Gant's best friends.

But seeing the brick-red face of Alec Ramsay, the mountainous figure of Mike Fogarty, suddenly with a sense of disbelief, and almost terrified revelation of the truth, she thought: "Why-why-why—these men are really the closest friends he's got—not rich men like Uncle Will or Uncle Jim or even Mr. Sluder—but men like Mike Fogarty—and Jannadeau—and Mr. Duncan—and Alec Ramsay—and Ernest Pegram—and Ollie Gant—but—but—good heavens, no!" she thought, almost desperately—"surely these are not his closest friends—why-why—of course, they're decent people—they're honest men—but they're only common people—I've always considered them as just *working* men—and-and-and—my God!" she thought, with that terrible feeling of discovery we have when we suddenly see ourselves as others see us—"do you suppose that's the way people in this town think of Papa? Do you suppose they have always thought of him as just a common working man—oh, no! but of course not!" she went on impatiently, trying to put the troubling thought out of her mind. "Papa's not a working man—Papa is a *business* man—a well thought of business man in this community. Papa has always owned property since he came here—he has always had his own shop"—she did not like the sound of the word shop, and in her mind she hastily amended it to "place"—"he always had his own place, up on the public square—he's—he's rented places to other people—he's—he's—oh, of course not!—Papa is different from men like Ernest Pegram, and Ollie, and Jannadeau and Alec Ramsay—why, they're just working men—they work with their hands—Ollie's just an ordinary plasterer—and-and—Mr. Ramsay is nothing but a stone-cutter."

And a small insistent voice inside her said most quietly: "And your father?"

And suddenly Helen remembered Gant's great hands of power and strength, and how they now lay quietly beside him on the bed, and lived and would not die, even when the rest of him had died, and she remembered the thousands of times she had gone to his shop in the afternoon and found the stonecutter in his long striped apron bending with delicate concentration over a stone inscription on a trestle, holding in his great hands the chisel and the heavy wooden mallet the stonecutters use, and remembering, the whole rich and living compact of the past came back to her, in a rush of tenderness and joy and terror, and on that flood a proud and bitter honesty returned. She thought: "Yes, he was a stonecutter, no different from these other men, and these men were his real friends."

And going directly to old Alec Ramsay she grasped his blunt thick fingers, the nails of which were always whitened a little with stone dust, and greeted him in her large and spacious way:

"Mr. Ramsay," she said, "I want you to know how glad we are that you could come. And that goes for all of you—Mr. Jannadeau, and Mr. Duncan, and Mr. Fogarty, and you, Ernest, and you, too, Ollie—you are the best friends Papa has, there's no one he thinks more of, and no one he would rather see."

Mr. Ramsay's brick-red face and brick-red neck became even redder before he spoke, and beneath his grizzled brows his blue eyes suddenly were smoke blue. He put his blunt hand to his mustache for a moment, and tugged at it, then he said in his gruff, quiet, and matter-of-fact voice:

"I guess we know Will about as well as any one, Miss Helen. I've worked for him off and on for thirty years."

At the same moment, she heard Ollie Gant's easy, deep, and powerful laugh, and saw him slowly lift his cigarette in his coarse paw; she saw Jannadeau's great yellow face and massive domy brow, and heard him laugh with guttural pleasure, saying, "Ah-h! I tell you vat! Dat girl has alvays looked out for her datty—she's de only vun dat coult hantle him; efer since she vas ten years olt it has been de same." And she was overwhelmingly conscious of that immeasurable mountain of a man, Mike Fogarty, beside her, the sweet clarity of his blue eyes, and the almost purring music of his voice as he gently laid his mutton of a hand upon her shoulder for a moment, saying,

"Ah, Miss Helen, I don't know how Will could have got along all these years without ye—for he has said the same himself a thousand times—aye! that he has!"

And instantly, having heard these words, and feeling the strong calm presences of these powerful men around her, it seemed to Helen she had somehow re-entered a magic world that she thought was gone forever. And she was immensely content.

At the same moment, with a sense of wonder, she discovered an astonishing thing, that she had never noticed before, but that she must have heard a thousand times;—this was that of all these people, who knew Gant best, and had a deep and true affection for him, there were only two—Mr. Fogarty and Mr. Ramsay—who had ever addressed him by his first name. And so far as she could now remember, these two men, together with Gant's mother, his brothers, his sister Augusta, and a few of the others who had known him in his boyhood in Pennsylvania, were the only people who ever had. And this revelation cast a strange, a lonely and a troubling light upon the great gaunt figure of the stonecutter, which moved her powerfully and which she had never felt before. And most strange of all was the variety of names by which these various people called her father.

As for Eliza, had any of her children ever heard her address her husband as anything but "Mr. Gant"—had she ever called him by one of his first names—their anguish of shame and impropriety would have been so great that they could hardly have endured it. But such a lapse would have been incredible: Eliza could no more have addressed Gant by his first name, than she could have quoted Homer's Greek; had she tried to address him so, the muscles of her tongue would have found it physically impossible to pronounce the word. And in this fact there was somehow, now that Gant was dying, an enormous pathos. It gave to Eliza's life with him a pitiable and moving dignity, the compensation of a proud and wounded spirit for all the insults and injuries that had been heaped upon it. She had been a young country woman of twenty-four when she had met him, she had been ignorant of life, and innocent of the cruelty, the violence, the drunkenness and abuse of which men are capable, she had borne this man fifteen children, of whom eight had come to life, and had for forty years eaten the bread of blood and tears and joy and grief and terror, she had wanted affection and had been given taunts, abuse, and curses, and somehow her proud and wounded spirit had endured with an anguished but unshaken fortitude all the wrongs and cruelties and injustices of which he had been guilty toward her. And now at the very end her pride still had this pitiable distinction, her spirit still preserved this last integrity: she had not betrayed her wounded soul to a shameful familiarity, he had remained to her—in mind and heart and living word—what he had been from the first day that she met him! the author of her grief and misery, the agent of her suffering, the gaunt and lonely stranger who had come into her hills from a strange and a distant people—that furious, gaunt, and lonely stranger with whom by fatal accident her destiny—past hate or love or birth or death or human error and confusion—had been insolubly enmeshed, with whom for forty years she had lived, a wife, a mother, and a stranger—and who would to the end remain to her a stranger—"Mr. Gant."

What was it? What was the secret of this strange and bitter mystery of life that had made of Gant a stranger to all men, and most of all a stranger to his wife? Perhaps some of the answer might have been found in Eliza's own unconscious words when she described her meeting with him forty years before:

"It was not that he was old," she said,—"he was only thirty-three —but he _looked_ old—his _ways_ were old—he had lived so much among old people.—Pshaw!" she continued, with a little puckered smile, "if any one had told me that night I saw him sitting there with Lydia and old Mrs. Mason—that was the very day they moved into the house, the night he gave the big dinner—and Lydia was still alive and, of course, she was ten years older than he was, and that may have had something to do with it—but I got to studying him as he sat there, of course, he was tired and run down and depressed and worried over all that trouble that he'd had in Sidney before he came up here, when he lost everything, and he knew that Lydia was dying, and that was preyin' on his mind—but he _looked_ old, thin as a rake you know, and sallow and run down, and with those _old_ ways he had acquired, I reckon, from associatin' with Lydia and old Mrs. Mason and people like that—but I just sat there studying him as he sat there with them and I said—'Well, you're an old man, aren't you, sure enough?'—pshaw! if any one had told me that night that some day I'd be married to him I'd have laughed at them—I'd have considered that I was marrying an old man—and that's just exactly what a lot of people thought, sir, when the news got out that I was goin' to marry him—I know Martha Patton came running to me, all excited and out of breath—said, 'Eliza! You're not going to marry that old man—you know you're not!'—you see, his _ways_ were old, he _looked_ old, _dressed_ old, _acted_ old—everything he did was old; there was always, it seemed, something strange and old-like about him, almost like he had been born that way."

And it was at this time that Eliza met him, saw him first—"Mr. Gant"—an immensely tall, gaunt, cadaverous-looking man, with a face stern and sad with care, lank, drooping mustaches, sandy hair, and cold-gray staring eyes—"not so old, you know—he was only thirty-three—but he _looked_ old, he _acted_ old, his _ways_ were old— he had lived so much among older people he seemed older than he was—I thought of him as an old man."

This, then, was "Mr. Gant" at thirty-three, and since then, although his fortunes and position had improved, his character had changed little. And now Helen, faced by all these working men, who had known, liked, and respected him, and had now come to see him again before he died—suddenly knew the reason for his loneliness, the reason so few people—least of all, his wife—had ever dared address him by his first name. And with a swift and piercing revelation, his muttered words, which she had heard him use a thousand times when speaking of his childhood—"We had a tough time of it —I tell you what, we did!"—now came back to her with the unutterable poignancy of discovery. For the first time she understood what they meant. And suddenly, with the same swift and nameless pity, she remembered all the pictures which she had seen of her father as a boy and a young man. There were a half dozen of them in the big family album, together with pictures of his own and Eliza's family: they were the small daguerreotypes of fifty years before, in small frames of faded plush, with glass covers, touched with the faint pale pinks with which the photographers of an earlier time tried to paint with life the sallow hues of their photography. The first of these pictures showed Gant as a little boy; later, a boy of twelve, he was standing in a chair beside his brother Wesley, who was seated, with a wooden smile upon his face. Later, a picture of Gant in the years in Baltimore, standing, his feet crossed, leaning elegantly upon a marble slab beside a vase; later still, the young stonecutter before his little shop in the years at Sidney; finally, Gant, after his marriage with Eliza, standing with gaunt face and lank drooping mustaches before his shop upon the square, in the company of Will Pentland, who was at the time his business partner.

And all these pictures, from first to last, from the little boy to the man with the lank drooping mustaches, had been marked by the same expression: the sharp thin face was always stern and sad with care, the shallow cold-gray eyes always stared out of the bony cage-formation of the skull with a cold mournfulness—the whole impression was always one of gaunt sad loneliness. And it was not the loneliness of the dreamer, the poet, or the misjudged prophet, it was just the cold and terrible loneliness of man, of every man, and of the lost American who has been brought forth naked under immense and lonely skies, to "shift for himself," to grope his way blindly through the confusion and brutal chaos of life as naked and unsure as he, to wander blindly down across the continent, to hunt forever for a goal, a wall, a dwelling place of warmth and certitude, a light, a door.

And for this reason, she now understood something about her

father, this great gaunt figure of a stonecutter that she had never understood or thought about before: she suddenly understood his order, sense of decency and dispatch; his love of cleanness, roaring fires, and rich abundance, his foul drunkenness, violence, and howling fury, his naked shame and trembling penitence, his good clothes of heavy monumental black that he always kept well pressed, his clean boiled shirts, wing collars, and his love of hotels, ships, and trains, his love of gardens, new lands, cities, voyages. She knew suddenly that he was unlike any other man that ever lived, and that every man that ever lived was like her father. And remembering the cold and mournful look in his shallow staring eyes of cold hard gray, she suddenly knew the reason for that look, as she had never known it before, and understood now why so few men had ever called him by his first name—why he was known to all the world as "Mr. Gant."

Having joined this group of working men, Helen immediately felt an indefinable but powerful sense of comfort and physical well-being which the presence of such men as these always gave to her. And she did not know why; but immediately, once she had grasped Mr. Ramsay by the hand, and was aware of Mike Fogarty's mountainous form and clear-blue eye above her, and Ollie Gant's deep and lazy laugh, and the deliberate and sensual languor with which he raised his cigarette to his lips with his powerful plasterer's hand, drawing the smoke deep into his strong lungs and letting it trickle slowly from his nostrils as he talked—she was conscious of a feeling of enormous security and relief which she had not known in years.

And this feeling, as with every person of strong sensuous perceptions, was literal, physical, chemical, astoundingly acute. She not only felt an enormous relief and joy to get back to these working people, it even seemed to her that everything they did—the way Mr. Duncan held his strong cheap cigar in his thick dry fingers, the immense satisfaction with which he drew on it, the languid and sensual trickling of cigarette smoke from Ollie Gant's nostrils, his deep, good-natured, indolently lazy laugh, even the perceptible bulge of tobacco-quid in Alec Ramsay's brick-red face, his barely perceptible rumination of it—all these things, though manlike in their nature, seemed wonderfully good and fresh and living to her—

the whole plain priceless glory of the earth restored to her—and gave her a feeling of wonderful happiness and joy.

And later that night when all these men, her father's friends, had gone into his room, filling it with their enormous and full-blooded vitality, as she saw him lying there, wax-pale, bloodless, motionless, yet with a faint grin at the edge of his thin mouth as he received them, as she heard their deep full-fibered voices, Mike Fogarty's lilting Irish, Mr. Duncan's thick Scotch burr, Ollie Gant's deep and lazy laugh, and the humor of Alec Ramsay's deep, gruff and matter-of-fact tone, relating old times—"God, Will!" he said, "at your worst, you weren't in it compared to Wes! He was a holy terror when he drank! Do you remember the day he drove his fist through your plate-glass window right in the face of Jannadeau—and went home then and tore all the plumbing out of the house and pitched the bathtub out of the second-story window into Orchard Street— God! Will!—you weren't in it compared to Wes"—as she heard all this, and saw Gant's thin grin and heard his faint and rusty cackle, his almost inaudible "E'God! Poor Wes!"—she could not believe that he was going to die, the great full-blooded working men filled the room with the vitality of a life which had returned in all its rich and living flood, and seemed intolerably near and familiar—and she kept thinking with a feeling of wonderful happiness and dis- belief: "Oh, but Papa's not going to die! It's not possible! He can't! He can't!"

The dying man himself was no longer to be fooled and duped by hope; he knew that he was done for, and he no longer cared. Rather, as if that knowledge had brought him a new strength—the immense and measureless strength that comes from resignation, and that has vanquished terror and despair—Gant had already consigned himself to death, and now was waiting for it, without weariness or anxiety, and with a perfect and peaceful acquiescence.

This complete resignation and tranquillity of a man whose life had been so full of violence, protest, and howling fury stunned and silenced them, and left them helpless. It seemed that Gant, knowing that often he had lived badly, was now determined to die well. And in this he succeeded. He accepted every ministration, every visit, every stammering reassurance, or frenzied activity, with a passive gratefulness which he seemed to want every one to know. On the evening of the day after his first hemorrhage, he asked for food and Eliza, bustling out, pathetically eager to do something, killed a chicken and cooked it for him.

And as if, from that infinite depth of death and silence from which he looked at her, he had seen, behind the bridling brisk activity of her figure, forever bustling back and forth, saying confusedly—"Why, yes! The very thing! This very minute, sir!"—had seen the white strained face, the stricken eyes of a proud and sensitive woman who had wanted affection all her life, had received for the most part injury and abuse, and who was ready to clutch at any crust of comfort that might console or justify her before he died—he ate part of the chicken with relish, and then looking up at her, said quietly:

"I tell you what—that was a good chicken."

And Helen, who had been sitting beside him on the bed, and feeding him, now cried out in a tone of bantering and good-humored challenge:

"What! Is it better than the ones *I* cook for you! You'd better not say it is—I'll beat you if you do."

And Gant, grinning feebly, shook his head, and answered:

"Ah-h! Your mother is a good cook, Helen. You're a good cook, too—but there's no one else can cook a chicken like your mother!"

And stretching out his great right hand, he patted Eliza's worn fingers with his own.

And Eliza, suddenly touched by that word of unaccustomed praise and tenderness, turned and rushed blindly from the room at a clumsy bridling gait, clasping her hands together at the wrist, her weak eyes blind with tears—shaking her head in a strong convulsive movement, her mouth smiling a pale tremulous smile, ludicrous, touching, made unnatural by her false teeth, whispering over and over to herself, "Poor fellow! Says, 'There's no one else can cook a chicken like your mother.' Reached out and patted me on the hand, you know. Says 'I tell you what, there's no one who can cook a chicken like your mother.' I reckon he wanted to let me know, to tell me, but says, 'The rest of you have all been good to me, Helen's a good cook, but there's no one else can cook like your mother.' "

"Oh, here, here, here," said Helen, who, laughing uncertainly had followed her mother from the room when Eliza had rushed out, and had seized her by the arms, and shook her gently, "good heavens! *Here!* You mustn't carry on like this! You mustn't take it this way! Why, he's all right!" she cried out heartily and shook Eliza again. "Papa's going to be all right! Why, what are you crying for?" she laughed. "He's going to get well now—don't you know that?"

And Eliza could say nothing for a moment but kept smiling that false trembling and unnatural smile, shaking her head in a slight convulsive movement, her eyes blind with tears.

"I tell you what," she whispered, smiling tremulously again and shaking her head, "there was something about it—you know, the way he said it—says, 'There's no one who can come up to your mother' —there was something in the way he said it! Poor fellow, says, 'None of the rest of you can cook like her'—says, 'I tell you what, that was certainly a good chicken'—Poor fellow! It wasn't so much what he said as the way he said it—there was something about it that went through me like a knife—I tell you what it did!"

"Oh, here, here, here!" Helen cried again, laughing. But her own eyes were also wet, the bitter possessiveness that had dominated all her relations with her father, and that had thrust Eliza away from him, was suddenly vanquished. At that moment she began to feel an affection for her mother that she had never felt before, a deep and nameless pity and regret, and a sense of sombre satisfaction.

"Well," she thought, "I guess it's all she's had, but I'm glad she's got that much to remember. I'm glad he said it: she'll always have that now to hang on to."

And Gant lay looking up from that sunken depth of death and silence, his great hands of living power quiet with their immense and passive strength beside him on the bed.

Towards one o'clock that night Gant fell asleep and dreamed that he was walking down the road that led to Spangler's Run. And although he had not been along that road for fifty years everything was as fresh, as green, as living and familiar as it had ever been to him. He came out on the road from Schaefer's farm, and on his left he passed by the little white frame church of the United Brethren, and the graveyard about the church where his friends and family had been buried. From the road he could see the line of family gravestones which he himself had carved and set up after he had returned from serving his apprenticeship in Baltimore. The stones were all alike: tall flat slabs of marble with plain rounded tops, and there was one for his sister Susan, who had died in infancy, and one for his sister Huldah, who had died in childbirth while the war was on, and one for Huldah's husband, a young farmer named Jake Lentz who had been killed at Chancellorsville, and one for the husband of his oldest sister, Augusta, a man named Martin, who had been an itinerant photographer and had died soon after the war, and finally one for Gant's own father. And since there were no stones for his brother George or for Elmer or for John, and none for his mother or Augusta, Gant knew that he was still a young man, and had just recently come home. The stones which he had put up were still white and new, and in the lower right hand corner of each stone, he had carved his own name: W. O. Gant.

It was a fine morning in early May and everything was sweet and green and as familiar as it had always been. The graveyard was carpeted with thick green grass, and all around the graveyard and the church there was the incomparable green velvet of young wheat. And the thought came back to Gant, as it had come to him a thousand times, that the wheat around the graveyard looked greener and richer than any other wheat that he had ever seen. And beside him on his right were the great fields of the Schaefer farm, some richly carpeted with young green wheat, and some ploughed, showing great bronze-red strips of fertile nobly swelling earth. And behind him on the great swell of the land, and commanding that sweet and casual scene with the majesty of its incomparable lay was Jacob Schaefer's great red barn and to the right the neat brick house with the white trimming of its windows, the white picket fence, the green yard with its rich tapestry of flowers and lilac bushes and the massed leafy spread of its big maple trees. And behind the house the hill rose, and all its woods were just greening into May, still smoky, tender and unfledged, gold-yellow with the magic of young green. And before the woods began there was the apple orchard halfway up the hill; the trees were heavy with the blossoms and stood there in all their dense still bloom incredible.

And from the greening trees the bird-song rose, the grass was thick with the dense gold glory of the dandelions, and all about

him were a thousand magic things that came and went and never
could be captured. Below the church, he passed the old frame house
where Elly Spangler, who kept the church keys, lived, and there
were apple trees behind the house, all dense with bloom, but the
house was rickety, unpainted and dilapidated as it had always been,
and he wondered if the kitchen was still buzzing with a million flies,
and if Elly's half-wit brothers, Jim and Willy, were inside. And
even as he shook his head and thought, as he had thought so many
times "Poor Elly," the back door opened and Willy Spangler, a man
past thirty wearing overalls, and with a fond, foolish witless face,
came galloping down across the yard toward him, flinging his arms
out in exuberant greeting, and shouting to him the same welcome
that he shouted out to every one who passed, friends and strangers
all alike—"I've been lookin' fer ye! I've been lookin' fer ye, Oll,"
using, as was the custom of the friends and kinsmen of his Pennsylvania boyhood, his second name—and then, anxiously, pleadingly,
again the same words that he spoke to every one: "Ain't ye goin' to
stay?"

And Gant, grinning, but touched by the indefinable sadness and
pity which that kind and witless greeting had always stirred in him
since his own childhood, shook his head, and said quietly:

"No, Willy. Not to-day. I'm meeting some one down the road"—
and straightway felt, with thudding heart, a powerful and nameless
excitement, the urgency of that impending meeting—why, where,
with whom, he did not know—but all-compelling now, inevitable.

And Willy, still with wondering, foolish, kindly face followed
along beside him now, saying eagerly, as he said to every one:

"Did ye bring anythin' fer me? Have ye got a chew?"

And Gant, starting to shake his head in refusal, stopped suddenly, seeing the look of disappointment on the idiot's face, and putting
his hand in the pocket of his coat, took out a plug of apple-tobacco,
saying:

"Yes. Here you are, Willy. You can have this."

And Willy, grinning with foolish joy, had clutched the plug of
tobacco and, still kind and foolish, had followed on a few steps
more, saying anxiously:

"Are ye comin' back, Oll? Will ye be comin' back real soon?"

And Gant, feeling a strange and nameless sorrow, answered:

"I don't know, Willy"—for suddenly he saw that he might never come this way again.

But Willy, still happy, foolish, and contented, had turned and galloped away toward the house, flinging his arms out and shouting as he went:

"I'll be waitin' fer ye. I'll be waitin' fer ye, Oll."

And Gant went on then, down the road, and there was a nameless sorrow in him that he could not understand, and some of the brightness had gone out of the day.

When he got to the mill, he turned left along the road that went down by Spangler's run, crossed by the bridge below, and turned from the road into the wood-path on the other side. A child was standing in the path, and turned and went on ahead of him. In the wood the sunlight made swarming moths of light across the path, and through the leafy tangle of the trees: the sunlight kept shifting and swarming on the child's gold hair, and all around him were the sudden noises of the wood, the stir, the rustle, and the bullet thrum of wings, the cool broken sound of hidden water.

The wood got denser, darker as he went on and coming to a place where the path split away into two forks, Gant stopped, and turning to the child said, "Which one shall I take?" And the child did not answer him.

But some one was there in the wood before him. He heard footsteps on the path, and saw a footprint in the earth, and turning took the path where the footprint was, and where it seemed he could hear some one walking.

And then, with the bridgeless instancy of dreams, it seemed to him that all of the bright green-gold around him in the wood grew dark and sombre, the path grew darker, and suddenly he was walking in a strange and gloomy forest, haunted by the brown and tragic light of dreams. The forest shapes of great trees rose around him, he could hear no bird-song now, even his own feet on the path were soundless, but he always thought he heard the sound of some one walking in the wood before him. He stopped and listened; the steps were muffled, softly thunderous, they seemed so near that he thought that he must catch up with the one he followed in another second, and then they seemed immensely far away, receding in the dark mystery of that gloomy wood. And again he stopped and listened, the footsteps faded, vanished, he shouted, no one answered. And suddenly he knew that he had taken the wrong path, that he was lost. And in his heart there was an immense and quiet sadness, and the dark light of the enormous wood was all around him; no birds sang.

Gant awoke suddenly and found himself looking straight up at Eliza who was seated in a chair beside the bed.

"You were asleep," she said quietly with a grave smile, looking at him in her direct and almost accusing fashion.

"Yes," he said, breathing a little hoarsely, "what time is it?"

It was a few minutes before three o'clock in the morning. She looked at the clock and told him the time: he asked where Helen was.

"Why," said Eliza quickly, "she's right here in this hall room: I reckon she's asleep, too. Said she was tired, you know, but that if you woke up and needed her to call her. Do you want me to get her?"

"No," said Gant. "Don't bother her. I guess she needs the rest, poor child. Let her sleep."

"Yes," said Eliza, nodding, "and that's exactly what you must do, too, Mr. Gant. You try to go on back to sleep now," she said coaxingly, "for that's what we all need. There's no medicine like sleep— as the fellow says, it's Nature's sovereign remedy," said Eliza, with that form of sententiousness that she was very fond of—"so you go on, now, Mr. Gant, and get a good night's sleep, and when you wake up in the morning, you'll feel like a new man. That's half the battle —if you can get your sleep, you're already on the road to recovery."

"No," said Gant, "I've slept enough."

He was breathing rather hoarsely and heavily and she asked him if he was comfortable and needed anything. He made no answer for a moment, and then muttered something under his breath that she could not hear plainly, but that sounded like "little boy."

"Hah? What say? What is it, Mr. Gant?" Eliza said. "Little boy?" she said sharply, as he did not answer.

"Did you see him?" he said.

She looked at him for a moment with troubled eyes, then said:

"Pshaw, Mr. Gant, I guess you must have been dreaming."

He did not answer, and for a moment there was no sound in the room but his breathing, hoarse, a little heavy. Then he muttered:

"Did some one come into the house?"

She looked at him sharply, inquiringly again, with troubled eyes:

"Hah? What say? Why, no, I think not," she said doubtfully, "unless you may have heard Gilmer come in an' go up to his room."

And Gant was again silent for several moments, breathing a little heavily and hoarsely, his hands resting with an enormous passive strength, upon the bed. Presently he said quietly:

"Where's Bacchus?"

"Hah? Who's that?" Eliza said sharply, in a startled kind of tone. "Bacchus? You mean Uncle Bacchus?"

"Yes," said Gant.

"Why, pshaw, Mr. Gant!" cried Eliza laughing—for a startled moment she had wondered if "his mind was wanderin'," but one glance at his quiet eyes, the tranquil sanity of his quiet tone, reassured her——

"Pshaw!" she said, putting one finger up to her broad nose-wing and laughing slyly. "You must have been havin' queer dreams, for a fact!"

"Is he here?"

"Why, I'll vow, Mr. Gant!" she cried again. "What on earth is in your mind? You know that Uncle Bacchus is way out West in Oregon—it's been ten years since he came back home last—that summer of the reunion at Gettysburg."

"Yes," said Gant. "I remember now."

And again he fell silent, staring upward in the semi-darkness, his hands quietly at rest beside him, breathing a little hoarsely, but without pain. Eliza sat in the chair watching him, her hands clasped loosely at her waist, her lips pursed reflectively, and a puzzled look in her eyes: "Now I wonder what ever put that in his mind?" she thought, "I wonder what made him think of Bacchus. Now his mind's not wanderin'— that's one thing sure. He knows what he's doing just as well as I do—I reckon he must have dreamed it—that Bacchus was here—but that's certainly a strange thing, that he should bring it up like this."

He was so silent that she thought he might have gone to sleep again, he lay motionless with his eyes turned upward in the semi-darkness of the room, his hands immense and passive at his side. But suddenly he startled her again by speaking, a voice so quiet and low that he might have been talking to himself.

"Father died the year before the war," he said, "when I was nine years old. I never got to know him very well. I guess Mother had a hard time of it. There were seven of us—and nothing but that little place to live on—and some of us too young to help her much—and George away at war. She spoke pretty hard to us sometimes—but I guess she had a hard time of it. It was a tough time for all of us," he muttered, "I tell you what, it was."

"Yes," Eliza said, "I guess it was. I know she told me—I talked to her, you know, the time we went there on our honeymoon— whew! what about it?" she shrieked faintly, and put her finger up to her broad nose-wing with the same sly gesture—"it was all I could do to keep a straight face sometimes—why, you know, the way she had of talkin'—the expressions she used—oh! came right out with it, you know—sometimes I'd have to turn my head away so she wouldn't see me laughin'—says, you know, 'I was left a widow with seven children to bring up, but I never took charity from no one; as I told 'em all, I've crawled under the dog's belly all my life; now I guess I can get over its back.' "

"Yes," said Gant with a faint grin. "Many's the time I've heard her say that."

"But she told it then, you know," Eliza went on in explanatory fashion, "about your father and how he'd done hard labor on a farm all his life and died—well, I reckon you'd call it consumption."

"Yes," said Gant. "That was it."

"And," Eliza said reflectively, "I never asked—of course, I didn't want to embarrass her—but I reckon from what she said, he may have been—well, I suppose you might say he was a drinkin' man."

"Yes," said Gant, "I guess he was."

"And I know she told it on him," said Eliza, laughing again, and passing one finger slyly at the corner of her broad nose-wing, "how he went to town that time—to Brant's Mill, I guess it was—and how she was afraid he'd get to drinkin', and she sent you and Wes along to watch him and to see he got home again—and how he met up with some fellers there and, sure enough, I guess he started drinkin' and stayed away too long—and then, I reckon he was afraid of what she'd say to him when he got back—and that was when he bought the clock—it's that very clock upon the mantel, Mr. Gant— but that was when he got the clock, all right—I guess he thought it would pacify her when she started out to scold him for gettin' drunk and bein' late."

"Yes," said Gant, who had listened without moving, staring at the ceiling, and with a faint grin printed at the corners of his mouth, "well do I remember: that was it, all right."

"And then," Eliza went on, "he lost the way comin' home—it had been snowin', and I reckon it was getting dark, and he had been drinkin'—and instead of turnin' in on the road that went down by your place he kept goin' on until he passed Jake Schaefer's farm— an' I guess Wes and you, poor child, kept follerin' where he led, thinkin' it was all right—and when he realized his mistake he said he was tired an' had to rest a while and—I'll vow! to think he'd go and do a thing like that," said Eliza, laughing again—"he lay right down in the snow, sir, with the clock beside him—and went sound to sleep."

"Yes," said Gant, "and the clock was broken."

"Yes," Eliza said, "she told me about that too—and how she heard you all come creepin' in real quiet an' easy-like about nine o'clock that night, when she and all the children were in bed—an' how she could hear him whisperin' to you and Wes to be quiet—an' how she heard you all come creepin' up the steps—and how he came tip-toein' in real easy-like an' laid the clock down on the bed—I reckon the glass had been broken out of it—hopin' she'd see it when she woke up in the morning an' wouldn't scold him then for stayin' out——"

"Yes," said Gant, still with the faint attentive grin, "and then the clock began to strike."

"Whew-w!" cried Eliza, putting her finger underneath her broad nose-wing—"I know she had to laugh about it when she told it to me—she said that all of you looked so sheepish when the clock be-gan to strike that she didn't have the heart to scold him."

And Gant, grinning faintly again, emitted a faint rusty cackle that sounded like "E'God!" and said: "Yes, that was it. Poor fellow."

"But to think," Eliza went on, "that he would have no more sense

than to do a thing like that—to lay right down there in the snow
an' go to sleep with you two children watchin' him. And I know
how she told it, how she questioned you and Wes next day, and I
reckon started in to scold you for not takin' better care of him, and
how you told her, 'Well, Mother, I thought that it would be all
right. I kept steppin' where he stepped, I thought he knew the way.'
And said she didn't have the heart to scold you after that—poor
child, I reckon you were only eight or nine years old, and boy-like
thought you'd follow in your father's footsteps and that everything
would be all right."

"Yes," said Gant, with the faint grin again, "I kept stretchin' my
legs to put my feet down in his tracks—it was all I could do to
keep up with him. . . . Ah, Lord," he said, and in a moment said
in a faint low voice, "how well I can remember it. That was just
the winter before he died."

"And you've had that old clock ever since," Eliza said. "That very
clock upon the mantel, sir—at least, you've had it ever since I've
known you, and I reckon you had it long before that—for I know
you told me how you brought it South with you. And that clock
must be all of sixty or seventy years old—if it's a day."

"Yes," said Gant, "it's all of that."

And again he was silent, and lay so still and motionless that there
was no sound in the room except his faint and labored breathing,
the languid stir of the curtains in the cool night breeze, and the
punctual tocking of the old wooden clock. And presently, when she
thought that he might have gone off to sleep again, he spoke, in
the same remote and detached voice as before:

"Eliza,"—he said—and at the sound of that unaccustomed word,
a name he had spoken only twice in forty years—her white face
and her worn brown eyes turned toward him with the quick and
startled look of an animal—"Eliza," he said quietly, "you have had
a hard life with me, a hard time. I want to tell you that I'm sorry."

And before she could move from her white stillness of shocked
surprise, he lifted his great right hand and put it gently down
across her own. And for a moment she sat there bolt upright,
shaken, frozen, with a look of terror in her eyes, her heart drained
of blood, a pale smile trembling uncertainly and foolishly on her
lips. Then she tried to withdraw her hand with a clumsy movement,

she began to stammer with an air of ludicrous embarrassment, she bridled, saying—"Aw-w, now, Mr. Gant. Well, now, I reckon,"—and suddenly these few simple words of regret and affection did what all the violence, abuse, drunkenness and injury of forty years had failed to do. She wrenched her hand free like a wounded creature, her face was suddenly contorted by that grotesque and pitiable grimace of sorrow that women have had in moments of grief since the beginning of time, and digging her fist into her closed eye quickly with the pathetic gesture of a child, she lowered her head and wept bitterly:

"It was a hard time, Mr. Gant," she whispered, "a hard time, sure enough. . . . It wasn't all the cursin' and the drinkin'—I got used to that. . . . I reckon I was only an ignorant sort of girl when I met you and I guess," she went on with a pathetic and unconscious humor, "I didn't know what married life was like . . . but I could have stood the rest of it . . . the bad names an' all the things you called me when I was goin' to have another child . . . but it was what you said when Grover died . . . accusin' me of bein' responsible for his death because I took the children to St. Louis to the Fair—" and at the words as if an old and lacerated wound had been re-opened raw and bleeding, she wept hoarsely, harshly, bitterly—"that was the worst time that I had—sometimes I prayed to God that I would not wake up—he was a fine boy, Mr. Gant, the best I had—like the write-up in the paper said he had the sense an' judgment of one twice his age . . . an' somehow it had grown a part of me, I expected him to lead the others—when he died it seemed like everything was gone . . . an' then to have you say that I had—" her voice faltered to a whisper, stopped: with a pathetic gesture she wiped the sleeve of her old frayed sweater across her eyes and already ashamed of her tears, said hastily:

"Not that I'm blamin' you, Mr. Gant. . . . I reckon we were both at fault . . . we were both to blame . . . if I had it to do all over I know I could do better . . . but I was so young and ignorant when I met you, Mr. Gant . . . knew nothing of the world . . . there was always something strange-like about you that I didn't understand."

Then, as he said nothing, but lay still and passive, looking at the ceiling, she said quickly, drying her eyes and speaking with a brisk and instant cheerfulness, the undaunted optimism of her ever-hopeful nature:

"Well, now, Mr. Gant, that's all over, and the best thing we can do is to forget about it. . . . We've both made our mistakes—we wouldn't be human if we didn't—but now we've got to profit by experience—the worst of all this trouble is all over—you've got to think of getting well now, that's the only thing you've got to do, sir," she said pursing her lips and winking briskly at him—"just set your mind on getting well—that's all you've got to do now, Mr. Gant—and the battle is half won. For half our ills and troubles are all imagination," she said sententiously, "and if you'll just make up your mind now that you're going to get well—why, sir, you'll do it," and she looked at him with a brisk nod. "And we've both got years before us, Mr. Gant—for all we know, the best years of our life are still ahead of us—so we'll both go on and profit by the mistakes of the past and make the most of what time's left," she said. "That's just exactly what we'll do!"

And quietly, kindly, without moving, and with the impassive and limitless regret of a man who knows that there is no return, he answered:

"Yes, Eliza. That is what we'll do."

"And now," she went on coaxingly, "why don't you go on back to sleep now, Mr. Gant? There's nothin' like sleep to restore a man to health—as the feller says, it's Nature's sovereign remedy, worth all the doctors and all the medicine on earth," she winked at him, and then concluded on a note of cheerful finality, "so you go on and get some sleep now, and tomorrow you will feel like a new man."

And again he shook his head in an almost imperceptible gesture of negation:

"No," he said, "not now. Can't sleep."

He was silent again, and presently, his breath coming somewhat hoarse and labored, he cleared his throat, and put one hand up to his throat, as if to relieve himself of some impediment.

Eliza looked at him with troubled eyes and said:

"What's the matter, Mr. Gant? There's nothing hurtin' you?"

"No," he said. "Just something in my throat. Could I have some water?"

"Why, yes sir! That's the very thing!" She got up hastily, and looking about in a somewhat confused manner, saw behind her a pitcher of water and a glass upon his old walnut bureau, and saying "This very minute, sir!" started across the room.

And at the same moment, Gant was aware that some one had entered the house, was coming towards him through the hall, would soon be with him. Turning his head towards the door he was conscious of something approaching with the speed of light, the instancy of thought, and at that moment he was filled with a sense of inexpressible joy, a feeling of triumph and security he had never known. Something immensely bright and beautiful was converging in a flare of light, and at that instant, the whole room blurred around him, his sight was fixed upon that focal image in the door, and suddenly the child was standing there and looking towards him.

And even as he started from his pillows, and tried to call his wife he felt something thick and heavy in his throat that would not let him speak. He tried to call to her again but no sound came, then something wet and warm began to flow out of his mouth and nostrils, he lifted his hands up to his throat, the warm wet blood came pouring out across his fingers: he saw it and felt joy.

For now the child—or some one in the house was speaking, calling to him; he heard great footsteps, soft but thunderous, imminent, yet immensely far, a voice well-known, never heard before. He called to it, and then it seemed to answer him; he called to it with faith and joy to give him rescue, strength, and life, and it answered him and told him that all the error, old age, pain and grief of life was nothing but an evil dream; that he who had been lost was found again, that his youth would be restored to him and that he would never die, and that he would find again the path he had not taken long ago in a dark wood.

And the child still smiled at him from the dark door; the great steps, soft and powerful, came ever closer, and as the instant imminent approach of that last meeting came intolerably near, he cried out through the lake of jetting blood, "Here, Father, here!" and heard a strong voice answer him, "My son!"

At that instant he was torn by a rending cough, something was wrenched loose in him, the death gasp rattled through his blood, and a mass of greenish matter foamed out through his lips. Then the world was blotted out, a blind black fog swam up and closed above his head, some one seized him, he was held, supported in two arms, he heard some one's voice saying in a low tone of terror and of pity, "Mr. Gant! Mr. Gant! Oh, poor man, poor man! He's gone!" And his brain faded into night. Even before she lowered him back upon the pillows, she knew that he was dead.

PROFESSOR HATCHER'S CELEBRATED COURSE

EUGENE was now a member of Professor Hatcher's celebrated course for dramatists, and although he had come into this work by chance, and would in the end discover that his heart and interest were not in it, it had now become for him the rock to which his life was anchored, the rudder of his destiny, the sole and all-sufficient reason for his being here. It now seemed to him that there was only one work in life which he could possibly do, and that this work was writing plays, and that if he could not succeed in this work he had better die, since any other life than the life of the playwright and the theatre was not to be endured.

Accordingly every interest and energy of his life was now fastened on this work with a madman's passion; he thought, felt, breathed, ate, drank, slept, and lived completely in terms of plays. He learned all the jargon of the art-playwriting cult, read all the books, saw all the shows, talked all the talk, and even became a kind of gigantic eavesdropper upon life, prowling about the streets with his ears constantly straining to hear all the words and phrases of the passing crowd, as if he might hear something that would be rare and priceless in a play for Professor Hatcher's celebrated course.

Professor James Graves Hatcher was a man whose professional career had been made difficult by two circumstances: all the professors thought he looked like an actor and all the actors thought he looked like a professor. In reality, he was wholly neither one, but in character and temper, as well as in appearance, he possessed some of the attributes of both.

His appearance was imposing: a well-set-up figure of a man of fifty-five, somewhat above the middle height, strongly built and verging toward stockiness, with an air of vital driving energy that was always filled with authority and a sense of sure purpose, and that never degenerated into the cheap exuberance of the professional hustler. His voice, like his manner, was quiet, distinguished, and controlled, but always touched with the suggestions of great latent power, with reserves of passion, eloquence, and resonant sonority.

His head was really splendid: he had a strong but kindly-looking face touched keenly, quietly by humor; his eyes, beneath his glasses, were also keen, observant, sharply humorous, his mouth was wide and humorous but somewhat too tight, thin and spinsterly for a man's, his nose was large and strong, his forehead shapely and able-looking, and he had neat wings of hair cut short and sparse and lying flat against the skull.

He wore eye-glasses of the pince-nez variety, and they dangled in a fashionable manner from a black silk cord: it was better than going to a show to see him put them on, his manner was so urbane, casual, and distinguished when he did so. His humor, although suave, was also quick and rich and gave an engaging warmth and humanity to a personality that sometimes needed them. Even in his display of humor, however, he never lost his urbane distinguished manner—for example, when some one told him that one of his women students had referred to another woman in the course, an immensely tall angular creature who dressed in rusty brown right up to the ears, as "the queen of the angleworms," Professor Hatcher shook all over with sudden laughter, removed his glasses with a distinguished movement, and then in a rich but controlled voice, remarked:

"Ah, she has a very pretty wit. A very pretty wit, indeed!"

Thus, even in his agreeable uses of the rich, subtle and immensely pleasant humor with which he had been gifted, Professor Hatcher was something of an actor. He was one of those rare people who really "chuckle," and although there was no doubting the spontaneity and naturalness of his chuckle, it is also probably true that Professor Hatcher somewhat fancied himself as a chuckler.

The Hatcherian chuckle was just exactly what the word connotes: a movement of spontaneous mirth that shook his stocky shoulders and strong well-set torso with a sudden hearty tremor. And although he could utter rich and sonorous throat-sounds indicative of hearty mirth while this chuckling process was going on, an even more characteristic form was completely soundless, the tight lips firmly compressed, the edges turned up with the convulsive inclination to strong laughter, the fine distinguished head thrown back, while all the rest of him, throat, shoulders, torso, belly, arms —the whole man—shook in the silent tremors of the chuckle.

It could also be said with equal truth that Professor Hatcher was one of the few men whose eyes could really "twinkle," and it is likewise true that he probably fancied himself as somewhat of a twinkler.

Perhaps one fact that made him suspect to professors was his air of a distinguished and mature, but also a very worldly, urbanity. His manner, even in the class room, was never that of the scholar or the academician, but always that of the cultured man of the world, secure in his authority, touched by fine humor and fine understanding, able, knowing and assured. And one reason that he so impressed his students may have been that he made some of the most painful and difficult labors in the world seem delightfully easy.

For example, if there were to be a performance by a French club at the university of a French play, produced in the language of its birth, Professor Hatcher might speak to his class in his assured, yet casual and urbanely certain tones, as follows:

"I understand *Le Cercle Français* is putting on De Musset's *Il faut qu'une porte soit ouverte ou fermée* on Thursday night. If you are doing nothing else, I think it might be very well worth your while to brush up on your French a bit and look in on it. It is, of course, a trifle and perhaps without great significance in the development of the modern theatre, but it is De Musset in rather good form and De Musset in good form is charming. So it might repay you to have a look at it."

What was there in these simple words that could so impress and captivate these young people? The tone was quiet, pleasant and urbanely casual, the manner easy yet authoritative, what he said about the play was really true. But what was so seductive about it was the flattering unction which he laid so casually to their young souls—the easy off-hand suggestion that people "brush up on their French a bit" when most of them had no French at all to brush up on, that if they had "nothing else to do," they might "look in" upon De Musset's "charming trifle," the easy familiarity with De Musset's name and the casual assurance of the statement that it was "De Musset in rather good form."

It was impossible for a group of young men, eager for sophistication and emulous of these airs of urbane wordliness, not to be impressed by them. As Professor Hatcher talked they too became easy, casual and urbane in their manners, they had a feeling of being delightfully at ease in the world and sure of themselves, the words "brush up on your French a bit" gave them a beautifully comfortable feeling that they would really be able to perform this remarkable accomplishment in an hour or two of elegant light labor. And when he spoke of the play as being "De Musset in rather good form" they nodded slightly with little understanding smiles as if De Musset and his various states of form were matters of the most familiar knowledge to them.

What was the effect, then, of this and other such-like talk upon these young men eager for fame and athirst for glory in the great art-world of the city and the theatre? It gave them, first of all, a delightful sense of being in the know about rare and precious things, of rubbing shoulders with great actors and actresses and other celebrated people, of being expert in all the subtlest processes of the theatre, of being travelled, urbane, sophisticated and assured.

When Professor Hatcher casually suggested that they might "brush up on their French a bit" before going to a performance of a French play, they felt like cosmopolites who were at home in all the great cities of the world. True, "their French had grown a little rusty"—it had been some time since they were last in Paris—a member of the French Academy, no doubt, might detect a few slight flaws in their pronunciation—but all that would arrange itself by a little light and easy "polishing"—"tout s'arrange, hein?" as we say upon the boulevards.

Again, Professor Hatcher's pleasant and often delightfully gay anecdotes about the famous persons he had known and with whom he was on such familiar terms—told always casually, apropos of some topic of discussion, and never dragged in or labored by pretense—"The last time I was in London, Pinero and I were having lunch together one day at the Savoy"—or "I was spending the week-end with Henry Arthur Jones"—or "It's very curious you should mention that. You know, Barrie was saying the same thing to me the last time I saw him—" or—"Apropos of this discussion, I have a letter here from 'Gene O'Neill which bears on that very point. Perhaps you would be interested in knowing what he has to say about it."—All this, of course, was cakes and ale to these young people—it made them feel wonderfully near and intimate with all these celebrated people, and with the enchanted world of art and of the theatre in which they wished to cut a figure.

It gave them also a feeling of amused superiority at the posturings and antics of what, with a slight intonation of disdain, they called "the commercial producers"—the Schuberts, Belascos, and others of this kind. Thus, when Professor Hatcher told them how he had done some pioneer service in Boston for the Russian Players and had received a telegram from the Jewish producer in New York who was managing them, to this effect: "You are the real wonder boy"— they were instantly able to respond to the sudden Hatcherian chuckle with quiet laughter of their own.

Again, he once came back from New York with an amusing story of a visit he had paid to the famous producer, David Belasco. And he described drolly how he had followed a barefoot, snaky-looking female, clad in a long batik gown, through seven gothic chambers mystical with chimes and incense. And finally he told how he had been ushered into the presence of the great ecclesiastic who sat at the end of a cathedral-like room beneath windows of church glass, and how he was preceded all the time by Snaky Susy who swept low in obeisance as she approached, and said in a silky voice—"One is here to see you, Mahster," and how she had been dismissed with Christ-like tone and movement of the hand—"Rise, Rose, and leave us now." Professor Hatcher told this story with a quiet drollery that was irresistible, and was rewarded all along by their shouts of astounded laughter, and finally by their smiling and astonished faces, lifting disbelieving eyebrows at each other, saying, "Simply incredible! It doesn't seem possible! . . . *Marvellous!*"

Finally, when Professor Hatcher talked to them of how a Russian actress used her hands, of rhythm, tempo, pause, and timing, of lighting, setting, and design, he gave them a language they could use with a feeling of authority and knowledge, even when authority and knowledge was lacking to them. It was a dangerous and often very trivial language—a kind of jargonese of art that was coming into use in the world of those days, and that seemed to be coincident with another jargonese—that of science—"psychology," as they called it—which was also coming into its brief hour of idolatry at about the same period, and which bandied about its talk of "complexes," "fixations," "repressions," "inhibitions," and the like, upon the lips of any empty-headed little fool that came along.

But although this jargon was perhaps innocuous enough when rattled off the rattling tongue of some ignorant boy or rattle-pated girl, it could be a very dangerous thing when uttered seriously by men who were trying to achieve the best, the rarest, and the highest life on earth—the life which may be won only by bitter toil and knowledge and stern living—the life of the artist.

And the great danger of this glib and easy jargon of the arts was this: that instead of knowledge, the experience of hard work and patient living, they were given a formula for knowledge; a language that sounded very knowing, expert and assured, and yet that knew nothing, was experienced in nothing, was sure of nothing. It gave to people without talent and without sincerity of soul or integrity of purpose, with nothing, in fact, except a feeble incapacity for the shock and agony of life, and a desire to escape into a glamorous and unreal world of make believe—a justification for their pitiable and base existence. It gave to people who had no power in themselves to create anything of merit or of beauty—people who were the true Philistines and enemies of art and of the artist's living spirit—the language to talk with glib knowingness of things they knew nothing of—to prate of "settings," "tempo," "pace," and "rhythm," of "boldly stylized conventions," and the wonderful way some actress "used her hands." And in the end, it led to nothing but falseness and triviality, to the ghosts of passions, and the spectres of sincerity, to the shoddy appearances of conviction and belief in people who had no passion and sincerity, and who were convinced of nothing, believed in nothing, were just the disloyal apes of fashion and the arts.

"I think you ought to go," says one. "I really do. I really think you might be interested."

"Yes," says number two, in a tone of fine, puzzled, eyebrow-lifting protest, "but I hear the play is pretty bad. The reviews were rather awful—they really were, you know."

"Oh, the play!" the other says, with a slight start of surprise, as if it never occurred to him that any one might be interested in the play—"the play, the play *is* rather terrible. But my dear fellow, no one goes to see the *play* . . . the play is nothing," he dismisses it with a contemptuous gesture—"It's the *sets!*" he cries—"the *sets* are really quite remarkable. You ought to go, old boy, just to see the *sets!* They're very good—they really are."

"H'm!" the other says, stroking his chin in an impressed manner. "Interesting! In that case, I shall go!"

The *sets!* The *sets!* One should not go to see the play; the only thing that matters is the sets. And this is the theatre—the magic-maker and the world of dreams; and these the men that are to fashion for it—with their trivial ape's talk about "sets." Did any one ever hear such damned stuff as this since time began?

False, trivial, glib, dishonest, empty, without substance, lacking faith—is it any wonder that among Professor Hatcher's young men few birds sang?

The purposes of Professor Hatcher's celebrated school for dramatists seemed, as stated, to be plain and reasonable enough. Professor Hatcher himself prudently forebore from making extravagant claims concerning the benefits to be derived from his course. He did not say that he could make a dramatist out of any man who came to take his course. He did not predict a successful career in the professional theatre for every student who had been a member of his class. He did not even say he could teach a student how to write plays. No. He made, in fact, no claims at all. Whatever he said about his course was a very reasonably, prudently, and temperately put: it was impossible to quarrel with it.

All Professor Hatcher said about his course was that, if a man had a genuine dramatic and theatric talent to begin with, he might be able to derive from the course a technical and critical guidance which it would be hard for him to get elsewhere, and which he might find for himself only after years of painful and even wasteful experiment.

Certainly this seemed reasonable enough. Moreover, Professor

Hatcher felt that the artist would benefit by what was known as the "round table discussion"—that is by the comment and criticism of the various members of the class, after Professor Hatcher had read them a play written by one of their group. He felt that the spirit of working together, of seeing one's play produced and assisting in the production, of being familiar with all the various "arts" of the theatre—lighting, designing, directing, acting, and so on—was an experience which should be of immense value to the young dramatist of promise and of talent. In short, although he made no assertion that he could create a talent where none was, or give life by technical expertness to the substance of a work that had no real life of its own. Professor Hatcher did feel that by the beneficent influence of this tutelage he might trim the true lamp to make it burn more brightly.

And though it was possible to take issue with him on some of his beliefs—that, for example, the comment and criticism of "the group," and a community of creative spirits was good for the artist —it was impossible to deny that his argument was reasonable, temperate, and conservative in the statement of his purposes.

And he made this plain to every member of his class. Each one was made to understand that the course made no claims of magic alchemy—that he could not be turned into an interesting dramatist if the talent was not there.

But although each member of the class affirmed his understanding of this fundamental truth, and readily said that he accepted it, most of these people, at the bottom of their hearts, believed—pitiably and past belief—that a miracle would be wrought upon their sterile, unproductive spirits, that for them, for *them,* at least, a magic transformation would be brought about in their miserable small lives and feeble purposes—and all because they now were members of Professor Hatcher's celebrated class.

The members of Professor Hatcher's class belonged to the whole lost family of the earth, whose number is uncountable, and for this reason, they could never be forgotten.

And, first and foremost, they belonged to that great lost tribe of people who are more numerous in America than in any other country in the world. They belonged to that unnumbered horde who think that somehow, by some magic and miraculous scheme or rule

or formula, "something can be done for them." They belonged to
that huge colony of the damned who buy thousands of books that
are printed for their kind, telling them how to run a tea shop, how
to develop a pleasing personality, how to acquire "a liberal education," swiftly and easily and with no anguish of the soul, by fifteen
minutes' reading every day, how to perform the act of sexual intercourse in such a way that your wife will love you for it, how to
have children, or to keep from having children, how to write short-
stories, novels, plays, and verses which are profitably salable, how
to keep from having body odor, constipation, bad breath, or tartar
on the teeth, how to have good manners, know the proper fork to
use for every course, and always do the proper thing—how, in
short, to be beautiful, "distinguished," "smart," "chic," "forceful,"
and "sophisticated"—finally, how to have "a brilliant personality"
and "achieve success."

Yes, for the most part, the members of Professor Hatcher's class
belonged to this great colony of the lost Americans. They belonged
to that huge tribe of all the damned and lost who feel that everything is going to be all right with them if they can only take a
trip, or learn a rule, or meet a person. They belonged to that futile,
desolate, and forsaken horde who felt that all will be well with
their lives, that all the power they lack themselves will be supplied,
and all the anguish, fury, and unrest, the confusion and the dark
damnation of man's soul can magically be healed if only they eat
bran for breakfast, secure an introduction to a celebrated actress,
get a reading for their manuscript by a friend of Sinclair Lewis, or
win admission to Professor Hatcher's celebrated class of dramatists.

And, in a curious way, the plays written by the people in Professor Hatcher's class, illustrated, in one form or another, this desire.
Few of the plays had any intrinsic reality, for most of these people
were lacking in the first, the last, the foremost quality of the artist,
without which he is lost: the ability to get out of his own life the
power to live and work by, to derive from his own experience—as
a fruit of all his seeing, feeling, living, joy and bitter anguish—the
palpable and living substance of his art.

Few of the people in Professor Hatcher's class possessed this
power. Few of them had anything of their own to say. Their lives
seemed to have grown from a stony and a fruitless soil and, as a

consequence, the plays they wrote did not reflect that life, save by a curious and yet illuminating indirection.

Thus, in an extraordinary way, their plays—unreal, sterile, imitative, and derivative as most of them indubitably were—often revealed more about the lives of the people who wrote them than better and more living work could do. For, although few of the plays showed any contact with reality—with that passionate integument of blood and sweat and pain and fear and grief and joy and laughter of which this world is made—most of them did show, in one way or another, what was perhaps the basic impulse in the lives of most of these people—the impulse which had brought them here to Professor Hatcher's class.

The impulse of the people in the class was not to embrace life and devour it, but rather to escape from it. And in one way or another most of the plays these people wrote were illustrative of this desire. For in these plays—unnatural, false, and imitative, as they were—one could discern, in however pale and feeble a design, a picture of the world not as its author had seen and lived and known it, but rather as he wished to find it, or believe in it. And, in all their several forms—whether sad, gay, comic, tragic, or fantastical— these plays gave evidence of the denial and the fear of life.

The wealthy young dawdler from Philadelphia, for example, wrote plays which had their setting in a charming little French Café. Here one was introduced to all the gay, quaint, charming Frenchmen—to Papa Duval, the jolly proprietor, and Mama Duval, his rotund and no less jolly spouse, as well as to all the quaint and curious habitués that are so prolific in theatrical establishments of this order. One met, as well, that fixture of these places: old Monsieur Vernet, the crusty, crotchety, but kindly old gentleman who is the café's oldest customer and has had the same table in the corner by the window for more than thirty years. One saw again the familiar development of the comic situation—the day when Monsieur Vernet enters at his appointed time and finds at his table a total stranger, sacrilege! Imprecations! Tears, prayers, and entreaties on the part of Papa Duval and his wife, together with the stubborn refusal of the imperious stranger to move! Climax: old Monsieur Vernet storming out of the café, swearing that he will never return. Resolution of conflict: the efforts of Papa and Mamma

Duval to bring their most prized customer back into the fold again, and their final success, the pacification and return of Monsieur Vernet amid great rejoicing, thanks to a cunning stratagem on the part of Henri, the young waiter, who wins a reward for all these efforts, the hand of Mimi, Papa Duval's charming daughter, from whom he has been separated by Papa Duval's stern decree.

Thus, custom is restored, and true love re-united by one brilliant comic stroke!

And all this pretty little world, the contribution of a rich young man who came from Philadelphia! How perfectly God-damn delightful it all was, to be sure!

The plays of old Seth Flint, the sour and withered ex-reporter, were, if of a different coloring, cut from the same gaudy cloth of theatric unreality. For forty years old Seth had pounded precincts as a newsman, and had known city-rooms across the nation. He had seen every crime, ruin, and incongruity of which man's life is capable. He was familiar with every trait of graft, with every accursed smell and smear of the old red murder which ineradicably fouled the ancient soul of man, and the stench of man's falseness, treachery, cruelty, hypocrisy, cowardice, and injustice, together with the look of brains and blood upon the pavements of the nation, was no new thing to old Seth Flint.

His skin had been withered, his eyes deadened, his heart and spirit burdened wearily, his faith made cynical, and his temper soured by the black picture of mankind which he had seen as a reporter—and because of this, in spite of this, he had remained or become—how, why, in what miraculous fashion no one knew—a curiously honest, sweet, and generous person, whose life had been the record of a self-less loyalty. He had known poverty, hardship, and self-sacrifice, and endured all willingly without complaint: he had taken the savings of a lifetime to send the two sons of his widowed sister to college, he had supported this woman and her family for years, and now, when his own life was coming to its close, he was yielding to the only self-indulgence he had ever known—a year away from the city-room of a Denver newspaper, a year away in the rare ether, among the precious and æsthetic intellects of Professor Hatcher's celebrated course, a year in which to realize the dream of a life-time, the vision of his youth—a year in which to write the plays he had always dreamed of writing. And what kind of plays did he write?

Alas! Old Seth did exactly what he set out to do, he succeeded perfectly in fulfilling his desire—and, by a tragic irony, his failure lay in just this fact. The plays which he produced with an astounding and prolific ease— ("Three days is enough to write a play," the old man said in his sour voice. "You guys who take a year to write a play give me a pain. If you can't write a play a week, you can't write anything; the play's no good")—these plays were just the plays which he had dreamed of writing as a young man, and therein was evident their irremediable fault.

For Seth's plays—so neat, brisk, glib, and smartly done—would have been good plays in a commercial way, as well, if he had only done them twenty years before. He wrote, without effort and with unerring accuracy, a kind of play which had been immensely popular at the beginning of the twentieth century, but which people had grown tired of twenty years before. He wrote plays in which the babies got mixed up in the maternity ward of a great hospital, in which the rich man's child goes to the family of a little grocer, and the grocer's child grows up as the heir to an enormous fortune, with all the luxuries and securities of wealth around him. And he brought about the final resolution of this tangled scheme, the meeting of these scrambled children and their bewildered parents, with a skill of complication, a design of plot, a dexterity that was astonishing. His characters—all well-known types of the theatre, as of nurse tough-spoken, shop-girl slangy, reporter cynical, and so on— were well conceived to fret their purpose, their lives well-timed and apt and deftly made. He had mastered the formula of an older type of "well-made play" with astonishing success. Only, the type was dead, the interest of the public in such plays had vanished twenty years before.

So here he was, a live man, writing, with amazing skill, dead plays for a theatre that was dead, and for a public that did not exist.

"Chekhov! Ibsen!" old Seth would whine sourly with a dismissing gesture of his parched old hand, and a scornful contortion of his bitter mouth in his old mummy of a face. "You guys all make me tired the way you worship them!" he would whine out at some of the exquisite young temperaments in Professor Hatcher's class.

"Those guys can't write a play! Take Chekhov, now!" whined Seth. "That guy never wrote a real play in his life! He never knew how to write a play! He couldn't have written a play if he tried! He never learned the rules for writing a play!—that *Cherry Orchard* now," whined old Seth with a sour sneering laugh, "—that *Cherry Orchard* that you guys are always raving about! That's not a play!" he cried indignantly. "What ever made you think it was a play? I was trying to read it just the other day," he rasped, "and there's nothing there to hold your interest! It's got no *plot!* There's no story in it! There's no suspense! Nothing happens in it. All you got is a lot of people who do nothing but talk all the time. You never get anywhere," said Seth scornfully. "And yet to hear you guys rave about it, you'd think it was a great play."

"Well, what do you call a great play, then, if *The Cherry Orchard* isn't one?" one of the young men said acidly. "Who wrote the great plays that you talk about?"

"Why George M. Cohan wrote some," whined Seth instantly. "That's who. Avery Hopwood wrote some great plays. We've had plenty of guys in this country who wrote great plays. If they'd come from Russia you'd get down and worship 'em," he said bitterly. "But just because they came out of this country they're no good!"

In the relation of the class towards old Seth Flint, it was possible to see the basic falseness of their relation towards life everywhere around them. For here was a man—whatever his defects as a playwright might have been—who had lived incomparably the richest, most varied and dangerous, and eventful life among them; as he was himself far more interesting than any of the plays they wrote, and as dramatists they should have recognized and understood his quality. But they saw none of this. For their relation towards life and people such as old Seth Flint was not one of understanding. It was not even one of burning indignation—of that indignation which is one of the dynamic forces in the artist's life. It was rather one of supercilious scorn and ridicule.

They felt that they were "above" old Seth, and most of the other people in the world, and for this reason they were in Professor Hatcher's class. Of Seth they said:

"He's really a misfit, terribly out of place here. I wonder why he came."

And they would listen to an account of one of Seth's latest errors in good taste with the expression of astounded disbelief, the tones of stunned incredulity which were coming into fashion about that time among elegant young men.

"Not really! . . . But he never really said *that*. . . . You *can't* mean it."

"Oh, but I assure you, he did!"

". . . It's simply past belief! . . . I can't believe he's as bad as *that*."

"Oh, but he *is!* It's incredible, I know, but you've no idea what he's capable of." And so on.

And yet old Seth Flint was badly needed in that class: his bitter and unvarnished tongue caused Professor Hatcher many painful moments, but it had its use—oh, it had its use, particularly when the play was of this nature:

Irene (slowly with scorn and contempt in her voice). So—it has come to this! This is all your love amounts to—a little petty selfish thing! I had thought you were bigger than that, John.

John (desperately). But—but, my God, Irene—what am I to think? I found you in bed with him—my best friend! *(with difficulty).* You know—that looks suspicious, to say the least!

Irene (softly—with amused contempt in her voice). You poor little man! And to think I thought your love was *so big.*

John (wildly). But I do love you, Irene. That's just the point.

Irene (with passionate scorn). Love! You don't know what love means! Love is bigger than that! Love is big enough for all things, all people. *(She extends her arms in an all-embracing gesture.)* My love takes in the world—it embraces all mankind! It is glamorous, wild, free as the wind, John.

John (slowly). Then you have had other lovers?

Irene: Lovers come, lovers go. *(She makes an impatient gesture.)* What is that? Nothing! Only love endures—my love which is greater than all.

Eugene would writhe in his seat, and clench his hands convulsively. Then he would turn almost prayerfully to the bitter, mummied face of old Seth Flint for that barbed but cleansing vulgarity that always followed such a scene:

"Well?" Professor Hatcher would say, putting down the manuscript he had been reading, taking off his eye-glasses (which were attached to a ribbon of black silk) and looking around with a quizzical smile, an impassive expression on his fine, distinguished face. "Well?" he would say again urbanely, as no one answered. "Is there any comment?"

"What is she?" Seth would break the nervous silence with his rasping snarl. "Another of these society whores? You know," he continued, "you can find plenty of her kind for three dollars a throw without any of that fancy palaver."

Some of the class smiled faintly, painfully, and glanced at each other with slight shrugs of horror; others were grateful, felt pleasure well in them and said underneath their breath exultantly:

"Good old Seth! Good old Seth!"

"Her love is big enough for all things, is it?" said Seth. "I know a truck driver out in Denver I'll match against her any day."

Eugene and Ed Horton, a large and robust aspirant from the Iowa cornlands, roared with happy laughter, poking each other sharply in the ribs.

"Do you think the play will act?" some one said. "It seems to me that it comes pretty close to closet drama."

"If you ask me," said Seth, "it comes pretty close to water-closet drama. . . . No," he said sourly. "What that boy needs is a little experience. He ought to go out and get him a woman and get all this stuff off his mind. After that, he might sit down and write a play."

For a moment there was a very awkward silence, and Professor Hatcher smiled a trifle palely. Then, taking his eyeglasses with a distinguished movement, he looked around and said:

"Is there any other comment?"

When Oswald Ten Eyck left his $8000 job on the Hearst Syndicate and came to Cambridge to enroll in Professor Hatcher's celebrated course for dramatists, he had saved a sum rare in the annals of journalism—$700. When he got through paying the tuition, admission, and other accessory fees that would entitle him to a membership in good standing in the graduate school of the university, something less than $500 remained. Oswald got an attic room in Cambridge, in a square, smut-gray frame house which was the home of an Irish family named Grogan. To reach his room, he had to mount a rickety flight of stairs that was almost as steep as a ladder, and when he got there, he had to manage his five feet five of fragile stature carefully in order to keep from cracking his head upon the sloping white-washed walls that followed the steep pitch of the roof with painful fidelity. The central part of Oswald's room, which was the only place in which the little man could stand erect, was not over four feet wide: there was a single window at the front where stood his writing table. He had a couple of straight chairs, a white iron cot pushed in under the eave of the left side, a few bookshelves pushed in under the eave of the right. It could literally be said that the playwright crawled to bed, and when he read he had to approach the poets as a poet should—upon his knees.

For this austere cell, Professor Hatcher's dramatist paid Mrs. Mary Grogan fifteen dollars every month. Therefore, when the primary fees of tuition and matriculation and the cell in Mrs. Grogan's house had been accounted for, Oswald Ten Eyck had all of $300 left to take care of clothing, food, tobacco, books, and plays during the ensuing period of nine months. This sum perhaps was adequate, but it was not grand, and Ten Eyck, poet though he was, was subject to all those base cravings of sensual desire that 100 pounds of five feet five is heir to.

This weakness of the flesh was unhappily reflected in the artist's work. During the brief period of his sojourn in Professor Hatcher's class, his plays were numerous but for the most part low. Ten Eyck turned them out with the feverish haste which only a trained newspaper man can achieve when driven on by the cherished ambition of a lifetime and the knowledge that art is long and $300 very fleeting. He had started out most promisingly in the fleshless ethers of mystic fantasy, but he became progressively more sensual until at the end he was practically wallowing in a trough of gluttony.

The man, in fact, became all belly when he wrote—and this was strange in a frail creature with the large burning eyes of a religious zealot, hands small-boned, fleshless as a claw, and a waist a rubber band would have snapped round comfortably. He seemed compact of flame and air and passion and an agonizing shyness. Professor Hatcher had great hopes for him—the whole atom was framed, Professor Hatcher thought, for what the true Hatcherian called "the drama of revolt," but the flaming atom fooled him, fooled him cruelly. For after the brilliant promise of that first beginning—a delicate, over-the-hills-and-far-away fantasy reminiscent of Synge, Yeats, and the Celtic Dawn—brain bowed to belly, Ten Eyck wrote of food.

His second effort was a one-act play whose action took place on the sidewalk in front of a Childs restaurant, while a white-jacketed attendant deftly flipped brown wheat-cakes on a plate. The principal character, and in fact the only speaker in this play, was a starving poet who stood before the window and delivered himself of a twenty-minute monologue on a poet's life and the decay of modern society, in the course of which most of the staple victuals on the Childs menu were mentioned frequently and with bitter relish.

Professor Hatcher felt his interest waning: he had hoped for finer things. Yet a wise caution learned from errors in the past had taught him to forbear. He knew that out of man's coarse earth the finer flowers of his spirit sometimes grew. Some earlier members of his class had taught him this, some who had written coarsely of coarse things. They wrote of sailors, niggers, thugs, and prostitutes, of sunless lives and evil strivings, of murder, hunger, rape, and incest, a black picture of man's life unlighted by a spark of grace, a ray of hope, a flicker of the higher vision. Professor Hatcher had not always asked them to return—to "come back for a second year," which was the real test of success and future promise in the Hatcherian world. And yet, unknighted by this accolade, some had gone forth and won renown: their grim plays had been put on everywhere and in all languages. And the only claim the true Hatcherian could make of them was: "Yes, they were with us but not of us: they were not asked to come back for a second year."

There were some painful memories, but Professor Hatcher had derived from them a wise forbearance. His hopes for Oswald Ten Eyck were fading fast, but he had determined to hold his judgment in abeyance until Oswald's final play. But, as if to relieve his distinguished tutor from a painful choice, Ten Eyck himself decided it. After his third play there was no longer any doubt of the decision. For that play, which Oswald called "Dutch Fugue," would more aptly have been titled "No Return."

It was a piece in four acts dealing with the quaintly flavored life and customs of his own people, the Hudson River Dutch. The little man was hotly proud of his ancestry, and always insisted with a slight sneer of aristocratic contempt: "Not the Pennsylvania Dutch —Good God, no! *They're* not Dutch but German: the *real* Dutch, the *old* Dutch, *Catskill* Dutch!" And if Ten Eyck's interest in food had been uncomfortably pronounced in his earlier work, in this final product of his curious genius, his sensual appetities became indecent in their unrestraint. It is doubtful if the long and varied annals of the stage have ever offered such a spectacle: the play became a sort of dramatic incarnation of the belly, acted by a cast of fourteen adults, male and female, all of whom were hearty eaters.

The central events of that extraordinary play, which were a birth, a death, a wedding, were all attended by eating, drinking, and the noises of the feast. Scene followed scene with a kaleidoscopic swiftness: the jubilant merry-making of the christening had hardly died away before the stage was set, the trestles groaning, with the more sombre, sober and substantial victuals of the funeral; and the wheels of the hearse had hardly echoed away into the distance before the scene burst out in all the boisterous reel and rout and feasting of the wedding banquet. Of no play that was ever written could it be more aptly said that the funeral baked meats did coldly furnish forth the marriage tables, and what is more, they almost furnished forth the casket and the corpse as well. Finally, the curtain fell as it had risen, upon a groaning table surrounded by the assembled cast of fourteen famished gluttons—a scene in which apparently the only sound and action were provided by the thrust of jowl and smack of lip, a kind of symphonic gluttony of reach and grab, cadenced by the stertorous breathing of the eaters, the clash of crockery, and the sanguinary drip of rare roast beef—the whole a prophetic augury that flesh was grass and man's days fleeting, that life would change and reappear in an infinite succession of births and deaths and marriages, but that the holy rites of eating and the divine permanence of good dinners and roast beef were indestructible and would endure forever.

Ten Eyck read the play himself one Friday afternoon to Professor Hatcher and his assembled following. He read in a rapid high-pitched voice, turning the pages with a trembling claw, and thrusting his long fingers nervously through his disordered mop of jet-black hair. As he went on, the polite attention of the class was changed insensibly to a paralysis of stupefaction. Professor Hatcher's firm thin lips became much firmer, thinner, tighter. A faint but bitter smile was printed at the edges of his mouth. Then, for a moment, when the playwright finished, there was silence: Professor Hatcher slowly raised his hand, detached his gold-rimmed glasses from his distinguished nose, and let them fall and dangle on their black silk cord. He looked around the class; his cultivated voice was low, controlled, and very quiet.

"Is there any comment?" Professor Hatcher said.

No one answered for a moment. Then Mr. Grey, a young patrician from Philadelphia, spoke:

"I think," he said with a quiet emphasis of scorn, "I think he might very well get it produced in the Chicago Stock Yards."

Mr. Grey's remark was ill-timed. For the Stock Yards brought to Ten Eyck's mind a thought of beef, and beef brought back a memory of his palmy days with Mr. Hearst when beef was plenty and the paychecks fat, and all these thoughts brought back the bitter memory of the day before which was the day when he had eaten last: a single meal, a chaste and wholesome dinner of spaghetti, spinach, coffee, and a roll. And thinking, Ten Eyck craned his scrawny neck convulsively along the edges of his fraying collar, looked desperately at Professor Hatcher, who returned his gaze inquiringly; ducked his head quickly, bit his nails and craned again. Then, suddenly, seeing the cold patrician features of young Mr. Grey, his blue shirt of costly madras, his limp crossed elegance of legs and pleated trousers, the little man half rose, scraping his chair back from the table round which the class was sitting, and with an inclusive gesture of his claw-like hand, screamed incoherently:

"These! These! . . . We have the English. . . . As for the Russians. . . . Take the Germans—Toller—Kaiser—the Expressionists. . . . But the Dutch, the Dutch, the *Catskill* Dutch. . . ." Pointing a trembling finger towards Mr. Grey, he shrieked: "The Philadelphia Cricket Club. . . . God! God!" he bent, racked with soundless laughter, his thin hands pressed against his sunken stomach. "That it should come to this!" he said, and suddenly, catching Professor Hatcher's cold impassive eye upon him, he slumped down abruptly in his seat, and fell to biting his nails: "Well, I don't know," he said with a foolish little laugh. "Maybe—I guess . . ." his voice trailed off, he did not finish.

"Is there any other comment?" said Professor Hatcher.

There was none.

"Then," said Professor Hatcher, "the class is dismissed until next Monday."

Professor Hatcher did not look up as Ten Eyck went out.

When Oswald got out into the corridor, he could hear the last footfalls of the departing class echoing away around the corner. For a moment, he leaned against the wall: he felt hollow, weak, and dizzy: his knees bent under him like rubber, and his head, after its recent flood of blood and passion, felt swollen, light, and floating as a toy balloon. Suddenly he remembered that it was Friday. Saturday, the day on which he could next allow himself to take a little from his dwindling hoard—for such was the desperate resolution made at the beginning and adhered to ever since—Saturday shone desperately far away, a small and shining disc of light at the black mouth of an interminable tunnel, and all giddy, weak, and hollow as he was, he did not see how he could wait! So he surrendered. He knew that if he hurried now he would be just in time for old Miss Potter's Friday afternoon. And torn between hunger and disgust, Ten Eyck gave in again to hunger as he had done a score of times before, even when he knew that he must face again that crowning horror of modern life, the art party.

Miss Potter was a curious old spinster of some property, and she lived, with a companion, in a pleasant house on Garden Street, not far from the University. Miss Potter's companion was also an aged spinster: her name was Miss Flitcroft; the two women were inseparable. Miss Potter was massively constructed: a ponderous woman who moved heavily and with wheezing difficulty, and whose large eyes bulged comically out of a face on which a strange fixed grin was always legible.

Miss Flitcroft was a wren of a woman, with bony little hands, and an old withered, rather distinguished-looking face: she wore a band of velvet around her stringy neck. She was not only a companion, she was also a kind of nurse to Miss Potter, and she could give relief and comfort to the other woman as no one else could.

For Miss Potter was really very ill: she had a savage love of life, a desperate fear of death, and she knew that she was dying. But even the woman's sufferings, which were obviously intense, were touched by that grotesque and ridiculous quality that made Ten Eyck want to howl with explosive laughter, even when he felt a rending pity for her. Thus, at table sometimes, with all her tribe of would-be poets, playwrights, composers, novelists, painters, critics, and enfeebled litterateurs gathered around her, putting away the delicious food she had so abundantly provided, Miss Potter would suddenly begin to choke, gasp, and cough horribly; her eyes would bulge out of her head in a fish-like stare, and looking desperately at Miss Flitcroft with an expression of unutterable terror, she would croak: . . . "Dying! Dying! I tell you I'm dying!"

"Nonsense!" Miss Flitcroft would answer tartly, jumping up and running around behind Miss Potter's chair. "You're no such thing! . . . You've only choked yourself on something you have eaten! There!" and she would deliver herself straightway of a resounding whack upon Miss Potter's meaty, mottled back (for on these great Friday afternoons, Miss Potter came out sumptuously in velvet, which gave ample glimpses of her heavy arms and breasts and the broad thick surface of her shoulders).

"If you didn't eat so fast these things would never happen!" Miss Flitcroft would say acidly, as she gave Miss Potter another resounding whack on her bare shoulders. "Now you get over this nonsense!" . . . whack! "There's nothing wrong with you—do you hear?" . . . whack! "You're frightened half out of your wits," . . . whack! . . . "just because you've tried to stuff everything down your throat at once!" whack! whack!

And by this time, Miss Potter would be on the road to recovery, gasping and panting more easily now, as she continued to look up with a fixed stare of her bulging eyes at Miss Flitcroft, with an expression full of entreaty, dawning hopefulness, apology, and pitiable gratitude.

As for Ten Eyck, his pain and embarrassment when one of these catastrophes occurred were pitiable. He would scramble to his feet, stand helplessly, half-crouched, casting stricken glances toward the most convenient exit as if contemplating the possibility of a sudden and inglorious flight. Then he would turn again toward the two old women, his dark eyes fixed on them in a fascinated stare in which anguish, sympathy, helplessness and horror were all legible.

For several years, in spite of her ill health, Miss Potter had fiddled around on the edges of Professor Hatcher's celebrated course at the university. She had written a play or two herself, took a passionate interest in what she called "the work," was present at the performances of all the plays, and was a charter member of Professor Hatcher's carefully selected and invited audiences. Now, whether by appointment or self-election, she had come to regard herself as a kind of embassadress for Professor Hatcher's work and was the chief sponsor of its social life.

The grotesque good old woman was obsessed by that delusion which haunts so many wealthy people who have no talent and no understanding, but who are enchanted by the glamour which they think surrounds the world of art. Miss Potter thought that through these Friday afternoons she could draw together all the talent, charm, and brilliance of the whole community. She thought that she could gather here not only Professor Hatcher's budding dramatists and some older representatives of the established order, but also poets, painters, composers, philosophers, "radical thinkers," people "who did interesting things," of whatever kind and quality. And she was sure that from this mad mélange every one would derive a profitable and "stimulating" intercourse.

Here, from the great "art community" of Cambridge and Boston, came a whole tribe of the feeble, the sterile, the venomous and inept—the meagre little spirits of no talent and of great pretensions: the people who had once got an essay printed in *The Atlantic Monthly* or published "a slender volume" of bad verse; the composers who had had one dull academic piece performed a single time by the Boston Symphony; the novelists, playwrights, painters, who had none of the "popular success" at which they sneered and which they pretended to despise, but for which each would have sold his shabby little soul; the whole wretched poisonous and embittered crew of those who had "taken" some one's celebrated course, or had spent a summer at the MacDowell Colony—in short, the true Philistines of art—the true enemies of the artist's living spirit, the true defilers and betrayers of creation—the impotent fumbling little half men of the arts whose rootless, earthless, sunless lives have grown underneath a barrel, and who bitterly nurse their fancied injuries, the swollen image of their misjudged worth, and hiss and sting in all the impotent varieties of their small envenomed hate; who deal the stealthy traitor's blow in darkness at the work and talent of far better men than they.

Usually, when Ten Eyck went to Miss Potter's house he found several members of Professor Hatcher's class who seemed to be in regular attendance on all these Friday afternoons. These others may have come for a variety of reasons: because they were bored, curious, or actually enjoyed these affairs, but the strange, horribly shy and sensitive little man who bore the name of Oswald Ten Eyck came from a kind of desperate necessity, the ravenous hunger of his meagre half-starved body, and his chance to get his one good dinner of the week.

It was evident that Ten Eyck endured agonies of shyness, boredom, confusion, and tortured self-consciousness at these gatherings but he was always there, and when they sat down at the table he ate with the voracity of a famished animal. The visitor to Miss Potter's reception room would find him, usually backed into an inconspicuous corner away from the full sound and tumult of the crowd, nervously holding a tea-cup in his hands, talking to some one in the strange blurted-out desperate fashion that was characteristic of him, or saying nothing for long periods, biting his nails, thrusting his slender hands desperately through his mop of black disordered hair, breaking from time to time into a shrill, sudden, almost hysterical laugh, blurting out a few volcanic words, and then relapsing into his desperate hair-thrusting silence.

The man's agony of shyness and tortured nerves was painful to watch: it made him say and do sudden, shocking and explosive things that could suddenly stun a gathering such as this, and plunge him back immediately into a black pit of silence, self-abasement and despair. And as great as his tortured sensitivity was, it was greater for other people than for himself. He could far better endure a personal affront, a wounding of his own quick pride, than see another person wounded. His anguish, in fact, when he saw this kind of suffering in other people would become so acute that he was no longer responsible for his acts: he was capable of anything on such an occasion.

And such occasions were not lacking at Miss Potter's Friday afternoons. For even if the entire diplomatic corps had gathered there in suavest mood, that good grotesque old woman with her unfailing talent for misrule, would have contrived to set every urbane minister of grace snarling for the other's blood before an hour had passed. And with that museum collection of freaks, embittered æsthetes and envenomed misfits of the arts, that did gather there, she never failed. Her genius for confusion and unrest was absolute.

If there were two people in the community who had been destined from birth and by every circumstance of education, religious belief, and temperament, to hate each other with a murderous hatred the moment that they met, Miss Potter would see to it instantly that the introduction was effected. If Father Davin, the passionate defender of the faith, and the foe of modernism in all its hated forms, had been invited to one of Miss Potter's Friday afternoons, he would find himself shaking hands before he knew it with Miss Shanksworth, the militant propagandist for free love, sterilization of the unfit, and the unlimited practice of birth control by every one, especially the lower classes.

If the editor of *The Atlantic Monthly* should be present, he would find himself, by that unerring drawing together of opposites which Miss Potter exercised with such accuracy, seated next to the person of one Sam Shulemovitch, who as a leader and chief editorial writer of an organ known as *Red Riot* or *The Worker's Dawn,* had said frequently and with violence that the sooner *The Atlantic Monthly* was extinguished, and its writers, subscribers, and editorial staff embalmed and put on exhibition in a museum, the better it would be for every one.

If the radical leader who had just served a sentence in prison for his speeches, pamphlets, and physical aggressions against the police, or members of the capitalist class, should come to one of Miss Potter's Friday afternoons, he would find himself immediately debating the merits of the present system and the need for the swift extinction of the wealthy parasite with a maiden lady from Beacon Street who had a parrot, two Persian kittens, and a Pekinese, three maids, a cook, a butler, chauffeur and motor car, a place at Marblehead, and several thousand shares of Boston and Maine.

And so it went, all up and down the line, at one of Miss Potter's Friday afternoons. There, in her house, you could be sure that if the lion and the lamb did not lie down together their hostess would seat them in such close proximity to each other that the ensuing slaughter would be made as easy, swift, and unadorned as possible.

And as the sound of snarl and curse grew louder in the clamorous tumult of these Friday afternoons, as the face grew livid with its hate, as the eye began to glitter, and the vein to swell upon the temple, Miss Potter would look about her with triumphant satisfaction, seeing that her work was good, thinking with delight:

"How stimulating! How fine it is to see so many interesting people together—people who are really doing things! To see the flash and play of wit, to watch the clash of brilliant intellects, to think of all these fine young men and women have in common, and of the mutual benefits they will derive from contact with one another!—ah-ha! What a delightful thing to see—but who is this that just came—" she would mutter, peering toward the door, for she was very near-sighted—"who? *Who?*—O-oh! Professor Lawes of the Art Department—oh, Professor Lawes, I'm so glad you could come. We have the most *interesting* young man here today—Mr. Wilder, who painted that picture every one's talking about—"Portrait of a Nude Falling Upon Her Neck in a Wet Bathroom"—Mr. Wilder, this is Doctor Lawes, the author of *Sanity and Tradition in the Renaissance*—I know you're going to find *so* much in common."

And having done her duty, she would wheeze heavily away, looking around with her strange fixed grin and bulging eyes to see if she had left anything or anyone undone or whether there was still hope of some new riot, chaos, brawl, or bitter argument.

And yet there was a kind of wisdom in her too, that few who came there to her house suspected: a kind of shrewdness in the fixed bulging stare of her old eyes that sometimes saw more than the others knew. Perhaps it was only a kind of instinct of the old woman's warm humanity that made her speak to the fragile little man with burning eyes more gently than she spoke to others, to seat him on her right hand at the dinner table, and to say from time to time: "Give Mr. Ten Eyck some more of that roast beef. Oh, Mr. Ten Eyck, *do*—you've hardly eaten anything."

And he, stretched out upon the rack of pride and all the bitter longing of his hunger, would crane convulsively at his collar and laugh with a note of feeble protest, saying "Well—I don't know . . . I really think . . . if you want me to. . . . Oh! all right then," as a plate smoking with her lavish helping was placed before him, and would straightway fall upon it with the voracity of a famished wolf.

When Ten Eyck reached Miss Potter's on that final fateful Friday, the other guests were already assembled. Miss Thrall, a student of the woman's section of Professor Hatcher's course, was reading her own translation of a German play which had only recently been produced. Miss Potter's reception rooms—which were two large gabled rooms on the top floor of her house, ruggedly festooned with enormous fishing nets secured from Gloucester fishermen—were crowded with her motley parliament, and the whole gathering was discreetly hushed while the woman student read her play.

It was a scene to warm the heart of any veteran of æsthetic parties. The lights were soft, shaded, quietly and warmly subdued: the higher parts of the room were pools of mysterious gloom from which the Gloucester fishing nets depended, but within the radius of the little lamps, one could see groups of people tastefully arranged in all the attitudes of rapt attentiveness. Some of the young women slouched dreamily upon sofas, their faces and bodies leaning toward the reader with a yearning movement, other groups could be vaguely discerned leaning upon the grand piano, or elegantly slumped against the walls with tea-cups in their hands. Mr. Cram, the old composer, occupied a chosen seat on a fat sofa; he drew voluptuously on a moist cigarette which he held daintily between his dirty fingers, his hawk-like face turned meditatively away into the subtle mysteries of the fishing nets. From time to time he would thrust one dirty hand through the long sparse locks of his gray hair, and then draw deeply, thoughtfully on his cigarette.

Some of the young men were strewn about in pleasing postures on the floor, in attitudes of insouciant grace, gallantly near the ladies' legs. Ten Eyck entered, looked round like a frightened rabbit, ducked his head, and then sat down jack-knife fashion beside them.

Miss Thrall sat on the sofa with the old composer, facing her audience. The play that she was reading was one of the new German Expressionist dramas, at that time considered one of "the most vital movements in the world theatre," and the young lady's translation of the play which bore the vigorous title of *You Shall Be Free When You Have Cut Your Father's Throat,* ran somewhat in this manner:

Elektra: (advancing a step to the top of the raised dais, her face blue with a ghastly light, and her voice low and hoarse with passion as she addresses the dark mass of men below her.) Listen, man! To you it is now proper that I speak must. Do you by any manner of means know who this woman who now before you speaking stands may be? (With a sudden swift movement she, the purple-reddish silk-stuff of the tunic which she wearing is, asunder in two pieces rips, her two breasts exposing.)

(A low swiftly-growing-and-to-the-outer-edges-of-the-crowd-thunder-becoming mutter of astonishment through the great crowd surges.)

Elektra: (Thunder louder becomes, and even with every moment growing yet) Elektra! (The sound to a mighty roar arisen has, and now from every throat is in a single shout torn.) ELEKTRA!

Elektra: (quietly) Ja! Man, thou hast said it. I am Elektra!

The Crowd: (with from their throats an even-stronger roar yet) E L E K- T R A. It is E l e k t r a !

Elektra: (her voice even lower and more hoarse becoming, her eyes with the red blood-pains of all her heart-grief with still greater love-sorrow at the man-mass gleaming.) Listen, man. Slaves, workers, the of your fathers' sons not yet awakened—hear! Out of the night-dark of your not yet born souls to deliver you have I come! So, hear! (Her voice even lower with the low blood-pain heart-hate hoarse becoming.) Tonight must you your old with-crime-blackened and by-ignorance-blinded father's throat cut! I have spoken: so must it be.

A Voice, Homunculus: (from the crowd, pleadingly, with protest.) Ach! Elektra! Spare us! Please! With the blood-lust malice-blinded your old father's throat to cut not nice is.

Elektra: (raising her arm with a cold imperious gesture of command.) As I have spoken, must it be! Silence!

(Homunculus starts to interrupt: again she speaks, her voice more loud and stern becoming.) Silence! Silence!

At this moment there was a loud and sibilant hiss from the door. Miss Potter, who had been on the point of entering the room, had been halted by the sight of Miss Thrall's arm uplifted in command and by the imperious coldness of her voice as she said "Silence!" Now as Miss Thrall stopped and looked up in a startled manner, Miss Potter, still hissing loudly, tip-toed ponderously into the room.

The old woman advanced with the grace of a hydroptic hippopotamus, laying her finger to her lips as she came on, looking all around her with her fixed grin and bulging eyes, and hissing loudly for the silence she had thus violently disrupted every time she laid her finger to her lips.

Every one *stared* at her in a moment of blank and horrible fascination. As for Miss Thrall, she gaped at her with an expression of stupefaction which changed suddenly to a cry of alarm as Miss Potter, tiptoeing blindly ahead, barged squarely into the small crouched figure of Oswald Ten Eyck, and went plunging over him to fall to her knees with a crash that made the fish-nets dance, the pictures swing, and even drew a sympathetic resonant vibration from the polished grand piano.

Then, for one never-to-be-forgotten moment, while every one *stared* at her in a frozen paralysis of horrified astonishment, Miss Potter stayed there on her knees, too stunned to move or breathe, her eyes bulging from her head, her face turned blindly upward in an attitude of grotesque devotion. Then as she began to gasp and cough with terror, Ten Eyck came to life. He fairly bounded off the floor, glanced round him like a startled cat, and spying a pitcher on a tray, rushed toward it wildly, seized it in his trembling hands, and attempted to pour a glass of water, most of which spilled out. He turned, still clutching the glass in his hands, and panting out "Here! Here! . . . Take this!" he rushed toward Miss Potter. Then, terrified by her apoplectic stare, he dashed the contents of the glass full in her face.

A half dozen young men sprang to her assistance and lifted her to her feet. The play was forgotten, the whole gathering broke into excited and clamorous talk, above which could be heard Miss Flitcroft's tart voice, saying sharply, as she whacked the frightened and dripping old woman on the back:

"Nonsense! You're not! You're no such thing! . . . You're just frightened out of your wits, that's all that's the matter with you— If you ever stopped to look where you were going, these things would never happen!"

Whack!

Both Oswald and Miss Potter had recovered by the time the guests were assembled round the table. As usual, Oswald found he had been seated on Miss Potter's right hand: and the feeling of security this gave him, together with the maddening fragrance of food, the sense of ravenous hunger about to be appeased, filled him with an almost delirious joy, a desire to shout out, to sing. Instead, he stood nervously beside his chair, looking about with a shy and timid smile, passing his fingers through his hair repeatedly, waiting for the other guests to seat themselves. Gallantly, he stood behind Miss Potter's chair, and pushed it under her as she sat down. Then, with a feeling of jubilant elation, he sat down beside her and drew his chair up. He wanted to talk, to prove himself a brilliant conversationalist, to surprise the whole gathering with his wit, his penetration, his distinguished ease. Above all, he wanted to eat and eat and eat! His head felt light and drunk and giddy, but gloriously so—he had never been so superbly confident in his life. And in this mood, he unfolded his napkin, and smiling brightly, turned to dazzle his neighbor on his right with the brilliant effervescence of wit that already seemed to sparkle on his lips. One look, and the bright smile faded, wit and confidence fell dead together, his heart shrank instantly and seemed to drop out of his very body like a rotten apple. Miss Potter had not failed. Her unerring genius for calamity had held out to the finish. He found himself staring into the poisonous face of the one person in Cambridge that he hated most—the repulsive visage of the old composer, Cram.

An old long face, yellowed with malevolence, a sudden fox-glint of small eyes steeped in a vitriol of ageless hate, a beak of cruel nose, and thin lips stained and hardened in a rust of venom, the whole craftily, slantingly astare between a dirty frame of sparse lank locks. Cackling with malignant glee, and cramming crusty bread into his mouth, the old composer turned and spoke:

"Heh! Heh! Heh!"—Crunch, crunch—"It's *Mister* Ten Eyck, isn't it? The man who wrote that play Professor Hatcher put on at his last performance—that mystical fantasy kind of thing. That was *your* play, wasn't it?"

The old yellow face came closer, and he snarled in a kind of gloating and vindictive whisper: "Most of the audience *hated* it! They thought it very *bad,* sir—very bad!" Crunch, crunch. "I am only telling you because I think you ought to know—that you may profit by the criticism."

And Ten Eyck, hunger gone now, shrank back as if a thin poi-

soned blade had been driven in his heart and twisted there. "I—I—
I thought some of them rather liked it. Of course I don't know—
I can't say—" he faltered hesitantly, "but I—I really thought some
of the audience—liked it."

"Well, they *didn't,*" the composer snarled, still crunching on his
crust of bread. "Every one that I saw thought that it was terrible.
Heh! Heh! Heh! Heh! Except my wife and I—" Crunch, crunch.
"We were the only ones who thought that it was any good at all,
the only ones who thought there would ever be any *hope* for you.
And we found parts of it—a phrase or sentence here and there—
now and then a scene—that we *liked.* As for the rest of them," he
suddenly made a horrible downward gesture with a clenched fist
and pointing thumb, "it was *thumbs down,* my boy! Done for! No
good. . . . That's what they thought of *you,* my boy. And that," he
snarled suddenly, glaring round him, "*that* is what they've thought
of *me* all these years—of *me,* the greatest composer that they have,
the man who has done more for the cause of American music than
all the rest of them combined—*me! me! me!* the prophet and the
seer!" he fairly screamed, "*thumbs down!* Done for! No good any
more!"

Then he grew suddenly quiet, and leaning toward Ten Eyck
with a gesture of horrible clutching intimacy, he whispered: "And
that's what they'll always think of you, my boy—of any one who
has a grain of talent—Heh! Heh! Heh! Heh!" Peering into Ten
Eyck's white face, he shook him gently by the arm, and cackled
softly a malevolent tenderness, as if the evidence of the anguish
that his words had caused had given him a kind of paternal affection for his victim. "That's what they said about your play, all
right, but don't take it too seriously. It's live and learn, my boy,
isn't it—profit by criticism—a few hard knocks will do you no harm.
Heh! Heh! Heh! Heh! Heh!"

And turning, satisfied with the anguish he had caused, he thrust
out his yellowed face with a vulture's movement of his scrawny
neck, and smacking his envenomed lips with relish, drew noisily
inward with slobbering suction on a spoon of soup.

As for Ten Eyck, all hunger now destroyed by his sick shame and
horror and despair, he turned, began to toy nervously with his food,

and forcing his pale lips to a trembling and uncertain smile, tried desperately to compel his brain to pay attention to something that was being said by the man across the table who was the guest of honor for the day, and whose name was Hunt.

Hunt had been well-known for his belligerent pacifism during the war, had been beaten by the police and put in jail more times than he could count, and now that he was temporarily out of jail, he was carrying on his assault against organized society with more ferocity than ever. He was a man of undoubted courage and deep sincerity, but the suffering he had endured, and the brutal intolerance of which he had been the victim, had left its mutilating mark upon his life. His face was somehow like a scar, and his cut, cruel-looking mouth could twist like a snake to the corner of his face when he talked. And his voice was harsh and jeering, brutally dominant and intolerant, when he spoke to any one, particularly if the one he spoke to didn't share his opinions.

On this occasion, Miss Potter, with her infallible talent for error, had seated next to Hunt a young Belgian student at the university, who had little English, but a profound devotion to the Roman Catholic Church. Within five minutes, the two were embroiled in a bitter argument, the Belgian courteous, but desperately resolved to defend his faith, and because of his almost incoherent English as helpless as a lamb before the attack of Hunt, who went for him with the rending and pitiless savagery of a tiger. It was a painful thing to watch: the young man, courteous and soft-spoken, his face flushed with embarrassment and pain, badly wounded by the naked brutality of the other man's assault.

As Ten Eyck listened, his spirit began to emerge from the blanket of shame and sick despair that had covered it, a spark of anger and resentment, hot and bright, began to glow, to burn, to spread. His large dark eyes were shining now with a deeper, fiercer light than they had had before, and on his pale cheeks there was a flush of angry color. And now he no longer had to force himself to listen to what Hunt was saying: anger had fanned his energy and his interest to a burning flame, he listened tensely, his ears seemed almost to prick forward on his head, from time to time he dug his fork viciously into the table cloth. Once or twice, it seemed that he would interrupt. He cleared his throat, bent forward, nervously clutching the table with his claw-like hands, but each time ended up thrusting his fingers through his mop of hair, and gulping down a glass of wine.

As Hunt talked, his voice grew so loud in its rasping arrogance that every one at the table had to stop and listen, which was what he most desired. And there was no advantage, however unjust, which the man did not take in this bitter argument with the young Belgian. He spoke jeeringly of the fat priests of the old corrupt church, fattening themselves on the blood and life of the oppressed workers; he spoke of the bigotry, oppression, and superstition of religion, and of the necessity for the workers to destroy this monster which was devouring them. And when the young Belgian, in his faltering and painful English, would try to reply to these charges, Hunt would catch him up on his use of words, pretend to be puzzled at his pronunciation, and bully him brutally in this manner:

"You think *what?* . . . *What?* . . . I don't understand what you're saying half the time. . . . It's very difficult to talk to a man who can't speak decent English."

"I—vas—say—ink," the young Belgian would answer slowly and painfully, his face flushed with embarrassment—"—vas—say—ink —zat—I sink—zat you—ex—ack—sher—ate—"

"That I *what?—What?* What is he trying to say, anyway?" demanded Hunt, brutally, looking around the table as if hoping to receive interpretation from the other guests. "Oh-h!" he cried suddenly, as if the Belgian's meaning had just dawned on him. *"Exaggerate!* That's the word you're trying to say!" and he laughed in an ugly manner.

Oswald Ten Eyck had stopped eating and turned white as a sheet. Now he sat there, looking across in an agony of tortured sympathy at the Young Belgian, biting his nails nervously, and thrusting his hands through his hair in a distracted manner. The resentment and anger that he had felt at first had now burned to a white heat of choking, murderous rage. The little man was taken out of himself entirely. Suddenly his sense of personal wrong, the humiliation and pain he had himself endured, was fused with a white-hot anger of resentment for every injustice and wrong that had ever been done to the wounded soul of man. United by that agony to a kind of savage fellowship with the young Belgian, with the insulted and the injured of the earth, of whatsoever class or creed, that burning coal of five feet five flamed in one withering blaze of wrath, and hurled the challenge of its scorn at the oppressor.

The thing happened like a flash. At the close of one of Hunt's jeering tirades, Ten Eyck jumped from his chair, and leaning half across the table, cried out in a high shrill voice that cut into the silence like a knife:

"Hunt! You are a swine, and every one who ever had anything to do with you is likewise a swine!" For a moment he paused, breathing hard, clutching his napkin in a bony hand. Slowly his feverish eyes went round the table, and suddenly, seeing the malevolent stare of the old composer Cram fixed upon him, he hurled the wadded napkin down and pointing a trembling finger at that hated face, he screamed: "And that goes for you as well, you old bastard! . . . It goes for all the rest of you," he shrieked, gesturing wildly. "Hunt . . . Cram! *Cram!* . . . God!" he cried, shaking with laughter. "*There's* a name for you! . . . It's perfect. . . . Yes, you! You swine!" he yelled again, thrusting his finger at Cram's yellowed face so violently that the composer scrambled back with a startled yelp. "And all the rest of you!" he pointed towards Miss Thrall—"You—the Expressionist!" And he paused, racked terribly again by soundless laughter—"The Greeks—the Russians—Oh, how we love in Spain! —and fantasy—why, Goddam my soul to hell, but it's delightful!" he fairly screamed, and then pointing a trembling finger at several in succession he yelled "You?—And you?—And you?—What the hell do you know about anything? . . . Ibsen—Chekov—the Celtic Dawn —*Balls!*" he snarled, "Food! Food! Food!—you Goddam fools! . . . That's all that matters." He picked up a morsel of his untouched bread and hurled it savagely upon the table—"Food! Food!—Ask Cram—he knows. . . . Now," he said, panting for breath and pointing a trembling finger at Miss Potter—"Now," he panted, "I want to tell *you* something."

"Oh . . . Mr. . . . Ten . . . Eyck," the old woman faltered in a tone of astonished reproach, "I . . . never . . . believed it possible . . . you could——"

Her voice trailed off helplessly, and she looked at him.

And Ten Eyck, suddenly brought to himself by the bulging stare of that good old creature fixed on him with wounded disbelief, suddenly laughed again, shrilly and hysterically, thrust his fingers through his hair, looked about him at the other people whose eyes were fixed on him in a stare of focal horror, and said in a confused, uncertain tone: "Well, I don't know—I'm always—I guess I said something that—oh, damn it, what's the use!" and with a desperate, stricken laugh, he slumped suddenly into his chair, craned convulsively at his collar, and seizing a decanter before him poured out a glass of wine with trembling haste and gulped it down.

Meanwhile, all around the table people began to talk with that kind of feverish eagerness that follows a catastrophe of this sort, and Hunt resumed his arguments, but this time in a much quieter tone, and with a kind of jeering courtesy, accompanying his remarks from time to time with a heavy sarcasm directed toward Ten Eyck—"If I may say so—since, of course, Mr. Ten Eyck considers me a swine" or "if you will pardon such a remark from a swine like me"—or—"as Mr. Ten Eyck has told you I am nothing but a swine," and so on.

The upshot of it was that Ten Eyck gulped down glass after glass of the strong wine, which raced instantly through his frail starved body like a flame.

He got disgracefully drunk, sang snatches of bawdy songs, screamed with maudlin laughter, and began to pound enthusiastically on the table, shaking his head to himself and shouting from time to time:

"You're right, Hunt! . . . God-damn it, man, you're right! . . . Go on! . . . Go on! I agree with you! You're right! Everybody else is wrong but Hunt and Cram! . . . Words by Hunt, music by Cram . . . no one's right but Hunt and Cram!"

They tried to quiet him, but in vain. Suddenly Miss Potter began to cough and choke and gasp, pressed both hands over her heart, and gasped out in a terror-stricken voice:

"Oh, my God, I'm dying!"

Miss Flitcroft jumped to her feet and came running to her friend's assistance, and then while Miss Flitcroft pounded the old woman on her back, and the guests scrambled up in a general disruption of the party, Oswald Ten Eyck staggered to the window, flung it open, and looking out across one of the bleak snow-covered squares of Cambridge, screamed at the top of his voice:

"Relentless! . . . Relentless! . . . Juh sweez un art-e-e-este!" Here
he beat on his little breast with a claw-like hand and yelled with
drunken laughter, "And, Goddam it, I will always be relentless . . .
relentless . . . relentless!"

The cool air braced him with its cleansing shock: for a moment,
the fog of shame and drunkenness shifted in his brain, he felt a
vacancy of cold horror at his back, and turning suddenly found
himself confronted by the frozen circle of their faces, fixed on him.
And even in that instant glimpse of utter ruin, as the knowledge
of this final castastrophe was printed on his brain, over the rim of
frozen faces he saw the dial-hands of a clock. The time was seven-
fifty-two: he knew there was a train at midnight for New York—
and work, food, freedom, and forgetfulness. He would have four
hours to go home and pack: if he hurried he could make it.

Little was heard of him thereafter. It was rumored that he had
gone back to his former lucrative employment with Mr. Hearst:
and Professor Hatcher smiled thinly when he heard the news; the
young men looked at one another with quiet smiles.

And yet he could not wholly be forgotten: occasionally some one
mentioned him.

"A strange case, wasn't it?" said Mr. Grey. "Do you remember
how he looked? Like . . . like . . . really, he was like some mediæval
ascetic. I thought he had something. I thought he would do something . . . I really did, you know! And then—heavens!—that last
play!" He tossed his cigarette away with a movement of dismissal.
"A strange case," he said with quiet finality. "A man who looked as
if he had it and who turned out—all belly and no brain."

There was silence for a moment while the young men smoked.

"I wonder what it was," another said thoughtfully at length.
"What happened to him? I wonder why."

There was no one there who knew the answer. The only one on
earth, perhaps, who could have given it was that curious old spinster named Miss Potter. For blind to many things that all these
clever young men knew, that good grotesque old empress of confusion still had a wisdom that none of them suspected. But Miss Potter
was no longer there to tell them, even if she could. She had died
that spring.

Later it seemed to Gene that the cold and wintry light of desolation—the red waning light of Friday in the month of March—shone forever on the lives of all the people. And forever after, when he thought of them, their lives, their faces and their words—all that he had seen and known of them—would be fused into a hopeless, joyless image which was somehow consonant to that accursed wintry light that shone upon it. And this was the image:

He was standing upon the black and grimy snow of winter before Miss Potter's house, saying good-bye to a group of her invited guests. The last red wintry light of Friday afternoon fell on their lives and faces as he talked to them, and made them hateful to him, and yet he searched those faces and talked desperately to see if he could find there any warmth or love or joy, any ring of hope for himself which would tell him that his sick heart and leaden spirit would awake to life and strength again, that he would get his hands again on life and love and labor, and that April would come back again.

But he found nothing in these cold and hateful faces but the lights of desolation, the deadly and corrupt joy that took delight in its own death, and breathed, without any of the agony and despair he felt, the poisonous ethers of its own dead world. In those cold hateful faces as that desolate and wintry light fell on them he could find no hope for his own life or the life of living men. Rather, he read in their pale faces, and in their rootless and unwholesome lives, which had come to have for him the wilted yellow pallor of nameless and unuseful plants such as flourish under barrels, a kind of cold malicious triumph, a momentary gleam in pale fox eyes, which said that they looked upon his desperate life and knew the cause of his despair, and felt a bitter triumph over it. The look on their cold faces and in their fox eyes said to him that there was no hope, no work, no joy, no triumph, and no love for such as he, that there could be nothing but defeat, despair and failure for the living of this world, that life had been devoured and killed by such as these, and had become rat's alley, death-in-life forever.

And yet he searched their hated faces desperately in that cold red light, he sought frantically in their loathed faces for a ray of hope, and in his drowning desolation shameful words were wrenched from him against his will—words of entreaty, pleading,

pitiful begging for an alms of mercy, a beggarly scrap of encouragement, even a word of kindly judgment on his life, from these cold
and hateful faces that he loathed.

"But my work—this last work that I did—don't you think—
didn't it seem to you that there was something good in it—not
much, perhaps, but just enough to give me hope? . . . Don't you
think if I go on I may do something good some day—for God's
sake, tell me if you do?—or must I die here in this barren and
accursed light of Friday afternoon, must I drown and smother in
this poisonous and lifeless air, wither in this rootless, yellow, barren
earth below the barrel, die like a mad-dog howling in the wilderness, with the damned, cold, hateful sneer of your impotent lives
upon me?

"Tell me, in God's name, man, is there no life on earth for such
as I? Has the world been stripped for such as you? Have all joy,
hope, health, sensual love, and warmth and tenderness gone out of
life—are living men the false men, then, and is all truth and work
and wisdom owned by rat's alley and the living dead such as yourself?—for God's sake, tell me if there is no hope for me! Let me
have the worst, the worst, I beg of you. Is there nothing for me now
but the gray gut, the sick heart, and the leaden spirit? Is there nothing now but Friday afternoon in March, Miss Potter's parties, and
your damned poisonous, sterile, cold, life-hating faces? For God's
sake tell me now if I am no good, am false while you, the living
dead, are true—and had better cut my throat or blow my brains out
than stay on longer in this world of truth, where joy is dead, and
only the barren rootless lives of dead men live!—In God's name, tell
me now, if this is true—or do you find a rag of hope for me?"

"Ah," the old composer Cram would answer, arranging the folds
of his dirty scarf, and peering out malevolently underneath his
sparse lank webs of dirty gray, as the red and wintry light fell hopelessly on his poisonous old face. "—Ah-h," he rasped bitterly, "—my
wife and I liked some things in that play of yours that Professor
Hatcher put on in his Playshop. . . . My wife and I liked one or two
speeches in that play," he rasped, "but"—for a moment a fox's glittering of malevolent triumph shone in his eyes as he drove the fine
blade home "—no one else did!—No one else thought it was any
good at all!" he cackled malevolently. "I heard people saying all

around me that they *hated* it," he gloated, "—that you had no talent, no ability to write, and had better go back where you came from—live some other kind of life—or *kill* yourself," he gloated— "That's the way it is, my boy!—Nothing but defeat and misery and despair for such as you in life! . . . That has been my lot, too," he cackled vindictively, rubbing his dry hands in glee. "They've always hated what I did—if I ever did anything good I was lucky if I found two people who liked it. The rest of them *hated* it," he whispered wildly. "There's no hope for you—so *die, die, die,*" he whispered, and cackling with malevolent triumph, he rubbed his dry hands gleefully.

"Meeker, for God's sake," the boy cried, turning to the elegant figure of the clergyman, who would be carefully arranging around his damned luxurious neck the rich folds of a silk blue scarf— "Meeker, do you feel this way about it, too? . . . Is that your opinion? . . . Do you find nothing good in what I do?"

—"You see, old chap, it's this way," Meeker answered, in his soft voice, and drew with languor on one of his expensive straw-tipped cigarettes—"You have lots of ability, I am sure"—here he paused to inhale meditatively again—"but don't you think, old boy, it's critical rather than creative?—now with Jim here it's different," he continued, placing one hand affectionately on Hogan's narrow shoulders—"Jim here's a great genius—like Shelley—with a great gift waiting for the world"—Here Hogan lowered his pale weak face with a simpering smile of modesty, but not before the boy had seen the fox's glitter of vindictive triumph in his pale dull eyes—"but you have nothing of that sort to give. Why don't you try to make the best of what you have?" he said with hateful sympathetic urbanity and put the cigarette to elegant and reflective lips again.

"Hogan," the boy cried hoarsely, turning to the poet,"—is that your answer, too? Have you no word of hope for me?—but no, you damned, snivelling, whining upstart—you are gloating at your rotten little triumph, aren't you? I'd get nothing out of you, would I?"

"Come on, Jim," said Meeker quietly. "He's becoming abusive. . . . The kind of attack you make is simply stupid," he now said. "It will get you nowhere."

"And so raucous—so raucous," said Hogan, smirking nervously. "It means nothing."

And the three hated forms of death would go away then rapidly, snickering among themselves, and he would turn again, filled with the death of life, the end of joy, again, again, to prowl the wintry, barren, and accursed streets of Friday night.

One Sunday morning early in the month of May, Starwick and Eugene had crossed the bridge that led to the great stadium, and turned right along a path that followed the winding banks of the Charles River. Spring had come with the sudden, almost explosive loveliness that marks its coming in New England: along the banks of the river the birch trees leaned their slender, white and beautiful trunks, and their boughs were coming swiftly into the young and tender green of May.

That spring—which, for Eugene, would be the second and last of his years in Cambridge—Starwick had become more mannered in his dress and style than ever before. During the winter, much to Professor Hatcher's concern—a concern which constantly became more troubled and which he was no longer able to conceal—the darling protégé on whom his bounty and his favor had been lavished, and to whom, he had fondly hoped, he would one day pass on the proud authorities of his own position when he himself should become too old to carry on "the work," had begun to wear spats and carry a cane and be followed by a dog.

Now, with the coming of spring, Frank had discarded the spats, but as they walked along beside the Charles, he twirled his elegant light stick with an air of languid insouciance, interrupting his conversation with his friend now and then to speak sharply to the little dog that frisked and scampered along as if frantic with the joy of May, crying out to the little creature sharply, commandingly, and in a rather womanish tone from time to time:

"Heel, Tang! Heel, I say!"

And the dog, a shaggy little terrier—the gift of some wealthy and devoted friends of Frank's on Beacon Hill—would pause abruptly in its frisking, turn its head, and look towards its owner with the attentive, puzzled, and wistfully inquiring look that dogs and little children have, as if to say: "What is it, master? Are you pleased with me or have I done something that was wrong?"

And in a moment, in response to Frank's sharper and more peremptory command, the little dog, with a crestfallen and somewhat apologetic look, would scamper back from its wild gaieties along the green banks of the Charles, to trot meekly along the path behind the two young men, until its exuberant springtime spirits got the best of it again.

From time to time, they would pass other students, in pairs or groups, striding along the pleasant path; and when these young men saw Starwick twirling his stick and speaking to the little dog, they would grin broadly at each other, and stare curiously at Starwick as they passed.

Once Starwick paused to call "Heel!" sharply to the little dog at the very moment it had lifted its leg against a tree, and the dog, still holding its leg up, had looked inquiringly around at Starwick with such a wistful look that some students who were passing had burst out in hearty laughter. But Starwick, although the color of his ruddy face deepened a shade, had paid no more attention to these ruffians than if they had been scum in the gutter. Rather, he snapped his fingers sharply, and cried, "Heel!" again, at which the little dog left its tree and came trotting meekly back to its obedient position.

Suddenly, while one of these episodes was being enacted, Eugene heard the bright wholesome tones of a familiar voice, and turning around with a startled movement, found himself looking straight into the broad and beaming countenance of Effie Horton, and her husband Ed.

"*Well!*" Effie was saying in her rich bright voice of Iowa. "Look who's here! I *thought* those long legs looked familiar," she went on in her tone of gay and lightsome, and yet wholesome, banter, "even from a distance! I told Pooly—" this, for an unknown reason, was the affectionate nick-name by which Horton was known to his wife, and all his friends from Iowa—"I told Pooly that there was only one pair of legs as long as that in Cambridge. 'It *must* be Eugene,' I said. —Yes, sir!" she went on brightly, shaking her head with a little bantering movement, her broad and wholesome face shining with good nature all the time. "It *is* Eugene—and *my! my! my!*—I just wish you'd look at him," she went on gaily, in her tones of full rich fellowship and banter in which, however, a trace of something ugly, envious, and mocking was evident—"all dressed up in his Sunday-go-to-meeting clothes out for a walk this fine morning just to give the pretty girls a treat! Yes, sir!" she cried again, shaking her head in wondering admiration, and with an air of beaming satisfaction, "I'll *bet* you that's *just* what he's going to do."

He flushed, unable to think of an apt reply to this good-natured banter, beneath whose hearty good-fellowship he felt the presence of something that was false, ugly, jeering and curiously tormented, and while he was blundering out a clumsy greeting, Horton, laughing with lazy good-nature at his confusion, slapped him on the back and said:

"How are yuh, kid? . . . Where the hell have you been keeping yourself, anyway?"

The tone was almost deliberately coarse and robust in its hearty masculinity, but beneath it one felt the same false and spurious quality that had been evident in the woman's tone.

—"And here is *Mister* Starwick!" Effie now cried brightly. "—And I *wish* you'd *look!*" she went on, as if enraptured by the spectacle— "all dressed up with a walking stick and a dog—and yes, *sir!*" she exclaimed ecstatically, after an astonished examination of Frank's sartorial splendor—"wearing a *bee-yew-teeful* brown tweed suit that looks as if it just came out of the shop of a London tailor! . . . *My! My! My!* . . . I tell *you!*" she went on admiringly—"I just wish the folks back home could see us now, Pooly——"

Horton laughed coarsely, with apparent good nature, but with an ugly jeering note in his voice.

"—I just wish they could see us now!" she said. "It's not every one can say they knew two London swells—and here they are—Mr. Starwick with his cane and his dog—and Eugene with his new suit —yes, *sir!*—and talking to us just as if we were their equals."

Eugene flushed, and then with a stiff and inept sarcasm, said:

"I'll try not to let it make any difference between us, Effie."

Horton laughed coarsely and heartily again, with false good nature, and then smote the boy amiably on the back, saying:

"Don't let her kid you, son! Tell her to go to hell if she gets fresh with you!"

"—And how is Mr. Starwick these fine days!" cried Effie gaily, now directing the artillery of her banter at his unworthy person—

"Where is that great play we've all been waiting for so eagerly for lo these many years! I tell *you!*" she exclaimed with rich conviction —"I'm going to be right there on the front row the night it opens up on Broadway!—I know that a play that has taken any one so many years will be a masterpiece—every word pure gold—I don't want to miss a *word* of it."

"Quite!" said Starwick coldly, in his mannered and affected tone. His ruddy face had flushed crimson with embarrassment; turning, he called sharply and coldly to the little dog, in a high and rather womanish voice:

"Heel, Tang! Heel, I say!"

He snapped his fingers and the little dog came trotting meekly toward him. Before Starwick's cold and scornful impassivity, Effie's broad and wholesome face did not alter a jot from its expression of radiant good-will, but suddenly her eyes, which, set in her robust and friendly countenance, were the tortured mirror of her jealous, envious, possessive, and ravenously curious spirit, had grown hard and ugly, and the undernote of malice in her gay tones was more apparent than ever when she spoke again:

"Pooly," she said laughing, taking Horton affectionately by the arm, and drawing close to him with the gesture of a bitterly jealous and possessive female, who, by the tortured necessity of her own spirit, must believe that "her man" is the paragon of the universe, and herself the envy of all other women, who lust to have him, but must gnash their teeth in vain—"Pooly," she said lightly, and drawing close to him—"maybe that's what's wrong with us! . . . Maybe that's what it takes to make you write a great play! . . . Yes, *sir!*" she said gaily, "I believe that's it! . . . I believe I'll save up all my spending money until I have enough to buy you a bee-yew-teeful tailored suit just like the one that Mr. Starwick has on. . . . Yes, *sir!*" she nodded her head emphatically in a convinced manner. "That's just *exactly* what I'm going to do! . . . I'm going to get Mr. Starwick to give me the address of his tailor—and have him make you a *bee-yew-teeful* new suit of English clothes—and then, maybe, you'll turn into a great genius like Mr. Starwick and Eugene!"

"The hell you will!" he said coarsely and heartily. "What's wrong with the one I got on? I only had it three years—why, it's as good as the day I bought it." And he laughed with hearty, robust masculinity.

"Why, Poo-o-ly!" she said reproachfully. "It's turning *green!* And I do so want you to get dressed up and be a *genius* like Mr. Starwick!"

"Nope!" he said in his tone of dominant finality. "I'll wear this pair of pants till it falls off me. Then I'll go into Filene's bargain basement and buy another pair. Nope! You can't make an æsthete out of me! I can write just as well with a hole in the seat of my britches as not." And laughing coarsely, with robust and manly good nature, he smote Eugene on the back again, and rasped out heartily:

"Ain't that right, kid?"

"Oh, *Pooly!*" cried Effie reproachfully—"And I do *so* want you to be a genius—like Mr. Starwick!"

"Now, wait a minute! Wait a minute!" he rasped, lifting a commanding hand, as he joined with her in this ugly banter. "That's different! Starwick's an artist—I'm nothing but a writer. They don't understand the way we artists work—do they, Starwick? Now an artist is sensitive to all these things," he went on in a jocose explanatory tone to his wife. "He's got to have the right *atmosphere* to work in. Everything's got to be just right for we artists—doesn't it, Starwick?"

"Quite!" said Starwick coldly.

"Now with me it's different," said Horton heavily. "I'm just one of those big crude guys who can write anywhere. I get up in the morning and write, whether I feel like it or not. But it's different with us artists, isn't it, Starwick? Why, with a real honest-to-God-dyed-in-the-wool *artist* like Starwick, his whole life would be ruined for a *month* if his pants didn't fit, or if his necktie was of the wrong shade. . . . Ain't that right, Starwick?"

And he laughed heavily, apparently with robust fellowship, hearty good nature, but his eyes were ugly, evil, jeering, as he spoke.

"Quite!" said Starwick as before; and, his face deeply flushed, he called sharply to his dog, and then, turning inquiringly to Eugene, said quietly: "Are we ready?"

"Oh, I *see*, I *see!*" cried Effie, with an air of gay enlightenment. "That's what every one is all dressed up about!—You're out for a walk, aren't you—all among the little birdies, and the beeses, and the flowers! *My! My!* How I wish I could go along! Pooly!" she said coaxingly, "why don't you take *me* for a walk sometime? I'd love to

346 THE THOMAS WOLFE READER

hear the little birdies sing! Come on, dear. Won't you?" she said
coaxingly.

"Nope!" he boomed out finally. "I walked you across the bridge
and I walked to the corner this morning for a paper. That's all the
walking that I'm going to do today. If you want to hear the little
birdies sing, I'll buy you a canary." And turning to Eugene, he
smote him on the shoulder again, and laughing with coarse laziness,
said:

"You know me, kid. . . . You know how I like exercise, don't you?"

"Well, then, if we can't go along to hear the little birdies sing to
Mr. Starwick and Eugene, I suppose we'll have to say good-bye,"
said Effie regretfully. "We've got no right to keep them from the
little birdies any longer—have we, dear? And think what a treat it
will be for all the little birdies. . . . And you, Eugene!" she cried out
gaily and reproachfully, but now with real warmth and friendship
in her voice. "We haven't seen you at our home in a-a-ages! What's
wrong with you? . . . You come up soon or I'll be mad at you."

"Sure," Horton came out in his broad Iowa accent, putting his
hand gently on the boy's shoulder. "Come up to see us, kid. We'll
cook some grub and chew the rag a while. You know, I'm not coming back next year—" for a moment Horton's eyes were clear,
gray, luminous, deeply hurt, and full of pride and tenderness.
"We're going to New Hampshire with Jim Madden. So come up,
kid, as soon as you can: we ought to have one more session before
I go."

And the boy, suddenly touched and moved, felt the genuine affection, the real friendliness—an animal-like warmth and kindliness
and affection that was the truest and most attractive element in
Horton's personality.

And nodding his head, suddenly feeling affection for them both
again, he said:

"All right, Ed. I'll see you soon. So long, Effie. Good-bye. Good-
bye, Ed."

"Good-bye, kid. So long, Starwick," Horton said in a kindly tone.
"We'll be looking for you, 'Gene— So long!"

Then they parted, in this friendly manner, and Starwick and
Eugene continued their walk along the river. Starwick walked
quietly, saying nothing; from time to time he called sharply to the
little dog, commanding him to come to "heel" again.

The two young men had not seen each other for two months, save at Professor Hatcher's class, and then their relations had been formal, cold, and strained. Now Starwick, with a quick friendly and generous spontaneity, had broken through the stubborn and resentful pride of the other youth, had made the first advance towards reconciliation, and, as he was able to do with every one when and where he pleased, had instantly conquered his friend's resentful feelings, and won him back with the infinite grace, charm, and persuasiveness of his own personality.

Yet, during the first part of their walk along the river their conversation, while friendly, had almost been studiously detached and casual, and was the conversation of people still under the constraint of embarrassment and diffidence, who are waiting for the moment to speak things in which their lives and feelings are more intimately concerned.

At length, they came to a bending in the river where there was a bank of green turf on which in the past they had often sat and smoked and talked while that small and lovely river flowed before them. Seated here again, and provided with cigarettes, a silence came between them, as if each was waiting for the other one to speak.

Presently when Eugene looked towards his companion, Starwick's pleasant face with the cleft chin was turned towards the river in a set stare, and even as the other young man looked at him, his ruddy countenance was contorted by the animal-like grimace swift and instant, which the other boy had often seen before, and which had in it, somehow, a bestial and inarticulate quality, a kind of unspeakable animal anguish that could find no release.

In a moment, lowering his head, and staring away into the grassy turf, Starwick said quietly:

"Why have you not been in to see me these last two months?"

The other young man flushed, began to speak in a blundering and embarrassed tone and then, angered by his own confusion, burst out hotly:

"Look here, Frank—why have you got to be so damned mysterious and secretive in everything you do?"

"Am I?" said Starwick quietly.

"Yes, you are! You've been that way ever since I met you."

"In what way?" Starwick asked.

"Do you remember the first time I met you?" the other one demanded.

"Perfectly," Starwick said. "It was during your first year in Cambridge, a few days after you arrived. We met for dinner at the Cock Horse Tavern."

"Yes," the other said excitedly. "Exactly. You had written me a note inviting me to dinner, and asking me to meet you there. Do you remember what was in that note?"

"No. What was it?"

"Well, you said: 'Dear Sir—I should be pleased if you will meet me for dinner at seven-thirty Wednesday evening at the Cock Horse Tavern on Brattle Street.' And the note was signed, 'Francis Starwick.'"

"Well?" Starwick demanded quietly. "And what was wrong with that?"

"Nothing!" the other young man cried, his face flushing to a darker hue, and the excitement of his manner growing. "Nothing, Frank! Only, if you were going to invite a stranger—some one you had never met before—to dinner—why the hell couldn't you have told him who you are, and the purpose of the meeting?"

"I should think the purpose of the meeting was self-evident," said Starwick calmly. "The purpose was to have dinner together. Does that demand a whole volume of explanation? No," he said coldly, "I confess I see nothing extraordinary about that at all."

"Of course there wasn't!" the other youth exclaimed with vehement excitement. "Of course there was nothing extraordinary about it! Why, then, did you attempt, Frank, to make something extraordinary out of it?"

"It seems to me that you're the one who's doing that!" Starwick answered.

"Yes, but, damn it, man," the other cried angrily "—don't you see the point? You're that way with everything you do! You try to surround the simplest act with this great air of mystery and secrecy," he said bitterly. "Inviting me to dinner was all right—it was fine!" he shouted. "I was a green kid of twenty who knew no one here, and I was scared to death. It was wonderful to get an invitation from some one asking me to dinner. But when you sent the invitation, why couldn't you have added just a word or two by way of explanation? Why couldn't you have stated one or two simple facts that would have made the reason for your invitation clear?"

"For example?" Starwick said.

"Why, Frank, simply that you were Professor Hatcher's assistant in the course, and that this thing of inviting people out to dinner was just a way you and Professor Hatcher had of getting acquainted with the new people," the other youth said angrily. "After all, you can't get an invitation to dinner from some one you don't know without wondering what it's all about."

"And yet you came," said Starwick.

"Yes, of course I came! I think I would have come if I had never heard of you before—I was so bewildered and rattled by this new life, and so overwhelmed by living in a big city for the first time in my life that I would have accepted any kind of invitation—jumped at the chance of meeting any one! However, I already knew who you were when your invitation came. I had heard that a man named Starwick was Hatcher's assistant. I figured therefore that the invitation had something to do with your connection with Professor Hatcher and the course—that you were inviting me to make me feel more at home up here, to establish a friendly relation, to give me what information you could, to help the new people out in any way you could. But when I met you, what happened?" he went on indignantly. "Never a word about the course, about Professor Hatcher, about your being his assistant—you pumped me with questions as if I were a prisoner on the witness stand and you the prosecuting lawyer. You told me nothing about yourself and asked a thousand questions about me—and then you shook hands coldly, and departed!—Always this air of secrecy and mystery, Frank!" the boy went on angrily. "That's always the way it is with you—in everything you do! And yet you wonder why people are surprised at your behavior! For weeks at a time I see you every day. We get together in your rooms and talk and argue about everything on earth. You come and yell for me in my place at midnight and then we walk all over Cambridge in the dead of night. We go over to Masillippo's place in Boston and eat and drink and get drunk together, and when you pass out, I bring you home and carry you upstairs and put you to bed. Then the next day, when I come around again," the boy cried bitterly, "what has happened? I ring the bell. Your voice comes through the place as cold as hell—'Who is it?' you say. 'Why,' I say, 'it's your old friend and drunken companion, Eugene Gant, who brought you home last night.'—'I'm sorry,' you say, in a tone that would freeze a polar bear— 'I can't see you. I'm busy now'—and then you hang up in my face. The season of the great mystery has now begun," he went on sarcastically. "The great man is closeted in his sanctum *composing*," he sneered. "Not *writing*, mind you, but *composing* with a gold-tipped quill plucked from the wing of a Brazilian condor—so, out, out, damned spot—don't bother me, Gant—begone, you low fellow—on your way, bum!—the great master, Signor Francis Starwick, is upstairs in a purple cloud, having a few immortal thoughts today with Amaryllis, his pet muse——"

"Gene! Gene!" said Starwick laughing, a trace of the old mannered accent returning to his voice again. "You are *most* unfair! You really are, you know!"

"No—but Frank, that's just the way you act," the other said. "You can't see enough of some one for weeks at a time and then you slam the door in his face. You pump your friends dry and tell them nothing about yourself. You try to surround everything you do with this grand romantic air of mysterious secrecy—this there's-more-to-this-than-meets-the-eye manner. Frank, who the hell do you think you are, anyway, with these grand airs and mysterious manners that you have? Is it that you're not the same as other men?" he jeered. "Is it that like Caesar you were from your mother's womb untimely ripped! Is it that you are made from different stuff than the damned base clay of blood and agony from which the rest of us have been derived?"

"What have I ever done," said Starwick flushing, "to give you the impression that I think of myself that way?"

"For one thing, Frank, you act sometimes as if the world exists solely for the purpose of being your oyster. You sometimes act as if friendship, the affection of your friends, is something that exists solely for your pleasure and convenience and may be turned on and off at will like a hot-water faucet—that you can use their time, their lives, their feelings when they amuse and interest you—and send them away like whipped dogs when you are bored, tired, indifferent, or have something else it suits you better to do."

"I am not aware that I have ever done that," said Starwick quietly. "I am sorry if you think I have."

"No, but, Frank—what can you expect your friends to think? I have told you about my life, my family, the kind of place and people I came from—but you have told me nothing. You are the best friend I have here in Cambridge—I think," the boy said slowly, flushing, and with some difficulty, "one of the best friends I have ever had. I have not had many friends—I have known no one like you—no one of my own age to whom I could talk as I have talked to you. I think I enjoy being with you and talking to you more than to any one I have ever known. This friendship that I feel for you has now become a part of my whole life and has got into everything I do. And yet, at times, I run straight into a blank wall. I could no more separate my friendship for you from the other acts and meetings of my life than I could divide into two parts of my body my father's and my mother's blood. With you it's different. You seem to have all your friend's partitioned off and kept separate from one another in different cells and sections of your life. I know now that you have three or four sets of friends and yet these different groups of people never meet one another. You go about your life with all these different sets of people in this same secret and mysterious manner that characterizes everything you do. You have these aunts and cousins here in Cambridge that you see every week, and who, like every one else, lay themselves out to do everything they can to make your life comfortable and pleasant. You know these swells over on Beacon Hill in Boston, and you have some grand, mysterious and wealthy kind of life with them. Then you have another group here at the university—people like Egan, and Hugh Dodd and myself. And at the end, Frank," the boy said almost bitterly—"what is the purpose of all this secrecy and separation among your friends? There's something so damned arrogant and cold and calculating about it—it's almost as if you were one of these damned, wretched, self-centered fools who have their little time and place for everything—an hour for social recreation and an hour for useful reading, another hour for healthy exercise, and then four hours for business, an hour for the concert and an hour for the play, an hour for "business contacts" and an hour for friendship—Surely to God, Frank, you of all people on earth are not one of these damned, smug, vain, self-centred egotists—who would milk this earth as if it were a great milk cow here solely for their enrichment, and who, at the end, in spite of all their damned, miserable, self-seeking profit for themselves remain nothing but the God-damned smug, sterile, misbegotten set of impotent and life-hating bastards that they are— Surely to God, you, of all people in the world are not one of these," he fairly yelled, and sat there panting, exhausted by the tirade, and glaring at the other youth with wild, resentful eyes.

"Eugene!" cried Starwick sharply, his ruddy features darkened with an angry glow. "You are being most unjust! What you are saying simply is not true." He was silent a moment, his face red and angry-looking, as he stared out across the river—"If I had known that you felt this way," he went on quietly, "I should have introduced you to my other friends—what you call these separate groups of people—long ago. You may meet them any time you wish," he concluded. "It simply never occurred to me that you would be interested in knowing them."

"Oh, Frank, I'm not!" the other boy cried impatiently, with a dismissing movement of the hand. "I don't want to meet them—I don't care who they are—or how rich and fashionable or 'artistic' they may be. The thing I was kicking about was what seemed to me to be your air of secrecy—the mysterious manner in which you go about things: it seemed to me that there was something deliberately calculating and secretive in the way you shut one part of your life off from the people who know and like you best."

Starwick made no answer for a moment, but sat looking out across the river. And for a moment, the old grimace of bestial, baffled pain passed swiftly across his ruddy features, and then he said, in a quiet and weary tone:

"Perhaps you are right. I had never thought about it in that way. Yes, I can see now that you have told me much more about yourself —your family, your life before you came here, than I have told you about mine. And yet it never occurred to me that I was being mysterious or secretive. I think it is easier for you to speak about these things than it is for me. There is a great river of energy in you and it keeps bursting over and breaking loose. You could not hold it back if you tried. With me, it's different. I have not got that great well of life and power in me, and I could not speak as you do if I tried. Yet, Gene, if there is anything you want to know about my life before I came here, or what kind of people I came from I would tell you willingly."

"I have wanted to know more about you, Frank," the other young man said. "All that I know about your life before you came here is that you come from somewhere in the Middle West, and yet are completely different from any one I ever knew who came from there."

"Yes," said Starwick quietly. "From Horton, for example?" his tone was still quiet, but there was a shade of irony in it.

"Well," the other boy said, flushing, but continuing obstinately, "—yes, from Horton. He is from Iowa, you can see, smell, read, feel Iowa all over him, in everything he says and does——"

"It's—a—*darn—good—yarn,*'" said Starwick, beginning to burble with laughter as he imitated the heavy, hearty, sonorous robustiousness of Horton's voice when he pronounced his favorite judgment.

"Yes," said Eugene, laughing at the imitation, "that's it, all right —'it's a *darn good yarn.*' Well, Frank, you couldn't be more different from Horton if you had come from the planet Mars, and yet the place you come from out there in the Middle West, the kind of life you knew when you were growing up—could not have been so different from Ed Horton's."

"No," said Starwick quietly. "As a matter of fact, I know where he is from—it's not over fifty miles from the town I was born in, which is in Illinois, and the life in both places is much the same."

He was silent a moment longer, as he stared across the river, and then continued in a quiet voice that had a calm, weary, and almost inert detachment that characterized these conversations with his friend, and that was almost entirely free of mannered speech:

"As to the kind of people that we came from," he continued, "I can't say how different they may be, but I should think it very likely that Horton's people are much the same kind of people as my own——"

"His father is a Methodist minister," the other young man quickly interposed. "He told me that."

"Yes," said Starwick in his quiet and inert voice—"and Horton is the rebel of the family." His tone had not changed apparently in its quality by an atom, yet the quiet and bitter irony with which he spoke was evident.

"How did you know that?" the other youth said in a surprised

.

tone. "Yes—that's true. His wife told me that Ed and his father are scarcely on speaking terms—the old man prays for the salvation of Ed's soul three times a day, because he is trying to write plays and wants to get into the theatre. Effie Horton says Ed's father still writes Ed letters begging him to repent and mend his ways before his soul is damned forever: she says the old man calls the theatre the Devil's Workshop."

"Yes," said Starwick in his quiet and almost lifeless tone that still had curiously the cutting edge of a weary and detached sarcasm —"and Horton has bearded the Philistines in their den, hasn't he, and given all for art?"

"Isn't that a bit unjust? I know you don't think very highly of Ed Horton's ability, but, after all, the man must have had some genuine desire to create something—some real love for the theatre—or he would not have broken with his family, and come here."

"Yes. I suppose he has. Many people have that desire," said Starwick wearily. "Do you think it is enough?"

"No, I do not. And yet I think a man who has it is better off—will have a better life, somehow—than the man who does not have it at all."

"Do you?" Starwick answered in a dead tone. "I wish I thought so, too."

"But don't you, Frank? Surely it is better to have some kind of talent, however small, than none at all."

"Would you say, then," Starwick answered, "that it was better to have some kind of child—however puny, feeble, ugly, and diseased —as King Richard said about himself, brought into the world 'scarce half made up'—than to have no child at all?"

"I would not think so. No."

"Have you ever thought, Eugene, that the great enemy of life may not be death, but life itself?" Starwick continued. "Have you never noticed that the really evil people that one meets—the people who are filled with hatred, fear, envy, rancour against life—who wish to destroy the artist and his work—are not figures of satanic darkness, who have been born with a malignant hatred against life, but rather people who have had the seeds of life within themselves, and been destroyed by them? They are the people who have been given just enough to get a vision of the promised land—however brief and broken it may be——"

"But not enough to get there? Is that what you mean?"

"Exactly," Starwick answered. "They are left there in the desert, maddened by the sight of water they can never reach, and all the juices of their life then turn to gall and bitterness—to envy and malignant hate. They are the old women in the little towns and villages with the sour eyes and the envenomed flesh who have so poisoned the air with their envenomed taint that everything young and beautiful and full of joy that lives there will sicken and go dead and vicious and malignant as the air it breathes. They are the lecherous and impotent old men of the world, those foul, palsied creatures with small rheumy eyes who hate the lover and his mistress with the hate of hell and eunuchry—who try to destroy love with their hatred, and the slanderous rumor of their poisoned tongues. And, finally, they are the eunuchs of the arts—the men who have the lust, without the power, for creation, and whose life goes dead and rotten with its hatred of the living artist and the living man."

"And you think that Horton will be one of these?"

Again Starwick was silent for a moment, staring out across the river. When he spoke again, he did not answer his companion's question directly, but in a quiet and inert tone in which the cutting edge of irony was barely evident, he said:

"My *God,* Eugene"—his voice was so low and wearily passionate with revulsion that it was almost inaudible—"if ever you may come to know, as I have known all my life, the falseness in a hearty laugh, the envy and the malice in a jesting word, the naked hatred in a jeering eye, and all the damned, warped, poisonous constrictions of the heart—the horrible fear and cowardice and cruelty, the naked shame, the hypocrisy, and the pretense, that is masked there behind the full hearty tones, the robust manliness of the Hortons of this earth . . ." He was silent a moment longer, and then went on in a quiet, matter-of-fact tone—"I was the youngest in a family of nine children—the same kind of family that you will find everywhere. I was the only delicate flower among them," he went on with a cold impassive irony. "We were not rich people . . . a big family growing up with only a small income to support us. They were all good people," he said quietly. "My father was superintendent of a small farm-machinery plant, and before that they were farming people, but they sent me to school, and after that to college. I was the 'bright boy' of the town"—again the weary irony of his voice was

evident—"the local prodigy, the teacher's pet. . . . Perhaps that is
my destiny; to have something of the artist's heart, his soul, his
understanding, his perceptions—never to have his power, the hand
that shapes, the tongue that can express—oh, God! Eugene! is *that*
to be my life—to have all that I know and feel and would create rot
still-born in my spirit, to be a wave that breaks forever in mid-ocean,
the shoulder of a strength without the wall—my God! My God! to
come into this world scarce half made up, to have the spirit of the
artist and to lack his hide, to feel the intolerable and unspeakable
beauty, mystery, loveliness, and terror of this immortal land—this
great America—and a skin too sensitive, a hide too delicate and rare
—" his voice was high and bitter with his passion—"to declare its
cruelty, its horror, falseness, hunger, the warped and twisted soul of
it frustration, and lacking hide and toughness, born without a skin,
to make an armor, school a manner, build a barrier of my own
against its Hortons——"

"And is that why—?" the other boy began, flushed, and quickly
checked himself.

"Is that why—what?" said Starwick turning, looking at him. Then
as he did not answer, but still remained silent, flushed with embarrassment, Starwick laughed, and said: "Is that why I am an affected
person—a poseur—what Horton calls a 'damned little æsthete'—
why I speak and act and dress the way I do?"

The other flushed miserably and muttered:

"No, I didn't say that, Frank!"

Starwick laughed suddenly, his infectious and spontaneous laugh,
and said:

"But why not? Why shouldn't you say it? Because it is the truth.
It really is, you know," and almost mockingly at these words, his
voice assumed its murmured and affected accent. Then he said
quietly again:

"Each man has his manner—with each it comes for his own
reason—Horton's, so that his hearty voice and robust way may hide
the hatred in his eyes, the terror in his heart, the falseness and
pretense in his pitiable warped small soul. He has his manner, I have
mine—his for concealment, mine for armor, because my native hide
was tender and my skin too sensitive to meet the Hortons of the earth
—and somewhere, down below our manner, stands the naked man."
Again he was silent and in a moment he continued quietly:

"My father was a fine man and we never got to know each other very well. The night before I went to college he 'took me to one side' and talked to me—he told me how they had their hearts set on me, and he asked me to become a good and useful man—a good American."

"And what did you say, Frank?"

"Nothing. There was nothing I could say. . . . Our house stands on little butte above the river," he went on quietly in a moment, "and when he had finished talking I went out and stood there looking at the river."

"What river, Frank?"

"There is only one," he answered. "The great slow river—the dark and secret river of the night—the everlasting flood—the unceasing Mississippi. . . . It is a river that I know so well, with all my life that I shall never tell about. Perhaps you will some day—perhaps you have the power in you— And if you do—" he paused.

"And if I do?"

"Speak one word for a boy who could not speak against the Hortons of this land, but who once stood above a river—and who knew America as every other boy has known it." He turned, smiling: "If thou did'st ever hold me in thy heart, absent thee from felicity awhile, and in this harsh world draw thy breath in pain, to tell my story."

In a moment he got up, and laughing his infectious laugh, said: "Come on, let's go."

And together they walked away.

A PORTRAIT OF ABRAHAM JONES

AT THE end of his classes, the final end, when all had spoken, when that hot wave of life and turbulence had withdrawn, the last clattering footfalls had echoed away along the corridors, the last loud aggressive voices had faded into silence, leaving, it seemed, an odor of exhaustion, use, and weariness even in the walls, boards and benches of the room, so that the empty classroom had a tired but living presence of fatigue, the indefinable but sharply felt character of a room with people absent from it, and seemed somehow to relax, settle, and respire with relief and weariness—at this final, fagged, and burned-out candle-end of day, Abraham Jones, as relentless as destiny, would be there waiting for Eugene. He waited there, grim, gray, unsmiling, tortured-looking behind an ominous wink of glasses, a picture of Yiddish melancholy and discontent, and as Eugene looked at him his heart went numb and dead; he hated the sight of him. He sat there now in the front rows of the class like a nemesis of scorn, a merciless censor of Eugene's ignorance and incompetence: the sight of his dreary discontented face, with its vast gray acreage of a painful Jewish and involuted intellectualism, was enough, even at the crest of a passionate burst of inspiration, to curdle his blood, freeze his heart, stun and deaden the fiery particle of his brain, and thicken his tongue to a faltering, incoherent mumble. Eugene did not know what Abe wanted, what he expected, what kind of teaching he thought worthy of him: he only knew that nothing he did suited him, that the story of his inadequacy and incompetence was legible in every line of that gray, dreary, censorious face. He thought of it at night with a kind of horror: the ghoulish head which craned out of a vulture's body swept after him through all the fields of a distressful sleep, a taloned fury filled with croakings of hoarse doom. Never before had Eugene been driven through desperation to such exhausting intensities of work: night by night he sweated blood over great stacks and sheaves of their dull, careless, trivial papers—he read, re-read, and triple-read them, putting in all commas, colons, periods, correcting all faults of spelling, grammar, punctuation that he knew, writing long, laborious comments and criticisms on the back and rising suddenly out of a haunted tortured sleep to change a grade. And at the end, the inexorable end, he was always faced with the menace of Abe's weekly paper: with dread and quaking he tackled it. He wrote the best papers that Eugene got: the grammar was flawless, the spelling impeccable, the vocabulary precise and extensive, the sentences cleanly and forcibly shaped. The thought was sound, subtle, and coherent—by every standard the work was of an extraordinary grade and quality, its merit was unmistakable, and yet Eugene approached a four-page paper with fear and trembling, before he had gone beyond the first paragraph great sobs and groans of weariness and despair were wrung from him, he stamped across the floor with it like a man maddened by an aching tooth; he began again, he flung himself upon the bed, got up and walked again, doused his head in basins of cold water—but it was no use: to read the paper to the end, as he did and must, was weariness and travail of the spirit—it was like eating chalk or trying to suck sweetness out of paving brick, or being drowned in an ocean of dishwater, or forced to gorge oneself on boiled unseasoned spinach. Abe wrote on a great range and variety of subjects and everything he wrote was good: he wrote about the plays of Pirandello, of "Six Characters in Search of an Author," and of "three planes of reality" therein: he estimated and analyzed those three planes with the power of a philosopher, the delicacy of a subtle-souled psychologist, and all of this to Eugene was as weeping and wailing and gnashing of teeth, because it was so good, and he did not know what was wrong, and he could not endure to read it. He could not write upon his papers that he found them intolerably dull unless he knew wherein the reason for that dullness lay, and he did not know the reason: accordingly the highest grade he ever gave to any one—the grade of "A"—was week by week wrung from trembling and reluctant fingers. But no matter what the grade was, or how flattering the comment, Abe protested. Gray, dreary, tortured, discontented, Yiddish, he would be waiting for Eugene at the end of every class, clutching his paper in his impatient fingers, armed and eager for the combat of dispute that was to follow.

The class met at night and they would walk rapidly away together along the empty echoing corridors, and turning clatter down the stairs that led to the main entrance. The vast building was deserted and full of weary echoes: they could hear the solitary clang of an elevator door, and the dynamic hum of its machinery as it mounted. Some one was walking in the big corridor downstairs: they heard the echoing ring of his footsteps on the slick marble flags, and the noisy rattle of a cleaner's bucket on the floor. The whole building was charged with a weary electric quality—with the quality of a light which has gone dim. And the taste and the smell of this weariness was in Eugene's mouth and nostrils; it was as if he had stuck his tongue against a warm but burned-out storage battery; it was like the smell that comes from the wheels of a street car when they have ground around a curve, or like the odor from a smoking hot-box on the fast express. His body also had this feeling of electric weariness, as if the vital currents were exhausted: his flesh felt dry and juiceless, his back was tired, his loins were sterile, the acrid burned-out flavor filled him.

The big ugly building breathed slowly with the fatigue of inanimate objects which have been overcharged with human energy: it was haunted with its tired emptiness, with the absence of the thousands of people who had swarmed through its every part that day with such a clamorous, hot and noisy life. The lifeless air in its passages had been breathed and rebreathed again and again: the walls, the furniture, the floors—every part of the building—seemed to exude this sense of nervous depletion.

As he hurried down the stairs on such an evening with his unshakable companion, his implacable disputant, he hated the building more than he had ever hated any building before: it seemed to be soaked in all the memories of fruitless labor and harsh strife, of fear and hate and weariness, of ragged nerves and pounding heart and tired flesh: the building brooded there, charged with its dreadful burden of human pain, encumbered with its grief; and his hatred for the building was the hatred of a man for the place where he has met some terrible humiliation of the flesh or spirit, or for the room in which a man has seen his brother die, or for the dwelling from which love and the beloved have departed. The ghosts of pain and darkness sat in the empty chairs, the spirits of venom and sterility brooded over the desks: dry hatred and the poison of the brain were seated in the chairs of the instructors; fear trembled in their seats, it made a hateful cold around the heart, it made the bowels queasy, it made swallowing hard, it slithered at the edges of the desk, it fell and crawled and wobbled like a boneless thing. And the gray-faced Jew beside Eugene made the weary lights burn dim: he gave a tongue to weariness, a color to despair.

They hurried down the steps and left the building almost as if they were in flight. The heavy door clanged to behind them making echoes in the halls, they reached the pavement at the Square, and immediately they halted. Here, they were in another world, and their weary bodies drank in a new vitality. Sometimes, on a cold still night in winter, the sky had the peculiarly frosty clarity that comes from a still, biting cold. Above the great vertical radiance and cold Northern passion of New York, it was a-glitter with magnificent stars, it was a-glitter with small pollens, with a jewelled dust of stars that seemed to have been sown drunkenly through heaven, and as Eugene looked his weariness was cleansed out of him at once, he was filled with an overwhelming desire to possess beauty and all things else, and to include all things in him. He would learn to be all things: he would be an artist and he would find a way of living in the maelstrom. The darkness filled him with a sense of power and possession: his spirit soared out over the city, and over the earth, he was no longer afraid of the gray-faced Jew beside him, peace and power and certitude possessed him. He drank the air into his veins in great gulps, he saw the huge walled cliff of the city ablaze with its jewelry of hard sown lights, he knew he could possess it all, and a feeling of joy and victory rushed through his senses.

Under the furious goad of desperation, a fear of failure and disgrace, a sense of loneliness and desolation, and a grim determination to go down into the dust of ruin only when he could no longer lift a hand or draw a breath, he learned his job, and found his life again, he did the labor of a titan, the flesh wasted from his bones, he became a mad, driven zealot, but he was a good teacher, and the day came when he knew he need no longer draw his breath in fear of shame, that he had paid his way and earned his wage and could meet them eye to eye. He took those swarthy swarming classes and looted his life clean for them: he bent over them, prayed, sweated, and exhorted like a prophet, a poet, and a priest—he poured upon them the whole deposit of his living, feeling, reading, the whole store of poetry, passion and belief: he went into the brain of a dullard like a surgeon, and he blew some spark of fire into a glow in even the least and worst of them, but that gray-faced Yiddish inquisitor hung doggedly to his heels, the more he gave, the more Abe wanted; he fed on Eugene's life, enriching his grayness with an insatiate and vampiric gluttony, and yet he never had a word of praise, a sentence of thanks, a syllable of commendation.

Instead he became daily more open in his surly discontent, his sour depreciation; his insolence, unchecked, grew by leaps and bounds, he exulted in a feeling of cruel crowing Jewish mastery over Eugene's bent aching spirit, he walked away with him day by day and his conversation now was one long surly indictment of his class, his teaching, and his competence. Why didn't Eugene give them better topics for their themes? Why didn't they use another volume of essays instead of the one they had, which was no good? Why, in the list of poems, plays, biographies and novels which Eugene had assigned, and which were no good, had he omitted the names of Jewish writers such as Lewisohn and Sholem Asch? Why did he not give each student private "conferences" more frequently, although he had conferred with them until his brain and heart were sick and weary. Why did they not write more expository, fewer descriptive themes; more argument, less narration? Why, in short, did he not do everything in a different way?—the indictment, merciless, insistent, unrelenting, piled up day by day and meanwhile resentment, anger, resolution began to blaze and burn in Eugene, a conviction grew that this could no longer be endured, that no life, no wage, no position was worth this thankless toil and trouble, and that he must make an end of a situation which had become intolerable.

One night, when Abe had accompanied Eugene from the class to the entrance of the hotel, and as he was in the full course and tide of his surly complaint, Eugene stopped him suddenly and curtly, saying: "You don't like my class, do you, Jones? You don't think much of the way I teach, do you?"

Abe was surprised at the question, because his complaint had always had a kind of sour impersonality: it had never wholly dared a final accusatory directness.

"Well," he said in a moment, with a surly and unwilling tone, "I never said that. I don't think we're getting as much out of the class as we should. I think we could get a lot more out of it than we're getting. That's all I said."

"And you have a few thousand suggestions to make, that would improve it? Is that it?"

"Well, I had to tell you how I felt about it," Abe said doggedly. "If you don't like it, I'm sorry. You know we fellows down there have got to pay tuition. And they charge you plenty for it, too! . . . Don't let them kid you!" he said with a derisive and scornful laugh. "That place is a gold mine for some one! The trustees are getting rich on it!"

"Well, I'm not getting rich on it," Eugene said. "I get $150 a month out of it. Apparently you think it's too much."

"Well, we've got a right to expect the best we can get," he said. "That's what we're there for. That's what we're paying out our dough for. You know, the fellows down there are not rich guys like the fellows at Yale and Harvard. A dollar means something to them. . . . We don't get everything handed to us on a silver platter. Most of us have got to work for everything we get, and if some guy who's teaching us is not giving us the best he's got we got a right to kick about it. . . . That's the way I feel about it."

"All right," Eugene said, "I know where you stand now. Now, I'll tell you where I stand. I've been giving you the best I've got, but you don't think it's good enough. Well, it's all I've got and it's all you're going to get from me. Now, I tell you what you're going to do, Jones. You're going out of my class. Do you understand?" he shouted. "You're going now. I never want to see you in my class again. I'll get you transferred, I'll have you put in some other instructor's class, but you'll never come into my room again."

"You can't do that," Abe said. "You've got no right to do that. You've got no right to change a fellow to another class in the middle of the term. I've done my work," he said resentfully, "you're not going to change me. . . . I'll take it to the faculty committee if you do."

Eugene could stand no more: in misery and despair he thought of all he had endured because of Abe, and the whole choking wave of resentment and fury which he had been gathering in his heart for months burst out upon him.

"Why, damn you!" he said. "Go to the faculty committee or any other damned place you please, but you'll never come back to any room where I'm teaching again. If they send you back, if they say I've got to have you in my class, I quit. Do you hear me, Jones?" he shouted. "I'll not have you! If they try to force me, I'm through! To hell with such a life! I'll get down and clean out sewers before I have you in my class again. . . . Now, you damned rascal," his voice had grown so hoarse and thick he could hardly speak, and the blind motes were swimming drunkenly before him. ". . . I've had all I can stand from you. . . . Why, you damned dull fellow. . . . Sitting there and sneering at me day after day with your damned Jew's face. . . .

What are you but a damned dull fellow, anyway? ... Why, damn you, Jones, you didn't deserve any one like me. . . . You should get down on your knees and thank God you had a teacher half as good as me. ... You ... damned ... *fellow*. . . . You! ... To think I sweat blood over you! . . . Now, get away from here!" . . . he yelled. "To hell with you! . . . I never want to see your face again!"

He turned and started toward the hotel entrance: he felt blind and weak and dizzy, but he did not care what happened now: after all these weeks of heavy misery a great wave of release and freedom was coursing through his veins. Before he had gone three steps Abe Jones was at his side, clutching at his sleeve, beseeching, begging, pleading: "Say! . . . You've got the wrong idea! Honest you have! . . . Say! I never knew you felt like that! Don't send me out of there," he begged earnestly, and suddenly Eugene saw that his shining glasses had grown misty and that his dull weak eyes blinked with tears. "I don't want to leave your class," he said. "Why, that's the best class I've got! . . . Honest it is! No kiddin'! . . . All the fellows feel the same way about it."

He begged, beseeched, and almost wept: finally, when good will had again been restored between them, he wrung Eugene's hand, laughed painfully and shyly, and then took off his misted glasses and began to shine and polish them with a handkerchief. His gray ugly face as he stood there polishing his glasses had that curiously naked, inept, faded and tired wistful look that is common to people with weak eyes when they remove their spectacles; it was a good and ugly face, and suddenly Eugene began to like Abe very much. He left him and went up to his room with a feeling of such relief, ease and happiness as he had not known for months; and that night, unhaunted, unashamed, unpursued by fears and furies and visions of his ruin and failure for the first time in many months, he sank dreamlessly, sweetly, deliciously, into the depths of a profound and soundless sleep.

And from that moment, through every change of fortune, all absence, all return, all wandering, and through the whole progress of his city life, through every event of triumph, ruin, or madness, this Jew, Abe Jones, the first manswarm atom he had come to know in all the desolation of the million-footed city—had been his loyal friend.

It was not the golden city he had visioned as a child, and the gray reptilian face of that beak-nosed Jew did not belong among the company of the handsome, beautiful and fortunate people that he had dreamed about, but Abe was made of better stuff than most dreams are made of. His spirit was as steady as a rock, as enduring as the earth, and like the flash of a light, the sight of his good, gray ugly face could always evoke for Eugene the whole wrought fabric of his life in the city, the whole design of wandering and return, with a thousand memories of youth and hunger, of loneliness, fear, despair, of glory, love, exultancy and joy.

Man's youth is a wonderful thing: It is so full of anguish and of magic and he never comes to know it as it is, until it has gone from him forever. It is the thing he cannot bear to lose, it is the thing whose passing he watches with infinite sorrow and regret, it is the thing whose loss he must lament forever, and it is the thing whose loss he really welcomes with a sad and secret joy, the thing he would never willingly re-live again, could it be restored to him by any magic.

Why is this? The reason is that the strange and bitter miracle of life is nowhere else so evident as in our youth. And what is the essence of that strange and bitter miracle of life which we feel so poignantly, so unutterably, with such a bitter pain and joy, when we are young? It is this: that being rich, we are so poor; that being mighty, we can yet have nothing, that seeing, breathing, smelling, tasting all around us the impossible wealth and glory of this earth, feeling with an intolerable certitude that the whole structure of the enchanted life—the most fortunate, wealthy, good, and happy life that any man has ever known—is ours—is ours at once, immediately and forever, the moment that we choose to take a step, or stretch a hand, or say a word—we yet know that we can really keep, hold, take, and possess forever—nothing. All passes; nothing lasts: the moment that we put our hand upon it it melts away like smoke, is gone forever, and the snake is eating at our heart again; we see then what we are and what our lives must come to.

A young man is so strong, so mad, so certain, and so lost. He has everything and he is able to use nothing. He hurls the great shoulder of his strength forever against phantasmal barriers, he is a wave whose power explodes in lost mid-oceans under timeless skies, he reaches out to grip a fume of painted smoke; he wants all, feels the thirst and power for everything, and finally gets nothing. In the end, he is destroyed by his own strength, devoured by his own hunger, impoverished by his own wealth. Thoughtless of money or the accumulation of material possessions, he is none the less defeated in the end by his own greed—a greed that makes the avarice of King Midas seem paltry by comparison.

And that is the reason why, when youth is gone, every man will look back upon that period of his life with infinite sorrow and regret. It is the bitter sorrow and regret of a man who knows that once he had a great talent and wasted it, of a man who knows that once he had a great treasure and got nothing from it, of a man who knows that he had strength enough for everything and never used it.

All youth is bound to be "mis-spent"; there is something in its very nature that makes it so, and that is why all men regret it. And that regret becomes more poignant as the knowledge comes to us that this great waste of youth was utterly unnecessary, as we discover with a bitter irony of mirth, that youth is something which only young men have, and which only old men know how to use. And for that reason, in later years, we all look back upon our youth with sorrow and regret—seeing what a wealth was ours if we had used it—remembering Weisberg, Snodgrass, and O'Hare—finally remembering with tenderness and joy the good bleak visage of the pavement cipher who was the first friend we ever knew in the great city—in whose gray face its million strange and secret mysteries were all compact—and who was our friend, our brother, and this earth's nameless man. And so Eugene recalled Abraham Jones.

This ugly, good, and loyal creature had almost forgotten his real name: the "Jones," of course, was one of those random acquisitions which, bestowed in some blind, dateless moment of the past, evoked a picture of those nameless hordes of driven and frightened people who had poured into this country within the last half-century, and whose whole lives had been determined for them by the turn of a word, the bend of a street, the drift of the crowd, or a surly and infuriated gesture by some ignorant tyrant of an official. In such a way, Abe Jones's father, a Polish Jew, without a word of Yankee English in his throat, had come to Castle Garden forty years before and, stunned and frightened by the moment's assault of some furious little swine of a customs inspector, had stood dumbly while the man snarled and menaced him: "What's yer name? . . . Huh? . . . Don't yuh know what yer name is . . . Huh? . . . Ain't you got a name? . . . Huh?" To all this the poor Jew had no answer but a stare of stupefaction and terror: at length a kind of frenzy seized him—a torrent of Polish, Jewish, Yiddish speech poured from his mouth, but never a word his snarling inquisitor could understand. The Jew begged, swore, wept, pleaded, prayed, entreated—a thousand tales of horror, brutal violence and tyranny swept through his terror-stricken mind, the whole vast obscene chronicle of immigration gleaned from the mouths of returned adventurers or from the letters of those who had triumphantly passed the gates of wrath: he showed his papers, he clasped his hands, he swore by all the oaths he knew that all was as it should be, that he had done all he had been told to do, that there was no trick or fraud or cheat in anything he did or said, and all the time, the foul, swollen, snarling face kept thrusting at him with the same maddening and indecipherable curse: "Yer name! . . . Yer name! . . . Fer Christ's sake don't yuh know yer own name? . . . All right!" he shouted suddenly, furiously, "If yuh ain't got a name I'll give yuh one! . . . If yuh ain't got sense enough to tell me what yer own name is, I'll find one for yuh!" The snarling face came closer: "Yer name's Jones! See! J-o-n-e-s. Jones! That's a good Amurrican name. See? I'm giving yuh a good honest Amurrican name that a lot of good decent Amurricans have got. Yuh've gotta try to live up to it and desoive it! See? Yer in Amurrica now, Jones. . . . See? . . . Yuh've gotta t'ink fer yerself, Jones. In Amurrica we know our own name. We've been trained to t'ink for ourselves over here! . . . See? Yer not one of them foreign dummies any more! . . . Yer Jones—Jones— Jones!" he yelled. "See!"—and in such a way, on the impulsion of brutal authority and idiot chance, Abe's father had been given his new name. Eugene did not know what Abe's real name was: Abe had told him once, and he remembered it as something pleasant, musical, and alien to our tongue, difficult for our mouths to shape and utter.

Already, when he had first met Abe Jones in the first class he taught, the process of mutation had carried so far that he was trying to rid himself of the accursed "Abraham," reducing it to an ambiguous initial, and signing his papers with a simple unrevealing "A. Jones," as whales are said to have lost through atrophy the use of legs with which they once walked across the land, but still to carry upon their bodies the rudimentary stump. Now, in the last year, he had dared to make a final transformation, shocking, comical, pitifully clumsy in its effort at concealment and deception: when Eugene had tried to find his name and number in the telephone directory a month before, among the great gray regiment of Joneses, the familiar, quaint, and homely "Abe" had disappeared—at length he found him coyly sheltered under the gentlemanly obscurity of A. Alfred Jones. The transformation, thus, had been complete: he was now, in name, at any rate, a member of the great Gentile aristocracy of Jones; and just as "Jones" had been thrust by violence upon his father, so had Abe taken violently, by theft and rape, the "Alfred." There was something mad and appalling in the bravado, the effrontery, and the absurdity of the attempt: what did he hope to do with such a name? What reward did he expect to win? Was he engaged in some vast conspiracy in which all depended on the *sound* and not the *appearance* of deception? Was he using the mails in some scheme to swindle or defraud? Was he carrying on by correspondence an impassioned courtship of some ancient Christian maiden with one tooth and a million shining dollars? Or was it part of a gigantic satire on Gentile genteelness, country-club Christianity, a bawdy joke perpetrated at the expense of sixty thousand anguished and protesting Social Registerites? That he should hope actually to palm himself off as a Gentile was unthinkable, because one look at him revealed instantly the whole story of his race and origin: if all the Polish-Russian Jews that ever swarmed along the ghettoes of the earth had been compacted in a single frame the physical result might have been something amazingly like Eugene's friend, Abraham Jones.

The whole flag and banner of his race was in the enormous putty-colored nose that bulged, flared and sprouted with the disproportionate extravagance of a caricature or a dill-pickle over his pale, slightly freckled and rather meagre face; he had a wide, thin, somewhat cruel-looking mouth, dull weak eyes that stared, blinked, and grew misty with a murky, somewhat slimily ropy feeling behind his spectacles, a low, dull, and slanting forehead, almost reptilian in its ugliness, that sloped painfully back an inch or two into the fringes of unpleasantly greasy curls and coils of dark, short, screwy hair. He was about the middle height, and neither thin nor fat: his figure was

rather big-boned and angular, and yet it gave an impression of mea-
greness, spareness, and somewhat tallowy toughness which so many
city people have, as if their ten thousand days and nights upon the
rootless pavement had dried all juice and succulence out of them, as
if asphalt and brick and steel had got into the conduits of their blood
and spirit, leaving them with a quality that is tough, dry, meagre,
tallowy, and somewhat calloused.

What earth had nourished him? Had he been born and grown
there among the asphalt lilies and the pavement wheat? What corn
was growing from the cobblestones? Or was there never a cry of earth
up through the beaten and unyielding cement of the streets? Had he
forgotten the immortal and attentive earth still waiting at the roots
of steel?

No. Beneath that cone of neat gray felt, behind the dreary, tal-
lowed pigment of his face, which had that thickened, stunned, and
deadened look one often sees upon the faces of old bruisers, as if the
violent and furious assault of stone and steel, the million harsh
metallic clangors, the brutal stupefaction of the streets, at length had
dried the flesh and thickened the skin, and blunted, numbed and
calloused the aching tumult of the tortured and tormented senses—
there still flowed blood as red and wet as any which ever swarmed
into the earth below the laurel bush. He was a part, a drop, an indecipherable fraction of these gray tides of swarming tissue that
passed in ceaseless weft and counter-weft upon the beaten pavements,
at once a typical man-swarm atom and a living man. Indistinguish-
able in his speech, gait, dress, and tallowy pigmentation from the
typical cell-and-pavement article, at the same time, although ugly,
meagre, toughened, gnarled and half-articulate, angular as brick and
spare as steel webbing, with little juice and succulence, he was honest, loyal, somehow good and memorable, grained with the life and
movement of a thousand streets, seasoned and alert, a living character, a city man. In that horrible desperation of drowning and atomic
desolation among the numberless hordes that swept along the rootless pavements, in Eugene's madness to know, own, intrude behind
the million barriers of brick, to root and entrench himself in the
hive, he seized upon that dreary, gray and hopeless-looking Jew.

This was his history:

Abraham Jones was one of the youngest members of a large family. In addition to two brothers, younger than himself, there were three older brothers, and two sisters. The family life was close, complex, and passionate, torn by fierce dislikes and dissensions, menaced by division among some of its members, held together by equally fierce loyalties and loves among the others. Abe disliked his father and hated one of his older brothers. He loved one of his sisters and was attached to the other one by a kind of loyalty of silence.

She, Sylvia, was a woman of perhaps thirty-five years when Eugene first saw her, she had not lived at home for ten years, she was a febrile, nervous, emaciated, highly enamelled city woman—a lover of what was glittering and electric in life, caught up in the surge of a furious and feverish life, and yet not content with it, dissonant, irritable and impatient. Like the rest of her family she had been forced to shift for herself since childhood: she had been first a salesgirl, then a worker in a millinery shop, and now, through her own cleverness, smartness, and ability, she had achieved a very considerable success in business. She ran a hat shop on Second Avenue, which Abe told him was the Broadway of the lower East Side: she had a small, elegant, glittering jewel of a shop there, blazing with hard electric light and smartly and tastefully dressed with windows filled with a hundred jaunty styles in women's hats. She did a thriving business and employed several assistants.

The first time Eugene met her, one day when Abe had taken him home to the flat where he lived with his mother, two of his brothers, and Sylvia's child, he thought she had the look and quality of an actress much more than of a business woman. There was a remarkably electric glitter and unnaturalness about her: it seemed as if the only light that had ever shone upon her had been electric light, the only air she could breathe with any certitude and joy, the clamorous and electric air of Broadway. Her face belonged, indeed, among those swarms of livid, glittering, night-time faces that pour along the street, with that mysterious fraternity of night-time people who all seem to speak a common language and to be bound together by some central interest and communication, who live mysteriously and gaudily without discoverable employments, in a world remote and alien. Sylvia was a woman of middling height, but of a dark and almost bird-like emaciation: all the flesh seemed to have been starved, wasted, and consumed from her by this devil of feverish and electric unrest and discontent that glittered with almost a drugged brilliance in her large dark eyes. Every visible portion of her body, hair, eyebrows, lashes, lips, skin and nails was greased, waved, leaded, rouged, plucked, polished, enamelled and varnished with the conventional extravagance of a ritualistic mask until now it seemed that all of the familiar qualities of living tissue had been consumed, and were replaced by the painted image, the varnished mask of a face, designed in its unreality to catch, reflect, and realize effectively the thousand lurid shifting lights and weathers of an electric, nocturnal, and inhuman world. Moreover, she was dressed in the most extreme and sharpest exaggeration of the latest style, her thin long hands, which were unpleasantly and ominously veined with blue, and her fragile wrists, which were so thin and white that light made a pink transparency in them when she lifted them, were covered, loaded—one vast encrusted jewelled glitter of diamond rings and bracelets: a fortune in jewelry blazed heavily and shockingly on her bony little hands.

Her life had been hard, painful, difficult, full of work and sorrow. Ten years before, when she was twenty-five years old, she had had her first—and probably her last—love affair. She had fallen in love with an actor at the Settlement Guild—a little East Side theatre maintained by the donations of two rich æsthetic females. She had left her family and become his mistress: within less than a year the man deserted her, leaving her pregnant.

Her child was a boy: she had no maternal feeling and her son, now nine years old, had been brought up by Abe's mother and by Abe. Sylvia rarely saw her son: she had long ago deserted the orthodoxy of Jewish family life, she had a new, impatient, driving, feverish city life of her own, she visited her family every month or so, and it was then, and only then, that she saw her child. This boy, Jimmy, was a bright, quick, attractive youngster, with a tousled sheaf of taffy-colored hair, and with the freckled, tough, puggish face and the cocky mutilated pavement argot and assurance of the city urchin: he was nevertheless excellently clothed, schooled, and cared for, for the old woman, Abe's mother, watched and guarded over him with the jealous brooding apprehension of an ancient hen, and Sylvia herself was most generous in her expenditures and benefactions, not only for the child, but also for the family.

The relation between Sylvia and her illegitimate child, Jimmy, was remarkable. He never called her "mother"; in fact neither seemed to have a name for the other, save an impersonal and rather awkward "You." Moreover, the attitude of both mother and child was marked by a quality that was hard, knowing, and cynical in its conversation: when she spoke to him her tone and manner were as cold and impersonal as if the child had been a stranger or some chance acquaintance and this manner was also touched by a quality that was resigned, and somewhat mocking—with a mockery which seemed to be directed toward herself, more than toward any one, as if in the physical presence of the boy she saw the visible proof and living evidence of her folly, the bitter fruit of the days of innocence, love, and guileless belief, and as if she was conscious that a joke had been played on both her and her child. And the boy seemed to understand and accept this feeling with a sharp correspondence of feeling, almost incredible in a child. And yet they did not hate each other: their conversations were cynically wise and impersonal and yet curiously honest and respectful. She would look at him for a moment with an air of cold and casual detachment, and that faint smile of mockery when, on one of her visits home, he would come in, panting and dishevelled, a tough and impish urchin, from the street.

"Come here, you," she would say at length, quietly, harshly. "Whatcha been doin' to yourself?" she would ask, in the same hard tone, as deftly she straightened and re-knotted his tie, smoothed out his rumpled sheaf of oaken-colored hair. "You look as if yuh just crawled out of some one's ash can."

"Ah!" he said in his tough, high city-urchin's voice, "a coupla guys tried to get wise wit' me an' I socked one of 'em. Dat's all!"

"Oh-ho-ho-ho!"—Abe turned his gray grinning face prayerfully to heaven and laughed softly, painfully.

"Fightin', huh?" said Sylvia. "Do you remember what I told you last time?" she said in a warning tone. "If I catch yuh fightin' again there's goin' to be no more ball games. *You'll stay home* next time."

"Ah!" he cried again in a high protesting tone. "What's a guy gonna do? Do you t'ink I'm gonna let a coupla mugs like dat get away wit' moidah?"

"Oh-ho-ho-ho!"—cried Abe, lifting his great nose prayerfully again: then with a sudden shift to reproof and admonition, he said sternly: "What kind of talk do you call that? Huh? Didn't I tell you not to say 'mugs'?"

"Ah, what's a guy gonna say?" cried Jimmy. "I neveh could loin all dem big woids, noway."

"My God! I wish you'd listen to 'm," his mother said in a tone of hard and weary resignation. "I suppose that's what I'm sendin' him to school for! *Loin, woids, noway, t'ink!* Is *that* the way to talk?" she demanded harshly. "Is *that* what they teach yuh?"

"Say *think!*" commanded Abe.

"I *did* say it," the child answered evasively.

"Go on! You *didn't!* You didn't say it right. I'll bet you can't say it right. Come on! Let's hear you: *think!*"

"T'ink," Jimmy answered immediately.

"Oh-ho-ho-ho!"—and Abe lifted his grinning face heavenward, saying, "Say! This is rich!"

"Can you beat it?" the woman asked.

And, for a moment, she continued to look at her son with a glance that was quizzical, tinged with a mocking resignation, and yet with a cold, detached affection. Then her long blue-veined hands twitched nervously and impatiently until all the crusted jewels on her wrists and fingers blazed with light: she sighed sharply and, looking away, dismissed the child from her consideration.

Although the boy saw very little of his mother, Abe watched and guarded over him as tenderly as if he had been his father. If the child was late in coming home from school, if he had not had his lunch before going out to play, if he remained away too long Abe showed his concern and distress very plainly, and he spoke very sharply and sternly at times to other members of the family if he thought they had been lax in some matter pertaining to the boy.

"Did Jimmy get home from school yet?" he would ask sharply. "Did he eat before he went out again? . . . Well, why did you let him get away, then, before he had his lunch? . . . For heaven's sake! You're here all day long: you could at least do that much—I can't be here to watch him all the time, you know—don't you know the kid ought never to go out to play until he's had something to eat?"

Eugene saw the child for the first time one day when Abe had taken him home for dinner: Abe, in his crisp neat shirt-sleeves, was seated at the table devouring his food with a wolfish and prowling absorption, and yet in a cleanly and fastidious way, when the child entered. The boy paused in surprise when he saw Eugene: his wheaten sheaf of hair fell down across one eye, one trouser leg had come unbanded at the knee and flapped down to his ankle, and for a moment he looked at Eugene with a rude frank stare of his puggish freckled face.

Abe, prowling upward from his food, glanced at the boy and grinned; then, jerking his head sharply toward Eugene, he said roughly:

"Whatcha think of this guy? Huh?"

"Who is he?" the boy asked in his high tough little voice, never moving his curious gaze from Eugene.

"He's my teacher," Abe said. "He's the guy that teaches me."

"Ah, g'wan!" the child answered in a protesting tone, still fixing Eugene with his steady and puzzled stare.

"Whatcha handin' me? He's *not!*"

"Sure he is! No kiddin'!" Abe replied. "He's the guy that teaches me English."

"Ah, he's *not!*" the boy answered decisively. "Yuh're bein' wise."

"What makes you think he's not?" Abe asked.

"If he's an English teacher," Jimmy said triumphantly, "w'y don't he say somet'ing? W'y don't he use some of dose woids?"

"Oh-ho-ho-ho!" cried Abe lifting his great bleak nose aloft. "Say! ... This is good! ... This is swell! ... Say, that's some kid!" he said when the boy had departed. "There's not much gets by *him!*" And lifting his gray face heavenward again, he laughed softly, painfully, in gleeful and tender reminiscence.

Thus, the whole care and government of the boy had been entrusted to Abe and his mother: Sylvia herself, although she paid liberally all her child's expenses, took no other interest in him. She was a hard, feverish, bitter, and over-stimulated woman, and yet she had a kind of harsh loyalty to her family: she was, in a fierce and smouldering way, very ambitious for Abe, who seemed to be the most promising of her brothers: she was determined that he should go to college and become a lawyer, and his fees at the university, in part at any rate, were paid by his sister—in part only, not because Sylvia would not have paid all without complaint, but because Abe insisted on paying as much as he could through his own labor, for Abe, too, had embedded in him a strong granite of independence, the almost surly dislike, of a strong and honest character, of being beholden to any one for favors. On this score, indeed, he had the most sensitive and tender pride of any one Eugene had ever known.

At home, Abe had become, by unspoken consent, the head of a family which now consisted only of his mother, two brothers, and his sister's illegitimate child, Jimmy. Two of his older brothers, who were in business together, had married and lived away from home, as did Sylvia, and another sister, Rose, who had married a musician in a theatre orchestra a year or two before; she was a dark, tortured and sensitive Jewess with a big nose and one blind eye. Her physical resemblance to Abe was marked. She was a very talented pianist, and once or twice he took Eugene to visit her on Sunday afternoons: she played for them in a studio room in which candles were burning and she carried on very technical and knowing conversations about the work of various composers with her brother. Abe listened to the music when she played with an obscure and murky smile: he seemed to know a great deal about music: it awakened a thousand subtle echoes in his Jewish soul, but for Eugene, somehow, the music, and something arrogant, scornful, and secretive in their knowingness, together with the dreary consciousness of a winter's Sunday afternoon outside, the barren streets, the harsh red waning light of day, and a terrible sensation of thousands of other knowing Jews—the men with little silken mustaches—who were coming from concerts at that moment, awakened in him vague but powerful emotions of nakedness, rootlessness, futility and misery, which even the glorious memory of the power, exultancy and joy of poetry could not conquer or subdue. The scene evoked for him suddenly a thousand images of a sterile and damnable incertitude, in which man groped indefinitely along the smooth metallic sides of a world in which there was neither warmth, nor depth, nor door to enter, nor walls to shelter him: he got suddenly a vision of a barren Sunday and a gray despair, of ugly streets, and of lights beginning to wink and flicker above cheap moving-picture houses and chop-suey restaurants, and of a raucous world of cheap and flashy people, as trashy as their foods, as trivial and infertile as their accursed amusements, and finally of the Jews returning through a thousand streets, in that waning and desolate light, from symphony concerts, an image, which, so far from giving a note of hope, life, and passionate certitude and joy to the worldless horror of this damned and blasted waste of Dead-Man's Land, seemed to enhance it rather, and to give it a conclusive note of futility and desolation.

Abe and his sister did not seem to feel this: instead the scene, the time, the day, the waning light, the barren streets, the music, awakened in them something familiar and obscure, a dark and painful joy, a certitude Eugene did not feel. They argued, jibed, and sneered harshly and arrogantly at each other: their words were sharp and cutting, impregnated with an aggressive and unpleasant intellectualism, they called each other fools and sentimental ignoramuses, and yet they did not seem to be wounded or offended by this harsh intercourse: they seemed rather to derive a kind of bitter satisfaction from it.

Already, the first year Eugene had known him he had discovered this strange quality in these people: they seemed to delight in jeering and jibing at one another; and at the same time their harsh mockery had in it an element of obscure and disquieting affection. At this time Abe was carrying on, week by week, a savage correspondence with another young Jew who had been graduated with him from the same class in high school. He always had in his pocket at least one of the letters this boy had written him, and he was forever giving it to Eugene to read, and then insisting that he read his answer. In these letters, they flew at each other with undisciplined ferocity, they hurled denunciation, mockery, and contempt at each other, and they seemed to exult in it. The tone of their letters was marked by an affectation of cold impersonality and austerity, and yet this obviously was only a threadbare cloak to the furious storm of personal insult and invective, the desire to crow over the other man and humiliate him, which seemed to delight them. "In your last letter," one would write, "I see that the long-expected débâcle has now occurred. In our last year at high school I saw occasional gleams of adult intelligence in your otherwise infantile and adolescent intellect, and I had some hope of saving you, but I now see my hopes were wasted—your puerile remarks on Karl Marx, Anatole France, et al, show you up as the fat-headed bourgeois you always were, and I accordingly wash my hands of you. You reveal plainly that your intellect is incapable of grasping the issues involved in modern socialism: you are a romantic individualist and you will find everything you say elegantly embalmed in the works of the late Lord Byron which is where you belong also: your mother should dress you up in a cowboy suit and give you a toy pistol to play with before you hurt yourself playing around with great big rough grown-up men."

Abe would read Eugene one of these letters, grinning widely with Kike delight, lifting his grinning face and laughing softly, "Oh-ho-ho-ho-ho!" as he came to some particularly venomous insult.

"But who wrote you such a letter?" Eugene demanded.

"Oh, a guy I went to school with," he answered, "a friend of mine!"

"A friend of yours! Is that the kind of letter that your friends write you!"

"Sure," he said. "Why not? He's a good guy. He doesn't mean anything by it. He's got bats in the belfry, that's all. But wait till you see what I wrote *him!*" he cried, grinning exultantly as he took his own letter from his pocket. "Wait till you see what I call *him!* Oh-ho-ho-ho-ho!"—softly, painfully, he laughed. "Say, this is rich!" and gleefully he would read his answer: five closely typed pages of bitter insult and vituperation.

Another astonishing and disquieting circumstance of this brutal correspondence was now revealed: this extraordinary "friend" of Abe's, who wrote him these insulting letters, had not gone abroad, nor did he live in some remote and distant city. When Eugene asked Abe where this savage critic lived, he answered: "Oh, a couple of blocks from where I live."

"But do you ever see him?"

"Sure. Why not?" he said, looking at Eugene in a puzzled way. "We grew up together. I see him all the time."

"And yet you write this fellow letters and he writes you, when you live only a block apart and see each other all the time?"

"Sure. Why not?" said Abe.

He saw nothing curious or unusual in the circumstance, and yet there was something disturbing and unpleasant about it: in all these letters Eugene had observed, below the tirades of abuse, an obscure, indefinable, and murky emotionalism that was somehow ugly.

Within a few months, however, this strange communication with his Jewish comrade ceased abruptly: Eugene began to see Abe, in the halls and corridors of the university, squiring various Jewish girls around with a sheepish and melancholy look. His lust for letter-writing still raged with unabated violence, although now the subjects of his correspondence were women. His attitude towards girls had always been cold and scornful: he regarded their cajoleries and

enticements with a fishy eye, and with a vast Jewish caution and sus-
piciousness, and he laughed scornfully at any one who allowed himself to be ensnared. Like many people who feel deeply, and who are
powerfully affected by the slightest and remotest changes in their
emotions, he had convinced himself that he was a creature whose
every action was governed by the operations of cool reason, and accordingly now that his feelings were powerfully and romantically involved in thoughts about several of these warm and luscious-looking
Jewish wenches, he convinced himself that he "cared only for their
minds" and that what he really sought from them was the stimulation of intellectual companionship. Accordingly, the love-letters
which this great-nosed innocent now wrote to them, and read to Eugene, were extraordinary and unwitting productions of defense and
justification.

"... I think I observe in your last letter," Abe would write, "traces
of that romantic sentimentality which we have both seen so often in
these childish lives around us but from which you and I long ago
freed ourselves. As you know, Florence, we both agreed at the beginning that we would not spoil our friendship by the intrusion of a
puerile and outmoded romanticism. Sex can play no part in our relations, Florence: it is at best a simple biological necessity, the urge
of the hungry animal which should be recognized as such and satisfied without intruding on the higher faculties. Have you read Have-
lock Ellis yet? If not, you must read him without further delay. . . .
So Myrtle Goldberg really thought I was in earnest that night of the
dance. . . . Ye Gods! It is to laugh! Ha-ha! What fools these mortals
be . . . I laugh, and yet I do not laugh . . . I laugh and observe my
laughter, and then there is yet another level of reality which observes my laughter at my laughter. . . . I play the clown with an ironic
heart and put on the grinning mask these fools wish to see. . . . O
tempora! O mores!"— et cetera.

And yet these same letters, in which he protested the cold detachment of his spirit, his freedom from the romantic fleshliness
which degraded the lives of lesser men, were invariably tagged and
embellished by little verses of his own contriving, all of them inspired
by the emotion he pretended to despise. He always had a number of
these little poems written down in a small note-book of black leather
which he carried with him, and in which, at this time, with a precise

and meticulous hand, he noted down his rarest thoughts, excerpts from books he had been reading, and these brief poems. At this time Abe was in a state of obscure and indefinable evolution: it was impossible to say what he would become, or what form his life would take, nor could he have told, himself. He walked along at a stooping loping gait, his face prowling around mistrustfully and with a glance full of tortured discontent: he was tormented by a dozen obscure desires and purposes and by a deep but murky emotionalism: his flesh was ugly, bowed, and meagre—conscious of a dreary inferiority (thus, in later and more prosperous years, he confessed to Eugene that he loved to abuse and "order around" brusquely the waiters in restaurants, because of the feeling of power and authority it gave him) , but his spirit was sustained by an immense and towering vanity, a gloomy egotism which told him he was not as other men, that his thoughts and feelings were too profound and rare to be understood and valued by the base world about him. At the same time he was secretly and fiercely ambitious, although the energy of his ambition was scattered in a half dozen directions and could fasten on no purpose: by turn, he wanted to be a teacher and a great investigator in the sciences—and in this he might have succeeded, for he showed a brilliant aptness in biology and physics—or an economist, a critic of literature, an essayist, a historian, a poet, or a novelist. His desire was high: at this time he did not want to make money, he regarded a life that was given up to money-making with contempt, and although he sometimes spoke of the study of medicine, he looked at the profession of law, which was the profession his sister and his family wanted him to follow, with horror and revulsion: he shrank with disgust from the prospect of joining the hordes of beak-nosed shysters, poured out of the law school year by year and who were adept in every dodge of dishonorable trickery, in working every crooked wire, or squirming through each rat's hole of escape and evasion the vast machinery of the law afforded them.

Such a man was Abe Jones when Eugene first knew him: dreary, tortured, melancholy, dully intellectual and joylessly poetic, his spirit gloomily engulfed in a great cloud of Yiddish murk, a gray pavement cipher, an atom of the slums, a blind sea-crawl in the drowning tides of the man-swarm, and yet, pitifully, tremendously, with a million other dreary Hebrew yearners, convinced that he was the messiah for which the earth was groaning. Such was he in the state of becoming, an indefinable shape before necessity and his better parts—the hard, savage, tough and honest city sinew, hardened the mould—made a man of him,—this was Abe at this time, an obscure and dreary chrysalis, and yet a dogged, loyal, and faithful friend, the salt of the earth, a wonderfully good, rare, and high person.

If the hard and rugged lineaments of Abe's character had not at this time emerged out of the glutinous paste of obscure yearnings, there was no such indecision and uncertainty in the character of his mother. It was as legible as gold, as solid as a rock.

Abe's mother was an old woman, with the powerful and primitive features of the aged Jewess: she was almost toothless, a solitary blackened tooth stood mournfully in the centre of her strong ruined mouth, she had a craggy worn face, seamed and furrowed by a countless sorrow, a powerful beaked nose, and a strong convulsive mouth, a mask which was like a destiny since it seemed to have been carved and fashioned for the dirge-like wailing of eternal grief. The face of the old woman might have served not only as the painting of the whole history of her race, but as the painting of the female everywhere—not the female with her ephemeral youth, her brief snares of hair and hide, her succulent burst of rose-lips and flowing curve—but the female timeless, ageless, fixed in sorrow and fertility, as savage, as enduring, and as fecund as the earth. The old woman's face was like a worn rock at which all the waves of life had smashed and beaten: it was unmistakably the face of an old Jewess and yet the powerful and craggy features bore an astonishing resemblance to the face of a pioneer woman or of an old Indian chief.

Her life, moreover, had the agelessness of the earth, the timelessness of her race and destiny: she had not been touched at all by the furious and savage life of the city with its sensational brevities, its hard, special, temporal qualities of speech, fashion, and belief, its million ephemeral enthusiasms, briefly held and forgotten, the stunned oblivion of its memory, which, in the brutal stupefaction of a thousand days, can hold to nothing, so that even the memory of love and death cannot endure there and a man may forget his dead brother ere his flesh grow rotten in the grave.

The old woman did not forget: for her, as for the God she worshipped, the passing of seven thousand years was like the passing of
a single day; yesterday, tomorrow, and forever, a moment at the
heart of love and memory. Thus, once when Eugene had called Abe
upon the telephone, a full year after the death of his oldest brother,
Jacob, the old woman had answered: the old voice came feebly,
brokenly, indecipherably, and was like a wail. He asked for Abe,
she could not understand, she began to talk in an excited, toothless
mumble—a torrent of Yiddish broken here and there by a few
mangled words and scraps of English—all she knew. At length Eugene made her understand he wanted to speak to Abe: suddenly
she recognized his voice and remembered him. Then, instantly, as
if it had happened only the day before, and as if he had been a friend
of her dead son, although he had never known him, the old woman
began to wail, faintly and rhythmically, across the wire: "Jakie! . . .
My Jakie! . . . Mein Sohn Jakie! . . . He is dead."

A few days later Eugene had gone home with Abe for dinner: he
lived with his mother, two brothers, and Jimmy, his sister's illegitimate child, in a flat which occupied the second floor of an old four-
storey red-brick house in Twelfth Street, near Second Avenue, on the
East Side. The old woman had prepared a good meal for them: a
thick rich soup, chopped chicken livers, chicken, cake, and a strong
sweet wine: she served them but would not sit and eat with them: she
came in briefly and shook hands shyly and awkwardly, mumbling
incoherently, a mangled jargon of Yiddish and English. Suddenly,
however, as if she had briefly mastered herself by a strong effort her
old and sorrowful face was twisted by a convulsion of powerful and
incurable grief, and a long, terrible, savagely wailing cry was torn
from her throat: she turned blindly, and with a movement of natural
and primitive sorrow, she suddenly seized the edges of her apron in
her gnarled and worn hands and flung it up over her head and
rushed toward the door at a blind, lunging, reeling step. She was like
one demented by sorrow: the old woman began to beat her withered
breasts and pull at her wispy gray hair, meanwhile running and
stumbling blindly around her kitchen in a horrible and savage de-
mentia and drunkenness of grief. Abe followed her out, and Eugene
could hear his voice, low, urgent, and tender, as he spoke to her persuasively in Yiddish, and her long wailing cries subsided and he

returned. His face was sad and weary-looking and in a moment he said: "Mama's breaking up fast. She's never been able to get over my brother's death. She thinks about it all the time: she can't get it off her mind."

"How long has he been dead, Abe?"

"He died over a year ago," Abe said. "But that doesn't matter: I know her—she'll never forget it now as long as she lives. She'll always feel the same about it."

This terrible and savage picture of grief was carved upon Eugene's memory unforgettably: it became a tremendous and formidable fact, a fact as ancient, timeless, and savage as the earth, a fact which neither the stupefying oblivion of the city's life, the furious chaos of the streets, the savage glare of ten thousand blind and dusty days could touch. The old woman's grief was taller than their tallest towers, and more enduring than all their steel and stone: it would last forever when all the city's bones were dust, and it was like the grief of all the women who had ever beat their breasts and flung their aprons across their heads and run, wailing, with a demented and drunken step: it filled him with horror, anger, a sense of cruelty, disgust, and pity.

She was the fertile and enduring earth from which they sprung, and all of them, transformed so sharply and so curiously by the city's tone and life, drew in to her with devotion and respect: Abe, with his dreary gray face of the man-swarm cipher, Sylvia with her feverish, electric night-time glitter, all of the brothers and sisters, with all that was new, sharp, alien, flashy, trivial, or material in speech, dress, manner, and belief—all of them returned to her with love, loyalty, and reverence as to some great broodhen of the earth. The old woman's life was rooted in the soil of two devotions: the synagogue and the home, and all that happened beyond the limits of this devotion was phantom and remote: this soil was ageless, placeless, everlasting.

Abe loved his mother dearly: whenever he spoke of her, even casually, his voice was touched with a hush of respect and affection. But he disliked his father: the few times Eugene heard him mention him he spoke of him in a hard and bitter voice, referring to him as "that guy," or "that fellow," as if he were a stranger. Eugene never saw the father: the children all felt bitterly towards him and had sent him away to room alone. Abe told Eugene that the man was a shoemaker, and apparently improvident and thriftless. He had never been able to earn enough to support his family, and in addition, Abe said, he was a petty family tyrant. Abe's childhood had been scarred by memories of privation, tyranny and poverty—the mother and the children had had a bitter struggle for existence, and Abe had worked since his eighth year at a variety of hard, gray, shabby and joyless employments: he had been a newsboy, a grocer's delivery boy, an office boy in a broker's office, a typist in a collection agency endlessly writing out form letters, the office man and secretary for the head-professor of the architectural school, and one of these pallid, swarthy, greasily sweating youths of the fur and garment house districts who ceaselessly propel through swarming and kaleidoscopic streets of trade small wheel-trucks piled high with dresses, garments, furs, and clothes or with the thousand travelling varieties of all that horrible nondescript junk known under the indecisive name of "novelties." Once, also, he had spent part of a summer in New Jersey unloading freight cars filled with Georgia watermelons, and for a considerable time he had driven a truck for his two oldest brothers, who had a zinc business in the "gas-house district" of the East Side, between Avenue A and the river and North of Fourteenth Street.

Here, once, Eugene had accompanied him at noon of a flashing day in spring, a glitter of light and flashing waters, a sparkle of gold and blue: in a large bare space near factories they had seen a ring of young thugs throwing dice, and near the river were the immense and ugly turrets of the gas tanks, and then the wharves, the great odorous piers, and the flashing waters—the vast exultant play and traffic of the river life, the powerful little tugs, the ships, and the barges laden with their strings of rusty freight cars.

As they walked away through the powerful ugliness and devastation of that district, with its wasteland rusts and rubbish, its slum-like streets of rickety tenement and shabby brick, its vast raw thrust of tank, glazed glass and factory building, and at length its clean, cold, flashing strength and joy of waters—a district scarred by that horror of unutterable desolation and ugliness and at the same time lifted by a powerful rude exultancy of light and sky and sweep and water, such as is found only in America, and for which there is yet no language—as they walked away along a street, the blue wicked shells of empty bottles began to explode on the pavements all around them: when they looked around to see from what quarter this attack was coming, the street was empty save for a young thug who leaned against the rotting edge of a closed door, hands thrust in pockets, and a look of pustulate and evil innocence upon his thin tough Irish face. The street was evil and silent and empty, but when they turned and went on again, the exploding bottles began to drop around them on the pavement in splinters of sinister blue.

Abe grinned toughly: he did not seem at all surprised or perturbed by the murderous stealth and secrecy of the attack, its obscene and cowardly uselessness. He explained that the district had been one of the worst in the city and the headquarters for one of the most criminal gangs: time and again the gangsters had broken into his brother's zinc shop and robbed it, and Abe and all his brothers, being Jews, had had to fight it out since childhood, foot and fist and tooth and nail, and club and stone, with the young Irish toughs and gangsters who infested the district. Such had been his childhood: he told Eugene many stories of bloody fights waged back and forth across these pavements, of young boys maimed, crippled, or blinded in these savage fights, of one boy who had his eye torn out of his head by his enemy's gouging thumb in a fight to a finish on one of the piers, and of another whose brains had been smashed out on the pavement below the elevated structure by a rock hurled by an enemy's hand in a fight of the neighborhood gangs. Thus, in pier and alley, on street and roof, children had learned the arts of murder, the smell of blood, the odor of brains upon the pavement. Abe told how one of his older brothers, Barney—a thickly set powerful-looking man with short thick hands and a tough meaty-looking fighter's face, gray, square, and good-humored—had to fight it out step by step with the gangsters, who had come to his shop, again and again, with demands for money—money which the merchants of the district paid them meekly and regularly for "protection"—a euphemism for graft and menace, a bribe for being left alone and for the assurance that one's shop would not be entered and one's stock smashed or stolen in the night. Barney had met all these menaces with a hard cold eye and two rock-like fists with which time and again he had beaten into a pulp the thugs who came to threaten him: he was a good man and a savage fighter and he had learned the arts of combat in the sternest and most brutal arena on earth—the city streets.

"And—oh-ho-ho-ho!"—softly, painfully, Abe lifted his widely grinning face and laughed, "how that guy loves it! Say! they picked the
wrong one when they picked on him! Oh-ho-ho-ho-ho! *Can* he fight!
Does he love it! Say! do you know what I saw him do to two of them
one time—oh-ho-ho-ho-ho-ho! Gee! it was rich! They came in there
to shake him down and—Oh! Ho-ho!—ho! You shoulda seen it! He
picks up a keg of zinc that weighs 200 pounds and he *breaks* it—oh-
ho-ho-ho!—over the first guy's head."

"And what became of the second guy?"

"Oh-ho-ho-ho! . . . Gee, it was rich! You shoulda seen that other
guy get out of there! Say! He almost tore the door down in his
hurry—oh-ho-ho-ho!"

Such were the various members of this family as Eugene came to
know about them: each of them in his own way was marked by a
decisive individuality and independence of spirit which told of their
lives of combat, toil and struggle in the city streets, and yet, although
indelibly marked, scarred and hardened by his life, none of them had
been brutalized by it. In fact, as Eugene thought of all these people
later, an extraordinary quality in them became evident. It was this:
here was a family of poor East Side Jews, the children of an immi-
grant and thriftless shoemaker and an old orthodox Jewish woman.
These children had all had to make their own way, to fight and
struggle bitterly for a living: now some of them were tough, rugged
and unlettered merchants, traders and mechanics, some were successful milliners and designers, and some were talented musicians,
students of science, people of extraordinary intelligence and ability.
And all of them, even the most unlettered, seemed to have a completely natural unaffected interest and respect for the arts, or for
scholarly and intellectual attainment. This circumstance—this remarkable fusion in one poor Jewish family of elements which would
have seemed almost incredible in the families of poor laboring or
country people Eugene had known before—this combination of the
manual, the commercial, the artistic and the scholarly in one poor
family—seemed so natural both to him and to them that Eugene
never found it strange or wonderful until years later.

THE HOUSE OF THE FAR
AND THE LOST

IN THE fall that year, Eugene lived about a mile out from town in a house set back from the Ventnor Road. The house was called a "farm"—Hill-top Farm, or Far-end Farm, or some such name as that —but it was really no farm at all. It was a magnificent house of the weathered gray stone they have in that country, as if in the very quality of the wet heavy air there is the soft thick gray of time itself, sternly yet beautifully soaking down forever on you—and enriching everything it touches—grass, foliage, brick, ivy, the fresh moist color of the people's faces, and old gray stone, with the incomparable weathering of time.

The house was set back off the road at a distance of several hundred yards, possibly a quarter of a mile, and one reached it by means of a road bordered by rows of tall trees which arched above the road, and which made Eugene think of home, at night when the stormy wind howled in their tossed branches. On each side of the road were the rugby fields of two of the colleges and in the afternoon he could look out and down and see the fresh moist green of the playing fields, and watch young college fellows, dressed in their shorts and jerseys, and with their bare knees scurfed with grass and turf as they twisted, struggled, swayed, and scrambled for a moment in the scrimmage-circle, and then broke free, running, dodging, passing the ball as they were tackled, filling the moist air with their sharp cries of sport. They did not have the desperate, the grimly determined, the almost professional earnestness that the college teams at home have; their scurfed and muddy knees, their swaying scrambling scrimmages, the swift breaking away and running, their panting breath and crisp clear voices gave them the appearance of grown-up boys.

Once when Eugene had come up the road in afternoon while they were playing, the ball got away from them and came bounding out into the road before him, and he ran after it to retrieve it, as he used to do when passing a field where boys were playing baseball. One of the players came over to the edge of the field and stood there waiting with his hands upon his hips while Eugene got the ball: he was panting hard, his face was flushed, and his blond hair tousled, but when

Eugene threw the ball to him, he said "Thanks very much!" crisply and courteously—getting the same sound into the word *"very"* that they got in *"American,"* a sound that always repelled Eugene a little because it seemed to have some scornful aloofness and patronage in it.

For a moment Eugene watched him as he trotted briskly away on to the field again: the players stood there waiting, panting, casual, their hands upon their hips; he passed the ball into the scrimmage, the pattern swayed, rocked, scrambled, and broke sharply out in open play again, and everything looked incredibly strange, near, and familiar.

Eugene felt that he had always known it, that it had always been his, and that it was as familiar to him as everything he had seen or known in his childhood. Even the texture of the earth looked familiar, and felt moist and firm and springy when he stepped on it, and the stormy howling of the wind in that avenue of great trees at night, was wild and desolate and demented as it had been when he was eight years old and would lie in his bed at night and hear the great oaks howling on the hill above his father's house.

The name of the people in the house was Coulson: he made arrangements with the woman at once to come and live there: she was a tall, weathered-looking woman of middle age, they talked together in the hall. The hall was made of marble flags and went directly out onto a gravelled walk.

The woman was crisp, cheerful, and worldly-looking. She was still quite handsome. She wore a well-cut skirt of woollen plaid, and a silk blouse: when she talked she kept her arms folded because the air in the hall was chilly, and she held a cigarette in the fingers of one hand. A shaggy brown dog came out and nosed upward toward her hand as she was talking and she put her hand upon its head and scratched it gently. When Eugene told her he wanted to move in the next day, she said briskly and cheerfully:

"Right you are! You'll find everything ready when you get here!" Then she asked if he was at the university. He said no, and added, with a feeling of difficulty and naked desolation, that he was a "writer," and was coming there to work. He was twenty-four years old.

"Then I am sure that what you do will be *very, very* good!" she said cheerfully and decisively. "We have had several Americans in the house before and all of them were very clever! All the Americans we have had here were very clever people," said the woman. "I'm sure that you will like it." Then she walked to the door with him to say good-bye. As they stood there, there was the sound of a small motor-car coming to a halt and in a moment a girl came swiftly across the gravel space outside and entered the hall. She was tall, slender, very lovely, but she had the same bright hard look in her eye that the woman had, the same faint, hard smile around the edges of her mouth.

"Edith," the woman said in her crisp curiously incisive tone, "this young man is an American—he is coming here tomorrow." The girl looked at Eugene for a moment with her hard bright glance, thrust out a small gloved hand, and shook hands briefly, a swift firm greeting.

"Oh! How d'ye do!" she said. "I hope you will like it here." Then she went on down the hall, entered a room on the left, and closed the door behind her.

Her voice had been crisp and certain like her mother's, but it was also cool, young, and sweet, with music in it, and later as Eugene went down the road, he could still hear it.

That was a wonderful house, and the people there were wonderful people. Later, he could not forget them. He seemed to have known them all his life, and to know all about their lives. They seemed as familiar to him as his own blood and he knew them with a knowledge that went deep below the roots of thought or memory. They did not talk together often, or tell any of their lives to one another. It is very hard to tell about it—the way they felt and lived together in that house—because it was one of those simple and profound experiences of life which people seem always to have known when it happens to them, but for which there is no language.

And yet, like a child's half-captured vision of some magic country he has known, and which haunts his days with strangeness and the sense of imminent, glorious re-discovery, the word that would unlock it all seemed constantly to be almost on their lips, waiting, just outside the gateway of their memory, just a shape, a phrase, a sound away, the moment that they chose to utter it—but when they tried to say the thing, something faded within their minds like fading light, and something melted within their grasp like painted smoke, and something went forever when they tried to touch it.

The nearest Eugene could come to it was this: In that house he sometimes felt the greatest peace and solitude that he had ever known. But he always knew the other people in the house were there. He could sit in his sitting-room at night and hear nothing but the stormy moaning of the wind outside in the great trees, the small gaseous flare and jet from time to time of the coal fire burning in the grate—and silence, strong living lonely silence that moved and waited in the house at night—and he would always know that they were there.

He did not have to hear them enter or go past his door, nor did he have to hear doors close or open in the house, or listen to their voices: if he had never seen them, heard them, spoken to them, it would have been the same—he would have known they were there.

It was somthing he had always known, and he had known it would happen to him, and now it was there with all the strangeness and dark mystery of an awaited thing. He knew them, felt them, lived among them with a familiarity that had no need of sight or word or speech. And the memory of that house and of his silent fellowship with all the people there was somehow mixed with an image of dark time. It was one of those sorrowful and unchanging images which, among all the blazing stream of images that passed constantly their stream of fire across his mind, was somehow fixed, detached, and everlasting, full of a sorrow, certitude, and mystery that he could not fathom, but that wore forever on it the old sad light of waning day— a light from which all the heat, the violence, and the substance of furious dusty day had vanished, and which was itself like time, un-earthly-of-the-earth, remote, detached, and everlasting.

And that fixed and changeless image of dark time was this: In an old house of time Eugene lived alone, and yet had other people all around him, and they never spoke to him, or he to them. They came and went like silence in the house, but he always knew that they were there. He would be sitting by a window in a room, and he would know then that they were moving in the house, and darkness, sorrow, and strong silence dwelt within them, and their eyes were quiet, full of sorrow, peace, and knowledge, and their faces dark, their tongues silent, and they never spoke. Eugene could not remember how their faces looked, but they were all familiar to him as his father's face, and they had known one another forever, and they lived together in the ancient house of time, dark time; and silence, sorrow, certitude, and peace were in them. Such was the image of dark time that was to haunt his life thereafter, and into which, somehow, his life among the people in that house had passed.

In the house that year there lived, besides Eugene and Morison, the Coulsons, father and mother, and their daughter, and three men who had taken rooms together, and who were employed in a factory where motor-cars were made, two miles from town.

Perhaps the reason that Eugene could never forget these people later and seemed to know them all so well was that there was in all of them something ruined, lost, or broken—some precious and irretrievable quality which had gone out of them and which they could never get back again. Perhaps that was the reason that he liked them all so much, because with ruined people it is either love or hate: there is no middle way. The ruined people that we like are those who desperately have died, and lost their lives because they loved life dearly, and had that grandeur that makes such people spend prodigally the thing they love the best, and risk and lose their lives because life is so precious to them, and die at length because the seeds of life are in them. It is only the people that love life who die in this way—and these are the ruined people that we like.

The people in the house were people who had lost their lives because they loved the earth too well, and somehow had been slain by their hunger. And for this reason Eugene liked them all, and could not forget them later: there seemed to have been some magic which had drawn them all together to that house, as if the house itself were a magnetic centre for lost people.

Certainly, the three men who worked at the motor-car factory had been drawn together for this reason. Two were still young men in their early twenties. The third man was much older. He was a man past forty, his name was Nicholl, he had served in the army during the war and had attained the rank of captain.

He had the spare, alert, and jaunty figure that one often finds in army men, an almost professional military quality that somehow seemed to set his figure upon a horse as if he had grown there, or had spent a lifetime in the cavalry. His face also had the same lean, bitten, professional military quality: his speech, although good-natured and very friendly, was clipped, incisive, jerky, and sporadic, his lean weather-beaten face was deeply, sharply scarred and sunken in the flanks, and he wore a small cropped mustache, and displayed long frontal teeth when he smiled—a spare, gaunt, toothy, yet attractive smile.

His left arm was withered, shrunken, almost useless, part of his hand and two of the fingers had been torn away by the blast or explosion which had destroyed his arm, but it was not this mutilation of the flesh that gave one the sense of a life that had been ruined, lost, and broken irretrievably. In fact, one quickly forgot his physical injury: his figure looked so spare, lean, jaunty, well-conditioned in its energetic fitness that one never thought of him as a cripple, nor pitied him for any disability. No: the ruin that one felt in him was never of the flesh, but of the spirit. Something seemed to have been torn away from his life—it was not the nerve-centres of his arm, but of his soul, that had been destroyed. There was in the man somewhere a terrible dead vacancy and emptiness, and the spare, lean figure that he carried so well seemed only to surround this vacancy like a kind of shell.

He was always smartly dressed in clothes that sat well on his trim spruce figure. He was always in good spirits, immensely friendly in his clipped spare way, and he laughed frequently—a rather metallic cackle which came suddenly and ended as swiftly as it had begun. He seemed, somehow, to have locked the door upon dark care and worry, and to have flung the key away—to have lost, at the same time that he lost more precious things, all the fretful doubts and perturbations of conscience that most men know.

Now, in fact, he seemed to have only one serious project in his life. This was to keep himself amused, to keep himself constantly amused, to get from his life somehow the last atom of entertainment it could possibly yield, and in this project the two young men who lived with him joined in with an energy and earnestness which suggested that their employment in the motor-car factory was just a necessary evil which must be borne patiently because it yielded them the means with which to carry on a more important business, the only one in which their lives were interested—the pursuit of pleasure.

And in the way in which they conducted this pursuit, there was an element of deliberate calculation, concentrated earnestness, and focal intensity of purpose that was astounding, grotesque, and unbelievable, and that left in the mind of one who saw it a formidable and disquieting memory because there was in it almost the madness of desperation, the deliberate intent to seek oblivion, at any cost of effort, from some hideous emptiness of the soul.

Captain Nicholl and his two young companions had a little motorcar so small that it scuttled up the road, shot around and stopped in the gravel by the door with the abruptness of a wound-up toy. It was astonishing that three men could wedge themselves into this midget of a car, but wedge themselves they did, and used it to the end of its capacity, scuttling away to work in it in the morning, and scuttling back again when work was done, and scuttling away to London every Saturday, as if they were determined to wrest from this small motor, too, the last ounce of pleasure to be got from it.

Finally, Captain Nicholl and his two companions had made up an orchestra among them, and this they played in every night when they got home. One of the young men, who was a tall fellow with blond hair which went back in even corrugated waves across his head as if it had been marcelled, played the piano, the other, who was slight and dark, and had black hair, performed upon a saxophone, and Captain Nicholl himself took turns at thrumming furiously on a banjo, or rattling a tattoo upon the complex arrangement of trap drums, bass drums, and clashing cymbals that surrounded him.

They played nothing but American jazz music or sobbing crooner's rhapsodies or nigger blues. Their performance was astonishing. Although it was contrived solely for their own amusement, they hurled themselves into it with all the industrious earnestness of professional musicians employed by a night-club or dance hall to furnish dance music for the patrons. The little dark fellow who played the saxophone would bend and weave prayerfully with his grotesque instrument, as the fat gloating notes came from its unctuous throat, and from time to time he would sway in a half circle, or get up and prance forward and back in rhythm to the music, as the saxophone players in dance orchestras sometimes do.

Meanwhile the tall blond fellow at the piano would sway and bend above the keys, glancing around from time to time with little nods and smiles as if he were encouraging an orchestra of forty pieces or beaming happily at a dance floor crowded with paying customers.

While this was going on, Captain Nicholl would be thrumming madly on the strings of a banjo. He kept the instrument gripped some-how below his withered arm, fingering the end strings with his two good fingers, knocking the tune out with his good right hand, and keeping time with a beating foot. Then with a sudden violent movement he would put the banjo down, snatch up the sticks of the trap drum, and begin to rattle out a furious accompaniment, beating the bass drum with his foot meanwhile, and reaching over to smash cymbals, chimes, and metal rings from time to time. He played with a kind of desperate fury, his mouth fixed in a strange set grin, his bright eyes burning with a sharp wild glint of madness.

They sang as they played, bursting suddenly into the refrain of some popular song with the same calculated spontaneity and spurious enthusiasm of the professional orchestra, mouthing the words of Negro blues and jazz with an obvious satisfaction, with an accent which was remarkably good, and yet which had something foreign and inept in it that made the familiar phrases of American music sound almost as strange in their mouths as if an orchestra or skilful patient Japanese were singing them.

They sang:

> "Yes, sir! That's my baby
> Yes, sir! Don't mean maybe
> Yes, sir! That's my baby now!"

or:

> "Oh, it ain't gonna rain no more, no more
> It ain't gonna rain no more"

or:

> " I got dose blu-u-ues"—

the young fellow at the piano rolling his eyes around in a ridiculous fashion, and mouthing out the word "blues" extravagantly as he sang it, the little dark fellow bending forward in an unctuous sweep as the note come gloating fatly from the horn, and Captain Nicholl swaying sideways in his chair as he strummed upon the banjo strings, and improvising a mournful accompaniment of his own, somewhat as follows: "I got dose blu-u-ues! Yes, suh! Oh! I got dose blues! Yes,

suh! I sure have got 'em—dose blu-u-ues—blu-u-ues—blu-u-ues!—"
his mouth never relaxing from its strange fixed grin, nor his eyes
from their bright set stare of madness as he swayed and strummed
and sang the words that came so strangely from his lips.

It was a weird scene, an incredible performance, and somehow it
pierced the heart with a wild nameless pity, an infinite sorrow and
regret.

Something precious, irrecoverable had gone out of them, and they
knew it. They fought the emptiness in them with this deliberate,
formidable, and mad intensity of a calculated gaiety, a terrifying
mimicry of mirth, and the storm-wind howled around them in dark
trees, and Eugene felt that he had known them forever, and had no
words to say to them—and no door.

There were four in the Coulson family: the father, a man of fifty
years, the mother, somewhere in the middle forties, a son, and a
daughter, Edith, a girl of twenty-two who lived in the house with
her parents. Eugene never met the son: he had completed his course
at Oxford a year or two before, and had gone down to London where
he was now employed. During the time Eugene lived there the son
did not come home.

They were a ruined family. How that ruin had fallen on them,
what it was, Eugene never knew, for no one ever spoke to him about
them. But the sense of their disgrace, of a shameful inexpiable dishonor, for which there was no pardon, from which there could never
be redemption, was overwhelming. In the most astonishing way Eugene found out about it right away, and yet he did not know what
they had done, and no one ever spoke a word against them.

Rather, the mention of their name brought silence, and in that
silence there was something merciless and final, something that belonged to the temper of the country, and that was far more terrible
than any open word of scorn, contempt, or bitter judgment could
have been, more savage than a million strident, whispering, or abusive tongues could be, because the silence was unarguable, irrevocable, complete, as if a great door had been shut against their
lives forever.

Everywhere Eugene went in town, the people knew about them,
and said nothing—saying everything—when he spoke their names.

He found this final, closed, relentless silence everywhere—in tobacco, wine, and tailor shops, in book stores, food stores, haberdashery stores —wherever he bought anything and gave the clerk the address to which it was to be delivered, they responded instantly with this shut finality of silence, writing the name down gravely, sometimes saying briefly, "Oh! Coulson's!" when he gave them the address, but more often saying nothing.

But whether they spoke or simply wrote the name down without a word, there was always this quality of instant recognition, this obdurate, contemptuous finality of silence, as if a door had been shut— a door that could never again be opened. Somehow Eugene disliked them more for this silence than if they had spoken evilly: there was in it something ugly, knowing, and triumphant that was far more evil than any slyly whispering confidence of slander, or any open vituperation of abuse, could be. It seemed somehow to come from all the vile and uncountable small maggotry of the earth, the cautious little hatreds of a million nameless ciphers, each puny, pallid, trivial in himself, but formidable because he added his tiny beetle's ball of dung to the mountainous accumulation of ten million others of his breed.

It was uncanny how these clerk-like faces, grave and quiet, that never spoke a word, or gave a sign, or altered their expression by a jot, when Eugene gave them the address, could suddenly be alive with something secret, foul; and sly, could be more closed and secret than a door, and yet instantly reveal the naked, shameful, and iniquitous filth that welled up from some depthless source. He could not phrase it, give a name to it, or even see a certain sign that it was there, any more than he could put his hand upon a wisp of fading smoke, but he always knew when it was there, and somehow when he saw it his heart went hard and cold against the people who revealed it, and turned with warmth and strong affection towards the Coulson family.

There was, finally, among these grave clerk-like faces, one face that Eugene could never forget thereafter, a face that seemed to resume into its sly suave surfaces all of the nameless abomination of evil in the world, for which he had no name, for which there was no handle he could grasp, no familiar places or edges he could get his hands upon, which slid phantasmally, oilily, and smokily away whenever he tried to get his hands upon it. But it was to haunt his life for years in dreams of hatred, madness, and despair that found no frontal wall for their attack, no word for their vituperation, no door for the shoulder of his hate—an evil world of phantoms, shapes, and whispers that was yet as real as death, as ever-present as man's treachery, but that slid away from him like smoke whenever he tried to meet, or curse, or strangle it.

This face was the face of a man in a tailor shop, a fitter there, and Eugene could have battered that foul face into a bloody pulp, distilled the filthy refuse of that ugly life out of the fat swelling neck and through the murderous grip of his fingers if he could only have found a cause, a logic, and a provocation for doing it. And yet he never saw the man but twice, and briefly, and there had been nothing in his suave, sly careful speech to give offense.

Edith Coulson had sent Eugene to the tailor's shop: he needed a suit and when he asked her where to go to have it made, she had sent him to this place because her brother had his suits made there and liked it. The fitter was a heavy shambling man in his late thirties: he had receding hair, which he brushed back flat in a thick pompadour; yellowish, somewhat bulging eyes; a coarse heavy face, loose-featured, red, and sensual; a sloping meaty jaw, and large discolored buckteeth which showed unpleasantly in a mouth that was always half open. It was, in fact, the mouth that gave his face its sensual, sly, and ugly look, for a loose and vulgar smile seemed constantly to hover about its thick coarse edges, to be deliberately, slyly restrained, but about to burst at any moment into an open, evil, foully sensual laugh. There was always about his mouth this ugly suggestion of a loose, corrupt, and evilly jubilant mirth, and yet he never laughed or smiled.

The man's speech had this same quality. It was suave and courteous, but even in its most urbane assurances, there was something non-committal, sly, and jeering, something that slid away from you, and was never to be grasped, a quality that was faithless, tricky and unwholesome. When Eugene came for the final fitting it was obvious that he had done as cheap and shoddy a job as he could do; the suit was vilely botched and skimped, sufficient cloth had not been put into it, and now it was too late to remedy the defect.

Yet, the fitter gravely pulled the vest down till it met the trousers, tugged at the coat, and pulled the thing together where it stayed until Eugene took a breath or moved a muscle, when it would all come apart again, the collar bulging outward from the shoulder, the skimpy coat and vest crawling backward from the trousers, leaving a hiatus of shirt and belly that could not now be remedied by any means.

Then, gravely he would pull the thing together again, and in his suave, yet oily, sly, and non-committal phrases say:

"Um! Seems to fit you very well."

Eugene was choking with exasperation, and knew that he had been done, because he had foolishly paid them half the bill already, and now knew no way out of it except to lose what he had paid, and get nothing for it, or take the thing, and pay the balance. He was caught in a trap, but even as he jerked at the coat and vest speechlessly, seized his shirt, and thrust the gaping collar in the fitter's face, the man said smoothly,

"Um! Yes! The collar. Should think all that will be all right. Still needs a little alteration." He made some chalk marks on Eugene. "Should think you'll find it fits you very well when the tailor makes the alterations."

"When will the suit be ready?"

"Um. Should think you ought to have it by next Tuesday. Yes. I think you'll find it ready by Tuesday."

The sly words slid away from the boy like oil: there was nothing to pin him to or grasp him by, the yellowed eyes looked casually away and would not look at Eugene, the sensual face was suavely grave, the discolored buck-teeth shone obscenely through the coarse loose mouth, and the suggestion of the foul loose smile was so pronounced now that it seemed that at any moment the man would have to turn away with heavy trembling shoulders, and stifle the evil jeering laugh that was welling up in him. But he remained suavely grave and non-committal to the end, and when Eugene asked him if he should come again to try it on, he said, in the same oily tone, never looking at him:

"Um. Shouldn't think that would be necessary. Could have it delivered to you when it's ready. What's your address?"

"The Far End Farm—it's on the Ventnor Road."

"Oh! Coulson's!" He never altered his expression, but the suggestion of the obscene smile was so pronounced that now it seemed he would have to come out with it. Instead, he only said:

"Um. Yes. Should think it could be delivered to you there on Tuesday. If you'll just wait a moment I'll ask the tailor."

Gravely, suavely, he took the coat from Eugene and walked back towards the tailor's room with the coat across his arm. In a moment, the boy heard sly voices whispering, laughing slyly, then the tailor saying:

"Where does he live?"

"Coulson's!" said the fitter chokingly, and now the foul awaited laugh did come—high, wet, slimy, it came out of that loose mouth, and choked and whispered wordlessly, and choked again, and mingled then with the tailor's voice in sly, choking, whispering intimacy, and then gasped faintly, and was silent. When the man came out again his coarse face was red and swollen with foul secret merriment, his heavy shoulders trembled slightly, he took out his handkerchief and wiped it once across his loose half-opened mouth, and with that gesture wiped the slime of laughter from his lips. Then he came toward Eugene suave, grave, and courteous, evilly composed, as he said smoothly:

"Should think we'll have that for you by next Tuesday, sir."

"Can the tailor fix it so it's going to fit?"

"Um. Should think you'll find that everything's all right. You ought to have it Tuesday afternoon."

He was not looking at Eugene: the yellowish bulging eyes were staring casually, indefinitely, away, and his words again had slid away from the boy like oil. He could not be touched, approached, or handled: there was nothing to hold him by, he had the impregnability of smoke or a ball of mercury.

As Eugene went out the door, the tailor began to speak to some one in the shop, Eugene heard low words and whispered voices, then, gasping, the word "Coulson's!" and the slimy, choking, smothered laughter as the street-door closed behind him. He never saw the man again. He never forgot his face.

That was a fine house: the people in it were exiled, lost, and ruined people, and Eugene liked them all. Later, he never knew why he felt so close to them, or remembered them with such warmth and strong affection.

He did not see the Coulsons often and rarely talked to them. Yet he felt as familiar and friendly with them all as if he had known them all his life. The house was wonderful as no other house he had ever known because they all seemed to be living in it together with this strange speechless knowledge, warmth, and familiarity, and yet each was as private, secret, and secure in his own room as if he occupied the house alone.

Coulson himself Eugene saw least of all: they sometimes passed each other going in or out the door, or in the hall: Coulson would grunt "Morning," or "Good Day," in a curt blunt manner, and go on, and yet he always left Eugene with a curious sense of warmth and friendliness. He was a stocky well-set man with iron-gray hair, bushy eyebrows, and a red weathered face which wore the open color of the country on it, but also had the hard dull flesh of the steady heavy drinker.

Eugene never saw him drunk, and yet he was never sober: he was one of those men who have drunk themselves past any hope of drunkenness, who are soaked through to the bone with alcohol, saturated, tanned, weathered in it so completely that it could never be distilled out of their blood again. Yet, even in this terrible excess one felt a kind of grim control—the control of a man who is enslaved by the very thing that he controls, the control of the opium eater who cannot leave his drug but measures out his dose with a cold calculation, and finds the limit of his capacity, and stops there, day by day.

But somehow this very sense of control, this blunt ruddy style of the country gentleman which distinguished his speech, his manner, and his dress, made the ruin of his life, the desperate intemperance of drink that smouldered in him like a slow fire, steadily, nakedly apparent. It was as if, having lost everything, he still held grimly to the outer forms of a lost standard, a ruined state, when the inner substance was destroyed.

And it was this way with all of them—with Mrs. Coulson and the girl, as well: their crisp, clipped friendly speech never deviated into intimacy, and never hinted at any melting into confidence and admission. Upon the woman's weathered face there hovered, when she talked, the same faint set grin that Captain Nicholl had, and her eyes were bright and hard, a little mad, impenetrable, as were his. And the girl, although young and very lovely, sometimes had this same look when she greeted any one or paused to talk. In that look there was nothing truculent, bitter, or defiant: it was just the look of three people who had gone down together, and who felt for one another neither bitterness nor hate, but that strange companionship of a common disgrace, from which love has vanished, but which is more secret, silent, and impassively resigned to its fatal unity than love itself could be.

And that hard bright look also said this plainly to the world: "We ask for nothing from you now, we want nothing that you offer us. What is ours is ours, what we are we are, you'll not intrude nor come closer than we let you see!"

Coulson might have been a man who had been dishonored and destroyed by his women, and who took it stolidly, saying nothing, and drank steadily from morning until night, and had nothing for it now but drink and silence and acceptance. Yet Eugene never knew for certain that this was so, it just seemed inescapable, and was somehow legible not only in the slow smouldering fire that burned out through his rugged weathered face, but also in the hard bright armor of the women's eyes, the fixed set grin around their lips when they were talking—a grin that was like armor, too. And Morison, who had referred to Coulson, chuckling, as a real "bottle-a-day-man," had added quietly, casually, in his brief, indefinite, but blurted-out suggestiveness of speech:

"I think the old girl's been a bit of a bitch in her day. . . . Don't know, of course, but has the look, hasn't she?" In a moment he said quietly, "Have you talked to the daughter yet?"

"Once or twice. Not for long."

"Ran into a chap at Magdalen other day who knows her," he said casually. "He used to come out here to see her." He glanced swiftly, slyly at Eugene, his face reddening a little with laughter. "Pretty hot, I gather," he said quietly, smiling, and looked away. It was night: the fire burned cheerfully in the grate, the hot coals spurting in small gaseous flares from time to time. The house was very quiet all around them. Outside they could hear the stormy wind in the trees along the road. Morison flicked his cigarette into the fire, poured out a drink of whiskey into a glass, saying as he did so: "I say, old chap, you don't mind if I take a spot of this before I go to bed, do you?" Then he shot some seltzer in the glass, and drank. And Eugene sat there, without a word, staring sullenly into the fire, dumbly conscious of the flood of sick pain and horror which the casual foulness of the man's suggestion had aroused, stubbornly trying to deny now that he was thinking of the girl all the time.

One night, as Eugene was coming home along the dark road that went up past the playing field to the house, and that was bordered on each side by grand trees whose branches seemed to hold at night all the mysterious and demented cadences of storm, he came upon her suddenly standing in the shadow of a tree. It was one of the grand wild nights that seemed to come so often in the autumn of that year: the air was full of a fine stinging moisture, not quite rain, and above the stormy branches of the trees he could see the sky, wild, broken, full of scudding clouds through which at times the moon drove in and out with a kind of haggard loneliness. By that faint, wild, and broken light, he could see the small white oval of the girl's face—somehow even more lovely now just because he could not see it plainly. And he could see as well the rough gleaming bark of the tree against which she leaned.

As he approached, he saw her thrust her hand into the pocket of her overcoat, a match flared, and for a moment he saw Edith plainly, the small flower of her face framed in the wavering light as she lowered her head to light her cigarette.

The light went out, he saw the small respiring glow of her cigarette before the white blur of her face, he passed her swiftly, head bent, without speaking, his heart filled with the sense of strangeness and wonder which the family had roused in him.

Then he walked on up the road, muttering to himself. The house was dark when he got there, but when he entered his sitting-room the place was still warmly and softly luminous with the glow of hot coals in the grate. He turned the lights on, shut the door behind him, and hurled several lumps of coal upon the bedded coals. In a moment the fire was blazing and crackling cheerfully, and getting a kind of comfort and satisfaction from this activity, he flung off his coat, went over to the sideboard, poured out a stiff drink of scotch from a bottle there, and coming back to the fire, flung himself into a chair, and began to stare sullenly into the dancing flames.

How long he sat there in this stupor of sullen and nameless fury, he did not know, but he was sharply roused at length by footsteps light and rapid on the gravel, shocked into a start of surprise by a figure that appeared suddenly at one of the French windows that opened directly from his sitting-room onto the level sward of velvet lawn before the house.

He peered through the glass for a moment with an astonished stare before he recognized the face of Edith Coulson. He opened the doors at once, she came in quickly, smiling at his surprise, and at the glass which he was holding foolishly, half-raised, in his hand.

He continued to look at her with an expression of gape-mouthed astonishment and in a moment became conscious of her smiling glance, the cool sweet assurance of her young voice.

"I say!" she was saying cheerfully, "what a lucky thing to find you up! I came away without any key—I should have had to wake the whole house up—so when I saw your light!" she concluded briskly, "—what luck! I hope you don't mind."

"Why no-o, no," Eugene stammered foolishly, still staring dumbly at her. "No—no-o—not at all," he blundered on. Then suddenly coming to himself with a burst of galvanic energy, he shut the windows, pushed another chair before the fire, and said:

"Won't you sit down and have a drink before you go?"

"Thanks," she said crisply. "I will—yes. What a jolly fire you have." As she talked she took off her coat and hat swiftly and put them on a chair. Her face was flushed and rosy, beaded with small particles of rain, and for a moment she stood before the mirror arranging her hair, which had been tousled by the wind.

The girl was slender, tall, and very lovely with the kind of beauty they have when they are beautiful—a beauty so fresh, fair, and delicate that it seems to be given to just a few of them to compensate for all the grimly weathered ugliness of the rest. Her voice was also lovely, sweet, and musical, and when she talked all the notes of tenderness and love were in it. But she had the same hard bright look in her eye that her mother had, the faint set smile around her mouth: as they stood there talking she was standing very close to him, and he could smell the fragrance of her hair, and felt an intolerable desire to put his hand upon hers and was almost certain she would not draw away. But the hard bright look was in her eye, the faint set smile around her mouth, and he did nothing.

"What'll you have?" Eugene said. "Whiskey?"

"Yes, thank you," she said with the same sweet crisp assurance with which she always spoke, "and a splash of soda." He struck a match and held it for her while she lit the cigarette she was holding in her hand, and in a moment returned to her with the drink. Then she sat down, crossed her legs, and for a moment puffed thoughtfully at her cigarette as she stared into the fire. The storm wind moaned in the great trees along the road, and near the house, and suddenly a swirl of rain and wind struck the windows with a rattling blast. The girl stirred a little in her chair, restlessly, shivered:

"Listen!" she said. "What a night! Horrible weather we have here, isn't it?"

"I don't know. I don't like the fog and rain so well. But this—the way it is tonight—" he nodded toward the window— "I like it."

She looked at him for a moment.

"Oh," she said non-committally. "You do." Then, as she sipped her drink, she looked curiously about the room, her reflective glance finally resting on his table, where there was a great stack of the ledgers in which he wrote.

"I say," she cried again, "what are you doing with all those big books there?"

"I write in them."

"Really?" she said, in a surprised tone. "I should think it'd be an awful bother carrying them around when you travel?"

"It is. But it's the best way I've found of keeping what I do together."

"Oh," she said, as before, and continued to stare curiously at him with her fair, lovely young face, the curiously hard, bright, and unrevealing glance of her eye. "I see. . . . But why do you come to such a place as this to write?" she said presently. "Do you like it here?"

"I do. As well as any place I've ever known."

"Oh! . . . I should think a writer would want a different kind of place."

"What kind?"

"Oh—I don't know—Paris—London—some place like that, where there is lots of life—people—fun—I should think you'd work better in a place like that."

"I work better here."

"But don't you get awfully fed up sitting in here all day long and writing in those enormous books?"

"I do, yes."

"I should think you would . . . I should think you'd want to get away from it sometimes."

"Yes. I do want to—every day—almost all the time."

"Then why don't you?" she said crisply. "Why don't you go off some week-end for a little spree? I should think it'd buck you up no end."

"It would—yes. Where should I go?"

"Oh, Paris, I suppose. . . . Or London! London!" she cried. "London is quite jolly if you know it."

"I'm afraid I don't know it."

"But you've *been* to London," she said in a surprised tone.

"Oh, yes. I lived there for several months."

"Then you know London," she said impatiently. "Of course you do."

"I'm afraid I don't know it very well. I don't know many people there—and after all, that's the thing that counts, isn't it?"

She looked at Eugene curiously for a moment, with the faint hard smile around the edges of her lovely mouth.

"—Should think that might be arranged," she said with a quiet, an enigmatic humor. Then, more directly, she added. "That shouldn't be difficult at all. Perhaps I could introduce you to some people."

"That would be fine. Do you know many people there?"

"Not many," she said. "I go there—whenever I can." She got up with a swift decisive movement, put her glass down on the mantel and cast her cigarette into the fire. Then she faced Eugene, looking at him with a curiously bold, an almost defiant directness, and she fixed him with this glance for a full moment before she spoke.

"Good-night," she said. "Thanks awfully for letting me in—and for the drink."

"Good-night," Eugene said, and she was gone before he could say more, and he had closed the door behind her, and he could hear her light swift footsteps going down the hall and up the steps. And then there was nothing in the house but sleep and silence, and storm and darkness in the world around him.

Mrs. Coulson came into Eugene's room just once or twice while he was there. One morning she came in, spoke crisply and cheerfully, and walked over to the window, looking out upon the velvet lawn and at the dreary, impenetrable gray of foggy air. Although the room was warm, and there was a good fire burning in the grate, she clasped her arms together as she looked, and shivered a little:

"Wretched weather, isn't it?" she said in her crisp tones, her gaunt weathered face, and toothy mouth touched by the faint fixed grin as she looked out with her bright hard stare. "Don't you find it fright-fully depressing? Most Americans do," she said, getting a sharp disquieting sound into the word.

"Yes. I do, a little. We don't have this kind of weather very often. But this is the time of year you get it here, isn't it? I suppose you're used to it by now?"

"Used to it?" she said crisply, turning her gaze upon him. "Not at all. I've known it all my life but I'll never get used to it. It is a wretched climate."

"Still, you wouldn't feel at home anywhere else, would you? You wouldn't want to live outside of England?"

"No?" she said, staring at him with the faint set grin around her toothy mouth. "Why do you think so?"

"Because your home is here."

"My home? My home is where they have fine days, and where the sun is always shining."

"I wouldn't like that. I'd get tired of sunlight all the time. I'd want some gray days and some fog and snow."

"Yes, I suppose you would. But then, you've been used to having fine days all your life, haven't you? With us, it's different. I'm so fed up with fog and rain that I could do without it nicely, thank you, if I never saw it again. . . . I don't think you could ever under-stand how much the sunlight means to us," she said slowly. She turned, and for a moment looked out the window. "Sunlight—warmth—fine days forever! Warmth everywhere—in the earth, the sky, in the lives of the people all around you, nothing but warmth and sunlight and fine days!"

"And where would you go to find all that? Does it exist?"

"Oh, of course!" she said crisply and good-naturedly, turning to him again. "There's only one place to live—only one country where I want to live."

"Where is that?"

"Italy," she said. "That's my real home. . . . I'd live the rest of my life there if I could." For a moment longer she looked out the window, then turned briskly, saying:

"Why don't you run over to Paris some week-end? After all, it's only seven hours from London: if you left here in the morning you'd be there in time for dinner. It would be a good change for you. I should think a little trip like that would buck you up tremendously."

Her words gave him a wonderful feeling of confidence and hope: she had travelled a great deal, and she had the casual, assured way of speaking of a voyage that made it seem very easy, and filled one with a sense of joy and adventure when he spoke about it. When Eugene tried to think of Paris by himself it had seemed very far away and hard to reach: London stood between it and him, and when he thought of the huge smoky web of London, the soft gray skies above him, and the enormous weight of lives that were hidden somewhere in that impenetrable fog, a gray desolation and weariness of the spirit filled him. It seemed to him that he must draw each breath of that soft gray air with heavy weary effort, and that every mile of his journey would be a ghastly struggle through some viscous and material substance, that weighted down his steps, and filled his heart with desolation.

But when Mrs. Coulson spoke to him about it, suddenly it all seemed wonderfully easy and good. England was magically small, the channel to be taken in a stride, and all the thrill, the joy, the mystery of Paris his again—the moment that he chose to make it his.

He looked at her gaunt weathered face, the hard bright armor of her eyes, and wondered how anything so clear, so sharp, so crisp, and so incisive could have been shaped and grown underneath these soft and humid skies that numbed him, mind and heart and body, with their thick dull substance of gray weariness and desolation.

A day or two before he left, Edith came into his room one afternoon bearing a tray with tea and jam and buttered bread. He was sitting in his chair before the fire, and had his coat off: when she came in he scrambled to his feet, reached for the coat and started to put it on. In her young crisp voice she told him not to, and put the tray down on the table, saying that the maid was having her afternoon off.

Then for a moment she stood looking at him with her faint and enigmatic smile.

"So you're leaving us?" she said presently.

"Yes. Tomorrow."

"And where will you go from here?" she said.

"To Germany, I think. Just for a short time—two or three weeks."

"And after that?"

"I'm going home."

"Home?"

"Back to America."

"Oh," she said slowly. "I see." In a moment, she added, "We shall miss you."

He wanted to talk to her more than he had ever wanted to talk to any one in his life, but when he spoke, all that he could say, lamely, muttering, was:

"I'll miss you, too."

"Will you?" She spoke so quietly that he could scarcely hear her. "I wonder for how long?" she said.

"Forever," he said, flushing miserably at the sound of the word, and yet not knowing any other word to say.

The faint hard smile about her mouth was a little deeper when she spoke again.

"Forever? That's a long time, when one is young as you," she said.

"I mean it. I'll never forget you as long as I live."

"We shall remember you," she said quietly. "And I hope you think of us sometimes—back here, buried, lost, in all the fog and rain and ruin of England. How good it must be to know that you are young in a young country—where nothing that you did yesterday matters very much. How wonderful it must be to know that none of the failure of the past can pull you down—that there will always be another day for you—a new beginning. I wonder if you Americans will ever know how fortunate you are," the girl said.

"And yet you couldn't leave all this?" Eugene said with a kind of desperate hope. "This old country you've lived in, known all your life. A girl like you could never leave a place like this to live the kind of life we have in America."

"*Couldn't* I?" she said with a quiet but unmistakable passion of conviction. "There's nothing I'd like better."

Eugene stared at her blindly, dumbly for a moment; suddenly all that he wanted to say, and had not been able to say, found release in a movement of his hands. He gripped her by the shoulders and pulled her to him, and began to plead with her:

"Then why don't you? I'll take you there!—Look here—" his words were crazy and he knew it, but as he spoke them, he believed all he said—"Look here! I haven't got much money—but in America you can make it if you want to! I'm going back there. You come, too—I'll take you when I go!"

She had not tried to free herself; she just stood there passive, unresisting, as he poured that frenzied proposal in her ears. Now, with the same passive and unyielding movement, the bright armor of her young eyes, she stepped away, and stood looking at him silently for a moment. Then slowly, with an almost imperceptible movement, she shook her head. "Oh, you'll forget all about us," she said quietly. "You'll forget about our lives here—buried in fog—and rain—and failure—and defeat."

"Failure and defeat won't last forever."

"Sometimes they do," she said with a quiet finality that froze his heart.

"Not for you—they won't!" Eugene said, and took her by the hand again with desperate entreaty. "Listen to me—" he blundered on incoherently, with the old feeling of nameless shame and horror. "You don't need to tell me what it is—I don't want to know—but whatever it is—for you, it doesn't matter—you can get the best of it."

She said nothing, but just looked at him through that hard bright armor of her eyes, the obdurate finality of her smile.

"Good-bye," she said, "I'll not forget you either." She looked at him for a moment curiously before she spoke again. "I wonder," she said slowly, "if you'll ever understand just what it was you did for me by coming here?"

"What was it?"

"You opened a door that I thought had been closed forever," she said, "a door that let me look in on a world I thought I should never see again—a new bright world, a new life and a new beginning—for us all. And I thought that was something which would never happen to any one in this house again."

"It will to you," Eugene said, and took her hand again with desperate eagerness. "It can happen to you whenever you want it to. It's yours, I'll swear it to you, if you'll only speak."

She looked at him, with an almost imperceptible movement of her head.

"I tell you I know what I'm talking about."

Again she shook her head.

"You don't know," she said. "You're young. You're an American. There are some things you'll never be old enough to know.—For some of us there's no return.—Go back," she said, "go back to the life you know—the life you understand—where there can always be a new beginning—a new life."

"And you—" Eugene said dumbly, miserably.

"Good-bye, my dear," she said so low and gently he could scarcely hear her. "Think of me sometimes, won't you—I'll not forget you." And before he could speak she kissed him once and was gone, so light and swift that he did not know it, until the door had closed behind her. And for some time, like a man in a stupor, he stood there looking out the window at the gay wet light of England.

The next day he went away, and never saw any of them again, but he could not forget them. Although he had never passed beyond the armor of their hard bright eyes, or breached the wall of their crisp, friendly, and impersonal speech, or found out anything about them, he always thought of them with warmth, with a deep and tender affection, as if he had always known them—as if, somehow, he could have lived with them or made their lives his own had he only said a word, or turned the handle of a door—a word he never knew, a door he never found.

THE SUN AND THE RAIN

WHEN he awoke in Chartres he was filled with a numb excitement. It was a gray wintry day with snow in the air, and he expected something to happen. He had this feeling often in the country, in France: it was a strange, mixed feeling of desolation and homelessness, of wondering with a ghostly emptiness why he was there—and of joy, and hope, and expectancy, without knowing what it was he was going to find.

In the afternoon he went down to the station and took a train that was going to Orléans. He did not know where Orléans was. The train was a mixed train, made up of goods cars and passenger compartments. He bought a third-class ticket and got into one of the compartments. Then the shill little whistle blew, and the train rattled out of Chartres into the countryside, in the abrupt and casual way a little French train has, and which was disquieting to him.

There was a light mask of snow on the fields, and the air was smoky: the whole earth seemed to smoke and steam, and from the windows of the train one could see the wet earth and the striped, cultivated pattern of the fields, and now and then, some farm buildings. It did not look like America: the land looked fat and well kept, and even the smoky wintry woods had this well-kept appearance. Far off sometimes one could see tall lines of poplars and knew that there was water there.

In the compartment he found three people—an old peasant and his wife and daughter. The old peasant had sprouting mustaches, a seamed and weather-beaten face, and small rheumy-looking eyes. His hands had a rock-like heaviness and solidity, and he kept them clasped upon his knees. His wife's face was smooth and brown, there were fine webs of wrinkles around her eyes, and her face was like an old brown bowl. The daughter had a dark sullen face and sat away from them next the window as if she was ashamed of them. From time to time when they spoke to her she would answer them in an infuriated kind of voice without looking at them.

The peasant began to speak amiably to him when he entered the compartment. He smiled and grinned back at the man, although he did not understand a word he was saying, and the peasant kept on talking then, thinking he understood.

The peasant took from his coat a package of the cheap, powerful tobacco—the 'bleu—which the French government provides for a few cents for the poor, and prepared to stuff his pipe. The young man pulled a package of American cigarettes from his pocket, and offered them to the peasant.

"Will you have one?"

"My faith, yes!" said the peasant.

He took a cigarette clumsily from the package and held it between his great, stiff fingers, then he held it to the flame the young man offered, puffing at it in an unaccustomed way. Then he fell to examining it curiously, revolving it in his hands to read the label. He turned to his wife, who had followed every movement of this simple transaction with the glittering intent eyes of an animal, and began a rapid and excited discussion with her.

"It's American—this."

"Is it good?"

"My faith, yes—it's of good quality."

"Here, let me see! What does it call itself?"

They stared dumbly at the label.

"What do you call this?" said the peasant to the young man.

"Licky Streek," said the youth, dutifully phonetical.

"L-l-leek-ee—?" they stared doubtfully. "What does that wish to say, in French?"

"Je ne sais pas," he answered.

"Where are you going?" the peasant said, staring at the youth with rheumy little eyes of fascinated curiosity.

"Orléans."

"How?" the peasant asked, with a puzzled look on his face.

"Orléans."

"I do not understand," the peasant said.

"Orléans! Orléans!" the girl shouted in a furious tone. "The gentleman says he is going to Orléans."

"Ah!" the peasant cried, with an air of sudden illumination. *"Orléans!"*

It seemed to the youth that he had said the word just the same way the peasant said it, but he repeated it.

"Yes, Orléans."

"He is going to Orléans," the peasant said, turning to his wife.

"Ah-h!" she cried knowingly, with a great air of illumination, then both fell silent, and began to stare at the youth with curious, puzzled eyes again.

"What region are you from?" the peasant asked presently, still intent and puzzled, staring at him with his small eyes.

"How's that? I don't understand."

"I say—what region are you from?"

"The gentleman is not French!" the girl shouted furiously, as if exasperated by their stupidity. "He is a foreigner. Can't you see that?"

"Ah-h!" the peasant cried, after a moment, with an air of astounded enlightenment. Then, turning to his wife, he said briefly, "He is not French. He is a stranger."

"Ah-h!"

And then they both turned their small, round eyes on him and regarded him with a fixed, animal-like curiosity.

"From what country are you?" the peasant asked presently. "What are you?"

"I am an American."

"Ah-h! An American. . . . He is an American," he said, turning to his wife.

"Ah-h!"

The girl made an impatient movement, and continued to stare furiously and sullenly out the window.

Then the peasant, with the intent, puzzled curiosity of an animal began to examine his companion carefully from head to foot. He looked at his shoes, his clothes, his overcoat, and finally lifted his eyes in an intent and curious stare to the young man's valise on the rack above his head. He nudged his wife and pointed to the valise.

"That's good stuff, eh?" he said in a low voice. "It's real leather."

"Yes, it's good, that."

And both of them looked at the valise for some time and then turned their curious gaze upon the youth again. He offered the peasant another cigarette, and the old man took one, thanking him.

"It's very fine, this," he said, indicating the cigarette. "That costs dear, eh?"

"Six francs."

"Ah-h! . . . That's very dear," and he began to look at the cigarette with increased respect.

"Why are you going to Orléans?" he asked presently. "Do you know some one there?"

"No, I am just going there to see the town."

"How?" the peasant blinked at him stupidly, uncomprehendingly. "You have business there?"

"No. I am going just to visit—to see the place."

"How?" the peasant said stupidly in a moment, looking at him. "I do not understand."

"The gentleman says he is going to see the town," the girl broke in furiously. Can't you understand anything?"

"I do not understand what he is saying," the old man said to her. "He does not speak French."

"He speaks very well," the girl said angrily. "I understand him very well. It is you who are stupid—that's all.

The peasant was silent for some time now, puffing at his cigarette, and looking at the young man with friendly, puzzled eyes.

"America is very large—eh?" he said at length—making a wide gesture with his hands.

"Yes, it is very large. Much larger than France."

"How?" the peasant said again with a puzzled, patient look. "I do not understand."

"He says America is much larger than France," the girl cried in an exasperated tone. "I understand all he says."

Then, for several minutes, there was an awkward silence: nothing was said. The peasant smoked his cigarette, seemed on the point of speaking several times, looked puzzled and said nothing. Outside, rain had begun to fall in long slanting lines across the fields, and beyond, in the gray blown sky, there was a milky radiance where the sun should be, as if it were trying to break through. When the peasant saw this, he brightened, and leaning forward to the young man in a friendly manner, he tapped him on the knee with one of his great, stiff fingers, and then pointing towards the sun, he said very slowly and distinctly, as one might instruct a child:

"Le so-leil."

And the young man obediently repeated the word as the peasant had said it:

"Le so-leil."

The old man and his wife beamed delightedly and nodded their approval, saying, "Yes. Yes. Good. Very good." Turning to his wife for confirmation, the old man said:

"He said it very well, didn't he?"

"But, yes! It was perfect!"

Then, pointing to the rain, and making a down-slanting movement with his great hands, he said again, very slowly and patiently:

"La pluie."

"La pluie," the young man repeated dutifully, and the peasant nodded vigorously, saying:

"Good, good. You are speaking very well. In a little time you will speak good French." Then, pointing to the fields outside the train, he said gently:

"La terre."

"La terre," the young man answered.

"I tell you," the girl cried angrily from her seat by the window, "he knows all these words. He speaks French very well. You are too stupid to understand him—that's all."

The old man made no reply to her, but sat looking at the young man with a kind, approving face. Then, more rapidly than before, and in succession, he pointed to the sun, the rain, the earth, saying:

"Le soleil . . . la pluie . . . la terre."

The young man repeated the words after him, and the peasant nodded vigorously with satisfaction. Then, for a long time, no one spoke, there was no sound except for the uneven rackety-clack of the little train, and the girl continued to look sullenly out the window. Outside, the rain fell across the fertile fields in long slanting lines.

Late in the afternoon, the train stopped at a little station, and every one rose to get out. This was as far as the train went: to reach Orléans it was necessary to change to another train.

The peasant, his wife and his daughter collected their bundles and got out of the train. On another track another little train was waiting, and the peasant pointed to this with his great, stiff finger, and said to the young man:

"Orléans. That's your train there."

The youth thanked him, and gave the old man the remainder of the package of cigarettes. The peasant thanked him effusively and before they parted he again pointed rapidly towards the sun, the rain, and the earth, saying with a kind and friendly smile:

"Le soleil . . . la pluie . . . la terre."

And the young man nodded to show that he understood, repeated what the old man had said. And the peasant shook his head with vigorous approval, saying:

"Yes, yes. It's very good. You will learn fast."

At these words, the girl, who with the same sullen, aloof, and shamed look had walked on ahead of her parents, now turned, and cried out in a furious and exasperated tone:

"I tell you, the gentleman knows all that! . . . Will you leave him alone now! . . . You are only making a fool of yourself!"

But the old man and old woman paid no attention to her, but stood looking at the young man, with a friendly smile, and shook hands warmly and cordially with him as he said good-bye.

Then he walked on across the tracks and got up into a compartment in the other train. When he looked out the window again, the peasant and his wife were standing on the platform looking towards him with kind and eager looks on their old faces. When the peasant caught his eye, he pointed his great finger at the sun again, and called out:

"Le so-leil."

"Le so-leil," the young man answered.

"Yes! Yes!" the old man shouted, with a laugh. "It's very good."

Then the daughter looked toward the young man sullenly, gave a short and impatient laugh of exasperation, and turned angrily away. The train began to move, then, but the old man and woman stood looking after him as long as they could. He waved to them, and the old man waved his great hand vigorously and, laughing, pointed towards the sun. And the young man nodded his head and shouted, to show that he had understood. Meanwhile, the girl had turned her back angrily and was walking away around the station.

Then they were lost from sight, the train swiftly left the little town behind, and now there was nothing but the fields, the earth, the smoky and mysterious distances. The rain fell steadily.

THE DREAM OF TIME

PLAY us a tune on an unbroken spinet, and let the bells ring, let the bells ring! Play music now: play us a tune on an unbroken spinet. Do not make echoes of forgotten time, do not strike music from old broken keys, do not make ghosts with faded tinklings on the yellowed board; but play us a tune on an unbroken spinet, play lively music when the instrument was new, let us see Mozart playing in the parlor, and let us hear the sound of the ladies' voices. But more than that; waken the turmoil of forgotten streets, let us hear their sounds again unmuted, and unchanged by time, throw the light of Wednesday morning on the Third Crusade, and let us see Athens on an average day. Let us hear the sound of the voices of the Greeks, and observe closely if they were all wise and beautiful at ten o'clock in the morning; let us see if their limbs were all perfect, and their gestures grave and stately, also let us smell their food and observe them eating, and hear, if only once, the sound of a wheel in a street, the texture of just four forgotten moments.

Give us the sounds of Egypt on a certain day; let us hear the voice of King Menkaura and some of the words of the Lady Sennuwy; also the voices of the cotton-farmers. Let us hear the vast and casual sound of life, in these old peoples: their greetings in the street, the voices of the housewives of the merchants. And let us hear the laughter of a woman in the sixteenth century.

The cry of the wolf would always be the same; the sound of the wheel will always be the same; and the hoof of the horse on the roads of every time will be the same. But play us a tune on an unbroken spinet; and let us hear the voices of the knights at dinner. The cry of a man to his dog, and the barking of the dog; the call of the plow-driver to his horse, and the sound of the horse; the noise of the hunt, and the sound of the flowing water, will always be the same.

By the waters of life, by time, by time, play us a tune on an unbroken spinet, and let us hear the actual voices of old fairs; let us move backward through our memories, and through the memory of the race, let us relive the million forgotten moments of our lives, and let us see poor people sitting in their rooms in 1597, and let us see the rich man standing with his back before the fire, in the Middle Ages, and his wife knitting by the table, and let us hear their casual words.

Let us see the men who built the houses of Old Frankfort; let us see how they worked, and let us see them sitting on hewn timbers when they ate their lunches; let us hear their words, the sound of their voices. Unwind the fabric of lost time out of our entrails, repair the million little threads of actual circumstance until the seconds grow gray, bright and dusty with the living light, and we see the plain unfabled faces of the people; let us awake, and hear the people in the streets, and see Tobias Smollett pass our window.

Then, play us a tune on the unbroken spinet, let time be as the road to London and we a traveller on it; and let us enter London and find out what year it is there in the Mile End Road; let it be dark, and let us enter London in the dark, and hear men's voices, and let us see if we could understand them; and let us then find out what year it is, a lodging for the night, and see if they read mystery on us, or would fly away from us.

But there are times that are stranger yet, there are times that are stranger than the young knights and the horses, and the sounds of the eating taverns. The far time is the time of yesterday: it is the time of early America, it is the voices of the people on Broadway in 1841, it is the sounds of the streets in Des Moines in 1887, it is the engines of the early trains at Baltimore in 1853, it is the faces and voices of the early American people, who are lapped up in the wilderness, who are hid from us, whose faces are in mystery, whose lives are more dark and strange than the lives of the Saxon thanes.

The time that is lovely is the time of the fatness and of the bright colors; it is the elfin time of the calendars, and the sad and mysterious time of the early photographs. It is the time of the early lithographs, it is the time when the world was green and red and yellow. It is the time of the red barn and the windmill, and the house of the seven thousand gables; it is the time of the green lawn and the blue sky and the white excursion-steamer in the river, and the flags, the streamers, and gay brown-and-white buntings, the brass bands and the tumult of all the people who cry out Hurray, hurray!

It is the time of the boy rolling his hoop down the pink path, and of Mama in a bonnet and with a muff, and a stuck-out bottom, and Papa with a derby; it is the time of peace and plenty and the fair stripes of color, and the iron stag. It is the time of the lightning-rod salesman and the summer boarder, it is the time of Farmer Hayseed and of Dusty Rhodes the tramp, it is the time when boys started on the downward path through cigarettes; it is a lovely time. It is the time of the lures and snares of the wicked city and of the Great White Way; it is the time of pitfalls that await the innocent country girl with a whaleboned collar and a small waist; it is the time of Palaces of Sin or the Devil in Society; it is the time of the Tenderloin, of the nests of vice; it is the time of the gilded resorts with mirrors and soft carpets, where the mechanical piano played and you bought champagne, and of the High Class places and the Madam who would not stand for any ungentlemanly behavior, the time of the girls who wore evening dresses and were Perfect Ladies.

It is the time of the opera and theatre parties, and the Horse Show, and of late jolly suppers in the walnut dining-rooms; it is the time of elegant ladies with long gloves on naked arms, and Welsh rarebit in the chafing-dish; it is the time of the Four Hundred, and the great names of the millionaires—the Vanderbilts, the Astors, and the Goulds—it is the time of the powdered flunkies and the twenty-dollar favors; it is the time of Newport, and the canopied red-carpeted sidewalks, and the great mansions on Fifth Avenue, and the splendid gilt and plush marble halls, and the time of the fortune-hunting foreign noblemen (London papers please copy).

It is the time of the effeminate fop, and the lisping ass (Oh, Percy! I'll slap you on your wrist, you rough, rude thing, you!) ; it is the time of the Damned Dude who wears English clothes and has cuffs on his trousers (Hey, mister! Is it raining in London?) , and he never did anything in his life but spend his old man's money, he never did an honest lick of work in his life, he's not worth powder enough to kill him, and if the son-of-a-bitch comes fooling around any sister of mine I'll beat the everlasting tar out of him.

When the songs that they sang were old and sweet, when the songs that they sang were like beauty's from afar, and when people sitting on their porches in the dusk could hear (O sweet and low!) the corner quartette sing, "Sweet Adeline"; when the songs that they sang were "Daisy, Daisy, Give Me Your Answer True."

It is the time of the wharves and the tangled shipping, the horse-cars by the docks, of piled-up casks and kegs of rum and molasses. There are forgotten fume-flaws of bright smoke above Manhattan; where are the lost faces that came towards us over Brooklyn bridge, where are the parted ripples and the proud forgotten ships?

By the waters of life, before we knew that we must die, before we had seen our father's face, before we had sought the print of his foot: by the waters of time (the tide! the tide!) , before we had seen the shadows in the haunted woods, before lost moments lived again, before the shades were fleshed. Who are we, that must follow in the footsteps of the king? Who are we, that had no kings to follow? We are the unkinged men. Have we left shadows on forgotten walls? Have we crossed running water and lived for seven timeless years with the enchantress, and shall we find our son who is ourself, and will he know us?

Shall your voices unlock the gates of my brain? Shall I know you, though I have never seen your face? Will you know me, and will you call me "son"? Father, I know that you live, though I have never found you.

In the old town of Tours he quickly found lodging in an ancient hotel or tavern—really a congeries of old, whited buildings with separate doors, looking out on a cobbled courtyard through whose gate, in former times perhaps, the horses and post-chaise of weary travellers had often clattered. In a cold, little room in one of the buildings facing on the court, he now settled down, and there began for him one of the most extraordinary and phantasmal time-experiences of his life. Day passed into night, night merged into day again like the unbroken weaving of a magic web, and he stayed on, week after week, plunged in a strange and legendary spell of time that seemed suspended and detached from the world of measurable event, fixed in unmoving moment, unsilent silence, changeless change.

Later, it seemed to him that that strange revery and dream of time, in which his life was now so strangely fixed, had been induced by a series of causes, easy to understand in the light of experience, and almost logical in their consequence. It was five months since he had left America. After the overwhelming impact of impression and event which a new world, a new life, had brought to him in so many varied, chance, and unexpected ways—after the ship, the voyage, the enormous isolation, the whole earth-detachment of the sea (itself a life, a world, a universe of new experience) , after the weeks in England, the huge web of London, the brief but poignantly illuminating days in Bristol, Bath, and Devonshire, with fleeting glimpses of something so strange, yet so familiar, so near, yet never to be touched, that it seemed to him he was looking in through a lighted window at a life which he had always known, but which he could never make his own; after the terrific impact of France and Paris—the month of bewildered, desperate and almost terror-stricken isolation in a new and hostile world—an atom, wordless, tongueless, almost drowned among the strange, dark faces of the Frenchmen; after all the confusion, grief, and error of that month—the night-time kaleidoscope of cafés, brothels, alcohol, and women, the frenzied day-time prowling through museums, bookstalls, thronging streets—the thousand monuments of alien culture, the million faces of an alien race, until every atom of him was wrung, trembling, maddened and exhausted, sick with loss and hopelessness, weary with despair—after the huge first shock and flood-tide of immersion in an alien life—had come his meeting with Starwick, Elinor, and Ann, the brief, fatal, furious weeks of their relation, the bitter loss and waste and rankling pain of parting; and finally the sweltering and incurable ache, the blind and driven aimlessness of wandering, the chance encounter with the Countess, and the brief interlude of forgetfulness and oblivion that had come to him while he was with her—and now, blank, silent loneliness again, the blind fortuity of chance, the arbitrary halt and desperate entrenchment of his spirit in this town of Tours.

Now, after the savage kaleidoscope of these months of hope and grief and ecstacy, of desolation and despair, of passion, love, and suffering, of maddened hunger and infuriate desire, after all the restless and insatiable seeking of his goaded, driven, and unresting soul, he had come at last to a place of quietness and pause; and suddenly he was like a desperate and bewildered man who has come in from the furious street of life to seek sanctuary and repose in the numb stillness of a tomb.

Day and night now, from dawn to dark, from sleeping until waking, in that strange spell of time and silence that was neither dream nor sleep nor waking vision, but that like an enchantment was miraculously composed of all, obsessed as a man exiled, banished, or condemned by fate to live upon a desert island without possibility of escape or return—he thought of home.

In that enchanted spell of time and silence, as men who gaze in visions across misty and illimitable seas, with the terrible homelessness of a man for whom there can never be return, with the terrible homelessness of a man who longs for home and has no home—with the impossible, hopeless, incurable and unutterable homesickness of the American, who is maddened by a longing for return, and does not know to what he can return, whose brain burns night and day with the maddened hope, whose heart aches night and day with the smothering and incurable ache of the houseless, homeless, and forsaken atom of the earth who has no goal or ending for his hunger, no final dwelling-place for his desire—he thought of home.

What was it? It was the furious desire, unceasing, unassuaged, of wandering and forsaken man—the lost American, who longs forever for return—and who has no door to enter, no room to dwell in, no single handsbreadth of certain, consecrated earth upon that continent of wild houseless space, to which he can return.

An astounding—an almost incredible thing—now happened. He had come to Tours, telling himself that now at last, at last, he was going "to settle down and write," that he was going to justify his voyage by the high purpose of creation. In his mind there swarmed various projects, cloudy, vague, and grandiose in their conception, of plays, books, stories, essays he must write: with desperate resolve he sat down grimly now to shape these grand designs into the stern and toilsome masonry of words. A few impatient, fragmentary beginnings, the opening pages of a story, the beginning speeches of a play —all crumpled in a wad and impatiently tossed aside—were the final results of this ambitious purpose.

And yet, write he did. Useless, fragmentary, and inchoate as were these first abortive efforts, he began to write now like a madman—as only a madman could write—driven by an insanity of sense and soul and feeling which he no longer could master or control, tranced in a hypnosis by whose fatal and insatiate compulsions he was forced, without will, to act. Gripped by that ungovernable desire, all ordered plans, designs, coherent projects for the work he had set out to do went by the board, were burned up in the flame of a quenchless passion, like a handful of dry straw. Seated at a table in his cold, little room that overlooked the old cobbled court of the hotel, he wrote ceaselessly from dawn to dark, sometimes from darkness on to dawn again—hurling himself upon the bed to dream, in a state of comatose awareness, strange sleeping-wakeful visions, dreams mad and terrible as the blinding imagery that now swept constantly across his brain its blaze of fire.

The words were wrung out of him in a kind of bloody sweat, they poured out of his finger tips, spat out of his snarling throat like writhing snakes; he wrote them with his heart, his brain, his sweat, his guts; he wrote them with his blood, his spirit; they were wrenched out of the last secret source and substance of his life.

And in those words was packed the whole image of his bitter homelessness, his intolerable desire, his maddened longing for return. In those wild and broken phrases was packed the whole bitter burden of his famished, driven, over-laden spirit—all the longing of the wanderer, all the impossible and unutterable homesickness that the American, or any man on earth, can know.

They were all there—without coherence, scheme, or reason—flung down upon paper like figures blasted by the spirit's lightning stroke, and in them was the huge chronicle of the billion forms, the million names, the huge, single, and incomparable substance of America.

At morning, in a foreign land, whether upon the mournful plains of Hungary, or in some quiet square of Georgian houses, embedded in the immensity of sleeping London, he awakes, and thinks of home; or in some small provincial town of France, he starts up from his sleep at night, he starts up in the living, brooding stillness of the night, for suddenly he thinks that he has heard there the sounds of America and the wilderness, the things that are in his blood, his heart, his brain, in every atom of his flesh and tissue, the things for which he draws his breath in labor, the things that madden him with an intolerable and nameless pain.

And what are they? They are the whistle-wail of one of the great American engines as it thunders through the continent at night, the sound of the voices of the city streets—those hard, loud, slangy voices, full of violence, humor, and recklessness, now stronger and more remote than the sounds of Asia—the sounds that come up from the harbor of Manhattan in the night—that magnificent and thrilling music of escape, mystery, and joy, with the mighty orchestration of the transatlantics, the hoarse little tugs, the ferryboats and lighters, those sounds that well up from the gulf and dark immensity of night and that pierce the entrails of the listener.

For this will always be one of the immortal and living things about the land, this will be an eternal and unchanging fact about that city whose only permanence is change: there will always be the great rivers flowing around it in the darkness, the rivers that have bounded so many nameless lives, those rivers which have moated in so many changes, which have girdled the wilderness and so much hard, brilliant, and sensational living, so much pain, beauty, ugliness, so much lust, murder, corruption, love, and wild exultancy.

They'll build great engines yet, and grander towers, but always the rivers run, in the day, in the night, in the dark, draining immensely their imperial tides out of the wilderness, washing and flowing by the coasts of the fabulous city, by all the little ticking sounds of time, by all the million lives and deaths of the city. Always the rivers run, and always there will be great ships upon the tide, always great horns are baying at the harbor's mouth, and in the night a thousand men have died while the river, always the river, the dark eternal river, full of strange secret time, washing the city's stains away, thickened and darkened by its dumpings, is flowing by us, by us to the sea.

He awakes at morning in a foreign land, and he thinks of home. He cannot rest, his heart is wild with pain and loneliness, he sleeps, but then he knows he sleeps, he hears the dark and secret spell of time about him; in ancient towns, thick tumbling chimes of the cathedral bells are thronging through the dark, but through the passages of his diseased and unforgetful sleep the sounds and memory of America make way: now it is almost dawn, a horse has turned into a street and in America, there is the sound of wheels, the lonely clop-clop of the hooves upon deserted pavements, silence, then the banging clatter of a can.

He awakes at morning in a foreign land, he draws his breath in labor in the wool-soft air of Europe: the wool-gray air is all about him like a living substance; it is in his heart, his stomach, and his entrails; it is in the slow and vital movements of the people; it soaks down from the sodden skies into the earth, into the heavy buildings, into the limbs and hearts and brains of living men. It soaks into the spirit of the wanderer; his heart is dull with the gray weariness of despair, it aches with hunger for the wilderness, the howling of great winds, the bite and sparkle of the clear, cold air, the buzz, the tumult and the wild exultancy. The wet, woolen air is all about him, and there is no hope. It was there before William the Conquerer; it was there before Clovis and Charles "the Hammer"; it was there before Attila; it was there before Hengist and Horsa; it was there before Vercingetorix and Julius Agricola.

It was there now; it will always be there. They had it in Merry

England and they had it in Gay Paree; and they were seldom merry, and they were rarely gay. The wet, woolen air is over Munich; it is over Paris; it is over Rouen and Madame Bovary; it soaks into England; it gets into boiled mutton and the Brussels sprouts; it gets into Hammersmith on Sunday; it broods over Bloomsbury and the private hotels and the British Museum; it soaks into the land of Europe and keeps the grass green. It has always been there; it will always be there. His eyes are mad and dull; he cannot sleep without the hauntings of phantasmal memory behind the eyes; his brain is overstretched and weary, it gropes ceaselessly around the prison of the skull, it will not cease.

The years are walking in his brain, his father's voice is sounding in his ears, and in the pulses of his blood the tom-tom's beat. His living dust is stored with memory: two hundred million men are walking in his bones; he hears the howling of the wind around forgotten eaves; he cannot sleep. He walks in midnight corridors; he sees the wilderness, the moon-drenched forests; he comes to clearings in the moonlit stubble, he is lost, he has never been here, yet he is at home. His sleep is haunted with the dreams of time; wires throb above him in the whiteness, they make a humming in the noonday heat.

The rails are laid across eight hundred miles of golden wheat, the rails are wound through mountains, they curve through clay-yellow cuts, they enter tunnels, they are built up across the marshes, they hug the cliff and follow by the river's bank, they cross the plains with dust and thunder, and they leap through flatness and the dull scrub-pine to meet the sea.

Then he awakes at morning in a foreign land, and thinks of home.

For we have awaked at morning in a foreign land and heard the bitter curse of their indictment, and we know what we know, and it will always be the same.

"One time!" their voices cried, leaning upon a bar the bitter weight of all their discontent. "One time! I've been back one time— just once in seven years," they said, "and Jesus that was plenty! One time was enough! To hell with that damned country! What have they got now but a lot of cheap spaghetti joints and skyscrapers?" they said. "If you want a drink, you sneak down three back-alleyways, get the once-over from a couple of ex-prize fighters, and then plank down

a dollar for a shot of varnish that would rot the guts out of a goat!
. . . And the women!"—the voices rose here with infuriated scorn—
"What a nice lot of cold-blooded gold-digging bastards *they've*
turned out to be! . . . I spent thirty dollars taking one of 'em to a
show, and to a night-club afterward! When bedtime came do you
think I got anything out of it? . . . 'You may kiss my little hand,' she
says. . . . 'You may kiss my little—that's what you may do,'" the
voices snarled with righteous bitterness. "When I asked her if she was
goin' to come through she started to yell for the cops! . . . A woman
who tried to pull one like that over here would get sent to Siberia!
. . . A nice country, I don't think! . . . Now, get this! *Me,* I'm a
Frenchman, see!" the voice said with a convincing earnestness.
"These guys know how to *live,* see! This is my country where I belong, see! . . . Johnny luh même chose pour mwah et m'seer! . . . Fill
'em up again, kid."

"Carpen-*teer!*" the voices then rose jeeringly, in true accents of
French pugnacity. "Sure, I'm a Frenchman—but Carpen-*teer!* Where
do yuh get that stuff? Christ, Dempsey could 'a' took that frog the
best day he ever saw! . . . An accident!" the voices yelled. "Whattya
mean—an accident? Didn't I see the whole thing with my own eyes?
Wasn't I back there then? . . . Wasn't I talkin' t' Jack himself an hour
after the fight was over? . . . An accident! Jesus! The only accident
was that he let him last four rounds. 'I could have taken him in the
first if I wanted to,' Jack says to me. . . . Sure, I'm a Frenchman!" the
voice said with belligerent loyalty. "But Carpen*teer!* Jesus! Where
do you get that stuff?"

And, brother, I have heard the voices you will never hear, discuss-
ing the graces of a life more cultured than any you will ever know—
and I know and I know, and yet it is still the same.

Bitterly, bitterly Boston one time more! the flying leaf, the broken
cloud—"I think," said they, "that we will live here now. I think,"
they said, "that we are running down to Spain next week so Francis
can do a little writing. . . . And really," their gay yet cultivated tones
continued, "it's wonderful what you can do here if you only have a
little money. . . . *Yes,* my dear!" their refined accents continued in a
tone of gay conviction. "It's really quite incredible, you know. . . . I
happen to know of a real honest-to-goodness château near Blois that
can be had for something less than $7000! . . . It's all rather incredi-

ble, you know," those light, half-English tones went on, "when you consider what it takes to live in Brookline! . . . Francis has always felt that he would like to do a little writing, and I feel somehow the atmosphere is better here for all that sort of thing—it really is, you know. Don't you think so?" said those gay and cultivated tones of Boston which you, my brother, never yet have heard. "And after all," those cultivated tones went on in accents of a droll sincerity, "you see all the people here you really *care* to see, I *mean,* you know! They all come to Paris at one time or another—I *mean,* the trouble really is in getting a little time alone for yourself. . . . Or do you find it so?" the voices suavely, lightly, asked. . . . "Oh, look! look at that—there!" they cried with jubilant elation, "I mean that boy and his girl there, walking along with their arms around each other! . . . Don't you just a-do-o-re it? . . . Isn't it too *ma-a-rvelous?*" those refined and silvery tones went on, with patriotic tenderness. "I mean, there's something so perfectly sweet and un-self-conscious about it all!" the voices said with all the cultivated earnestness of Boston! "Now *where?*—where? —would you see anything like that at home?" the voices said triumphantly.

(Seldom in Brookline, lady. Oh, rarely, seldom, almost never in the town of Brookline, lady. But on the Esplanade—did you ever go out walking on the Esplanade at night-time, in the hot and sultry month of August, lady? They are not Frenchmen, lady: they are all Jews and Irish and Italians, lady, but the noise of their kissing is like the noise the wind makes through a leafy grove—it is like the great hooves of a hundred thousand cavalry being pulled out of the marshy places of the earth, dear lady.)

". . . I *mean*—these people really understand that sort of thing so much better than we do. . . . They're so much *simpler* about it. . . . I mean, so much more graceful with that kind of thing. . . . Il faut un peu de sentiment, n'est-ce pas? . . . Or do you think so?" said those light, those gay, those silvery, and half-English tones of cultivated Boston, which you, my brother, never yet have heard.

(I got you, lady. That was French. I know. . . . But if I felt your leg, if I began by fondling gracefully your leg, if in a somewhat graceful Gallic way I felt your leg, and said, "Chérie! Petite chérie!"— would you remember, lady, this is Paris?)

Oh, bitterly, bitterly, Boston one time more: their silvery voices speak an accent you will never know, and of their loins is marble made, but, brother, there are corn-haired girls named Neilsen out in Minnesota, and the blonde thighs of the Lundquist girl could break a bullock's back.

Oh, bitterly, bitterly, Boston one time more: the French have little ways about them that we do not have, but brother, they're still selling cradles down in Georgia, and in New Orleans their eyes are dark, their white teeth bite you to the bone.

Oh, bitterly, bitterly, Boston, one time more, and of their flesh is codfish made. Big Brother's still waiting for you with his huge, red fist, behind the barn up in the State of Maine, and they're still having shotgun marriages at home.

Oh, brother, there are voices you will never hear—ancestral voices prophesying war, my brother, and rare and radiant voices that you know not of, as they have read us into doom. The genteel voices of Oxenford broke once like chimes of weary, unenthusiastic bells across my brain, speaking to me compassionately its judgment on our corrupted lives, gently dealing with the universe, my brother, gently and without labor—gently, brother, gently, it dealt with all of us, with easy condescension and amused disdain:

"I'm afraid, old boy," the genteel voice of Oxenford remarked, "you're up against it over thöh. . . . I really am. . . . Thöh's no place thö faw the individual any longah,"—the genteel voice went on, unindividual brother. "Obviously," that tolerant voice instructed me, "obviously, thöh can be no cultuah in a country so completely lackin' in tradition as is yoähs. . . . It's all so objective—if you see what I main—thöh's no place left faw innah life," it said, oh, outward brother! ". . . We Europeans have often obsöhved (it's *very* curious, you know) that the *Ameri*can is incapable of any real feelin'—it seems quite impawsible faw him to distinguish between true emotion an' sentimentality—an' he invayably chooses the lattah! . . . *Curious, isn't it?*—or do you think so, brother? Of co'se, thöh is yoäh beastly dreadful sex-prawblem. . . . Yoäh women! . . . Oh, deah, deah! . . . Perhaps we'd bettah say no moah . . . but, thöh you *ah!*"—right in the eye, my brother. "Yoäh country is a matriahky, my deah fellah . . . it really is, you know." . . . if you can follow us, dear brother. "The women have the men in a state of complete subjection . . . the male is rapidly becomin' moah sexless an' emasculated"—that gen-teel voice of doom went on—"No!—Decidedly you have quite a prawblem befoah you. . . . Obviously thöh can be no cultuah while such a condition puhsists. . . . *That* is why when my friends say to me, 'You ought to see *America*, . . . you really ought, you know.' . . . I say, 'No, thanks. . . . If you don't mind, I'd rathah not. . . . I think I'll stay at home . . . I'm sorry,' " the compassionate tones of Oxenford went on, "but that's the way I feel—it really is, you know. . . . Of co'se, I know you couldn't undahstand my feelin'—faw aftah all, you ah a Yank—but thöh you ah! Sorry!" it said regretfully, as it spoke its courteous but inexorable judgments of eternal exile, brother, and removed forever the possibility of your ever hearing it. "But that's the way I feel! I hope you don't mind," the voice said gently, with compassion.

No, sir, I don't mind. We don't mind, he, she, it, or they don't mind. Nobody minds, sir, nobody minds. Because, just as you say, sir, oceans are between us, seas have sundered us, there is a magic in you that we cannot fathom—a light, a flame, a glory—an impalpable, in-definable, incomprehensible, undeniable, something-or-other, some-thing which I can never understand or measure because—just as you say, sir—with such compassionate regret, I am—I am—a Yank.

'Tis true, my brother, we are Yanks. Oh, 'tis true, 'tis true! I am a Yank! Yet, wherefore Yank, good brother? Hath not a Yank ears? Hath not a Yank lies, truths, bowels of mercy, fears, joys, and lusts? Is he not warmed by the same sun, washed by the same ocean, rotted by the same decay, and eaten by the same worms as a German is? If you kill him, does he not die? If you sweat him, does he not stink? If you lie with his wife or his mistress, does she not whore, lie, forni-cate and betray, even as a Frenchman's does? If you strip him, is he not naked as a Swede? Is his hide less white than Baudelaire's? Is his breath more foul than the King of Spain's? Is his belly bigger, his neck fatter, his face more hoggish, and his eye more shiny than a Munich brewer's? Will he not cheat, rape, thieve, whore, curse, hate, and murder like any European? Aye—Yank! But wherefore, where-fore Yank—good brother?

Brother, have we come then from a fated stock? Augured from birth, announced by two dark angels, named in our mother's womb? And for what? For what? Father-less, to grope our feelers on the sea's dark bed, among the polyped squirms, the blind sucks and crawls and sea-valves of the brain, loaded with memory that will not die? To cry our love out in the wilderness, to wake always in the night, smiting the pillow in some foreign land, thinking forever of the myriad sights and sounds of home?

"While Paris Sleeps!"—By God, while Paris sleeps, to wake and walk and not to sleep; to wake and walk and sleep and wake, and sleep again, seeing dawn come at the window-square that cast its wedge before our glazed, half-sleeping eyes, seeing soft, hated foreign light, and breathing soft, dull languid air that could not bite and tingle up the blood, seeing legend and lie and fable wither in our sight as we saw what we saw, knew what we knew.

Sons of the lost and lonely fathers, sons of the wanderers, children of hardy loins, the savage earth, the pioneers, what had we to do with all their bells and churches? Could we feed our hunger on portraits of the Spanish king? Brother, for what? For what? To kill the giant of loneliness and fear, to slay the hunger that would not rest, that would not give us rest.

Of wandering forever, and the earth again. Brother, for what? For what? For what? For the wilderness, the immense and lonely land. For the unendurable hunger, the unbearable ache, the incurable loneliness. For the exultancy whose only answer is the wild goat-cry. For a million memories, ten thousand sights and sounds and shapes and smells and names of things that only we can know.

For what? For what? Not for a nation. Not for a people, not for an empire, not for a thing we love or hate.

For what? For a cry, a space, an ecstacy. For a savage and nameless hunger. For a living and intolerable memory that may not for a second be forgotten, since it includes all the moments of our lives, includes all we do and are. For a living memory; for ten thousand memories; for a million sights and sounds and moments; for something like nothing else on earth; for something which possesses us.

For something under our feet, and around us and over us; something that is in us and part of us, and proceeds from us, that beats in all the pulses of our blood.

Brother, for what?

First for the thunder of imperial names, the names of men and battles, the names of places and great rivers, the mighty names of the States. The name of The Wilderness; and the names of Antietam, Chancellorsville, Shiloh, Bull Run, Fredericksburg, Cold Harbor, the Wheat Fields, Ball's Bluff, and the Devil's Den; the names of Cowpens, Brandywine, and Saratoga; of Death Valley, Chickamauga, and the Cumberland Gap. The names of the Nantahalahs, the Bad Lands, the Painted Desert, the Yosemite, and the Little Big Horn; the names of Yancey and Cabarrus counties; and the terrible name of Hatteras.

Then, for the continental thunder of the States: the names of Montana, Texas, Arizona, Colorado, Michigan, Maryland, Virginia, and the two Dakotas; the names of Oregon and Indiana, of Kansas and the rich Ohio; the powerful name of Pennsylvania, and the name of Old Kentucky; the undulance of Alabama; the names of Florida and North Carolina.

In the red-oak thickets, at the break of day, long hunters lay for bear—the rattle of arrows in laurel leaves, the war-cries round the painted buttes, and the majestical names of the Indian Nations: the Pawnees, the Algonquins, the Iroquois, the Comanches, the Black-feet, the Seminoles, the Cherokees, the Sioux, the Hurons, the Mohawks, the Navajos, the Utes, the Omahas, the Onondagas, the Chippewas, the Crees, the Chickasaws, the Arapahoes, the Catawbas, the Dakotas, the Apaches, the Croatans, and the Tuscaroras; the names of Powhatan and Sitting Bull; and the name of the Great Chief, Rain-In-The-Face.

Of wandering forever, and the earth again: in red-oak thickets, at the break of day, long hunters lay for bear. The arrows rattle in the laurel leaves, and the elmroots thread the bones of buried lovers. There have been war-cries on the Western trails, and on the plains the gunstock rusts upon a handful of bleached bones. The barren earth? Was no love living in the wilderness?

The rails go westward in the dark. Brother, have you seen starlight on the rails? Have you heard the thunder of the fast express?

Of wandering forever, and the earth again—the names of the mighty rails that bind the nation, the wheeled thunder of the names that net the continent: the Pennsylvania, the Union Pacific, the Santa Fé, the Baltimore and Ohio, the Chicago and Northwestern, the Southern, the Louisiana and Northern, the Seaboard Air Line, the Chicago, Milwaukee and Saint Paul, the Lackawanna, the New York, New Haven and Hartford, the Florida East Coast, the Rock Island, and the Denver and Rio Grande.

Brother, the names of the engines, the engineers, and the sleeping-cars: the great engines of the Pacific type, the articulated Mallets with three sets of eight-yoked driving-wheels, the 400-ton thunder-bolts with J. T. Cline, T. J. McRae, and the demon hawk-eyes of H. D. Campbell on the rails.

The names of the great tramps who range the nation on the fastest trains: the names of the great tramps Oklahoma Red, Fargo Pete, Dixie Joe, Iron Mike, The Frisco Kid, Nigger Dick, Red Chi, Ike the Kike, and The Jersey Dutchman.

By the waters of life, by time, by time, Lord Tennyson stood among the rocks, and stared. He had long hair, his eyes were deep and sombre, and he wore a cape; he was a poet, and there was magic and mystery in his touch, for he had heard the horns of Elfland faintly blowing. And by the waters of life, by time, by time, Lord Tennyson stood among the cold, gray rocks, and commanded the sea to break—break—break! And the sea broke, by the waters of life, by time, by time, as Lord Tennyson commanded it to do, and his heart was sad and lonely as he watched the stately ships (of the Hamburg-American Packet Company, fares forty-five dollars and up, first-class) go on to their haven under the hill, and Lord Tennyson would that his heart could utter the thoughts that arose in him.

By the waters of life, by time, by time: the names of the mighty rivers, the alluvial gluts, the drains of the continent, the throats that drink America (Sweet Thames, flow gently till I end my song). The names of the men who pass, and the myriad names of the earth that abides forever: the names of the men who are doomed to wander, and the name of that immense and lonely land on which they wan-der, to which they return, in which they will be buried—America! The immortal earth which waits forever, the trains that thunder on the continent, the men who wander, and the women who cry out, "Return!"

Finally, the names of the great rivers that are flowing in the dark-ness (Sweet Thames, flow gently till I end my song).

By the waters of life, by time, by time: the names of great mouths, the mighty maws, the vast, wet, coiling, never-glutted and unending snakes that drink the continent. Where, sons of men, and in what other land will you find others like them, and where can you match the mighty music of their names?—The Monongahela, the Colorado, the Rio Grande, the Columbia, the Tennessee, the Hudson (Sweet Thames!) ; the Kennebec, the Rappahannock, the Delaware, the Penobscot, the Wabash, the Chesapeake, the Swannanoa, the Indian River, the Niagara (Sweet Afton!) ; the Saint Lawrence, the Susquehanna, the Tombigbee, the Nantahala, the French Broad, the Chattahoochee, the Arizona, and the Potomac (Father Tiber!) —these are a few of their princely names, these are a few of their great, proud, glittering names, fit for the immense and lonely land that they inhabit.

Oh, Tiber! Father Tiber! You'd only be a suckling in that mighty land! And as for you, sweet Thames, flow gently till I end my song: flow gently, gentle Thames, be well-behaved, sweet Thames, speak softly and politely, little Thames, flow gently till I end my song.

By the waters of life, by time, by time, and of the yellow cat that smites the nation, of the belly of the snake that coils across the land —of the terrible names of the rivers in flood, the rivers that foam and welter in the dark, that smash the levees, that flood the lowlands for two thousand miles, that carry the bones of the cities seaward on their tides: of the awful names of the Tennessee, the Arkansas, the Missouri, the Mississipi, and even the little mountain rivers, brothers, in the season of the floods.

Delicately they dive for Greeks before the railway station: the canoe glides gently through the portals of the waiting-room (for whites) . Full fathom five the carcass of old man Lype is lying (of his bones is coral made) and delicately they dive for lunch-room Greeks before the railway station.

Brother, what fish are these? The floatage of sunken rooms, the sodden bridal-veils of poverty, the slime of ruined parlor plush, drowned faces in the family album; and the blur of long-drowned eyes, blurred features, whited, bloated flesh.

Delicately they dive for Greeks before the railway station. The stern, good, half-drowned faces of the brothers Trade and Mark survey the tides. Cardui! Miss Lillian Leitzell twists upon one arm above the flood; the clown, half-sunken to his waist, swims upward

out of swirling yellow; the tiger bares his teeth above the surges of a
river he will never drink. The ragged tatters of the circus posters are
plastered on soaked boards. And delicately they dive for Greeks before the railway station.

Have we not seen them, brother?

For what are we, my brother? We are a phantom flare of grieved
desire, the ghostling and phosporic flicker of immortal time, a brevity of days haunted by the eternity of the earth. We are an unspeakable utterance, an insatiable hunger, an unquenchable thirst; a lust
that bursts our sinews, explodes our brains, sickens and rots our guts,
and rips our hearts asunder. We are a twist of passion, a moment's
flame of love and ecstasy, a sinew of bright blood and agony, a lost
cry, a music of pain and joy, a haunting of brief, sharp hours, an
almost captured beauty, a demon's whisper of unbodied memory.
We are the dupes of time.

For, brother, what are we?

We are the sons of our father, whose face we have never seen, we
are the sons of our father, whose voice we have never heard, we
are the sons of our father, to whom we have cried for strength and
comfort in our agony, we are the sons of our father, whose life like
ours was lived in solitude and in the wilderness, we are the sons of
our father, to whom only can we speak out the strange, dark burden
of our heart and spirit, we are the sons of our father, and we shall
follow the print of his foot forever.

Time, please, time. . . . What time is it? . . . Gentlemen, it's closing time. . . . Time, gentlemen . . . that time of year thou may'st in
me behold. . . . In the good old summer-time. . . . I keep thinking
of you all the time . . . all the time . . . and all the time. . . . A long
time ago the world began. . . . There goes the last bell, run, boy, run:
you'll just have time. . . . There are times that make you ha-a-ap-py,
there are times that make you sa-a-ad. . . . Do you remember the
night you came back to the University: it was that time right after
your brother's death, you had just come back that night, I know I
was coming across the campus before Old East when I saw you coming up the path with a suitcase in your hand. It was raining but we
both stopped and began to talk there—we stepped in under one of

the oak-trees because it was raining. I can still remember the old, wet, shining bark of the tree—the reason I can remember is that you put your hand out and leaned against the tree as you talked to me and I kept thinking how tall you were—of course you didn't notice it, you weren't conscious of it but you had your head up and it must have been about eight feet above the ground. But I can remember everything we said that night—it was that time when you came back just after your brother's death: that's when it was all right, I guess that's why I can remember it so well. . . . It's time all little boys were in bed. . . . Now, boy, I'll tell you when it was: it was that time your Papa made that trip to California—the reason that I know is I had just got a letter from him that morning written from Los Angeles telling me how he had seen John Balch and old Professor Truman, and how they had both gone into the real-estate business out there, and both of them getting rich by leaps and bounds—but that's just exactly when it was, sir, the time he made that trip out there in 1906, along towards the end of February, and I had just finished reading his letter when—well as I say now . . . Garfield, Arthur, Harrison and Hayes . . . time of my father's time, life of his life. "Ah, Lord," he said, "I knew them all—and all of them are gone. I'm the only one that's left. By God, I'm getting old." . . . In the year that the locusts came, something that happened in the year the locusts came, two voices that I heard there in that year. . . . Child! Child! It seems so long ago since the year the locusts came, and all of the trees were eaten bare: so much has happened, and it seems so long ago. . . .

"To keep time with!"—To Eugene Gant, Presented to Him on the Occasion of His Twelfth Birthday, by His Brother, B. H. Gant, Oct. 3, 1912. . . . "To keep time with!" . . . Up on the mountain, down in the valley, deep, deep in the hill, Ben, cold, cold, cold.

"Ces arbres——"

"Monsieur?" a thin, waxed face of tired Gaul, professionally attentive, the eyebrows arched perplexedly above old tired eyes, the waiter's fatigued napkin on the arm.

"—Monsieur——?"

"Ces arbres—" he stammered, pointing helplessly— "J'ai—j'ai—mais je les ai vu—avant——"

"Monsieur?"—the eyebrows still more patient, puzzled and concerned, the voice wrought with attention—"vous dites, monsieur?"

"J'ai dit que—ces arbres—je les ai vu—" he blundered helplessly, and suddenly muttered with a face gone sullen and ashamed—"Ça ne fait rien—l'addition, s'il vous plaît."

The waiter stared at him a moment with courteous, slightly pained astonishment, then smiled apologetically, shrugged his shoulders slightly in a movement of defeat, and saying, "Bien, monsieur," took the ten-franc note upon the table, counted the racked saucers, and made change for him.

When the waiter had gone, he sat for a moment staring at the trees. It was in the month of April, it was night, he was alone on the café terrace, and yet the chill air was touched with a fragrance that was soft, thrilling and mysterious—a citrous fume, the smell of unknown flowers, or perhaps not even this—but only the ghost of a perfume, the thrilling, barren, and strangely seductive odor of Provence.

It was a street in the little town of Arles, at night—an old, worn, rutted, curiously dirty-looking street, haunted by the trunks of immense and dusty-looking trees. He had never been here before, the scene was strange and haunting as a dream, and yet it was instantly and intolerably familiar. It was, somehow, he thought, like a street he had been to in some small town in the hot South at the faded end of summer—a South Carolina town, he thought it must be, and he was sure that he would hear the sound of familiar, unknown voices, the passing of feet, the rustling of quiet, tired leaves. And then he saw again how strange it was, and could see the tired waiter racking chairs and tables for the night, and in the café tired lights and emptiness, and the white, tired light upon the old dusty street, the huge haunting boles of the great trees; and he knew that he had never been along that way before.

Then he got up and walked away, and put his hand upon the trunk of one of the old trees: it was white and felt smooth to the touch, and was somewhat like the sycamores at home—and yet it was not this that haunted him with troubling memory. He felt, intolerably, that the place, the scene, the great wreathed branches of the trees, were something he had seen before—that he had seen it here from the same spot where now he sat—but *when, when, when?*

And suddenly, with a thrill of recognition that flashed across his brain like an electric spark, he saw that he was looking at the same trees that Van Gogh had painted in his picture of the roadmenders at their work in Arles, that the scene was the same, that he was sitting where the painter had sat before. And he noted that the trees had tall, straight, symmetrical trunks, and remembered that the trees that Vincent had painted had great, tendoned trunks that writhed and twisted like creatures in a dream—and yet were somehow more true than truth, more real than this reality. And the great vinelike trunks of these demented trees had wound and rooted in his heart, so that now he could not forget them, nor see this scene in any other way than that in which Van Gogh had painted it.

When he got up, the waiter was still racking chairs upon the tables, and the white and quiet light from the café fell like a tired stillness on the dusty street, and he walked away, haunted by unfathomed memories of home, and with something in his heart he could not utter.

In all the dreams and visions that now swarmed across his sleep, dreams and visions which can only be described as haunted fatally by the sense of time—his mind seemed to exercise the same complete control it ever had shown in all the operations of its conscious memory. He slept, and knew he slept, and saw the whole vast structure of the sleeping world about him as he slept; he dreamed, and knew he dreamed, and like a sorcerer, drew upward at his will, out of dark deeps and blue immensities of sleep, the strange, dark fish of his imagining.

Sometimes they came with elfish flakings of a hoary light, sometimes they came like magic and the promise of immortal joy, they came with victory and singing and a shout of triumph in his blood, and again he felt the strange and deathless joy of voyages: he was a passenger upon great ships again, he walked the broad, scrubbed decks exultantly, and smelled the hot, tarred roofs of powerful and ugly piers, he smelled the spermy sea-wrack of the harbor once again, the wastes of oil, the sharp, acrid and exultant smoke from busy little tugs, the odor of old, worn plankings, drenched with sunlight, and the thousand strange compacted spices of the laden piers. Again he felt the gold and sapphire loveliness of a Saturday in May, and drank the glory of the earth into his heart, and heard in lucent and lyrical air the heavy shattering "baugh" of the great ship's whistle, as it spoke gloriously, of springtime, new lands and departure. Again he saw ten thousand faces, touched with their strange admixture of sorrow and joy, swarm past the openings of the pier, and again he saw the flashing tides that girdled the city, whitened around the prows of a hundred boats, and gleaming with a million iridescent points of light. Again the great walled cliff, the crowded isle, the fabulous spires and ramparts of the city, as delicate as the hues of light that flashed around them, slid away from him, and one by one, the great ships, with the proud sweep of their breasts of white, their opulent storied superstructure, their music of power and speed, fell into line at noon on Saturday. And now, like bridled horses held in rein, with princely chafe and curvetings, they breach the mighty harbor, nose the narrows, circle slowly to brief pauses at the pilot's boat, and then, like racers set loose from the barriers, they are sent away, their engines tremble to a mighty stroke, the ships are given to the sea, to solitude, and to their proper glory once more.

And again he walked the decks, he walked the decks alone, and saw the glittering sea-flung city melt within his sight, and watched the sandy edges of the land fade away, and felt the incredible gold and sapphire glory of the day, the sparkle of dancing waters, and smelled salt, sea-borne air again, and saw upon the decks the joyful and exultant faces of the passengers, their looks of wonder, hope, and speculation, as they looked into the faces of strange men and women, now by the miracle of the voyage and chance isled with them in the loneliness of water, upon the glorious prison of a ship. And again he saw the faces of the lovely women, and saw the lights of love and passion in their eyes, and again he felt the plangent and depthless undulance, the unforgettable feeling of the fathomless might of the sea beneath a ship; a wild cry was torn from his throat, and a thousand unutterable feelings of the voyage, of white coasts and sparkling harbors and the creaking, eerie cries of gulls, of the dear, green dwelling of the earth again, and of strange, golden cities, potent wines, delicious foods, of women, love, and amber thighs spread amorously in ripe golden hay, of discovery and new lands, welled up in him like deathless song and certitude.

But just as these visions of delight and joy thronged upward through the deep marine of sleep, so, by the same fiat, the same calm order of an imperial will, the visions of a depthless shame, a faceless abomination of horror, an indefinable and impalpable corruption, returned to haunt his brain with their sentences of inexpiable guilt and ruin: under their evil spell he lay tranced upon his bed in a hypnosis of acquiescent horror, in a willing suspension of all his forces of resistance, like some creature held captive before the hypnotic rhythm of a reptile's head, the dull, envenomed fascination of its eye.

He moved on ceaselessly across a naked and accursed landscape and beneath a naked and accursed sky, an exile in the centre of a planetary vacancy that, like his guilt and shame, had neither place among things living nor among things dead, in which there was neither vengeance of lightning, nor mercy of burial, in which there was neither shade nor shelter, curve nor bend, nor hill, nor tree, nor hollow, in which—earth, air, sky, and limitless horizon—there was only one vast naked eye, inscrutable and accusing, from which there was no escape, and which bathed his naked soul in its fathomless depths of shame.

And then the vision faded, and suddenly, with the bridgeless immediacy of a dream, he found himself within the narrow canyon of a street, pacing interminably along on endless pavements where there was neither face nor footfall save his own, nor eye, nor window, nor any door that he might enter.

He thought he was walking through the harsh and endless continuity of one of those brownstone streets of which most of the city was constructed fifty years ago, and of which great broken lengths and fragments still remain. These streets, even if visited by some one in his waking hours, by some stranger in the fulness of health and sanity, and under the living and practical light of noon or, more particularly, by some man stunned with drink, who came there at some desolate and empty hour of night, might have a kind of cataleptic horror, a visionary unreality, as if some great maniac of architecture had conceived and shaped the first, harsh, ugly pattern of brown angularity, and then repeated it, without a change, into an infinity of illimitable repetition, with the mad and measureless insistence of an idiot monotony.

And forever he walked the street, under the brown and fatal light that fell upon him. He walked the street, and looked for a house there that was his own, for a door he knew that he must enter, for some one who was waiting for him in the house, and for the merciful dark wall and door that would hide and shelter him from the immense and naked eye of shame that peered upon him constantly. Forever he walked the street and searched the bleak, untelling façades for the house he knew and had forgotten, forever he prowled along before the endless and unchanging façades of the street, and he never found it, and at length he became aware of a vast sibilant whispering, of an immense conspiracy of subdued and obscene laughter, and of the mockery of a thousand evil eyes, that peered in silence from these bleak façades, and that he could never find or see; and forever he walked the streets alone, and heard the immense and secret whisperings and laughter, and was bathed in the bottomless depths of a wordless shame, and could never find the house he had lost, the door he had forgotten.

Among the dreams that returned to haunt his waking, watchful sleep during the strange, living vision of that green spring, as he lay hearted at the pulse of time, there was one which remained ever after in his memory.

He was striding along a wide and sandy beach and by the side of a calm and tranquilly flowing sea. The waves broke quietly and evenly in a long, low roll upon the beach, rushing up the sand in small hissing eddies of foam and water. Below his feet the firm, brown sand sprang back with an elastic vitality, a warm and vital wind was blowing, and he drew into his lungs exultantly the smell of the sea, and of the warm, wet, fragrant beach, ribbed evenly with braided edges of brown seaweed.

He did not recognize the scene as one which he had ever visited before, and yet he felt an instant and complete familiarity with it, as if he had known it forever. Behind him, drumming evenly upon the hard, elastic sand, and fading away into the distance with a hard, wooden thunder of wheels, he heard the furious rhythm of pounding hooves of driven horses. He knew that he had just descended from a ship, and that he was living in one of the antique and early ages of the earth; and all of this he knew with joy and wonder, and without surprise, with the thrill of recovering something he had always known and had lost forever.

It was a scene out of the classic period of the earth, and yet it was wholly different from every image he had ever had about this earth, in his imagination. For where, in every vision of his mind and reading, that earth had come to him in a few sharp and radiant colors, in a structure of life as glowing and proportionate as one of its faultless temples, as remote from the world he lived in as all its fables, myths, and legends, this earth he now walked on was permeated with the living tones and weathers of life.

The world of Homer was the world of first light, sunlight, and of morning: the sea was wine-dark, a gold and sapphire purity of light fell on the walls of Troy, a lucent depthless purity of light welled from the eyes of Helen, as false, fatal, and innocently corrupt a woman as ever wrought destruction on the earth. The light that fell on Nausicaa and her maidens was all gold and crystal like the stream they bathed in, as lucent in purity as their limbs, as radiant as joy and morning on the earth; and even the lights of vengeance and the rout of the dread furies that fell upon the doomed and driven figure of Orestes were as fatal as blood, as relentless as an antique tragedy, as toneless as a destiny.

And in his pictures of a later time, of Athens in the period of recorded history, of Pericles and Plato and the time of the wars with Sparta, the scenes of history were bathed in these radiant and perfect lights and weathers. He knew these men were made of living, breathing flesh and subject to the errors and imperfections of mortal men, and yet when he tried to think of a slum in Athens, of people with bad teeth, blemished skins, muddy complexions—of disease, filth, and squalor among them, and of the million weary, beaten, dusty, sweating moments of their lives, he could not. Even human grief, pain, and trouble took on a color of classical perfection, of tragic grandeur, and the tortured and distressful skein of human life, with all that is ugly, trivial, and disgusting in it, took on the logical pattern of design and ordered destiny.

The light that fell upon them was of gold and sapphire, and of singing, or as ominous and fatal as a certain and inexorable doom; but now he walked this beach in one of the classical periods of the earth, and nothing was as he had tried to picture it, and yet all was as familiar as if he had known it forever.

There was no gold nor sapphire in the air: it was warm and sultry, omened with some troubling, variable and exultant menace, fraught with the sulphurous promise of a storm, pregnant with mystery and discovery, touched with a hundred disturbing elements and weathers of man's soul, and scented with a thousand warm and spermy odors of the land and sea, that touched man's entrails with delight and prophecy.

And the sea also was neither lyrical with gold and blue, or wine-dark in its single harmony: the sea was dark and sultry as the sky that bent above it; murked greenly, thickly, milkily, as it rolled quietly and broke upon the beach; as omened with impalpable prophecy as the earth and air.

He did not know the reason for his being there, and yet he knew beyond a doubt that he had come there for a purpose, that some one was waiting for him there, that the greatest joy and triumph he had ever known was impending in this glorious meeting.

That year, in June, he was sitting one day at a table before a little café that looked out across a quiet, cobbled square in the ancient city of Dijon. He was on his way to Paris from Italy and Switzerland and he had stopped here on impulse, remembering that the town was the capital of the old kingdom of Burgundy—a name which, in some way, since childhood, had flourished in his mind with a green magic, evoking images of a fair, green country, noble wine and food, a golden, drowsy legendry of old wars and heroes, women, gallantry, and knightly acts.

And he had not been disappointed. The old town with its ancient palaces—the worn and age-grimed façades of a forgotten power, a storied architecture—and the fair, green earth, the deep, familiar green of the intimate and yet enchanted hills, awoke in him all the old drowsy gold of legendry, the promise of a fair and enfabled domain, fat with plenty.

He had been here three days now, flooded with living green and gold, a willing captive in the spell of time, drinking the noblest wine, eating some of the noblest cookery he had ever known. After the dull Swiss food, the food and wine of Burgundy were good beyond belief; and everything—old town, the fair, green country and the hills—made a music in him again which was like all the green-gold magic of his childhood dream of France.

Now, he sat there at a table before a little café, already meditating with slow, lustful revery his noon-day meal at an ancient, famous inn where for eighteen francs one was served a stupendous meal—a succession of succulent native dishes such as he had dreamed about but had never thought that he would find outside of dreams or legends, in a town so small as this.

As he thought of this gourmet's heaven with a feeling of wonder and disbelief, the memory of a hundred little towns and cities in America returned to him, with the hideous and dyspeptic memory of their foods—the greasy, rancid, sodden, stale, dead, and weary foods of the Greek restaurants, of the lunchrooms, coffee shops and railroad cafeterias—hastily bolted and washed down to the inevitable miseries of dyspepsia with gulping swallows of sour, weak coffee.

Yes, even the noble food and wine had made a magic in this ancient place, and suddenly he was pierced again by the old hunger that haunts and hurts Americans—the hunger for a better life—an end of rawness, newness, sourness, distressful and exacerbated misery, the taking from the great plantation of the earth and of America our rich inheritance of splendor, ease, and abundance—good food, and sensual love, and noble cookery—the warmth of radiant color and of wine—pulse of the blood—an end of misery, bitterness, hunger and unrest upon the breast of everlasting plenty—the inheritance of exultancy and joy forever, which some foul, corrosive poison in our lives—bitter enigma that it is!—has taken from us.

Now, as he thought these things, sitting before the café and looking across the quiet square of whitened cobbles, a bell struck, and noon came. Slowly a great clock began to strike in the old town. In a cool, dark church, which he had seen the day before, a bell-rope, knotted at the ends, hung down before the altar-steps from an immense distance in the ceiling. The moment the town bell had finished its deep reverberation, a sexton walked noisily across the old flagged church-floor and took the bell-cord in his hands. Slowly, with a gentle rhythm, he began to swing upon the rope, and one could hear at first an old and heavy creaking from the upper air, but as yet no bell.

Then the sexton's body stiffened in its rhythm, he hung hard upon the knotted rope in punctual sway, and there began, far up in the church, the upper air of that old place, a sweet and ponderous beating of the bells. At first they beat in threes—ding-dong-dong; ding-dong-dong; then swiftly the man changed his rhythm, and the bells began to beat a faster double measure.

And now the youth remembered old, distant chimes upon a street at night; and the memory of his own bells came back into his heart. He remembered the great bell at college that rang the boys to classes, and how the knotted bell-rope came down into the room of the student who rang it; and how often he had rung the bell himself, and how at first there was the creaking noise in the upper air of the bell tower, there as here; and how, as the great bell far above him swung into its rhythm, he would be carried off the floor by that weight of thronging bronze; and he remembered still the lift and power of the old college bell, as he swung at the knotted rope, and the feeling of joy and power that surged up in him as he was lifted on the mighty upward stroke, and heard above him in the tower, the dark music of the grand old bell and the students running on the campus paths below the window, and then the loose rope, the bell tolling brokenly away to silence, the creaking sound again, and finally nothing but silence, the day's green spell and golden magic of the drowsy campus in the month of May.

And now the memory of that old bell, with all its host of long-forgotten things, swarmed back with living and intolerable pungency, as he sat there at noon in the old French town, and heard the sexton swinging on the bell of the old church.

He thought of home.

And now, with the sound of that old bell, everything around him burst into instant life. Although the structure of that life was foreign to him, and different from anything he had known as a child, everything instantly became incredibly living, near, and familiar, like something he had always known.

The little café before which he was sitting, was old and small, and had a warm, worn look of use and comfort. Inside, in the cool, dark depth of the place, were two old men sitting at a table playing cards —with a faded, green cloth upon the table; and two waiters. One of the old men had long, pointed mustaches, and a thin, distinguished face; the other was more ruddy and full-fleshed and had a beard. They played quietly, bending over the old, green cloth with studious deliberation, making each play slowly. Sometimes they spoke quietly to each other, only a few words at a time; sometimes the ruddy old man's thick shoulders would heave and tremble, and his face would flush rosily, with satisfaction; but the other one laughed thinly, quietly, in a more gentle, weary way.

The two waiters were polishing up the silverware, and getting the tables set and put in order for the mid-day meal. One of the waiters was an old man with the sprouting, energetic mustaches one sees so often in France, and with the weary, hawk-like, cynical, yet not ill-natured face that one often sees on old waiters. The other—really just a bus-boy—was a young, clumsy, thick-fingered and thick-featured country lad, with the wine-dark, vital, sanguinary coloring some Frenchmen have.

The young fellow was full of exuberant good spirits; he was polishing up the knives and forks and spoons with enthusiastic gusto, humming the snatches of a song as he did so, and slamming each piece of silver down into a drawer with such vigor, when he had finished, that it was obvious that he got great pleasure from the musical jingle thus created.

Meanwhile the old waiter moved quietly, softly, and yet wearily about, setting the tables. At length, however, at the end of a particularly violent and enthusiastic jingle of silverware from his polishing companion, he looked up, with a slight cynical arching of his eyebrows, and then, without ill-nature but with perfect urbanity, he said ironically:

"Ah! On fait la musique!"

This was all, but one saw the young fellow's face flush and redden with exuberant laughter; his thick shoulders rose and for a moment trembled convulsively, then he went on polishing, singing to himself, and hurling the noisy silverware into the drawer with more enthusiasm than ever.

And that brief, pleasant, and somehow poignantly unforgettable scene now seemed, like everything else, to be intolerably near and familiar to the youth, and something he had always known.

Before him, the quiet, faded, strangely pleasant square was waking briefly to its moment of noon-day life. Far off he could hear the little shrill fifing whistle of a French locomotive, and the sound of slow trains; an ice-wagon, with a tin interior and large, delicately carved cakes of ice, clattered across the cobbles of the square; and he remembered how he had seen, the day before, some barge people eating on a barge beneath the trees. From where he sat he could see workmen, wearing shapeless caps and baggy corduroy trousers streaked with lime and cement, and talking in hoarse, loud, disputatious voices as they leaned above their drinks on the zinc bar of a little bistro on the corner.

Some young, dull-looking women, wearing light-colored stockings, and light, gray-tannish overcoats, came by, with domesticity written in every movement that they made, looking, somehow, their wedded propriety, and the stern dullness of provincial places everywhere.

And then the lost, the irrevocable, the lonely sounds which he had not heard for fifteen years awoke there in the square, and suddenly he was a child, and it was noon, and he was waiting in his father's house to hear the slam of the iron gate, the great body stride up the high porch steps, knowing his father had come home again.

At first, before him, in that little whitened square, it was just the thring of the bicycle bells, the bounding of the light-wired wheels. And at first he could see some French army officers riding home upon their bicycles. They were proper and assured-looking men, with solid, wine-dark faces, and they rode solidly and well, driving the light-wired wheels beneath them with firm propulsions of their solid legs.

Then, with a thring of bells, an army sergeant came by, riding fast and smoothly on his way home to dinner. And then, with sudden rush, the thring of bells, the thrum of wheels increased: the clerks, the bank clerks, the bookkeepers—the little proper and respectable people of all sorts—were riding home across the quiet little square at noon.

On the other side of the square he could see two workmen who were still at work upon a piece of stone; one was holding an iron spike, and one a sledge, and they worked slowly, with frequent pauses.

A young buck, with a noisy, sporty little car, sped over the square, and vanished; and the youth wondered if he was one of the daring blades of Dijon, and what young women of the town's best families he had taken out in the car, and if he boasted to other young town blades in cafés of his prowess at seduction, as did the bucks before Wood's Pharmacy at home.

Then, for a moment there was a brooding silence in the square again, and presently there began the most lonely, lost and unforgettable of all sounds on earth—the solid, liquid leather-shuffle of footsteps going home one way, as men had done when they came home to lunch at noon some twenty years ago, in the green-gold and summer magic of full June, before he had seen his father's land, and when the kingdoms of this earth and the enchanted city still blazed there in the legendary magic of his boyhood vision.

They came with solid, lonely, liquid shuffle of their decent leather, going home, the merchants, workers, and good citizens of that old town of Dijon. They streamed across the cobbles of that little square; they passed, and vanished, and were gone forever—leaving silence, the brooding hush and apathy of noon, a suddenly living and intolerably memory, instant and familiar as all this life around him, of a life that he had lost, and that could never die.

It was the life of twenty years ago in the quiet, leafy streets and little towns of lost America—of an America that had been lost beneath the savage roar of its machinery, the brutal stupefaction of its days, the huge disease of its furious, ever-quickening and incurable unrest, its flood-tide horror of gray, driven faces, stolid eyes, starved, brutal nerves, and dull, dead flesh.

The memory of the lost America—the America of twenty years ago, of quiet streets, the time-enchanted spell and magic of full June, the solid, lonely, liquid shuffle of men in shirt-sleeves coming home, the leafy fragrance of the cooling turnip-greens, and screens that slammed, and sudden silence—had long since died, had been drowned beneath the brutal flood-tide, the fierce stupefaction of that roaring surge and mechanic life which had succeeded it.

And now, all that lost magic had come to life again here in the little whitened square, here in this old French town, and he was closer to his childhood and his father's life of power and magnificence than he could ever be again in savage new America; and as the knowledge of these strange, these lost yet familiar things returned to him, his heart was filled with all the mystery of time, dark time, the mystery of strange, million-visaged time that haunts us with the briefness of our days.

He thought of home.

FROM

FROM DEATH TO MORNING

IN 1935 WOLFE assembled most of the stories, sketches, and short novels which he had been publishing in the period between the appearance of *Look Homeward, Angel* and *Of Time and the River* and issued them in the volume *From Death to Morning* (New York: Charles Scribner's Sons, 1935). The book contained two short novels—"Death the Proud Brother" and "The Web of Earth"— and twelve short stories and sketches. He believed that it represented some of his very best writing and was disappointed that it received little attention and sold poorly.

The five short stories here reprinted from the collection not only indicate that his judgment was correct but also show both his range of interests and his command of the short story medium.

"The Face of War," which was originally published in the *Modern Monthly,* June, 1935, was probably material written for *Look Homeward, Angel* and excised from that manuscript. Its juxtaposition of incidents bound by a common theme represents one of Wolfe's favorite structural devices.

"Only the Dead Know Brooklyn," originally published in the *New Yorker,* June 15, 1935, is the best known of Wolfe's several sketches of city life and city people.

"Dark in the Forest, Strange as Time," originally published in *Scribner's Magazine,* November, 1934, is one of Wolfe's two most successful uses of his experiences in Germany. The other is the short novel *"I Have a Thing To Tell You,"* and it, too, is laid on a train.

"The Far and the Near," was originally published under the title "Cottage by the Tracks" in *Cosmopolitan Magazine,* July, 1935. It is interesting not only as an example of Wolfe's efforts at the "short-short story," but also as an elaboration of one of those moments in which images are imprisoned in the imagination through being glimpsed from a train. Such moments occur again and again throughout Wolfe's work.

"In the Park," originally published in *Harper's Bazaar,* June, 1935, was first written in 1930 as a portion of the early life of Esther Jacks for the novel "The October Fair," a work which was abandoned but large portions of which were used in *The Web and the Rock*. Wolfe's sharp evocation, through memory, of time and place— and, above all, of feeling—was never more successful than in this story.

The text of "The Face of War" is from *From Death to Morning,* pages 71-90; that of "Only the Dead Know Brooklyn," pages 91-97; that of "Dark in the Forest, Strange as Time," pages 98-113; that of "The Far and the Near," pages 164-168; and that of "In the Park," pages 169-184.

THE FACE OF THE WAR

. . . HEAT-BRUTAL August the year the war ended: here are four moments from the face of the war. One—at Langley Field: a Negro retreating warily out of one of the rude shed-like offices of the contracting company on the flying field, the white teeth bared in a horrible grimace of fear and hatred, the powerful figure, half-crouched, ape-like, ready to leap or run, the arms, the great black paws, held outward defensively as he retreats under the merciless glazed brutality of the August sun, over the barren, grassless horror of hard dry clay, the white eyeballs fixed with an expression of mute unfathomable hatred, fear and loathing upon the slouchy, shambling figure of a Southern white—a gang boss or an overseer—who advances upon him brandishing a club in his meaty hand, screaming the high thick throat-scream of blood-lust and murder: "I'll stomp the guts out of you, you God-damned black bastard! I'll beat his God-damn brains out!"—and smashing brutally with his club, coming down across the Negro's skull with the sickening resilient thud, heard clear across the field, of wood on living bone. Behind the paunch-gut white, an office clerk, the little meager yes-man of the earth, a rat in shirt-sleeves, quick as a rat to scamper to its hiding, quick as a rat to come in to the kill when all is safe, with rat's teeth bared—advancing in the shambling wake of his protector, fear's servile seconder, murder's cringing aide, coming in behind with rat's teeth bared, the face white as a sheet, convulsed with fear and with the coward's lust to kill without mercy or reprisal, the merciless sun blazing hot upon the arm-band buckles on the crisp shirt sleeve, and with a dull metallic glint upon the barrel of the squat blue automatic that he clutches with a trembling hand, offering it to his blood-mad master, whispering frantically—"Here! . . . Here, Mister Bartlett! . . . Shoot the bastard if he tries to hit you!"

Meanwhile, the Negro retreating slowly all the time, his terrible white stare of fear and hatred no longer fixed upon his enemy, but on the evil glint of that cylinder of blue steel behind him, his arms thrust blindly, futilely before him as his hated foe comes on, his black face, rilled and channelled first with lacings of bright red, then beaten to a bloody pulp as the club keeps smashing down with its sickening and resilient crack:

"You . . . God-damn . . . black . . . son-of-a-bitch!" the voice, thick, high, phlegmy, choked with murder. "I'll teach ye—" Smash! the cartilage of the thick black nose crunches and is ground to powder by the blow "—if a God-damned Nigger can talk back to a white man!"— Smash. A flailing, horribly clumsy blow across the mouth which instantly melts into a bloody smear through which the Negro, eyes unmoving from the blue glint of the steel, mechanically spits the shattered fragments of his solid teeth—"I'll bash in his God-damned head—the damned black bastard—I'll show him if he can—" Smash! Across the wooly center of the skull and now, the scalp ripped open to the base of the low forehead, the powerful black figure staggering drunkenly, bending at the knees, the black head sagging, going down beneath the blows, the arms still blindly thrust before him, upon one knee now on the barren clay-baked earth, the head sunk down completely on the breast, blood over all, the kneeling figure blindly rocking, swaying with the blows, the arms still out until he crashes forward on the earth, his arms outspread, face to one side and then, the final nausea of horror—the murderous kick of the shoe into the blood-pulp of the unconscious face, and then silence, nothing to see or hear now but the heavy, choked and labored breathing of the paunch-gut man, the white rat-face behind him with the bared rat's fangs of terror, and the dull blue wink of the envenomed steel.

Again, the coward's heart of fear and hate, the coward's lust for one-way killing, murder without danger to himself, the rat's salvation from the shipwreck of his self-esteem—armed with a gun now, clothed in khaki, riding the horse of his authority, as here. Three boys, all employed by the contracting company, are walking after supper on the borders of the flying field in the waning light of evening, coming dark. They are walking down near the water's edge, across the flat marshy land, they are talking about their homes, the towns and cities they have known and come from, their colleges and schools, their plans for an excursion to the beach at the week-end, when they draw their pay. Without knowing it, they have approached a hangar where one of the new war-planes with which the government is experimenting has been housed. Suddenly, the soldier who is there on guard has seen them, advances on them now, one hand upon the revolver in his holster, his little furtive eyes narrowed into slits. Face of the city rat, dry, gray, furtive, pustulate, the tallowy lips, the rasping voice, the scrabble of a few harsh oaths, the stoney gravel of a sterile, lifeless, speech:

"What are ya doin' here ya f—little bastards!—Who told ya t'come f—round duh hangah?"

One of the boys, a chubby red-cheeked youngster from the lower South, fair-haired, blue-eyed, friendly and slow of speech, attempts to answer:

"Why, mister, we just thought—"

Quick as a flash, the rat has slapped the boy across the mouth, the filthy finger-tips have left their mottled print upon the boy's red cheek, have left their loathsome, foul and ineradicable print upon the visage of his soul forever:

"I don't give a f— what ya t'ought, ya little p—! Anuddeh woid out a ya f—trap an' I'll shoot the s— outa ya!" He has the gun out of its holster now, ready in his hand; the eyes of the three boys are riveted on the dull wink of its blue barrel with a single focal intensity of numb horror, fascinated disbelief.

"Now get t' f— hell outa here!" the hero cries, giving the boy he has just slapped a violent shove with his free hand. "Get t' f— hell away from heah, all t'ree of youse! Don't f— aroun' wit me, ya little p—," the great man snarls now, eyes a-glitter, narrow as a snake's, as he comes forward with deadly menace written in his face. "Annuddeh woid outa ya f— traps, an' I'll shoot t' s— outa youse! On yuh way, now, ya p—! Get t' hell away from me befoeh I plug yah!"

And the three boys, stunned, bewildered, filled with shame, and sickened out of all the joy and hope with which they had been speaking of their projects just a moment before, have turned, and are walking silently away with the dull shame, the brutal and corrosive hatred which the war has caused, aching and rankling in their hearts.

Again, an image of man's naked desire, brutal and imperative, stripped down to his raw need, savage and incurious as the harsh pang of a starved hunger which takes and rends whatever food it finds—as here: Over the bridge, across the railway track, down in the Negro settlement of Newport News—among the dives and stews and rusty tenements of that grimy, dreary and abominable section, a rude shack of unpainted pine boards, thrown together with the savage haste which war engenders, to pander to a need as savage and insatiate as hunger, as old as life, the need of friendless, un-housed men the world over.

The front part of this rawly new, yet squalid place, has been par-titioned off by rude pine boards to form the semblance of a lunch room and soft drink parlor. Within are several tables, furnished with a few fly-specked menu cards, on which half a dozen items are recorded, and at which none of the patrons ever look, and a wooden counter, with its dreary stage property of luke-warm soda pop, a few packages of cigarettes and a box of cheap cigars beneath a dingy little glass case; and beneath a greasy glass humidor, a few stale ham and cheese sandwiches, which have been there since the place was opened, which will be there till the war is done.

Meanwhile, all through the room, the whores, in their thin and meager mummers, act as waitresses, move patiently about among the crowded tables and ply their trade. The men, who are seated at the tables, belong for the most part to that great group of un-classed creatures who drift and float, work, drift, and starve, are now in jail, now out again, now foul, filthy, wretched, hungry, out of luck, riding the rods, the rusty box cars of a freight, snatching their food at night from the boiling slum of hoboes' jungle, now swaggering with funds and brief prosperity—the floaters, drifters, and half-bums, that huge nameless, houseless, rootless and anomalous class that swarm across the nation.

They are the human cinders of the earth. Hard, shabby, scarred and lined of face, common, dull and meager of visage as they are, they have the look of having crawled that morning from the box car in the train yard of another city or of having dropped off a day coach in the morning, looking casually and indifferently about them, carrying a cardboard suitcase with a shirt, two collars and a tie. Yet a legend of great distances is written on them—a kind of atomic desolation. Each is a human spot of moving rust naked before the desolation of the skies that bend above him, unsheltered on the huge and savage wilderness of the earth, across which he is hurled—a spot of grimy gray and dingy brown, clinging to the brake-rods of a loaded freight.

He is a kind of human cinder hurled through space, naked, rootless, nameless, with all that was personal and unique in its one life almost emptied out into that huge vacancy of rust and iron and waste, and lonely and incommunicable distances, in which it lives, through which it has so often been bombarded.

And this atom finds its end at length, perhaps, at some unknown place upon the savage visage of the continent, exploded, a smear of blood on the rock ballast, a scream lost in the roar of pounding wheels, a winding of entrails round the axle rods, a brief indecipherable bobbing of blood and bone and brains upon the wooden ties, or just a shapeless bundle of old soiled brown and gray slumped down at morning in a shabby doorway, on a city street, beneath the elevated structure, a bundle of rags and bone, now cold and lifeless, to be carted out of sight by the police, nameless and forgotten in its death as in its life.

Such, for the most part, were the men who now sat at the tables in this rude house of pleasure, looking about them furtively, warily, with an air of waiting calculation, or indecision, and sometimes glancing at one another with sly, furtive, rather sheepish smiles.

As for the women who attended them, they were prostitutes recruited, for the most part, from the great cities of the North and Middle-West, brutally greedy, rapacious, weary of eye, hard of visage, over-driven, harried and exhausted in their mechanical performance of a profession from which their only hope was to grasp and clutch as much as they could in as short a time as possible. They had the harsh, rasping and strident voices, the almost deliberately exaggerated and inept extravagance of profanity and obscenity, the calculated and over-emphasized style of toughness which one often finds among poor people in the tenement sections of great cities—which one observes even in small children—the constant oath, curse, jeer, threat, menace, and truculent abuse, which really comes from the terrible fear in which they live, as if, in that world of savage aggression and brute rapacity, from which they have somehow to wrest their bitter living, they are afraid that any betrayal of themselves into a gentler, warmer and more tolerant kind of speech and gesture, will make them suspect to their fellows, and lay them open to the assaults, threats, tyrannies, and dominations they fear.

So was it with these women now: one could hear their rasping voices everywhere throughout the smoke-filled room, their harsh jeering laughter, and the extravagant exaggeration and profusion with which they constantly interlarded their strident speech with a few oaths and cries repeated with a brutal monotony—such phrases as "Christ!"—"Jesus!"—"What t' God-damn hell do I care?"— "Come on! Whatcha goin' t' do now! I got no time t'— around wit' yuh! If ya want t'—come on an' pay me—if ya don't, get t' God-damn hell outa here"—being among the expressions one heard most frequently.

Yet, even among these poor, brutally exhausted and fear-ridden women, there was really left, like something pitiably living and indestructible out of life, a kind of buried tenderness, a fearful, almost timid desire to find some friendship, gentleness, even love among the rabble-rout of lost and ruined men to whom they ministered.

And this timid, yet inherent desire for some warmer and more tender relation even in the practice of their profession, was sometimes almost ludicrously apparent as they moved warily about among the tables soliciting patronage from the men they served. Thus, if a man addressed them harshly, brutally, savagely, with an oath— which was a customary form of greeting—they would answer him in kind. But if he spoke to them more quietly, or regarded them with a more kindly smiling look, they might respond to him with a pathetic and ridiculous attempt at coquetry, subduing their rasping voices to a kind of husky, tinny whisper, pressing against him intimately, bending their bedaubed and painted faces close to his, and cajoling him with a pitiable pretense at seductiveness, somewhat in this manner:

"Hello there, big boy! . . . Yuh look lonesome sittin' there all by yourself. . . . Whatcha doin' all alone? . . . Yuh want some company? Huh?"—whispered hoarsely, with a ghastly leer of the smeared lips, and pressing closer—"Wanta have some fun, darling? . . . Come on!"—coaxingly, imperatively, taking the patron by the hand— "I'll show yuh a big time."

It was in response to some such blandishment as this that the boy had got up from his table, left the smoke-filled room accompanied by the woman, and gone out through a door at one side into the corridor that led back to the little partitioned board compartments of the brothel.

Here, it was at once evident that there was nothing to do but wait.

A long line of men and women that stretched from one end of the hallway to another stood waiting for their brief occupancies of the little compartments at the other end, all of which were now obviously and audibly occupied.

As they came out into the hall, the woman with the boy called out to another woman at the front end of the line: "Hello, May! . . . Have ya seen Grace?"

"Aah!" said the woman thus addressed, letting cigarette smoke coil from her nostrils as she spoke, and speaking with the rasping, exaggerated and brutal toughness that has been described: "I t'ink she's in number Seven here havin' a—."

And having conveyed the information in this delicate manner, she then turned to her companion, a brawny, grinning seaman in the uniform of the United States Navy, and with a brisk, yet rather bantering humor, demanded:

"Well, whatcha say, big boy? . . . Gettin' tired of waitin'? . . . Well, it won't be long now . . . Dey'll be troo in dere in a minute an' we're next."

"Dey better had be!" the sailor replied with a kind of jocular savagery. "If dey ain't, I'll tear down duh—joint! . . . Christ!" he cried in an astounded tone, after listening attentively for a moment. "Holy Jeez!" he said with a dumbfounded laugh. "What t' hell are dey doin' in deh all dis time? Who is dat guy, anyway?—A whole regiment of duh Marines, duh way it sounds t' me! Holy *Je-sus!*" he cried with an astounded laugh, listening again—"Christ!"

"Ah, c'mon, Jack!" the woman said with a kind of brutal, husky tenderness, snuggling close to his brawny arm meanwhile, and lewdly proposing her heavy body against his. "Yuh ain't gonna get impatient on me now, are yuh? . . . Just hold on a minute moeh and I'll give ya somet'ing ya neveh had befoeh!—"

"If yuh do," the gallant tar said tenderly, drawing his mighty fist back now in a gesture of savage endearment that somehow seemed to please her, "I'll come back here and smack yuh right in duh puss, yuh son-of-a-bitch!" he amorously whispered, and pulled her to him.

Similar conversations and actions were to be observed all up and down the line: there were lewd jests, ribald laughter, and impatiently shouted demands on the noisy occupants of the little compartments to "come on out an' give some of duh rest of us a chanct, f'r Chris' sake!" and other expressions of a similar nature.

It was a brutally hot night in the middle of August: in the hall-way the air was stifling, weary, greasily humid. The place was thick, dense, stale and foul with tobacco smoke, the stench of the men, the powder and cheap perfume of the women and over all, unforgettable, overpowering, pungent, resinous, rude and raw as savage nature and man's naked lust, was the odor of the new, unpainted, white-pine lumber of which the whole shambling and haphazard place had been constructed.

Finally, after a long and weary wait in that stifling place, during which time the door of the compartments had opened many times, and many men and women had come out, and many more gone in, the boy and the woman with him had advanced to the head of the line, and were next in the succession of that unending and vocifer-ous column.

Presently, the door of the room for which they waited opened, a man came out, shut the door behind him, and then went quickly down the hall. Then for a moment there was silence, impatient mutters in the line behind them, and at length the woman with the boy, muttering:

"I wondeh what t' hell she's doin' all dis time!—Hey!" she cried harshly, and hammered on the door, "Who's in dere? . . . Come on out, f'r Chris' sake! . . . Yuh're holding up duh line!"

In a moment, a woman's voice answered wearily:

"All right, Fay! . . . Just a moment, dear. . . . I'll be there."

"Oh," the woman with the boy said, in a suddenly quiet, strangely tender kind of voice. "It's Margaret. . . . I guess she's worn out, poor kid." And knocking at the door again, but this time gently, almost timidly, she said in a quiet voice:

"How are yuh, kid? . . . D'ya need any help?"

"No, it's all right, Fay," the girl inside said in the same tired and and utterly exhausted tone. "I'll be out in a moment. . . . Come on in, honey."

The woman opened the door softly and entered the room. The only furnishings of the hot, raw, and hideous little place, besides a chair, an untidy and rumpled looking bed, and a table, was a cheap dresser on which was a doll girdled with a soiled ribbon of pink silk, tied in a big bow, a photograph of a young sailor in-scribed with the words, "To Margaret, the best pal I ever had—Ed"
—and a package of cigarettes. An electric fan, revolving slowly from

left to right, droned incessantly, and fanned the close stale air with a kind of sporadic and sweltering breeze.

And from moment to moment, as it swung in its half-orbit, the fan would play full upon the face and head of the girl, who was lying on the bed in an attitude of utter pitiable weariness. When this happened, a single strand of her shining hair, which was straight, lank, fine-spun as silk, and of a lovely red-bronze texture, would be disturbed by the movement of the fan and would be blown gently back and forth across her temple.

The girl, who was tall, slender, and very lovely was, save for her shoes and stockings, naked, and she lay extended at full length on the untidy bed, with one arm thrust out in a gesture of complete exhaustion, the other folded underneath her shining hair, and her face, which had a fragile, transparent, almost starved delicacy, turned to one side and resting on her arm, the eyelids closed. And the eyelids also had this delicacy of texture, were violet with weariness, and so transparent that the fine net-work of the veins was plainly visible.

The other woman went softly over to the bed, sat down beside her, and began to speak to her in a low and tender tone. In a moment the girl turned her head towards the woman, opened her eyes, and smiled, in a faint and distant way, as of some one who is just emerging from the drugged spell of an opiate:

"What? . . . What did you say, darling? . . . No, I'm all right," she said faintly, and sitting up, with the other woman's help, she swiftly pulled on over her head the cheap one-piece garment she was wearing, which had been flung back over the chair beside the bed. Then smiling, she stood up, took a cigarette out of the package on the dresser, lighted it, and turning to the boy, who was standing in the door, said ironically, with something of the rasping accent which the other women used, beneath which, however, her pleasant rather husky tone was plainly evident.

"All right, 'Georgia'! Come on in!"

He went in slowly, still looking at her with an astounded stare. He had known her the first moment he had looked at her. She was a girl from the little town where the state university, at which he was a student, was situated, a member of a family of humble decent people, well known in the town: she had disappeared almost two years before, there had been rumor at the time that one of the students had "got her in trouble," and since that time he had neither seen nor heard of her.

"How are all the folks down home?" she said. "How's every one in Hopewell?"

Her luminous smoke-gray eyes were hard and bright as she spoke, her mouth, in her thin young face, was hard and bitter as a blade, and her voice was almost deliberately hard and mocking. And yet, beneath this defiant scornfulness, the strange, husky tenderness of the girl's tone persisted, and as she spoke, she put her slender hand lightly on his arm, with the swift, unconscious tenderness of people in a world of strangers who suddenly meet some one they know from home.

"They're all right," he stammered in a confused and bewildered tone, his face beginning to smoulder with embarrassment as he spoke.

"Well, if you see any one I know," she said in the same ironic tone, "say hello for me. . . . Tell 'em that I sent my love."

"All right," he blurted out stupidly. "I—I—certainly will."

"And I'm mad at you, 'Georgia,' " she said with a kind of mocking reproachfulness, "I'm mad at you for not telling me you were here. . . . The next time you come here you'd better ask for me— or I'll be mad! . . . We homefolks have got to stick together. . . . So you ask for Margaret—or I'll be mad at you—do you hear?"

"All right!" he stammered confusedly again, "I certainly will."

She looked at him a moment longer with her hard bright stare, her bitter, strangely tender smile. Then thrusting her fingers swiftly through his hair, she turned to the other woman and said:

"Be nice to him, Fay. . . . He's one of the folks from down my way. . . . Good-bye, 'Georgia.' . . . When you come back again you ask for Margaret."

"Good-bye," he said, and she was gone, out the door and down that stifling little hall of brutal, crowding, and imperative desire, into the market-place again, where for the thousandth time she would offer the sale of her young slender body to whoever would be there to buy; to solicit, take, accept the patronage of any of the thousand nameless and unknown men that the huge cylinder of chance and of the night might bring to her.

He never saw her after that. She was engulfed into the great vortex of the war, and the huge dark abyss and thronging chaos of America, the immense, the cruel, the indifferent and the magic land, where all of us have lived and walked as strangers, where all of us have been so small, so lonely, and forsaken, which has engulfed us all at length, and in whose dark and lonely breast so many lost and nameless men are buried and forgotten.

This, then, was the third visage of calamity, the image of desire, the face of war.

Again, the speed, haste, violence, savage humor and the instant decisiveness of war:—A sweltering noon on one of the great munition piers at Newport News where now the boy is working as material checker. Inside the great shed of the pier, a silent, suffocating heat of one hundred ten degrees, a grimy, mote-filled air, pollenated with the golden dust of oats which feed through a gigantic chute into the pier in an unending river, and which are stacked and piled in tremendous barricades all up and down the length of that enormous shed.

Elsewhere upon the pier, the towering geometries of war munitions: the white hard cleanliness of crated woods containing food and shot provender of every sort—canned goods, meat, beans, dried fruits, and small arms ammunitions—the enormous victualling of life and death fed ceaselessly into the insatiate and receiving maw of distant war.

The sweltering air is impregnated with the smells of all these things—with smells of oats and coarse brown sacking, with the clean fresh pungency of crated boxes, and with the huge, drowsy and nostalgic compact of a pier—the single blend of a thousand multiform and mixed aromas, the compacted fragrance of the past, sharp, musty, thrilling, unforgettable, as if the savor of the whole huge earth's abundance had slowly stained, and worn through, and soaked its mellow saturation into the massive and encrusted timbers.

But now all work has ceased: all of the usual sounds of work— the unceasing rumble of the trucks, the rattling of winches and the hard, sudden labor of the donkey engines on the decks of ships, the great nets swinging up and over with their freight of boxes, the sudden rattling fall, and rise again, the shouts and cries of the black sweating stevedores, the sharp commands of the gang bosses, overseers, and loading men—all this has stopped, has for the moment given over to the measured stamp of marching men, the endless streams of men in khaki uniforms who have all morning long, since early light, been tramping through the pier and filing up a gang-plank into the side of a great transport which waits there to en-gulf them.

The Negro stevedores sprawl lazily on loaded oat sacks round the grain chute, the checkers doze upon the great walled pile of grain or, kneeling in a circle down behind some oaty barricade, they gamble feverishly with dice.

Meanwhile, the troops come through. The sweltering brown col-umns tramp in, pause, are given rest, wearily shift the brutal im-pediment of the loaded knapsacks on their shoulders, take off their caps, wipe their sleeves across their red sweating faces, curse quietly among themselves, and then wait patiently for the lines to move again.

Down by the ship-side, at the gangplank's end, a group of officers are seated at a table as the troops file by them, examining each man's papers as he comes to them, passing them on from hand to hand, scrawling signatures, filing, recording, putting the stamp of their approval finally on the documents that will release each little khaki figure to its long-awaited triumph of the ship, the voyage, the new land, to all the joy and glory it is panting for, and to the uncon-sidered perils of battle, war, and death, disease or mutilation, and the unknown terror, horror, and disgust.

But now a column of black troops is coming by. They are a por-tion of a Negro regiment from Texas, powerful big men, naïve and wondering as children, incorrigibly unsuited to the military dis-cipline. Something, in fact, is missing, wrong, forgotten, out of place, with every one's equipment: one has lost his cap, another is without a belt, another is shy two buttons on his jacket, still another has mislaid his canteen, one is shy a good part of his knapsack equip-men, and dumbly, ignorantly bewildered at his loss—every one has lost something, left something behind, done something wrong, now misses something which he has to have.

And now, in one of the pauses of their march along the pier, each one of them pours out the burden of his complaint; into the swelter-ing misery of the heated air, the babel of black voices mounts. And the target of their bewilderment, the object on whom this whole burden of mischance and error is now heaped, the over-burdened and exhausted ruler to whom each now turns in his distress, and, with the naïve and confident faith of a child, asks for an instant solution of the tangled web of error in which he is enmeshed—is an infuriated little bullock of a white man, a first lieutenant, their commander, who during the mountainous accumulations of that catastrophic morning has been driven completely out of his head.

Now he stamps up and down the pier like a maddened animal, the white eyeballs, and the black, sweat-rilled faces follow him back and forth on his stamping and infuriated lunges with the patient, dutiful, and all-confiding trustfulness of children.

His red solid little face is swollen with choked fury and exasperation: as the unending chronicle of their woes mounts up he laughs insanely, clutches violently at the neck-band of his coat as if he is strangling, and stamps drunkenly and blindly about like a man maddened with the toothache.

And still they petition him, with the confident hope and certitude of trusting children that one word from their infallible governor will settle everything:—one tells about his missing belt, another of his forgotten canteen, another of his lost cap, his depleted and half-furnished knapsack—affectionately, incorrigibly, they address him as "Boss!" in spite of his curses, threats, entreaties, his final maddened screams that they must address him in a military manner, and the man stamps up and down, out of his wits with choking and unutterable exasperation, cursing vilely:

"You God-damned black bone-headed gang of sausage-brained gorillas!" he yells chokingly, and clutches at his throat—"Oh, you damned thick-skulled solid-ivory idiot brothers of a one-eyed mule! You sweet stinking set of ape-faced sons of bitches, you! If your brains were made of dynamite you wouldn't have enough to blow your nose, you poor dumb suffering second cousins of an owl! . . . Oh, you just wait, you ink-complected bastards, you!" he now shouts with a kind of fiendish and anticipatory pleasure. "Just wait until I get you in the front line trenches—I'll line you up there till those German bastards shoot you full of daylight if it's the last thing I ever live to do, you . . . damned . . . ignorant . . . misbegotten . . . cross . . . between a . . . a . . . a . . . wall-eyed possum and a camel's hump—why, you low-down, ignorant bunch of . . . of—"

"Boss?"

"Don't call me Boss!" in a high, choking, almost strangled gurgle. "You dumb son-of-a-bitch, how often have I got to tell you not to call me BOSS!" he yells.

"I know, Boss—" in a plaintive tone—"but my belt-buckle's busted. Is you got a piece of string?"

"*A piece of string!*" he chokes. "Why you damned—you—you— a piece of string!" he squeaks, and finally defeated, he takes off his cap, throws it on the floor and, sobbing, stamps upon it.

But an even greater affliction is in store for this unhappy man. Down at the ship-side, where the examining officers are sitting at the table, there has come a sudden pause, a disturbing interruption in the swift and mechanical dispatch with which the troops have been filing in before them. Six of the big black soldiers in a group have been stopped, sharply questioned, and then brusquely motioned out of line.

The officer picks up his cap, yells, "What in Christ's name is the matter now?" and rushes down to where they stand, in an attitude of crushed dejection, with tears rolling down their ebony cheeks. A moment's excited interrogation of the officers seated at the table informs him of the trouble: the six Negroes, all of whom are members of his command, have been under treatment for venereal diseases, but have somehow managed to sneak away from camp without a clean bill of health. Now their delinquency and stratagem of escape has been discovered, they have been denied their embarkation papers and weeping and begging, with the pitiable confidence which all these blacks put in their commanding officer, they are fairly grovelling before him, pleading with him that they be allowed to take ship with the rest of their companions.

"We ain't done nothin', Boss!" their leader, a huge ape of a man, black as ebony, is sniffling, pawing at the officer's sleeve. "Dey ain't nothin' wrong with us!"—"We don't want to stay heah in dis Gawd-damn hole, Boss!" another sniffles. "We want to go to France wheah you is! . . . Don't leave us behind, Boss! . . . We'll do anyt'ing you say if you'll jest take us along wid you!—"

"Why, you black clappy bastards!" he snarls—"I wish you were in hell, the lot of you! . . . How the hell do you expect *me* to do anything now at the last moment?" he yells, and filled with a frenzy that can find no stay or answer he goes stamping back and forth like a man gone mad with the very anguish of exasperation and despair. He charges into the midst of that small group of tainted and dejected blacks like a maddened little bull. He raves at them, he reviles them and curses them most foully, for a moment it seems that he is going to assault them physically. And they gather around him, weeping, entreating, crying, begging him for rescue and release, until at length, as if driven frantic by their clamor, he claps both hands to his ears and screaming, "All right, all right, all right!—I'll try—but if they let you go I hope they kill every clappy son-of-a-bitch in the first attack"—he rushes away to the table where the examining officers are seated at their work, engages them long and earnestly in a passionate and persuasive debate and finally wins them over to his argument.

It is decided that the infected Negroes shall be given a physical examination here and now upon the pier and a tall medical officer, delegated for this task, rises from the table, signs briefly to the rejected men, and accompanied by their red-faced little officer, marches them away behind the concealing barrier of the great wall of sacked oats.

They are gone perhaps ten minutes: when they return the Negroes are cavorting with glee, their black faces split by enormous ivory grins, and they are scraping around their little officer like frantic children. They fairly fawn upon him, they try to kiss his hands, they pat his shoulders with their great black paws—the story of their triumphant restoration to the fold is legible in every move they make, in everything they do.

The tall medical officer marches sternly ahead, but with a faint grin playing round the corners of his mouth, and the little red-faced officer is still cursing bitterly, but in his curses now there is a gentler note, the suggestion almost of a lewd tenderness.

And at length that brown, enormous, apparently interminable column has filed into the ship's great side, and there is nothing on the pier now but far lost sounds and silence, the breath of coolness, evening, the on-coming, undulant stride of all-enfolding and deep-breasted night.

ONLY THE DEAD KNOW BROOKLYN

DERE'S no guy livin' dat knows Brooklyn t'roo an' t'roo, because it'd take a guy a lifetime just to find his way aroun' duh f— town.

So like I say, I'm waitin' for my train t' come when I sees dis big guy standin' deh—dis is duh foist I eveh see of him. Well, he's lookin' wild, y'know, an' I can see dat he's had plenty, but still he's holdin' it; he talks good an' is walkin' straight enough. So den, dis big guy steps up to a little guy dat's standin' deh, an' says, "How d'yuh get t' Eighteent' Avenoo an' Sixty-sevent' Street?" he says.

"Jesus! Yuh got me, chief," duh little guys says to him. "I ain't been heah long myself. Where is duh place?" he says. "Out in duh Flatbush section somewhere?"

"Nah," duh big guy says. "It's out in Bensonhoist. But I was neveh deh befoeh. How d'yuh get deh?"

"Jesus," duh little guy says, scratchin' his head, y'know—yuh could see duh little guy didn't know his way about—"yuh got me, chief. I neveh hoid of it. Do any of youse guys know where it is?" he says to me.

"Sure," I says. "It's out in Bensonhoist. Yuh take duh Fourt' Avenoo express, get off at Fifty-nint' Street, change to a Sea Beach local deh, get off at Eighteent' Avenoo an' Sixty-toid, an' den walk down foeh blocks. Dat's all yuh got to do," I says.

"G'wan!" some wise guy dat I neveh seen befoeh pipes up. "Whatcha talkin' about?" he says—oh, he was wise, y'know. "Duh guy is crazy! I tell yuh what yuh do," he says to duh big guy. "Yuh change to duh West End line at Toity-sixt'," he tells him. "Get off at Noo Utrecht an' Sixteent' Avenoo," he says. "Walk two blocks oveh, foeh blocks up," he says, "an' you'll be right deh." Oh, a *wise* guy, y'know.

"Oh, yeah?" I says. "Who told *you* so much?" He got me sore because he was so wise about it. "How long you been livin' heah?" I says.

"All my life," he says. "I was bawn in Williamsboig," he says. "An' I can tell you t'ings about dis town you neveh hoid of," he says.

"Yeah?" I says.

"Yeah," he says.

"Well, den, you can tell me t'ings about dis town dat nobody else has eveh hoid of, either. Maybe you make it all up yoehself at night," I says, "befoeh you go to sleep—like cuttin' out papeh dolls, or somp'n."

"Oh, yeah?" he says. "You're pretty wise, ain't yuh?"

"Oh, I don't know," I says. "Duh boids ain't usin' my head for Lincoln's statue yet," I says. "But I'm wise enough to know a phony when I see one."

"Yeah?" he says. "A wise guy, huh? Well, you're so wise dat some one's goin' t'bust yuh one right on duh snoot some day," he says. "Dat's how wise *you* are."

Well, my train was comin' or I'da smacked him den and dere, but when I seen duh train was comin', all I said was, "All right, mugg! I'm sorry I can't stay to take keh of you, but I'll be seein' yuh sometime, I hope, out in duh cemetery." So den I says to duh big guy, who'd been standin' deh all duh time, "You come wit me," I says. So when we gets onto duh train I says to him, "Where yuh goin' out in Bensonhoist?" I says. "What numbeh are yuh lookin' for?" I says. *You* know—I t'ought if he told me duh address I might be able to help him out.

"Oh," he says, "I'm not lookin' for no one. I don't know no one out deh."

"Then whatcha goin' out deh for?" I says.

"Oh," duh guy says, "I'm just goin' out to see duh place," he says. "I like duh sound of duh name—Bensonhoist, y'know—so I t'ought I'd go out an' have a look at it."

"Whatcha tryin' t'hand me?" I says. "Whatcha tryin' t'do—kid me?" *You* know, I t'ought duh guy was bein' wise wit me.

"No," he says, "I'm tellin' yuh duh troot. I like to go out an' take a look at places wit nice names like dat. I like to go out an' look at all kinds of places," he says.

"How'd yuh know deh was such a place," I says, "if yuh neveh been deh befoeh?"

"Oh," he says, "I got a map."

"A *map?*" I says.

"Sure," he says, "I got a map dat tells me about all dese places. I take it wit me every time I come out heah," he says.

And Jesus! Wit dat, he pulls it out of his pocket, an' so help me,

but he's *got* it—he's tellin' duh troot—a big map of duh whole f—
place with all duh different pahts mahked out. You know—Canarsie
an' East Noo Yawk an' Flatbush, Bensonhoist, Sout' Brooklyn, duh
Heights, Bay Ridge, Greenpernt—duh whole goddam layout, he's
got it right deh on duh map.

"You been to any of dose places?" I says.

"Sure," he says, "I been to most of 'em. I was down in Red Hook
just last night," he says.

"Jesus! Red Hook!" I says. "Whatcha do down deh?"

"Oh," he says, "nuttin' much. I just walked aroun'. I went into
a coupla places an' had a drink," he says, "but most of the time I
just walked aroun'."

"Just walked aroun'?" I says.

"Sure," he says, "just lookin' at t'ings, y'know."

"Where'd yuh go?" I asts him.

"Oh," he says, "I don't know duh name of duh place, but I could
find it on my map," he says. "One time I was walkin' across some
big fields where deh ain't no houses," he says, "but I could see ships
oveh deh all lighted up. Dey was loadin'. So I walks across duh
fields," he says, "to where duh ships are."

"Sure," I says, "I know where you was. You was down to duh Erie
Basin."

"Yeah," he says, "I guess dat was it. Dey had some of dose big
elevators an' cranes an' dey was loadin' ships, an' I could see some
ships in drydock all lighted up, so I walks across duh fields to where
dey are," he says.

"Den what did yuh do?" I says.

"Oh," he says, "nuttin' much. I came on back across duh fields
after a while an' went into a coupla places an' had a drink."

"Didn't nuttin' happen while yuh was in dere?" I says.

"No," he says. "Nuttin' much. A coupla guys was drunk in one of
duh places an' started a fight, but dey bounced 'em out," he says,
"an' den one of duh guys stahted to come back again, but duh bar-
tender gets his baseball bat out from under duh counteh, so duh
guy goes on."

"Jesus!" I said. "Red Hook!"

"Sure," he says. "Dat's where it was, all right."

"Well, you keep outa deh," I says. "You stay away from deh."

"Why?" he says. "What's wrong wit it?"

"Oh," I says, "it's a good place to stay away from, dat's all. It's a good place to keep out of."

"Why?" he says. "Why is it?"

Jesus! Whatcha gonna do wit a guy as dumb as dat? I saw it wasn't no use to try to tell him nuttin', he wouldn't know what I was talkin' about, so I just says to him, "Oh, nuttin'. Yuh might get lost down deh, dat's all."

"Lost?" he says. "No, I wouldn't get lost. I got a map," he says. A map! Red Hook! Jesus!

So den duh guy begins to ast me all kinds of nutty questions: how big was Brooklyn an' could I find my way aroun' in it, an' how long would it take a guy to know duh place.

"Listen!" I says. "You get dat idea outa yoeh head right now," I says. "You ain't neveh gonna get to know Brooklyn," I says. "Not in a hundred yeahs. I been livin' heah all my life," I says, "an' I don't even know all deh is to know about it, so how do you expect to know duh town," I says, "when you don't even live heah?"

"Yes," he says, "but I got a map to help me find my way about."

"Map or no map," I says, "yuh ain't gonna get to known Brooklyn wit no map," I says.

"Can you swim?" he says, just like dat. Jesus! By dat time, y'know, I begun to see dat duh guy was some kind of a nut. He'd had plenty to drink, of course, but he had dat crazy look in his eye I didn't like. "Can you swim?" he says.

"Sure," I says. "Can't you?"

"No," he says. "Not more'n a stroke or two. I neveh loined good."

"Well, it's easy," I says. "All yuh need is a little confidence. Duh way I loined, me older bruddeh pitched me off duh dock one day when I was eight yeahs old, cloes an' all. 'You'll swim,' he says. 'You'll swim all right—or drown.' An', believe me, I *swam*! When yuh know yuh got to, you'll do it. Duh only t'ing yuh need is confidence. An' once you've loined," I says, "you've got nuttin' else to worry about. You'll neveh forget it. It's somp'n dat stays wit yuh as long as yuh live."

"Can yuh swim good?" he says.

"Like a fish," I tells him. "I'm a regulah fish in duh wateh," I says. "I loined to swim right off duh docks wit all duh oddeh kids," I says.

"What would you do if yuh saw a man drownin'?" duh guy says. "Do? Why, I'd jump in an' pull him out," I says. "Dat's what I'd do."

"Did yuh eveh see a man drown?" he says.

"Sure," I says. "I see two guys—bot' times at Coney Island. Dey got out too far, an' neider one could swim. Dey drowned befoeh any one could get to 'em."

"What becomes of people after dey've drowned out heah?" he says.

"Drowned out where?" I says.

"Out heah in Brooklyn."

"I don know whatcha mean," I says. "Neveh hoid of no one drownin' heah in Brooklyn, unless you mean a swimmin' pool. Yuh can't drown in Brooklyn," I says. "Yuh gotta drown somewhere else—in duh ocean, where dere's wateh."

"Drownin'," duh guy says, lookin' at his map. "Drownin'." Jesus! I could see by den he was some kind of nut, he had dat crazy expression in his eyes when he looked at you, an' I didn't know what he might do. So we was comin' to a station, an' it wasn't my stop, but I got off anyway, an' waited for duh next train.

"Well, so long, chief," I says. "Take it easy, now."

"Drownin'," duh guy says, lookin' at his map. "Drownin'."

Jesus! I've t'ought about dat guy a t'ousand times since den an' wondered what eveh happened to 'm goin' out to look at Bensonhoist because he liked duh name! Walkin' aroun' t'roo Red Hook by himself at night an' lookin' at his map! How many people did I see get drowned out heah in Brooklyn! How long would it take a guy wit a good map to know all deh was to know about Brooklyn!

Jesus! What a nut *he* was! I wondeh what eveh happened to 'im, anyway! I wondeh if some one knocked him on duh head, or if he's still wanderin' aroun' in duh subway in duh middle of duh night wit his little map! Duh poor guy! Say, I've got to laugh, at dat, when I t'ink about him! Maybe he's found out by now dat he'll neveh live long enough to know duh whole of Brooklyn. It'd take a guy a lifetime to know Brooklyn t'roo an' t'roo. An' even den, yuh wouldn't know it all.

DARK IN THE FOREST,
STRANGE AS TIME

SOME years ago, among the people standing on one of the platforms of the Munich railway station, beside the Swiss express, which was almost ready to depart, there were a woman and a man—a woman so lovely that the memory of her would forever haunt the mind of him who saw her, and a man on whose dark face the legend of a strange and fatal meeting was already visible.

The woman was at the flawless summit of a mature and radiant beauty, packed to the last red ripeness of her lip with life and health, a miracle of loveliness in whom all the elements of beauty had combined with such exquisite proportion and so rhythmical a balance that even as one looked at her he could scarcely believe the evidence of his eyes.

Thus, although not over tall, she seemed at times to command a superb and queenly height, then to be almost demurely small and cosy as she pressed close to her companion. Again, her lovely figure seemed never to have lost the lithe slenderness of girlhood, yet it was ripe, lavish, undulant with all the voluptuous maturity of womanhood, and every movement she made was full of seductive grace.

The woman was fashionably dressed; her little toque-like hat fitted snugly down over a crown of coppery reddish hair, and shaded her eyes which had a smoke-blue and depthless quality that could darken almost into black, and change with every swiftest shade of feeling that passed across her face. She was talking to the man in low and tender tones, smiling a vague voluptuous smile as she looked at him. She spoke eagerly, earnestly, gleefully to him, and from time to time burst into a little laugh that came welling low, rich, sensual, and tender from her throat.

As they walked up and down the platform talking, the woman thrust her small gloved hand through the arm of his heavy overcoat and snuggled close to him, sometimes nestling her lovely head, which was as proud and graceful as a flower, against his arm. Again they would pause, and look steadfastly at each other for a moment. Now she spoke to him with playful reproof, chided him, shook him tenderly by the arms, pulled the heavy furred lapels of his overcoat together, and wagged a small gloved finger at him warningly.

And all the time the man looked at her, saying little, but devouring her with large dark eyes that were burning steadily with the fires of death, and that seemed to feed on her physically, with an insatiate and voracious tenderness of love. He was a Jew, his figure immensely tall, cadaverous, and so wasted by disease that it was lost, engulfed, forgotten in the heavy and expensive garments that he wore.

His thin white face, which was wasted almost to a fleshless integument of bone and skin, converged to an immense hooked nose, so that his face was not so much a face as a great beak of death, lit by two blazing and voracious eyes and colored on the flanks with two burning flags of red. Yet, with all its ugliness of disease and emaciation it was a curiously memorable and moving face, a visage somehow nobly tragic with the badge of death.

But now the time had come for parting. The guards were shouting warnings to the passengers, all up and down the platform there were swift serried movements, hurried eddyings among the groups of friends. One saw people embracing, kissing, clasping hands, crying, laughing, shouting, going back for one hard swift kiss, and then mounting hastily into their compartments. And one heard in a strange tongue the vows, oaths, promises, the jests and swift allusions, that were secret and precious to each group and that sent them off at once in the roars of laughter, the words of farewell that are the same the whole world over.

"Otto! Otto! . . . Have you got what I gave you? . . . Feel! Is it still there?" He felt, it was still there: fits of laughter.

"Will you see Else?"

"How's that? Can't hear"—shouting, cupping hand to ear, and turning head sideways with a puzzled look.

"I—say—will—you—see—Else?" fairly roared out between cupped palms above the tumult of the crowd.

"Yes. I think so. We expect to meet them at St. Moritz."

"Tell her she's got to write."

"Hey? I can't hear you." Same pantomime as before.

"I—say—tell—her—she's got—to write"—another roar.

"Oh, yes! Yes!" Nodding quickly, smiling, "I'll tell her."

"—or I'll be mad at her!"

"What? Can't hear you for all this noise"—same business as before.

"I—say—tell—her—I'll—be—mad—if she—doesn't—write" roared out again deliberately at the top of his lungs.

Here, a man who had been whispering slyly to a woman, who was trembling with smothered laughter, now turned with grinning face to shout something at the departing friend, but was checked by the woman who seized him by the arm and with a face reddened by laughter, gasped hysterically.

"No! No!"

But the man, still grinning, cupped his hands around his mouth and roared:

"Tell Uncle Walter he has got to wear his——"

"How's that? Can't hear!"—cupping ear and turning head to one side as before.

"I—say," the man began to roar deliberately.

"No! No! No! Sh-h!" the woman gasped frantically, tugging at his arm.

"—to—tell—Uncle Walter—he—must—wear—his woolen——"

"No! No! No!—Heinrich! . . . Sh-h!" the woman shrieked.

"—The—heavy—ones—Aunt—Bertha embroidered with his—initials!" the man went on relentlessly.

Here the whole crowd roared, and the woman screamed with laughter, shrieking protests, and saying:

"Sh-h! Sh-h!" loudly.

"Ja—I'll tell him!" the grinning passenger yelled back at him as soon as they had grown somewhat quieter. "Maybe—he hasn't—got —'em any—more," he shouted as a happy afterthought. Maybe—one —of—the—Fräuleins—down—there—" he gasped and choked with laughter.

"Otto!" the woman shrieked. "Sh-h!"

"Maybe—one—of—the—Fräuleins—got them—away—from"—he began to gasp with laughter.

"O-o-o-t-to! . . . Shame on you—Sh-h!" the woman screamed.

"Souvenir—from—old—München," roared back his fellow wit, and the whole group was convulsed again. When they had recovered somewhat, one of the men began in a wheezing and faltering tone, as he wiped his streaming eyes:

"Tell—Else"—here his voice broke off in a feeble squeak, and he had to pause to wipe his eyes again.

"What?"—the grinning passenger yelled back at him.

"Tell—Else," he began again more strongly, "that Aunt—Bertha

—oh! my God!" he groaned weakly again, faltered, wiped his streaming eyes, and was reduced to palsied silence.

"What?—What?" shouted the grinning passenger sharply, clapping his hand to his attentive ear. "Tell Else what?"

"Tell—Else—Aunt—Bertha—is—sending—her—recipe—for—layer—cake," the man fairly screamed now as if he would get it out at any cost before his impending and total collapse. The effect of that apparently meaningless reference to Aunt Bertha's layer cake was astonishing: nothing that had gone before could approach the spasmodic effect it had upon this little group of friends. They were instantly reduced to a shuddering paralysis of laughter, they staggered drunkenly about, clasped one another feebly for support, tears streamed in torrents from their swollen eyes, and from their wide-open mouths there came occasionally feeble wisps of sound, strangled gasps, faint screams from the women, a panting palsied fit of mirth from which they finally emerged into a kind of hiccoughing recovery.

What it was—the total implication of that apparently banal reference which had thrown them all into such a convulsive fit of merriment—no stranger could ever know, but its effect upon the other people was infectious; they looked toward the group of friends, and grinned, laughed, and shook their heads at one another. And so it went all up and down the line. Here were people grave, gay, sad, serious, young, old, calm, casual, and excited; here were people bent on business and people bent on pleasure; here people sharing by every act, word, and gesture the excitement, joy, and hope which the voyage wakened in them, and people who looked wearily and indifferently about them, settled themselves in their seats and took no further interest in the events of the departure—but everywhere it was the same.

People were speaking the universal language of departure, that varies not at all the whole world over—that language which is often banal, trivial, and even useless, but on this account curiously moving, since it serves to hide a deeper emotion in the hearts of men, to fill the vacancy that is in their hearts at the thought of parting, to act as a shield, a concealing mask to their true feeling.

And because of this there was for the youth, the stranger, and the alien who saw and heard these things, a thrilling and poignant quality in the ceremony of the train's departure. As he saw and heard these familiar words and actions—words and actions that beneath the guise of an alien tongue were identical to those he had seen and known all his life, among his own people—he felt suddenly, as he had never felt before, the overwhelming loneliness of familiarity, the sense of the human identity that so strangely unites all the people in the world, and that is rooted in the structure of man's life, far below the tongue he speaks, the race of which he is a member.

But now that the time had come for parting, the woman and the dying man said nothing. Clasped arm to arm they looked at each other with a stare of burning and voracious tenderness. They embraced, her arms clasped him, her living and voluptuous body drew toward him, her red lips clung to his mouth as if she could never let him go. Finally, she fairly tore herself away from him, gave him a desperate little push with her hands, and said, "Go, go! It's time!"

Then the scarecrow turned and swiftly climbed into the train, a guard came by and brutally slammed the door behind him, the train began to move slowly out of the station. And all the time the man was leaning from a window in the corridor looking at her, and the woman was walking along beside the train, trying to keep him in sight as long as she could. Now the train gathered motion, the woman's pace slowed, she stopped, her eyes wet, her lips murmuring words no one could hear, and as he vanished from her sight she cried, "Auf Wiedersehn!" and put her hand up to her lips and kissed it to him.

For a moment longer the younger man, who was to be this specter's brief companion of the journey, stood looking out the corridor window down the platform toward the great arched station sheds, seeming to look after the group of people departing up the platform, but really seeing nothing but the tall, lovely figure of the woman as she walked slowly away, head bent, with a long, deliberate stride of incomparable grace, voluptuous undulance. Once she paused to look back again, then turned and walked on slowly as before.

Suddenly she stopped. Some one out of the throng of people on the platform had approached her. It was a young man. The woman paused in a startled manner, lifted one gloved hand in protest, started to go on, and the next moment they were locked in a savage embrace, devouring each other with passionate kisses.

When the traveller returned to his seat, the dying man who had already come into the compartment from the corridor and had fallen back into the cushions of his seat, breathing hoarsely, was growing calmer, less exhausted. For a moment the younger man looked intently at the beak-like face, the closed weary eyes, wondering if this dying man had seen that meeting on the station platform, and what knowledge such as this could now mean to him. But that mask of death was enigmatic, unrevealing; the youth found nothing there that he could read. A faint and strangely luminous smile was playing at the edges of the man's thin mouth, and his burning eyes were now open, but far and sunken and seemed to be looking from an unspeakable depth at something that was far away. In a moment, in a profound and tender tone, he said:

"Zat vas my vife. Now in ze vinter I must go alone, for zat iss best. But in ze spring ven I am better she vill come to me."

All through the wintry afternoon the great train rushed down across Bavaria. Swiftly and powerfully it gathered motion, it left the last scattered outposts of the city behind it, and swift as dreams the train was rushing out across the level plain surrounding Munich.

The day was gray, the sky impenetrable and somewhat heavy, and yet filled with a strong, clean Alpine vigor, with that odorless and yet exultant energy of cold mountain air. Within an hour the train had entered Alpine country, now there were hills, valleys, the immediate sense of soaring ranges, and the dark enchantment of the forests of Germany, those forests which are something more than trees—which are a spell, a magic, and a sorcery, filling the hearts of men, and particularly those strangers who have some racial kinship with that land, with a dark music, a haunting memory, never wholly to be captured.

It is an overwhelming feeling of immediate and impending discovery, such as men might have who come for the first time to their father's country. It is like coming to that unknown land for which our spirits long so passionately in youth, which is the dark side of our soul, the strange brother and the complement of the land we have known in our childhood. And it is revealed to us instantly the moment that we see it with a powerful emotion of perfect recognition and disbelief, with that dream-like reality of strangeness and familiarity which dreams and all enchantment have.

What is it? What is this wild fierce joy and sorrow swelling in our hearts? What is this memory that we cannot phrase, this instant recognition for which we have no words? We cannot say. We have no way to give it utterance, no ordered evidence to give it proof, and scornful pride can mock us for a superstitious folly. Yet we will know the dark land at the very moment that we come to it, and though we have no tongue, no proof, no utterance for what we feel, we have what we have, we know what we know, we are what we are.

And what are we? We are the naked men, the lost Americans. Immense and lonely skies bend over us, ten thousand men are marching in our blood. Where does it come from—the sense of strangeness, instant recognition, the dream-haunted, almost captured, memory? Where does it come from, the constant hunger and the rending lust, and the music, dark and solemn, elfish, magic, sounding through the wood? How is it that this boy, who is American, has known this strange land from the first moment that he saw it?

How is it that from his first night in a German town he has understood the tongue he never heard before, has spoken instantly, saying all he wished to say, in a strange language which he could not speak, speaking a weird argot which was neither his nor theirs, of which he was not even conscious, so much did it seem to be the spirit of a language, not the words, he spoke, and instantly, in this fashion, understood by every one with whom he talked?

No. He could not prove it, yet he knew that it was there, buried deep in the brain and blood of man, the utter knowledge of this land and of his father's people. He had felt it all, the tragic and insoluble admixture of the race. He knew the terrible fusion of the brute and of the spirit. He knew the nameless fear of the old barbaric forest, the circle of barbaric figures gathered round him in their somber and unearthly ring, the sense of drowning in the blind forest horrors of barbaric time. He carried all within himself, the slow gluttony and lust of the unsated swine, as well as the strange and powerful music of the soul.

He knew the hatred and revulsion from the never-sated beast—the beast with the swine-face and the quenchless thirst, the never-ending hunger, the thick, slow, rending hand that fumbled with a smouldering and unsated lust. And he hated the great beast with the hate of hell and murder because he felt and knew it in himself and was himself the prey of its rending, quenchless, and obscene desires. Rivers of wine to drink, whole roast oxen turning on the spit, and through the forest murk, the roaring wall of huge beast-bodies and barbaric sound about him, the lavish flesh of the great blonde women, in brutal orgy of the all-devouring, never-sated maw of the huge belly, without end or surfeit—all was mixed into his blood, his spirit, and his life.

It had been given to him somehow from the dark time-horror of the ancient forest together with all that was magical, glorious, strange and beautiful: the husky horn-notes sounding faint and elfin through the forests, the infinite strange weavings, dense mutations of the old Germanic soul of man. How cruel, baffling, strange, and sorrowful was the enigma of the race: the power and strength of the incorruptible and soaring spirit rising from the huge corrupted beast with such a radiant purity, and the powerful enchantments of grand music, noble poetry, so sorrowfully and unalterably woven and inwrought with all the blind brute hunger of the belly and the beast of man.

It was all his, and all contained in his one life. And it could, he knew, never be distilled out of him, no more than one can secrete from his flesh his father's blood, the ancient and immutable weavings of dark time. And for this reason, as he now looked out the window of the train at that lonely Alpine land of snow and dark enchanted forest he felt the sense of familiar recognition instantly, the feeling that he had always known this place, that it was home. And something dark, wild, jubilant, and strange was exulting, swelling in his spirit like a grand and haunting music heard in dreams.

And now, a friendly acquaintance having been established, the specter, with the insatiate, possessive curiosity of his race, began to ply his companion with innumerable questions concerning his life, his home, his profession, the journey he was making, the reason for that journey. The young man answered readily, and without annoyance. He knew that he was being pumped unmercifully, but the dying man's whispering voice was so persuasive, friendly, gentle, his manner so courteous, kind, and insinuating, his smile so luminous and winning, touched with a faint and yet agreeable expression of weariness, that the questions almost seemed to answer themselves.

The young man was an American, was he not? . . . Yes. And how long had he been abroad—two months? Three months? No? Almost a year! So long as that! Then he liked Europe, yes? It was his first trip? No? His fourth?—The specter lifted his eyebrows in expressive astonishment, and yet his sensitive thin mouth was touched all the time by his faint, wearily cynical smile.

Finally, the boy was pumped dry: the specter knew all about him. Then for a moment he sat staring at the youth with his faint, luminous, subtly mocking, and yet kindly smile. At last, wearily, patiently, and with the calm finality of experience and death, he said:

"You are very young. Yes. Now you vant to see it all, to haf it all— but you haf nothing. Zat iss right—yes?" he said with his persuasive smile. "Zat will all change. Some day you vill vant only a little— maybe, den, you *haf* a little—" and he flashed his luminous, winning smile again. "Und zat iss better—Yes?" He smiled again, and then said wearily, "I know. I know. Myself I haf gone eferyvere like you. I haf tried to see eferyt'ing—und I haf had nothing. Now I go no more. Eferyvere it iss ze same," he said wearily, looking out the window, with a dismissing gesture of his thin white hand. "Fields, hills, mountains, riffers, cities, peoples—you vish to know about zem all. Vun field, vun hill, vun riffer," the man whispered, "zat iss enough!"

He closed his eyes for a moment: when he spoke again his whisper was almost inaudible—"Vun life, vun place, vun time."

Darkness came, and the lights in the compartment were turned on. Again that whisper of waning life made its insistent, gentle, and implacable demand upon the youth. This time it asked that the light in the compartment be extinguished, while the specter stretched himself out upon the seat to rest. The younger man consented willingly and even gladly: his own journey was near its end and outside, the moon, which had risen early, was shining down upon the Alpine forests and snows with a strange, brilliant, and haunting magic which gave to the darkness in the compartment some of its own ghostly and mysterious light.

The specter lay quietly stretched out on the cushions of the seat, his eyes closed, his wasted face, on which the two bright flags of burning red now shone with vermilion hue, strange and ghastly in the magic light as the beak of some great bird. The man scarcely seemed to breathe: no sound or movement of life was perceptible in the compartment except the pounding of the wheels, the leathery stretching and creaking sound of the car, and all that strange-familiar and evocative symphony of sounds a train makes—that huge symphonic monotone which is itself the sound of silence and forever.

For some time held in that spell of magic light and time, the youth sat staring out the window at the enchanted world of white and black that swept grandly and strangely past in the phantasmal radiance of the moon. Finally he got up, went out into the corridor, closing the door carefully behind him, and walked back down the narrow passageway through car after car of the rocketing train until he came to the dining car.

Here all was brilliance, movement, luxury, sensual warmth and gaiety. All the life of the train now seemed to be concentrated in this place. The waiters, surefooted and deft, were moving swiftly down the aisle of the rocketing car, pausing at each table to serve people from the great platters of well-cooked food which they carried on trays. Behind them the *sommelier* was pulling corks from tall frosty bottles of Rhine wine: he would hold the bottle between his knees as he pulled, the cork would come out with an exhilarating pop, and he would drop the cork then into a little basket.

At one table a seductive and beautiful woman was eating with a jaded-looking old man. At another a huge and powerful-looking German, with a wing collar, a shaven skull, a great swine face and a forehead of noble and lonely thought, was staring with a concentrated look of bestial gluttony at the tray of meat from which the waiter served him. He was speaking in a guttural and lustful tone, saying, "Ja! . . . Gut! . . . und etwas von diesem hier auch. . . ."

The scene was one of richness, power and luxury, evoking as it did the feeling of travel in a crack European express, which is different from the feeling one has when he rides on an American train. In America, the train gives one a feeling of wild and lonely joy, a sense of the savage, unfenced, and illimitable wilderness of the country through which the train is rushing, a worldless and unutterable hope as one thinks of the enchanted city toward which he is speeding; the unknown and fabulous promise of the life he is to find there.

In Europe, the feeling of joy and pleasure is more actual, ever present. The luxurious trains, the rich furnishings, the deep maroons, dark blues, the fresh, well-groomed vivid colors of the cars, the good food and the sparkling, heady wine, and the worldly, wealthy, cosmopolitan look of the travellers—all of this fills one with a power-ful sensual joy, a sense of expectancy about to be realized. In a few hours' time one goes from country to country, through centuries of history, a world of crowded culture and whole nations swarming with people, from one famous pleasure-city to another.

And, instead of the wild joy and nameless hope one feels as he looks out the window of an American train, one feels here (in Europe) an incredible joy of realization, an immediate sensual gratification, a feeling that there is nothing on earth but wealth, power, luxury, and love, and that one can live and enjoy this life, in all the infinite varieties of pleasure, forever.

When the young man had finished eating, and paid his bill, he began to walk back again through corridor after corridor along the length of the rocketing train. When he got back to his compartment, he saw the specter lying there as he had left him, stretched out upon the seat, with the brilliant moonlight still blazing on the great beak of his face.

The man had not changed his position by an inch, and yet at once the boy was conscious of some subtle, fatal change he could not de-fine. What was it? He took his seat again and for some time stared fixedly at the silent ghostly figure opposite him. Did he not breathe? He thought, he was almost sure, he saw the motion of his breathing, the rise and fall of the emaciated breast, and yet he was not sure. But what he plainly saw now was that a line, vermilion in its moon-dark hue, had run out of the corner of the firm set mouth and that there was a large vermilion stain upon the floor.

What should he do? What could be done? The haunted light of the fatal moon seemed to have steeped his soul in its dark sorcery, in the enchantment of a measureless and inert calmness. Already, too, the train was slackening its speed, the first lights of the town ap-peared, it was his journey's end.

And now the train was slowing to a halt. There were the flare of rails, the switch-lights of the yard, small, bright, and hard, green, red, and yellow, poignant in the dark, and on other tracks he could see the little goods cars and the strings of darkened trains, all empty, dark, and waiting with their strange attentiveness of recent life. Then the long station quays began to slide slowly past the windows of the train, and the sturdy goat-like porters were coming on the run, eagerly saluting, speaking, calling to the people in the train who had already begun to pass their baggage through the window.

Softly the boy took his overcoat and suit-case from the rack above his head and stepped out into the narrow corridor. Quietly he slid the door of the compartment shut behind him. Then, for a moment, still unsure, he stood there looking back. In the semi-darkness of the compartment the spectral figure of the cadaver lay upon the cushions, did not move.

Was it not well to leave all things as he had found them, in silence, at the end? Might it not be that in his great dream of time in which we live and are the moving figures, there is no greater certitude than this: that, having met, spoken, known each other for a moment, as somewhere on this earth we were hurled onward through the darkness between two points of time, it is well to be content with this, to leave each other as we met, letting each one go alone to his appointed destination, sure of this only, needing only this—that there will be silence for us all and silence only, nothing but silence, at the end?

Already the train had come to a full stop. The boy went down the corridor to the end, and in a moment, feeling the bracing shock of the cold air upon his flesh, breathing the vital and snow-laden air into his lungs, he was going down the quay with a hundred other people, all moving in the same direction, some toward certitude and home, some toward a new land, hope, and hunger, the swelling pre-science of joy, the promise of a shining city. He knew that he was going home again.

THE FAR AND THE NEAR

ON THE outskirts of a little town upon a rise of land that swept back from the railway there was a tidy little cottage of white boards, trimmed vividly with green blinds. To one side of the house there was a garden neatly patterned with plots of growing vegetables, and an arbor for the grapes which ripened late in August. Before the house there were three mighty oaks which sheltered it in their clean and massive shade in summer, and to the other side there was a border of gay flowers. The whole place had an air of tidiness, thrift, and modest comfort.

Every day, a few minutes after two o'clock in the afternoon, the limited express between two cities passed this spot. At that moment the great train, having halted for a breathing-space at the town near by, was beginning to lengthen evenly into its stroke, but it had not yet reached the full drive of its terrific speed. It swung into view deliberately, swept past with a powerful swaying motion of the engine, a low smooth rumble of its heavy cars upon pressed steel, and then it vanished in the cut. For a moment the progress of the engine could be marked by heavy bellowing puffs of smoke that burst at spaced intervals above the edges of the meadow grass, and finally nothing could be heard but the solid clacking tempo of the wheels receding into the drowsy stillness of the afternoon.

Every day for more than twenty years, as the train had approached this house, the engineer had blown on the whistle, and every day, as soon as she heard this signal, a woman had appeared on the back porch of the little house and waved to him. At first she had a small child clinging to her skirts, and now this child had grown to full womanhood, and every day she, too, came with her mother to the porch and waved.

The engineer had grown old and gray in service. He had driven his great train, loaded with its weight of lives, across the land ten thousand times. His own children had grown up and married, and four times he had seen before him on the tracks the ghastly dot of tragedy converging like a cannon ball to its eclipse of horror at the boiler head—a light spring wagon filled with children, with its clustered row of small stunned faces; a cheap automobile stalled upon the tracks, set with the wooden figures of people paralyzed with fear; a battered hobo walking by the rail, too deaf and old to hear the whistle's warning; and a form flung past his window with a scream— all this the man had seen and known. He had known all the grief, the joy, the peril and the labor such a man could know; he had grown seamed and weathered in his loyal service, and now, schooled by the qualities of faith and courage and humbleness that attended his labor, he had grown old, and had the grandeur and the wisdom these men have.

But no matter what peril or tragedy he had known, the vision of the little house and the women waving to him with a brave free motion of the arm had become fixed in the mind of the engineer as something beautiful and enduring, something beyond all change and ruin, and something that would always be the same, no matter what mishap, grief or error might break the iron schedule of his days.

The sight of the little house and of these two women gave him the most extraordinary happiness he had ever known. He had seen them in a thousand lights, a hundred weathers. He had seen them through the harsh bare light of wintry gray across the brown and frosted stubble of the earth, and he had seen them again in the green luring sorcery of April.

He felt for them and for the little house in which they lived such tenderness as a man might feel for his own children, and at length the picture of their lives was carved so sharply in his heart that he felt that he knew their lives completely, to every hour and moment of the day, and he resolved that one day, when his years of service should be ended, he would go and find these people and speak at last with them whose lives had been so wrought into his own.

That day came. At last the engineer stepped from a train onto the station platform of the town where these two women lived. His years upon the rail had ended. He was a pensioned servant of his company, with no more work to do. The engineer walked slowly through the station and out into the streets of the town. Everything was as strange to him as if he had never seen this town before. As he walked on, his sense of bewilderment and confusion grew. Could this be the town he had passed ten thousand times? Were these the same houses he had seen so often from the high windows of his cab? It was all as unfamiliar, as disquieting as a city in a dream, and the perplexity of his spirit increased as he went on.

Presently the houses thinned into the straggling outposts of the town, and the street faded into a country road—the one on which the women lived. And the man plodded on slowly in the heat and dust. At length he stood before the house he sought. He knew at once that he had found the proper place. He saw the lordly oaks before the house, the flower beds, the garden and the arbor, and farther off, the glint of rails.

Yes, this was the house he sought, the place he had passed so many times, the destination he had longed for with such happiness. But now that he had found it, now that he was here, why did his hand falter on the gate; why had the town, the road, the earth, the very entrance to this place he loved turned unfamiliar as the landscape of some ugly dream? Why did he now feel this sense of confusion, doubt and hopelessness?

At length he entered by the gate, walked slowly up the path and in a moment more had mounted three short steps that led up to the porch, and was knocking at the door. Presently he heard steps in the hall, the door was opened, and a woman stood facing him.

And instantly, with a sense of bitter loss and grief, he was sorry he had come. He knew at once that the woman who stood there looking at him with a mistrustful eye was the same woman who had waved to him so many thousand times. But her face was harsh and pinched and meager; the flesh sagged wearily in sallow folds, and the small eyes peered at him with timid suspicion and uneasy doubt. All the brave freedom, the warmth and the affection that he had read into her gesture, vanished in the moment that he saw her and heard her unfriendly tongue.

And now his own voice sounded unreal and ghastly to him as he tried to explain his presence, to tell her who he was and the reason he had come. But he faltered on, fighting stubbornly against the horror of regret, confusion, disbelief that surged up in his spirit, drowning all his former joy and making his act of hope and tenderness seem shameful to him.

At length the woman invited him almost unwillingly into the house, and called her daughter in a harsh shrill voice. Then, for a brief agony of time, the man sat in an ugly little parlor, and he tried to talk while the two women stared at him with a dull, bewildered hostility, a sullen, timorous restraint.

And finally, stammering a crude farewell, he departed. He walked away down the path and then along the road toward town, and suddenly he knew that he was an old man. His heart, which had been brave and confident when it looked along the familiar vista of the rails, was now sick with doubt and horror as it saw the strange and unsuspected visage of an earth which had always been within a stone's throw of him, and which he had never seen or known. And he knew that all the magic of that bright lost way, the vista of that shining line, the imagined corner of that small good universe of hope's desire, was gone forever, could never be got back again.

IN THE PARK

THAT year I think we were living with Bella; no, we weren't, I guess we were living with Auntie Kate—well, maybe we were staying with Bella: I don't know, we moved around so much, and it's so long ago. It gets all confused in my mind now; when Daddy was acting he was always on the go, he couldn't be still a minute; sometimes he was playing in New York, and sometimes he went off on a tour with Mr. Mansfield and was gone for months.

Anyway, that night when the show was over we went out onto the street and turned up Broadway. We were both so happy and excited that we fairly bounded along, and that was the way it was that night. It was one of the first fine days in spring, the air was cool and delicate and yet soft, and the sky was of a velvety lilac texture, and it was glittering with great stars. The streets outside the theatre were swarming with hansoms, four-wheelers, private carriages and victorias; they kept driving up in front of the theatre all the time and people kept getting into them.

All of the men looked handsome, and all of the women were beautiful: every one seemed to be as happy and elated as we were, it seemed as if a new world and new people had burst out of the earth with the coming of spring—everything ugly, dull, sour, and harsh had vanished—the streets were flashing with life and sparkle. I saw all of it, I felt myself a part of it all, I wanted to possess it all, and there was something I wanted to say so much it made my throat ache, and yet I could not say it because I could not find the words I wanted. I could not think of anything else to say—it sounded foolish, but suddenly I seized my father's arm and cried: "Oh, to be in April, now that England's there."

"Yes!" he shouted, "Also in Paris, Naples, Rome, and Dresden! Oh, to be in Budapest!" cried Daddy, "now that April's here and the frost is on the pumpkin, and the dawn comes up like thunder out of the night that covers me."

He seemed to have grown young again; he was the way he used to be when I was a little girl and I would knock at his study door and he would call out in a wonderful actor's voice, "Enter, Daughter of Des-o-la-tion, into this abode of mis-er-ee."

His eyes sparkled, and he threw back his head and laughed his wild and happy laugh.

I think that must have been the year before he died; I was about eighteen: I was a beauty—I was like peaches and cream——

In those days when he was acting I used to meet him after the theater and we would go somewhere to eat. *There* was a fellow after your heart: the very best was *just* about good enough for him. New York was awfully nice in those days. They had such nice places to go to—I don't know, they didn't have all this noise and confusion; it seems like another world sometimes. You could go to White's or Martin's or Delmonico's—there were a lot of nice places. There was also a place called Mock's; I never went there, but one of the first things I remember as a child was hearing Daddy come home late at night and say he'd been to Mock's. When he came home, I would listen at the grating of the heater in my room and I could hear him and the other actors talking to my mother: it was fascinating; and sometimes it was all about Mock's. "Oh, have you been to Mock's?" I thought I heard my mother say. "Oh, yes! I have been to Mock's," my father said. "And what did you have at Mock's?" my mother said. "Oh, I had some oysters and a glass of beer and some mock-turtle soup at Mock's," my father said.

We used to go to White's almost every night after the show, with two priests who were friends of Daddy's: Father Dolan and Father Chris O'Rourke. Father Dolan was a big man with the bluest eyes I ever saw, and Father Chris O'Rourke was a little man with a swarthy and greasy face: it was all full of black marks, it was one of the strangest faces I ever saw; but there was something very powerful and sweet about it. Father Dolan was a very fine, high sort of man: he was very kind and jolly, but he also had a fine mind and he was very outspoken and honest. He loved the theatre, he knew a great many actors, a great many of them went to his Church, and he loved my father. He was a great scholar, he knew the plays of Shakespeare almost by heart—he and Daddy used to tag each other's lines, to see who knew the most. I never knew my father to catch him up but once and that was on a line from "King Lear," "The prince of darkness is a gentleman"—Father Dolan said it came from "As You Like It."

How those fellows loved to eat and drink: if one of them had to say Mass the next day we had to hurry, because you can't eat or drink after midnight if you are saying Mass the next day. Because of this, both these priests would immediately take out their watches and lay them on the table before them when they sat down. Father Chris O'Rourke drank nothing but beer and as soon as he sat down a waiter would bring him a half-dozen glasses which he would drink at once. But if these two priests had a glass of beer on the table before them when midnight came, they left it: no matter what it was, no matter whether they'd finished eating or drinking or not, when the stroke of midnight came these fellows quit, if they were going to say Mass the morning after.

Father Chris O'Rourke would eat and drink for almost an hour as if his life depended on it: he was very nearsighted, he wore thick glasses, and from time to time he would seize his watch and bring it right under his nose while he peered and squinted at it. Because of his own hurry to get through before twelve o'clock, he thought every one else must be the same way: he was afraid some one would not get fed, and he was always urging and belaboring people to hurry up and eat. Father Dolan loved to eat, too, but he was a great talker: sometimes he would get to talking to Daddy and forget to eat: when he did this Father Chris O'Rourke would almost go out of his head, he would keep nudging and poking at Father Dolan and pointing at his watch with a look of agony on his face, leaning over and muttering at him in an ominous sort of way, "You're going to be *late!* It's almost *twelve!*"

"Bedad, then!" said Father Dolan, "I'll be late!" He was a big man, but he had a funny little Irish voice; it was very crisp and jolly and had a little chuckling lilt in it, and it seemed to come from a long way off. "I never saw a man like ye, Chris, to be always thinkin' of his belly! Did the great Saints of the Church spend their time guzzlin' and crammin', or did they spend it in meditatin' and prayin' an' mortifyin' their flesh? Did ye never hear of the sin of gluttony?"

"Yis," said Father Chris O'Rourke, "that I have, an' I've also heard of the wicked sin of wanton waste. Shame on ye, Dan Dolan, wit yer talk about the great Saints of the Church: there was niver a great Saint yit that would praise a man for wastin' what the Lord had set before him. Do ye think I'll sit here an' see good food go to waste whin there's poor people all over the world tonight that's goin' without?"

"Well," said Father Dolan, "I've read most of the argyments of the learned reasoners of the Church, as well as the damnable heresies of the infidels, all the way from St. Thomas Aquinas to Spinozey, an' in me young days I could split a hair meself wit the best of them, but in all me life I niver heard the beat of that one: it makes Aristotle look like Wordsworth's Idiot Boy. Bedad, if ye can prove what ye're doin' wit yer gorgin' is feedin' the poor all over the earth, I won't put anything past yer powers of reasonin', Chris—ye could show the Pope that Darwin was a Jesuit, an' he'd believe ye!"

Well, as I say, when we got to the restaurant the first thing Father Chris O'Rourke would do was to lay his watch upon the table, and the first thing Daddy would do was to order two or three bottles of champagne: they used to know we were coming and it would be waiting for us in great silver buckets full of ice. Then Daddy would pick up the menu—it was a great big card simply covered with the most delicious things to eat, and he would frown and look serious and clear his throat, and say to Father Dolan, "What does the pontificial palate crave, Dan?"

After the play, that night, we went to White's and these two priests were waiting for us when we got there. A little later Mr. Gates came in—he's still alive, I saw him on the street the other day, he's getting quite old. He was married to one of the most beautiful women you ever saw, and she was burned to death in an automobile accident. He saw the thing happen right under his eyes: isn't that the most horrible thing you ever heard of? Well, you could tell by the way Mr.

Gates walked that he was awfully excited about something: he was another of those great fat fellows, and you could see his old jowls quivering as he came.

"Good God!" said Daddy, "here comes Bunny with a full head of steam on!"

Mr. Gates began to speak to Daddy half across the room, all of the people stopped and stared at him.

"Joe! Joe!" he said—he had a funny hoarse kind of voice, one of those foggy whiskey voices; I think he drank a good deal. "Joe, do you know what I've done? I've just bought a horseless carriage. Come on! You're going for a ride with me!"

"Now, wait! Wait! Wait!" said Daddy, holding up his hand just like an actor. "Not so fast, Bunny! Sit down and have a bite to eat first, and tell us about it. When did you do this desperate deed?"

"Today," Mr. Gates said in a sort of hoarse whisper. "Do you suppose I've done right?"

He looked around at us with his old eyes simply bulging out of his head and with a sort of scared look on his face. Oh! We laughed so much about it: Father Dolan began to laugh, and Daddy had to pound him on the back, he got to coughing so!

Mr. Gates was an awfully nice man: he was a great fat fellow, but he was so handsome; there was something so delicate about him, his mouth kept trembling and twitching so when he was excited and wanted to say something. I think that was why they called him Bunny.

So Daddy said, "Sit down and have something to eat and then we'll see."

Mr. Gates said, "Say, Joe, I've got the mechanic outside here, and I don't know what to do with him."

"You mean you hired him for keeps?" Daddy said.

"Yes," Mr. Gates said, "and I'm damned if I'm not embarrassed! I don't know what to do with him. I mean, what is his social standing?"

"Does he wash?" Daddy said.

"Well," said Mr. Gates, looking at Father Dolan, "I think he uses holy water."

"Oh, Mr. Gates!" I said. "How awful! Right before Father Dolan, too!"

But Father Dolan laughed just as I knew he would: he was another great fat fellow, he was an awfully nice man. Father Chris O'Rourke laughed, too, but I don't think he liked it so much.

"I mean," Mr. Gates said, "I don't know how to treat the man. Is he above me, or below me, or what?"

"It looks to me," Daddy said, "as if he were on top of you. I think you've gone and got yourself saddled with a black elephant."

Daddy was so wonderful like that, everybody loved him. Mr. Gates was so worried about the driver: it all seems so funny now to think back on it—he didn't know whether the man was to eat at the table with his family, and be treated like one of them, or what. There was something so delicate about Mr. Gates: he was big and fat, but a very sensitive, fine person.

"It looks like a neat little problem in social etiquette, Bunny," Daddy said. "Well, let's have him in here for a bite to eat. We'll see what he looks like."

So Mr. Gates went out and got him, and pretty soon he came back with him, and he was really an awfully nice young fellow: he had a little mustache, and he wore a Norfolk jacket and a flat cap, and everybody stared so, and nudged each other, he was awfully embarrassed. But Daddy was wonderful with people, he made him feel right at home. He said, "Sit down, young fellow. If we're going to run an engine we've got to feed the driver."

So he sat down, and we had a wonderful meal: you'd get great juicy chops in that place, cooked in butter, and steaks an inch thick, and the most marvellous oysters and sea food.

I know it was pretty late in the season, but we started off with oysters and champagne: I don't think the young fellow was used to drinking. Daddy kept filling up the young fellow's glass, and he got quite drunk. He was awfully funny, he kept talking about his responsibility.

"It's a terrible responsibility to know that all these lives are dependent on you," he said; then Daddy would fill up his glass again.

"A moment's hesitation in a crisis," he said, "and all is lost."

"A truer word was never spoken," said Daddy, and he filled his glass up again.

"A man must have a clear brain and a steady hand," he said.

"Right you are," said Daddy. "This will make you so steady, son, that you will get practically paralyzed."

Mr. Gates and Father Dolan laughed so much that the tears began to trickle down their cheeks. Oh, we had an awfully good time in those days, there was something so innocent about everything.

Then we all got up to go, and I was really quite nervous: the poor kid could hardly stand up, and I didn't know what was going to happen. Daddy was so happy and excited, there was something so wild about him, his eyes danced like devils, and he threw back his head and laughed, and you could hear him all over the place.

Father Chris O'Rourke had to hold Mass the next morning, and he left us, but Father Dolan came along. We all went outside, with the young man being helped along by Daddy and Mr. Gates, and every one in the restaurant followed us outside, and Mr. Gates told me to sit up front beside the driver. God, I was proud! And Daddy and Mr. Gates and Father Dolan got in behind; how they ever did it I don't know, it must have been awfully small—I think Daddy must have sat on Father Dolan's lap. Oh, yes! I know he did.

And everybody cheered as we started off: the actors followed us out of the restaurant and stood looking after us as we drove off into the lilac and velvet darkness, and I can still remember how I looked back and saw their smiling and unnatural faces, their bright masks, their lonely and haunted eyes. They kept shouting funny things at Daddy and asking if he had any last messages, and De Wolfe Hopper was there and he ran around pretending to be a horse and neighing, and trying to climb up a lamp-post. Oh, it was thrilling!

So Mr. Gates said, "Whither away, Joe?"

And Daddy said, "To the Golden Gate and may she never stop!"

Then Daddy said to the young fellow who was driving, "How fast can she go, son?" and the young fellow said, "She can do twenty miles an hour without any trouble."

"Downhill, you mean," said Daddy just to tease him, so we started to go, and God! I was thrilled! It seemed to me we were flying. I suppose he did go twenty miles an hour, but it seemed like a hundred would now and we passed a policeman on a horse and the horse got frightened and tried to run away and God! the cop was so mad: he came galloping after us and shouted for us to stop, and Daddy laughed just like a crazy man and said, "Go on, son! Go on! There's not a horse in the world can catch you!"

But the young fellow was scared and he slowed down and then the cop came up and said what did we mean, and where did we think we were, and he'd a good mind to put us all under arrest for disturbing the peace at that hour of night, with "that thing"; he kept calling it "that thing" in such a scornful way, and I got so angry at him, I thought it was so beautiful, it was painted the richest kind of winey red, it looked good enough to eat, and I was so mad to think the man should talk that way.

I don't know why it made me mad, but I think the reason must have been that the car didn't seem to me like a thing at all. It's hard to tell you how it was, but it was almost as if the car were some strange and beautiful and living creature which we had never known before but which now gave to all our lives a kind of added joy and warmth and wonder. And I believe that was the way it was with those first motor cars. Somehow each one of them seemed different from all the others, each one seemed to have a different name, a separate life and personality; and although I know they would look crude and funny and old-fashioned now, it was all different then. We had never seen or known them in the world before, we had only dreamed or heard they could exist, and now that I was riding in one, it all seemed unbelievable and yet gloriously real and strange, as every beautiful thing is when it first happens to you. The car was as magical to me as if it had come out of some other world like Mars, and yet the very moment that I saw it I seemed to have known about it always, and it seemed to belong to that day, that hour, that year, somehow to be a part of all that happened that night; to belong to Daddy and the priests and Mr. Gates, the young mechanic and all the haunted faces of the actors, and to all the songs we sang that year, the things we did and said, and something strange and innocent and lost and long ago.

I can remember now the way the old car looked, so well that I could close my eyes and draw it for you. I can remember its rich wine color, its great polished lamps of brass, the door that opened in its round, fat back, and all its wonderful and exciting smells— the strong and comforting smell of its deep leather, and the smells of gasoline and oil and grease that were so strong and warm and pungent that they seemed to give a kind of thrilling life and ecstasy to everything in the whole world. They seemed to hold the unknown promise of something wonderful and strange that was about to happen and that belonged to the night, and to the mystery and joy of life, the ecstasy of the lilac dark, as all the smells of flowers and leaf and grass and earth belonged to them.

So I guess that was the reason that I got so mad when I heard the policeman call the car "that thing," although I did not know the reason then. It looked as if the cop were going to run us in, but then Daddy got up out of Father Dolan's lap, and when the cop saw Father Dolan of course he got very nice to us: and Mr. Gates talked to him and gave him some money, and Daddy joked with him and made him laugh, and then Daddy showed him his police badge and asked him if he knew Big Jake Dietz at police headquarters, and told him he was one of Jake's best friends, and then I was so proud to see the way the cop came round.

And the cop said for us all to go into Central Park and we could ride all we damn please for all he cared, but you wouldn't catch him in one of those things, they'd blow up on you at any moment and then where'd you all be? And Daddy said he hoped we'd all be in Heaven, and what's more we'd take our own priest with us, so there'd be no hitch in any of the formalities, and we all got so tickled and began to laugh and the cop did too, and then he began to brag about his horse, and God! it *was* a beautiful horse, and he said give him a horse always, that they'd never make one of those things that could go faster than a horse. The poor fellow! I wonder what he'd say now!

And Daddy teased him and said the time would come when you'd have to go to the zoo to see a horse, and the policeman said by that time you'd have to go to a junk-shop to see a motor-car, and Daddy said, "The trouble with us is that we're anachronisms." And the policeman said, well, he didn't know about that, but he wished us luck and hoped we all got out of it alive.

So he rode off and we drove into Central Park and started off as hard as we could go and began to climb a hill, when sure enough, we broke down just as the policeman said we would. I guess the young fellow may have had too much to drink, he seemed wild and excited, but anyway we saw a hansom halfway up the hill in front of us and he cried out, "Watch me pass them," and did something to the car, and just as we got up even with them and were trying to go by, the car coughed and spluttered and stood still. Well, we could hear the people in the hansom laughing, and one of them shouted something back to us about the tortoise and the hare. And I felt so mad at them and so humiliated and so sorry for our driver, and Daddy said, "Never mind, son, the race may not always be to the swift, but even the hare will sometimes have his day."

But our young fellow felt so bad he couldn't say a word. He got out of the car and walked round and round it, and finally he began to explain to us the way it happened and how it could never happen again in a hundred years. And well, you see it was this way, and well, you see it was that. And we didn't understand a word of what he was saying, but we felt so sorry for him that we told him he was right. So he began to poke around inside of it, and then he would turn something here and twist something there, and grab the crank and whirl it round and round until I was afraid he was going to wring his arm off. Then he would get down on his back and crawl in under it and bang and hammer at something underneath. And nothing happened. Then he would get up and walk round and round the car again and mutter to himself. Finally, he gave up and said he was afraid we'd have to get out of the car and take a hansom if we wanted to get home without walking. So we started to get out, and the mechanic was so mad and so embarrassed at the way his car had acted that he grabbed it and shook it as if it were a brat. And nothing happened.

He gave it one last try. He grabbed the crank like a crazy man and began to whirl it round and round until he was exhausted. And when nothing happened he suddenly shouted out, "Oh, damn that thing," kicked it in the tire as hard as he could, and collapsed across the radiator, sobbing as if his heart would break. And I don't know what that did to it or how it happened, but suddenly the car began to chug and wheeze again, and there we were ready to go, and the young fellow with a grin that stretched from ear to ear.

So we went on up that hill and coasted down the next, and now we really seemed to fly. It was like soaring through the air, or finding wings you never knew you had before. It was like something we had always known about and dreamed of finding, and now we had it like a dream come true. And I suppose we must have gone the whole way round the park from one end to another, but none of us really knew how far we went or where we were going. It was like that kind of flight you make in dreams, and sure enough, just like something you are waiting for in a dream, we came tearing around a curve in the road and there before us we could see the same hansom we had tried to pass upon the hill. And the minute that I saw it I knew that it was bound to happen, it seemed too good to be true, and yet I had felt sure all the time that it was going to turn out just this way. And that was the way it was with all of us, we threw back our heads and roared with laughter, we yelled and waved our hands at all the people in the cab, we went tearing by them as if they were rooted to the earth, and as we passed them Daddy turned and shouted back at them, "Cheer up, my friends, they also serve who only stand and wait."

So we passed them by and left them far behind us and they were lost; and now there was nothing all around us but the night, the blazing stars, the lilac darkness in the park, and God! but it was beautiful. It was just the beginning of May and all the leaves and buds were coming out, they had that tender feathery look, and there was just a little delicate shaving of moon in the sky, and it was so cool and lovely, with the smell of the leaves, and the new grass, and all the flowers bursting from the earth till you could hear them grow: it seemed to me the loveliest thing that I had ever known, and when I looked at my father, his eyes were full of tears and he cried out, "Glory! Oh, glory! Glory!" and then he began in his magnificent voice, "What a piece of work is a man! how noble in reason! how infinite in faculty! in form and moving how express and admirable! in action how like an angel! in apprehension how like a god!"

And the words were so lovely, the music was so grand, that somehow it made me want to cry, and when he had finished he cried out, "Glory!" once again, and I saw his wild and beautiful brow there in the darkness, and I turned my eyes up toward the sky and there were the tragic and magnificent stars, and a kind of fate was on his head and in his eyes, and suddenly as I looked at him I knew that he was going to die.

And he cried, "Glory! Glory!" and we rode all through the night, and round and round the park, and then dawn came, and all of the birds began to sing. And now the bird-song broke in the first light, and suddenly I heard each sound the bird-song made. It came to me like music I had always heard, it came to me like music I had always known, the sounds of which I never yet had spoken, and now I heard the music of each sound as clear and bright as gold, and the music of each sound was this: at first it rose above me like a flight of shot, and then I heard the sharp, fast skaps of sound the bird-song made. And now they were smooth drops and nuggets of bright gold, and now with chittering bicker and fast-fluttering skirrs of sound the palmy, honied bird-cries came. And now the bird-tree sang, all filled with lutings in bright air; the thrum, the lark's wing, and tongue-trilling chirrs arose. And now the little brainless cries arose, with liquorous, liquefied lutings, with lirruping chirp, plum-bellied smoothness, sweet lucidity. And now I heard the rapid kweet-kweet-kweet-kweet-kweet of homely birds, and then their pwee-pwee-pwee: others had thin metallic tongues, a sharp cricketing stitch, and high shrew's caws, with eery rasp, with hard, far calls—these were the sounds the bird-cries made. All birds that are awake in the park's woodland tangles; and above them passed the whirr of hidden wings, the strange lost cry of the unknown birds in full light now in the park, the sweet confusion of their cries was mingled. "Sweet is the breath of morn, her rising sweet with charm of earliest birds," and it was just like that, and the sun came up, and it was like the first day of the world, and that was the year before he died and I think we were staying at Bella's then, but maybe we were staying at the old hotel, or perhaps we had already moved to Auntie Kate's: we moved around so much, we lived so many places, it seems so long ago, that when I try to think about it now it gets confused and I cannot remember.

FROM

THE WEB AND THE ROCK

THE MASS OF manuscript which Wolfe delivered to Edward C. Aswell in May, 1938, and from which Aswell fashioned the posthumously published books represented an ordering of material on which Wolfe had been working but not a book or series of books prepared for the press. Wolfe estimated that at least a year's work would be required before the first volume of the new work would be ready. The first of the three books which Aswell extracted from the manuscript was *The Web and the Rock* (New York: Harper and Brothers, 1939).

In this novel the protagonist is George Webber, who is physically quite different from Eugene Gant but whose life story and emotional and intellectual characteristics are very close to those of the earlier figure. *The Web and the Rock* tells the story of Webber from his childhood in Libya Hill, in the mountains of Old Catawba, through his years at Pine Rock College, to his mature life in New York City. There he falls in love with Esther Jack, and the affair is a tormented and tempestuous one. At the conclusion of the book he is in Munich and is brought to a kind of self-knowledge through a fight at the October Fair.

Although Aswell had to do a major job of assembling and weaving material together in making *The Web and the Rock*, the general pattern of the completed work is very close to what Wolfe would probably have made it had he lived, even though the last 200 pages are in his earlier and more extravagant style rather than the sparser style of the opening sections.

The selections which follow from *The Web and the Rock* are representative of the childhood experiences of George Webber in "The Child by Tiger," of his early days as a dreaming provincial in the city in "Alone," and of his experiences at the Munich Fair and the self-knowledge that comes from them in "Oktoberfest."

"The Child by Tiger," one of Wolfe's very best short stories, was originally published in the *Saturday Evening Post* on September 11, 1937. It is a powerfully symbolic tale of the child's awareness of evil, based very closely upon an event which had occurred in Asheville when Wolfe was six years old.

"Alone" is an almost archetypal expression of the dreams of the American small-town boy in the great city, on "the Enfabled Rock," dreaming of endless and fantastic conquest. It is illuminating to compare that vision of the city and its promise with the picture of "The Hollow Men" that comes later in *You Can't Go Home Again*.

The selection here entitled "Oktoberfest" consists of Chapter 47, "A Visit to the Fair" (originally published under the title "Oktoberfest" in *Scribner's Magazine,* June, 1937) , Chapter 48, "The Hospital," and Chapter 50, "The Looking Glass." It presents a powerfully evocative picture of the Munich October Fair and, in the final dialogue of body and soul, a statement of George Webber's reconciliation to the conditions of earth.

The text of "The Child by Tiger" is from *The Web and the Rock,* pages 132-156; that of "Alone," pages 273-293; and that of "Oktoberfest," pages 662-679, 689-695.

THE CHILD BY TIGER

ONE DAY after school, Monk and several of the boys were playing with a football in the yard at Randy Shepperton's. Randy was calling signals and handling the ball. Nebraska Crane was kicking it. Augustus Potterham was too clumsy to run or kick or pass, so they put him at center where all he'd have to do would be to pass the ball back to Randy when he got the signal. To the other boys, Gus Potterham was their freak child, their lame duck, the butt of their jokes and ridicule, but they also had a sincere affection for him; he was something to be taken in hand, to be protected and cared for.

There were several other boys who were ordinarily members of their group. They had Harry Higginson and Sam Pennock, and two boys named Howard Jarvis and Jim Redmond. It wasn't enough to make a team, of course. They didn't have room enough to play a game even if they had had team enough. What they played was really a kind of skeletonized practice game, with Randy and Nebraska back, Gus at center, two other fellows at the ends, and Monk and two or three more on the other side, whose duty was to get in and "break it up" if they could.

It was about four o'clock in the afternoon, late in October, and there was a smell of smoke, of leaves, of burning in the air. Bras had just kicked to Monk. It was a good kick too—a high, soaring punt that spiraled out above Monk's head, behind him. He ran back and tried to get it, but it was far and away "over the goal line" —that is to say, out in the street. It hit the street and bounded back and forth with that peculiarly erratic bounce a football has.

The ball rolled away from Monk down towards the corner. He was running out to get it when Dick Prosser, Shepperton's new Negro man, came along, gathered it up neatly in his great black paw, and tossed it to him. Dick turned in then, and came on around the house, greeting the boys as he came. He called all of them "Mister" except Randy, and Randy was always "Cap'n"—"Cap'n Shepperton." This formal address—"Mr." Crane, "Mr." Potterham, "Mr." Webber, "Cap'n" Shepperton—pleased them immensely, gave them a feeling of mature importance and authority.

"Cap'n Shepperton" was splendid! It was something more to all of them than a mere title of respect. It had a delightful military association, particularly when Dick Prosser said it. Dick had served a long enlistment in the U.S. army. He had been a member of a regiment of crack Negro troops upon the Texas border, and the stamp of the military man was evident in everything he did. It was a joy just to watch him split up kindling. He did it with a power, a clean precision, a kind of military order, that was astounding. Every stick he cut seemed to be exactly the same length and shape as every other. He had all of them neatly stacked against the walls of the Shepperton basement with such regimented faultlessness that it almost seemed a pity to disturb their symmetry for the use for which they were intended.

It was the same with everything else he did. His little whitewashed basement room was as spotless as a barracks room. The bare board floor was always cleanly swept, a plain, bare table and a plain, straight chair were stationed exactly in the center of the room. On the table there was always just one object—an old Bible with a limp cover, almost worn out by constant use, for Dick was a deeply religious man. There was a little cast-iron stove and a little wooden box with a few lumps of coal and a neat stack of kindling in it. And against the wall, to the left, there was an iron cot, always precisely made and covered cleanly with a coarse grey blanket.

The Sheppertons were delighted with him. He had come there looking for work just a month or two before, "gone around to the back door" and modestly presented his qualifications. He had, he said, only recently received his discharge from the army, and was eager to get employment, at no matter what wage. He could cook, he could tend the furnace, he could do odd jobs, he was handy at carpentry, he knew how to drive a car—in fact, it seemed to the boys that there was very little that Dick Prosser could not do.

He could certainly shoot. He gave a modest demonstration of his prowess one afternoon, with Randy's "twenty-two, that left them gasping. He just lifted that little rifle in his powerful black hands as if it were a toy, without seeming to take aim, pointed it towards a strip of tin on which they had crudely marked out some bull's-eye circles, and he simply peppered the center of the bull's eye, putting twelve holes through a space one inch square, so fast they could not even count the shots.

He knew how to box, too. Randy said he had been a regimental champion. At any rate, he was as cunning and crafty as a cat. He never boxed with the boys, of course, but Randy had two sets of gloves, and Dick used to coach them while they sparred. There was something amazingly tender and watchful about him. He taught them many things, how to lead, to hook, to counter, and to block, but he was careful to see that they did not hurt each other. Nebraska, who was the most powerful of the lot, could hit like a mule. He would have killed Gus Potterham in his simple, honest way if he had ever been given a free hand. But Dick, with his quick watchfulness, his gentle and persuasive tact, was careful to see this did not happen.

He knew about football, too, and that day, as Dick passed the boys, he paused, a powerful, respectable-looking Negro of thirty years or more, and watched them for a moment as they played.

Randy took the ball and went up to him.

"How do you hold it, Dick?" he said. "Is this right?"

Dick watched him attentively as he gripped the ball and held it back above his shoulder. The Negro nodded approvingly and said:

"That's right, Cap'n Shepperton. You've got it. Only," he said gently, and now took the ball in his own powerful hand, "when you gits a little oldah, yo' handses gits biggah and you gits a bettah grip."

His own great hand, in fact, seemed to hold the ball as easily as if it were an apple. And, holding it so a moment, he brought it back, aimed over his outstretched left hand as if he were pointing a gun, and rifled it in a beautiful, whizzing spiral thirty yards or more to Gus. He then showed them how to kick, how to get the ball off of the toe in such a way that it would rise and spiral cleanly.

He showed them how to make a fire, how to pile the kindling, where to place the coal, so that the flames shot up cone-wise, cleanly, without smoke or waste. He showed them how to strike a match with the thumbnail of one hand and keep and hold the flame in the strongest wind. He showed them how to lift a weight, how to "tote" a burden on their shoulders in the easiest way. There was nothing that he did not know. They were all so proud of him. Mr. Shepperton himself declared that Dick was the best man he'd ever had, the smartest darky that he'd ever known.

And yet? He went too softly, at too swift a pace. He was there upon them sometimes like a cat. Looking before them sometimes, seeing nothing but the world before them, suddenly they felt a shadow at their back, and, looking up, would find that Dick was there. And there was something moving in the night. They never saw him come or go. Sometimes they would waken, startled, and feel that they had heard a board creak, the soft clicking of a latch, a shadow passing swiftly. All was still.

"Young white fokes—O young white gentlemen"—his soft voice ending in a moan, a kind of rhythm in his lips—"O young white fokes, I'se tellin' *you*—" that soft, low moan again—"you gotta love each othah like a brothah." He was deeply religious and went to church three times a week. He read his Bible every night.

Sometimes Dick would come out of his little basement room and his eyes would be red, as if he had been weeping. They would know, then, that he had been reading his Bible. There would be times when he would almost moan when he talked to them, a kind of hymnal chant, a religious ecstasy, that came from some deep intoxication of the spirit, and that transported him. For the boys, it was a troubling and bewildering experience. They tried to laugh it off and make jokes about it. But there was something in it so dark and strange and full of a feeling they could not fathom that their jokes were hollow, and the trouble in their minds and in their hearts remained.

Sometimes on these occasions his speech would be made up of some weird jargon of Biblical phrases and quotations and allusions, of which he seemed to have hundreds, and which he wove together in the strange pattern of his emotion in a sequence that was mean-ingless to them but to which he himself had the coherent clue.

"O young white fokes," he would begin, moaning gently, "de dry bones in de valley. I tell you, white fokes, de day is comin' when He's comin' on dis earth again to sit in judgment. He'll put de sheep upon de right hand and de goats upon de left—O white fokes, white fokes—de Armageddon day's a-comin, white fokes—an' de dry bones in de valley."

Or again, they could hear him singing as he went about his work, in his deep, rich voice, so full of warmth and strength, so full of Africa, singing hymns that were not only of his own race, but that were familiar to them all. They didn't know where he learned them. Perhaps they were remembered from his army days. Perhaps he had learned them in the service of former masters. He drove the Sheppertons to church on Sunday morning, and would wait for them throughout the service. He would come up to the side door of the church while the service was going on, neatly dressed in his good, dark suit, holding his chauffeur's hat respectfully in his hand, and stand there humbly and listen during the course of the entire sermon.

And then when the hymns were sung, and the great rich sound would swell and roll out into the quiet air of Sunday, Dick would stand and listen, and sometimes he would join quietly in the song. A number of these favorite hymns the boys heard him singing many times in a low, rich voice as he went about his work around the house. He would sing "Who Follows in His Train?"—or "Alexander's Glory Song," or "Rock of Ages," or "Onward, Christian Soldiers."

And yet? Well, nothing happened—there was just "a flying hint from here and there"—and the sense of something passing in the night.

Turning into the Square one day, as Dick was driving Mr. Shepperton to town, Lon Pilcher skidded murderously around the corner, side-swiped Dick, and took the fender off. The Negro was out of the car like a cat and got his master out. Mr. Shepperton was unhurt. Lon Pilcher climbed out and reeled across the street, drunk as a sot in mid-afternoon. He swunk viciously, clumsily, at the Negro, smashed him in the face. Blood trickled from the fat black nostrils and from the thick, liver-colored lips. Dick did not move. But suddenly the whites of his eyes were shot with red, his bleeding lips bared for a moment over the white ivory of his teeth. Lon smashed at him again. The Negro took it full in the face again; his hands twitched slightly but he did not move. They collared the drunken sot and hauled him off and locked him up. Dick stood there for a moment, then he wiped his face and turned to see what damage had been done to the car. No more now, but there were those who saw it, who remembered later how the eyes went red.

Another thing. The Sheppertons had a cook named Pansy Harris. She was a comely Negro wench, young, plump, black as the ace of spades, a good-hearted girl with a deep dimple in her cheeks and faultless teeth, bared in a most engaging smile. No one ever saw

Dick speak to her. No one ever saw her glance at him, or him at her—and yet that dimpled, plump, and smilingly good-natured wench became as mournful-silent and as silent-sullen as midnight pitch. She sang no more. No more was seen the gleaming ivory of her smile. No more was heard the hearty and infectious exuberance of her warm, full-throated laugh. She went about her work as mournfully as if she were going to a funeral. The gloom deepened all about her. She answered sullenly now when spoken to.

One night towards Christmas she announced that she was leaving. In response to all entreaties, all efforts to find the reason for her sudden and unreasonable decision. She had no answer except a sullen repetition of the assertion that she had to leave. Repeated questionings did finally wring from her a statement that her husband wanted her to quit, that he needed her at home. More than this she would not say, and even this excuse was highly suspected, because her husband was a Pullman porter, home only two days a week, and well accustomed to do himself such housekeeping tasks as she might do for him.

The Sheppertons were fond of her. The girl had been with them for several years. They tried again to find the reason for her leaving. Was she dissatisfied? "No'm"—an implacable monosyllable, mournful, unrevealing as the night. Had she been offered a better job elsewhere? "No'm"—as untelling as before. If they offered her more wages, would she stay with them? "No'm"—again and again, sullen and unyielding; until finally the exasperated mistress threw her hands up in a gesture of defeat and said: "All right then, Pansy. Have it your own way, if that's the way you feel. Only for heaven's sake, don't leave us in the lurch. Don't leave us until we get another cook."

This, at length, with obvious reluctance, the girl agreed to. Then, putting on her hat and coat, and taking the paper bag of "leavings" she was allowed to take home with her at night, she went out the kitchen door and made her sullen and morose departure.

This was on Saturday night, a little after eight o'clock.

That same afternoon Randy and Monk had been fooling around the Shepperton basement, and, seeing that Dick's door was slightly ajar, they stopped at the opening and looked in to see if he was there. The little room was empty, and swept and spotless as it had always been.

But they did not notice that! That saw *it!* At the same moment their breaths caught sharply in a gasp of startled wonderment. Randy was the first to speak.

"Look!" he whispered. "Do you see it?"

See it? Monk's eyes were glued upon it. Had he found himself staring suddenly at the flat head of a rattlesnake his hypnotized surprise could have been no greater. Squarely across the bare boards of the table, blue-dull, deadly in its murderous efficiency, lay an automatic army rifle. They both knew the type. They had seen them all when Randy went to buy his little "twenty-two" at Uncle Morris Teitlebaum's. Beside it was a box containing one hundred rounds of ammunition, and behind it, squarely in the center, face downward, open on the table, was the familiar cover of Dick's old, worn Bible.

Then he was on them like a cat. He was there like a great, dark shadow before they knew it. They turned, terrified. He was there above them, his thick lips bared above his gums, his eyes gone small and red as rodents'.

"Dick!" Randy gasped, and moistened his dry lips. "Dick!" he fairly cried now.

It was all over like a flash. Dick's mouth closed. They could see the whites of his eyes again. He smiled and said softly, affably, "Yes suh, Cap'n Shepperton. Yes suh! You gent-mum lookin' at my riflle?"—and he stepped across the sill into the room.

Monk gulped and nodded his head and couldn't say a word, and Randy whispered. "Yes." And both of them still stared at him with an expression of appalled and fascinated interest.

Dick shook his head and chuckled. "Can't do without my rifle, white fokes. No suh!" He shook his head good-naturedly again. "Ole Dick, he's—he's—he's an ole *ahmy* man, you know. He's gotta have his rifle. If they take his rifle away from him, why that's jest lak takin' candy away from a little baby. Yes suh!" he chuckled again, and picked the weapon up affectionately. "Ole Dick felt Christmas comin' on—he—he—I reckon he must have felt it in his bones," he chuckled, "so I been savin' up my money—I jest thought I'd hide this heah and keep it as a big surprise fo' the young white fokes," he said. "I was jest gonna put it away heah and keep it un-twill Christmas morning. Then I was gonna take the young white fokes out an show 'em how to shoot."

They had begun to breathe more easily now, and, almost as if they were under the spell of the Pied Piper of Hamelin, they had followed him step by step into the room.

"Yes suh," Dick chuckled, "I was jest fixin' to hide this gun away and keep it hid twill Christmas day, but Cap'n Shepperton—hee!" he chuckled heartily and slapped his thigh—"you can't fool ole Cap'n Shepperton! He was too quick fo' me. He jest musta've smelled this ole gun right out. He comes right in and sees it befo' I has a chance to tu'n around. . . . Now, white fokes," Dick's voice fell to a tone of low and winning confidence, "Ah's hopin' that I'd git to keep this gun as a little surprise fo' you. Now that you's found out, I'll tell you what I'll do. If you'll jest keep it a surprise from the other white fokes twill Christmas day, I'll take all you gent'mun out and let you shoot it. Now cose," he went on quietly, with a shade of resignation, "if you want to tell on me you can—but"—here his voice fell again, with just the faintest yet most elo-quent shade of sorrowful regret—"Ole Dick was lookin' fahwad to this. He was hopin' to give all the white fokes a surprise Christmas day."

They promised earnestly that they would keep his secret as if it were their own. They fairly whispered their solemn vow. They tip-toed away out of the little basement room, as if they were afraid their very footsteps might betray the partner of their confidence.

This was four o'clock on Saturday afternoon. Already, there was a somber moaning of the wind, grey storm clouds sweeping over. The threat of snow was in the air.

Snow fell that night. It began at six o'clock. It came howling down across the hills. It swept in on them from the Smokies. By seven o'clock the air was blind with sweeping snow, the earth was carpeted, the streets were numb. The storm howled on, around houses warm with crackling fires and shaded light. All life seemed to have withdrawn into thrilling isolation. A horse went by upon the street with muffled hoofs.

George Webber went to sleep upon this mystery, lying in the

darkness, listening to that exultancy of storm, to that dumb wonder, that enormous and attentive quietness of snow, with something
dark and jubilant in his soul he could not utter.

Snow in the South is wonderful. It has a kind of magic and a
mystery that it has nowhere else. And the reason for this is that it
comes to people in the South not as the grim, unyielding tenant of
the Winter's keep, but as a strange and wild visitor from the secret
North. It comes to them from darkness, to their own special and
most secret soul there in the South. It brings to them the thrilling
isolation of its own white mystery. It brings them something that
they lack, and that they have to have; something that they have lost,
but now have found; something that they have known utterly, but
had forgotten until now.

In every man there are two hemispheres of light and dark, two
worlds discrete, two countries of his soul's adventure. And one of
these is the dark land, the other half of his heart's home, the unvisited domain of his father's earth.

And this is the land he knows the best. It is the earth unvisited—
and it is his, as nothing he has seen can ever be. It is the world
intangible that he has never touched—yet more his own than something he has owned forever. It is the great world of his mind, his
heart, his spirit, built there in his imagination, shaped by wonder
and unclouded by the obscuring flaws of accident and actuality,
the proud, unknown earth of the lost, the found, the never-here,
the ever-real America, unsullied, true, essential, built there in the
brain, and shaped to glory by the proud and flaming vision of a
child.

Thus, at the head of those two poles of life will lie the real, the
truthful image of its immortal opposite. Thus, buried in the dark
heart of the cold and secret North, abides forever the essential
image of the South; thus, at the dark heart of the moveless South,
there burns forever the immortal splendor of the North.

So had it always been with George. The other half of his heart's
home, the world unknown that he knew the best, was the dark
North. And snow swept in that night across the hills, demonic visi-
tant, to restore that land to him, to sheet it in essential wonder.
Upon this mystery he fell asleep.

A little after two o'clock next morning he was awakened by the ringing of a bell. It was the fire bell of the City Hall, and it was beating an alarm—a hard, fast stroke that he had never heard before. Bronze with peril, clangorous through the snow-numbed silence of the air, it had a quality of instancy and menace he had never known before. He leaped up and ran to the window to look for the telltale glow against the sky. But it was no fire. Almost before he looked, those deadly strokes beat in upon his brain the message that this was no alarm for fire. It was a savage, brazen tongue calling the town to action, warning mankind against the menace of some peril—secret, dark, unknown, greater than fire or flood could ever be.

He got instantly, in the most overwhelming and electric way, the sense that the whole town had come to life. All up and down the street the houses were beginning to light up. Next door, the Shepperton house was ablaze with light, from top to bottom. Even as he looked Mr. Shepperton, wearing an overcoat over his pajamas, ran down the steps and padded out across the snow-covered walk towards the street.

People were beginning to run out of doors. He heard excited cries and shouts and questions everywhere. He saw Nebraska Crane come pounding up the middle of the street. He knew that he was coming for him and Randy. As Bras ran by Shepperton's he put his fingers to his mouth and whistled piercingly. It was a signal they all knew.

Monk was already almost dressed by the time he came running in across the front yard. He hammered at the door; Monk was already there. They both spoke at once. He had answered Monk's startled question before he got it out.

"Come on!" he said, panting with excitement, his Cherokee black eyes burning with an intensity Monk had never seen before. "Come on!" he cried. They were halfway out across the yard by now. "It's that nigger! He's gone crazy and is running wild!"

"Wh-wh-what nigger?" Monk gasped, pounding at his heels.

Even before he spoke Monk had the answer. Mr. Crane had already come out of his house and crossed the street, buttoning his heavy policeman's overcoat and buckling his girdle as he came. He had paused to speak for a moment to Mr. Shepperton, and Monk heard Mr. Shepperton say quickly, in a low voice:

"Which way did he go?"

Then he heard somebody cry, "It's that nigger of Shepperton's!"

Mr. Shepperton turned and went quickly back across his yard towards the house. His wife and two girls stood huddled in the open doorway. The snow had drifted in across the porch. The three women stood there, white, trembling, holding themselves together, their arms thrust in the wide sleeves of their kimonos.

The telephone in Shepperton's house was ringing like mad but no one was paying any attention to it. Monk heard Mrs. Shepperton say quickly as her husband ran up the steps, "Is it Dick?" He nodded and passed her brusquely, going towards the phone.

At this moment, Nebraska whistled piercingly again upon his fingers, and Randy Shepperton ran past his mother and sped down the steps. She called sharply to him. He paid no attention to her. When he came up, Monk saw that his fine, thin face was white as a sheet. He looked at Monk and whispered:

"It's—it's Dick!" And in a moment, "They say he's killed four people!"

"With—?" Monk couldn't finish.

Randy nodded dumbly, and they both stared there for a minute, two white-faced boys, aware now of the full and murderous significance of the secret they had kept, the confidence they had not violated, with a sudden sense of guilt and fear as if somehow the crime lay on their shoulders.

Across the street a window banged up in the parlor of Suggs' house and the Old Man Suggs appeared in the window clad only in his nightgown, his brutal old face inflamed with excitement, his shock of silvery white hair awry, his powerful shoulders and his thick hands gripping his crutches.

"He's coming this way!" he bawled to the world in general. "They say he lit out across the Square! He's heading out in this direction!"

Mr. Crane paused to yell back impatiently over his shoulder, "No, he went down South Main Street. He's heading for Wilton and the river. I've already heard from headquarters."

Automobiles were beginning to roar and sputter all along the

street. Even at that time, over half the people on the street had
them. Across the street Monk could hear Mr. Potterham sweating
with his Ford. He would whirl the crank a dozen times or more,
the engine would catch for a moment, cough and splutter, and then
die again. Gus ran out of doors with a kettle of boiling water and
began to pour it feverishly down the radiator spout.

Mr. Shepperton was already dressed. They saw him run down the
back steps towards the carriage house. Randy, Bras, and Monk
streaked down the driveway to help him. They got the old wooden
doors open. He went in and cranked the car. It was a new Buick. It
responded to their prayers and started up at once. Mr. Shepperton
backed out into the snowy drive. They all clambered up onto the
running board. He spoke absently, saying:

"You boys stay here. Randy, your mother's calling you."

But they all tumbled in and he didn't say a word.

He came backing down the driveway at top speed. They turned
into the street and picked up Mr. Crane. As they took the corner
into Charles Street, Fred Sanford and his father roared past them
in their Oldsmobile. They lit out for town, going at top speed.
Every house along Charles Street was lighted up. Even the hospital
was ablaze with light. Cars were coming out of alleys everywhere.
They could hear people shouting questions and replies at one another. Monk heard one man shout, "He's killed six men!"

Monk didn't know how fast they went, but it was breakneck
speed with streets in such condition. It didn't take them over five
minutes to reach the Square, but when they got there it seemed as
if the whole town was there ahead of them. Mr. Shepperton pulled
the car up and parked in front of the City Hall. Mr. Crane leaped
out and went pounding away across the Square without another
word to them.

Everyone was running in the same direction. From every corner,
every street that led into the Square, people were streaking in. One
could see the dark figures of running men across the white carpet
of the Square. They were all rushing in to one focal point.

The southwest corner of the Square where South Main Street
came into it was like a dog fight. Those running figures streaking
towards that dense crowd gathered there made Monk think of nothing else so much as a fight between two boys upon the playgrounds

of the school at recess time. The way the crowd was swarming in was just the same.

But then he *heard* a difference. From that crowd came a low and growing mutter, an ugly and insistent growl, of a tone and quality he had never heard before, but, hearing it now, he knew instantly what it meant. There was no mistaking the blood note in that foggy growl. And the three of them, the three boys, looked at one another with the same question in the eyes of all.

Nebraska's coal black eyes were shining now with a savage sparkle even they had never had before. The awakened blood of the Cherokee was smoking in him. "Come on," he said in a low tone, exultantly. "They mean business this time, sure. Let's go!" And he darted away towards the dense and sinister darkness of the crowd.

Even as they followed him they heard behind them, at the edge of Niggertown, coming towards them now, growing, swelling at every instant, one of the most savagely mournful and terrifying sounds that night can know. It was the baying of the hounds as they came up upon the leash from Niggertown. Full-throated, howling deep, the savagery of blood was in it, and the savagery of man's guilty doom was in it, too.

They came up swiftly, fairly baying at the boys' heels as they sped across the snow-white darkness of the Square. As they got up to the crowd they saw that it had gathered at the corner where Mark Joyner's hardware store stood. Monk's uncle had not yet arrived but they had phoned for him; he was already on the way. But Monk heard Mr. Shepperton swear beneath his breath in vexation: "Damn, if I'd only thought—we could have taken him!"

Facing the crowd which pressed in on them so close and menacing that they were almost flattened out against the glass, three or four men were standing with arms stretched out in a kind of chain, as if trying to protect with the last resistance of their strength and eloquence the sanctity of private property.

George Gallatin was Mayor at that time, and he was standing there shoulder to shoulder and arm to arm with Hugh McPherson. Monk could see Hugh, taller by half a foot than anyone around him, his long, gaunt figure, the gaunt passion of his face, even the attitude of his outstretched bony arms, strangely, movingly Lincoln-

esque, his one good eye (for he was blind in the other) blazing in
the cold glare of the corner lamp with a kind of cold, inspired,
Scotch passion.

"Wait a minute! Stop! You mean wait a minute!" he cried. His
words cut out above the shouts and clamor of the mob like an electric spark. "You'll gain nothing, you'll help nothing if you do this
thing."

They tried to drown him out with an angry and derisive roar.
He shot his big fist up into the air and shouted at them, blazed at
them with that cold single eye, until they had to hear. "Listen to
me!" he cried. "This is no time for mob law. This is no case for
lynch law. This is a time for law and order. Wait till the sheriff
swears you in. Wait until Mark Joyner comes. Wait—"

He got no further. "Wait, hell!" cried someone. "We've waited
long enough! We're going to get that nigger!"

The mob took up the cry. The whole crowd was writhing angrily
now, like a tormented snake. Suddenly there was a flurry in the
crowd, a scattering. Somebody yelled a warning at Hugh McPherson. He ducked quickly, just in time. A brick whizzed past him,
smashing the plate-glass window into fragments.

And instantly a bloody roar went up. The crowd surged forward,
kicked the fragments of jagged glass away. In a moment the whole
mob was storming into the dark store. Mark Joyner got there just
too late. He said later that he heard the smash of broken glass just
as he turned the corner to the Square from College Street. He arrived in time to take out his keys and open the front doors, but as
he grimly remarked, with a convulsive movement of his lips, it was
like closing the barn doors after the horse had been stolen.

The mob was in and they looted him. They helped themselves
to every rifle they could find. They smashed open cartridge boxes
and filled their pockets with the loose cartridges. Within ten minutes they had looted the store of every rifle, every cartridge in the
stock. The whole place looked as if a hurricane had hit it. The mob
was streaming out into the street, was already gathering around
the dogs a hundred feet or so away, who were picking up the scent
at that point, the place where Dick had halted last before he had
turned and headed south, downhill along South Main Street,
towards the river.

The hounds were scampering about, tugging at the leash, moaning softly with their noses pointed to the snow, their long ears flattened down. But in that light and in that snow it almost seemed no hounds were needed to follow Dick. Straight down the middle, in a snow-white streak, straight as a string right down the center of the sheeted car tracks, the Negro's footsteps led away. By the light of the corner lamps one could follow them until they vanished downhill in the darkness.

But now, although the snow had stopped, the wind was swirling through the street and making drifts and eddies in the snow. The footprints were fading rapidly. Soon they would be gone.

The dogs were given their head. They went straining on, softly, sniffing at the snow; behind them the dark masses of the mob closed in and followed. The three boys stood there watching while they went. They saw them go on down the street and vanish. But from below, over the snow-numbed stillness of the air, the vast, low mutter of the mob came back to them.

Men were clustered now in groups. Mark Joyner stood before his shattered window, ruefully surveying the ruin. Other men were gathered around the big telephone pole at the corner, measuring, estimating its width and thickness, pointing out two bullet holes that had been drilled cleanly through.

And swiftly, like a flash, running from group to group, like a powder train of fire, the full detail of that bloody chronicle of night was pieced together.

This was what had happened.

Somewhere between nine and ten o'clock that night, Dick Prosser had gone to Pansy Harris' shack in Niggertown. Some said he had been drinking when he went there. At any rate, the police had later found the remnants of a gallon jug of raw corn whiskey in the room.

What had happened in the shack from that time on was never clearly known. The woman evidently had protested, had tried to keep him out, but eventually, as she had done before, succumbed. He went in. They were alone. What happened then, what passed between them, was never known. And, besides, no one was greatly interested. It was a crazy nigger with a nigger wench. She was "another nigger's woman"; probably she had "gone with" Dick. This was the general assumption, but no one cared. Adultery among Negroes was assumed.

At any rate, some time after ten o'clock that night—it must have been closer to eleven, because the train of the Negro porter, Harris, was late and did not pull into the yards until 10:20—the woman's husband appeared upon the scene. The fight did not start then. According to the woman, the real trouble did not come until an hour or more after his return.

The men drank together. Each was in an ugly temper. Dick was steadily becoming more savagely inflamed. Shortly before midnight they got into a fight. Harris slashed at Dick with a razor. In a second they were locked together, rolling about and fighting like two madmen on the floor. Pansy Harris went screaming out of doors and across the street into a dingy little grocery store.

A riot call was telephoned at once to police headquarters at the City Hall. The news came in that a crazy nigger had broken loose on Valley Street in Niggertown, and to send help at once. Pansy Harris ran back across the street towards her little shack.

As she got there, her husband, with blood streaming from his face, staggered out across the little lean-to porch into the street, with his hands held up protectively behind his head in a gesture of instinctive terror. At the same moment, Dick Prosser appeared in the doorway of the shack, deliberately took aim with his rifle, and shot the fleeing Negro squarely through the back of the head. Harris dropped forward on his face into the snow. He was dead before he hit the ground. A huge dark stain of blood-soaked snow widened out around him. Dick Prosser took one step, seized the terrified Negress by the arm, hurled her into the shack, bolted the door, pulled down the shades, blew out the lamp, and waited.

A few minutes later, two policemen arrived from town. They were a young constable named Willis, who had but recently got on the force and John Grady, a lieutenant. The policemen took one look at the bloody figure in the snow, questioned the frightened keeper of the grocery store, and then, after consulting briefly, produced their weapons and walked out into the street.

Young Willis stepped softly down onto the snow-covered porch of the shack, flattened himself against the wall between the window and the door, and waited. Grady went around to the side, produced his flashlight, flashed it against the house and through the window, which on this side was shadeless. At the same moment Grady said in a loud voice:

"Come out of there!"

Dick's answer was to shoot him cleanly through the wrist. At the same moment Willis kicked the door in with a powerful thrust of his foot, and, without waiting, started in with pointed revolver. Dick shot him just above the eyes. The policeman fell forward on his face.

Grady came running out around the house, crossed the street, rushed into the grocery store, pulled the receiver of the old-fashioned telephone off the hook, rang frantically for headquarters, and yelled out across the wire that a crazy nigger had killed Sam Willis and a Negro man, and to send help.

At this moment Dick, coatless and without a hat, holding his rifle crosswise in his hands, stepped out across the porch into the street, aimed swiftly through the dirty window of the dingy little store and shot John Grady as he stood there at the phone. Grady fell dead with a bullet that entered just below his left temple and went out on the other side.

Dick, now moving in a long, unhurried stride that covered the ground with catlike speed, turned up the snow-covered slope of Valley Street and began his march towards town. He moved right up the center of the street, shooting cleanly from left to right as he went. Halfway up the hill, the second-story window of a Negro tenement flew open. An old Negro man, the janitor of an office building in the Square, stuck out his ancient head of cotton wool. Dick swiveled and shot casually from his hip. The shot tore the top of the old Negro's head off.

By the time Dick reached the head of Valley Street, they knew he was coming. He moved steadily along, leaving his big tread cleanly in the middle of the sheeted street, shifting a little as he walked, swinging his gun crosswise before him. This was the Negro Broadway of the town, the center of the night life of the Negro settlement. But where those pool rooms, barber shops, drug stores, and fried-fish places had been loud with dusky life ten minutes before, they were now silent as the ruins of Egypt. The word was flaming through the town that a crazy nigger was on the way. No one showed his head.

Dick moved on steadily, always in the middle of the street, reached the end of Valley Street and turned into South Main— turned right, uphill, in the middle of the car tracks, and started towards the Square. As he passed the lunchroom on the left he took a swift shot through the window at the counter man. The fellow ducked behind the counter. The bullet crashed into the wall above his head.

Meanwhile, the news that Dick was coming was crackling through the town. At the City Club on Sondley Street, three blocks away, a group of the town's leading gamblers and sporting men was intent in a haze of smoke above a green baize table and some stacks of poker chips. The phone rang. The call was for Wilson Redmond, the police court magistrate.

Wilson listened for a moment, then hung the phone up casually. "Come on, Jim," he said in casual tones to a crony, Jim McIntyre, "there's a crazy nigger loose. He's shooting up the town. Let's go get him." And with the same nonchalance he thrust his arms into the overcoat which the white-jacketed Negro held for him, put on his tall silk hat, took up his cane, pulled out his gloves, and started to depart. Wilson, like his comrade, had been drinking.

As if they were going to a wedding party, the two men went out into the deserted, snow-white streets, turned at the corner by the post office, and started up the street towards the Square. As they reached the Square and turned into it they heard Dick's shot into the lunchroom and the crash of glass.

"There he is, Jim!" said Wilson Redmond happily. "Now I'll have some fun. Let's go get him." The two gentlemen moved rapidly across the Square and into South Main Street.

Dick kept coming on, steadily, at his tireless, easy stride, straight up the middle of the street. Wilson Redmond started down the street to get him. He lifted his gold-headed cane and waved it at Dick Prosser.

"You're under arrest!" Wilson Redmond said.

Dick shot again, and also from the hip, but something faltered this time by the fraction of an inch. They always thought it was Wilson Redmond's tall silk hat that fooled him. The bullet drilled a hole right through the top of Judge Redmond's tall silk hat, and it went flying away. Wilson Redmond faded into the doorway of a building and fervently wished that his too, too solid flesh would melt.

Jim McIntyre was not so lucky. He started for the doorway but Wilson got there first. Dick shot cleanly from the hip again and blew Jim's side in with a fast shot. Poor Jim fell sprawling to the ground, to rise and walk again, it's true, but ever thereafter with a cane. Meanwhile, on the other side of the Square, at police headquarters, the sergeant had sent John Chapman out to head Dick off. Mr. Chapman was perhaps the best-liked man on the force. He was a pleasant, florid-faced man of forty-five, with curling brown mustaches, congenial and good-humored, devoted to his family, courageous, but perhaps too kindly and too gentle for a good policeman.

John Chapman heard the shots and ran forward. He came up to the corner by Joyner's hardware store just as Dick's shot sent poor Jim McIntyre sprawling to the ground. Mr. Chapman took up his position there at the corner behind the telephone pole. From this vantage point he took out his revolver and shot directly at Dick Prosser as he came up the street.

By this time Dick was not over thirty yards away. He dropped quietly upon one knee and aimed. Mr. Chapman shot again and missed. Dick fired. The high-velocity bullet bored through the post a little to one side. It grazed the shoulder of John Chapman's uniform and knocked a chip out of the monument sixty yards or more behind him in the center of the Square.

Mr. Chapman fired again and missed. And Dick, still cooly poised upon his knee, as calm and steady as if he were engaging in a rifle practice, fired again, drilled squarely through the center of the pole, and shot John Chapman through the heart. Mr. Chapman dropped dead. Then Dick rose, pivoted like a soldier in his tracks, and started back down the street, right down the center of the car tracks, straight as a string, right out of town.

This was the story as they got it, pieced together like a train of fire among the excited groups of men that clustered there in trampled snow before the shattered glass of Joyner's store.

And the rifle? Where did he get it? From whom had he purchased it? The answer to this, too, was not long in coming.

Mark Joyner denied instantly that the weapon had come from his store. At this moment there was a flurry in the crowd and Uncle Morris Teitlebaum, the pawnbroker, appeared, gesticulating volubly, clinging to a policeman. Baldheaded, squat, with the face of an old monkey, he protested shrilly, using his hands eloquently, and displaying craggy nuggins of gold teeth as he spoke.

"Vell," he said, "vhat could I do? His moaney vas good!" he said plaintively, lifting his hands and looking around with an expression of finality. "He comes with his moaney, he pays it down like everybodies—I should say no?" he cried, with such an accent of aggrieved innocence that, in spite of the occasion, a few people smiled.

Uncle Morris Teitlebaum's pawn shop, which was on the right-hand side of South Main Street, and which Dick had passed less than an hour before in his murderous march towards town, was, unlike Joyner's hardware store, securely protected at night by strong bars over the doors and show windows.

But now, save for these groups of talking men, the town again was silent. Far off, in the direction of the river and the Wilton Bottoms, they could hear the low and mournful baying of the hounds. There was nothing more to see or do. Mark Joyner stooped, picked up some fragments of the shattered glass, and threw them in the window. A policeman was left on guard, and presently all five of them—Mr. Shepperton, Mark Joyner, and the three boys—walked back across the Square and got into the car and drove home again.

But there was no more sleep for anyone that night. Black Dick had murdered sleep. Toward daybreak snow began to fall again. It continued through the morning. It was piled deep in gusting drifts by noon. All footprints were obliterated. The town waited, eager, tense, wondering if the man could get away.

They did not capture him that day, but they were on his trail. From time to time throughout the day news would drift back to them. Dick had turned east along the river to the Wilton Bottoms and, following the river banks as closely as he could, he had gone out for some miles along the Fairchilds road. There, a mile or two from Fairchilds, he crossed the river at the Rocky Shallows.

Shortly after daybreak a farmer from the Fairchilds section had seen him cross a field. They picked the trail up there again and followed it across the field and through a wood. He had come out on the other side and got down into the Cane Creek section, and there, for several hours, they lost him. Dick had gone right down into the icy water of the creek and walked upstream a mile or so. They brought the dogs down to the creek, to where he broke the trail, took them over to the other side and scented up and down.

Towards five o'clock that afternoon they picked the trail up on the other side, a mile or more upstream. From that point on they began to close in on him. He had been seen just before nightfall by several people in the Lester township. The dogs followed him across the fields, across the Lester road, into a wood. One arm of the posse swept around the wood to head him off. They knew they had him. Dick, freezing, hungry, and unsheltered, was hiding in that wood. They knew he couldn't get away. The posse ringed the wood and waited until morning.

At seven-thirty the next morning he made a break for it. He almost got away. He got through the line without being seen, crossed the Lester road, and headed back across the fields in the direction of Cane Creek. And there they caught him. They saw him plunging through the snowdrift of a field. A cry went up. The posse started after him.

Part of the posse was on horseback. The men rode in across the field. Dick halted at the edge of the wood, dropped deliberately upon one knee, and for some minutes held them off with rapid fire. At two hundred yards he dropped Doc Lavender, a deputy, with a bullet through the throat.

The posse came in slowly, in an encircling, flank-wise movement. Dick got two more of them as they closed in, and then, as slowly and deliberately as a trained soldier retreating in good order, still firing as he went, he fell back through the wood. At the other side he turned and ran down through a sloping field that bordered on Cane Creek. At the creek edge he turned again, knelt once more in the snow, and aimed.

It was Dick's last shot. He didn't miss. The bullet struck Wayne Foraker, another deputy, dead center in the forehead and killed him in his saddle. Then the posse saw the Negro aim again, and nothing happened. Dick snapped the cartridge breech open savagely, then hurled the gun away. A cheer went up. The posse came charging forward. Dick turned, stumblingly, and ran the few remaining yards that separated him from the cold and rock-bright waters of the creek.

And here he did a curious thing—a thing that in later days was a subject of frequent and repeated speculation, a thing that no one ever wholly understood. It was thought that he would make one final break for freedom, that he would wade the creek and try to get away before they got to him. Instead, arrived at the creek, he sat down calmly on the bank, and, as quietly and methodically as if he were seated on his cot in an army barracks, he unlaced his shoes, took them off, placed them together neatly at his side, and then stood up like a soldier, erect, in his bare feet, and faced the mob.

The men on horseback reached him first. They rode up around him and discharged their guns into him. He fell forward in the snow, riddled with bullets. The men dismounted, turned him over on his back, and all the other men came in and riddled him. They took his lifeless body, put a rope around his neck, and hung him to a tree. Then the mob exhausted all their ammunition on the riddled carcass.

By nine o'clock that morning the news had reached the town. Around eleven o'clock the mob came back, along the river road. A good crowd had gone out to meet it at the Wilton Bottoms. The sheriff rode ahead. Dick's body had been thrown like a sack and tied across the saddle of the horse of one of the deputies he had killed.

It was in this way, bullet-riddled, shot to pieces, open to the vengeful and the morbid gaze of all, that Dick came back to town. The mob came back right to its starting point in South Main Street. They halted there before an undertaking parlor, not twenty yards away from where Dick had halted last and knelt to kill John Chapman. They took that ghastly mutilated thing and hung it in the window of the undertaker's place, for every woman, man, and child in town to see.

And it was so they saw him last. Yes, they all had their look. In the end, they had their look. They said they wouldn't look,

Randy and Monk. But in the end they went. And it has always been the same with people. It has never changed. It never will. They protest. They shudder. And they say they will not go. But in the end they always have their look.

Nebraska was the only one of the boys who didn't lie about it. With that forthright honesty that was part of him, so strangely wrought of innocence and brutality, of heroism, cruelty, and tenderness, he announced at once that he was going, and then waited impatiently, spitting briefly and contemptuously from time to time, while the others argued out their own hypocrisy.

At length they went. They saw it—that horrible piece of torn bait—tried wretchedly to make themselves believe that once this thing had spoken to them gently, had been partner to their confidence, object of their affection and respect. And they were sick with nausea and fear, for something had come into their lives they could not understand.

The snow had stopped. The snow was going. The streets had been pounded into dirty mush, and before the shabby undertaking place the crowd milled and jostled, had their fill of horror, could not get enough.

Within, there was a battered roll-top desk, a swivel chair, a cast-iron stove, a wilted fern, a cheap diploma cheaply framed, and, in the window, that ghastly relic of man's savagery, that horrible hunk of torn bait. The boys looked and whitened to the lips, and craned their necks and looked away, and brought unwilling, fascinated eyes back to the horror once again, and craned and turned again, and shuffled in the slush uneasily, but could not go. And they looked up at the leaden reek of day, the dreary vapor of the sky, and, bleakly, at these forms and faces all around them—the people come to gape and stare, the pool-room loafers, the town toughs, the mongrel conquerors of earth—and yet, familiar to their lives and to the body of their whole experience, all known to their landscape, all living men.

And something had come into life—into their lives—that they had never known about before. It was a kind of shadow, a poisonous blackness filled with bewildered loathing. The snow would go, they knew; the reeking vapors of the sky would clear away. The leaf, the blade, the bud, the bird, then April, would come back

again—and all of this would be as if it had never been. The homely
light of day would shine again familiarly. And all of this would
vanish as an evil dream. And yet not wholly so. For they would
still remember the old dark doubt and loathing of their kind, of
something hateful and unspeakable in the souls of men. They knew
that they would not forget.

Beside them a man was telling the story of his own heroic accom-
plishments to a little group of fascinated listeners. Monk turned
and looked at him. He was a little ferret-faced man with a furtive
and uneasy eye, a mongrel mouth, and wiry jaw muscles.

"I was the first one to git in a shot," he said. "You see that hole
there?" He pointed with a dirty finger. "That big hole right above
the eye?"

They turned and goggled with a drugged and feeding stare.

"That's mine," the hero said, and turned briefly to the side and
spat tobacco juice into the slush. "That's where I got him. Hell,
after that he didn't know what hit him. The son-of-a-bitch was dead
before he hit the ground. We all shot him full of holes then. The
whole crowd came and let him have it. But that first shot of mine
was the one that got him. But, boy!" he paused a moment, shook
his head, and spat again. "We sure did fill him full of lead. Why,
hell yes," he declared positively, with a decisive movement of his
head, "we counted up to 287. We must have put 300 holes in him."

And Nebraska, fearless, blunt, outspoken, as he always was,
turned abruptly, put two fingers to his lips and spat between them,
widely and contemptuously.

"Yeah—*we!*" he grunted. *We* killed a big one! *We*—we killed a
b'ar, we did! . . . Come on, boys," he said gruffly, "let's be on our
way!"

And, fearless and unshaken, untouched by any terror or any
doubt, he moved away. And two white-faced, nauseated boys went
with him.

A day or two went by before anyone could go into Dick's room
again. Monk went in with Randy and his father. The little room
was spotless, bare, and tidy as it had always been. Nothing had been
changed or touched. But even the very bare austerity of that little
room now seemed terribly alive with the presence of its recent black

tenant. It was Dick's room. They all knew that. And somehow they all knew that no one else could ever live there again.

Mr. Shepperton went over to the table, picked up Dick's old Bible that still lay there, open and face downward, held it up to the light and looked at it, at the place that Dick had marked when he last read in it. And in a moment, without speaking to them, he began to read in a quiet voice:

"The Lord is my shepherd; I shall not want. He maketh me to lie down in green pastures: He leadeth me beside the still waters. He restoreth my soul: He leadeth me in the paths of righteousness for His name's sake. Yea, though I walk through the valley of the shadow of death, I will fear no evil: for Thou are with me. . . ."

Then Mr. Shepperton closed the book and put it down upon the table, the place where Dick had left it. And they went out the door, he locked it, and they went back into that room no more, forever.

The years passed, and all of them were given unto time. They went their ways. But often they would turn and come again, these faces and these voices of the past, and burn there in George Webber's memory again, upon the muted and immortal geography of time.

And all would come again—the shout of the young voices, the hard thud of the kicked ball, and Dick moving, moving steadily, Dick moving, moving silently, a storm-white world and silence, and something moving, moving in the night. Then he would hear the furious bell, the crowd a-clamor and the baying of the dogs, and feel the shadow coming that would never disappear. Then he would see again the little room, the table and the book. And the pastoral holiness of that old psalm came back to him, and his heart would wonder with perplexity and doubt.

For he had heard another song since then, and one that Dick, he knew, had never heard and would not have understood, but one whose phrases and whose imagery, it seemed to him, would suit Dick better:

> *Tiger! Tiger! burning bright*
> *In the forests of the night,*
> *What immortal hand or eye*
> *Could shape thy fearful symmetry?*

* * *

What the hammer? What the chain?
In what furnace was thy brain?
What the anvil? what dread grasp
Dare its deadly terrors clasp?

When the stars threw down their spears,
And water'd heaven with their tears,
Did he smile his work to see?
Did he who made the Lamb make thee?

What the hammer? *What* the chain? No one ever knew. It was a mystery and a wonder. It was unexplained. There were a dozen stories, a hundred clues and rumors; all came to nothing in the end. Some said that Dick had come from Texas, others that his home had been in Georgia. Some said it was true that he had been enlisted in the army, but that he had killed a man while there and served a term at Leavenworth. Some said he had served in the army and had received an honorable discharge, but had later killed a man and had served a term in the state prison in Louisiana. Others said that he had been an army man but that he had "gone crazy," that he had served a period in an asylum when it was found that he was insane, that he had escaped from this asylum, that he had escaped from prison, that he was a fugitive from justice at the time he came to them.

But all these stories came to nothing. Nothing was ever proved. Nothing was ever found out. Men debated and discussed these things a thousand times—who and what he had been, what he had done, where he had come from—and all of it came to nothing. No one knew the answer.

He came from darkness. He came out of the heart of darkness, from the dark heart of the secret and undiscovered South. He came by night, just as he passed by night. He was night's child and partner, a token of the wonder and the mystery, the other side of man's dark soul, his nighttime partner, and his nighttime foal, a symbol of those things that pass by darkness and that still remain, of something still and waiting in the night that comes and passes and that will abide, a symbol of man's evil innocence, and the token of his mystery, a projection of his own unfathomed quality, a friend, a brother, and a mortal enemy, an unknown demon—our loving friend, our mortal enemy, two worlds together—a tiger and a child.

ALONE

GEORGE went to live by himself in a little room he rented in a house downtown near Fourteenth Street. Here he worked feverishly, furiously, day by day, week by week, and month by month, until another year went by—and at the end of it there was nothing done, nothing really accomplished, nothing finished, in all that plan of writing which, begun so modestly the year before, had spread and flowered like a cancerous growth until now it had engulfed him. From his childhood he could remember all that people said or did, but as he tried to set it down his memory opened up enormous vistas and associations, going from depth to limitless depth, until the simplest incident conjured up a buried continent of experience, and he was overwhelmed by a project of discovery and revelation that would have broken the strength and used up the lives of a regiment of men.

The thing that drove him on was nothing new. Even in early childhood some stern compulsion, a burning thirst to know just how things were, had made him go about a duty of observing people with such fanatical devotion that they had often looked at him resentfully, wondering what was wrong with him, or them. And in his years at college, under the same relentless drive, he had grown so mad and all-observing that he had tried to read ten thousand books, and finally had begun to stare straight through language like a man who, from the very fury of his looking, gains a superhuman intensity of vision, so that he no longer sees merely the surfaces of things but seems to look straight through a wall. A furious hunger had driven him on day after day until his eye

seemed to eat into the printed page like a ravenous mouth. Words—
even the words of the greatest poets—lost all the magic and the
mystery they had had for him, and what the poet said seemed only
a shallow and meager figuration of what he might have said, had
some superhuman energy and desperation of his soul, greater than
any man had ever known or attempted, driven him on to empty out
the content of the ocean in him.

And he had felt this even with the greatest sorcerer of words the
earth has ever known. Even when he read Shakespeare, that ravenous eye of his kept eating with so desperate a hunger into the substance of his lives that they began to look grey, shabby, and almost
common, as they had never done before. George had been assured
that Shakespeare was a living universe, an ocean of thought whose
shores touched every continent in the world, a fathomless cosmos
which held in it the full and final measure of all human life. But
now it did not seem to him that this was true.

Rather, as if Shakespeare himself had recognized the hopelessness
of ever putting down the millionth part of what he had seen and
known about this earth, or of ever giving wholly and magnificently
the full content of one moment in man's life, it now seemed that
his will had finally surrendered to a genius which he knew was so
soaring, so far beyond the range of any other man, that it could
overwhelm men with its power and magic even when its owner
knew he had shirked the desperate labor of mining from his entrails
the huge substance of all life he really had within him.

Thus, even in the great passage in *Macbeth* in which he speaks of
time—

> *. . . . that but this blow*
> *Might be the be-all and the end-all here,*
> *But here, upon this bank and shoal of time,*
> *We'd jump the life to come. . . .*

—in this tremendous passage where he mounts from power to
power, from one incredible magic to another, hurling in twenty
lines at the astounded earth a treasure that would fill out the works
and make the fame of a dozen lesser men—it seemed to George
that Shakespeare had not yet said the thousandth part of all he
knew about the terror, mystery, and strangeness of time, dark time,

nor done more than sketch the lineaments of one of time's million faces, depending on the tremendous enchantments of his genius to cover the surrender of his will before a labor too great for human flesh to bear.

And now as time, grey time, wore slowly, softly, and intolerably about him, rubbing at the edges of his spirit like a great unfathomable cloud, he thought of all these things. And as he thought of them, grey time washed over him, and drowned him in the sea-depths of its unutterable horror, until he became nothing but a wretched and impotent cipher, a microscopic atom, a bloodless, eyeless grope-thing crawling on the sea-floors of the immense, without strength or power ever to know a hand's breadth of the domain in which he dwelt, and with no life except a life-in-death, a life of drowning horror, as he scuttled, headless, eyeless, blind and ignorant and groping, his way to the grey but merciful extinction of death. For, if the greatest poet that had ever lived had found the task too great for him, what could one do who had not a fraction of his power, and who could not conceal the task, as he had done, behind the enchantments of an overwhelming genius?

It was a desperate and lonely year he lived there by himself. He had come to the city with a shout of triumph and of victory in his blood, and the belief that he would conquer it, be taller and more mighty than its greatest towers. But now he knew a loneliness unutterable. Alone, he tried to hold all the hunger and madness of the earth within the limits of a little room, and beat his fists against the walls, only to hurl his body savagely into the streets again, those terrible streets that had neither pause nor curve, nor any door that he could enter.

In the blind lashings of his fury, he strove with all the sinews of his heart and spirit trying to master, to devour, and utterly to possess the great, the million-footed, the invincible and unceasing city. He almost went mad with loneliness among its million faces. His heart sank down in atomic desolation before the overwhelming vision of its immense, inhuman, and terrific architectures. A terrible thirst parched his burning throat and hunger ate into his flesh with a vulture's beak as, tortured by the thousand images of glory, love, and power which the city holds forever to a starving man, he thought that he would perish—only a hand's breadth off from love if he could span it, only a moment away from friendship if he knew it, only an inch, a door, a word away from all the glory of the earth, if he only knew the way.

Why was he so unhappy? The hills were beautiful as they had always been, the everlasting earth was still beneath his feet, and April would come back again. Yet he was wretched, tortured, and forlorn, filled with fury and unrest, doing the ill thing always when the good lay ready to his hand, choosing the way of misery, torment, waste, and madness, when joy, peace, certitude, and power were his, were his forever, if only he would take and use them for his own.

Why was he so unhappy? Suddenly he remembered the streets of noon some dozen years ago, and the solid, lonely, liquid leather shuffle of men's feet as they came home at noon to dinner; the welcoming shout of their children, the humid warmth and fragrance of the turnip greens, the sound of screen doors being slammed, and then the brooding hush and peace and full-fed apathy of noon again.

Where were they now? And where was all that ancient certitude and peace: the quietness of summer evenings, and people talking on their porches, the smell of the honeysuckles, roses, and the grapes that ripened in thick leaves above the porch, the dew-sweet freshness and repose of night, the sound of a street car stopping on the corner of the hill above them, and the lonely absence of departure that it left behind it when it had gone, far sounds and laughter, music, casual voices, all so near and far, so strange and so familiar, the huge million-noted ululation of the night, and Aunt Maw's voice droning in the darkness of the porch; finally the sound of voices going, people leaving, streets and houses settling into utter quietness; and sleep, then, sleep—the sweet, clean mercy and repose of healthful sleep—had these things vanished from the earth forever?

Why was he so unhappy? Where had it come from—this mad coil and fury of his life? It was, he knew, in everyone, not only in himself, but in people everywhere. He had seen and known it in a thousand streets, a million faces: it had become the general weather of their lives. Where had it come from—this fury of unrest and longing, driven flight and agonized return, terrific speed and smashing movement that went nowhere?

Each day they swarmed into the brutal stupefaction of a million streets, were hurled like vermin through the foul, fetid air of roaring tunnels, and swarmed up out of the earth like rats to thrust, push, claw, sweat, curse, cringe, menace, or contrive, in a furious round of dirty, futile, little efforts that got them nowhere, brought them nothing.

At night they rushed out again with the idiot and unwearied pertinacity of a race that was damned and lost, and gutted of the vital substance of its life, to seek, with a weary, frenzied, exacerbated fury, new pleasures and sensations that, when found, filled them with weariness, boredom, and horror of the spirit, and that were viler and baser than the pleasures of a dog. Yet, with this weary hopelessness of hope, this frenzied longing of despair, they would swarm back into their obscene streets of night again.

And for what? For what? To push, thrust, throng, and jostle up and down past the thousand tawdry pomps and dreary entertainments of those streets. To throng back and forth incessantly on the grimy, grey, weary pavements, filling the air with raucous jibe and jeer, and with harsh, barren laughter, from which all the blood and life of mirth and cheer, the exultant, swelling goat-cry of their youth, or the good, full guffaw of the belly-laugh, had died!

For what? For what? To drive the huge exasperation of their weary bodies, their tortured nerves, their bewildered, overladen hearts, back to those barren, furious avenues of night again, spurred on forever by this fruitless hopelessness of hope. To embrace again the painted shell of the old delusion, hurling themselves onward towards that huge, sterile shine and glitter of the night as feverishly as if some great reward of fortune, love, or living joy was waiting for them there.

And for what? For what? What was the reward of all this frenzied searching? To be shone on lividly by the lights of death, to walk with jaunty swagger and a knowing wink past all the gaudy desolations of the hot-dog, fruit-drink stands, past the blazing enticements, the trickster's finery of the eight-foot hole-in-the-wall Jew shops, and to cram their dead grey jaws in the gaudy restaurants with the lifeless husks of dead grey food. Proudly to thrust their way into the lurid maws, the dreary, impotent escapes, the feeble, half-hid nastiness of the moving picture shows, and then to thrust and swagger it upon the streets again. To know nothing, yet to look with knowing looks upon the faces of their fellow nighttime dead, to look at them with sneering lips and scornful faces, and with hard, dark, slimy eyes, and jeering tongues. Each night to see and be seen— oh, priceless triumph!—displaying the rich quality of their wit, the keen humor of their fertile minds, with such gems of repartee as:

"Jesus!"

"*Ho*-ly Chee!"

"Oh, yeah?"

"Yeah!"

"*Wich* guy?"

"*Dat* guy! Nah—not *him!* Duh *otheh* guy!"

"*Dat* guy? *Je*-sus! Is dat duh guy yuh mean?"

"Wich guy?"

"Duh guy dat said he was a friend of yours."

"A *friend* of mine! *Je*-sus! Who said he was a friend of mine?"

"He said so."

"*G'wan!* Where d'yah get dat stuff? Dat son-of-a-bitch ain't no friend of mine!"

"No?"

"No."

"Holy *Chee!*"

"*Je*-sus!"

Oh, to hurl that stony gravel of their barren tongues forever, forever, with a million million barren repetitions into the barren ears of their fellow dead men, into the livid, sterile wink of night, hating their ugly, barren lives, their guts, and the faces of their fellow dead men—hating, hating, always hating and unhappy! And then, having prowled the streets again in that ancient, fruitless, and unceasing quest, having hugged the husks of desolation to the bone, to be hurled back into their cells again, as furiously as they had come!

Oh, dear friends, is that not the abundant life of glory, power, and wild, exultant joy, the great vision of the shining and enchanted city, the fortunate and happy life, and all the heroic men and lovely women, that George Webber dreamed of finding in his youth?

Then why was he unhappy? Great God, was it beyond their power—a race that flung up ninety-story buildings in the air, and shot projectiles bearing twenty thousand men through tunnels at every moment of the day—to find a little door that he could enter? Was it beyond the power of people who had done these gigantic things to make a chair where he could sit, a table where he might be fed on food and not on lifeless husks, and a room, a room of peace, repose, and certitude, where for a little moment he could pause from all the anguish, fury, and unrest of the world around him, drawing his breath calmly for a moment without agony, weariness, and damnation of the soul!

At other times his mood would change, and he would walk the swarming streets for hours at a time and find in the crowds that thronged about him nothing but delight, the promise of some glorious adventure. At such a time he would sink himself wholly and exultantly into the city's life. The great crowds stirred him with a feeling of ecstasy and anticipation. With senses unnaturally absorptive, he drank in every detail of the mighty parade, forever alert for the pretty face and seductive figure of a woman. Every woman with a well-shaped leg, or with a strong, attractive, sexual energy in her appearance, was invested at once with the glamorous robe of beauty, wisdom, and romance which he threw around her.

He had a hundred unspoken meetings and adventures in a day. Each passed and was lost in the crowd, and the brevity of that meeting and departure pierced him with an intolerable sense of pain and joy, of triumph and of loss. Into each lovely mouth he put words of tenderness and understanding. A sales girl in a department store became eloquent and seductive with poignant and beautiful speech; the vulgar, loose mouth of an Irish waitress uttered enchanted music for him when it spoke. In these adventures of his fancy, it never occurred to him that he would have any difficulty in winning the admiration of these beauties—that he was nothing but an ungainly youth, with small features, large shoulders, legs too short, a prowling, simian look about the out-thrust head, and an incredible length of flailing arms. No: instead he cut a very handsome and heroic figure in these fantasies, and dreamed of an instant marriage of noble souls, of an immediate and tremendous seduction, ennobled by a beautiful and poetic intensity of feeling.

Sometimes, in these golden fantasies, it was a great lady who yielded herself to him—a lady rich, twenty-four or five years of age (for he could not stand them younger than he was) , and widowed recently from an old man that she did not love but had been forced to marry by some bitter constraint and hard occasion dear. The circumstances of his meeting with her varied from repelling with a single annihilating blow of the fist the proffered violence of some Irish thug, to finding quite by accident in the gutter, already half obscured by the dead leaves of Autumn, a wallet or a mesh-bag containing not only ten or twenty thousand dollars in bank notes of huge denominations, but also a rope of pearls, some loose, uncut gems, an emerald of great size mounted on a ring, and a number of stocks or bonds, together with letters of the most valuable and distressing privacy. This form of meeting he preferred to any other, for, although it deprived him of heroism, it enabled him to show equivalent virtues of honesty and manly dignity. Also by means of it he could pay his way.

Thus, having picked up the bag on a lonely walk in Central Park, he would see at once the value of its contents—so huge as to make even a modest reward a substantial thing—and, thrusting it quickly into his pocket, he would go at once, though by a rather circuitous route which he had all planned out, to his room, where carefully and exactly he would itemize everything upon the back of an envelope, noting that the initials upon the clasp agreed with the name upon the visiting card he should find within.

This done, he would summon a taxicab and drive at once and at great speed to the indicated address. It would be a modest house in the East Sixties, or again it would be a large, grim pile on Fifth Avenue. He preferred the modest house, high storied, but with a narrow façade, not glaringly obtrusive, but almost gloomily mellow and dark. The furnishings would be masculine, the house still bearing the mark of its dead master's character—walnut and mahogany, with heavy, worn leather cushions on the chairs. To the right of the entrance hall would be the library, a gloomy room in walnut, completely lined up to its high ceiling with ten or fifteen thousand books save for the interstices of recessed, narrow windows.

Having arrived before the house, he would dismiss the taxicab and mount the steps. The door would be opened by a maid, a well-made girl of twenty-one or two, who obviously bathed frequently, and who wore expensive black-silk stockings—which her mistress gave her—on her heavy but shapely legs. Smiling, she would usher him into the library, pausing, before she went in to inform her mistress, to poke up the glowing coals in a small grate, revealing as she bent before him, the heavy white flesh of her under leg, just above the knee, where her garters of ruffled green silk (probably a gift from her mistress) furrowed deeply into the smooth column of her thigh. Then she would depart, one side of her face prettily flushed by the heat, casting him a swift and provocative glance as she went, while he grew conscious of the rhythmical undulations of her heavy breasts.

Presently he would hear the maid's low voice upstairs, and the nervous, irritable voice of another woman:

"Oh, who is it? Some young man? Tell him I can't see him today! I'm much too upset by this whole affair!"

Ablaze with fierce but righteous anger at this unhandsome return for his labor and honesty, he would stride to the foot of the stairway in time to find the maid descending, and to address her in a proud, harsh voice, not loud but almost metallic—a voice of great carrying power.

"Tell your mistress that it is imperative she give me the honor of her attendance. If I am intruding here, it is certainly against my will, and at a cost of considerable anxiety, care, and labor to myself. But I have information concerning a loss she may have sustained, which I believe may be of the greatest interest to her."

He would get no further. There would be a sharp cry above, and she would come down the stairs regardless of safety, her tense face very pale, her voice almost stricken. She would seize him so fiercely with her small, strong hands that she made a white circle around his wrists, speaking in a tone that was no more than a trembling breath:

"What is it? You must tell me at once, do you hear? Have you found it?"

Gently, soothingly, but with implacable firmness, he would answer:

"I have found something which may be your property. But so serious are the possibilities of this matter, to me, that I must ask you first of all to submit yourself to a few questions that I am going to ask you."

"Anything—anything you like!"

"You have suffered a loss. Describe that loss—the time and the place."

"I lost a silver mesh-bag two days ago between 8:20 and 8:35 in the morning, while riding in Central Park, just back of the Museum. The bag had been put in the righthand pocket of my riding jacket; it was dislodged during my ride."

"Describe as carefully and exactly as you can the contents of the bag."

"There were $16,400 in bank notes—140 hundred dollar bills, the rest in fifties and twenties. There was also a necklace with a platinum clasp, containing ninety-one pearls of graduated size, the largest about the size of a large grape; a plain gold ring set with a diamond-shaped emerald—"

"Of what size?"

"About the size of a lump of sugar. There were, in addition, eight Bethlehem Steel stock certificates, and, what I value most of all, several letters written by friends and business associates to my late husband, which contain matter of the most private sort."

Meanwhile he would be checking the list off, envelope in hand. Now he would say quietly, taking the bag from his pocket and presenting it to her:

"I think you will find your property intact."

Seizing the bag with a cry, she would sink quickly upon a leather divan, opening it with trembling fingers and hastily counting through the contents. He would watch her with nervous constraint, conscious of the personal risk he took, the unanswerable suspicion that might be attached to him if everything was not there. But everything would be!

Finally looking up, her voice filled with fatigue and unutterable relief, she would say:

"Everything is here! Everything! Oh! I feel as if I had been born again!"

Bowing coldly and ironically, he would answer:

"Then, madam, you will pardon me the more willingly if I leave you now to enjoy the first happy hours of your childhood alone."

And, taking his battered but adventurous-looking old hat from a table, he would start for the door. She would follow immediately and interrupt his passage, seizing him again by the arms in her excitement:

"No, you *shall not* go yet. You shall *not* go until you tell me what your name is. What is your name? You *must* tell me your name!"

Very coldly he would answer:

"The name would not matter to you. I am not known yet. I am only a poor writer."

She would see, of course, from his ragged clothing—the same suit he was now wearing—that he was neither a wealthy nor fashionable person, but she would also see, from the great sense of style with which his frame carried these rags, as if indifferent or unconscious of them, that there was some proud royalty of nature in him that had no need of worldly dignities. She would say:

"Then, if you're a poor writer, there is one thing I can do—one very small return I can make for your splendid honesty. You must accept the reward that I have offered."

"Reward?" He would say in an astounded tone. "Is there a *reward?"*

"Five thousand dollars. I—I—hope—if you wouldn't mind—" she would falter, frightened by the stern frown on his forehead.

"I accept, of course," he would answer, harshly and proudly. "The service I rendered was worth it. I am not ashamed to take my wage. At any rate, it is better invested with me than it would be among a group of Irish policemen. Let me congratulate you on what you have done today for the future of art."

"I am so glad—so happy—that you'll take it—that it will be of any help to you. Won't you come to dinner tonight? I want to talk to you."

He would accept.

Before he left they would have opportunity to observe each other more closely. He would see that she was rather tall for a woman— about five feet six or seven inches, but giving the impression of being somewhat taller. She would have a heavy weight of rather blondish hair, but perhaps with a reddish tint in it, also—perhaps it would be the color of very pale amber. It would be piled compactly and heavily upon her head, so as to suggest somewhat a molten or malleable weight, and it would be innumerably various with little winking lights.

This weight would rest like a heavy coronal above a small, delicately-moulded face, remarkably but not unhealthily pale, and saved from unpleasant exoticism by the rapid and boyish daring of its movements, a smile like a flick of golden light across a small, full, incredibly sensitive mouth—a swift, twisted smile, revealing small, milk-white but not too even teeth. The face would usually be cast in an intense, slightly humorous earnestness. Her conversation would be boyishly direct and sincere, delivered half while looking seriously at the auditor, and half with the eyes turned thoughtfully away; at the conclusion of each remark, however, the eyes, of a luminous blue-grey depth, a catlike health and sensuousness, would steal thievishly sideways up to the face of the listener.

She would be dressed in a close-fitting blouse of knitted green silk, with pockets into which she occasionally thrust her small, brown, competent hands (unjeweled). Her breasts would not be like the slow, rich melons of the maid, but eager and compact—each springing forward lithely and passionately, their crisp and tender nozzles half defined against the silk. She would wear a short, straight skirt of blue serge; her long, graceful legs would be covered with silk hose; her small feet sheathed in velvet shoes clasped by old buckles.

Before he left, she would tell him that he must come as often as he liked—daily, if possible—to use the library: it was rarely used now, and that he might have it all to himself. He would depart, the door being closed behind him by the voluptuous and softly smiling maid.

Then, in a fever of excitement and rapt contemplation, he would walk, a furnace of energy, through the streets and up the broad promenade in the middle of Central Park. It would be a slate-colored day in late Autumn, dripping with small, cold rain, pungent with smoke, and as inchoate as Spring with unknown prophecy and indefinable hope. A few lone, wet, withered leaves would hang from bare boughs; occasionally he would burst into a bounding run, leaping high in the air and tearing with tooth or hand at some solitary leaf.

Finally, late in the afternoon, he would become conscious of delightful physical exhaustion, which, ministered by the golden wine of his fancy, could easily be translated into voluptuous ease, just as the flesh of certain fowl becomes more dainty when slightly old. Then turning towards Lexington Avenue, his face chill with beaded rain, he would take the subway to Fourteenth Street, go home to his room, enjoy the soaking luxury of a hot bath, shave, put on clean underwear, socks, shirt, and tie; and then wait with trembling limbs and a heart thudding with strong joy for the impending meeting.

Then, at half-past eight, he would present himself at her door again. The rain would fall coldly and remotely from bare branches, and from all the eaves. The first floor of the house would be dark, but behind drawn curtains the second floor would be warm with mellow light. Again the maid would open the door for him, leading him past the dark library, up the broad, carpeted stars, where a single dim lamp was burning at the landing. He would follow, not too close, but a step or two behind, in order to watch the pleasant rhythm of her hips and the slipping back and forth of her rather tight skirt up her comely but somewhat heavy legs.

At the top of the stairs, waiting to greet him, the lady would be waiting. Taking him quickly by the hand with a warm, momentary pressure, and drawing him slightly towards her, she led the way into the living room, probably without saying a word, but with only the liquid stealth of the eyes. There would be none of that cold, remote, well-bred iciness of courtesy that chills and freezes up the warm glow of affection, such as "I'm *so* glad you could come!" or "It's *so* nice of you to come"—they would have begun almost instantly with a natural and casual intimacy, full of dignity and ease and beauty.

The boyishness of her morning garb and manner would have disappeared entirely. In unadorned but costly evening dress, of heavy, pearl-colored silk, with silver hose, and black, jeweled slippers, she would reveal an unsuspected maturity, depth of breast, and fullness of limb. Her sloping shoulders, round, firm arms, and long throat, in which a pulse would be beating slowly and warmly, in that light would be pearl-tinted, suffused, however, with a delicate bone color.

The living room would be a high, spacious room, masculine in its dimensions, but touched by her delicate taste, as the library had not been, into a room which was, although not frillishly, obviously, or offensively so, feminine.

There would be a huge divan, a chaise longue, several large, deep chairs, luxuriously upholstered and covered with a dull, flowered pattern of old satin. A warm, bright fire of coals would be burning in a hearth of small dimensions, with a sturdy and sensible alignment of shovels, pokers, and tongs to one side, their brass very highly polished, and with no revolting antiquey-ness of pesudo-Revolutionary bed warmers. The mantel would be an unadorned piece of creamy marble; above, extending the entire distance to the ceiling, there would be an eighteenth-century French mirror, with a simple gilded border, somewhat mottled with small brown patches at the lower edges. The sole object upon the mantel would be an ornate, gilded, eighteenth-century clock, very feminine and delicate. All of the furniture would have strong but delicate proportions. There would be a table behind the divan—a round leaf of polished walnut. Scattered about its surface would be several periodicals and magazines: a copy of *The Dial, Vanity Fair,* which he might pick up without comment, tossing them back carelessly with a slight ironical lifting of the eyebrows, copies of *The Century, Harper's,* and *Scribner's,* but none of *The Atlantic Monthly.* There would also be copies of *Punch,* of *Sketch, The Tatler,* or sporting and dramatic magazines, filled with pictures of hunt and chase, and many small photographs showing members of the English aristocracy, gaunt, toothy men and women, standing, talking, tailored into squares and checks with the toes of their large feet turned inwards, or caught walking, with their open mouths awry, and an arm or leg cutting angularly the air, with such legends below as, "Captain Mc-Dingle and the Lady Jessica Houndsditch caught last week enjoying a chat at the Chipping-Sodbury Shoot."

On a small table at one end of the divan there would be materials for making various kinds of cocktails and iced drinks—a rich, squat bottle of mellow rum, a bottle of Kentucky Bourbon whiskey matured for more than twenty years in oaken casks, and pungent gin, faintly nostalgic with orange bitters. There would be as well a cocktail shaker, a small bucket of cracked ice, and dishes of olives and salted almonds.

After drinking a chill and heady liquor, infused with her own certain intoxication, he would have another, his senses roused to controlled ecstasy, his brain leaping with a fiery and golden energy. Then they would go in to dinner.

The dining room, on the same floor, would be in semi-darkness, save for the golden light that bathed a round table, covered with a snowy and capacious cover, and two small, shaded lamps upon a huge buffet, gleaming with glassware, and various bottles containing whiskey, wines, liqueurs, vermouth, and rum. They would be attended at table by the maid. There would be only one other servant, the cook, a middle-aged New Hampshire woman, who had added to her native art things she had learned when the family had spent the Summer on Cape Cod, or in Paris, where the lady would have lived for several years. In the daytime there would be a man as well, who tended the furnace and did the heavier chores.

This would be all the service. The estate would not be unhappily and laboriously wealthy, extending into several millions of dollars: there would only be seven or eight hundred thousand dollars, solidly founded in tax-free bonds, yielding an annual income of twenty or twenty-five thousand, the whole intention and purpose of the fortune being total expenditure of the income for simple luxury.

The dishes would be few in number; the food would be man's food, simply and incomparably cooked. They would begin with a heavy tomato soup, the color of mahogany, or with a thick pea soup of semi-solid consistency, or with a noble dish of onion soup with a solid crust of toasted bread and cheese upon it, which she had made herself. There would be no fish, but, upon a huge silver platter, a thick sirloin or porterhouse, slightly charred and printed with the grid at the edges and center. Small pats of butter previously mixed with chopped mint and a dash of cinnamon would be dissolving visibly upon its surface. She would carve the steak into tender three-inch strips, revealing the rich, juicy, but not pasty, red of its texture. Then she would help his plate to mealy fried potatoes and tender, young boiled onions, exfoliating their delicate and pungent skins evenly at the touch of a fork. She would cover them with a rich butter sauce, touched with paprika.

There would be as well a salad—a firm heart of lettuce, or an artichoke, or, better still, crisp white endive. She would prepare the dressing in a deep mixing bowl, cutting small fragments of mint or onion into the vinegar, oil, and mustard to give it pungency. Finally, there would be deep-dish apple pie, spiced with nutmeg and cinnamon, and gummed with its own syrups along its crisped, wavy crust; this would be served with a thick hunk of yellow American cheese. They would have also a large cup of strong, fragrant coffee, with heavy cream. He would watch the cream coil through the black surface like thick smoke, changing finally into mellow brown. He would say little during the course of the meal. He would eat his food decently, but with enthusiastic relish, looking up from time to time to find her eyes fastened upon him with a subtly humorous and yet tender look.

Later, in the living room, they would sit before the fire, he in a deep upholstered chair, she on the chaise longue, where they would have small cups of black coffee, a glass of green Chartreuse, or of Grand Marnier, and cigarettes. He would smoke fragrant, toasted, loose-drawing Lucky Strikes; she would smoke Melachrinos. From time to time she would move her limbs slightly, and her silken calves, sliding gently apart or together, would cause an audible and voluptuous friction.

There would be little other sound save the enveloping and quieting drip of rain from eaves and boughs, a brief gaseous spurt from the red coals, and the minute ticking of the little clock. From time to time he would hear the maid clearing the table in the dining room. Presently she would appear, ask if anything more was wanted, say good-night, and mount the stairs to her room on the top floor. Then they would be left alone.

They would begin to talk at first, if not with constraint, at least with some difficulty. She would speak of her education—in a convent—of her life abroad, of stupid and greedy parents, now dead, of her great devotion to an aunt, a wise and kindly woman, her only friend against her family in her difficult youth, and of her marriage at twenty to a man in his late forties, good, devoted, but vacant of any interest for her. He had died the year before.

Then she would ask him about his life, his home, his childhood, his age, and his ambition. Then he would talk, at first in short spurts and rushes. At length, language bursting like a torrent at the gates of speech, he would make a passionate avowal of what he had done, believed, felt, loved, hated, and desired, of all he wanted to do and be. Then he would light another cigarette, get up restlessly before the fire, sit down again beside her on the chaise longue, and take her hand in a natural and casual way, at which she would give a responsive squeeze to his. Then, throwing his cigarette into the grate, he would put his arms around her quite naturally and easily, and kiss her, first for about forty seconds upon the mouth, then in a circle upon the cheeks, eyes, forehead, nose, chin, and throat, about the place where the pulse was beating. After this, he would gently insinuate his hand into her breasts, beginning near the deep and fragrant channel that parted them. Meanwhile, she would ruffle his hair gently and stroke his face with her delicate fingers. Their passion would have them chained in a silent drunkenness; she would submit to every action of his embrace without thought of resistance.

Lying beside her now, wound in her long arms, he would pass his hand along her silken, swelling hips, down the silken seam of her calf, and gently up her thigh below her skirt, lingering for a moment upon the tender, heavy flesh of her under leg. Then he would loosen one breast over the neck of her gown, holding its tender weight and teat gently and lovingly in one hand. The nipples of her firm breast would not be leathery, stained brown, and flaccid, like those of a woman who has borne children; they would end briefly in a tender pink bud, as did those of the ladies in old French paintings—those of Boucher, for example.

Then he would lift her arms, observing the delicate silken whorls and screws of blonde hair in the arm pits. He would kiss and perhaps bite her tender shoulder haunch, and smell the pungent but not unpleasant odor, already slightly moist with passion. And this odor of an erotic female would have neither the rank stench of a coarse-bodied woman, nor some impossible and inhuman bouquet, disgusting to a healthy taste. It would be delicately vulgar: the odor of a healthy woman and a fine lady, who has not only been housed, clothed, fed, and attended with the simple best, but has been derived from ancestral loins similarly nourished, so that now the marrow of her bones, the substance of her flesh, the quality of her blood, the perspiration of her skin, the liquor of her tongue, the moulding of her limbs—all the delicate joinings and bindings of ligament and muscle, and the cementing jellies, the whole incorporate loveliness of her body—were of rarer, subtler, and more golden stuff than would be found elsewhere the world over.

And lying thus, warmed by the silent, glowing coals, he would perform on her the glorious act of love. He would dedicate to her the full service of his love and energy, and find upon her mouth double oblivion.

Later, reviving slowly, he would lie in her embrace, his head heavily sunk upon her neck, feel the slow, unsteady respiration of her breast, and hear, his senses somewhat drugged, the faint, incessant beating of the rain.

And he would stay with her that night, and on many nights thereafter. He would come to her in the darkness, softly and quietly, although there was no need for silence, conscious that in the dark there was waiting a central energy of life and beauty; in the darkness they would listen to the million skipping feet of rain.

Shortly after this night, he would come and live with her in the house. This would be all right because he would insist on paying for his board. He would pay, against all protests, fifteen dollars a week, saying:

"This is all I can afford—this is what I would pay elsewhere. I could not eat and drink and sleep as I do here, but I could live. Therefore, take it!"

His days would be spent in the library. There he would do stupendous quantities of reading, going voraciously and completely through those things he desired most to know, but effecting combinations, mélanges, woven fabrics of many other books, keeping a piled circle about him and tearing chunks hungrily from several at random.

The library would be based solidly, first, on five or six thousand volumes, which would cover excellently but not minutely the range of English and American literature. There would be standard editions of Thackeray, the Cruickshank and Phiz Dickenses, Meredith, James, Sir Walter Scott, and so on. In addition to the well-known literature of the Elizabethans, such as Shakespeare, the handy Mermaid collection of the dramatists, and the even more condensed anthologies with Jonson's *Volpone, The Alchemist* and *Bartholomew Fair*, Dekker's *Shoemaker's Holiday*, Chapman's *Bussy d'Ambois*, there would be several hundred of the lesser-known plays, bad, silly, and formless as they were, but filled with the bawdy, beautiful, and turbulent speech of that time.

There would be prose pamphlets, such as the romances after Bandello of Robert Greene, the dramatist, or his quarrel with

Gabriel Harvey, or his confessions, Dekker's *Guls Horne-booke,* the remnants of Jonson's *Sad Shepherd,* his *Underwoods.* There would be such books as Coleridge's *Anima Poetae,* the *Biographia Literaria, The Table Talk of S. T. C.,* and the sermons of the Puritan divines, particularly of Jonathan Edwards. There would be books of voyages, Hakluyt, Purchas, Bartram's *Travels in North America.*

And there would be facsimile reproductions of all the scientific manuscripts of Leonardo da Vinci, the great *Codice Atlantico,* written backwards and reversed across the page, scribbled with hundreds of drawings, including his flying machines, canals, catapults, fire towers, spiral staircases, anatomical dissections of human bodies, diagrams of the act of copulation while standing erect, researches in the movement of waves, fossilized remains, sea shells on a mountain side, notes of the enormous antiquity of the world, the leafless and blasted age of the earth which he put in the background of his paintings—as he did in Mona Lisa. With the aid of mirrors and of Italian grammars and dictionaries, he would spell out the words and translate them, using as a guide the partial deciphering already made by a German. Then, in his spare moments between writing novels, he would show how Leonardo regarded painting only as a means of support for his investigation into all movement, all life, and was only incidentally an artist and an engineer, and how what he was really doing was tracing with a giant's brush the map of the universe, showing the possibility of Man becoming God.

There would also be books of anatomical drawings, besides those of Leonardo, of the fifteenth and sixteenth centuries, showing ladies lying on divans, gazing wistfully through their open bellies at their entrails, and maps out of the medieval geographers, compounded of scraps of fact, hypothesis, and wild imaginings, with the different quarters of the sea people by various monsters, some without heads, but with a single eye and with a mouth between the shoulders.

Then there would be some of those books that Coleridge "was deep in" at the time he wrote *The Ancient Mariner,* such as Iamblichus, Porphyry, Plotinus, Josephus, Jeremy Taylor, "the English Metaphysicum"—the whole school of the neoplatonists; all the works that could be collected on the histories of demons, witches, fairies, elves, gnomes, witches' sabbaths, black magic, alchemy, spirits—all the Elizabethans had to say about it, particularly

Reginald Scott; and all the works of Roger Bacon; all legends and books of customs and superstition whatever, and works of quaint and learned lore, Burton's *Anatomy of Melancholy,* Frazer's *Golden Bough, The Encyclopædia Britannica,* in which, when he was tired of other reading, he could plunge luxuriously—picking out first the plums, such as Stevenson on Bérenger, or Theodore Watts-Dunton on poetry, or Carlyle, if any of him was left, on various things, or Swinburne on Keats, Chapman, Congreve, Webster, Beaumont and Fletcher.

He would have the *Magnalia* of Cotton Mather, the *Voyage of Dr. Syntax,* with illustrations, Surtees' sporting novels. He would have the complete works of Fielding, Smollett, Sterne, and Richardson, and everything of Daniel Defoe's he could lay his hands on. He would have the entire corpus of Greek and Latin literature, so far as it might be obtained in Loeb's library and in the coffee-colored india paper Oxford classical texts, with footnotes and introduction all in Latin, as well as cross-references to all the manuscripts. And he would have several editions each of the *Carmina* of Catullus (with Lamb's translations and settings to verse) ; Plato, with Jowett's great rendering—in particular, of the *Apology* and the *Phaedo;* the histories of Herodotus, and in general all lying and entertaining histories and voyages whatever, as Strabo, Pausanias, Froissart, Josephus, Holinshed, Marco Polo, Swift, Homer, Dante, Xenophon in his *Anabasis,* Chaucer, Sterne, Voltaire in his voyage to England, *With Stanley in Africa,* Baron Munchausen.

There would be as well the Oxford and Cambridge University texts of the poets, with other editions when lacking for men like Donne, Crashaw, Herbert, Carew, Herrick, Prior. And in the drama there would be several hundred volumes besides the Elizabethans, including everyone from the early Greeks to the liturgical plays of the Middle Ages, to the great periods in France, Germany, Spain, Italy, Scandinavia, Russia, including all newer dramatists of the art theatre—Ibsen, Shaw, Chekhov, Benavente, Molnar, Toller, Wedekind, the Irish, Pirandello, O'Neill, Sardou, Romains, including others from the Bulgarian, Peruvian, and Lithuanian never heard of. There would also be complete bound editions of *Punch, Blackwood's Harper's Weekly, L'Illustration, The Police Gazette, The Literary Digest,* and *Frank Leslie's Illustrated Weekly.*

Walled by these noble, life-giving books, he would work furiously throughout the day, drawing sustenance and courage, when not reading them, from their presence. Here in the midst of life, but of life flowing in regular and tranquil patterns, he could make his rapid and violent sorties into the world, retiring when exhausted by its tumult and fury to this established place.

And at night again, he would dine with rich hunger and thirst, and, through the hours of darkness, lie in the restorative arms of his beautiful mistress. And sometimes at night when the snow came muffling in its soft fall all of the noises of the earth and isolating them from all its people, they would stand in darkness, only a dying flicker of coal fire behind them, watching the transforming drift and flurry of white snow outside.

Thus, being loved and being secure, working always within a circle of comfort and belief, he would become celebrated as well. And to be loved and to be celebrated—was there more than this in life for any man?

After the success of his first book, he would travel, leaving her forever steadfast, while he drifted and wandered like a ghost around the world, coming unknown, on an unplanned journey, to some village at dusk, and finding there a peasant woman with large ox eyes. He would go everywhere, see everything, eating, drinking, and devouring his way across the earth, returning every year or so to make another book.

He would own no property save a small lodge with thirty acres of woodland, upon a lake in Maine or New Hampshire. He would not keep a motor—he would signal a taxi whenever he wanted to go anywhere. His clothing, laundry, personal attentions, and, when he was alone at the lodge, his cooking, would be cared for by a Negro man, thirty-five years old, black, good-humored, loyal, and clean.

When he was himself thirty or thirty-five years old, having used up and driven out all the wild frenzy and fury in him by that time, or controlled it somehow by flinging and batting, eating and drinking and whoring his way about the world, he would return to abide always with the faithful woman, who would now be deep-breasted and steadfast like the one who waited for Peer Gynt.

And they would descend, year by year, from depth to depth in each other's spirit; they would know each other more completely than two people ever had before, and love each other better all the time. And as they grew older, they would become even younger in spirit, triumphing above all the weariness, dullness, and emptiness of youth. When he was thirty-five he would marry her, getting on her blonde and fruitful body two or three children.

He would wear her love like a most invulnerable target over his heart. She would be the heart of his desire, the well of all his passion. He would triumph over the furious welter of the days during the healing and merciful nights: he would be spent, and there would always be sanctuary for him; weary, a place of rest; sorrowful, a place of joy.

So was it with him during that year, when, for the first time and with their full strength, the elements of fury, hunger, thirst, wild hope, and savage loneliness worked like a madness in the adyts of his brain. So was it when, for the first time, he walked the furious streets of life, a manswarm atom, a nameless cipher, who in an instant could clothe his life with all the wealth and glory of the earth. So was it with him that year when he was twenty-three years old, and when he walked the pavements of the city—a beggar and a king.

Has it been otherwise with any man?

OKTOBERFEST

SEPTEMBER was advancing to its close and the season of the Oktoberfest was at hand. Everywhere throughout Munich he saw posters announcing the event, and wherever he went people were talking about it. In the pension in the Theresienstrasse the table guests spoke to him about it with that elaborate jocoseness that men use towards a child—or a foreigner who speaks the language badly. His mind was busy with conjectures and images, but he could get no very clear picture of the approaching carnival. But the affair began to take on in his mind a ritualistic significance. He began to feel that at last he was to come close to the heart of this people—as if, after a voyage through the old barbaric forest, he would come suddenly upon them at their altars in a cleared ring.

One Sunday afternoon, early in October, a day or two after the carnival had opened, Monk made his way, accompanied by Heinrich Bahr, to the Theresian Fields, on the eastern edges of the city, where the Fair was now going on. As they walked along past the railway station and towards the carnival grounds, the street, and all the streets that led to it, began to swarm with people. Most of them were native Müncheners, but a great number were also Bavarian country people. These Bavarians were brawny men and women who stained the crowd brilliantly with the rich dyes of their costume—the men in their elaborately-embroidered holiday shorts and stockings, the women in their bright dresses and lace bodices, marching briskly along with the springy step of the mountaineer. These peasants had the perfect flesh and the sound teeth of animals. Their smooth, round faces wore only the markings of the sun and the wind: they were unworn by the thought and pain that waste away man's strength. Monk looked at them with a pang of regret and of envy—their lives were so strong and so confident, and, having missed so much, they seemed to have gained so greatly. Their lives were limited to one or two desires. Most of them had never read a book, a visit to this magic city of Munich was to them a visit to the heart of the universe, and the world that existed beyond their mountains had no real existence for them at all.

As they neared the Theresien Fields, the crowd became so thick that movement was impeded and slowed down. The huge noises of the Fair came to them now, and Monk could see the various buildings. His first feeling as he entered the Fields was one of overwhelming disappointment. What lay before him and around him seemed to be only a smaller and less brilliant Coney Island. There were dozens of booths and sheds filled with cheap dolls, teddy bears, candy wrappers, clay targets, etc., with all the accompanying claptrap of two-headed monsters, crazy houses, fat ladies, dwarfs, palmists, hypnotists, as well as all the elaborate machinery for making one dizzy: whirling carriages and toy automobiles that spun about on an electrified floor, all filled with people who screamed with joy when the crazy vehicles crashed together and were released again by the attendant.

Heinrich Bahr began to laugh and stare like a child. The child-like capacity of all these people for amusement was astonishing. Like children, they seemed never to grow weary of the whole gaudy show. Great fat fellows with shaven heads and creased necks rode on the whirling and whipping machines, or rode round and round, again and again, on the heaving wooden horses of the merry-go-rounds. Heinrich was fascinated. Monk rode with him several times on the breathless dip-and-dive of the great wooden trestlelike railway, and then was whipped and spun dizzy in several of the machines.

Finally Heinrich was content. They moved slowly along down the thronging central passage of the Fair until they came to a more open space at the edge of the Fields. Here, from a little platform, a man was haranguing the crowd in harsh, carnival barker's German. Beside him on the platform stood a young man whose body and arms were imprisoned in a sleeveless canvas jacket and manacled with a chain. Presently the barker stopped talking, the young man thrust his feet through canvas loops, and he was hauled aloft, feet first, until he hung face downward above the staring mob. Monk watched him as he began his desperate efforts to free himself from the chain and jacket that fettered him, until he saw his face turn purple, and the great veins stand out in ropes upon his forehead. Meanwhile a woman passed through the crowd soliciting contributions, and when she had got all the money that the crowd would yield, the young man, whose swollen face was now almost black with blood, freed himself very quickly and was lowered to the earth. The crowd dispersed, almost, it seemed to Monk, with a kind of sullenness as if the thing which they had waited to see had now happened but had somehow disappointed them, and while the barker began his harangue again, the young man sat in a chair recovering himself, with his hand before his eyes. Meanwhile the woman who had collected money stood by him anxiously, looking at him, and in a moment spoke to him. And somehow, just by their nearness to each other and by no other outward sign, there was communicated to Monk a sense of tenderness and love.

His mind was reeling from all the clamorous confusion of the Fair and this last exhibition, coming as a climax of an unceasing program of monsters and animal sensations, touched him with a sense of horror. For a moment it seemed to him that there was something evil and innate in men that blackened and tainted even their most primitive pleasures.

Late afternoon had come; the days were now shortening rapidly, and the air was already that of Autumn—it was crisp and chill, meagerly warmed by a thin red sunshine. Over all the Fair there rose the dense and solid fabric of a hundred thousand voices. Heinrich, whose interest in the shows of the Fair had been for the time appeased, now began to think of beer. Taking Monk by the arm, he joined in the vast oscillation of the crowd that jammed the main avenue of the carnival in an almost solid wedge.

The Germans moved along slowly and patiently, with that tremendous massivity that seems to be an essence of their lives, accepting the movement of the crowd with enormous contentment as they lost themselves and became a part of the great beast around them. Their heavy bodies jostled and bumped against one another awkwardly and roughly, but there was no anger among them. They roared out greetings or witticisms to one another and to everyone; they moved along in groups of six or eight, men and women all together with arms linked.

Heinrich Bahr had become eager and gay; he laughed and chuckled to himself constantly; presently, slipping his hand through Monk's arm with a friendly and persuasive movement, he said:

"Come! Let us go and see the Roasted Ox."

And immediately at these words the enormous hunger woke in Monk again, a hunger for flesh such as he had never known—he wanted not only to see the Roasted Ox, he wanted to devour great pieces of it. He had already noticed one characteristic of this Fair that distinguished it from any other he had ever seen. This was the great number of booths, large and small, given over to the sale of hot and cold meats. Great sausages hung in ropes and festoons from the walls of some of these places, while in others there was a constant exhalation from steaming and roasting viands of all kinds and sizes. The fragrance and the odor were maddening. And it seemed to him that above this dense mass of people that swayed along so slowly, there hovered forever in the thin, cold air an odor of slaughtered flesh.

But now they found themselves before a vast, long shed, gaily colored in front, and bearing above its doors a huge drawing of an ox. This was the Oxen Roastery (Ochsen-Braterei), but so dense was the crowd within that a man stood before the doors with his arms out, keeping back the people who wanted to enter, and telling them they must wait another fifteen minutes. Heinrich and Monk joined the crowd and waited docilely with all the others: to Monk there was communicated some of the enormous patience of this crowd, which waited and which did not try to thrust past barriers. Presently the doors were opened and they all went in.

Monk found himself in a vast, long shed, at the end of which, through the dense cloud of tobacco smoke which thickened the atmosphere almost to the consistency of a London fog, he could see the carcasses of two great animals revolving slowly on iron spits over troughs of red-hot coals.

The place, after the chill bite of the October air, was warm—warm with a single unmistakable warmth: the warmth of thousands of bodies crowded together in an enclosed place. And mingled with this warmth, there was an overpowering odor of food. At hundreds of tables people were sitting together devouring tons of flesh—ox flesh, great platters of sliced cold sausages, huge slabs of veal and pork—together with the great stone mugs that foamed with over a liter of the cold and strong October beer. There was a heavy and incessant rumble of voices full of food, an enormous and excessive clatter of heavy pottery and knives, that rose and fell in brittle waves. Down the central aisles and around the sides moved and jostled constantly another crowd looking restlessly over the densely packed area for a vacant place. And the brawny peasant women who acted as waitresses plunged recklessly through this crowd, bearing platters of food or a half-dozen steins of beer in one hand, and brusquely thrusting human impediments out of their way with the other.

Heinrich and Monk moved with the crowd slowly down the central aisle. The feeders, it seemed to Monk, were for the most part great, heavy people who already had in their faces something of the bloated contentment of swine. Their eyes were dull and bleared with food and beer, and many of them stared at the people around them in a kind of stupefaction, as if they had been drugged. And indeed the air itself, which was so thick and strong it could be cut with a knife, was sufficient to drug one's senses, and he was therefore glad when, having arrived at the end of the aisle and stared for a moment at the great carcass of the ox that was turning brown as it revolved slowly before them, Heinrich suggested that they go elsewhere.

The sharp air lifted him at once from his lethargy, and he began to look about him quickly and eagerly again. The crowd was growing denser as evening approached, and he knew now that the evening was to be dedicated solidly to food and beer.

Distributed among the innumerable smaller buildings of the Fair, like lions couched among a rabble of smaller beasts, there rose about them the great beer halls erected by the famous breweries. And as thick as the crowd had been before the booths and shows, it seemed small compared to the crowd that filled these vast buildings —enormous sheds that each held several thousand people. Before them now, and at a distance, Monk could see the great red façade of the Löwenbrau brewery, with its proud crest of two royal lions, rampant. But when they came near the vast roaring of sound the hall enclosed, they saw that it would be impossible to find a seat there. Thousands of people were roaring over their beer at the tables, and hundreds more milled up and down incessantly, looking for an opening.

They tried several other of the great beer halls of the breweries with no better success, but at length they found one which had a few tables set about on a small graveled space before the hall and screened from the swarming crowd outside by a hedge. A few people were sitting at some of the tables, but most of them were vacant. Darkness was now approaching, the air was sharp and frosty, and there was almost a frantic eagerness to enter the fetid human warmth and the howling tempest of noise and drunkenness that the great hall contained. But both of them were now tired, fatigued by the excitement, by the crowd, by the huge kaleidoscope of noise, of color and sensation they had experienced.

"Let us sit down here," Monk said, indicating one of the vacant tables before the hall.

And Heinrich, after peering restlessly through one of the windows

at the smoky chaos within, through which dark figures pushed and
jostled like spirits lost in fog, in the vapors of Valhalla, consented
and took a seat, but with a disappointment he was unable to conceal. "It is beautiful in there," he said. "You cannot afford to
miss it."

Then a peasant woman bore down upon them, swinging in each
of her strong hands six foaming steins of the powerful October beer.
She smiled at them with ready friendliness and said, "The light or
the dark?"

They answered, "Dark."

Almost before they had spoken she had set two foaming mugs
before them on the table and was on her way again.

"But beer?" Monk said. "Why beer? Why have they come here to
drink beer? Why have all these great sheds been built here by the
famous breweries when all Munich is renowned for beer and there
are hundreds of beer restaurants in the city?"

"Yes," Heinrich answered, *"but—"* he smiled and emphasized the
word—"this is October beer. It is almost twice as strong as ordinary
beer."

Then they seized their great stone mugs, clinked them together
with a smiling "Prosit," and in the frosty, sharp exhilaration of that
air they drank long and deep the strong, cold liquor that sent
tingling through their veins its potent energy. All about them
people were eating and drinking. Near by at another table, some
peasant people in gay clothes had ordered beer, and now, unwrap-
ping several paper bundles that they were carrying with them, they
set out on the table a prodigious quantity of food and began to eat
and drink stolidly. The man, a brawny fellow with thick mustaches
and white woolen stockings that covered his powerful calves but
left his feet and knees bare pulled from his pocket a large knife and
cut the heads from several salt fish, which shone a beautiful golden
color in the evening light. The woman produced several rolls, a
bunch of radishes, and a big piece of liver sausage from another
paper and added them to the general board. Two children, a boy
and a girl, the girl with braided hanks of long, blond hair falling
before her over the shoulders, both watchful and blue-eyed with
the intent and focused hunger of animals, stared silently at the food
as their parents cut it and apportioned it. In a moment, with this

same silent and voracious attentiveness, all of them were eating and drinking.

Everyone was eating; everyone was drinking. A ravenous hunger—an insane hunger that knew no appeasement, that wished to glut itself on all the roasted ox flesh, all the sausages, all the salt fish in the world, seized Monk and held him in its teeth. In all the world there was nothing but Food—glorious Food. And Beer—October Beer. The world was one enormous Belly—there was no higher heaven than the Paradise of Cram and Gorge. All of the agony of the mind was here forgotten. What did these people know about books? What did they know about pictures? What did they know about the million tumults of the soul, the conflict and the agony of the spirit, the hopes, fears, hatreds, failures, and ambitions, the whole fevered complex of modern life? These people lived for nothing but to eat and drink—and Monk felt at that instant that they were right.

The doors of the great hall kept opening and shutting constantly as the incessant stream of beer drinkers pressed patiently in. And from within Monk heard the shattering blare of a huge brass band and the roar of five thousand beer-drunk voices, rocking together in the rhythms of "Trink, Trink, Brüderlein, Trink!"

Savage hunger was devouring Monk and Heinrich. They called out loudly to the bustling waitress as she passed them and were told that if they wanted hot food they must go within. But in a moment she sent another woman to their table who was carrying an enormous basket loaded with various cold foods. Monk took two sandwiches made most deliciously of onions and small salted fish, and an enormous slice of liver cheese with a crust about its edges. Heinrich also selected two or three sandwiches, and, having ordered another liter of dark beer apiece, they began to devour their food. Darkness had come on. All of the buildings and amusement devices of the Fair were now blazing with lights; from the vast irradiant murk of night there rose and fell in wavelike nodes the huge fused roar and mumble of the crowd.

When they had devoured their sandwiches and finished their beer, Heinrich suggested that they now make a determined effort to find seats within the hall, and Monk, who had heretofore felt a strong repulsion towards the thick air and roaring chaos of the hall, now found to his surprise that he was ready and eager to join the vast crowd of beer-fumed feeders. Obediently now he joined the line of patient Germans who were shuffling slowly through the doors and in a moment more he found himself enveloped by a cyclone of drunken sound, tramping patiently with a crowd that moved slowly around the great room looking for seats. Presently, peering through the veils and planes of shifting smoke that coiled and rose in the great hall like smoke above a battlefield, Heinrich spied two seats at a table near the center of the room, where, on the square wooden platform, fog-enveloped, forty men dressed in peasant costume were producing a deafening noise upon brass instruments. They plunged directly for the seats, jostling and half-falling over unprotesting bodies that were numb with beer.

And at last, dead center of that roaring tumult, they seated themselves triumphantly, panting victoriously, and immediately ordered two liters of dark beer and two plates of schweinwurstl and sauerkraut. The band was blaring for the strains of "Ein Prosit! Ein Prosit!" and all over the room people had risen from their tables and were standing with arms linked and mugs upraised while they roared out the great drinking song and swung and rocked rhythmically back and forth.

The effect of these human rings all over the vast and murky hall had in it something that was almost supernatural and ritualistic: something that belonged to the essence of a race was enclosed in those rings, something dark and strange as Asia, something older than the old barbaric forests, something that had swayed around an altar, and had made a human sacrifice, and had devoured burnt flesh.

The hall was roaring with their powerful voices, it shook to their powerful bodies, and as they swung back and forth it seemed to Monk that nothing on earth could resist them—that they must smash whatever they came against. He understood now why other nations feared them so; suddenly he was himself seized with a terrible and deadly fear of them that froze his heart. He felt as if he had dreamed and awakened in a strange, barbaric forest to find a ring of savage, barbaric faces bent down above him: blond-braided, blond-mustached, they leaned upon their mighty spear staves, rested on their shields of toughened hide, as they looked down. And he was surrounded by them, there was no escape. He thought of all that was familiar to him and it seemed far away, not only in another world but in another time, sea-sunken in eternity ages hence from the old, dark forest of barbaric time. And now he thought almost with warm friendliness of the strange, dark faces of the Frenchmen, their cynicism and dishonesty, their rapid and excited voices, their small scale, their little customs; even their light and trivial adulteries now seemed friendly and familiar, playful, charming, full of grace. And of the dogged English, with their pipes, their pubs, their bitter beer, their fog, their drizzle, their women with neighing voices and long teeth—all these things now seemed immensely warm, friendly and familiar to him, and he wished that he were with them.

But suddenly a hand was slipped through his arm, and through that roar and fog of sound he realized that someone was speaking to him. He looked down, and there beside him saw the jolly, flushed, and smiling face of a pretty girl. She tugged at his arm goodnaturedly and mischievously, spoke to him, nodded her head for him to look. He turned. Beside him was a young man, her companion; he, too, smiling, happy, held his arm for Monk to take. He looked across and saw Heinrich, his sallow, lonely, pitted face smiling and happy as he had never seen it before. He nodded to Monk. In an instant they were all linked together, swinging, swaying, singing in rhythm to the roar of those tremendous voices, swinging and swaying, singing all together as the band played "Ein Prosit!" Ended at length the music, but now all barriers broken through, all flushed and happy, smiling at one another, they added their own cheers to the crowd's great roar of approval when the song was ended. Then, laughing, smiling, talking, they all sat down again.

And now there was no strangeness any more. There were no barriers any more. They drank and talked and ate together. Monk drained liter after liter of the cold and heady beer. Its fumes mounted in his brain. He was jubilant and happy. He talked fearlessly in a broken jargon of his little German. Heinrich helped him out from time to time, and yet it did not matter. He felt that he had known all these people forever. The young girl with her jolly, pretty face eagerly tried to find out who he was and what he did. He teased her. He would not tell her. He told her a dozen things—that he was a business man, a Norwegian, an Australian, a carpenter, a sailor, anything that popped into his head, and Heinrich, smiling, aided and abetted him in all his foolishness. But the girl clapped her hands and gleefully cried out "No," that she knew what he was —he was an artist, a painter, a creative man. She and all the others turned to Heinrich, asking him if this was not true. And, smilingly, he half inclined his head and said that Monk was not a painter but that he was a writer—he called him a poet. And then all of them nodded their heads in satisfied affirmation, the girl gleefully clapped her hands together again and cried that she had known it. And now they drank and linked their arms and swayed and swung together in a ring again. And presently, now that it was growing late and people had begun to leave the hall, they too got up, the six of them, the girl, another girl, their two young men, and Heinrich and Monk, moved out among the singing, happy crowds again, and, arm in arm, linked all together, moved singing through the crowds.

And then Monk and Heinrich left them, finally, four young people from the mass of life and from the heart of Germany, whom Monk would never see again—four people, and the happy, flushed, and smiling face of a young girl. They left them, never having asked each other's names; they left and lost them, with warmth, with friendship, with affection in the hearts of all of them.

Monk and Heinrich went their way, and they went theirs. The great roar and clamor of the Fair suffused and faded far behind them, until it had become a vast and drowsy distant murmur. And presently, walking arm in arm together, they reached again the railway station and the ancient heart of Munich. They crossed the Karlsplatz and presently they had come to their dwelling in the Theresienstrasse.

And yet they found they were not tired, they were not ready to go in. The fumes of the powerful and heady beer, and, more than that, the fumes of fellowship and of affection, of friendship and of human warmth, had mounted to their brains and hearts. They knew it was a rare and precious thing, a moment's spell of wonder and of joy, that it must end, and they were loath to see it go.

It was a glorious night, the air sharp, frosty, and the street deserted, and far away, like time, like the ceaseless and essential murmur of eternity, the distant, drowsy, wavelike hum of the great Fair. The sky was cloudless, radiant, and in the sky there blazed a radiant blank of moon. And so they paused a moment at their dwelling, then as by mutual instinct walked away. They went along the streets, and presently they had arrived before the enormous, silent, and moon-sheeted blankness of the Old Pinakothek. They passed it, they entered on the grounds, they strode back and forth, their feet striking cleanly on clean gravel. Arm in arm they talked, they sang, they laughed together.

"A poet, yes," Heinrich cried, and looked exultantly at the blazing moon. "A poet, ja!" he cried again. "These people did know you and they said you were a poet. And you are."

And in the moonlight, his lonely, scarred, and pitted face was transfigured by a look of happiness. And they walked the streets, they walked the streets. They felt the sense of something priceless and unutterable, a world invisible that they must see, a world intangible that they must touch, a world of warmth, of joy, of imminent and impending happiness, of impossible delight, that was almost theirs. And so they walked the streets, they walked the streets. The moon blazed blank and cold out of the whited brilliance of the sky. And the streets were silent. All the doors were closed. And from the distance came the last and muted murmurs of the Fair. And they went home.

At night he lay and turned his ruined face up to the ceiling, and listened to the rain out in the garden, making sound. Save for the small and steady rain that beat upon the yellow mat of sodden leaves, there was no sound. It was a dreary and incessant monotone; unwearied, it was the weary reek of time; it was like waiting without hope for nothing, just listening to the rain on sodden leaves as he lay there.

Then there would come a momentary lull, and through the rain would come the distant noises of the Fair. Immense and murmurous, rising in drowsy waves and so subsiding, the broken music and the noises of the carnival would come in upon the rain, rise and subside, recede and vanish; and then there would be the steady reek of rain again. Sometimes, when it was late, outside the garden walls there would be voices and hoarse laughter and sounds of people going home. And he lay there upon his back and waited, listening to rain.

How had it happened? What had he done? Events as he remembered them were vague, confused, like half-lost, half-recalled contortions in a nightmare. He knew he had paid a visit to the Fair again, had drained stein after stein of the heady, cold October beer, its fumes had mounted in his head until the thousand beery faces all about him grew fantastic, ghostlike, in that fetid, smoke-fogged air. Again there had been the roaring tumult of the people rising from their tables, linking arms together with their mugs upraised, the rhythmic swinging, the rocking back and forth to the blaring of "Ein Prosit!" Again the ritualistic spell of all those human rings in swaying, roaring, one-voiced chant there in that vast and murky hall; again the image of the savage faces in the old dark forest of barbaric time; again the sudden fear of them that froze his heart. What happened then he did not know. In that quick instant of his drunken fear, had he swung out and smashed his great stone mug into the swine-like face, the red pig's eyes, of the hulking fellow next to him? He did not know, but there had been a fight—a murderous swinging of great mugs, a flash of knives, the sudden blinding fury of red, beer-drunk rage. And now he lay there in the hospital, his head all swathed in bandages; he lay upon his back and listened, listened to the rain.

The rain dripped down from roof and limb and spout, and as he listened to it he thought of all the glistening buildings of the Fair: within, the gorging, drinking, swaying, singing throngs, their faces gleaming redly in the body-heat of steaming, smoke-filled air; outside, the shambles of the mud and slime that must be there in all those lanes and passages that had been beaten, trampled, battered down beneath so many thousand feet. A clock struck out its measurement of mortal time with a solemn and final sweetness, and the rain drove in between him and that sound and made phantasmal readings of the news it bore. The news it bore to him was that another hour for all men living had gone by, and that all men living now were just that one hour closer to their death; and whether it was the silent presence of the ancient and eternal earth that lay about him—that ancient earth that lay here in the darkness like a beast now drinking steadily, relentlessly, unweariedly into its depth the rain that fell upon it—he did not know, but suddenly it seemed to him that all man's life was like one small tongue of earth that juts into the waters of time, and that incessantly, steadily, in the darkness, in the night, this tongue of earth was crumbling in the tide, was melting evenly in dark waters.

As he lay there looking at the ceiling, the door had opened silently and a nun, in her nurse's uniform and spotless linen and her bonnet with its enormous wings of stiff, starched white, came in to look at him. Her small white face, framed closely in its cowl of holiness, shone from the prison of her garments with a startling and almost indecent nakednes. She came and went so softly in that somber light of the shaded lamp that it was as if he had been visited by a ghost, and somehow he felt afraid of her.

But now he looked at her and saw that her face was pure and delicate; it was a good face, but for men it had neither mercy nor love nor passion in it. Her heart and love were fixed divinely and dwelt among the blessed of heaven. She passed her life upon this earth a shadow and an exile; the blood of the wounded, the pain of the suffering, the cry of sorrow, the terror of the dying, had made her neither hard nor pitying. She could not grieve as he did for the death of men, since what was death to him was life to her; what was the end of hope and joy and blessedness for him, for her was only the beginning.

She laid her cool hand on his forehead, spoke a few words to him which he did not hear, and then she left him.

When he had entered the clinic and Geheimrat Becker had examined the wounds upon his head, he had discovered two on the left side of the skull. They were each about an inch and a half in length and they crossed each other like an X. The Herr Geheimrat ordered his assistant to shave the hair away around the wounds, and this was done. Monk was left, therefore, with a fringe of abundant hair, and a ridiculous bald spot about the size of a saucer askew upon his skull.

At the first, while Geheimrat Becker's brutal fingers probed and pressed and sponged, Monk believed that there was another smaller wound lost in the thick luxuriance of hair at the back of his head which the doctor had not seen. But his fame was so great, his manner so authoritative, and his speech to Monk when he had mentioned it so gruff and so contemptuous, that Monk had said no further word, yielding to the man's authority and to that desire in all of us which leads us to try to escape trouble by ignoring it.

He had at no time been in any danger. His fears were phantoms of his dark imagining, and he knew this now. He had bled copiously and lost much blood, but his wounds were already healing. In time the hair would grow out again and cover the scars on his bald skull, and the only visible results of his injuries in the end might be a crooked set to his broken nose and the small scar of a knife across its fleshy tip.

So now at night there was nothing for him to do but lie and wait and look up at the ceiling.

The room had four white walls, a bed, a night-stand, and a lamp, a dresser, and a chair. The walls were high and square, the ceiling, too, was white, just like a blank of time and memory, and everything was very clean. At night, when just the lamp beside the bed was lighted, the high white walls and ceiling would be muted of their brightness, suffused and mellowed with a shade of somber light. And this, too, was like waiting, and the sound of rain.

Above the door there was a wooden crucifix, nailed with tormented claws, the splayed, nailed feet, the gaunt ribs, and the twisted thighs, the starved face, and the broken agony of Christ. And that image, so cruel in compassion, so starved, so twisted, and so broken in the paradox of its stern mercy, the fatal example of its suffering, was so alien to Pine Rock, to Joyners, and to Baptistry, to all the forms he knew, that it filled him with a sense of strangeness and uneasy awe.

Then there would come an impatient shift in this eternity of dreary waiting. He would hitch around in the hard sheets, and pound the pillow, jerk the covers, curse the hard discomfort of the sloping mattress wedge that always kept the upper body at a tilt. He would run his fingers over the shaved pate of his scarred head, feel the ridges of scabbed scars, and thrust his hand beneath the bandages, cursing where the hair was left, and at the throbbing of the one they *hadn't* got; and, roused to a sudden boil of blind, unreasonable fury, he would swing erect, stride to the door, and down the stillness of the sleeping hall, roar out:

"Johann! . . . Johann! Johann!"

And he would come, hastening along the green oiled matting of the hallway with a heavy limp. His limping, too, infuriated Monk, for Becker limped in the same way; he had been Becker's orderly, both had been wounded in the leg—the same leg, the same limp: "Do they *all* limp?" Monk thought, and the thought would fill him with a bitter rage.

"Johann."

He came up limping. His face, square, brown, and wide, full-nosed, plain, was full of protest, admonition, and bewildered concern:

"Was ist?" he said.

"The *Verbindung.*"

"Ach!" He looked, and then with reproachful accusation, "You moved it!"

"But I'm still verletzt! Look! Tell Becker there's a place he didn't find!" He put his finger on it, pointing.

He felt; then laughed and shook his head:

"Nein, it's only the Verbindung!" Johann said.

"I tell you I'm verletzt!" Monk cried.

Heel-tapping and unsleeping, brisk, along the oiled green hall-way of the night, her plain face pleated in her bonnet between enormous wings of starch, the Mother Superior of the night came in:

"Was ist?"

He pointed, mollified a little: "Here."

"It is nothing," Johann said to her. "It is the bandage, but he thinks it is a wound."

"Here! . . . Here!" Monk choked, and pointed.

She put her parsley fingers on the place:

"It is a wound," she said.

"Nein!" said Johann, amazed. "But Herr Geheimrat said—"

"There is a wound," she said.

Oh, sustained now by that reassurance as by the tidings of immediate victory—to know *that* butcher of a doctor was *one time* wrong! That brutal scorner with contemptuous tongue, that hog-necked contemner with the butcher's thumb—was wrong!—was *wrong!* By God!—ah, wounds, scars, and bandages—all was one to him! The limping butcher with the brutal thumb, for one time in his damned butcher's life—was *wrong!*

"Verletzt, ja! . . . And with fever!" gloatingly Monk said.

Between enormous wings of white, she laid her cool and parsley finger on his forehead; and said quietly:

"Kein Fieber!"

"I tell you that I have!"

"Fieber?" Johann turned his square and puzzled face to her. And she, stern-faced as ever, gentle, grave, implacable:

"Kein Fieber. Nein."

"I tell you that I have!" Monk cried. "And the Geheimrat—yes! the *great* Geheimrat Becker—" chokingly.

And with stern quietude, between enormous wings of starch, with stern reproach, she said:

"The *Herr* Geheimrat!"

"The *Herr* Geheimrat then!—he couldn't find it!"

Sternly, quietly:

"You have not fever. Now, go back to bed!" She went away.

"But the Geheimrat!" Monk now shouted.

Johann looked steadily at him. His plain German face was now severe in a quiet look of outraged decorum and protest.

"Please," he said. "The people are in bed."

"But the Geheimrat—?"

"The *Herr* Geheimrat—" quietly and pointedly—"the Herr Geheimrat also is in bed!"

"Then wake him, Johann! Tell him I have fever! He must come!" And suddenly, shaking with a feeling of outrage and insult, Monk shouted loudly down the hall:

"Geheimrat Becker! . . . Becker! . . . Where is Becker? . . . I want Becker! . . . Geheimrat Becker—O Geheimrat Becker—" jeeringly— "*great* Geheimrat Becker—are you there?"

His face a map of outraged decency, Johann took Monk by the arm and whispered:

Quiet! . . . Are you mad? . . . The Herr Geheimrat Becker is not here!"

"Not *here?*" Monk stared unbelievingly into the square face. "Not *here?*"

"Nein," implacably. "Not here."

Not *here!*—the limping butcher was not *here!*—in his own slaughter pen! The shaven butcher, with his scarred face, his shaven head, his creased neck—was not *here!*— where he was born to be, to limp along these halls, to probe thick fingers at a wound—in his own slaughter house, the butcher was not *here!*

"Then *where?*" the astounded questioner turned on Johann now. "Then where is he?"

"At home, of course," he answered with a patient accent of reproof. "Where should he be?"

"At *home?*" Monk stared at him. "He has a *home!* You mean to tell me *Becker* has a *home?*"

"But, ja, Natürlich," he said in a tone of patient weariness. "And wife, and kinder."

"A *wife!*" Monk looked blank. "And *children!* You mean to tell me *he* has *children?*"

"But naturally, of course. Four of them!"

The limping butcher with the brutal thumb has—

That the surly Becker with the short, thick fingers and the hairy hands, with his heavy limp, his bullet head, his stiff clipped brush of grey-black mustache, his bald skull with its ugly edge of shaved blue skin, and his coarse, pleated face scarred with old duelling wounds—that this creature had any existence apart from the life of the hospital had never occurred to Monk, and now it seemed fantastic. His presence possessed and dominated the place: he seemed an organism that was constantly buttoned to its thick, strong neck in butcher's robe of starched white, and no more to be imagined without this garment, in the ordinary clothing of citizenship, than one of the nuns in the high heels and trimmed skirts of a worldly woman. He was like the living spirit of these walls, a special creation waiting here to hurl himself upon the maimed and wounded of the earth, to force them roughly back upon a table as he had forced Monk back, and then to take their flesh and bones into his keeping, to press, probe, squeeze with brutal fingers, and if necessary, to chisel upon their skulls, to solder together their broken plates, even to cut down to the living convolutions of man's thought. . . .

Johann looked at Monk and shook his head, and then said quietly:

"Go back to bed. The Herr Geheimrat will be in to see you in the morning."

He limped away.

Monk went back and sat down on his bed.

Facing him, on the wall, was a mirror above the dresser, and he stared into it.

"Man's image in a broken looking glass." What of his broken image in a looking glass unbroken?

Out of the dark pool of the looking glass, the Thing hinged forward at the waist, the trunk foreshortened, the thick neck sunken in the hulking shoulders, the barrel contours of the chest, the big paw clasped around the knee. So was he made, so fashioned.

And what nature had invented, human effort had improved. In the dark pool of the mirror the Thing was more grotesque and simian than it had ever been. Denuded of its shock of hair, the rakishly tonsured skull between the big wings of its ears came close upon the corrugated shortness of the forehead into the bushy ridges of the brow; below this, the small, battered features, the short pug nose, uptilted, flattened towards the right (it had been broken at the center on the other side), the long upper lip, thick mouth, the general look of startled, quick attentiveness—it was a good job. Not since childhood had he looked so much the part the boys had made for him—the "Monk."

He looked at it now, and it at him, with a quizzical, detached objectiveness, not as a child looks in a mirror, at the silent eloquence of his pooled self, unspeaking, saying "I," but outside of it, and opposite, regardant, thinking, "Well, by God, *you* are a pretty sight!"—and meaning, not *Himself,* but *It.*

It looked back at him, breathing thickly through half-parted, swollen lips. (He could smell the odor of stale iodine, the dried-blood-wadded cotton in his nose.) He drew in hoarsely through the battered mouth, and in the looking glass the loosened teeth bared, caked with filaments of blood. Above the mouth, the nose smeared sideways on the face, the blood-injected eyes attentive now; below the eyes, the rainbow purple-green-and-yellow coloration of the face.

"Christ! What a mug!"

It grinned back crookedly through its battered mask; and suddenly—all pride and vanity destroyed—he laughed. The battered mask laughed with him, and at last his soul was free. He was a man.

"Well, Mug?"

"Love's Martyr?" it replied, grinning back.

"Nature's Masterpiece!"

"Art's Exile!"

"Darwin's Pet!"

"Who let *you* out?" his Body said quite pointedly.

"Who let me *out? Out,* hell! Who put me *in,* you mean?"

"Meaning *me?*" his Body said.

"Yes, *you!*"

"I thought the crack was so intended," said his Body. "Well?"

"Well?"

"If you hadn't been put *in,* where *would* you be?"

"In clover, my pug-nosed, thuggish-looking friend. In clover, Ape."

"That's what *you* think," his Body said sardonically.

"That's what I *know!* You gorilla, you! *You* don't belong! You're just an accident!"

"I am, hey? And *you?* I suppose you're something that was all planned out."

"Well—"

"And with pretty little feet," his Body said ironically. "And such fine hands—" it lifted its thick paws and looked at them—"with the long, tapering fingers of the artist—is that it?" his Body sneered.

"Now, Body, don't you sneer!"

"And six feet, two inches of lean American young manhood—"

"Now—"

"—but would compromise on six feet one, bless his little heart! And light blond hair, by nature curly!"

"Your nature, Body, is so coarse and low you can't appreciate—"

"The Finer Things," said Body dryly. "Yes, I know!—but to proceed: blue eyes, a Roman nose, a classic brow, the profile of a young Greek god—Byron, in short, without the limp or fatness—the ladies' darling, and a genius to boot!"

"Now, Body, damn your soul!"

"I have no soul," said Body dryly. "That's for '*Artists*'—is that the word?" it leered.

"Don't you sneer!"

"The soul is for Great Lovers," Body said. "My soul is suspended down below the waist. True, it has served you in your own more soulful flights—we won't go into that," said Body wryly. "I'm just a millstone round your neck—an accident."

And for a moment more they stared there at each other; then they grinned.

As he sat there staring at the image of his body in the mirror, the memory of their life together came back to pierce him with its poignant mystery. He thought of the millions of steps they had made together, of the millions of times they had drawn upon the air for breath and life, and of the thousands of times they had heard the clocks of time strike out below the timeless light of un- known skies. Yes, they had been long together, this body and he. They had lived alone so much, they had felt and seen and thought so much, and now they knew what they knew, they did not deny and regret each other, they were friends.

There had been a time, a child's time of wish and fable, when he had not seen his body as it was. Then he saw himself clothed in comely flesh. Together they were the hero of a thousand brave and romantic exploits, they were beautiful and brave together.

Then there had come a time when he had cursed and hated his body because he thought it was ugly and absurd and unworthy of him, because he thought it was a cause of all his trouble and grief, because he felt it had betrayed him and shut him away from the life he loved so well and wanted to belong to. He wanted to know all things and persons living, and constantly he wished to say to people:

"This grotesque figure that you see is nothing like me. Pay no attention to it. Forget about it. I am like one of you. I *am* one of you. Please try to see me as I really am. My blood bleeds and is red the same as yours. In every particular I am made from the same elements, born on the same earth, living the same life and hating the same death, as you. I am one of you in every way, and I *will* have my rightful place among you now!"

At that time he had been impatient and angry, and he hated his body because he knew it came between him and his most deep desires. He despised it because its powers of smell, taste, sight, sound, and touch let slip forever, as all flesh must, the final, potent, and completest distillation of life, the matchless ecstasy of living. So he had beaten and smashed at it in his madness, driven and abused it under the terrible lash of his insatiate thirst and hunger, made it the vessel of that mad lust of belly and brain and heart which for four thousand days and nights had never given him a moment's waking peace. He had cursed it because it could not do the inhuman task he set for it, hated it because its hunger could not match his hunger, which was for the earth and all things living in it.

But now he felt none of these things. As he sat there and saw the figure in the mirror, it was like some homely garment which he had worn all his days and which he had for a moment discarded. His naked spirit had stepped out of its rude residence, and this clothing of flesh and bone now stared back at it and awakened in it the emotion of friendship and respect with which we regard any old object—a shoe, a chair, a table, or a hat—which has shared our life and served us loyally.

Now, they had got a little wisdom for themselves. This flesh had not betrayed him. It had been strong, enduring, and enormously sensitive within the limitations of its senses. The arms were too long, the legs too short, the hands and feet a little closer to the simian than most men's are, but they belonged to the family of the earth, they were not deformed. The only deformity had been in the madness and bitterness of his heart. But now he had learned, through a wisdom of the body and the brain, that a spirit which thinks itself too fine for the rough uses of the world is too young and callow, or else too centered on itself, too inward-turning, too enamored of the beauties of its own artistic soul and worth to find itself by losing self in something larger than itself, and thus to find its place and do a man's work in the world—too fine for all of this, and hence defeated, precious, fit for nothing.

They had discovered the earth together, this flesh and he, they had discovered it alone, in secrecy, in exile, and in wandering, and far more than most men living they knew what they knew for themselves. Alone, by their hard labor, they got the cup into their hands and drank it. They learned the things most other men were lucky to have given to them. And now, for all their sweat and agony, what did they know? This: that they loved life and their fellow men and hated the death-in-life, and that it was better to live than die.

Now he looked at his body without falsehood or rancor, and with wonder that he dwelt there in this place. He knew and accepted now its limitations. He knew now that the demon of his mortal hunger would be inches and eternities from his grasp forever. He knew that we who are men are more than men, and less than spirit. What have we but the pinion of a broken wing to soar half-heavenward?

Yes! He knew as he looked at the grotesque figure in the mirror that he had done all with his hunger and his flesh that one man could. And he knew also, although the bleared and battered face might seem to be the visage of a madman, the spirit that dwelt behind this ruined mask now looked calmly and sanely forth upon the earth for the first time in ten years.

"Is it a man," he said, "that waits here so unsleeping in the ventricles of night?"

"Or, so unsleeping, is it not the Body that holds the man?"

"It is not true. Now, Body, let me sleep."

"It is. Now, Man, let me."

"No, Body; it's the brute, compulsive Worm that here, within the ventricles of night, keeps working always, and that will not let me sleep."

"The Worm is yours. There was no Worm when, in the years long past, the Body of your recent wrath and you lay down together."

"But there was the Worm."

"The Worm incipient, Worm progressive, Worm crawling in the blood, first stirring in the leaf."

"Somewhere, somewhere begun—*where? where?* Was that the Worm?"

"Long, long ago—where hatched, God knows, or in what particle of memory—perhaps with sunlight on the porch."

"Which was a good time then, for there were all the things that came and went, the steps, the basket, and the bright nasturtiums—"

"The immediate clackings of the sun-warm hens, the common crack of wake-a-day, and someone's voice in the Immediate, the skreaking halt upon the corner on the hill of street cars coming home for noon, and men and leather in the street, and yard-gates slammed and sudden greetings, the cold invigoration of sawn ice at noon—the hard black stench of funky niggers, and the ice tongs and linoleum—the coarse, sweet coolness of Crane's cow along the alleyway, along the hammocks of the backyard fence—"

"And were *you* there?"

"Aye! To the limits of mortality."

"And to the pits of time and memory?"

"Not so. That was *your* part—here were the first intrusions of the blind, compulsive Worm. But I was there, was *there*—aye, fat-legged in a wicker basket, feeling light."

"Lights going, lights returning—sadness, hope—"

"Yours, *yours*—the sickness of the Worm—not mine! Mine the sun!"

"But sorrow, Body, when it went away?"

"Discomfort sometimes—not regret. Regret's the Worm."

"Would howl?"

"Would howl, yes! When I was filthy and befouled, nasty, wet, sour-bellied,——upon! Would howl! Would howl!—Yes! Would howl for comfort, warmth, appeasement, a full belly, a warm-bottom—sun!"

"And then?"

"No more, no more. The plain Immediate. That was the good time then."

"The time that is good—"

"Is the time when once there was a tiny little boy," the Body said.

"That is the good time because it is the time the sunlight came and went upon the porch, and when there was a sound of people coming home at noon, earth loaming, grass spermatic, a fume of rope-sperm in the nostrils and the dewlaps of the throat, torpid, thick, and undelightful, the humid commonness of housewives turbaned with a dish-clout, the small dreariness of As-They-Are mixed in with humid turnip greens, and houses aired to morning, the turned mattress and the beaten rug, the warm and common mucus of the earth-nasturtium smells, the thought of parlors and the good stale smell, the sudden, brooding stretch of absence of the street car after it had gone, and a feeling touched with desolation hoping noon would come."

"That was your own—the turnings of the Worm," his Body said.

"And then Crane's cow again, and morning, morning in the thickets of the memory, and so many lives-and-deaths of life so long ago, together with the thought of Winter howling in the oak, so many sunlights that had come and gone since morning, morning, and all lost voices—'Son, where are you?"—of lost kinsmen in the mountains long ago. . . . That was a good time then."

"Yes," said Body. "But—you can't go home again."

YOU CAN'T GO HOME AGAIN

YOU CAN'T GO HOME AGAIN is the most loosely organized of Wolfe's novels. In assembling it, Edward C. Aswell had much less help from the manuscript than he had had in assembling *The Web and the Rock*. Indeed, this last novel of Wolfe's probably should be considered a bringing together, in a loose narrative frame, of blocks of material which Wolfe had completed but only partially arranged at the time of his death. In it George Webber returns from Europe, writes a book, returns to Libya Hill, travels in Europe again, discovers the emptiness of fame by observing Lloyd McHarg (Sinclair Lewis), travels to Germany and there becomes aware of the terror at the heart of Naziism, and writes a long letter setting forth his beliefs. What is most valuable about the book, however, is not this frame but the sharply drawn pictures of life to which Webber is witness and the deepening concern with social issues by which the book is marked. The most "objective" of his works in style, it is also the most socially oriented of his novels.

The passages here selected from it are reasonably self-contained units displaying Wolfe's critical interest in society. Each of them has had a life as a separate story or sketch.

"Nebraska Crane," which was published as a short story in *Harper's Magazine,* in August, 1940, introduces one of Wolfe's most effective characters, and apparently one without a real-life model. The story also illustrates Wolfe's great love for baseball. The material dramatically presented here would probably have filled three times this much space a few years earlier in his career.

"Boom Town" is a combination in greatly revised form of material from two stories, "Boom Town," published in the *American Mercury,* in May, 1934, and "The Company," published in *New Masses,* in January, 1938. The combined stories form a satiric attack on the standards of middle class America and an almost Marxist view of business tactics. In "Boom Town" and in the short novel *The Party at Jack's* (also included in *You Can't Go Home Again*) Wolfe made his sharpest comments on the America economic system.

"The Hollow Men" was published as a sketch in *Esquire* magazine in October, 1940. In it Foxhall Edwards, Webber's editor (whose prototype was Maxwell Perkins), while reading his newspaper, broods upon the death of a cipher in the city whose passing identifies "a single spot of all our general Nothingness with the unique passion, the awful terror, and the dignity of Death." In its witty and almost playful improvisation on a serious theme, the sketch is typical of Wolfe's late non-fictional expressions of dislike for the mechanization of life in the city.

"The Promise of America" was published as a prose poem in *Coronet* magazine in September, 1940. Here, in one of his most famous prose poems, Wolfe celebrates America and makes one of his strongest statements of democratic principle.

"Credo" is the concluding section of the long letter to Foxhall Edwards about his beliefs. As an ending to a novel, this letter is obviously unsatisfactory; as a statement of belief and of commitment to a doctrine of radical democracy, it is a moving and effective document. I have omitted the concluding paragraphs, which were originally written for a different context, and have reserved them for use at the end of this Reader.

All of the selections are from *You Can't Go Home Again* (New York: Harper and Brothers, 1940). "Nebraska Crane" appears on pages 55-69; "Boom Town" on pages 109-140; "The Hollow Men" on pages 460-482; "The Promise of America" on pages 505-508; and "Credo" on pages 739-743.

NEBRASKA CRANE

THE TRAIN had hurtled like a projectile through its tube beneath the Hudson River to emerge in the dazzling sunlight of a September afternoon, and now it was racing across the flat desolation of the Jersey meadows. George sat by the window and saw the smoldering dumps, the bogs, the blackened factories slide past, and felt that one of the most wonderful things in the world is the experience of being on a train. It is so different from watching a train go by. To anyone outside, a speeding train is a thunderbolt of driving rods, a hot hiss of steam, a blurred flash of coaches, a wall of movement and of noise, a shriek, a wail, and then just emptiness and absence, with a feeling of "There goes everybody!" without knowing who anybody is. And all of a sudden the watcher feels the vastness and loneliness of America, and the nothingness of all those little lives hurled pass upon the immensity of the continent. But if one is *inside* the train, everything is different. The train itself is a miracle of man's handiwork, and everything about it is eloquent of human purpose and direction. One feels the brakes go on when the train is coming to a river, and one knows that the old gloved hand of cunning is at the throttle. One's own sense of manhood and of mastery is heightened by being on a train. And all the other people, how real they are! One sees the fat black porter with his ivory teeth and the great swollen gland on the back of his neck, and one warms with friendship for him. One looks at all the pretty girls with a sharpened eye and an awakened pulse. One observes all the other passengers with lively interest, and feels that he has known them forever. In the morning most of them will be gone out of his life; some will drop out silently at night through the dark, drugged snoring of the sleepers; but now all are caught upon the wing and held for a moment in the peculiar intimacy of this pullman car which has become their common home for a night.

Two traveling salesmen have struck up a chance acquaintance in the smoking room, entering immediately the vast confraternity of their trade, and in a moment they are laying out the continent as familiarly as if it were their own backyard. They tell about running into So-and-So in St. Paul last July, and—

"Who do you suppose I met coming out of Brown's Hotel in Denver just a week ago?"

"You don't mean it! I haven't seen old Joe in years!"

"And Jim Withers—they've transferred him to the Atlanta office!"

"Going to New Orleans?"

"No, I'll not make it this trip. I was there in May."

With such talk as this one grows instantly familiar. One enters naturally into the lives of all these people, caught here for just a night and hurtled down together across the continent at sixty miles an hour, and one becomes a member of the whole huge family of the earth.

Perhaps this is our strange and haunting paradox here in America—that we are fixed and certain only when we are in movement. At any rate, that is how it seemed to young George Webber, who was never so assured of his purpose as when he was going somewhere on a train. And he never had the sense of home so much as when he felt that he was going there. It was only when he got there that his homelessness began.

At the far end of the car a man stood up and started back down the aisle toward the washroom. He walked with a slight limp and leaned upon a cane, and with his free hand he held onto the backs of the seats to brace himself against the lurching of the train. As he came abreast of George, who sat there gazing out the window, the man stopped abruptly. A strong, good-natured voice, warm, easy, bantering, unafraid, unchanged—exactly as it was when it was fourteen years of age—broke like a flood of living light upon his consciousness:

"Well I'll be dogged! Hi, there, Monkus! Where you goin'?"

At the sound of the old jesting nickname George looked up quickly. It was Nebraska Crane. The square, freckled, sunburned visage had the same humorous friendliness it had always had, and the tar-black Cherokee eyes looked out with the same straight, deadly fearlessness. The big brown paw came out and they clasped each other firmly. And, instantly, it was like coming home to a strong and friendly place. In another moment they were seated together, talking with the familiarity of people whom no gulf of years and distance could alter or separate.

George had seen Nebraska Crane only once in all the years since he himself had first left Libya Hill and gone away to college. But he had not lost sight of him. Nobody had lost sight of Nebraska Crane. That wiry, fearless little figure of the Cherokee boy who used to come down the hill on Locust Street with the bat slung over his shoulder and the well-oiled fielder's mitt protruding from his hip pocket had been prophetic of a greater destiny, for Nebraska had become a professional baseball player, he had crashed into the big leagues, and his name had been emblazoned in the papers every day.

The newspapers had had a lot to do with his seeing Nebraska that other time. It was in August 1925, just after George had returned to New York from his first trip abroad. That very night, in fact, a little before midnight, as he was seated in a Childs Restaurant with smoking wheatcakes, coffee, and an ink-fresh copy of next morning's *Herald-Tribune* before him, the headline jumped out at him: "Crane Slams Another Homer." He read the account of the game eagerly, and felt a strong desire to see Nebraska again and to get back in his blood once more the honest tang of America. Acting on a sudden impulse, he decided to call him up. Sure enough, his name was in the book, with an address way up in the Bronx. He gave the number and waited. A man's voice answered the phone, but at first he didn't recognize it.

"Hello! . . . Hello! . . . Is Mr. Crane there? . . . Is that you, Bras?"

"Hello." Nebraska's voice was hesitant, slow, a little hostile, touched with the caution and suspicion of mountain people when speaking to a stranger. "Who is that? . . . Who? . . . Is that *you,* Monk?"—suddenly and quickly, as he recognized who it was. "Well I'll be dogged!" he cried. His tone was delighted, astounded, warm with friendly greeting now, and had the somewhat high and faintly howling quality that mountain people's voices often have when they are talking to someone over the telephone: the tone was full, sonorous, countrified, and a little puzzled, as if he were yelling to someone on an adjoining mountain peak on a gusty day in autumn when the wind was thrashing through the trees. "Where'd you come from? How the hell are you, boy?" he yelled before George could answer. "Where you been all this time, anyway?"

"I've been in Europe. I just got back this morning."

"Well, I'll be dogged!"—still astounded, delighted, full of howling friendliness. "When am I gonna see you? How about comin' to the game tomorrow? I'll fix you up. And say," he went on rapidly, "if you can stick aroun' after the game, I'll take you home to meet the wife and kid. How about it?"

So it was agreed. George went to the game and saw Nebraska knock another home run, but he remembered best what happened afterwards. When the player had had his shower and had dressed, the two friends left the ball park, and as they went out a crowd of young boys who had been waiting at the gate rushed upon them. They were those dark-faced, dark-eyed, dark-haired little urchins who spring up like dragon seed from the grim pavements of New York, but in whose tough little faces and raucous voices there still remains, curiously, the innocence and faith of children everywhere. "It's Bras!" the children cried. "Hi, Bras! Hey, Bras!" In a moment they were pressing round him in a swarming horde, deafening the ears with their shrill cries, begging, shouting, tugging at his sleeves, doing everything they could to attract his attention, holding dirty little scraps of paper toward him, stubs of pencils, battered little notebooks, asking him to sign his autograph.

He behaved with the spontaneous warmth and kindliness of his character. He scrawled his name out rapidly on a dozen grimy bits of paper, skillfully working his way along through the yelling, pushing, jumping group, and all the time keeping up a rapid fire of banter, badinage, and good-natured reproof:

"All right—give it here, then! . . . Why don't you fellahs pick on somebody else once in a while? . . . Say, boy!" he said suddenly, turning to look down at one unfortunate child, and pointing an accusing finger at him—"What you doin' aroun' here again today? I signed my name fer you at least a dozen times!"

"No sir, Misteh Crane!" the urchin earnestly replied. "Honest—not me!"

"Ain't that right?" Nebraska said, appealing to the other children. "Don't this boy keep comin' back here every day?"

They grinned, delighted at the chagrin of their fellow petitioner. "Dat's right, Misteh Crane! Dat guy's got a whole book wit' nuttin' but yoeh name in it!"

"Ah-h!" the victim cried, and turned upon his betrayers bitterly. "What youse guys tryin' to do—get wise or somep'n? Honest, Misteh Crane!"—he looked up earnestly again at Nebraska—"Don't believe 'em! I jest want yoeh ottygraph! Please, Misteh Crane, it'll only take a minute!"

For a moment more Nebraska stood looking down at the child with an expression of mock sternness; at last he took the outstretched notebook, rapidly scratched his name across a page, and handed it back. And as he did so, he put his big paw on the urchin's head and gave it a clumsy pat; then, gently and playfully, he shoved it from him, and walked off down the street.

The apartment where Nebraska lived was like a hundred thousand others in the Bronx. The ugly yellow brick building has a false front, with meaningless little turrets at the corners of the roof, and a general air of spurious luxury about it. The rooms were rather small and cramped, and were made even more so by the heavy, overstuffed Grand Rapids furniture. The walls of the living room, painted a mottled, rusty cream, were bare except for a couple of sentimental colored prints, while the place of honor over the mantel was reserved for an enlarged and garishly tinted photograph of Nebraska's little son at the age of two, looking straight and solemnly out at all comers from a gilded oval frame.

Myrtle, Nebraska's wife, was small and plump, and pretty in a doll-like way. Her corn-silk hair was frizzled in a halo about her face, and her chubby features were heavily accented by rouge and lipstick. But she was simple and natural in her talk and bearing, and George liked her at once. She welcomed him with a warm and friendly smile and said she had heard a lot about him.

They all sat down. The child, who was three or four years old by this time, and who had been shy, holding onto his mother's dress and peeping out from behind her, now ran across the room to his father and began climbing all over him. Nebraska and Myrtle asked George a lot of questions about himself, what he had been doing, where he had been, and especially what countries he had visited in Europe. They seemed to think of Europe as a place so far away that anyone who had actually been there was touched with an unbelievable aura of strangeness and romance.

"Whereall did you go over there, anyway?" asked Nebraska.

"Oh, everywhere, Bras," George said—"France, England, Holland, Germany, Denmark, Sweden, Italy—all over the place."

"Well I'll be dogged!"—in frank astonishment. "You sure do git aroun', don't you?"

"Not the way *you* do, Bras. You're traveling most of the time."

"Who—*me?* Oh, hell, I don't git anywhere—just the same ole

places. Chicago, St. Looie, Philly—I seen 'em all so often I could find
my way blindfolded!" He waved them aside with a gesture of his
hand. Then, suddenly, he looked at George as though he were just
seeing him for the first time, and he reached over and slapped him
on the knee and exclaimed: "Well I'll be dogged! How you doin',
anyway, Monkus?"

"Oh, can't complain. How about you? But I don't need to ask that.
I've been reading all about you in the papers."

"Yes, Monkus," he said. "I been havin' a good year. But, boy!"—
he shook his head suddenly and grinned—"Do the ole dogs feel it!"

He was silent a moment, then he went on quietly:

"I been up here since 1919—that's seven years, and it's a long time
in this game. Not many of 'em stay much longer. When you been
shaggin' flies as long as that you may lose count, but you don't need
to count—your legs'll tell you."

"But, good Lord, Bras, *you're* all right! Why, the way you got
around out there today you looked like a colt!"

"Yeah," Nebraska said, "maybe I *looked* like a colt, but I felt like
a plough horse." He fell silent again, then he tapped his friend
gently on the knee with his brown hand and said abruptly: "No,
Monkus. When you been in this business as long as I have, you
know it."

"Oh, come on, Bras, quit your kidding!" said George, remembering that the player was only two years older than himself. "You're
still a young man. Why, you're only twenty-seven!"

"Sure, sure," Nebraska answered quietly. "But it's like I say. You
cain't stay in this business much longer than I have. Of course, Cobb
an' Speaker an' a few like that—they was up here a long time. But
eight years is about the average, an' I been here seven already. So
if I can hang on a few years more, I won't have no kick to make. . . .
Hell!" he said in a moment, with the old hearty ring in his voice,
"I ain't got no kick to make, no-way. If I got my release tomorrow,
I'd still feel I done all right. . . . Ain't that so, Buzz?" he cried genially
to the child, who had settled down on his knee, at the same time seizing the boy and cradling him comfortably in his strong arm. "Ole
Bras has done all right, ain't he?"

"That's the way me an' Bras feel about it," remarked Myrtle, who
during this conversation had been rocking back and forth, placidly
ruminating on a wad of gum. "Along there last year it looked once

or twice as if Bras might git traded. He said to me one day before the game, 'Well, ole lady, if I don't git some hits today somethin' tells me you an' me is goin' to take a trip.' So I says, 'Trip where?' An' he says, 'I don't know, but they're goin' to sell me down the river if I don't git goin', an' somethin' tells me it's now or never!' So I just looks at him," continued Myrtle placidly, "an' I says, 'Well, what do you want me to do? Do you want me to come today or not?' You know, gener'ly, Bras won't let me come when he ain't hittin'— he says it's bad luck. But he just looks at me a minute, an' I can see him sort of studyin' it over, an' all of a sudden he makes up his mind an' says, 'Yes, come on if you want to; I couldn't have no more bad luck than I been havin', no-way, an' maybe it's come time fer things to change, so you come on.' Well, I went—an' I don't know whether I brought him luck or not, but somethin' did," said Myrtle, rocking in her chair complacently.

"Dogged if she didn't!" Nebraska chuckled. "I got three hits out of four times up that day, an' two 'em was home runs!"

"Yeah," Myrtle agreed, "an' that Philadelphia fast-ball thrower was throwin' 'em, too."

"He sure was!" said Nebraska.

"I know," went on Myrtle, chewing placidly, "because I heard some of the boys say later that it was like he was throwin' 'em up there from out of the bleachers, with all them men in shirt-sleeves right behind him, an' the boys said half the time they couldn't even see the ball. But Bras must of saw it—or been lucky—because he hit two home runs off of him, an' that pitcher didn't like it, either. The second one Bras got, he went stompin' an' tearin' around out there like a wild bull. He sure did look mad," said Myrtle in her customary placid tone.

"Maddest man I ever seen!" Nebraska cried delightedly. "I thought he was goin' to dig a hole plumb through to China. . . . But that's the way it was. She's right about it. That was the day I got goin'. I know one of the boys said to me later, 'Bras,' he says, 'we all thought you was goin' to take a ride, but you sure dug in, didn't you?' That's the way it is in this game. I seen Babe Ruth go fer weeks when he couldn't hit a balloon, an' all of a sudden he lams into it. Seems like he just cain't miss from then on."

All this had happened four years ago. Now the two friends had met again, and were seated side by side in the speeding train, talking and catching up on one another. When George explained the reason for his going home, Nebraska turned to him with open-mouthed astonishment, genuine concern written in the frown upon his brown and homely face.

"Well, what d'you know about that!" he said. "I sure am sorry, Monk." He was silent while he thought about it, and embarrassed, not knowing what to say. Then, after a moment: "Gee!"—he shook his head—"your aunt was one swell cook! I never will fergit it! Remember how she used to feed us kids—every danged one of us in the whole neighborhood?" He paused, then grinned up shyly at his friend: "I sure wish I had a fistful of them good ole cookies of hers right this minute!"

Nebraska's right ankle was taped and bandaged; a heavy cane rested between his knees. George asked him what had happened.

"I pulled a tendon," Nebraska said, "an' got laid off. So I thought I might as well run down an' see the folks. Myrtle, she couldn't come —the kid's got to git ready fer school."

"How are they?" George asked.

"Oh, fine, fine. All wool an' a yard wide, both of 'em!" He was silent for a moment, then he looked at his friend with a tolerant Cherokee grin and said: "But I'm crackin' up, Monkus. Guess I cain't stan' the gaff much more."

Nebraska was only thirty-one now, and George was incredulous. Nebraska smiled good-naturedly again:

"That's an ole man in baseball, Monk. I went up when I was twenty-one. I been aroun' a long time."

The quiet resignation of the player touched his friend with sadness. It was hard and painful for him to face the fact that this strong and fearless creature, who had stood in his life always for courage and for victory, should now be speaking with such ready acceptance of defeat.

"But, Bras," he protested, "you've been hitting just as well this season as you ever did! I've read about you in the papers, and the reporters have all said the same thing."

"Oh, I can still hit 'em," Nebraska quietly agreed. "It ain't the hittin' that bothers me. That's the last thing you lose, anyway. Leastways, it's goin' to be that way with me, an' I talked to other fellahs who said it was that way with them." After a pause he went on in a low tone: "If this ole leg heals up in time, I'll go on back an' git in the game again an' finish out the season. An' if I'm lucky, maybe they'll keep me on a couple more years, because they know I can still hit. But, hell," he added quietly, "they know I'm through. They already got me all tied up with string."

As Nebraska talked, George saw that the Cherokee in him was the same now as it had been when he was a boy. His cheerful fatalism had always been the source of his great strength and courage. That was why he had never been afraid of anything, not even death. But, seeing the look of regret on George's face, Nebraska smiled again and went on lightly:

"That's the way it is, Monk. You're good up there as long as you're good. After that they sell you down the river. Hell, I ain't kickin'. I been lucky. I had ten years of it already, an' that's more than most. An' I been in three World's Serious. If I can hold on fer another year or two—if they don't let me go or trade me—I think maybe we'll be in again. Me an' Myrtle has figgered it all out. I had to help her people some, an' I bought a farm fer Mama an' the Ole Man—that's where they always wanted to be. An' I got three hundred acres of my own in Zebulon—all paid fer, too!—an' if I git a good price this year fer my tobacco, I stan' to clear two thousand dollars. So if I can git two years more in the League an' one more good World's Serious, why—" he turned his square face toward his friend and grinned his brown and freckled grin, just as he used to as a boy—"we'll be all set."

"And—you mean you'll be satisfied?"

"Huh? Satisfied?" Nebraska turned to him with a puzzled look. "How do you mean?"

"I mean after all you've seen and done, Bras—the big cities and the crowds, and all the people shouting—and the newspapers, and the headlines, and the World's Series—and—and—the first of March, and St. Petersburg, and meeting all the fellows again, and spring training——"

Nebraska groaned.

"Why, what's the matter?"

"Spring trainin'."

"You mean you don't like it?"

"Like it! Them first three weeks is just plain hell. It ain't bad when you're a kid. You don't put on much weight durin' the winter, an' when you come down in the spring it only takes a few days to loosen up an' git the kinks out. In two weeks' time you're loose as ashes. But wait till you been aroun' as long as I have!" He laughed loudly and shook his head. "Boy! The first time you go after a grounder you can hear your joints creak. After a while you begin to limber up—you work into it an' git the soreness out of your muscles. By the time the season starts, along in April, you feel pretty good. By May you're goin' like a house a-fire, an' you tell yourself you're good as you ever was. You're still goin' strong along in June. An' then you hit July, an' you git them double-headers in St. Looie! Boy, oh boy!" Again he shook his head and laughed, baring big square teeth. "Monkus," he said quietly, turning to his companion, and now his face was serious and he had his black Indian look—"you ever been in St. Looie in July?"

"No."

"All right, then," he said very softly and scornfully. "An' you ain't played *ball* there in July. You come up to bat with sweat bustin' from your ears. You step up an' look out there to where the pitcher ought to be, an' you see four of him. The crowd in the bleachers is out there roastin' in their shirt-sleeves, an' when the pitcher throws the ball it just comes from nowheres—it comes right out of all them shirt-sleeves in the bleachers. It's on top of you before you know it. Well, anyway, you dig in an' git a toe-hold, take your cut, an' maybe you connect. You straighten out a fast one. It's good fer two bases if you hustle. In the old days you could've made it standin' up. But now—boy!" He shook his head slowly. "You cain't tell me nothin' about that ball park in St. Looie in July! They got it all growed out in grass in April, but after July first—" he gave a short laugh—"hell! —it's paved with concrete! An' when you git to first, them dogs is sayin', 'Boy, let's stay here!' But you gotta keep on goin'—you know the manager is watchin' you—you're gonna ketch hell if you don't take that extra base, it may mean the game. An' the boys up in the press box, they got their eyes glued on you, too—they've begun to say old Crane is playin' on a dime—an' you're thinkin' about next year an' maybe gittin' in another Serious—an' you hope to God you don't git traded to St. Looie. So you take it on the lam, you slide into second like the Twentieth Century comin' into the Chicago yards—an' when you git up an' feel yourself all over to see if any of your parts is missin', you gotta listen to one of that second baseman's wisecracks: 'What's the hurry, Bras? Afraid you'll be late fer the Veterans' Reunion?' "

"I begin to see what you mean, all right," said George.

"See what I mean? Why, say! One day this season I ast one of the boys what month it was, an' when he told me it was just the middle of July, I says to him: 'July, hell! If it ain't September I'll eat your hat!' 'Go ahead, then,' he says, 'an' eat it, because it ain't September, Bras—it's July.' 'Well,' I says, 'they must be havin' sixty days a month this year—it's the longest damn July *I* ever felt!' An' lemme tell you, I didn't miss it fer, either—I'll be dogged if I did! When you git old in this business, it may be only July, but you think it's September." He was silent for a moment. "But they'll keep you in there, gener'ly, as long as you can hit. If you can smack that ole apple, they'll send you out there if they've got to use glue to keep you from fallin' apart. So maybe I'll git in another year or two if I'm lucky. So long's I can hit 'em, maybe they'll keep sendin' me out there till all the other players has to grunt every time ole Bras goes after a ground ball!" He laughed. "I ain't that bad yet, but soon's I'm am, I'm through."

"You won't mind it, then, when you have to quit?"

He didn't answer at once. He sat there looking out the window at the factory-blighted landscape of New Jersey. Then he laughed a little wearily:

"Boy, this may be a ride on the train to you, but to *me*—say!—I covered this stretch so often that I can tell you what telephone post we're passin' without even lookin' out the window. Why, hell yes!"— he laughed loudly now, in the old infectious way—"I used to have 'em numbered—now I got 'em *named!*"

"And you think you can get used to spending all your time out on the farm in Zebulon?"

"Git used to it?" In Nebraska's voice there was now the same note of scornful protest that it had when he was a boy, and for a moment he turned and looked at his friend with an expression of astonished disgust. "Why, what are you talkin' about? That's the greatest life in the world!"

"And your father? How is he, Bras?"

The player grinned and shook his head: "Oh, the Ole Man's happy as a possum. He's doin' what he wanted to all his life."

"And is he well?"

"If he felt any better he'd have to go to bed. Strong as a bull," said Nebraska proudly. "He could wrastle a bear right now an' bite his nose off! Why, hell yes!" the player went on with an air of conviction—"he could take any two men I know today an' throw 'em over his shoulder!"

"Bras, do you remember when you and I were kids and your father was on the police force, how he used to wrestle all those professionals that came to town? There were some good ones, too!"

"You're damn right there was!" said the player, nodding his head. "Tom Anderson, who used to be South Atlantic champion, an' that fellah Petersen—do you remember him?"

"Sure. They called him the Bone-Crushing Swede—he used to come there all the time."

"Yeah, that's him. He used to wrastle all over the country—he was way up there, one of the best in the business. The Ole Man wrastled him three times, an' throwed him once, too!"

"And that big fellow they called the Strangler Turk——"

"Yeah, an' he was good, too! Only he wasn't no Turk—he only called hisself one. The Ole Man told me he was some kind of Polack or Bohunk from the steel mills out in Pennsylvania, an' that's how he got so strong."

"And the Jersey Giant——"

"Yeah——"

"And Cyclone Finnegan——"

"Yeah——"

"And Bull Dakota—and Texas Jim Ryan—and the Masked Marvel? Do you remember the Masked Marvel?"

"Yeah—only there was a whole lot of them—guys cruisin' all over the country callin' theirselves the Masked Marvel. The Ole Man wrastled two of 'em. Only the real Masked Marvel never came to town. The Ole Man told me there *was* a real Masked Marvel, but he was too damn good, I guess, to come to Libya Hill."

"Do you remember the night, Bras, up at the old City Auditorium, when your father was wrestling one of these Masked Marvels, and we were there in the front row rooting for him, and he got a strangle hold on this fellow with the mask, and the mask came off—and the fellow wasn't the Masked Marvel at all, but only that Greek who used to work all night at the Bijou Café for Ladies and Gents down by the depot?"

"Yeah—haw-haw!" Nebraska threw back his head and laughed loudly. "I'd clean fergot that damn Greek, but that's who it was! The whole crowd hollered frame-up an' tried to git their money back.—I'll swear, Monk! I'm glad to see you!" He put his big brown hand on his companion's knee. "It don't seem no time, does it? It all comes back!"

"Yes, Bras—" for a moment George looked out at the flashing landscape with a feeling of sadness and wonder in his heart—"it all comes back."

BOOM TOWN

DURING the week that followed Aunt Maw's funeral George renewed his acquaintance with his home town, and it was a disconcerting experience. The sleepy little mountain village in which he had grown up—for it had been hardly more than that then—was now changed almost beyond recognition. The very streets that he had known so well, and had remembered through the years in their familiar aspect of early-afternoon emptiness and drowsy lethargy, were now foaming with life, crowded with expensive traffic, filled with new faces he had never seen before. Occasionally he saw somebody that he knew, and in the strangeness of it all they seemed to him like lights shining in the darkness of a lonely coast.

But what he noticed chiefly—and once he observed it he began watching for it, and it was always there—was the look on the people's faces. It puzzled him, and frightened him, and when he tried to find a word to describe it, the only thing he could think of was—

madness. The nervous, excited glitter in the eyes seemed to belong to nothing else but madness. The faces of natives and strangers alike appeared to be animated by some secret and unholy glee. And their bodies, as they darted, dodged, and thrust their way along, seemed to have a kind of leaping energy as if some powerful drug was driving them on. They gave him the impression of an entire population that was drunk—drunk with an intoxication which never made them weary, dead, or sodden, and which never wore off, but which incited them constantly to new efforts of leaping and thrusting exuberance.

The people he had known all his life cried out to him along the streets, seizing his hand and shaking it, and saying: "Hi, there, boy! Glad to see you home again! Going to be with us for a while now? Good! I'll be seeing you! I've got to go on now—got to meet a fellow down the street to sign some papers! Glad to see you, boy!" Then, having uttered this tempestuous greeting without a pause and without the loss of a stride, pulling and dragging him along with them as they wrung his hand, they vanished.

On all sides he heard talk, talk, talk—terrific and incessant. And the tumult of voices was united in variations of a single chorus—speculation and real estate. People were gathered in earnestly chattering groups before the drug stores, before the post office, before the Court House and the City Hall. They hurried along the pavements talking together with passionate absorption, bestowing half-abstracted nods of greeting from time to time on passing acquaintances.

The real estate men were everywhere. Their motors and busses roared through the streets of the town and out into the country, carrying crowds of prospective clients. One could see them on the porches of houses unfolding blueprints and prospectuses as they shouted enticements and promises of sudden wealth into the ears of deaf old women. Everyone was fair game for them—the lame, the halt, and the blind, Civil War veterans or their decrepit pensioned widows, as well as high school boys and girls, Negro truck drivers, soda jerkers, elevator boys, and bootblacks.

Everyone bought real estate; and everyone was "a real estate man" either in name or practice. The barbers, the lawyers, the grocers, the butchers, the builders, the clothiers—all were engaged now in this single interest and obsession. And there seemed to be only one rule, universal and infallible—to buy, always to buy, to pay whatever price was asked, and to sell again within two days at any price one chose to fix. It was fantastic. Along all the streets in town the ownership of the land was constantly changing; and when the supply of streets was exhausted, new streets were feverishly created in the surrounding wilderness; and even before these streets were paved or a house had been built upon them, the land was being sold, and then resold, by the acre, by the lot, by the foot, for hundreds of thousands of dollars.

A spirit of drunken waste and wild destructiveness was everywhere apparent. The fairest places in the town were being mutilated at untold cost. In the center of town there had been a beautiful green hill, opulent with rich lawns and lordly trees, with beds of flowers and banks of honeysuckle, and on top of it there had been an immense, rambling, old wooden hotel. From its windows one could look out upon the vast panorama of mountain ranges in the smoky distance.

George could remember its wide porches and comfortable rockers, its innumerable eaves and gables, its labyrinth of wings and corridors, its great parlors and their thick red carpets, and the lobby with its old red leather chairs, hollowed and shaped by the backs of men, and its smell of tobacco and its ice tinkle of tall drinks. It had a splendid dining room filled with laughter and quiet voices, where expert Negroes in white jackets bent and scraped and chuckled over the jokes of the rich men from the North as with prayerful grace they served them delicious foods out of old silver dishes. George could remember, too, the smiles and the tender beauty of the rich men's wives and daughters. As a boy he had been touched with the unutterable mystery of all these things, for these wealthy travelers had come great distances and had somehow brought with them an evocation of the whole golden and unvisited world, with its fabulous cities and its promise of glory, fame, and love.

It had been one of the pleasantest places in the town, but now it was gone. An army of men and shovels had advanced upon this beautiful green hill and had leveled it down to an ugly flat of clay, and had paved it with a desolate horror of white concrete, and had built stores and garages and office buildings and parking spaces— all raw and new—and were now putting up a new hotel beneath the very spot where the old one had stood. It was to be a structure of sixteen stories, of steel and concrete and pressed brick. It was being stamped out of the same mold, as if by some gigantic biscuit-cutter of hotels, that had produced a thousand others like it all over the country. And, to give a sumptuous—if spurious—distinction to its patterned uniformity, it was to be called The Libya-Ritz.

One day George ran into Sam Pennock, a boyhood friend and a classmate at Pine Rock College. Sam came down the busy street swiftly at his anxious, lunging stride, and immediately, without a word of greeting, he broke hoarsely into the abrupt and fragmentary manner of speaking that had always been characteristic of him, but that now seemed more feverish than ever:

"When did you get here? . . . How long are you going to stay? . . . What do you think of the way things look here?" Then, without waiting for an answer, he demanded with brusque, challenging, and almost impatient scornfulness: "Well, what do you intend to do—be a two thousand-dollar-a-year school teacher all your life?"

The contemptuous tone, with its implication of superiority—an implication he had noticed before in the attitude of these people, big with their inflated sense of wealth and achievement—stung George to retort sharply:

"There are worse things than teaching school! Being a paper millionaire is one of them! As for the two thousand dollars a year, you really get it, Sam! It's not real estate money, it's money you can spend. You can buy a ham sandwich with it."

Sam laughed. "You're right!" he said. "I don't blame you. It's the truth!" He began to shake his head slowly. "Lord, Lord!" he said. "They've all gone clean out of their heads here. . . . Never saw anything like it in my life. . . . Why, they're all crazy as a loon!" he exclaimed. "You can't talk to them. . . . You can't reason with them. . . . They won't listen to you. . . . They're getting prices for property here that you couldn't get in New York."

"Are they *getting* it?"

"Well," he said, with a falsetto laugh, "they get the first five hundred dollars. . . . You pay the next five hundred thousand on time."

"How much time?"

"God!" he said. "I don't know. . . . All you want, I reckon. . . .

Forever! . . . It doesn't matter. . . . You sell it next day for a million."

"On time?"

"That's it!" he cried, laughing. "You make half a million just like that."

"On time?"

"You've got it!" said Sam. "On time. . . . God! Crazy, crazy, crazy," he kept laughing and shaking his head. "That's the way they make it."

"Are you making it, too?"

At once his manner became feverishly earnest: "Why, it's the damnedest thing you ever heard of!" he said. "I'm raking it in hand over fist! . . . Made three hundred thousands dollars in the last two months. . . . Why, it's the truth! . . . Made a trade yesterday and turned around and sold the lot again not two hours later. . . . Fifty thousand dollars just like that!" he snapped his fingers. "Does your uncle want to sell that house on Locust Street where your Aunt Maw lived? . . . Have you talked to him about it? . . . Would he consider an offer?"

"I suppose so, if he gets enough."

"How much does he want?" he demanded impatiently. "Would he take a hundred thousand?"

"Could you get it for him?"

"I could get it within twenty-four hours," he said. "I know a man who'd snap it up in five minutes. . . . I tell you what I'll do, Monk, if you persuade him to sell—I'll split the commission with you. . . . I'll give you five thousand dollars."

"All right, Sam, it's a go. Could you let me have fifty cents on account?"

"Do you think he'll sell?" he asked eagerly.

"Really, I don't know, but I doubt it. That place was my grandfather's. It's been in the family a long time. I imagine he'll want to keep it."

"Keep it! What's the sense in keeping it? . . . Now's the time when things are at the peak. He'll never get a better offer!"

"I know, but he's expecting to strike oil out in the backyard any time now," said George with a laugh.

At this moment there was a disturbance among the tides of traffic in the street. A magnificent car detached itself from the stream of humbler vehicles and moved in swiftly to the curb, where it came to a smooth stop—a glitter of nickel, glass, and burnished steel. From it a gaudily attired creature stepped down to the pavement with an air of princely indolence, tucked a light Malacca cane carelessly under its right armpit, and slowly and fastidiously withdrew from its nicotined fingers a pair of lemon-colored gloves, at the same time saying to the liveried chauffeur:

"You may go, James. Call for me again in hal-luf an houah!"

The creature's face was thin and sunken. Its complexion was a death sallow—all except the nose, which was bulbous and glowed a brilliant red, showing an intricate network of enlarged purple veins. Its toothless jaws were equipped with such an enormous set of glittering false teeth that the lips could not cover them, and they grinned at the world with the prognathous bleakness of a skeleton. The whole figure, although heavy and shambling, had the tottering appearance which suggested a stupendous debauchery. It moved forward with its false, bleak grin, leaning heavily upon the stick, and suddenly George recognized that native ruin which had been known to him since childhood as Tim Wagner.

J. Timothy Wagner—the "J" was a recent and completely arbitrary addition of his own, appropriated, no doubt, to fit his ideas of personal grandeur, and to match the eminent position in the town's affairs to which he had belatedly risen—was the black sheep of one of the old, established families in the community. At the time George Webber was a boy, Tim Wagner had been for so long the product of complete disillusion that there was no longer any vestige of respect attached to him.

He had been preëminently the town sot. His title to this office was unquestioned. In this capacity he was even held in a kind of affection. His exploits were notorious, the subjects of a hundred stories. One night, for example, the loafers in McCormick's pharmacy had seen Tim swallow something and then shudder convulsively. This process was repeated several times, until the curiosity of the loafers was aroused. They began to observe him furtively but closely, and in a few minutes Tim thrust out his hand slyly, fumbled around in the gold fish bowl, and withdrew his hand with a wriggling little shape between his fingers. Then the quick swallow and the convulsive shudder were repeated.

He had inherited two fortunes before his twenty-fifth year and had run through them both. Hilarious stories were told of Tim's celebrated pleasure tour upon the inheritance of the second fortune. He had chartered a private car, stocked it plentifully with liquor, and selected as his traveling companions the most notorious sots, vagabonds, and tramps the community could furnish. The debauch had lasted eight months. This party of itinerant bacchuses had made a tour of the entire country. They had exploded their empty flasks against the ramparts of the Rocky Mountains, tossed their empty kegs into San Francisco Bay, strewn the plains with their beer bottles. At last the party had achieved a condition of exhausted satiety in the nation's capital, where Tim, with what was left of his inheritance, had engaged an entire floor at one of the leading hotels. Then, one by one, the exhausted wanderers had drifted back to town, bringing tales of bacchanalian orgies that had not been equaled since the days of the Roman emperors, and leaving Tim finally in solitary possession of the wreckage of empty suites.

From that time on he had slipped rapidly into a state of perpetual sottishness. Even then, however, he had retained the traces of an attractive and engaging personality. Everyone had had a tolerant and unspoken affection for him. Save for the harm he did himself, Tim was an inoffensive and good-natured creature.

His figure on the streets of the town at night had been a familiar one. From sunset on, he might be found almost anywhere. It was easy to tell what progressive state of intoxication he had reached simply by observing his method of locomotion. No one ever saw him stagger. He did not weave drunkenly along the pavement. Rather, when he approached the saturation point, he walked very straight, very rapidly, but with funny little short steps. As he walked he kept his face partly lowered, glancing quickly and comically from side to side, with little possumlike looks. If he approached complete paralysis, he just stood quietly and leaned against something—a lamp post or a doorway or the side of a building or the front of the drug store. Here he would remain for hours in a state of solemn immobility, broken only by an occasional belch. His face, already grown thin and flabby-jowled, with its flaming beacon of a nose, would at these times be composed in an expression of drunken gravity, and his whole condition would be characterized by a remarkable alertness, perceptiveness, and control. He rarely degenerated into complete collapse. Almost always he could respond instantly and briskly to a word of greeting.

Even the police had had a benevolent regard for him, and they had exercised a friendly guardianship over him. Through long experience and observation, every policeman on the force was thoroughly acquainted with Tim's symptoms. They could tell at a glance just what degree of intoxication he had reached, and if they thought he had crossed the final border line and that his collapse in doorway or gutter was imminent, they would take charge of him, speaking to him kindly, but with a stern warning:

"Tim, if you're on the streets again tonight, we're going to lock you up. Now you go on home and go to bed."

To this Tim would nod briskly, with instant and amiable agreement: "Yes, sir, yes, sir. Just what I was going to do, Captain Crane, when you spoke to me. Going home right this minute. Yes, sir."

With these words he would start off briskly across the street, his legs making their little fast, short steps and his eyes darting comically from side to side, until he had vanished around the corner. Within ten or fifteen minutes, however, he might be seen again, easing his way along cautiously in the dark shadow of a building, creeping up to the corner, and peeking around with a sly look on his face to see if any of the watchdogs of the law were in sight.

As time went on and his life lapsed more and more into total vagabondage, one of his wealthy aunts, in the hope that some employment might partially retrieve him, had given him the use of a vacant lot behind some buildings in the business section of the town, a short half block from Main Street. The automobile had now come in sufficient numbers to make parking laws important, and Tim was allowed by his aunt to use this lot as parking space for cars and to keep the money thus obtained. In this employment he succeeded far better than anyone expected. He had little to do except stay on the premises, and this was not difficult for him so long as he was plentifully supplied with corn whiskey.

During this period of his life some canvassers at a local election had looked for Tim to enroll him in the interest of their candidate, but they had been unable to find out where he lived. He had not lived, of course, with any member of his family for years, and investigation failed to disclose that he had a room anywhere. The question then began to go around: "Where does Tim Wagner live? Where does he sleep?" No one could find out. And Tim's own answers, when pressed for information, were slyly evasive.

One day, however, the answer came to light. The automobile had come, and come so thoroughly that people were even getting buried by motor car. The day of the horse-drawn hearse had passed forever. Accordingly, one of the local undertaking firms had told Tim he could have their old horse-drawn hearse if he would only take it off their premises. Tim had accepted the macabre gift and had parked the hearse in his lot. One day when Tim was absent the canvassers came back again, still persistent in their efforts to learn his address so they could enroll him. They noticed the old hearse, and, seeing that its raven curtains were so closely drawn that the interior was hidden from view, they decided to investigate. Cautiously they opened the doors of the hearse. A cot was inside. There was even a chair. It was completely furnished as a small but adequate bedroom.

So at last his secret had been found out. Henceforth all the town knew where he lived.

That was Tim Wagner as George had known him fifteen years ago. Since then he had been so constantly steeped in alcohol that his progressive disintegration had been marked, and he had lately adopted the fantastic trappings of a clown of royalty. Everyone knew all about him, and yet—the fact was incredible!—Tim Wagner had now become the supreme embodiment of the town's extravagant folly. For, as gamblers will stake a fortune on some moment's whimsey of belief, thrusting their money into a stranger's hand and bidding him to play with it because the color of his hair is lucky, or as race track men will rub the hump upon a cripple's back to bring them luck, so the people of the town now listened prayerfully to every word Tim Wagner uttered. They sought his opinion in all their speculations, and acted instantly on his suggestions. He had become—in what way and for what reason no one knew—the high priest and prophet of this insanity of waste.

They knew that he was diseased and broken, that his wits were always addled now with alcohol, but they used him as men once used divining rods. They deferred to him as Russian peasants once deferred to the village idiot. They now believed with an absolute and unquestioning faith that some power of intuition in him made all his judgments infallible.

It was this creature who had just alighted at the curb a little beyond George Webber and Sam Pennock, full of drunken majesty and bleary-eyed foppishness. Sam turned to him with a movement of feverish eagerness, saying to George abruptly:

"Wait a minute! I've got to speak to Tim Wagner about something! Wait till I come back!"

George watched the scene with amazement. Tim Wagner, still drawing the gloves off of his fingers with an expression of bored casualness, walked slowly over toward the entrance of McCormack's drug store—no longer were his steps short and quick, for he leaned heavily on his cane—while Sam, in an attitude of obsequious entreaty, kept at his elbow, bending his tall form toward him and hoarsely pouring out a torrent of questions:

". . . Property in West Libya. . . . Seventy-five thousand dollars. . . . Option expires tomorrow at noon. . . . Joe Ingram has the piece above mine. . . . Won't sell. . . . Holding for hundred fifty. . . . Mine's the best location. . . . But Fred Bynum says too far from main road. . . . What do you think, Tim? . . . Is it worth it?"

During the course of this torrential appeal Tim Wagner did not even turn to look at his petitioner. He gave no evidence whatever that he heard what Sam was saying. Instead, he stopped, thrust his gloves into his pocket, cast his eyes around slyly in a series of quick glances, and suddenly began to root into himself violently with a clutching hand. Then he straightened up like a man just coming out of a trance, and seemed to become aware for the first time that Sam was waiting.

"What's that? What did you say, Sam?" he said rapidly. "How much did they offer you for it? Don't sell, don't sell!" he said suddenly and with great emphasis. "Now's the time to buy, not to sell. The trend is upward. Buy! Buy! Don't take it. Don't sell. That's my advice!"

"I'm not selling, Tim," Sam cried excitedly. "I'm thinking of buying."

"Oh—yes, yes, yes!" Tim muttered rapidly. "I see, I see." He turned now for the first time and fixed his eyes upon his questioner.

"Where did you say it was?" he demanded sharply. "Deepwood? Good! Good! Can't go wrong! Buy! Buy!"

He started to walk away into the drug store, and the lounging idlers moved aside deferentially to let him pass. Sam rushed after him frantically and caught him by the arm, shouting:

"No, no, Tim! It's not Deepwood! It's the other way. . . . I've been telling you. . . . It's West Libya!"

"What's that?" Tim cried sharply. "West Libya? Why didn't you say so? That's different. Buy! Buy! Can't go wrong! Whole town's moving in that direction. Values double out there in six months. How much do they want?"

"Seventy-five thousand," Sam panted. "Option expires tomorrow. . . . Five years to pay it up."

"Buy! Buy!" Tim barked, and walked off into the drug store.

Sam strode back toward George, his eyes blazing with excitement.

"Did you hear him? Did you hear what he said?" he demanded hoarsely. "You heard him, didn't you? . . . Best damned judge of real estate that ever lived. . . . Never known to make a mistake! . . . 'Buy! Buy! Will double in value in six months!' . . . You were standing right here—" he said hoarsely and accusingly, glaring at George —"you heard what he said, didn't you?"

"Yes, I heard him."

Sam glanced wildly about him, passed his hand nervously through his hair several times, and then said, sighing heavily and shaking his head in wonder:

"Seventy-five thousand dollars' profit in one deal! . . . Never heard anything like it in my life! . . . Lord, Lord!" he cried. "What are we coming to?"

Somehow the news had gotten around that George had written a book and that it would soon be published. The editor of the local paper heard of it and sent a reporter to interview him, and printed a story about it.

"So you've written a book?" said the reporter. "What kind of a book is it? What's it about?"

"Why—I—I hardly know how to tell you," George stammered. "It—it's a novel——"

"A Southern novel? Anything to do with this part of the country?"

"Well—yes—that is—it's about the South, all right—about an Old Catawba family—but——"

LOCAL BOY WRITES ROMANCE OF THE OLD SOUTH

George Webber, son of the late John Webber and nephew of Mark Joyner, local hardware merchant, has written a novel with a Libya Hill background which the New York house of James Rodney & Co. will publish this fall.

When interviewed last night, the young author stated that his book was a romance of the Old South, centering about the history of a distinguished ante-bellum family of this region. The people of Libya Hill and environs will await the publication of the book with special interest, not only because many of them will remember the author, who was born and brought up here, but also because that stirring period of Old Catawba's past has never before been accorded its rightful place of honor in the annals of Southern literature.

"We understand you have traveled a great deal since you left home. Been to Europe several times?"

"Yes, I have."

"In your opinion, how does this section of the country compare with other places you have seen?"

"Why—why—er—why *good!* . . . I mean, *fine!* That is——"

LOCAL PARADISE COMPARES FAVORABLY

In answer to the reporter's question as to how this part of the country compared to other places he had seen, the former Libya man declared:

"There is no place I have ever visited—and my travels have taken me to England, Germany, Scotland, Ireland, Wales, Norway, Denmark, Sweden, to say nothing of the south of France, the Italian Riviera, and the Swiss Alps—which can compare in beauty with the setting of my native town.

"We have here," he said enthusiastically, "a veritable Paradise of Nature. Air, climate, scenery, water, natural beauty, all conspire to make this section the most ideal place in the whole world to live."

"Did you ever think of coming back here to live?"

"Well—yes—I *have* thought of it—but—you see——"

WILL SETTLE AND BUILD HERE

When questioned as to his future plans, the author said:

"For years, my dearest hope and chief ambition has been that one day I should be able to come back here to live. One who has ever known the magic of these hills cannot forget them. I hope, therefore, that the time is not far distant when I may return for good.

"Here, I feel, as nowhere else," the author continued wistfully, "that I will be able to find the inspiration that I must have to do my work. Scenically, climatically, geographically, and in every other way, the logical spot for a modern renaissance is right here among these hills. There is no reason why, in ten years' time, this community should not be a great artistic colony, drawing to it the great artists, the music and the beauty lovers, of the whole world, as Salzburg does now. The Rhododendron Festival is already a step in the right direction.

"It shall be a part of my purpose from now on," the earnest young author added, "to do everything in my power to further this great cause, and to urge all my writing and artistic friends to settle here—to make Libya Hill the place it ought to be—The Athens of America."

"Do you intend to write another book?"

"Yes—that is—I hope so. In fact——"

"Would you care to say anything about it?"

"Well—I don't know— it's pretty hard to say——"

"Come on, son, don't be bashful. We're all your home folks here. . . . Now, take Longfellow. *There* was a great writer! You know what a young fellow with your ability ought to do? He ought to come back here and do for this section what Longfellow did for New England. . . ."

PLANS NATIVE SAGA

When pressed for details about the literary work

he hopes to do hereafter, the author became quite
explicit:

"I want to return here," he said, "and commen-
orate the life, history, and development of Western
Catawba in a series of poetic legends comparable to
those with which the poet Longfellow commemo-
rated the life of the Acadians and the folklore of
the New England countryside. What I have in mind
is a trilogy that will begin with the early settlement
of the region by the first pioneers, among them my
own forebears, and will trace the steady progress of
Libya Hill from its founding and the coming of the
railroad right down to its present international promi-
nence and the proud place it occupies today as 'The
Gem City of the Hills.' "

George writhed and swore when he read the article. There was
hardly an accurate statement in it. He felt angry and sheepish and
guilty all at the same time.

He sat down and wrote a scathing letter to the paper, but when
he had finished he tore it up. After all, what good would it do? The
reporter had spun his story out of nothing more substantial than
his victim's friendly tones and gestures, a few words and phrases
which he had blurted out in his confusion, and, above all, his reti-
cence to talk about his work; yet the fellow had obviously been so
steeped in the booster spirit that he had been able to concoct this
elaborate fantasy—probably without quite knowing that it was a
fantasy.

Then, too, he reflected, people would take an emphatic denial of
the statements that had been attributed to him as evidence that he
was a sorehead, full of conceit about his book. You couldn't undo
the effect of a thing like this with a simple negative. If he gave the
lie to all that gush, everybody would say he was attacking the town
and turning against those who had nurtured him. Better let bad
enough alone.

So he did nothing about it. And after that, strangely enough, it
seemed to George that the attitude of people changed toward him.
Not that they had been unfriendly before. It was only that he now
felt they approved of him. This in itself gave him a quiet sense of

accomplishment, as if the stamp of business confirmation had been put upon him.

Like all Americans, George had been amorous of material success, so it made him happy now to know that the people of his home town believed he had got it, or at any rate was at last on the highroad to it. One thing about the whole affair was most fortunate. The publisher who had accepted his book had an old and much respected name; people knew the name, and would meet him on the street and wring his hand and say:

"So your book is going to be published by James Rodney & Co.?"

That simple question, asked with advance knowledge of the fact, had a wonderful sound. It had a ring, not only of congratulation that his book was being published, but also of implication that the distinguished house of Rodney had been fortunate to secure it. That was the way it sounded, and it was probably also the way it was meant. He had the feeling, therefore, that in the eyes of his own people he had "arrived." He was no longer a queer young fellow who had consumed his substance in the deluded hope that he was —oh, loaded word!—"a writer." He *was* a writer. He was not only a writer, but a writer who was about to be published, and by the ancient and honorable James Rodney & Co.

There is something good in the way people welcome success, or anything—no matter what—that is stamped with the markings of success. It is not an ugly thing, really. People love success because to most of them it means happiness, and, whatever form it takes, it is the image of what they, in their hearts, would like to be. This is more true in America than anywhere else. People put this label on the image of their heart's desire because they have never had an image of another kind of happiness. So, essentially, this love of success is not a bad thing, but a good thing. It calls forth a general and noble response, even though the response may also be mixed with self-interest. People are happy for *your* happiness because they want so much to be happy themselves. Therefore it's a good thing. The idea behind it is good, anyhow. The only trouble with it is that the direction is misplaced.

That was the way it seemed to George. He had gone through a long and severe period of probation, and now he was approved. It made him very happy. There is nothing in the world that will take the chip off of one's shoulder like a feeling of success. The chip was off now, and George didn't want to fight anybody. For the first time he felt that it was good to be home again.

Not that he did not have his apprehensions. He knew what he had written about the people and the life of his home town. He knew, too, that he had written about them with a nakedness and directness which, up to that time, had been rare in American fiction. He wondered how they would take it. Even when people congratulated him about the book he could not altogether escape a feeling of uneasiness, for he was afraid of what they would say and think after the book came out and they had read it.

These apprehensions took violent possession of him one night in a most vivid and horrible dream. He thought he was running and stumbling over the blasted heath of some foreign land, fleeing in terror from he knew not what. All that he knew was that he was filled with a nameless shame. It was wordless, and as shapeless as a smothering fog, yet his whole mind and soul shrank back in an agony of revulsion and self-contempt. So overwhelming was his sense of loathing and guilt that he coveted the place of murderers on whom the world had visited the fierceness of its wrath. He envied the whole list of those criminals who had reaped the sentence of mankind's dishonor—the thief, the liar, the trickster, the outlaw, and the traitor —men whose names were anathema and were spoken with a curse, but which *were* spoken; for *he* had committed a crime for which there was no name, *he* was putrescent with a taint for which there was neither comprehension nor cure, *he* was rotten with a vileness of corruption that placed him equally beyond salvation or vengeance, remote alike from pity, love, and hatred, and unworthy of a curse. Thus he flew across the immeasurable and barren heath beneath a burning sky, an exile in the center of a planetary vacancy which, like his own shameful self, had no place either among things living or among things dead, and in which there was neither vengeance of lightning nor mercy of burial; for in all that limitless horizon there was no shade or shelter, no curve or bend, no hill or tree or hollow: there was only one vast, naked eye—searing and inscrutable—from which there was no escape, and which bathed his defenseless soul in its fathomless depths of shame.

And then, with bright and sharp intensity, the dream changed, and suddenly he found himself among the scenes and faces he had known long ago. He was a traveler who had returned after many years of wandering to the place he had known in his childhood. The sense of his dreadful but nameless corruption still hung ominously above him as he entered the streets of the town again, and he knew that he had returned to the springs of innocence and health whence he came, and by which he would be saved.

But as he came into the town he became aware that the knowledge of his guilt was everywhere about him. He saw the men and women he had known in childhood, the boys with whom he had gone to school, the girls he had taken to dances. They were engaged in all their varied activities of life and business, and they showed their friendship toward one another, but when he approached and offered his hand in greeting they looked at him with blank stares, and in their gaze there was no love, hatred, pity, loathing, or any feeling whatsoever. Their faces, which had been full of friendliness and affection when they spoke to one another, went dead; they gave no sign of recognition or of greeting; they answered him briefly in toneless voices, giving him what information he asked, and repulsed every effort he made toward a resumption of old friendship with the annihilation of silence and that blank and level stare. They did not laugh or mock or nudge or whisper when he passed; they only waited and were still, as if they wanted but one thing—that he should depart out of their sight.

He walked on through the old familiar streets, past houses and places that lived again for him as if he had never left them, and by people who grew still and waited until he had gone, and the knowledge of wordless guilt was rooted in his soul. He knew that he was obliterated from their lives more completely than if he had died, and he felt that he was now lost to all men.

Presently he had left the town, and was again upon the blasted heath, and he was fleeing across it beneath the pitiless sky where flamed the naked eye that pierced him with its unutterable weight of shame.

George considered himself lucky to have the little room over the Shepperton garage. He was also glad that his visit had overlapped that of Mr. David Merrit, and that Mr. Merrit had been allowed to enjoy undisturbed the greater comfort of the Shepperton guest room, for Mr. Merrit had filled him with a pleasant glow at their first meeting. He was a ruddy, plump, well-kept man of forty-five or so, always ready with a joke and immensely agreeable, with pockets bulging with savory cigars which he handed out to people on the slightest provocation. Randy had spoken of him as "the Company's man," and, although George did not know what the duties of a "Company's man" were, Mr. Merrit made them seem very pleasant.

George knew, of course, that Mr. Merrit was Randy's boss, and he learned that Mr. Merrit was in the habit of coming to town every two or three months. He would arrive like a benevolent, pink-cheeked Santa Claus, making his jolly little jokes, passing out his fat cigars, putting his arm around people's shoulders, and, in general, making everyone feel good. As he said himself:

"I've got to turn up now and then just to see that the boys are behaving themselves, and not taking in any wooden nickels."

Here he winked at George in such a comical way that all of them had to grin. Then he gave George a big cigar.

His functions seemed to be ambassadorial. He was always taking Randy and the salesmen of the Company out to lunch or dinner, and, save for brief visits to the office, he seemed to spend most of his time inaugurating an era of good feeling and high living. He would go around town and meet everybody, slapping people on the back and calling them by their first names, and for a week after he had left the business men of Libya Hill would still be smoking his cigars. When he came to town he always stayed "out at the house," and one knew that Margaret would prepare her best meals for him, and that there would be some good drinks. Mr. Merrit supplied the drinks himself, for he always brought along a plentiful store of expensive beverages. George could see at their first meeting that he was the kind of man who exudes an aura of good fellowship, and that was why it was so pleasant to have Mr. Merrit staying in the house.

Mr. Merrit was not only a nice fellow. He was also "with the Company," and George soon realized that "the Company" was a vital and mysterious force in all their lives. Randy had gone with it as soon as he left college. He had been sent to the main office, up North somewhere, and had been put through a course of training. Then he had come back South and had worked his way up from salesman to district agent—an important member of the sales organization.

"The Company," "district agent," "the sales organization"—mysterious titles all of them, but most comforting. During the week George was in Libya Hill with Randy and Margaret, Mr. Merrit was usually on hand at meal times, and at night he would sit out on the front porch with them and carry on in his jolly way, joking and laughing and giving them all a good time. Sometimes he would talk shop with Randy, telling stories about the Company and about his own experiences in the organization, and before long George began to pick up a pretty good idea of what it was all about.

The Federal Weight, Scales, and Computing Company was a far-flung empire which had a superficial aspect of great complexity, but in its essence it was really beautifully simple. Its heart and soul—indeed, its very life—was its sales organization.

The entire country was divided into districts, and over each district an agent was appointed. This agent, in turn, employed salesmen to cover the various portions of his district. Each district also had an "office man" to attend to any business that might come up while the agent and his salesmen were away, and a "repair man" whose duty it was to overhaul damaged or broken-down machines. Together, these comprised the agency, and the country was so divided that there was, on the average, an agency for every unit of half a million people in the total population. Thus there were two hundred and sixty or seventy agencies through the nation, and the agents with their salesmen made up a working force of from twelve to fifteen hundred men.

The higher purposes of this industrial empire, which the employees almost never referred to by name, as who should speak of the deity with coarse directness, but always with a just perceptible lowering and huskiness of the voice as "the Company"—these higher purposes were also beautifully simple. They were summed up in the famous utterance of the Great Man himself, Mr. Paul S. Appleton, III, who invariably repeated it every year as a peroration to his hour-long address before the assembled members of the sales organization at their national convention. Standing before them at the close of each year's session, he would sweep his arm in a gesture of magnificent command toward an enormous map of the United States of America that covered the whole wall behind him, and say:

"There's your market! Go out and sell them!"

What could be simpler and more beautiful than this? What could more eloquently indicate that mighty sweep of the imagination which has been celebrated in the annals of modern business under the name of "vision"? The words had the spacious scope and austere directness that have characterized the utterances of great leaders in every epoch of man's history. It is Napoleon speaking to his troops in Egypt: "Soldiers, from the summit of yonder pyramids, forty centuries look down upon you." It is Captain Perry: "We have met the enemy, and they are ours." It is Dewey at Manila Bay: "You may fire when ready, Gridley." It is Grant before Spottsylvania Court House: "I propose to fight it out on this line, if it takes all summer."

So when Mr. Paul S. Appleton, III, waved his arm at the wall and said: "There's your market! Go out and sell them!"—the assembled captains, lieutenants, and privates in the ranks of his sales organization knew that there were still giants in the earth, and that the age of romance was not dead.

True, there had once been a time when the aspirations of the Company had been more limited. That was when the founder of the institution, the grandfather of Mr. Paul S. Appleton, III, had expressed his modest hopes by saying: "I should like to see one of my machines in every store, shop, or business that needs one, and that can afford to pay for one." But the self-denying restrictions implicit in the founder's statement had long since become so out of date as to seem utterly mid-Victorian. Mr. David Merrit admitted it himself. Much as he hated to speak ill of any man, and especially the founder of the Company, he had to confess that by the standards of 1929 the old gentleman had lacked vision.

"That's old stuff now," said Mr. Merrit, shaking his head and winking at George, as though to take the curse off of his treason to the founder by making a joke of it. "We've gone way beyond that!" he exclaimed with pardonable pride. "Why, if we waited nowadays to sell a machine to someone who *needs* one, we'd get nowhere." He was nodding now at Randy, and speaking with the seriousness of deep conviction. "We don't wait until he *needs* one. If he says he's getting along all right without one, we make him buy one anyhow. We make him *see* the need, don't we, Randy? In other words, we *create* the need."

This, as Mr. Merrit went on to explain, was what is known in more technical phrase as "creative salesmanship" or "creating the market." And this poetic conception was the inspired work of one man—none other than the present head of the Company, Mr. Paul S. Appleton, III, himself. The idea had come to him in a single blinding flash, born full-blown like Pallas Athene from the head of Zeus, and Mr. Merrit still remembered the momentous occasion as vividly as if it had been only yesterday. It was at one of the meetings of the assembled parliaments of the Company that Mr. Appleton, soaring in an impassioned flight of oratory, became so intoxicated with the grandeur of his own vision that he stopped abruptly in the middle of a sentence and stood there as one entranced, gazing out dreamily into the unknown vistas of magic Canaan; and when he at last went on again, it was in a voice surcharged with quivering emotion:

"My friends," he said, "the possibilities of the market, now that we see how to create it, are practically unlimited!" Here he was silent for a moment, and Mr. Merrit said that the Great Man actually paled and seemed to stagger as he tried to speak, and that his voice faltered and sank to an almost inaudible whisper, as if he himself could hardly comprehend the magnitude of his own conception. "My friends—" he muttered thickly, and was seen to clutch the rostrum for support—"my friends—seen properly—" he whispered, and moistened his dry lips—"seen properly—the market we shall create being what it is—" his voice grew stronger, and the clarion words now rang forth—"there is no reason why one of our machines should not be in the possession of every man, woman, and child in the United States!" Then came the grand, familiar gesture to the map: "There's your market, boys! Go out and sell them!"

Henceforth this vision became the stone on which Mr. Paul S. Appleton, III, erected the magnificent edifice of the true church and living faith which was called "the Company." And in the service of this vision Mr. Appleton built up an organization which worked with the beautiful precision of a locomotive piston. Over the salesman was the agent, and over the agent was the district supervisor, and over the district supervisor was the district manager, and over the district manager was the general manager, and over the general manager was—if not God himself, then the next thing to it, for the agents and salesmen referred to him in tones of proper reverence as "P. S. A."

Mr. Appleton also invented a special Company Heaven known as the Hundred Club. Its membership was headed by P. S. A., and all the ranks of the sales organization were eligible, down to the humblest salesman. The Hundred Club was a social order, but it was also a good deal more than that. Each agent and salesman had a "quota"—that is to say, a certain amount of business which was assigned to him as the normal average of his district and capacity. A man's quota differed from another's according to the size of his territory, its wealth, and his own experience and ability. One man's quota would be sixty, another's eighty, another's ninety or one hundred, and if he was a district agent, his quota would be higher than that of a mere salesman. Each man, however, no matter how small or how large his quota might be, was eligible for membership in the Hundred Club, the only restriction being that he must average one hundred per cent of his quota. If he averaged more—if he got, say, one hundred and twenty per cent of his quota—there were appropriate honors and rewards, not only social but financial as well. One could be either high up or low down in the Hundred Club, for it had almost as many degrees of merit as the Masonic order.

The unit of the quota system was "the point," and a point was forty dollars' worth of business. So if a salesman had a quota of eighty, this meant that he had to sell the products of the Federal Weight, Scales, and Computing Company to the amount of at least $3200 every month, or almost $40,000 a year. The rewards were high. A salesman's commission was from fifteen to twenty per cent of his sales; an agent's, from twenty to twenty-five per cent. Beyond this there were bonuses to be earned by achieving or surpassing his quota. Thus it was possible for an ordinary salesman in an average district to earn from $6000 to $8000 a year, while an agent could earn from $12,000 to $15,000, and even more if his district was an exceptionally good one.

So much for the rewards of Mr. Appleton's Heaven. But what would Heaven be if there were no Hell? So Mr. Appleton was forced by the logic of the situation to invent a Hell, too. Once a man's quota was fixed at any given point, the Company never reduced it. Moreover, if a salesman's quota was eighty points and he achieved it during the year, he must be prepared at the beginning of the new year to find that his quota had been increased to ninety points. One had to go onward and upward constantly, and the race was to the swift.

While it was quite true that membership in the Hundred Club was not compulsory, it was also true that Mr. Paul S. Appleton, III, was a theologian who, like Calvin, knew how to combine free will and predestination. If one did *not* belong to the Hundred Club, the time was not far distant when one would not belong to Mr. Appleton. Not to belong to it was, for agent or salesman, the equivalent of living on the other side of the railroad tracks. If one failed of admission to the Company Heaven, or if one dropped out, his fellows would begin to ask guardedly: "Where's Joe Klutz these days?" The answers would be vague, and in the course of time Joe Klutz would be spoken of no more. He would fade into oblivion. He was "no longer with the Company."

Mr. Paul S. Appleton, III, never had but the one revelation—the one which Mr. Merrit so movingly described—but that was enough, and he never let its glories and allurements grow dim. Four times a year, at the beginning of each quarter, he would call his general manager before him and say: "What's the matter, Elmer? You're not getting the business! The market is *there!* You know what you can do about it—or else . . .!" Thereupon the general manager would summon the district managers one by one and repeat to them the words and manner of P. S. A., and the district managers would reenact the scene before each of the district supervisors, who would duplicate it to the agents, who would pass it on to the salesmen, who, since they had no one below them, would "get out and hustle—or else!" This was called "keeping up the morale of the organization."

As Mr. David Merrit sat on the front porch and told of his many experiences with the Company, his words conveyed to George Webber a great deal more than he actually said. For his talk went on and on in its vein of mellow reminiscence, and Mr. Merrit made his little jokes and puffed contentedly at one of his own good cigars, and everything he said carried an overtone of "What a fine and wonderful thing it is to be connected with the Company!"

He told, for example, about the splendid occasion every year when all the members of the Hundred Club were brought together for what was known as "The Week of Play." This was a magnificent annual outing conducted "at the Company's expense." The meeting place might be in Philadelphia or Washington, or in the tropic opulence of Los Angeles or Miami, or it might be on board a chartered ship—one of the small but luxurious twenty-thousand-tonners that ply the transatlantic routes—bound to Bermuda or Havana. Wherever it was, the Hundred Club was given a free sweep. If the journey was by sea, the ship was theirs—for a week. All the liquor in the world was theirs, if they could drink it—and Bermuda's coral isles, or the unlicensed privilege of gay Havana. For that one week everything on earth that money could buy was at the command of the members of the Hundred Club, everything was done on the grand scale, and the Company—the immortal, paternal, and great-hearted Company—"paid for everything."

But as Mr. Merrit painted his glowing picture of the fun they had on these occasions, George Webber saw quite another image. It was an image of twelve or fifteen hundred men—for on these pilgrimages, by general consent, women (or, at any rate, wives) were debarred—twelve or fifteen hundred men, Americans, most of them in their middle years, exhausted, overwrought, their nerves frayed down and stretched to the breaking point, met from all quarters of the continent "at the Company's expense" for one brief, wild, gaudy week of riot. And George thought grimly what this tragic spectacle of business men at play meant in terms of the entire scheme of things and the plan of life that had produced it. He began to understand, too, the changes which time had brought about in Randy.

The last day of his week in Libya Hill, George had gone to the station to buy his return ticket and he stopped in at Randy's office a little before one o'clock to go home to lunch with him. The outer salesroom, with its shining stock of scales and computing machines imposingly arrayed on walnut pedestals, was deserted, so he sat down to wait. On one wall hung a gigantic colored poster. "August Was the Best Month in Federal History," it read. *"Make September a Better One! The Market's There, Mr. Agent. The Rest Is Up to You!"*

Behind the salesroom was a little partitioned space which served

Randy as an office. As George waited, gradually he became aware of mysterious sounds emanating from beyond the partition. First there was the rustle of heavy paper, as if the pages of a ledger were being turned, and occasionally there would be a quick murmur of hushed voices, confidential, ominous, interspersed with grunts and half-suppressed exclamations. Then all at once there were two loud bangs, as of a large ledger being slammed shut and thrown upon a desk or table, and after a moment's silence the voices rose louder, distinct, plainly audible. Instantly he recognized Randy's voice—low, grave, hesitant, and deeply troubled. The other voice he had never heard before.

But as he listened to that voice he began to tremble and grow white about the lips. For its very tone was a foul insult to human life, an ugly sneer whipped across the face of decent humanity, and as he realized that that voice, these words, were being used against his friend, he had a sudden blind feeling of murder in his heart. And what was so perplexing and so troubling was that this devil's voice had in it as well a curiously familiar note, as of someone he had known.

Then it came to him in a flash—it was Merrit speaking! The owner of that voice, incredible as it seemed, was none other than that plump, well-kept, jolly-looking man who had always been so full of hearty cheerfulness and good spirits every time he had seen him.

Now, behind that little partition of glazed glass and varnished wood, this man's voice had suddenly become fiendish. It was inconceivable, and as George listened he grew sick, as one does in some awful nightmare when he visions someone he knows doing some perverse and abominable act. But what was most dreadful of all was Randy's voice, humble, low, submissive, modestly entreating. Merrit's voice would cut across the air like a gob of rasping phlegm, and then Randy's voice—gentle, hesitant, deeply troubled—would come in from time to time in answer.

"Well, what's the matter? Don't you want the job?"

"Why—why, yes, you know I do, Dave—haw-w—" and Randy's voice lifted a little in a troubled and protesting laugh.

"What's the matter that you're not getting the business?"

"Why—haw-w!—" again the little laugh, embarrassed and troubled—"I *thought* I was——"

"Well, you're not!" that rasping voice cut in like a knife. "This district ought to deliver thirty per cent more business than you're getting from it, and the Company is going to have it, too—or else! You deliver or you go right out on your can! See? The Company doesn't give a damn about you! It's after the business! You've been around a long time, but you don't mean a damn bit more to the Company than anybody else! And you know what's happened to a lot of other guys who got to feeling they were too big for their job—don't you?"

"Why—why, yes, Dave—but—haw-w!" the little laugh again—"but—honestly, I never thought——"

"We don't give a damn what you never thought!" the brutal voice ripped in. "I've given you fair warning now! You get the business or out you go!"

The glazed glass door burst open violently and Merrit came striding out of the little partitioned office. When he saw George, he looked startled. Then he was instantly transformed. His plump and ruddy face became wreathed in smiles, and he cried out in a hearty tone:

"Well, well, well! Look who's here! If it's not the old boy himself!"

Randy had followed him out, and Merrit now turned and winked humorously at him, in the manner of a man who is carrying on a little bantering byplay:

"Randy," he said, "I believe George gets better looking from day to day. Has he broken any hearts yet?"

Randy tried to smile, grey-faced and haggardly.

"I bet you're burning them up in the Big Town," said Merrit, turning back to George. "And, say, I read that piece in the paper about your book. Great stuff, son! We're all proud of you!"

He gave George a hearty slap on the back and turned away with an air of jaunty readiness, picked up his hat, and said cheerfully:

"Well, what d'ya say, folks? What about one of Margaret's famous meals, out at the old homestead? Well, you can't hurt my feelings. I'm ready if you are. Let's go!"

And, smiling, ruddy, plump, cheerful, a perverted picture of amiable good will to all the world, he sauntered through the door. For a moment the two old friends just stood there looking at each other, white and haggard, with a bewildered expression in their eyes. In

Randy's eyes there was also a look of shame. With that instinct for loyalty which was one of the roots of his soul, he said:

"Dave's a good fellow. . . . You—you see, he's got to do these things. . . . He—He's with the Company."

George didn't say anything. For as Randy spoke, and George remembered all that Merrit had told him about the Company, a terrific picture flashed through his mind. It was a picture he had seen in a gallery somewhere, portraying a long line of men stretching from the Great Pyramid to the very portals of great Pharaoh's house, and great Pharaoh stood with a thonged whip in his hand and applied it unmercifully to the bare back and shoulders of the man in front of him, who was great Pharaoh's chief overseer, and in the hand of the overseer was a whip of many tails which he unstintedly applied to the quivering back of the wretch before him, who was the chief overseer's chief lieutenant, and in the lieutenant's hand a whip of rawhide which he laid vigorously on the quailing body of his head sergeant, and in the sergeant's hand a wicked flail with which he belabored a whole company of groaning corporals, and in the hands of every corporal a knotted lash with which to whack a whole regiment of slaves, who pulled and hauled and bore burdens and toiled and sweated and built the towering structure of the pyramid.

So George didn't say anything. He couldn't. He had just found out something about life that he had not known before.

"THE HOLLOW MEN"

FOX picks up the paper and settles back to read it with keen relish. The paper is the *Times*. (He read the *Tribune* late last night: waited up for it, would not miss it, has never missed it, could not sleep if he had not read it.) Morning now, Fox reads the *Times*.

How does he read the *Times*?

He reads it the way Americans have always read the paper. He also reads it as few Americans have ever read the paper—with nostrils sensitive, dilating with proud scorn, sniffing for the news behind the news.

He loves it—even loves the *Times*—loves Love unlovable—and don't we all? Ink-fresh papers, millions of them—ink-fresh with morning, orange juice, waffles, eggs and bacon, and cups of strong hot coffee. How fine it is, here in America, at ink-fresh, coffee-fragrant morning, to read the paper!

How often have we read the paper in America! How often have we seen it *blocked* against our doors! Little route-boys fold and block it, so to throw it—and so we find it and unfold it, crackling and ink-laden, at our doors. Sometimes we find it tossed there lightly with flat *plop;* sometimes we find it thrown with solid, whizzing *whack* against the clapboards (clapboards here, most often, in America) ; sometimes, as now in Turtle Bay, servants find just freshly folded sheets laid neatly down in doorways, and take them to the table for their masters. No matter how it got there, we always find it.

How we do love the paper in America! How we do love the paper, all!

Why do we love the paper in America? Why do we love the paper, all?

Mad masters, I will tell ye why.

Because the paper is "the news" here in America, and we love the *smell* of news. We love the smell of news that's "fit to print." We also love the smell of news *not* fit to print. We love, besides, the smell of *facts* that news is made of. Therefore we love the paper because the news is so fit-printable—so unprintable—and so fact-printable.

Is the news, then, like America? No, it's not—and Fox, unlike the rest of you, mad masters, turns the pages knowing it is just the news and not America that he reads there in his *Times*.

The *news* is not America, nor is America the *news*—the news is *in* America. It is a kind of light at morning, and at evening, and at midnight in America. It is a kind of growth and record and excrescence of our life. It is not good enough—it does not tell our story— yet it is the news!

Fox reads (proud nose sharp-sniffing with a scornful relish) :

An unidentified man fell or jumped yesterday at noon from the twelfth story of the Admiral Francis Drake Hotel, corner of Hay and Apple Streets, in Brooklyn. The man, who was about thirty-five years old, registered at the hotel about a week ago, according to the police, as C. Green. Police are of the opinion that this was an assumed name. Pending identification, the body is being held at the King's County Morgue.

This, then, is news. Is it also the whole story, Admiral Drake? No! Yet we do not supply the whole story—we who have known all the lights and weathers of America—as Fox supplies it now:

Well, then, it's news, and it happened in your own hotel, brave Admiral Drake. It didn't happen in the Penn-Pitt at Pittsburgh, nor the Phil-Penn at Philadelphia, nor the York-Albany at Albany, nor the Hudson-Troy at Troy, nor the Libya-Ritz at Libya Hill, nor the Clay-Calhoun at Columbia, nor the Richmond-Lee at Richmond, nor the George Washington at Easton, Pennsylvania, Canton, Ohio, Terre Haute, Indiana, Danville, Virginia, Houston, Texas, and ninety-seven other places; nor at the Abraham Lincoln at Springfield, Massachusetts, Hartford, Connecticut, Wilmington, Delaware, Cairo, Illinois, Kansas City, Missouri, Los Angeles, California, and one hundred and thirty-six other towns; nor at the Andrew Jackson, the Roosevelt (Theodore or Franklin—take your choice), the Jefferson Davis, the Daniel Webster, the Stonewall Jackson, the U. S. Grant, the Commodore Vanderbilt, the Waldorf-Astor, the Adams House, the Parker House, the Palmer House, the Taft, the McKinley, the Emerson (Waldo or Bromo), the Harding, the Coolidge, the Hoover, the Albert G. Fall, the Harry Daugherty, the Rockefeller, the Harriman, the Carnegie or the Frick, the Christopher Columbus or the Leif Ericsson, the Ponce-de-Leon or the Magellan, in the remaining eight hundred and forty-three cities of America—but at the Francis Drake, brave Admiral—your own hotel—so, of course, you'll want to know what happened.

"An unidentified man"—well, then, this man was an American. "About thirty-five years old" with "an assumed name"—well, then, call him C. Green as he called himself ironically in the hotel register. C. Green, the unidentified American, "fell or jumped," then, "yes-

terday at noon . . . in Brooklyn"—worth nine lines of print in today's
Times—one of seven thousand who died yesterday upon this continent—one of three hundred and fifty who died yesterday in this
very city (see dense, close columns of obituaries, page 15: begin with
"Aaronson," so through the alphabet to "Zorn"). C. Green came
here "a week ago"——

And came from where? From the deep South, or the Mississippi
Valley, or the Middle West? From Minneapolis, Bridgeport, Boston,
or a little town in Old Catawba? From Scranton, Toledo, St. Louis,
or the desert whiteness of Los Angeles? From the pine barrens of the
Atlantic coastal plain, or from the Pacific shore?

And so—was *what,* brave Admiral Drake? Had seen, felt, heard,
smelled, tasted—*what?* Had known—*what?*

Had known all our brutal violence of weather: the burned swelter
of July across the nation, the smell of the slow, rank river, the mud,
the bottom lands, the weed growth, and the hot, coarse, humid fragrance of the corn. The kind that says, "Jesus, but it's hot!"—pulls
off his coat, and mops his face, and goes in shirt-sleeves in St. Louis,
goes to August's for a Swiss on rye with mustard, and a mug of beer.
The kind that says, "Damn! It's hot!" in South Carolina, slouches in
shirt-sleeves and straw hat down South Main Street, drops into Evans
Drug Store for a dope, says to the soda jerker, "Is it hot enough fer
you today, Jim?" The kind that reads in the paper of the heat, the
deaths, and the prostrations, reads it with a certain satisfaction, hangs
on grimly day by day and loses sleep at night, can't sleep for heat,
is tired in the morning, says, "Jesus! It can't last forever!" as heat
lengthens into August, and the nation gasps for breath, and the green
that was young in May now mottles, fades and bleaches, withers,
goes heat-brown. Will boast of coolness in the mountains, Admiral
Drake. "Always cool at night! May get a little warm around the
middle of the day, but you'll sleep with blankets every night."

Then summer fades and passes, and October comes. Will smell
smoke then, and feel an unsuspected sharpness, a thrill of nervous,
swift elation, a sense of sadness and departure. C. Green doesn't know
the reason, Admiral Drake, but lights slant and shorten in the afternoon, there is a misty pollen of old gold in light at noon, a murky
redness in the lights of dusk, a frosty stillness, and the barking of
the dogs; the maples flame upon the hills, the gums are burning,

bronze the oak leaves, and the aspens yellow; then come the rains, the sodden dead-brown of the fallen leaves, the smoke-stark branches —and November comes.

Waiting for winter in the little towns, and winter comes. It is really the same in big towns and the cities, too, with the bleak enclosure of the winter multiplied. In the commerce of the day, engaged and furious, then darkness, and the bleak monotony of "Where shall we go? What shall we do?" The winter grips us, closes round each house—the stark, harsh light encysts us—and C. Green walks the streets. Sometimes hard lights burn on him, Admiral Drake, bleak faces stream beneath the lights, amusement signs are winking. On Broadway, the constant blaze of sterile lights; in little towns, no less the clustered raisins of hard light on Main Street. On Broadway, swarming millions up to midnight; in little towns, hard lights and frozen silence—no one, nothing, after ten o'clock. But in the hearts of C. Greens everywhere, bleak boredom, undefined despair, and "Christ! Where shall I go now? When will winter end?"

So longs for spring, and wishes it were Saturday, brave Admiral Drake.

Saturday night arrives with the thing that we are waiting for. Oh, it will come tonight; the thing that we have been expecting all our lives will come tonight, on Saturday! On Saturday night across America we are waiting for it, and ninety million Greens go mothwise to the lights to find it. Surely it will come tonight! So Green goes out to find it, and he finds—hard lights again, saloons along Third Avenue, or the Greek's place in a little town—and then hard whiskey, gin, and drunkenness, and brawls and fights and vomit.

Sunday morning, aching head.

Sunday afternoon, and in the cities the chop-suey signs wink on and flash their sterile promises of unborn joy.

Sunday night, and the hard stars, and the bleak enclosures of our wintry weather—the buildings of old rusty brick, in cold enclosed, the fronts of old stark brown, the unpainted houses, the deserted factories, wharves, piers, warehouses, and office buildings, the tormented shabbiness of Sixth Avenues; and in the smaller towns, bleak Main Streets, desolate with shabby store fronts and be-raisined clusters of lamp standards, and in the residential streets of wooden houses (dark by ten o'clock), the moaning of stark branches, the stiff lights, limb-bepatterned, shaking at street corners. The light shines there with wintry bleakness on the clapboard front and porch of a shabby house where the policeman lives—blank and desolate upon the stuffy, boxlike little parlor where the policeman's daughter amorously receives—and *almost*—not quite—*gives*. Hot, fevered, fearful, and insatiate, it is all too close to the cold street light—too creaking, panting, flimsy-close to others in the flimsy house—too close to the policeman's solid and slow-creaking tread—yet somehow valiant, somehow strong, somehow triumphant over the stale varnish of the little parlor, the nearness of the street, the light, the creaking boughs, and papa's tread—somehow triumphant with hot panting, with rose lips and tender tongue, white underleg and tight-locked thighs—by these intimacies of fear and fragrant hot desire will beat the ashen monotone of time and even the bleak and grey duration of the winter out.

Does this surprise you, Admiral Drake?

"But Christ!"—Green leaves the house, his life is bitter with desire, the stiff light creaks. "When will it end?" thinks Green. "When will spring come?"

It comes at last unhoped for, after hoping, comes when least expected, and when given up. In March there is a day that's almost in the eye in March. Raw days return, and blown light, and gusty moanings of the wind. Then April comes, and small, soaking rain. spring, and C. Green, strong with will to have it so, says, "Well, it's here"—and it is gone like smoke. You can't look spring too closely The air is wet and raw and chilled, but with a smell of spring now, a smell of earth, of grass exploding in small patches, here and there a blade, a bud, a leaf. And spring comes, marvelous, for a day or two—"It's here!" Green thinks. "It's here at last!"—and he is wrong again. It goes, chill days and greyness and small, soaking rains return. Green loses hope. "There is no spring!" he says. "You never get spring any more; you jump from winter into summer—we'll have summer now and the hot weather before you know it."

Then spring comes—explodes out of the earth in a green radiance —comes up overnight! It's April twenty-eighth—the tree there in the city backyard is smoke-yellow, feathered with the striplings of young leaf! It's April twenty-ninth—the leaf, the yellow, and the smoke have thickened overnight. April thirtieth—you can watch it grow and thicken with your eye! Then May the first—the tree's in leaf now, almost full and dense, young, feather-fresh! The whole spring has exploded from the earth!

All's explosive with us really, Admiral Drake—spring, the brutal summer, frost, October, February in Dakota with fifty-one below, spring floods, two hundred drowning along Ohio bottoms, in Missouri, in New England, all through Pennsylvania, Maryland, and Tennessee. Spring shot at us overnight, and everything with us is vast, explosive, floodlike. A few hundred dead in floods, a hundred in a wave of heat, twelve thousand in a year by murder, thirty thousand with the motor car—it all means nothing here. Floods like this would drown out France; death like this would plunge England in black mourning; but in America a few thousand C. Greens more or less, drowned, murdered, killed by motor cars, or dead by jumping out of windows on their heads—well, it just means nothing to us— the next flood, or next week's crop of death and killings, wash it out. We do things on a large scale, Admiral Drake.

The tar-smell in the streets now, children shouting, and the smell of earth; the sky shell-blue and faultless, a sapphire sparkle everywhere; and in the air the brave stick-candy whippings of a flag. C. Green thinks of the baseball games, the raw-hide arm of Lefty Grove, the resilient crack of ashwood on the horsehide ball, the waiting pockets of the well-oiled mitts, the warm smell of the bleachers, the shouted gibes of shirt-sleeved men, the sprawl and monotone of inning after inning. (Baseball's a dull game, really; that's the reason that it is so good. We do not love the game so much as we love the sprawl and drowse and shirt-sleeved apathy of it.) On Saturday afternoon, C. Green goes out to the ball park and sits there in the crowd, awaiting the sudden sharpness and the yell of crisis. Then the game ends and the crowd flows out across the green turf of the playing field. Sunday, Green spends the day out in the country in his flivver, with a girl.

Then summer comes again, heat-blazing summer, humid, murked with mist, sky-glazed with brutal weariness—and C. Green mops his face and sweats and says, "Jesus! Will it never end?"

This, then, is C. Green, "thirty-five years old"—"unidentified"— and an American. In what way an American? In what way different from the men *you* knew, old Drake?

When the ships bore home again and Cape St. Vincent blazed in

Spaniard's eye—or when old Drake was returning with his men, beating coastwise from strange seas abreast, past the Scilly Isles toward the slant of evening fields, chalk cliffs, the harbor's arms, the town's sweet cluster and the spire—where was Green?

When, in red-oak thickets at the break of day, coon-skinned, the huntsmen of the wilderness lay for bear, heard arrows rattling in the laurel leaves, the bullets' whining *plunk,* and waited with cocked musket by the tree—where was Green?

Or when, with strong faces turning toward the setting sun—hawk-eyed and Indian-visaged men bore gunstocks on the western trails and sternly heard the fierce war-whoops around the Painted Buttes —where, then, was Green?

Was never there with Drake's men in the evening when the sails stood in from the Americas! Was never there beneath the Spaniard's swarthy eye at Vincent's Cape! Was never there in the red-oak thicket in the morning! Was never there to hear the war-cries round the Painted Buttes!

No, no. He was no voyager of unknown seas, no pioneer of western trails. He was life's little man, life's nameless cipher, life's man-swarm atom, life's American—and now he lies disjected and exploded on a street in Brooklyn!

He was a dweller in mean streets, was Green, a man-mote in the jungle of the city, a resident of grimy steel and stone, a mole who burrowed in rusty brick, a stunned spectator of enormous salmon-colored towers, hued palely with the morning. He was a renter of shabby wooden houses in a little town, an owner of a raw new bungalow on the outskirts of the town. He was a waker in bleak streets at morning, an alarm-clock watcher, saying, "Jesus, I'll be late!"—a fellow who took short cuts through the corner lot, behind the advertising signs; a fellow used to concrete horrors of hot day and blazing noon; a man accustomed to the tormented hodgepodge of our architectures, used to broken pavements, ash cans, shabby store fronts, dull green paint, the elevated structure, grinding traffic, noise, and streets be-tortured with a thousand bleak and dismal signs. He was accustomed to the gas tanks going out of town, he was an atom of machinery in an endless flow, going, stopping, going to the winking of the lights; he tore down concrete roads on Sundays, past the hot-dog stands and filling stations; he would return at darkness;

hunger lured him to the winking splendor of chop-suey signs; and midnight found him in The Coffee Pot, to prowl above a mug of coffee, tear a coffee-cake in fragments, and wear away the slow grey ash of time and boredom with other men in grey hats and with skins of tallow-grey, at Joe the Greek's.

C. Green could read (which Drake could not), but not too accurately; could write, too (which the Spaniard couldn't), but not too well. C. Green had trouble over certain words, spelled them out above the coffee mug at midnight, with a furrowed brow, slow-shaping lips, and "Jesus!" when news stunned him—for he read the news. Preferred the news with pictures, too, girls with voluptuous legs crossed sensually, dresses above the knees, and plump dolls' faces full of vacant lechery. Green liked news "hot"—not as Fox knows it, not subtly sniffing with strange-scornful nostrils for the news *behind* the news—but straight from the shoulder—socko!—biff!—straight off the griddle, with lots of mustard, shapely legs, roadside wrecks and mutilated bodies, gangsters' molls and gunmen's hide-outs, tallow faces of the night that bluntly stare at flashlight lenses—this and talk of "heart-balm," "love-thief," "sex-hijacker"—all of this liked Green.

Yes, Green liked the news—and now, a bit of news himself (nine lines of print in *Times*), has been disjected and exploded on a Brooklyn pavement!

Well, such was our friend, C. Green, who read, but not too well; and wrote, but not too easily; who smelled, but not too strongly; felt, but not too deeply; saw, but not too clearly—yet had smelled the tar in May, smelled the slow, rank yellow of the rivers, and the clean, coarse corn; had seen the slants of evening on the hill-flanks in the Smokies, and the bronze swell of the earth, the broad, deep red of Pennsylvania barns, proud-portioned and as dominant across the fields as bulls; had felt the frost and silence in October; had heard the whistles of the train wail back in darkness, and the horns of New Year's Eve, and—"Jesus! There's another year gone by! What now?"

No Drake was he, no Spaniard, no coon-skin cap, no strong face burning west. Yet, in some remote and protoplasmic portion, he was a little of each of these. A little Scotch, perhaps, was Green, a little Irish, English, Spanish even, and some German—a little of each part, all compacted and exploded into nameless atom of America!

No. Green—poor little Green—was not a man like Drake. He was just a cinder out of life—for the most part, a thinker of base thoughts, a creature of unsharpened, coarse perceptions. He was meager in the hips, he did not have much juice or salt in him. Drake gnawed the beef from juicy bones in taverns, drank tankards of brown ale, swore salty curses through his whiskers, wiped his mouth with the back of his hard hand, threw the beef bone to his dog, and pounded with his tankard for more ale. Green ate in cafeterias, prowled at midnight over coffee and a doughnut or a sugar-coated bun, went to the chop-suey joint on Saturday nights and swallowed chow mein, noodle soup, and rice. Green's mouth was mean and thin and common, it ran to looseness and a snarl; his skin was grey and harsh and dry; his eyes were dull and full of fear. Drake was self-contained: the world his oyster, seas his pastures, mighty distances his wings. His eyes were sea-pale (like the eyes of Fox); his ship was England. Green had no ship, he had a motor car, and tore down concrete roads on Sunday, and halted with the lights against him with the million other cinders hurtling through hot space. Green walked on level concrete sidewalks and on pavements grey, through hot and grimy streets past rusty tenements. Drake set his sails against the west, he strode the buoyant, sea-washed decks, he took the Spaniard and his gold, and at the end he stood in to the sweet enfoldments of the spire, the clustered town, the emerald fields that slope to Plymouth harbor—then Green came!

We who never saw brave Drake can have no difficulty conjuring up an image of the kind of man he was. With equal ease we can imagine the bearded Spaniard, and almost hear his swarthy oaths. But neither Drake nor Spaniard could ever have imagined Green. Who could have foreseen him, this cipher of America, exploded now upon a street in Brooklyn?

Behold him, Admiral Drake! Observe the scene now! Listen to the people! Here is something strange as the Armadas, the gold-laden cargoes of the bearded Spaniards, the vision of unfound Americas! What do you see here, Admiral Drake?

Well, first, a building—your own hotel—such a building as the folk of Plymouth never saw. A great block of masonry, pale-hued, grimy-white, fourteen stories tall, stamped in an unvarying pattern with many windows. Sheeted glass below, the store front piled with medicines and toilet articles, perfumes, cosmetics, health contrivances. Within, a soda fountain, Admiral Drake. The men in white with monkey caps, soda jerkers sullen with perpetual overdriven irritation. Beneath the counter, pools of sloppy water, filth, and unwashed dishes. Across the counter, Jewesses with fat, rouged lips consuming ice cream sodas and pimento sandwiches.

Outside upon the concrete sidewalk lies the form of our exploded friend, C. Green. A crowd has gathered round—taxi drivers, passers-by, hangers-on about the subway station, people working in the neighborhood, and the police. No one has dared to touch exploded Green as yet—they stand there in a rapt and fascinated circle, looking at him.

Not much to look at either, Admiral Drake; not even those who trod your gory decks would call the sight a pretty one. Our friend has landed on his head—"taken a nose dive," as we say—and smashed his brains out at the iron base of the second lamp post from the corner. (It is the same lamp post as heretofore described, to be found throughout America—a "standard," standardized, supporting five hard grapes of frosted glass.)

So here Green lies, on the concrete sidewalk all disjected. No head is left, the head is gone now, head's exploded; only brains are left. The brains are pink, and almost bloodless, Admiral Drake. (There's not much blood here—we shall tell you why.) But brains exploded are somewhat like pale sausage meat, fresh-ground. Brains are stuck hard to the lamp post, too; there is a certain driven emphasis about them, as if they had been shot hydraulically out of a force-hose against the post.

The head, as we have said, is gone completely; a few fragments of the skull are scattered round—but of the face, the features, forehead —nothing! They have all been blown *out,* as by some inner explosion. Nothing is left but the back of the skull, which curiously remains, completely hollowed out and vacant, and curved over, like the rounded handle of a walking stick.

The body, five feet eight or nine of it, of middling weight, is lying —we were going to say "face downward"; had we not better say "stomach downward"?—on the sidewalk. It is well-dressed, too, in cheap, neatly pressed, machine-made clothes: tan shoes and socks with a clocked pattern, suit of a light texture, brownish red in hue, a neat canary-colored shirt with attached collar—obviously C. Green had a nice feeling for proprieties! As for the body itself, save for a certain indefinable and curiously "disjected" quality, one could scarcely tell that every bone in it is broken. The hands are still spread out, half-folded and half-clenched, with a still-warm and startling eloquence of recent life. (It happened just four minutes ago!)

Well, where's the blood, then, Drake? You're used to blood; you'd like to know. Well, you've heard of casting bread upon the waters, Drake, and having it return—but never yet, I'll vow, of casting blood upon the streets—and having it run away—and then come back to you! But here it comes now, down the street—down Apple Street, round the corner into Hay, across the street now toward C. Green, the lamp post, and the crowd!—a young Italian youth, blunt-featured, low-browed, and bewildered, his black eyes blank with horror, tongue mumbling thickly, arm held firmly by a policeman, suit and shirt all drenched with blood, and face be-spattered with it! A stir of sudden interest in the crowd, sharp nudges, low-toned voices whispering:

"Here he is! Th' guy that 'got it'! . . . Sure, that's him—you know him, that Italian kid that works inside in the newsstand—he was standin' *deh* beside the post! Sure, *that* the guy!—talkin' to anotheh guy—he got it all! *That's* the reason you didn't see more blood—*this* guy got it!—Sure! The guy just missed him by six inches!—Sure! I'm tellin' you I *saw* it, ain't I? I looked up an' saw him in the air! He'd a hit this guy, but when he saw that he was goin' to hit the lamp post, he put out his hands an' tried to keep away! *That's* the reason that he didn't hit this guy! . . . But this guy heard him when he hit, an' turned around—and zowie!—he got all of it right in his face!"

And another, whispering and nudging, nodding toward the horror-blank, thick-mumbling Italian boy: "Jesus! Look at th' guy, will yuh! . . . He don't know what he's doing! . . . He don't know yet what happened to him! . . . Sure! He got it *all*. I tell yuh! He was standin' deh beside the post, wit a package undehneath one ahm—an' when it happened—when he got it—he just stahted runnin' . . . He don't know yet what's happened! . . . That's what I'm tellin' yuh—th' guy just stahted runnin' when he got it."

And one policeman (to another) : ". . . Sure, I yelled to Pat to stop him. He caught up with him at Borough Hall. . . . He just kept on runnin'—he don't know yet what happened to him."

And the Italian youth, thick-mumbling: ". . . Jeez! W'at happened? . . . Jeez! . . . I was standin' talkin' to a guy—I heard it hit. . . . Jeez! . . . W'at happened, anyway? . . . I got it all oveh me! . . . Jeez! . . . I just stahted runnin'. . . . Jeez! I'm sick!"

Voices: "Here, take 'im into the drug store! . . . Wash 'im off! . . . That guy needs a shot of liquor! . . . Sure! Take him into the drug stoeh *deh!* . . . *They'll* fix him up!"

The plump, young, rather effeminate, but very intelligent young Jew who runs the newsstand in the corridor, talking to everyone around him, excitedly and indignantly: ". . . Did I *see* it? Listen! I saw *everything!* I was coming across the street, looked up, and saw him in the air! . . . *See* it? . . . *Listen!* If someone had taken a big ripe watermelon and dropped it on the street from the twelfth floor you'd have some idea what it was like! . . . *See* it! *I'll* tell the world I saw it! I don't want to see anything like *that* again!" Then excitedly, with a kind of hysterical indignation: "Shows no consideration for other people, that's all *I've* got to say! If a man is going to do a thing like that, why does he pick a place like *this*—one of the busiest corners in Brooklyn? . . . How did *he* know he wouldn't hit someone? Why, if that boy had been standing six inches nearer to the post, he'd have killed him, as sure as you live! . . . And here he does it right in front of all these people who have to look at it! It shows he had no consideration for other people! A man who'd do a thing like that. . . ."

(Alas, poor Jew! As if C. Green, now past considering, had considered nice "considerations.")

A taxi driver, impatiently: "That's what I'm tellin' yuh! . . . I watched him for five minutes before he jumped. He crawled out on the window sill an' stood there for *five* minutes, makin' up his mind! . . . Sure, I saw him! Lots of people saw him!" Impatiently, irritably: "Why didn't we *do* somethin' to stop him? F'r Chri' sake, what was there to do? A guy who'd do a thing like that is nuts to start with! You don't think he'd listen to anything *we* had to say, do you? . . . Sure, we *did* yell at him! . . . Jesus! . . . We was almost *afraid* to yell at him—we made motions to him to get back—tried to hold his attention while the cops sneaked round the corner into the hotel. . . .

Sure, the cops got there just a second after he jumped—I don't know if he jumped when he heard 'em comin', or what happened, but Christ!—he stood there gettin' ready for five minutes while we watched!"

And a stocky little Czech-Bohemian, who works in the delicatessen-fruit store on the corner, one block down: "Did I *hear* it! Say, you could have heard it for six blocks! Sure! *Everybody* heard it! The minute that I heard it, I knew what had happened, too! I come runnin'!"

People press and shuffle in the crowd. A man comes round the corner, presses forward to get a better look, runs into a little fat, bald-headed man in front of him who is staring at the Thing with a pale, sweating, suffering, fascinated face, by accident knocks off the little fat man's straw hat. The new straw hat hits the pavement dryly, the little fat, bald-headed man scrambles for it, clutches it, and turns around on the man who has knocked it off, both of them stammering frantic apologies:

"Oh, excuse me! . . . 'Scuse me! . . . 'Scuse me! . . . Sorry!"

"Quite all right. . . . All right! . . . All right."

Observe now, Admiral, with what hypnotic concentration the people are examining the grimy-white façade of your hotel. Watch their faces and expressions. Their eyes go traveling upward slowly—up—up—up. The building seems to widen curiously, to be distorted, to flare out wedgelike till it threatens to annihilate the sky, overwhelm the will, and crush the spirit. (These optics, too, American, Admiral Drake.) The eyes continue on past story after story up the wall until they finally arrive and come to rest with focal concentration on that single open window twelve floors up. It is no jot different from all the other windows, but now the vision of the crowd is fastened on it with a fatal and united interest. And after staring at it fixedly, the eyes come traveling slowly down again—down—down—down— the faces strained a little, mouths all slightly puckered as if something set the teeth on edge—and slowly, with fascinated measurement—down—down—down—until the eyes reach sidewalk, lamp post, and—the Thing again.

The pavement finally halts all, stops all, answers all. It is the American pavement, Admiral Drake, our universal city sidewalk, a wide, hard stripe of grey-white cement, blocked accurately with dividing lines. It is the hardest, coldest, cruellest, most impersonal pavement in the world: all of the indifference, the atomic desolation, the exploded nothingness of one hundred million nameless "Greens" is in it.

In Europe, Drake, we find worn stone, all hollowed out and rubbed to rounded edges. For centuries the unknown lives of men now buried touched and wore this stone, and when we see it something stirs within our hearts, and something strange and dark and passionate moves our souls, and—"They were here!" we say.

Not so, the streets, the sidewalks, the paved places of America. Has *man* been here? No. Only unnumbered nameless Greens have swarmed and passed here, and none has left a mark.

Did ever the eye go seaward here with searching for the crowded sail, with longing for the strange and unknown coasts of Spain? Did ever beauty here come home to the heart and eyes? Did ever, in the thrusting crowd, eye look to eye, and face to face, and heart to heart, and know the moment of their meeting—stop and pause, and be oblivious in this place, and make one spot of worn pavement sacred stone? You won't believe it, Admiral Drake, but it is so—these things *have* happened on the pavements of America. But, as you see yourself, they have not left their mark.

You, old Drake, when last your fellow townsmen saw you at the sailing of the ships, walked with the crowd along the quay, past the spire and cluster of the town, down to the cool lap of the water; and from your deck, as you put out, you watched the long, white, fading arm of your own coast. And in the town that you had left were streets still haunted by your voice. There was your worn tread upon the pavement, there the tavern table dented where you banged your tankard down. And in the evening, when the ships were gone, men waited for your return.

But no return is here among us in America. Here are no streets still haunted by departed men. Here is no street at all, as you knew streets. Here are just our cement Mobways, unannealed by time! No place in Mobway bids you pause, old Drake. No spot in Mobway bids you hold your mind a moment in reflection, saying: "He was here!" No square of concrete slab says: "Stay, for I was built by men." Mobway never knew the hand of man, as your streets did. Mobway was laid down by great machines, for one sole purpose—to unimpede and hurry up the passing of the feet.

Where did Mobway come from? What produced it?

It came from the same place where all our mob ways come from—from Standard Concentrated Production Units of America, No. 1. This is where all our streets, sidewalks, and lamp posts (like the one on which Green's brains are spattered) come from, where all our white-grimy bricks (like those of which your hotel is constructed) come from, where the red façades of our standard-unit tobacco stores (like the one across the street) come from, where our motor cars come from, where our drug stores and our drug store windows and displays come from, where our soda fountains (complete, with soda jerkers attached) come from, where our cosmetics, toilet articles, and the fat, rouged lips of our Jewesses come from, where our soda water, slops and syrups, steamed spaghetti, ice cream, and pimento sandwiches come from, where our clothes, our hats (neat, standard stamps of grey), our faces (also stamps of grey, not always neat), our language, conversation, sentiments, feelings, and opinions come from. All these things are made for us by Standard Concentrated Production Units of America, No. 1.

So here we are, then, Admiral Drake. You see the street, the sidewalk, the front of your hotel, the constant stream of motor cars, the drug store and the soda fountain, the tobacco store, the traffic lights, the cops in uniform, the people streaming in and out of the subway, the rusty, pale-hued jungle of the buildings, old and new, high and low. There is no better place to see it, Drake. For this is Brooklyn—which means ten thousand streets and blocks like this one. Brooklyn, Admiral Drake, is the Standard Concentrated Chaos No. 1 of the Whole Universe. That is to say, it has no size, no shape, no heart, no joy, no hope, no aspiration, no center, no eyes, no soul, no purpose, no direction, and no anything—just Standard Concentrated Units everywhere—exploding in all directions for an unknown number of square miles like a completely triumphant Standard Concentrated Blot upon the Face of the Earth. And here, right in the middle—no, that is wrong, for Standard Concentrated Blots don't have a middle—but, if not in the middle, at least right slap-bang out in the open, upon a minute portion of this magnificent Standard Concentrated Blot, where all the Standard Concentrated Blotters can stare at him, and with the brains completely out of him——

—Lies Green!

And this is bad—most bad—oh, *very* bad—and should not be

allowed! For, as our young Jewish friend has just indignantly proclaimed, it "shows no consideration for other people"—which means, for other Standard Concentrated Blotters. Green has no right to go falling in this fashion in a public place. He has no right to take unto himself any portion of this Standard Concentrated Blot, however small. He has no business *being* where he is at all. A Standard Concentrated Blotter is not supposed to *be* places, but to *go* places.

You see, dear Admiral, this is not a street to amble in, to ride along, to drift through. It is a channel—in the words of the Standard Concentrated Blotter-Press, an "artery." This means that it is not a place where one drives, but a place where one is driven—not really a street at all, but a kind of tube for a projectile, a kind of groove for millions and millions of projectiles, all driven past incessantly, all beetling onward, bearing briefly white slugged blurs of driven flesh.

As for the sidewalk, this Standard Concentrated Mobway is not a place to walk on, really. (Standard Concentrated Blotters have forgotten how to walk.) It is a place to swarm on, to weave on, to thrust and dodge on, to scurry past on, to crowd by on. It is not a place to stand on, either. One of the earliest precepts in a Concentrated Blotter's life is: "Move on there! Where th' hell d'you think you are, anyway—in a cow pasture?" And, most certainly, it is not a place to lie on, to sprawl out on.

But look at Green! Just *look* at him! No wonder the Jewish youth is angry with him!

Green has willfully and deliberately violated every Standard Concentrated Principle of Blotterdom. He has not only gone and dashed his brains out, but he has done it in a public place—upon a piece of Standard Concentrated Mobway. He has messed up the sidewalk, messed up another Standard Concentrated Blotter, stopped traffic, taken people from their business, upset the nerves of his fellow Blotters—and now *lies* there, all *sprawled* out, in a place where he has no right to *be*. And, to make his crime unpardonable, C. Green has——

—Come to Life!

Consider *that,* old Drake! We can understand some measure of *your* strangeness, because we heard you swearing in the tavern and saw your sails stand to the west. Can you now do the same for *us?* Consider strangeness, Drake—and look at Green! For you have heard it said by your own countryman, and in your living generation: "The times have been that, when the brains were out, the man would die." But now, old Drake, what hath Time wrought? There is surely here some strangeness in us that you could never have foretold. For the brains are "out" now—and the man has——

—Come to Life!

What's that, Admiral? You do not understand it? Small wonder, though it's really very simple:

For just ten minutes since, C. Green was a Concentrated Blotter like the rest of us. Ten minutes since, he, too, might hurry in and out of the subway, thrust and scurry on the pavement, go hurtling past with whited blur in one of our beetles of machinery, a nameless atom, cipher, cinder, swarming with the rest of us, just another "guy" like a hundred million other "guys." But now, observe him! No longer is he just "another guy"—already he has become a "special guy"—he has become *"The* Guy." C. Green at last has turned into a—*Man!*

Four hundred years ago, brave Admiral Drake, if we had seen you lying on your deck, your bronze gone pale and cold, imbrued in your own blood, and hewn to the middle by the Spaniards' steel, we could have understood that, for there was *blood* in you. But Green— this Concentrated Blotter of ten minutes since—made in our own image, shaped in our own dust, compacted of the same grey stuff of which our own lives are compacted, and filled, we thought, with the same Standard Concentration of embalming fluid that fills *our* veins —oh, Drake, we did not know the fellow had such *blood* in him! We could not have thought it was so red, so rich, and so abundant!

Poor, shabby, and corrupted cipher! Poor, nameless, and exploded atom! Poor little guy! He fills us Concentrated Blotters of the Universe with fear, with shame, with awe, with pity, and with terror— for we see ourselves in him. If he was a man with blood in him, then so are we! If he, in the midst of his always-driven life, could at last be driven to this final and defiant gesture of refusal to remain a Concentrated Blotter, then we, too, might be driven to a point of equal desperation! And there are other methods of defiance, other ways of ultimate refusal, other means of exercising one's last-remaining right of manhood—and some of them are no less terrifying to contemplate than this! So our fascinated eyes go up and up, past floor after floor of Standard Concentrated brick, and fasten on the open window where he stood—and suddenly we crane our necks along the ridges of our collars, look away with constricted faces, and taste the acrid bitterness of steel upon our lips!

It is too hard, and not to be endured—to know that little Green, speaking our own tongue and stuffed with our own stuffing, had yet concealed in him some secret, dark, and frightful thing more terrible than anything that we have ever known—that he bore within him some black and hideous horror, some depth of madness or of courage, and could stand *there*—upon the sheer and nauseating verge of that grey window ledge for five full minutes—and know the thing he was about to do—and tell himself he *must* now!—that he *had* to!—that the compulsion of every horror-fascinated eye down in the gulf below had *now* made escape impossible—and then, horror-sick past all regeneration, see, too, before he jumped, his fall, the downward-hurtling plunge, and his own exploded body—feel the bones crack and fly apart, and the brutal obliteration of the instant when his brains would shoot out against the lamp post—and even while his soul drew back from that sheer verge of imagined terror, shame, and unutterable self-loathing, crying, "I cannot do it!"—then jumped!

And *we*, brave Drake? We try to see it, but we cannot see. We try to fathom it, but we cannot plunge. We try to comprehend the hell of hells, the hundred lives of horror, madness, anguish, and despair that were exhausted *in five minutes* by that shabby creature crouched there on the window ledge. But we cannot understand, or look at it any longer. It is too hard, too hard, and not to be endured. We turn away with nausea, hollowness, blind fear, and unbelief within us.

One man stares, cranes his neck, wets his lips, and whispers: "Jesus! To do a thing like that takes *guts!*"

Another, harshly: "Nah! It don't take guts! A guy who'd do a thing like that is crazy! He don't know what he's doin' to begin with!"

And others, doubtfully, half-whispering, with eyes focused on the ledge: "But Jesus!"

A taxi driver, turning away and moving toward his cab, with an attempt at casual indifference that does not ring entirely true: "Oh, well! Just another guy, I guess!"

Then one man, turning to his companion with a little puckered smile: "Well, what about it, Al? You still feel like eating?"

And his companion, quietly: "Eating, hell! I feel like two or three stiff shots of rye! Come on, let's go around to Steve's!"

They go. The Concentrated Blotters of the World cannot abide it. They must somehow blot it out.

So a policeman comes around the corner now with an old tarpaulin, with which he covers the No-Head. The crowd remains. Then the green wagon from the morgue. The Thing, tarpaulin and all, is pushed into it. It drives away. A policeman with thick-soled boots scuffs and pushes skull-pieces and brain-fragments into the gutter. Someone comes with sawdust, strews it. Someone from the drug store with formaldehyde. Later, someone with a hose and water. From the subway come an adolescent boy and girl with the hard, tough faces of the city; they walk past it, deliberately and arrogantly step among it, look at the lamp post, then at each other, and laugh!

All's over now, all's gone, the crowd's departed. Something else remains. It cannot be forgotten. There's a sick, humid smell upon the air, what was light and clear and crystal has gone out of day, and something thick and glutinous—half taste, half smell, and all impalpable—remains upon your tongue.

There would have been a time and place for such a thing, brave Admiral Drake, if he, our fellow Green, had only fallen as a hollow man and landed dryly, or if he had opened to disperse a grey embalming fluid in the gutter. It would have been all right if he had just been blown away like an old paper, or if he had been swept aside like remnants of familiar litter, and then subsumed into the Standard Concentrated stuff from which he came. But C. Green would not have it so. He exploded to drench our common substance of viscous grey with the bright indecency of blood, to resume himself from number, to become before our eyes a Man, and to identify a single spot of all our general Nothingness with the unique passion, the awful terror, and the dignity of Death.

So, Admiral Drake—"an unidentified man fell or jumped yesterday at noon" from a window of your own hotel. That was the news. Now you've had the story.

We are "the hollow men, the hollow men"? Brave Admiral, do not be too sure.

THE PROMISE OF AMERICA

GO, SEEKER, if you will, throughout the land and you will find us burning in the night.

There where the hackles of the Rocky Mountains blaze in the blank and naked radiance of the moon, go make your resting stool upon the highest peak. Can you not see us now? The continental wall juts sheer and flat, its huge black shadow on the plain, and the plain sweeps out against the East, two thousand miles away. The great snake that you see there is the Mississippi River.

Behold the gem-strung towns and cities of the good, green East, flung like star-dust through the field of night. That spreading constellation to the north is called Chicago, and that giant wink that blazes in the moon is the pendant lake that it is built upon. Beyond, close-set and dense as a clenched fist, are all the jeweled cities of the eastern seaboard. There's Boston, ringed with the bracelet of its shining little towns, and all the lights that sparkle on the rocky indentations of New England. Here, southward and a little to the west, and yet still coasted to the sea, is our intensest ray, the splintered firmament of the towered island of Manhattan. Round about her, sown thick as grain, is the glitter of a hundred towns and cities. The long chain of lights there is the necklace of Long Island and the Jersey shore. Southward and inland, by a foot or two, behold the duller glare of Philadelphia. Southward further still, the twin constellations—Baltimore and Washington. Westward, but still within the borders of the good, green East, that nighttime glow and smolder of hell-fire is Pittsburgh. Here, St. Louis, hot and humid in the cornfield belly of the land, and bedded on the mid-length coil and fringes of the snake. There at the snake's mouth, southward six hundred miles or so, you see the jeweled crescent of old New Orleans. Here, west and south again, you see the gemmy glitter of the cities on the Texas border.

Turn now, seeker, on your resting stool atop the Rocky Mountains, and look another thousand miles or so across moon-blazing fiend-worlds of the Painted Desert and beyond Sierras' ridge. That magic congeries of lights there to the west, ringed like a studded belt around the magic setting of its lovely harbor, is the fabled town of

San Francisco. Below it, Los Angeles and all the cities of the California shore. A thousand miles to north and west, the sparkling towns of Oregon and Washington.

Observe the whole of it, survey it as you might survey a field. Make it your garden, seeker, or your backyard patch. Be at ease in it. It's your oyster—yours to open if you will. Don't be frightened, it's not so big now, when your footstool is the Rocky Mountains. Reach out and dip a hatful of cold water from Lake Michigan. Drink it—we've tried it—you'll not find it bad. Take your shoes off and work your toes down in the river oozes of the Mississippi bottom—it's very refreshing on a hot night in the summertime. Help yourself to a bunch of Concord grapes up there in northern New York State—they're getting good now. Or raid that watermelon patch down there in Georgia. Or, if you like, you can try the Rockyfords here at your elbow, in Colorado. Just make yourself at home, refresh yourself, get the feel of things, adjust your sights, and get the scale. It's your pasture now, and it's not so big—only three thousand miles from east to west, only two thousand miles from north to south—but all between, where ten thousand points of light prick out the cities, towns, and villages, there, seeker, you will find us burning in the night.

Here, as you pass through the brutal sprawl, the twenty miles of rails and rickets, of the South Chicago slums—here, in an unpainted shack, is a Negro boy, and, seeker, he is burning in the night. Behind him is a memory of the cotton fields, the flat and mournful pineland barrens of the lost and buried South, and at the fringes of the pine another nigger shack, with mammy and eleven little niggers. Farther still behind, the slave-driver's whip, the slave ship, and, far off, the jungle dirge of Africa. And before him, what? A roped-in ring, a blaze of lights, across from him a white champion; the bell, the opening, and all around the vast sea-roaring of the crowd. Then the lightning feint and stroke, the black panther's paw—the hot, rotating presses, and the rivers of sheeted print! O seeker, where is the slave ship now?

Or there, in the clay-baked piedmont of the South, that lean and tan-faced boy who sprawls there in the creaking chair among admiring cronies before the open doorways of the fire department, and tells them how he pitched the team to shut-out victory today. What visions burn, what dreams possess him, seeker of the night? The packed stands of the stadium, the bleachers sweltering with their unshaded hordes, the faultless velvet of the diamond, unlike the clay-baked outfields down in Georgia. The mounting roar of eighty thousand voices and Gehrig coming up to bat, the boy himself upon the pitching mound, the lean face steady as a hound's; then the nod, the signal, and the wind-up, the rawhide arm that snaps and crackles like a whip, the small white bullet of the blazing ball, its loud report in the oiled pocket of the catcher's mitt, the umpire's thumb jerked upward, the clean strike.

Or there again, in the East-Side Ghetto of Manhattan, two blocks away from the East River, a block away from the gas-house district and its thuggery, there in the swarming tenement, shut in his sweltering cell, breathing the sun-baked air through opened window at the fire escape, celled there away into a little semblance of privacy and solitude from all the brawling and vociferous life and argument of his family and the seething hive around him, the Jew boy sits and pores upon his book. In shirt-sleeves, bent above his table to meet the hard glare of a naked bulb, he sits with gaunt, starved face converging to his huge beaked nose, the weak eyes squinting painfully through his thick-lens glasses, his greasy hair roached back in oily scrolls above the slanting cage of his painful and constricted brow. And for what? For what this agony of concentration? For what this hell of effort? For what this intense withdrawal from the poverty and squalor of dirty brick and rusty fire escapes, from the raucous cries and violence and never-ending noise? For what? Because, brother, he is burning in the night. He sees the class, the lecture room, the shining apparatus of gigantic laboratories, the open field of scholarship and pure research, certain knowledge, and the world distinction of an Einstein name.

So, then, to every man his chance—to every man, regardless of his birth, his shining, golden opportunity—to every man the right to live, to work, to be himself, and to become whatever thing his manhood and his vision can combine to make him—this, seeker, is the promise of America.

CREDO

I HAVE never before made a statement of belief [George wrote in his conclusion to Fox], although I have believed in many things and said that I believed in them. But I have never stated my belief in concrete terms because almost every element of my nature has been opposed to the hard framework, the finality, of formulation.

Just as you are the rock of life, I am the web; just as you are Time's granite, so, I think, am I Time's plant. My life, more than that of anyone I know, has taken on the form of growth. No man that I have known was ever more deeply rooted in the soil of Time and Memory, the weather of his individual universe, than was I. You followed me through the course of that whole herculean conflict. For four years, as I lived and worked and explored the jungle depths of Brooklyn—jungle depths coincident with those of my own soul—you were beside me, you followed, and you stuck.

You never had a doubt that I would finish—make an end—round out the cycle—come to the whole of it. The only doubt was mine, enhanced, tormented by my own fatigue and desperation, and by the clacking of the feeble and malicious little tongues which, knowing nothing, whispered that I would never make an end again because I could not begin. We both knew how grotesquely false this was—so false and so grotesque that it was sometimes the subject of an anguished and exasperated laugh. The truth was so far different that my own fears were just the opposite: that I might never make an end to anything again because I could never get through telling what I knew, what I felt and thought and *had* to say about it.

That was a giant web in which I was caught, the product of my huge inheritance—the torrential recollectiveness, derived out of my mother's stock, which became a living, million-fibered integument that bound me to the past, not only of my own life, but of the very earth from which I came, so that nothing in the end escaped from its in-rooted and all-feeling explorativeness. The way the sunlight came and went upon a certain day, the way grass felt between bare toes, the immediacy of noon, the slamming of an iron gate, the halting skreak upon the corner of a street car, the liquid sound of shoe leather on the pavements as men came home to lunch, the smell of turnip greens, the clang of ice tongs, and the clucking of a hen—and then Time fading like a dream, Time melting to oblivion, when I was two years old. Not only this, but all lost sounds and voices, forgotten memories exhumed with a constant pulsing of the brain's great ventricle, until I live them in my dreams, carrying the stupendous and unceasing burden of them through the unresting passages of sleep. Nothing that had ever been was lost. It all came back in an endless flow, even the blisters of the paint upon the mantelpiece in my father's house, the smell of the old leather sofa with my father's print upon it, the smell of dusty bottles and of cobwebs in the cellar, the casual stomping of a slow, gaunt hoof upon the pulpy lumber of a livery stable floor, the proud lift and flourish of a whisking tail, and the oaty droppings. I lived again through all times and weathers I had known—through the fag-ends of wintry desolation in the month of March and the cold, bleak miseries of ragged red at sunset, the magic of young green in April, the blind horror and suffocation of concrete places in mid-summer sun where no limits were, and October with the smell of fallen leaves and wood smoke in the air. The forgotten moments and unnumbered hours came back to me with all the enormous cargo of my memory, together with lost voices in the mountains long ago, the voices of the kinsmen dead and never seen, and the houses they had built and died in, and the rutted roads they trod upon, and every unrecorded moment that Aunt Maw had told me of the lost and obscure lives they led long, long ago. So did it all revive in the ceaseless pulsings of the giant ventricle, so did the plant go back, stem by stem, root by root, and filament by filament, until it was complete and whole, compacted of the very earth that had produced it, and of which it was itself the last and living part.

You stayed beside me like the rock you are until I unearthed the plant, followed it back through every fiber of its pattern to its last and tiniest enrootment in the blind, dumb earth. And now that it is finished, and the circle come full swing—we, too, are finished, and I have a thing to say:

I believe that we are lost here in America, but I believe we shall be found. And this belief, which mounts now to the catharsis of knowledge and conviction, is for me—and I think for all of us—not only our own hope, but America's everlasting, living dream. I think the life which we have fashioned in America, and which has fashioned us—the forms we made, the cells that grew, the honeycomb that was created—was self-destructive in its nature, and must be destroyed. I think these forms are dying, and must die, just as I know that America and the people in it are deathless, undiscovered, and immortal, and must live.

I think the true discovery of America is before us. I think the true fulfillment of our spirit, of our people, of our mighty and immortal land, is yet to come. I think the true discovery of our own democracy is still before us. And I think that all these things are certain as the morning, as inevitable as noon. I think I speak for most men living when I say that our America is Here, is Now, and beckons on before us, and that this glorious assurance is not only our living hope, but our dream to be accomplished.

I think the enemy is here before us, too. But I think we know the forms and faces of the enemy, and in the knowledge that we know him, and shall meet him, and eventually must conquer him is also our living hope. I think the enemy is here before us with a thousand faces, but I think we know that all his faces wear one mask. I think the enemy is single selfishness and compulsive greed. I think the enemy is blind, but has the brutal power of his blind grab. I do not think the enemy was born yesterday, or that he grew to manhood forty years ago, or that he suffered sickness and collapse in 1929, or that we began without the enemy, and that our vision faltered, that we lost the way, and suddenly were in his camp. I think the enemy is old as Time, and evil as Hell, and that he has been here with us from the beginning. I think he stole our earth from us, destroyed our wealth, and ravaged and despoiled our land. I think he took our people and enslaved them, that he polluted the fountains of our life, took unto himself the rarest treasures of our own possession, took our bread and left us with a crust, and, not content, for the nature of the enemy is insatiate—tried finally to take from us the crust.

I think the enemy comes to us with the face of innocence and says to us:

"I am your friend."

I think the enemy deceives us with false words of lying phrases, saying:

"See, I am one of you—I am one of your children, your son, your brother, and your friend. Behold how sleek and fat I have become—and all because I am just one of you, and your friend. Behold how rich and powerful I am—and all because I am one of you—shaped in your way of life, of thinking, of accomplishment. What I am, I am because I am one of you, your humble brother and your friend. Behold," cries Enemy, "the man I am, the man I have become, the thing I have accomplished—and reflect. Will you destroy this thing? I assure you that it is the most precious thing you have. It is yourselves, the projection of each of you, the triumph of your individual lives, the thing that is rooted in your blood, and native to your stock, and inherent in the traditions of America. It is the thing that all of you may hope to be," says Enemy, "for—" humbly—"am I not just one of you? Am I not just your brother and your son? Am I not the living image of what each of you may hope to be, would wish to be, would desire for his own son? Would you destroy this glorious incarnation of your own heroic self? If you do, then," says Enemy, "you destroy yourselves—you kill the thing that is most gloriously American, and in so killing, kill yourselves."

He lies! And now we know he lies! He is not gloriously, or in any other way, ourselves. He is not our friend, our son, our brother. And he is not American! For, although he has a thousand familiar and convenient faces, his own true face is old as Hell.

Look about you and see what he has done.

FROM

THE HILLS BEYOND

AFTER EDWARD C. ASWELL had organized *The Web and the Rock* and *You Can't Go Home Again* from the mass of manuscript which Wolfe left at his death, he had a great deal of unused material. From it he extracted the work which seemed to warrant publication and presented it in the book *The Hills Beyond* (New York: Harper and Brothers, 1941). This volume contains ten short stories and sketches, many of them previously unpublished in any form, and the first ten chapters of an unfinished novel, *The Hills Beyond.*

The selections here presented are "The Lost Boy," one of Wolfe's finest short stories, and "God's Lonely Man," a revealing autobiographical sketch.

"The Lost Boy" was written in the spring of 1937 and first published in the November, 1937, issue of *Redbook* magazine. Its central event is the death of Wolfe's brother Grover while the family was at the St. Louis Exposition in 1904, and its immediate trigger seems to have been Wolfe's stopping off in St. Louis for a day when he was on his way back East from the West Coast in September, 1935 "to see where Grover died." The story makes an effective and dramatic statement of Wolfe's concept of three levels of time—simple chronology, past time existing in the present through the triggering of a concrete sensory perception that recalls the past, and "the eternal and unchanging universe of time."

"God's Lonely Man" is an autobiographical sketch which Wolfe wrote in 1930 and rewrote many times until his death. Loneliness was a primary fact of his existence and a persistent theme of much of his best work. In this moving essay he sees it as a portion of man's tragic condition and out of its contemplation arrives at a rare statement of religious concern and a final sense of "joy solemn and triumphant."

"The Lost Boy" appears on pages 1-42 of *The Hills Beyond,* and "God's Lonely Man" on pages 186-197.

THE LOST BOY

LIGHT came and went and came again, the booming strokes of three o'clock beat out across the town in thronging bronze from the courthouse bell, light winds of April blew the fountain out in rainbow sheets, until the plume returned and pulsed, as Grover turned into the Square. He was a child, dark-eyed and grave, birthmarked upon his neck—a berry of warm brown—and with a gentle face, too quiet and too listening for his years. The scuffed boy's shoes, the thick-ribbed stockings gartered at the knees, the short knee pants cut straight with three small useless buttons at the side, the sailor blouse, the old cap battered out of shape, perched sideways up on top of the raven head, the old soiled canvas bag slung from the shoulder, empty now, but waiting for the crisp sheets of the afternoon—these friendly, shabby garments, shaped by Grover, uttered him. He turned and passed along the north side of the Square and in that moment saw the union of Forever and of Now.

Light came and went and came again, the great plume of the fountain pulsed and winds of April sheeted it across the Square in a rainbow gossamer of spray. The fire department horses drummed on the floors with wooden stomp, most casually, and with dry whiskings of their clean, coarse tails. The street cars ground into the Square from every portion of the compass and halted briefly like wound toys in their familiar quarter-hourly formula. A dray, hauled by a bone-yard nag, rattled across the cobbles on the other side before his father's shop. The courthouse bell boomed out its solemn warning of immediate three, and everything was just the same as it had always been.

He saw that haggis of vexed shapes with quiet eyes—that hodge-podge of ill-sorted architectures that made up the Square, and he did not feel lost. For "Here," thought Grover, "here is the Square as it has always been—and papa's shop, the fire department and the City Hall, the fountain pulsing with its plume, the street cars coming in and halting at the quarter hour, the hardware store on the corner there, the row of old brick buildings on this side of the street, the people passing and the light that comes and changes and that always will come back again, and everything that comes and goes and changes in the Square, and yet will be the same again. And here," the boy thought, "is Grover with his paper bag. Here is old Grover, almost twelve years old. Here is the month of April, 1904. Here is the courthouse bell and three o'clock. Here is Grover on the Square that never changes. Here is Grover, caught upon this point of time.

It seemed to him that the Square, itself the accidental masonry of many years, the chance agglomeration of time and of disrupted strivings, was the center of the universe. It was for him, in his soul's picture, the earth's pivot, the granite core of changelessness, the eternal place where all things came and passed, and yet abode forever and would never change.

He passed the old shack on the corner—the wooden fire-trap where S. Goldberg ran his wiener stand. Then he passed the Singer place next door, with its gleaming display of new machines. He saw them and admired them, but he felt no joy. They brought back to him the busy hum of housework and of women sewing, the intricacy of stitch and weave, the mystery of style and pattern, the memory of women bending over flashing needles, the pedaled tread, the busy whir. It was women's work: it filled him with unknown associations of dullness and of vague depression. And always, also, with a moment's twinge of horror, for his dark eye would always travel toward that needle stitching up and down so fast the eye could never follow it. And then he would remember how his mother once had told him she had driven the needle through her finger, and always, when he passed this place, he would remember it and for a moment crane his neck and turn his head away.

He passed on then, but had to stop again next door before the music store. He always had to stop by places that had shining perfect things in them. He loved hardware stores and windows full of accurate geometric tools. He loved windows full of hammers, saws, and planing boards. He liked windows full of strong new rakes and hoes, with unworn handles, of white perfect wood, stamped hard and vivid with the maker's seal. He loved to see such things as these in the windows of hardware stores. And he would fairly gloat upon them and think that some day he would own a set himself.

Also, he always stopped before the music and piano store. It was a splendid store. And in the window was a small white dog upon his haunches, with head cocked gravely to one side, a small white dog that never moved, that never barked, that listened attentively at the flaring funnel of a horn to hear "His Master's Voice"—a horn for-ever silent, and a voice that never spoke. And within were many rich and shining shapes of great pianos, an air of splendor and of wealth.

And now, indeed, he *was* caught, held suspended. A waft of air, warm, chocolate-laden, filled his nostrils. He tried to pass the white front of the little eight-foot shop; he paused, struggling with con-science; he could not go on. It was the little candy shop run by old Crocker and his wife. And Grover could not pass.

"Old stingy Crockers!" he thought scornfully. "I'll not go there any more. But—" as the maddening fragrance of rich cooking choco-late touched him once again—"I'll just look in the window and see what they've got." He paused a moment, looking with his dark and quiet eyes into the window of the little candy shop. The window, spotlessly clean, was filled with trays of fresh-made candy. His eyes rested on a tray of chocolate drops. Unconsciously he licked his lips. Put one of them upon your tongue and it just melted there, like honeydew. And then the trays full of rich home-made fudge. He gazed longingly at the deep body of the chocolate fudge, reflectively at maple walnut, more critically, yet with longing, at the mints, the nougatines, and all the other dainties.

"Old stingy Crockers!" Grover muttered once again, and turned to go. "I wouldn't go in *there* again."

And yet he did not go away. "Old stingy Crockers" they might be; still, they did make the best candy in town, the best, in fact, that he had ever tasted.

He looked through the window back into the little shop and saw Mrs. Crocker there. A customer had gone in and had made a pur-chase, and as Grover looked he saw Mrs. Crocker, with her little wrenny face, her pinched features, lean over and peer primly at the scales. She had a piece of fudge in her clean, bony, little fingers, and as Grover looked, she broke it, primly, in her little bony hands. She dropped a morsel down into the scales. They weighted down alarm-ingly, and her thin lips tightened. She snatched the piece of fudge out of the scales and broke it carefully once again. This time the scales wavered, went down very slowly, and came back again. Mrs. Crocker carefully put the reclaimed piece of fudge back in the tray, dumped the remainder in a paper bag, folded it and gave it to the customer, counted the money carefully and doled it out into the till, the pennies in one place, the nickels in another.

Grover stood there, looking scornfully. "Old stingy Crocker—afraid that she might give a crumb away!"

He grunted scornfully and again he turned to go. But now Mr. Crocker came out from the little partitioned place where they made all their candy, bearing a tray of fresh-made fudge in his skinny hands. Old Man Crocker rocked along the counter to the front and put it down. He really rocked along. He was a cripple. And like his wife, he was a wrenny, wizened little creature, with bony hands, thin lips, a pinched and meager face. One leg was inches shorter than the other, and on this leg there was an enormous thick-soled boot, with a kind of wooden, rocker-like arrangement, six inches high at least, to make up for the deficiency. On this wooden cradle Mr. Crocker rocked along, with a prim and apprehensive little smile, as if he were afraid he was going to lose something.

"Old stingy Crocker!" muttered Grover. "Humph! He wouldn't give you anything!"

And yet—he did not go away. He hung there curiously, peering through the window, with his dark and gentle face now focused and intent, alert and curious, flattening his nose against the glass. Unconsciously he scratched the thick-ribbed fabric of one stockinged leg with the scuffed and worn toe of his old shoe. The fresh, warm odor of the new-made fudge was delicious. It was a little maddening. Half consciously he began to fumble in one trouser pocket, and pulled out his purse, a shabby worn old black one with a twisted clasp. He opened it and prowled about inside.

What he found was not inspiring—a nickel and two pennies and—he had forgotten them—the stamps. He took the stamps out and unfolded them. There were five twos, eight ones, all that remained of the dollar-sixty-cents' worth which Reed, the pharmacist, had given him for running errands a week or two before.

"Old Crocker," Grover thought, and looked somberly at the grotesque little form as it rocked back into the shop again, around the counter, and up the other side. "Well—" again he looked indefinitely at the stamps in his hand—"he's had all the rest of them. He might as well take these."

So, soothing conscience with this sop of scorn, he went into the shop and stood looking at the trays in the glass case and finally decided. Pointing with a slightly grimy finger at the fresh-made tray of chocolate fudge, he said, "I'll take fifteen cents' worth of this, Mr. Crocker." He paused a moment, fighting with embarrassment, then he lifted his dark face and said quietly, "And please, I'll have to give you stamps again."

Mr. Crocker made no answer. He did not look at Grover. He pressed his lips together primly. He went rocking away and got the candy scoop, came back, slid open the door of the glass case, put fudge into the scoop, and, rocking to the scales, began to weigh the candy out. Grover watched him as he peered and squinted, he watched him purse and press his lips together, he saw him take a piece of fudge and break it in two parts. And then old Crocker broke two parts in two again. He weighed, he squinted, and he hovered, until it seemed to Grover that by calling *Mrs.* Crocker stingy he had been guilty of a rank injustice. But finally, to his vast relief, the job was over, the scales hung there, quivering apprehensively, upon the very hair-line of nervous balance, as if even the scales were afraid that one more move from Old Man Crocker and they would be undone.

Mr. Crocker took the candy then and dumped it in a paper bag and, rocking back along the counter toward the boy, he dryly said: "Where are the stamps?" Grover gave them to him. Mr. Crocker relinquished his clawlike hold upon the bag and set it down upon the counter. Grover took the bag and dropped it in his canvas sack, and then remembered. "Mr. Crocker—" again he felt the old embarrassment that was almost like strong pain—"I gave you too much," Grover said. "There were eighteen cents in stamps. You—you can just give me three ones back."

Mr. Crocker did not answer. He was busy with his bony little hands, unfolding the stamps and flattening them out on top of the glass counter. When he had done so, he peered at them sharply for a moment, thrusting his scrawny neck forward and running his eye up and down, like a bookkeeper who totes up rows of figures.

When he had finished, he said tartly: "I don't like this kind of business. If you want candy, you should have the money for it. I'm not a post office. The next time you come in here and want anything, you'll have to pay me money for it."

Hot anger rose in Grover's throat. His olive face suffused with angry color. His tarry eyes got black and bright. He was on the verge of saying: "Then why did you take my other stamps? Why do you tell me now, when you have taken all the stamps I had, that you don't want them?"

But he was a boy, a boy of eleven years, a quiet, gentle, gravely thoughtful boy, and he had been taught how to respect his elders. So he just stood there looking with his tar-black eyes. Old Man Crocker, pursing at the mouth a little, without meeting Grover's gaze, took the stamps up in his thin, parched fingers and, turning, rocked away with them down to the till.

He took the twos and folded them and laid them in one rounded scallop, then took the ones and folded them and put them in the one next to it. Then he closed the till and started to rock off, down toward the other end. Grover, his face now quiet and grave, kept looking at him, but Mr. Crocker did not look at Grover. Instead he began to take some stamped cardboard shapes and fold them into boxes.

In a moment Grover said, "Mr. Crocker, will you give me the three ones, please?"

Mr. Crocker did not answer. He kept folding boxes, and he compressed his thin lips quickly as he did so. But Mrs. Crocker, back turned to her spouse, also folding boxes with her birdlike hands, muttered tartly: "Hm! *I'd* give him nothing!"

Mr. Crocker looked up, looked at Grover, said, "What are you waiting for?"

"Will you give me the three ones, please?" Grover said.

"I'll give you nothing," Mr. Crocker said.

He left his work and came rocking forward along the counter. "Now you get out of here! Don't you come in here with any more of those stamps," said Mr. Crocker.

"I should like to know where he gets them—that's what *I* should like to know," said Mrs. Crocker.

She did not look up as she said these words. She inclined her head a little to the side, in Mr. Crocker's direction, and continued to fold the boxes with her bony fingers.

"You get out of here!" said Mr. Crocker. "And don't you come back here with any stamps. . . . Where did you get those stamps?" he said.

"That's just what *I've* been thinking," Mrs. Crocker said. "*I've* been thinking all along."

"You've been coming in here for the last two weeks with those stamps," said Mr. Crocker. "I don't like the look of it. Where did you get those stamps?" he said.

"That's what *I've* been thinking," said Mrs. Crocker, for a second time.

Grover had got white underneath his olive skin. His eyes had lost their luster. They looked like dull, stunned balls of tar. "From Mr. Reed," he said. "I got the stamps from Mr. Reed." Then he burst out desperately: "Mr. Crocker—Mr. Reed will tell you how I got the stamps. I did some work for Mr. Reed, he gave me those stamps two weeks ago."

"Mr. Reed," said Mrs. Crocker acidly. She did not turn her head. "I call it mighty funny."

"Mr. Crocker," Grover said, "if you'll just let me have three ones——"

"You get out of here!" cried Mr. Crocker, and he began rocking forward toward Grover. "Now don't you come in here again, boy! There's something funny about this whole business! I don't like the look of it," said Mr. Crocker. "If you can't pay as other people do, then I don't want your trade."

"Mr. Crocker," Grover said again, and underneath the olive skin his face was gray, "if you'll just let me have those three——"

"You get out of here!" Mr. Crocker cried, rocking down toward the counter's end. "If you don't get out, boy——"

"*I'd* call a policeman, that's what I'd do," Mrs. Crocker said.

Mr. Crocker rocked around the lower end of the counter. He came rocking up to Grover. "You get out," he said.

He took the boy and pushed him with his bony little hands, and Grover was sick and gray down to the hollow pit of his stomach.

"You've got to give me those three ones," he said.

"You get out of here!" shrilled Mr. Crocker. He seized the screen door, pulled it open, and pushed Grover out. "Don't you come back in here," he said, pausing for a moment, and working thinly at the lips. He turned and rocked back in the shop again. The screen door slammed behind him. Grover stood there on the pavement. And light came and went and came again into the Square.

The boy stood there, and a wagon rattled past. There were some people passing by, but Grover did not notice them. He stood there blindly, in the watches of the sun, feeling this was Time, this was the center of the universe, the granite core of changelessness, and feeling, this is Grover, this the Square, this is Now.

But something had gone out of day. He felt the overwhelming, soul-sickening guilt that all the children, all the good men of the earth, have felt since Time began. And even anger had died down, had been drowned out, in this swelling tide of guilt, and "This is the Square"—thought Grover as before—"This is Now. There is my father's shop. And all of it is as it has always been—save I."

And the Square reeled drunkenly around him, light went in blind gray motes before his eyes, the fountain sheeted out to rainbow iridescence and returned to its proud, pulsing plume again. But all the brightness had gone out of day, and "Here is the Square, and here is permanence, and here is Time—and all of it the same as it has always been, save I."

The scuffed boots of the lost boy moved and stumbled blindly. The numb feet crossed the pavement—reached the cobbled street, reached the plotted central square—the grass plots, and the flower beds, so soon to be packed with red geraniums.

"I want to be alone," thought Grover, "where I cannot go near him. . . . Oh God, I hope he never hears, that no one ever tells him——"

The plume blew out, the iridescent sheet of spray blew over him. He passed through, found the other side and crossed the street, and —"Oh God, if papa ever hears!" thought Grover, as his numb feet started up the steps into his father's shop.

He found and felt the steps—the width and thickness of old lumber twenty feet in length. He saw it all—the iron columns on his father's porch, painted with the dull anomalous black-green that all such columns in this land and weather come to; two angels, fly-specked, and the waiting stones. Beyond and all around, in the stone-cutter's shop, cold shapes of white and marble, rounded stone, the languid angel with strong marble hands of love.

He went on down the aisle, the white shapes stood around him. He went on to the back of the workroom. This he knew—the little cast-iron stove in left-hand corner, caked, brown, heat-blistered, and the elbow of the long stack running out across the shop; the high and dirty window looking down across the Market Square toward

Niggertown; the rude old shelves, plank-boarded, thick, the wood not smooth but pulpy, like the strong hair of an animal; upon the shelves the chisels of all sizes and a layer of stone dust; an emery wheel with pump tread; and a door that let out on the alleyway, yet the alleyway twelve feet below. Here in the room, two trestles of this coarse spiked wood upon which rested gravestones, and at one, his father at work.

The boy looked, saw the name was Creasman: saw the carved analysis of John, the symmetry of the s, the fine sentiment that was being polished off beneath the name and date: "John Creasman, November 7, 1903."

Gant looked up. He was a man of fifty-three, gaunt-visaged, mustache cropped, immensely long and tall and gaunt. He wore good dark clothes—heavy, massive—save he had no coat. He worked in shirt-sleeves with his vest on, a strong watch chain stretching across his vest, wing collar and black tie, Adam's apple, bony forehead, bony nose, light eyes, gray-green, undeep and cold, and, somehow, lonely-looking, a striped apron going up around his shoulders, and starched cuffs. And in one hand a tremendous rounded wooden mallet like a butcher's bole; and in his other hand, a strong cold chisel.

"How are you, son?"

He did not look up as he spoke. He spoke quietly, absently. He worked upon the chisel and the wooden mallet, as a jeweler might work on a watch, except that in the man and in the wooden mallet there was power too.

"What is it, son?" he said.

He moved around the table from the head, started up on "J" once again.

"Papa, I never stole the stamps," said Grover.

Gant put down the mallet, laid the chisel down. He came around the trestle.

"What?" he said.

As Grover winked his tar-black eyes, they brightened, the hot tears shot out. "I never stole the stamps," he said.

"Hey? What is this?" his father said. "What stamps?"

"That Mr. Reed gave me, when the other boy was sick and I worked there for three days. . . . And Old Man Crocker," Grover said, "he took all the stamps. And I told him Mr. Reed had given them to me. And now he owes me three ones—and Old Man Crocker says he don't believe they were mine. He says—he says—that I must have taken them somewhere," Grover blurted out.

"The stamps that Reed gave you—hey?" the stonecutter said. "The stamps you had—" He wet his thumb upon his lips, threw back his head and slowly swung his gaze around the ceiling, then turned and strode quickly from his workshop out into the storeroom.

Almost at once he came back again, and as he passed the old gray painted-board partition of his office he cleared his throat and wet his thumb and said, "Now, I tell you——"

Then he turned and strode up toward the front again and cleared his throat and said, "I tell you now—" He wheeled about and started back, and as he came along the aisle between the marshaled rows of gravestones he said beneath his breath, "By God, now——"

He took Grover by the hand and they went out flying. Down the aisle they went by all the gravestones, past the fly-specked angels waiting there, and down the wooden steps and across the Square. The fountain pulsed, the plume blew out in sheeted iridescence, and it swept across them; an old gray horse, with a peaceful look about his torn lips, swucked up the cool mountain water from the trough as Grover and his father went across the Square, but they did not notice it.

They crossed swiftly to the other side in a direct line to the candy shop. Gant was still dressed in his long striped apron, and he was still holding Grover by the hand. He opened the screen door and stepped inside.

"Give him the stamps," Gant said.

Mr. Crocker came rocking forward behind the counter, with the prim and careful look that now was somewhat like a smile. "It was just—" he said.

"Give him the stamps," Gant said, and threw some coins down on the counter.

Mr. Crocker rocked away and got the stamps. He came rocking back. "I just didn't know—" he said.

The stonecutter took the stamps and gave them to the boy. And Mr. Crocker took the coins.

"It was just that—" Mr. Crocker began again, and smiled.

Gant cleared his throat: "You never were a father," he said. "You never knew the feelings of a father, or understood the feelings of a child; and that is why you acted as you did. But a judgment is upon you. God has cursed you. He has afflicted you. He has made you lame and childless as you are—and lame and childless, miserable as you are, you will go to your grave and be forgotten!"

And Crocker's wife kept kneading her bony little hands and said, imploringly, "Oh, no—oh don't say that, please don't say that."

The stonecutter, the breath still hoarse in him, left the store, still holding the boy tightly by the hand. Light came again into the day. "Well, son," he said, and laid his hand on the boy's back. "Well, son," he said, "now don't you mind."

They walked across the Square, the sheeted spray of iridescent light swept out on them, the horse swizzled at the water-trough, and "Well, son," the stonecutter said.

And the old horse sloped down, ringing with his hoofs upon the cobblestones.

"Well, son," said the stonecutter once again, "be a good boy."

And he trod his own steps then with his great stride and went back again into his shop.

The lost boy stood upon the Square, hard by the porch of his father's shop.

"This is Time," thought Grover. "Here is the Square, here is my father's shop, and here am I."

And light came and went and came again—but now not quite the same as it had done before. The boy saw the pattern of familiar shapes and knew that they were just the same as they had always been. But something had gone out of day, and something had come in again. Out of the vision of those quiet eyes some brightness had gone, and into their vision had come some deeper color. He could not say, he did not know through what transforming shadows life had passed within that quarter hour. He only knew that something had been lost—something forever gained.

Just then a buggy curved out through the Square, and fastened to the rear end was a poster, and it said "St. Louis" and "Excursion" and "The Fair."

II—THE MOTHER

As we went down through Indiana—you were too young, child, to remember it—but I always think of all of you the way you looked that morning, when we went down through Indiana, going to the Fair. All of the apple trees were coming out, and it was April; it was the beginning of spring in southern Indiana and everything was getting green. Of course we don't have farms at home like those in Indiana. The children had never seen such farms as those, and I reckon, kidlike, they had to take it in.

So all of them kept running up and down the aisle—well, no, except for you and Grover. *You* were too young, Eugene. You were just three, I kept you with me. As for Grover—well, I'm going to tell you about that.

But the rest of them kept running up and down the aisle and from one window to another. They kept calling out and hollering to each other every time they saw something new. They kept trying to look out on all sides, in every way at once, as if they wished they had eyes at the back of their heads. It was the first time any of them had ever been in Indiana, and I reckon that it all seemed strange and new.

And so it seemed they couldn't get enough. It seemed they never could be still. They kept running up and down and back and forth, hollering and shouting to each other, until—"I'll vow! You children! I never saw the beat of you!" I said. "The way that you keep running up and down and back and forth and never can be quiet for a minute beats all I ever saw," I said.

You see, they were excited about going to St. Louis, and so curious over everything they saw. They couldn't help it, and they wanted to see everything. But—"I'll vow!" I said. "If you children don't sit down and rest you'll be worn to a frazzle before we ever get to see St. Louis and the Fair!"

Except for Grover! He—no, sir! not him. Now, boy, I want to tell you—I've raised the lot of you—and if I do say so, there wasn't a numbskull in the lot. But *Grover*! Well, you've all grown up now, all of you have gone away, and none of you are children any more. . . . And of course, I hope that, as the fellow says, you have reached the dignity of man's estate. I suppose you have the judgment of grown men. . . . But *Grover*! *Grover* had it even then!

Oh, even as a child, you know—at a time when I was almost afraid to trust the rest of you out of my sight—I could depend on Grover. He could go anywhere, I could send him anywhere, and I'd always know he'd get back safe, and do exactly what I told him to!

Why, I didn't even have to tell him. You could send that child to market and tell him what you wanted, and he'd come home with *twice* as much as you could get yourself for the same money!

Now you know, I've always been considered a good trader. But *Grover!*—why, it got so finally that I wouldn't even tell him. Your papa said to me: "You'd be better off if you'd just tell him what you want and leave the rest to him. For," your papa says, "damned if I don't believe he's a better trader than you are. He gets more for the money than anyone I ever saw."

Well, I had to admit it, you know. I had to own up then. Grover, even as a child, was a far better trader than I was. . . . Why, yes, they told it on him all over town, you know. They said all of the market men, all of the farmers, knew him. They'd begin to laugh when they saw him coming—they'd say: "Look out! Here's Grover! Here's one trader you're not going to fool!"

And they were right! *That* child! I'd say, "Grover, suppose you run uptown and see if they've got anything good to *eat* today"—and I'd just wink at him, you know, but he'd know what I meant. I wouldn't let on that I *wanted* anything exactly, but I'd say, "Now it just occurs to me that some good fresh stuff may be coming in from the country, so suppose you take this dollar and just see what you can do with it."

Well, sir, that was all that was needed. The minute you told that child that you depended on his judgment, he'd have gone to the ends of the earth for you—and, let me tell you something, he wouldn't *miss*, either!

His eyes would get as black as coals—oh! the way that child would look at you, the intelligence and sense in his expression. He'd say: "Yes, *ma'am!* Now don't you worry, mama. You leave it all to me— and I'll do *good!*" said Grover.

And he'd be off like a streak of lightning and—oh Lord! As your father said to me, "I've been living in this town for almost thirty years," he said—"I've seen it grow up from a crossroads village, and I thought I knew everything there was to know about it—but that child—" your papa says—"he knows places that I never heard of!" . . . Oh, he'd go right down there to that place below your papa's shop where the drayman and the country people used to park their wagons—or he'd go down there to those old lots on Concord Street where the farmers used to keep their wagons. And, child that he was, he'd go right in among them, sir—*Grover* would!—go right in and barter with them like a grown man!

And he'd come home with things he'd bought that would make your eyes stick out. . . . Here he comes one time with another boy, dragging a great bushel basket full of ripe termaters between them. "Why, Grover!" I says. "How on earth are we ever going to use them? Why they'll go bad on us before we're half way through with them." "Well, mama," he says, "I know—" oh, just as solemn as a judge— "but they were the last the man had," he says, "and he wanted to go home, and so I got them for ten cents," he says. "They were so cheap," said Grover, "I thought it was a shame to let 'em go, and I figgered that what we couldn't eat—why," says Grover, "you could *put up!*" Well, the way he said it—so earnest and so serious—I had to laugh. "But I'll vow!" I said. "If you don't beat all!" . . . But that was *Grover!*—the way he was in *those* days! As everyone said, boy that he was, he had the sense and judgment of a grown man. . . . Child, child, I've seen you all grow up, and all of you were bright enough. There were no half-wits in *my* family. But for all-around intelligence, judgment, and general ability, Grover surpassed the whole crowd. I've never seen his equal, and everyone who knew him as a child will say the same.

So that's what I tell them now when they ask me about all of you. I have to tell the truth. I always said that *you* were smart enough, Eugene—but when they come around and brag to me about you, and about how you have got on and have a kind of name— I don't let on, you know. I just sit there and let them talk. I don't brag on you— if *they* want to brag on you, that's *their* business. I never bragged on one of my own children in my life. When father raised us up, we were all brought up to believe that it was not good breeding to brag about your kin. "If the others want to do it," father said, "well, let *them* do it. Don't ever let on by a word or sign that you know what they are talking about. Just let *them* do the talking, and say nothing."

So when they come around and tell me all about the things *you've* done—I don't let on to them, I never say a word. Why yes!—why, here, you know—oh, along about a month or so ago, this feller comes —a well-dressed man, you know—he looked intelligent, a good substantial sort of person. He said he came from New Jersey, or somewhere up in that part of the country, and he began to ask me all sorts of questions—what you were like when you were a boy, and all such stuff as that.

I just pretended to study it all over and then I said, "Well, yes"— real serious-like, you know—"well, yes—I reckon I ought to know a little something about him. Eugene was my child, just the same as all the others were. I brought him up just the way I brought up all the others. And," I says—oh, just as solemn as you please—"he wasn't a *bad* sort of a boy. Why," I says, "up to the time that he was twelve years old he was just about the same as any other boy—a good, average, normal sort of fellow."

"Oh," he says. "But didn't you notice something? Wasn't there something kind of strange?" he says—"something different from what you noticed in the other children?"

I didn't let on, you know—I just took it all in and looked as solemn as an owl—I just pretended to study it all over, just as serious as you please.

"Why no," I says, real slow-like, after I'd studied it all over. "As I remember it, he was a good, ordinary, normal sort of boy, just like all the others."

"Yes," he says—oh, all excited-like, you know— "But didn't you notice how brilliant he was? Eugene must have been more brilliant than the rest!"

"Well, now," I says, and pretended to study that all over too. "Now let me see. . . . Yes," I says—I just looked him in the eye, as solemn as you please—"he did pretty well. . . . Well, yes," I says, "I guess he was a fairly bright sort of a boy. I never had no complaints to make of him on that score. He was bright enough," I says. "The only trouble with him was that he was lazy."

"Lazy!" he says—oh, you should have seen the look upon his face, you know—he jumped like someone had stuck a pin in him. "Lazy!" he says. "Why, you don't mean to tell me——"

"Yes," I says—oh, I never cracked a smile—"I was telling him the same thing myself the last time that I saw him. I told him it was a mighty lucky thing for him that he had the gift of gab. Of course, he went off to college and read a lot of books, and I reckon that's where he got this flow of language they say he has. But as I said to him the last time that I saw him: 'Now look a-here,' I said. 'If you can earn your living doing a light, easy class of work like this you do,' I says, 'you're mighty lucky, because none of the rest of your people,' I says, 'had any such luck as that. They had to work hard for a living.' "

Oh, I told him, you know. I came right out with it. I made no bones about it. And I tell you what—I wish you could have seen his face. It was a study.

"Well," he says, at last, "you've got to admit this, haven't you—he was the brightest boy you had, now wasn't he?"

I just looked at him a moment. I had to tell the truth. I couldn't fool him any longer. "No," I says. "He was a good, bright boy—I got no complaint to make about him on that score—but the brightest boy I had, the one that surpassed all the rest of them in sense, and understanding, and in judgment—the best boy I had—the smartest boy I ever saw—was—well, it wasn't Eugene," I said. "It was another one."

He looked at me a moment, then he said, "Which boy was that?"

Well, I just looked at him, and smiled. I shook my head, you know. I wouldn't tell him. "I never brag about my own," I said. "You'll have to find out for yourself."

But—I'll have to tell *you*—and you know yourself, I brought the whole crowd up, I knew you all. And you can take my word for it— the best one of the lot was—*Grover!*

And when I think of Grover as he was along about that time, I always see him sitting there, so grave and earnest-like, with his nose pressed to the window, as we went down through Indiana in the morning, to the Fair.

All through that morning we were going down along beside the Wabash River—the Wabash River flows through Indiana, it is the river that they wrote the song about—so all that morning we were going down along the river. And I sat with all you children gathered about me as we went down through Indiana, going to St. Louis, to the Fair.

And Grover sat there, so still and earnest-like, looking out the window, and he didn't move. He sat there like a man. He was just eleven and a half years old, but he had more sense, more judgment, and more understanding than any child I ever saw.

So here he sat beside this gentleman and looked out the window. I never knew the man—I never asked his name—but I tell you what! He was certainly a fine-looking, well-dressed, good, substantial sort of man, and I could see that he had taken a great liking to Grover. And Grover sat there looking out, and then turned to this gentleman, as grave and earnest as a grown-up man, and says, "What kind of crops grow here, sir?" Well, this gentleman threw his head back and just hah-hahed. "Well, I'll see if I can tell you," says this gentleman, and then, you know, he talked to him, they talked together, and Grover took it all in, as solemn as you please, and asked this gentleman every sort of question—what the trees were, what was growing there, how big the farms were—all sorts of questions, which this gentleman would answer, until I said: "Why, I'll vow, Grover! You shouldn't ask so many questions. You'll bother the very life out of this gentleman."

The gentleman threw his head back and laughed right out. "Now you leave that boy alone. He's all right," he said. "He doesn't bother me a bit, and if I know the answers to his questions I will answer him. And if I don't know, why, then, I'll tell him so. But he's *all right*," he said, and put his arm round Grover's shoulders. "You leave him alone. He doesn't bother me a bit."

And I can still remember how he looked that morning, with his black eyes, his black hair, and with the birthmark on his neck—so grave, so serious, so earnest-like—as he sat by the train window and watched the apple trees, the farms, the barns, the houses, and the orchards, taking it all in, I reckon, because it was strange and new to him.

It was so long ago, but when I think of it, it all comes back, as if it happened yesterday. Now all of you have either died or grown up and gone away, and nothing is the same as it was then. But all of you were there with me that morning and I guess I should remember how the others looked, but somehow I don't. Yet I can still see Grover just the way he was, the way he looked that morning when we went down through Indiana, by the river, to the Fair.

III—THE SISTER

Can you remember, Eugene, how Grover used to look? I mean the birthmark, the black eyes, the olive skin. The birthmark always showed because of those open sailor blouses kids used to wear. But I guess you must have been too young when Grover died. . . . I was looking at that old photograph the other day. You know the one I mean—that picture showing mama and papa and all of us children before the house on Woodson Street. *You* weren't there, Eugene. *You* didn't get in. *You* hadn't arrived when that was taken. . . . You remember how mad you used to get when we'd tell you that you were only a dishrag hanging out in Heaven when something happened?

You were the baby. That's what you get for being the baby. You don't get in the picture, do you? . . . I was looking at that old picture just the other day. There we were. And, my God, what is it all about? I mean, when you see the way we were—Daisy and Ben and Grover, Steve and all of us—and then how everyone either dies or grows up and goes away—and then—look at us now! Do you ever get to feeling funny? You know what I mean—do you ever get to feeling *queer*— when you try to figure these things out? You've been to college and you ought to know the answer—and I wish you'd tell me if you know.

My Lord, when I think sometimes of the way I used to be—the dreams I used to have. Playing the piano, practicing seven hours a day, thinking that some day I would be a great pianist. Taking singing lessons from Aunt Nell because I felt that some day I was going to have a great career in opera. . . . Can you beat it now? Can you imagine it? *Me!* In grand opera! . . . Now I want to ask you. I'd like to know.

My Lord! When I go uptown and walk down the street and see all these funny-looking little boys and girls hanging around the drug store—do you suppose any of them have ambitions the way we did? Do you suppose any of these funny-looking little girls are thinking about a big career in opera? . . . Didn't you ever see that picture of us? I was looking at it just the other day. It was made before the old house down on Woodson Street, with papa standing there in his swallow-tail, and mama there beside him—and Grover, and Ben, and Steve, and Daisy, and myself, with our feet upon our bicycles. Luke, poor kid, was only four or five. *He* didn't have a bicycle like us. But there he was. And there were all of us together.

Well, there I was, and my poor old skinny legs and long white dress, and two pigtails hanging down my back. And all the funny-looking clothes we wore, with the doo-lolley business on them. . . . But I guess you can't remember. You weren't born.

But, well, we were a right nice-looking set of people, if I do say so.

And there was "86" the way it used to be, with the front porch, the grape vines, and the flower beds before the house—and "Miss Eliza" standing there by papa, with a watch charm pinned upon her waist. . . . I shouldn't laugh, but "Miss Eliza"—well, mama was a pretty woman then. Do you know what I mean? "Miss Eliza" was a right good-looking woman, and papa in his swallow-tail was a good-looking man. Do you remember how he used to get dressed up on Sunday? And how grand we thought he was? And how he let me take his money out and count it? And how rich we all thought he was? And how wonderful that dinkey little shop on the Square looked to us? . . . Can you beat it, now? Why we thought that papa was the biggest man in town and—oh, you can't tell me! You can't tell me! He had his faults, but papa was a wonderful man. You know he was!

And there was Steve and Ben and Grover, Daisy, Luke, and me lined up there before the house with one foot on our bicycles. And I got to thinking back about it all. It all came back.

Do you remember anything about St. Louis? You were only three or four years old then, but you must remember something. . . . Do you remember how you used to bawl when I would scrub you? How you'd bawl for Grover? Poor kid, you used to yell for Grover every time I'd get you in the tub. . . . He was a sweet kid and he was crazy about you—he almost brought you up.

That year Grover was working at the Inside Inn out on the Fair Grounds. Do you remember the old Inside Inn? That big old wooden thing inside the Fair? And how I used to take you there to wait for Grover when he got through working? And old fat Billy Pelham at the newsstand—how he always used to give you a stick of chewing gum?

They were all crazy about Grover. Everybody liked him. . . . And how proud Grover was of you! Don't you remember how he used to show you off? How he used to take you around and make you talk to Billy Pelham? And Mr. Curtis at the desk? And how Grover would try to make you talk and get you to say "Grover"? And you couldn't say it—you couldn't pronounce the "r." You'd say "Gova." Have you forgotten that? You shouldn't forget *that,* because—you were a *cute* kid, then—Ho-ho-ho-ho-ho—I don't know where it's gone to, but you were a big hit in those days. . . . I tell you, boy, you were Somebody back in those days.

And I was thinking of it all the other day when I was looking at that photograph. How we used to go and meet Grover there, and how he'd take us to the Midway. Do you remember the Midway? The Snake-Eater and the Living Skeleton, the Fat Woman and the Chute-the-chute, the Scenic Railway and the Ferris Wheel? How you bawled the night we took you up on the Ferris Wheel? You yelled your head off—I tried to laugh it off, but I tell you, I was scared myself. Back in those days, that was Something. And how Grover laughed at us and told us there was no danger. . . . My lord! poor little Grover. He wasn't quite twelve years old at the time, but he seemed so grown up to us. I was two years older, but I thought he knew it all.

It was always that way with him. Looking back now, it sometimes seems that it was Grover who brought us up. He was always looking after us, telling us what to do, bringing us something—some ice cream or some candy, something he had bought out of the poor little money he'd gotten at the Inn.

Then I got to thinking of the afternoon we sneaked away from home. Mama had gone out somewhere. And Grover and I got on the street car and went downtown. And my Lord, we thought that we were going Somewhere. In those days, that was what we called a *trip*. A ride in the street car was something to write home about in those days. . . . I hear that it's all built up around there now.

So we got on the car and rode the whole way down into the business section of St. Louis. We got out on Washington Street and walked up and down. And I tell you, boy, we thought that that was Something. Grover took me into a drug store and set me up to soda water. Then we came out and walked around some more, down to the Union Station and clear over to the river. And both of us half scared to death at what we'd done and wondering what mama would say if she found out.

We stayed down there till it was getting dark, and we passed by a lunchroom—an old one-armed joint with one-armed chairs and people sitting on stools and eating at the counter. We read all the signs to see what they had to eat and how much it cost, and I guess nothing on the menu was more than fifteen cents, but it couldn't have looked grander to us if it had been Delmonico's. So we stood there with our noses pressed against the window, looking in. Two skinny little kids, both of us scared half to death, getting the thrill of a lifetime out of it. You know what I mean? And smelling everything with all our might and thinking how good it all smelled. . . . Then Grover turned to me and whispered: "Come on, Helen. Let's go in. It says fifteen cents for pork and beans. And I've got the money," Grover said. "I've got sixty cents."

I was so scared I couldn't speak. I'd never been in a place like that before. But I kept thinking, "Oh Lord, if mama should find out!" I felt as if we were committing some big crime. . . . Don't you know how it is when you're a kid? It was the thrill of a lifetime. . . . I couldn't resist. So we both went in and sat down on those high stools before the counter and ordered pork and beans and a cup of coffee. I suppose we were too frightened at what we'd done really to enjoy anything. We just gobbled it all up in a hurry, and gulped our coffee down. And I don't know whether it was the excitement—I guess the poor kid was already sick when we came in there and didn't know it. But I turned and looked at him, and he was white as death. . . . And when I asked him what was the matter, he wouldn't tell me. He was too proud. He said he was all right, but I could see that he was sick as a dog. . . . So he paid the bill. It came to forty cents—I'll never forget *that* as long as I live. . . . And sure enough, we no more than got out the door—he hardly had time to reach the curb—before it all came up.

And the poor kid was so scared and so ashamed. And what scared him so was not that he had gotten sick, but that he had spent all that money and it had come to nothing. And mama would find out. . . . Poor kid, he just stood there looking at me and he whispered: "Oh Helen, don't tell mama. She'll be mad if she finds out." Then we hurried home, and he was still white as a sheet when we got there.

Mama was waiting for us. She looked at us—you know how "Miss Eliza" looks at you when she thinks you've been doing something that you shouldn't. Mama said, "Why, where on earth have you two children been?" I guess she was all set to lay us out. Then she took one look at Grover's face. That was enough for her. She said, "Why, child, what in the world!" She was white as a sheet herself. . . . And all that Grover said was—"Mama, I feel sick."

He was sick as a dog. He fell over on the bed, and we undressed him and mama put her hand upon his forehead and came out in the hall—she was so white you could have made a black mark on her face with chalk—and whispered to me, "Go get the doctor quick, he's burning up."

And I went chasing up the street, my pigtails flying, to Dr. Packer's house. I brought him back with me. When he came out of Grover's room he told mama what to do but I don't know if she even heard him.

Her face was white as a sheet. She looked at me and looked right through me. She never saw me. And oh, my Lord, I'll never forget the way she looked, the way my heart stopped and came up in my throat. I was only a skinny little kid of fourteen. But she looked as if she was dying right before my eyes. And I knew that if anything happened to him, she'd never get over it if she lived to be a hundred.

Poor old mama. You know, he always was her eyeballs—you know that, don't you?—not the rest of us!—no, sir! I know what I'm talking about. It always has been Grover—she always thought more of him than she did of any of the others. And—poor kid!—he was a sweet kid. I can still see him lying there, and remember how sick he was, and how scared I was! I don't know why I was so scared. All we'd done had been to sneak away from home and go into a lunchroom—but I felt guilty about the whole thing, as if it was my fault.

It all came back to me the other day when I was looking at that picture, and I thought, my God, we were two kids together, and I was only two years older than Grover was, and now I'm forty-six. . . . Can you believe it? Can you figure it out—the way we grow up and change and go away? . . . And my Lord, Grover seemed so grown-up to me. He was such a quiet kid—I guess that's why he seemed older than the rest of us.

I wonder what Grover would say now if he could see that picture. All my hopes and dreams and big ambitions have come to nothing, and it's all so long ago, as if it happened in another world. Then it comes back, as if it happened yesterday. . . . Sometimes I lie awake at night and think of all the people who have come and gone, and how everything is different from the way we thought that it would be. Then I go out on the street next day and see the faces of the people that I pass. . . . Don't they look strange to you? Don't you see something funny in people's eyes, as if all of them were puzzled about something? As if they were wondering what had happened to them since they were kids? Wondering what it is that they have lost? . . . Now am I crazy, or do you know what I mean? You've been to college, Gene, and I want you to tell me if you know the answer. Now do they look that way to you? I never noticed that look in people's eyes when I was a kid—did you?

My God, I wish I knew the answer to these things. I'd like to find out what is wrong—what has changed since then—and if we have the same queer look in our eyes, too. Does it happen to us all, to everyone? . . . Grover and Ben, Steve, Daisy, Luke, and me—all standing there before that house on Woodson Street in Altamont—there we are, and you see the way we were—and how it all gets lost. What is it, anyway, that people lose?

How is it that nothing turns out the way we thought it would be? It all gets lost until it seems that it has never happened—that it is something we dreamed somewhere. . . . You see what I mean? . . . It seems that it must be something we heard somewhere—that it happened to someone else. And then it all comes back again.

And suddenly you remember just how it was, and see again those two funny, frightened, skinny little kids with their noses pressed against the dirty window of that lunchroom thirty years ago. You remember the way it felt, the way it smelled, even the strange smell in the old pantry in that house we lived in then. And the steps before the house, the way the rooms looked. And those two little boys in sailor suits who used to ride up and down before the house on tricycles. . . . And the birthmark on Grover's neck. . . . The Inside Inn. . . . St. Louis, and the Fair.

It all comes back as if it happened yesterday. And then it goes away again, and seems farther off and stranger than if it happened in a dream.

IV—THE BROTHER

"*This* is King's Highway," the man said.

And then Eugene looked and saw that it was just a street. There were some big new buildings, a large hotel, some restaurants and "bar-grill" places of the modern kind, the livid monotone of neon lights, the ceaseless traffic of motor cars—all this was new, but it was just a street. And he knew that it had always been just a street, and nothing more—but somehow—well, he stood there looking at it, wondering what else he had expected to find.

The man kept looking at him with inquiry in his eyes, and Eugene asked him if the Fair had not been out this way.

"Sure, the Fair was out beyond here," the man said. "Out where the park is now. But this street you're looking for—don't you remember the name of it or nothing?" the man said.

Eugene said he thought the name of the street was Edgemont, but that he wasn't sure. Anyhow it was something like that. And he said the house was on the corner of that street and of another street.

Then the man said: "What was that other street?"

Eugene said he did not know, but that King's Highway was a block or so away, and that an interurban line ran past about half a block from where he once had lived.

"What line was this?" the man said, and stared at him.

"The interurban line," Eugene said.

Then the man stared at him again, and finally, "I don't know no interurban line," he said.

Eugene said it was a line that ran behind some houses, and that there were board fences there and grass before the tracks. But somehow he could not say that it was summer in those days and that you could smell the ties, a wooden, tarry smell, and feel a kind of absence in the afternoon after the car had gone. He only said the interurban line was back behind somewhere between the backyards of some houses and some old board fences, and that King's Highway was a block or two away.

He did not say that King's Highway had not been a street in those days but a kind of road that wound from magic out of some dim and haunted land, and that along the way it had got mixed in with Tom the Piper's son, with hot cross buns, with all the light that came and went, and with coming down through Indiana in the morning, and the smell of engine smoke, the Union Station, and most of all with voices lost and far and long ago that said "King's Highway."

He did not say these things about King's Highway because he looked about him and he saw what King's Highway was. All he could say was that the street was near King's Highway, and was on the corner, and that the interurban trolley line was close to there. He said it was a stone house, and that there were stone steps before it, and a strip of grass. He said he thought the house had had a turret at one corner, he could not be sure.

The man looked at him again, and said, "This is King's Highway, but I never heard of any street like that."

Eugene left him then, and went on till he found the place. And so at last he turned into the street, finding the place where the two corners met, the huddled block, the turret, and the steps, and paused a moment, looking back, as if the street were Time.

For a moment he stood there, waiting—for a word, and for a door to open, for the child to come. He waited, but no words were spoken; no one came.

Yet all of it was just as it had always been, except that the steps were lower, the porch less high, the strip of grass less wide, than he had thought. All the rest of it was as he had known it would be. A graystone front, three-storied, with a slant slate roof, the side red brick and windowed, still with the old arched entrance in the center for the doctor's use.

There was a tree in front, and a lamp post; and behind and to the side, more trees than he had known there would be. And all the slatey turret gables, all the slatey window gables, going into points, and the two arched windows, in strong stone, in the front room.

It was all so strong, so solid, and so ugly—and all so enduring and so good, the way he had remembered it, except he did not smell the tar, the hot and caulky dryness of the old cracked ties, the boards of backyard fences and the coarse and sultry grass, and absence in the afternoon when the street car had gone, and the twins, sharp-visaged in their sailor suits, pumping with furious shrillness on tricycles up and down before the house, and the feel of the hot afternoon, and the sense that everyone was absent at the Fair.

Except for this, it was all just the same; except for this and for King's Highway, which was now a street; except for this, and for the child that did not come.

It was a hot day. Darkness had come. The heat rose up and hung and sweltered like a sodden blanket in St. Louis. It was wet heat, and one knew that there would be no relief or coolness in the night. And when one tried to think of the time when the heat would go away, one said: "It cannot last. It's bound to go away," as we always say it in America. But one did not believe it when he said it. The heat soaked down and men sweltered in it; the faces of the people were pale and greasy with the heat. And in their faces was a patient wretchedness, and one felt the kind of desolation that one feels at the end of a hot day in a great city in America—when one's home is far away, across the continent, and he thinks of all that distance, all that heat, and feels, "Oh God! but it's a big country!"

And he feels nothing but absence, absence, and the desolation of America, the loneliness and sadness of the high, hot skies, and evening coming on across the Middle West, across the sweltering and heat-sunken land, across all the lonely little towns, the farms, the fields, the oven swelter of Ohio, Kansas, Iowa, and Indiana at the close of day, and voices, casual in the heat, voices at the little stations, quiet, casual, somehow faded into that enormous vacancy and weariness of heat, of space, and of the immense, the sorrowful, the most high and awful skies.

Then he hears the engine and the wheel again, the wailing whistle and the bell, the sound of shifting in the sweltering yard, and walks the street, and walks the street, beneath the clusters of hard lights, and by the people with sagged faces, and is drowned in desolation and in no belief.

He feels the way one feels when one comes back, and knows that he should not have come, and when he sees that, after all, King's Highway is—a street; and St. Louis—the enchanted name—a big, hot, common town upon the river, sweltering in wet, dreary heat, and not quite South, and nothing else enough to make it better.

It had not been like this before. He could remember how it would get hot, and how good the heat was, and how he would lie out in the backyard on an airing mattress, and how the mattress would get hot and dry and smell like a hot mattress full of sun, and how the sun would make him want to sleep, and how, sometimes, he would go down into the basement to feel coolness, and how the cellar smelled as cellars always smell—a cool, stale smell, the smell of cobwebs and of grimy bottles. And he could remember, when you opened the door upstairs, the smell of the cellar would come up to you—cool, musty, stale and dank and dark—and how the thought of the dark cellar always filled him with a kind of numb excitement, a kind of visceral expectancy.

He could remember how it got hot in the afternoons, and how he would feel a sense of absence and vague sadness in the afternoons, when everyone had gone away. The house would seem so lonely, and sometimes he would sit inside, on the second step of the hall stairs, and listen to the sound of silence and of absence in the afternoon. He could smell the oil upon the floor and on the stairs, and see the sliding doors with their brown varnish and the beady chains across the door, and thrust his hands among the beady chains, and gather them together in his arms, and let them clash, and swish with light beady swishings all around him. He could feel darkness, absence, varnished darkness, and stained light within the house, through the stained glass of the window on the stairs, through the small stained glasses by the door, stained light and absence, silence and the smell of floor oil and vague sadness in the house on a hot mid-afternoon. And all these things themselves would have a kind of life: would seem to wait attentively, to be most living and most still.

He would sit there and listen. He could hear the girl next door practice her piano lessons in the afternoon, and hear the street car coming by between the backyard fences, half a block away, and smell the dry and sultry smell of backyard fences, the smell of coarse hot grasses by the car tracks in the afternoon, the smell of tar, of dry caulked ties, the smell of bright worn flanges, and feel the loneliness of backyards in the afternoon and the sense of absence when the car was gone.

Then he would long for evening and return, the slant of light, and feet along the street, the sharp-faced twins in sailor suits upon their tricycles, the smell of supper and the sound of voices in the house again, and Grover coming from the Fair.

That is how it was when he came into the street, and found the place where the two corners met, and turned at last to see if Time was there. He passed the house: some lights were burning, the door was open, and a woman sat upon the porch. And presently he turned, came back, and stopped before the house again. The corner light fell blank upon the house. He stood looking at it, and put his foot upon the step.

Then he said to the woman who was sitting on the porch: "This house—excuse me—but could you tell me, please, who lives here in this house?"

He knew his words were strange and hollow, and he had not said what he wished to say. She stared at him a moment, puzzled.

Then she said: "I live here. Who are you looking for?"

He said, "Why, I am looking for——"

And then he stopped, because he knew he could not tell her what it was he was looking for.

"There used to be a house—" he said.

The woman was now staring at him hard.

He said, "I think I used to live here."

She said nothing.

In a moment he continued, "I used to live here in this house," he said, "when I was a little boy."

She was silent, looking at him, then she said: "Oh. Are you sure this was the house? Do you remember the address?"

"I have forgotten the address," he said, "but it was Edgemont Street, and it was on the corner. And I know this is the house."

"This isn't Edgemont Street," the woman said. "The name is Bates."

"Well, then, they changed the name of the street," he said, "but this is the same house. It hasn't changed."

She was silent a moment, then she nodded: "Yes. They did change the name of the street. I remember when I was a child they called it something else," she said. "But that was a long time ago. When was it that you lived here?"

"In 1904."

Again she was silent, looking at him. Then presently: "Oh. That was the year of the Fair. You were here then?"

"Yes." He now spoke rapidly, with more confidence. "My mother had the house, and we were here for seven months. And the house belonged to Dr. Packer," he went on. "We rented it from him."

"Yes," the woman said, and nodded, "this was Dr. Packer's house. He's dead now, he's been dead for many years. But this was the Packer house, all right."

"That entrance on the side," he said, "where the steps go up, that was for Dr. Packer's patients. That was the entrance to his office."

"Oh," the woman said, "I didn't know that, I've often wondered what it was. I didn't know what it was for."

"And this big room in front here," he continued, "that was the office. And there were sliding doors, and next to it, a kind of alcove for his patients——"

"Yes, the alcove is still there, only all of it has been made into one room now—and I never knew just what the alcove was for."

"And there were sliding doors on this side, too, that opened on the hall—and a stairway going up upon this side. And half-way up the stairway, at the landing, a little window of colored glass—and across the sliding doors here in the hall, a kind of curtain made of strings of beads."

She nodded, smiling. "Yes, it's just the same—we still have the sliding doors and the stained glass window on the stairs. There's no bead curtain any more," she said, "but I remember when people had them. I know what you mean."

"When we were here," he said, "we used the doctor's office for a parlor—except later on—the last month or two—and then we used it for—a bedroom."

"It is a bedroom now," she said. "I run the house—I rent rooms —all of the rooms upstairs are rented—but I have two brothers and they sleep in this front room."

Both of them were silent for a moment, then Eugene said, "My brother stayed there too.

"In the front room?" the woman said.

He answered, "Yes."

She paused, then said: "Won't you come in? I don't believe it's changed much. Would you like to see?"

He thanked her and said he would, and he went up the steps. She opened the screen door to let him in.

Inside it was just the same—the stairs, the hallway, the sliding doors, the window of stained glass upon the stairs. And all of it was just the same, except for absence, the stained light of absence in the afternoon, and the child who once had sat there, waiting on the stairs.

It was all the same except that as a child he had sat there feeling things were *Somewhere*—and now he *knew*. He had sat there feeling that a vast and sultry river was somewhere—and now he knew! He had sat there wondering what Kings' Highway was, where it began, and where it ended—now he knew! He had sat there haunted by the magic word "downtown"—now he knew!—and by the street car after it had gone—and by all things that came and went and came again, like the cloud shadows passing in a wood, that never could be captured.

And he felt that if he could only sit there on the stairs once more, in solitude and absence in the afternoon, he would be able to get it back again. Then would he be able to remember all that he had seen and been—the brief sum of himself, the universe of his four years, with all the light of Time upon it—that universe which was so short to measure, and yet so far, so endless, to remember. Then would he be able to see his own small face again, pooled in the dark mirror of the hall, and peer once more into the grave eyes of the child that he had been, and discover there in his quiet three-years' self the lone integrity of "I," knowing: "Here is the House, and here House listening; here is Absence, Absence in the afternoon; and here in this House, this Absence, is my core, my kernel—here am I!"

But as he thought it, he knew that even if he could sit here alone and get it back again, it would be gone as soon as seized, just as it had been then—first coming like the vast and drowsy rumors of the distant and enchanted Fair, then fading like cloud shadows on a hill, going like faces in a dream—coming, going, coming, possessed and held but never captured, like lost voices in the mountains long ago—and like the dark eyes and quiet face of the dark, lost boy, his brother, who, in the mysterious rhythms of his life and work, used to come into this house, then go, and then return again.

The woman took Eugene back into the house and through the hall. He told her of the pantry, told her where it was and pointed to the place, but now it was no longer there. And he told her of the backyard, and of the old board fence around the yard. But the old board fence was gone. And he told her of the carriage house, and told her it was painted red. But now there was a small garage. And the backyard was still there, but smaller than he thought, and now there was a tree.

"I did not know there was a tree," he said. "I do not remember any tree."

"Perhaps it was not there," she said. "A tree could grow in thirty years." And then they came back through the house again and paused at the sliding doors.

"And could I see this room?" he said.

She slid the doors back. They slid open smoothly, with a rolling heaviness, as they used to do. And then he saw the room again. It was the same. There was a window at the side, the two arched windows at the front, the alcove and the sliding doors, the fireplace, with the tiles of mottled green, the mantel of dark mission wood, the mantel posts, a dresser and a bed, just where the dresser and the bed had been so long ago.

"Is this the room?" the woman said. "It hasn't changed?"

He told her that it was the same.

"And your brother slept here where my brothers sleep?"

"This is his room," he said.

They were silent. He turned to go, and said, "Well, thank you. I appreciate your showing me."

She said that she was glad and that it was no trouble. "And when you see your family, you can tell them that you saw the house," she said. "My name is Mrs. Bell. You can tell your mother that a Mrs. Bell has the house now. And when you see your brother, you can tell him that you saw the room he slept in, and that you found it just the same."

He told her then that his brother was dead.

The woman was silent for a moment. Then she looked at him and said: "He died here, didn't he? In this room?"

He told her that it was so.

"Well, then," she said, "I knew it. I don't know how. But when you told me he was here, I knew it."

He said nothing. In a moment the woman said, "What did he die of?"

"Typhoid."

She looked shocked and troubled, and said involuntarily, "My two brothers——"

"That was a long time ago," he said. "I don't think you need to worry now."

"Oh, I wasn't thinking about that," she said. "It was just hearing that a little boy—your brother—was—was in this room that my two brothers sleep in now——"

"Well, maybe I shouldn't have told you then. But he was a good boy—and if you'd known him you wouldn't mind."

She said nothing, and he added quickly: "Besides, he didn't stay here long. This wasn't really his room—but the night he came back with my sister he was so sick—they didn't move him."

"Oh," the woman said, "I see." And then: "Are you going to tell your mother you were here?"

"I don't think so."

"I—I wonder how she feels about this room."

"I don't know. She never speaks of it."

"Oh. . . . How old was he?"

"He was twelve."

"You must have been pretty young yourself."

"I was not quite four."

"And—you just wanted to see the room, didn't you? That's why you came back."

"Yes."

"Well—" indefinitely—"I guess you've seen it now."

"Yes, thank you."

"I guess you don't remember much about him, do you? I shouldn't think you would."

"No, not much."

The years dropped off like fallen leaves: the face came back again —the soft dark oval, the dark eyes, the soft brown berry on the neck, the raven hair, all bending down, approaching—the whole appearing to him ghost-wise, intent and instant.

"Now say it—*Grover!*"

"Gova."

"No—not Gova—*Grover!* . . . Say it!"

"Gova."

"Ah-h—you didn't say it. You said Gova. *Grover*—now say it!"

"Gova."

"Look, I tell you what I'll do if you say it right. Would you like to go down to King's Highway? Would you like Grover to set you up? All right, then. If you say Grover and say it right, I'll take you to King's Highway and set you up to ice cream. Now say it right— *Grover!*"

"Gova."

"Ah-h, you-u. You're the craziest little old boy I ever did see. Can't you even say Grover?"

"Gova."

"Ah-h, you-u. Old Tongue-Tie, that's what you are. . . . Well, come on, then, I'll set you up anyway."

It all came back, and faded, and was lost again. Eugene turned to go, and thanked the woman and said good-bye.

"Well, then, good-bye," the woman said, and they shook hands. "I'm glad if I could show you. I'm glad if—" She did not finish, and at length she said: "Well, then, that was a long time ago. You'll find everything changed now, I guess. It's all built up around here now— and way out beyond here, out beyond where the Fair Grounds used to be. I guess you'll find it changed."

They had nothing more to say. They just stood there for a moment on the steps, and then shook hands once more.

"Well, good-bye."

And again he was in the street, and found the place where the corners met, and for the last time turned to see where Time had gone.

And he knew that he would never come again, and that lost magic would not come again. Lost now was all of it—the street, the heat, King's Highway, and Tom the Piper's son, all mixed in with the vast and drowsy murmur of the Fair, and with the sense of absence in the afternoon, and the house that waited, and the child that dreamed. And out of the enchanted wood, that thicket of man's memory, Eugene knew that the dark eye and the quiet face of his friend and brother—poor child, life's stranger, and life's exile, lost like all of us, a cipher in blind mazes, long ago—the lost boy was gone forever, and would not return.

GOD'S LONELY MAN

MY LIFE, more than that of anyone I know, has been spent in solitude and wandering. Why this is true, or how it happened, I cannot say; yet it is so. From my fifteenth year—save for a single interval—I have lived about as solitary a life as a modern man can have. I mean by this that the number of hours, days, months, and years that I have spent alone has been immense and extraordinary. I propose, therefore, to describe the experience of human loneliness exactly as I have known it.

The reason that impels me to do this is not that I think my knowledge of loneliness different in kind from that of other men. Quite the contrary. The whole conviction of my life now rests upon the belief that loneliness, far from being a rare and curious phenomenon, peculiar to myself and to a few other solitary men, is the central and inevitable fact of human existence. When we examine the moments, acts, and statements of all kinds of people—not only the grief and ecstasy of the greatest poets, but also the huge unhappiness of the average soul, as evidenced by the innumerable strident words of abuse, hatred, contempt, mistrust, and scorn that forever grate upon our ears as the manswarm passes us in the streets—we find, I think, that they are all suffering from the same thing. The final cause of their complaint is loneliness.

But if my experience of loneliness has not been different in kind from that of other men, I suspect it has been sharper in intensity. This gives me the best authority in the world to write of this, our general complaint, for I believe I know more about it than anyone of my generation. In saying this, I am merely stating a fact as I see it, though I realize that it may sound like arrogance or vanity. But before anyone jumps to that conclusion, let him consider how strange it would be to meet with arrogance in one who has lived alone as much as I. The surest cure for vanity is loneliness. For, more than other men, we who dwell in the heart of solitude are always the victims of self-doubt. Forever and forever in our loneliness, shameful feelings of inferiority will rise up suddenly to overwhelm us in a poisonous flood of horror, disbelief, and desolation, to sicken and corrupt our health and confidence, to spread pollution at the very root of strong, exultant joy. And the eternal paradox of it is that if a man is to know the triumphant labor of creation, he must for long periods resign himself to loneliness, and suffer loneliness to rob him of the health, the confidence, the belief and joy which are essential to creative work.

To live alone as I have lived, a man should have the confidence of God, the tranquil faith of a monastic saint, the stern impregnability of Gibraltar. Lacking these, there are times when anything, everything, all or nothing, the most trivial incidents, the most casual words, can in an instant strip me of my armor, palsy my hand, constrict my heart with frozen horror, and fill my bowels with the gray substance of shuddering impotence. Sometimes it is nothing but a shadow passing on the sun; sometimes nothing but the torrid milky light of August, or the naked, sprawling ugliness and squalid decencies of streets in Brooklyn fading in the weary vistas of that milky light and evoking the intolerable misery of countless drab and nameless lives. Sometimes it is just the barren horror of raw concrete, or the heat blazing on a million beetles of machinery darting through the torrid streets, or the cindered weariness of parking spaces, or the slamming smash and racket of the El, or the driven manswarm of the earth, thrusting on forever in exacerbated fury, going nowhere in a hurry.

Again, it may be just a phrase, a look, a gesture. It may be the cold, disdainful inclination of the head with which a precious, kept, exquisite princeling of Park Avenue acknowledges an introduction, as if to say: "You are nothing." Or it may be a sneering reference and dismissal by a critic in a high-class weekly magazine. Or a letter from a woman saying I am lost and ruined, my talent vanished, all my efforts false and worthless—since I have forsaken the truth, vision, and reality which are so beautifully her own.

And sometimes it is less than these—nothing I can touch or see or hear or definitely remember. It may be so vague as to be a kind of hideous weather of the soul, subtly compounded of all the hunger, fury, and impossible desire my life has ever known. Or, again, it may be a half-forgotten memory of the cold wintry red of waning Sunday afternoons in Cambridge, and of a pallid, sensitive, æsthetic face that held me once in earnest discourse on such a Sunday afternoon in Cambridge, telling me that all my youthful hopes were pitiful delusions and that all my life would come to naught, and the red and waning light of March was reflected on the pallid face with a desolate impotence that instantly quenched all the young ardors of my blood.

Beneath the evocations of these lights and weathers, and the cold, disdainful words of precious, sneering, and contemptuous people, all of the joy and singing of the day goes out like an extinguished candle, hope seems lost to me forever, and every truth that I have ever found and known seems false. At such a time the lonely man will feel that all the evidence of his own senses has betrayed him, and that nothing really lives and moves on earth but creatures of the death-in-life—those of the cold, constricted heart and the sterile loins, who exist forever in the red waning light of March and Sunday afternoon.

All this hideous doubt, despair, and dark confusion of the soul a lonely man must know, for he is united to no image save that which he creates himself, he is bolstered by no other knowledge save that which he can gather for himself with the vision of his own eyes and brain. He is sustained and cheered and aided by no party, he is given comfort by no creed, he has no faith in him except his own. And often that faith deserts him, leaving him shaken and filled with impotence. And then it seems to him that his life has come to nothing, that he is ruined, lost, and broken past redemption, and that morning—bright, shining morning, with its promise of new beginnings—will never come upon the earth again as it did once.

He knows that dark time is flowing by him like a river. The huge, dark wall of loneliness is around him now. It encloses and presses in upon him, and he cannot escape. And the cancerous plant of memory is feeding at his entrails, recalling hundreds of forgotten faces and ten thousand vanished days, until all life seems as strange and insubstantial as a dream. Time flows by him like a river, and he waits in his little room like a creature held captive by an evil spell. And he will hear, far off, the murmurous drone of the great earth, and feel that he has been forgotten, that his powers are wasting from him while the river flows, and that all his life has come to nothing. He feels that his strength is gone, his power withered, while he sits there drugged and fettered in the prison of his loneliness.

Then suddenly, one day, for no apparent reason, his faith and his belief in life will come back to him in a tidal flood. It will rise up in him with a jubilant and invincible power, bursting a window in the world's great wall and restoring everything to shapes of deathless brightness. Made miraculously whole and secure in himself, he will plunge once more into the triumphant labor of creation. All his old strength is his again: he knows what he knows, he is what he is, he has found what he has found. And he will say the truth that is in him, speak it even though the whole world deny it, affirm it though a million men cry out that it is false.

At such a moment of triumphant confidence, with this feeling in me, I dare now assert that I have known Loneliness as well as any man, and will now write of him as if he were my very brother, which he is. I will paint him for you with such fidelity to his true figure that no man who reads will ever doubt his visage with Loneliness comes to him hereafter.

The most tragic, sublime, and beautiful expression of human loneliness which I have ever read is the Book of Job; the grandest and most philosophical, Ecclesiastes. Here I must point out a fact which is so much at variance with everything I was told as a child concerning loneliness and the tragic underweft of life that, when I first discovered it, I was astounded and incredulous, doubting the overwhelming weight of evidence that had revealed it to me. But there it was, as solid as a rock, not to be shaken or denied; and as the years passed, the truth of this discovery became part of the structure of my life.

The fact is this: the lonely man, who is also the tragic man, is invariably the man who loves life dearly—which is to say, the joyful man. In these statements there is no paradox whatever. The one condition implies the other, and makes it necessary. The essence of human tragedy is in loneliness, not in conflict, no matter what the arguments of the theater may assert. And just as the great tragic writer (I say, "the tragic writer" as distinguished from "the writer of tragedies," for certain nations, the Roman and French among them, have had no great tragic writers, for Vergil and Racine were none, but rather great writers of tragedy) : just as the great tragic writer—Job, Sophocles, Dante, Milton, Swift, Dostoevski—has always been the lonely man, so has he also been the human who loved life best and had the deepest sense of joy. The real quality and substance of human joy is to be found in the works of these great tragic writers as nowhere else in all the records of man's life upon the earth. In proof of this, I can give here one conclusive illustration:

In my childhood, any mention of the Book of Job evoked instantly in my mind a long train of gloomy, gray, and unbrokenly dismal associations. This has been true, I suspect, with most of us. Such phrases as "Job's comforter," and "the patience of Job," and "the afflictions of Job," have become part of our common idiom and are used to refer to people whose woes seem uncountable and unceasing, who have suffered long and silently, and whose gloom has never been interrupted by a ray of hope or joy. All these associations had united to make for me a picture of the Book of Job that was grim, bleak, and constant in its misery. When I first read it as a child, it seemed to me that the record of Job's tribulations was relieved only by a kind of gloomy and unwilling humor—a humor not intended by the author, but supplied by my own exasperation, for my childish sense of proportion and justice was at length so put upon by this dreary tidal flood of calamities that I had to laugh in protest.

But any reader of intelligence and experience who has read that great book in his mature years will realize how false such a picture is. For the Book of Job, far from being dreary, gray, and dismal, is woven entire, more than any single piece of writing I can recall, from the sensuous, flashing, infinitely various, and gloriously papable material of great poetry; and it wears at the heart of its tremendous chant of everlasting sorrow the exulting song of everlasting joy.

In this there is nothing strange or curious, but only what is inevitable and right. For the tragic writer knows that joy is rooted at the heart of sorrow, that ecstasy is shot through with the sudden crimson thread of pain, that the knife-thrust of intolerable desire and the wild, brief glory of possession are pierced most bitterly, at the very instant of man's greatest victory, by the premonitory sense of loss and death. So seen and so felt, the best and worst that the human heart can know are merely different aspects of the same thing, and are interwoven, both together, into the tragic web of life.

It is the sense of death and loneliness, the knowledge of the brevity of his days, and the huge impending burden of his sorrow, growing always, never lessening, that makes joy glorious, tragic, and unutterably precious to a man like Job. Beauty comes and passes, is lost the moment that we touch it, can no more be stayed or held than one can stay the flowing of a river. Out of this pain of loss, this bitter ecstasy of brief having, this fatal glory of the single moment, the tragic writer will therefore make a song for joy. That, at least, he may keep and treasure always. And his song is full of grief, because he knows that joy is fleeting, gone the instant that we have it, and that is why it is so precious, gaining its full glory from the very things that limit and destroy it.

He knows that joy gains its glory out of sorrow, bitter sorrow, and man's loneliness, and that it is haunted always with the certainty of death, dark death, which stops our tongues, our eyes, our living breath, with the twin oblivions of dust and nothingness. Therefore a man like Job will make a chant for sorrow, too, but it will still be a song for joy as well, and one more strange and beautiful than any other that man has ever sung:

Hast thou given the horse strength? hast thou clothed his neck with thunder?

Canst thou make him afraid as a grasshopper? the glory of his nostrils is terrible.

He paweth in the valley, and rejoiceth in his strength: he goeth on to meet the armed men.

He mocketh at fear, and is not affrighted; neither turneth he back from the sword.

The quiver rattleth against him, the glittering spear and the shield.

He swalloweth the ground with fierceness and rage; neither believeth he that it is the sound of the trumpet.

He saith among the trumpets, Ha, ha; and he smelleth the battle afar off, the thunder of the captains, and the shouting.

That is joy—joy solemn and triumphant; stern, lonely, everlasting joy, which has in it the full depth and humility of man's wonder, his sense of glory, and his feeling of awe before the mystery of the universe. An exultant cry is torn from our lips as we read the lines about that glorious horse, and the joy we feel is wild and strange, lonely and dark like death, and grander than the delicate and lovely joy that men like Herrick and Theocritus described, great poets though they were.

Just as the Book of Job and the sermon of Ecclesiastes are, each in its own way, supreme histories of man's loneliness, so do all the books of the Old Testament, in their entirety, provide the most final and profound literature of human loneliness that the world has known. It is astonishing with what a coherent unity of spirit and belief the life of loneliness is recorded in those many books—how it finds its full expression in the chants, songs, prophecies, and chronicles of so many men, all so various, and each so individual, each revealing some new image of man's secret and most lonely heart, and all combining to produce a single image of his loneliness that is matchless in its grandeur and magnificence.

Thus, in a dozen books of the Old Testament—in Job, Ecclesiastes, and the Song of Solomon; in Psalms, Proverbs, and Isaiah; in words of praise and words of lamentation; in songs of triumph and in chants of sorrow, bondage, and despair; in boasts of pride and arrogant assertion, and in stricken confessions of humility and fear; in warning, promise, and in prophecy; in love, hate, grief, death, loss, revenge, and resignation; in wild, singing jubilation and in bitter sorrow—the lonely man has wrought out in a swelling and tremendous chorus the final vision of his life.

The total, all-contributory unity of this conception of man's loneliness in the books of the Old Testament becomes even more astonishing when we begin to read the New. For, just as the Old Testament becomes the chronicle of the life of loneliness, the gospels of the New Testament, with the same miraculous and unswerving unity, become the chronicle of the life of love. What Christ is saying always, what he never swerves from saying, what he says a thousand times and in a thousand different ways, but always with a central unity of belief, is this: "I am my Father's son, and you are my brothers." And the unity that binds us all together, that makes this earth a family, and all men brothers and the sons of God, is love.

The central purpose of Christ's life, therefore, is to destroy the life of loneliness and to establish here on earth the life of love. The evidence to support this is clear and overwhelming. It should be obvious to everyone that when Christ says: "Blessed are the poor in spirit: for theirs is the kingdom of heaven," "Blessed are they that mourn: for they shall be comforted," "Blessed are the meek: for they shall inherit the earth," "Blessed are they which do hunger and thirst after righteousness: for they shall be filled," "Blessed are the merciful: for they shall obtain mercy," and "Blessed are the pure in heart: for they shall see God"—Christ is not here extolling the qualities of humility, sorrow, meekness, righteousness, mercy,

and purity as virtues sufficient in themselves, but he promises to men
who have these virtues the richest reward that men were ever
offered.

And what is that reward? It is a reward that promises not only
the inheritance of the earth, but the kingdom of heaven as well. It
tells men that they shall not live and die in loneliness, that their
sorrow will not go unassuaged, their prayers unheard, their hunger
and thirst unfed, their love unrequited: but that, through love, they
shall destroy the walls of loneliness forever; and even if the evil and
unrighteous of this earth shall grind them down into the dust, yet
if they bear all things meekly and with love, they will enter into
a fellowship of joy, a brotherhood of love, such as no men on earth
ever knew before.

Such was the final intention of Christ's life, the purpose of his
teaching. And its total import was that the life of loneliness could
be destroyed forever by the life of love. Or such, at least, has been
the meaning which I read into his life. For in these recent years
when I have lived alone so much, and known loneliness so well, I
have gone back many times and read the story of this man's words
and life to see if I could find in them a meaning for myself, a way
of life that would be better than the one I had. I read what he had
said, not in a mood of piety or holiness, not from a sense of sin, a
feeling of contrition, or because his promise of a heavenly reward
meant very much to me. But I tried to read his bare words nakedly
and simply, as it seems to me he must have uttered them, and as I
have read the words of other men—of Homer, Donne, and Whitman, and the writer of Ecclesiastes—and if the meaning I have put
upon his words seems foolish or extravagant, childishly simple or
banal, mine alone or not different from what ten million other men
have thought, I have only set it down here as I saw it, felt it, found
it for myself, and have tried to add, subtract, and alter nothing.

And now I know that though the way and meaning of Christ's
life is a far, far better way and meaning than my own, yet I can
never make it mine; and I think that this is true of all the other
lonely men that I have seen or known about—the nameless, voice-
less, faceless atoms of this earth as well as Job and Everyman and
Swift. And Christ himself, who preached the life of love, was yet as
lonely as any man that ever lived. Yet I could not say that he was

mistaken because he preached the life of love and fellowship, and lived and died in loneliness; nor would I dare assert his way was wrong because a billion men have since professed his way and never followed it.

I can only say that I could not make his way my own. For I have found the constant, everlasting weather of man's life to be, not love, but loneliness. Love itself is not the weather of our lives. It is the rare, the precious flower. Sometimes it is the flower that gives us life, that breaches the dark walls of all our loneliness and restores us to the fellowship of life, the family of the earth, the brotherhood of man. But sometimes love is the flower that brings us death; and from it we get pain and darkness; and the mutilations of the soul, the maddening of the brain, may be in it.

How or why or in what way the flower of love will come to us, whether with life or death, triumph or defeat, joy or madness, no man on this earth can say. But I know that at the end, forever at the end for us—the houseless, homeless, doorless, driven wanderers of life, the lonely men—there waits forever the dark visage of our comrade, Loneliness.

But the old refusals drop away, the old avowals stand—and we who were dead have risen, we who were lost are found again, and we who sold the talent, the passion, and belief of youth into the keeping of the fleshless dead, until our hearts were corrupted, our talent wasted, and our hope gone, have won our lives back bloodily, in solitude and darkness; and we know that things will be for us as they have been, and we see again, as we saw once, the image of the shining city. Far flung, and blazing into tiers of jeweled light, it burns forever in our vision as we walk the Bridge, and strong tides are bound round it, and the great ships call. And we walk the Bridge, always we walk the Bridge alone with you, stern friend, the one to whom we speak, who never failed us. Hear:

"Loneliness forever and the earth again! Dark brother and stern friend, immortal face of darkness and of night, with whom the half part of my life spent, and with whom I shall abide now till my death forever—what is there for me to fear as long as you are with me? Heroic friend, blood-brother of my life, dark face—have we not gone together down a million ways, have we not coursed together the great and furious avenues of night, have we not crossed the stormy seas alone, and known strange lands, and come again to walk the continent of night and listen to the silence of the earth? Have we not been brave and glorious when we were together, friend? Have we not known triumph, joy, and glory on this earth— and will it not be again with me as it was then, if you come back to me? Come to me, brother, in the watches of the night. Come to me in the secret and most silent heart of darkness. Come to me as you always came, bringing to me again the old invincible strength, the deathless hope, the triumphant joy and confidence that will storm the earth again."

DEATH

THE FOLLOWING two selections are justly famous comments by Wolfe on death, and they form together a fitting conclusion to this Reader.

The first, "Toward Which," is an arrangement as verse of the paragraphs printed as a conclusion to *You Can't Go Home Again*. The arrangement is by John S. Barnes. This passage, in essentially the same language, first appeared as the conclusion to *"I Have a Thing to Tell You"*, a short novel serialized in the *New Republic*, March 10, 17, 24, 1937. There it was a part of a farewell to Germany. It was later added to the final page of *You Can't Go Home Again*, and there it appears to be a prophecy of his approaching death. The version here printed is from *A Stone, A Leaf, A Door*, Poems by Thomas Wolfe, arranged by John S. Barnes (New York: Charles Scribner's Sons, 1945), page 166.

The letter to Maxwell E. Perkins is from *The Letters of Thomas Wolfe*, edited by Elizabeth Nowell (New York: Charles Scribner's Sons, 1956), pages 777-778.

TOWARD WHICH

Something has spoken to me in the night,
Burning the tapers of the waning year;
Something has spoken in the night,
And told me I shall die, I know not where.

Saying:
"To lose the earth you know, for greater knowing;
To lose the life you have, for greater life;
To leave the friends you loved, for greater loving;
To find a land more kind than home, more large than
    earth—

"—Whereon the pillars of this earth are founded,
Toward which the conscience of the world is tending—
A wind is rising, and the rivers flow."

TO MAXWELL E. PERKINS

*The following note, written to Maxwell Perkins on August 12,
1938, when Wolfe first had intimations of death, was the last letter
which he was ever to write.*

Providence Hospital
Seattle, Washington
August 12, 1938

Dear Max:
   I'm sneaking this against orders, but "I've got a hunch"—and I
wanted to write these words to you.

I've made a long voyage and been to a strange country, and I've seen the dark man very close; and I don't think I was too much afraid of him, but so much of mortality still clings to me—I wanted most desperately to live and still do, and I thought about you all a thousand times, and wanted to see you all again, and there was the impossible anguish and regret of all the work I had not done, of all the work I had to do—and I know now I'm just a grain of dust, and I feel as if a great window has been opened on life I did not know about before—and if I come through this, I hope to God I am a better man, and in some strange way I can't explain, I know I am a deeper and a wiser one. If I get on my feet and out of here, it will be months before I head back, but if I get on my feet, I'll come back.

Whatever happens—I had this "hunch" and wanted to write you and tell you, no matter what happens or has happened, I shall always think of you and feel about you the way it was that Fourth of July day three years ago* when you met me at the boat, and we went out of the café on the river and had a drink and later went on top of the tall building, and all the strangeness and the glory and the power of life and of the city was below.

Yours always,
Tom

---

* The fourth of July, 1935, was the day on which Wolfe had returned to America to find *Of Time and the River* a great success.